DISQUIET
GODS

By Christopher Ruocchio:

THE SUN EATER SEQUENCE

Empire of Silence

Howling Dark

Demon in White

Kingdoms of Death

Ashes of Man

Disquiet Gods

DISQUIET GODS

THE SUN EATER BOOK SIX

CHRISTOPHER RUOCCHIO

An Ad Astra Book

First published in the US in 2024 by Baen Books

This edition first published in the UK in 2024 by Head of Zeus Ltd,
part of Bloomsbury Publishing Plc

9 7 5 3 4 6 8

A CIP catalogue record for this book is available
from the British Library.

ISBN (HB): 9781803287607
ISBN (E): 9781803287584

Map by Daniel Hasenbos

Printed and bound in Great Britain by
CPI Group (UK) Ltd, Croydon, CR0 4YY

Head of Zeus
First Floor East
5–8 Hardwick Street
London EC1R 4RG

WWW.HEADOFZEUS.COM

TO MY LITTLE GIRL.
I LOVED YOU AT ONCE.

CHAPTER 1

THE SHADOW OF THE EMPIRE

SONG.

A solitary voice rose up in song—as it did at the end of every watch of every day—from the parapet of the agiary temple that stood upon a spur of the black mountain at my back. I hardly heard it. After more than two hundred years of exile, the prayers of the fire priests of Jadd seemed to me no stranger than the sunset prayers of our Chantry, though they too rang hollow in my ears. Prince Aldia had told me many times—and my good Neema had echoed him—that their prayers were the source of ours. The worship of *Atash,* the holy fire, and of Ahura Mazda, the *Lord of Wisdom,* was older—far older—than the Imperial Cult of Earth.

Our ancestors worshipped the fire and Our Lord when men were children, the great prince told me often, voice quavering in his great-grandfatherly way. *Your ancestors did not worship the Earth until they burned her.*

I did not argue with him, though I might have pointed out that the manner of those prayers had come to his faith much later, in the clamor out of Earth, when they had needed ritual and song for comfort in the bitter, lightless years that had carried their people to new suns. So it was with all the old religions, though each claimed not to have changed at all.

Yet why should they not change?

If the god of the fire priests was real—and there are gods that are—then surely his part in the universal story is not ended. Surely there are new revelations at hand...and to come. That thought returned to me—who had received revelations of my own—time and again. In a younger man, the thought might have caught and kindled a fire of its own in my belly.

But I was old, and the wind that blew the words of the fire-priest's song back upon the mountain dragged my long and graying hair back with it, and stoked not the embers in my heart. It was midafternoon, the start of

1

Uziran, that watch which ran from midafternoon until evenfall. Looking up, I could see the acolytes in robes of Jaddian white and the neophytes of the Fire School in tunic and trousers of the same moving toward the agiary.

I did not move to join them, but gripped the iron rail. The metal was hot in the afternoon sun—red and huge as an apple in the pale sky—and I leaned my weight against it. I had started just after lunch, having dismissed Demetra for the day, and left my villa upon the sward above the beach of mingled black and white sand. As I always did, I'd set my sights upon Hephaistos, and walked the *Scala Aspara,* the White Stair, to the Fire School.

The Fire School.

All across the galaxy, songs are sung of its shining towers, its sweeping colonnades and intricately styled oriels. Legends are spun of duelists facing one another upon arched step bridges over steep-walled canals where the lavas of Hephaistos flow down to the sea, of odalisques oiled and clad in golden collars reclining for the delectation of their masters, of knives and whispers in the dark.

The songs are true, and legends mostly so.

The black mountain, which the first cartographers named Hephaistos— and which the Jaddians themselves called *Kauf Adar*—rose above all, its broken head cloud-crowned in the eggshell sky, its dark shoulders seeming frosted where the white towers and terraces gleamed. I had walked up the *Scala Aspara* earlier that afternoon, walked beneath the rows of date palms swaying in the wind and alongside the Grand Canal until I came to *Il Casa du Burkan,* the Volcano House, where the neophytes had their dormitories.

The mountain was always burning, casting up its fires from the belly of the world. The Jaddians had long ago tamed Hephaistos, directing its flows along canals and down cataracts where molten stone ran like water. To the men of Jadd, this was as ordinary as rain. Always I would pass students taking their lunch upon the embankment, or a pair of old men playing at druaja at a table overlooking the rivers of fire. Great columns of steam were always rising from the sea where fire and water met, and always there were boats dredging the lagoons to keep them from filling in.

For two hundred years and more, the island and the Fire School had been my home.

Adequately rested at last, I pushed myself off the rail and continued my walk, white shirt clinging to sweating flesh. I was feeling my age that afternoon, I well recall, in my knees and in the shoulder old Doctor Elkan had so painstakingly repaired.

A pair of acolytes hurried past me, late for the watch's prayers. One smiled at me and said, *"Buon pogevra, domi!"*

"Buon pogevra," I said in return, touching my forehead. *Good afternoon.*

As they hurried past, the other acolyte muttered to his companion in Jaddian. *"Itan quillo al Neroblis?"*

"Si," the first said. Then they were gone.

Al Neroblis, they called me. *The Black Devil.* I supposed I still looked the part. I still wore the high black boots of a military man, and the black trousers. My shirt was of plain white cotton, loose fitting, with laces at the neck in the fashion of Jaddian country lords. My hair was still more black than gray, even at six hundred and sixteen years of age, and though the creases at the corners of my eyes and mouth would no longer smooth away, a peasant might have marked me for a man of perhaps fifty standard years.

The Gray Devil might be more apt before long, I thought, almost muttering to myself as I began the walk back down. I had a mind to visit the library, where old Abdecalas maintained a collection nearly so fine as the Royal Library in Jaharrad, though it was a little thing when measured against the hoard at Colchis. Still, they had books out of Earth, kept in temperature-controlled vaults beneath the stacks. Cassandra would be at her practice, and would remain so until sundown, when the neophytes were released to the evening meal.

I left the terrace rail and went down an arcing stair of white marble onto an esplanade that overlooked the Grand Canal. Lava burbled in the channel below, flowing black and redly down its gentle incline at my left hand thirty feet below the level of the esplanade. A reflecting pool shimmered to my right, surrounded on three sides by a low building fronted by horseshoe-arched colonnades. A heron trilled in the water and took flight, disturbed by my appearance.

The entirety of the Fire School was built along the gentler, lower slopes of Hephaistos, bisected by the Grand Canal, which ran almost due west from the mountain down to the Varkanan Sea. When I'd ascended that afternoon, I'd traveled up the south side, climbing level by switchbacked level from Volcano House up nearly to the level of the Grand Agiary, the Atash Behram Jaddi, which was highest up the mountain. Now I was descending along the north side. There were twenty-five terraces on either side, each mirroring the other. The library stood opposite Volcano House on the lowest, each connected to the other by an arched bridge.

The sound of training swords clacked from a quadrangle to my right, but the duelists were hidden from my sight. There was always a fight somewhere, or a student reciting scripture, or his own verse. My hosts, the swordmasters, had permitted me to recite my own writings, and though they praised it and me, I think they humored me, in truth, and found my writings as unsophisticated as my sword work. Though I matched many of their masters one-to-one, they found my Imperial style clumsy and imprecise. Master Hydarnes had laughed when I first bested him, and called me *Al Brutan*—the Brute—and the masters had taken to calling me that when they did not call me *Al Neroblis*.

They rarely called me Hadrian.

As I reached the second terrace from the library, a flock of gulls rose from a gabled rooftop, and it was a minute before I realized what had startled them. I felt the shuttle's repulsors before I heard them, as a trembling in the air. Looking up, I saw the black shape sliding across the sky, its slim wings spread against the afternoon sun.

That was strange in itself. For all its galactic reputation, the Fire School rarely received visitors. Its students were expected to make pilgrimage by sea, and crossed the Varkanan by ship from the capital in Jaharrad. Occasionally the prince himself or some other dignitary would visit by air, taking one of the cetacean fliers so loved by the Jaddian people, with foil sails and filigreed hulls.

It was an Imperial shuttle, a black knife cutting the sky.

I hadn't seen one in nearly two hundred years. The Jaddians were jealous of their holy planet, not permitting foreign ships to make anchor. That had made it the perfect place to keep me safe all the long years. I had assaulted the Emperor, had struck him clean across the face for all his court to see... and in doing so I had forfeited my life. Only the intervention of Lorian Aristedes and Bassander Lin had saved my life.

Lorian and Bassander... and Prince Kaim, who was Olorin.

I squeezed the regrown fingers of my right hand with the hollow-boned fingers of my left, ran a hand along the scarred left forearm to the inside of the elbow, remembering the needles. Once, I had bought passage to Vorgossos with a vial of inhuman blood. I had bought a home on Jadd with a vial of my own. My genome lay now in the treasure vaults of House du Otranto, High Princes of Jadd. In a generation, perhaps, certain of my genes would be introduced to that august line. I imagined violet eyes peering out from the porcelain masks of Jaddian lords, or smiling through the chained veils of their ladies.

They imagined something more.

They had hoped to replicate my gifts. I knew that Aldia and Olorin both dreamed of Jaddian princes with the power to peer across time, to collapse the waves of potential into a chosen *now*. Olorin and the Emperor both had seen me slay Attavaisa in the bunker on Perfugium, watched me shatter the windows of the Cielcin ship with a thought.

The Jaddians had saved me, from the Emperor... and myself, but they had not done so wholly out of charity.

I watched the shuttle circle the Fire School, following the coastline. For a moment, I thought it was not going to land at all. But it circled back, lower this time, and I fancied that the hairs on my arms stood on end, though the ship was by then too far off for me to sense its repulsors. Its wings folded gracefully back and up as it settled on the square outside *Il Casa du Burkan,* trees bending in the wind.

An overwhelming urge to run kindled in me, and it took all my scholiast-trained composure not to act on it, not to find Cassandra at her lessons and run. They would look for me—if they *were* looking for me—at the villa.

Fear is a poison, I told myself, that ancient part of me that spoke in Gibson's voice still speaking after all the long centuries.

I let my hands fall to my side, and hurried down the slope to meet them.

"Just one man, sir?" said Neema, coming to stand beside me in the shadow of the villa's entryway. He offered a prim frown. "From your manner I thought we were expecting a battalion."

"Never mind that, Neema," I said. "You have my coat?"

"Yes, sir." The servant held up the garment, and I slid my arms into it. I had to wave him off as he orbited me and attempted to do up my buttons.

The coat was not quite the bridge coat of a Legion officer, though it hung past my knees. It was of Jaddian make, black gabardine lined with silk of scarlet paisley, high collared and silver buttoned. In it I looked half a soldier again, and half a lord.

"I wish they'd given us more time," Neema said. "No call ahead? Most irregular, lordship! Most irregular!"

I placed a hand on the Jaddian's shoulder, and stepped past him, out the tiled arch of the entryway, and stood upon the top step of the short stair that opened on the crushed marble path that led back up the slope toward the Fire School.

The villa which Prince Aldia had set aside for my use when I arrived on Jadd two centuries earlier had been a geological testing station initially, established on the island long before the Fire School itself was built. The geophysicists and planetologists who had tamed the mountain had lived in it long ago, when mankind was new to the holy planet. It had been they who carved the cataracts and the Grand Canal, and ensured the volcano would not erupt again. They had built their base right upon the seashore, and as I had asked the prince for a place on the water, it was perfect for me, though it was less grand than Maddalo House on Nessus and less dear than the pod I shared on Thessa with Gibson and Valka.

Valka...

I could just make out the crouched-bat shape of the shuttle on the landing yard beside Volcano House, but my eyes went to the man who had just reached the base of the stair and had turned to come toward us. A quartet of Jaddians were scurrying after him, one a master by the white half-robe she wore on her left side. I could hear them shouting over the pleasant crash of the waves. The wind guttered, blowing the steams where the lava flow hit the lagoon across the path between us, so that for a moment the five of them advanced through fog.

One black rook, one white knight, and pawns...

"You were told to wait, *sayido!*" cried the Maeskolos, chasing after the man in black. "Master Sasan was to send for Lord Marlowe!"

The Imperial emissary shouted back over his shoulder, "No need! It seems he knew to expect me!"

There was something familiar in his voice—though I was sure I had never heard it before. Perhaps it was only the accents of the Imperium, so different from the lilting music of Jadd.

"He's right," Neema sniffed from just behind me. "I say again, master: most irregular."

"Hush, Neema."

The servant went quiet.

The space immediately before the villa was clear of all but grass, and the man in black had reached the final bend in the path, and I marked him clearly through the parting curtains of mist, his Jaddian satellites dragged along in his wake. He was not palatine. He had neither the height nor the perfect symmetry of features. I guessed he was patrician. Second generation, perhaps, or third. He had no visible scars from the uplift procedures, as dear Pallino had. His black hair was cut short in the best Legion officer fashion, shaved close on the sides, oiled and neatly combed to the right on top. He wore an officer's black tunic buttoned up the left side, but neither collar tabs nor any badge of rank or office shone at shoulder or throat. His high boots might have been the twins of my own.

He wore a pair of spectacles—that was the strangest thing. No patrician so young should need such implements. They were rimmed in ivory, and flashed in the red sun as he came to a halt on the crushed marble. Beating his breast in salute, he clicked his heels. "Lord Hadrian Marlowe?"

I returned the gesture with cautious automation, unthinking. "Yes?"

Almost at once I wish I'd not saluted. I was not a soldier anymore, not a servant of the Emperor.

"I have been fighting for the last three years to get in to see you, lord," he said. "I am Lieutenant Edouard Albé, Imperial Intelligence. I am come on a matter of Special Security to the Imperium. May we speak privately?" He glanced at Neema, then back over his shoulder at the approaching Jaddians.

As if on cue, the Maeskolos—a tall, bronze woman with incongruously red hair—shouted, "Ten thousand pardons, *domi!* This man was told to await your coming in Volcano House! He would not wait!"

"I have waited long enough!" Edouard exclaimed, jostling with the woman and her attendants. "My lord, I *must* speak with you!"

My words had all deserted me, and I looked round at Neema, as if expecting an answer in the butler's studiously blank face. I was not certain what I had expected. An arrest? An assassin? I had been a guest of the Prince of Jadd so long that the Sollan Empire—which had been as Olympos to me; a gleaming, beckoning Erewhon—had diminished, become a mere shadow at the fringes of my mind. The shadow cast by the lieutenant's shuttle had been only a part of that greater shadow.

"Let him go, Anamara," I said to the swordmaster.

The red-haired woman released him only haltingly. Edouard brushed his tunic with his hands, straightened his belt and baldric. "Thank you," he said. "May I come in?"

"No," I said flatly. "Say what you have to say and be done."

The young lieutenant's brow furrowed. "My lord," he began to protest. "Mine are matters of grave security to the Imperium—"

"I am wanted by the Imperium, lieutenant!" I almost shouted, bulling over him.

She was only Tavrosi. The Emperor's words sounded fresh in my ears, as though it were William standing before me and not this poor lieutenant.

"I bring a pardon, lordship," said Edouard Albé, reaching into an inner pocket of his tunic.

"A pardon?" I sneered, surprised by my own anger. "Caesar should beg my pardon, sir."

Lieutenant Albé blinked up at me, and withdrew a packet wrapped in snowy vellum. He let his hands go to his side, not proffering the packet. "This is no joking matter, lord."

"No joking matter?" I said, and felt my brows arch. "Did he tell you what he did?"

"I have never met His Radiance," Edouard said.

"My *wife* was but lately dead, and he offered me another," I said. "She would have lived had he but listened to me, and left the field when I told him to." I could sense Neema's discomfort coming off the man in waves, and Anamara and the other Jaddians, too, seemed wrongfooted by my naked coldness.

She was only Tavrosi.

I left it to the lieutenant to respond, and he stood there a long moment, mouth half-open.

He lifted his free hand, dabbed delicately at an unseen bead of sweat at his hairline. "My lord," he said at last, advancing to the foot of the stairs between us, "we really should speak privately."

"You will speak now or not at all, lieutenant!" I said.

Edouard chewed his tongue, clearly frustrated by his long delay and by me. Three years he'd said he'd spent in orbit, waiting to be admitted to the planet of fire. The Jaddians were—as I have said—jealous of their world, and doubly so in those days, when the virus haunted the starways.

The Imperial embassy had learned of my presence some decades after my arrival on Jadd, and had spent many long years attempting to have me extradited to Forum to face the Emperor's justice. Prince Aldia's viziers had fought the Emperor's logothetes to a standstill, and eventually they had surrendered. They had tried to get at me several times, had sent many consuls and apostols to speak with me. Once, an Inquisitor of the Chantry had come and been turned away in the capital.

Why had this man been permitted when all those others were turned away?

Lieutenant Albé thrust the white packet toward me. "Since you will not hear me, I am bidden to tell you to recall Carteia, my lord."

My fingers—which had extended on reflex to take the man's letter—went suddenly numb. The packet slipped from my grasp and fell heavily upon the step.

"Carteia?"

A cold wind scoured the surface of my soul, carrying with it the swirl of snow, the stink of mold and ash, and the memory of a dining hall dominated by the headless statue of the Emperor.

You will receive a call, His Radiance had said. *We will find Dorayaica's god, and when we do . . . we will kill it, you and I.*

"They found one?" I asked, and hid my shaking hands behind my back. I did not stoop to take the packet. "One of the Watchers?" I understood then why the lieutenant had been so reluctant to speak in front of the Jaddians, though I myself found I did not care.

The call had come at last.

"You understand now why it is imperative you let me in to speak with you?" asked Lieutenant Albé.

I frowned down at him, still bothered by his voice. There was something in it, something about the man I could not place. It was as if I knew him—as indeed I would. I did not know it then, but Edouard was to become one of my last and dearest friends.

"For all I know you could be an assassin," I said. "Perhaps you mean to overpower me. I am an old man, lieutenant." I could feel the hilt of the sword in its thigh holster, its ivory hilt graven in the shape of a winged lion.

And yet, he had spoken of Carteia, of that cold day alone in the ruins of Rothsmoor with the Emperor and his Lord Chamberlain. Surely, he could only know about that meeting if word had come to him from Nicephorus or the Emperor himself? An Imperial assassin might know such things, but would the Emperor hand one of the galaxy's greatest secrets to a man certain to be captured by the Jaddians should he make his attempt—win or lose?

I thought not.

"I told you," the lieutenant said, "I'm Legion Intelligence."

"You're lying," I said, but did not say *You're HAPSIS.*

HAPSIS was the Emperor's own contact division. A secret intelligence corps tasked with uncovering the mysteries of the cosmos, of the ancient and long dead empires that—officially—did not exist.

"Lying?" the lieutenant made as if to remove his spectacles, but seemed to think better of it and let his hands fall.

"You're no lieutenant," I said, pointing to his shoulders. "You wear no badge."

For a moment, I thought the young man would speak plainly, but still it seemed the presence of the Jaddians held his tongue. "My lord, we came all this way..."

"We?" My eyes went to the pale heavens, as if I expected to spy his ship beyond the roof of the world.

His eyes went to the Master Anamara. "My lord, I am forbidden to speak with any man but yourself!"

"Then be silent."

"Can we not speak privately?" the lieutenant's voice rose in pitch as he stooped to collect his fallen packet.

I studied Edouard then for a long and silent moment. I could not decide what it was about the man's round, pale face that seemed so familiar to me. His haircut recalled that of Bassander Lin, but they were both military men. It was something else, something more singular. The spectacles? Bastien Durand had worn spectacles, but Durand had been as dark as this man was pale.

You will receive a call.

The Emperor's words echoed from the faded recesses of my mind, half-forgotten until that sunny afternoon. Cloudier shapes moved in recesses deeper still. Wings like the wings of bats. Eyes like glittering jewels. Countless hands of jointed bone. On the mountain, the Quiet had shown them to me. The Watchers. The Monumentals. Those vile gods of night.

Do what must be done.

"No," I said.

I was too old.

Once, I had dreamed of sailing the farther suns. Of visiting far-off worlds, of speaking with strange peoples and seeing strange sights. I had dreamed of seeing the Quiet's ruins at Athten Var, to the towers of the Menhir Dur. But I had dreamed of seeing them with Valka. And Valka was dead.

My dream had died with her.

In its place, there was only a black window, a square of night opening on nothing.

Between the emotion and the response...Falls the Shadow.

Life is very long...

"Wait!" A hand seized me by the wrist, and whirling I found the lieutenant clinging to my arm. Edouard realized his mistake an instant too late. I raised my free hand and struck the young officer sharply across the face.

For a moment, neither of us moved. Nothing moved, unless it was the guttering mists off the lagoon. Anamara took a step forward, but I stopped her with a glare. Edouard slowly raised his head to look at me. My ring had left a thin tear beneath his eye, and his spectacles had clattered to the crushed marble of the path, but he offered no complaint. Still not speaking, he straightened, and did the most remarkable thing I have ever seen a man so reprimanded do in all my life.

He raised his head, defiant, and presented his other cheek.

I almost laughed. Almost. But I shook my head, embarrassment sliding like egg down my face. I turned to go instead.

Before I had gone two paces, he raised his voice—his strangely familiar voice—and said, "My lord! Your father is dead!"

I froze, fearing in that moment that if I moved I would fall.

The galaxy had lost its center, as I had lost mine.

Too old, indeed.

My father is dead. The words echoed in my skull, my own thought mingling with Edouard's. *Your father is dead. My father is dead.*

Lord Alistair was dead.

I had not seen my father since I was a boy, and yet as shadows grow larger as the sun vanishes from the sky, so his absence from my life had made him grow in memory to a vague and slouching titan, his hulking silhouette cast like a pall across my childhood. Some part of me had, perhaps, been anchored to that childhood by the certain knowledge that he was out there, ruling from the black castle of my home—his life extended by so many long voyages offworld, just as the Emperor had extended his own life sailing round his provinces.

Your father is dead.

All these years, I expected to feel nothing. I had not seen the man in centuries, and he had never loved me—but I threw a hand to catch myself upon the delicately tiled arch, and turned to look back at the apostol. The hulking shadow was gone, and in its place...night had fallen. I had felt myself an old man before Edouard had spoken, but in that moment I felt truly aged.

I was an orphan at last, and so—in a sense—I was finally a man.

"How long?" The voice that asked the question sounded like my own.

"More than a century ago," Lieutenant Albé said, once more proffering his packet. "There's a holograph from your lord brother in here, along with the Emperor's pardon and the papers I was instructed to deliver. Lord Crispin gave it to me when I left Delos for the academy. He hoped I might find you. Now I have."

Neema advanced and took the apostol's envelope and withdrew on slippered feet, his head bowed.

"Delos?" I echoed the old name, and marked at last what it was about the young officer that seemed so familiar. "You're from Delos?"

His accent.

His voice had the clipped consonants and genteel polish of the Delian high style, an ancient mode. He sounded like the villain in a Eudoran masque.

He sounded like me. Or like I had done, so long ago.

"From Meidua," he said, and the recognition of a fellow countrymen in that distant country was an ache as sweet as the news of my father's death was sour. To hear the clean music of home once more intensified the sense of loss the man had piled on me mere moments before.

Of lost time.

"My family has served yours now for five generations, beginning shortly after you left. I'm the second to enter Imperial service." The man had not yet bent to collect his spectacles. Without them, his round and earnest face seemed almost the face of a child.

"Leave me," said the old soldier in the arch.

"Lord Marlowe, if you will but read the report. There is a letter from Sir Friedrich Oberlin. We will remain at anchor for some weeks yet while we resupply, we—"

"I said leave!" I practically bellowed the words. "The Lord Marlowe you came to find no longer exists, boy. Go back to your masters. Tell them he's dead."

"We need your help, lord!" the lieutenant said, "The Empire needs your help!"

"Damn the Empire!" I said. "What is the Empire to me?"

The man had no reply ready-made to that, and stammered, "Do you care so little for your own people?"

"My people are dead," I said, and thought *Save one, and she is safe here.* "Good day, lieutenant." I turned and reentered the house as Anamara and the neophytes laid hands on the lieutenant and led him—half-broken by the experience, I think—back along the path to Volcano House.

CHAPTER 2

THE PRINCE OF THE HOUSE OF THE MOON

THE PRINCE HAD MADE a fatal error.

I surveyed him over the petrified wood table between us, waiting to see if he had seen it. I searched Aldia's wrinkled visage, as if expecting to find the answer inscribed in the creases on his forehead. He looked like some fabulous sorcerer, his thick, white hair nearly so long as his snowy beard. He leaned upon one fist, studying the board, apparently heedless of his mistake.

Was that a smile on the papery lips? A sparkle in the deep black of his eyes?

"Are you going to make your move, *mi sadji?*" he asked, not lifting his eyes from the game.

"In a moment, Your Grace," I said, studying the labyrinth myself.

Druaja was an ancient game, and one I'd come to truly appreciate only late in life. I had learned it on Vorgossos, when I tarried in the halls of the Undying, waiting for an audience. But I had come to enjoy it only in my Jaddian captivity. When Prince Aldia came to visit the Fire School—and on the rarer occasions when I attended the Alcaz du Badr, as on that day—he and I would play and pass a watch in conversation.

He was better than this.

I had moved the walls three turns previous, lowering the white. By so doing I had cleared a path for my third centurion to make his circuit of the board. Aldia had advanced his king such that by simply moving the piece a quarter turn around the hexagonal board, I might place my centurion behind him, leaving him with nowhere to go. It was an elementary mistake—if perhaps not one obvious at a casual glance.

Lifting the sardonyx figure, I traced the quarter turn, placed the centurion on the appropriate onyx hexagon. "Shahmat, Your Grace."

"Is it?" The old man leaned back, chuckling. "Is it, indeed? Well played, my friend! Do you know, I'd forgotten you dropped the walls on me!" He collected his cobalt teacup with knobby fingers and drained it. "So simple a move! So direct! There is something sublime in such simplicity, do you not think?"

"Indeed, Your Grace," I said.

Prince Aldia's eyes narrowed over the rim of his teacup. "You are more somber even than your usual self, my funereal friend," he said. "Am I to assume your meeting with the Emperor's emissary left much to be desired?"

"You don't know?" I asked, looking up from the finished game board.

"My *Yahmazi* have ears to hear, but whatever their reputation, I am not in the habit of prying into the private matters of my friends."

The *Yahmazi* were the Jaddian secret police, and enjoyed a reputation as fearsome as that of Imperial Special Security. More fearsome perhaps, because they were even less talked about.

"My father is dead," I said flatly.

"Ah," Prince Aldia grew silent for a moment. *"Mis dolorossos, mi sadji."*

I opened my hand in a reflexive gesture of acceptance.

"Your father was an archon, yes?"

"He ruled a continent."

"Your brother is succeeding him?"

"I don't know," I said. I had not opened the lieutenant's packet. Some tired voice deep in my soul had whispered. *Let it lie. Let it lie until the lieutenant and his ship depart.*

I had heeded that voice, and so ignored Crispin's holograph along with the Emperor's pardon and whatever else lay inside. "I have a sister, as well— one I never met. Possibly she inherited the prefecture. I really don't know."

"We tried to keep him from getting in at you," Aldia said after a long silence. "The consulate applied every legal pressure. We threw everything we had at them: quarantine regulations, religious excuses, outright denials that you were even here."

"They've known I'm here for decades," I said.

"Since that business with the Oannosene, yes."

Oannos was one of the Small Kingdoms, a dominion of little more than a dozen suns on the fringes of Jaddian space, along the border they shared with the Lothrian Commonwealth. They had sent a delegation to Jadd to treat with the prince. They had tried to assassinate him instead, and might have succeeded were it not for Hadrian Marlowe, who had been masked and was quietly in attendance.

"They knew you were here well before the Oannos affair," Aldia said. "So it was for your father this messenger came?"

"You know it was not," I said.

Aldia studied me with his dimming eyes a moment before reaching out to pluck my winning centurion from the board. "You haven't read the letter."

"So you do know what it says?"

"I told you I do not," he said. "But I do know that your lieutenant has fought long and hard to get at you. They've been at dock more than three years."

"You didn't tell me sooner?"

"We had hoped the problem would resolve itself without the need to trouble your rest."

"What changed?"

A pained looked flickered across the old man's wizened face. "The Empire subsidizes our naval construction. In return we police the border with the Commonwealth. The consul threatened to ... renegotiate our arrangement." He closed his fist about the chessman. "The Lothrians have attacked our border worlds many times in the last half century. My admirals believe they will launch a full-scale invasion soon. We require Imperial funding to secure our border. I couldn't jeopardize our security for your peace of mind."

I told him I understood.

"It's getting bad out there, isn't it?"

Aldia weighed the chessman in his glittering hand as though it were his words. "Yes." He restored the piece to its hex, and reached for his articulated lapis mask. "You know our fleets prevented a number of foreign objects from striking the planet over the last several years."

"Foreign objects?" I looked sharply up at him. "Plague cannisters?"

"One assumes," the prince said, fitting his mask in place. "There's no way to be certain. They were vaporized." The azure plates of his *fersunan*, his mask, fitted smoothly over his face. The mask left his mouth and chin uncovered, so that his beard thrust out unencumbered. "Shall we go? You must be returning to the island, soon."

I nodded, and stood.

I'd heard reports of such attacks across the galaxy. Of small probes traveling at near light speed. Of how they would strike the upper airs of a world and fall to pieces, spreading their vile poison on the wind. The virus showed itself only slowly, incubated over the course of many days. The sorcerers of MINOS had done their black work well. Men and women might live apparently normal lives for weeks before the first growths showed.

Plagues were always falling out of heaven, carried by some poor unfortunate from some far-off world. They ravaged the plebeians mostly, for they had weaker immune systems than those of more exalted blood, and at any rate had no exposure to the animalcules of other worlds.

Such a monster had claimed poor Cat when I was just a boy.

This was something far worse, a demon hatched in glass cradles by arts black as hell.

LTH-81. Lymphotropic T-cell Human Retrovirus Mark-81.

I've heard it called many names. The Red Sleep. The Gasping Death. The Fleshing Plague. To many of the poorest beneath our stars it is simply *the Rot*. To the nobiles, it is *Lethe's Sickness*. To the scholiasts, the *lethovirus*.

I will call it what it is, what I called it when I discovered it in the Ganelon fortress.

Cancer as plague.

The bodies of the afflicted quickly developed tumorous growths. New organs formed, or half formed, beside the old. New bone—brittle and spongey—sprouted from joints until the human form was twisted half beyond recognition.

In the end, the afflicted was reduced to a mass of indolent flesh, unable even to move. Unable to do anything but shed the virus into the unwitting air. They had designed it to instill *terror*. And they had designed it perfectly.

It is out there, even now, though it has mutated into lesser form. There were beggars on Sun Street at Summerfair with misshapen faces and eyes swollen shut. There are lazarets in every city of the Empire now, built to house the sick and dying.

Even now, there is no cure. LTH-81 was a retrovirus, and as with all retroviruses, infection remains for life.

"Jadd is safe for now," Aldia continued. "By Atash, may it remain so."

His chair floated off the ground and moved toward the wooden lattice screen between the pillars beyond which stood the water garden. Twin servants—mamluks in chrome masks with silver armor flashing beneath their blue and white cloaks—moved like clockwork to roll back the sliding screen.

The prince floated through the arch and out into warm sunlight. Passing out after him, I felt the static cling of an energy field that separated the cool air of the chess room from the garden proper. I walked beside him, bootheels ringing on the mosaic tiled path. A pair of black swans waded in the nearest pool.

"They always remind me of young Olorin, those birds," the prince said, pointing. Peering up at me sidelong from his chair, he said, "All that black. Of course, you'd know a thing or two about that, would you not?" He flashed white teeth. I returned the smile more thinly. He must have marked the shallowness of my expression, for his own face fell, the plates of his *fersunan* clicking almost below hearing. "Why have you not read the Emperor's letter, Dom Hadrian?"

"I don't need his pardon," I said.

The Prince of Jadd looked up at me, lips compressed to a thin, white

line in his whiter beard. Presently he spoke, "They came all this way...
and waited so long...only to issue you a pardon?"

I in turn studied the elderly prince. Clad as he was in cerulean and
masked, he looked like some spirit of the clouds. Though I owed him
much—and had given more—I had never told him of the Watchers, not in
all our years of friendship. It was possible he knew of them already, just
as the Emperor had known, and yet I could not bring myself to speak,
sensing that to do so was to betray some secret covenant—not between
the Emperor and myself, he was no friend of mine, not any longer—but
between myself and the man I once had been.

The same embarrassment I had felt when I had struck the young lieutenant across his face returned that moment. Being old then and wise to the
workings of my heart, I understood the feeling almost at once. I was not
guarding any secret from the old prince. I was simply ashamed. Ashamed
because to admit the lieutenant had come to me upon so dire an errand,
and that I had sent him away, was to admit that I was faithless.

The call had come at last, and I'd refused it, was hiding from it even
then, as Mashya hid in paradise from the eyes of God, who saw all things.

Had I become a coward in old age? Hiding behind my pride and pain?

"They came to ask me to sail with them," I said, and turned my face
to the great red sun, feeling the warmth and the gentle breeze on my face.

"Will you go?" Aldia had not moved.

I looked down at him, unable to hide my shock. "You would let me?"

"You are not a prisoner," he said.

"I..." My eyes narrowed. I was not sure his words were precisely truth.
Not for the first time since Edouard's visit, I thought of the blood they had
taken when I first arrived, of the months I spent in a Jaddian military clinic,
allowing them to test me and scan my brain. "I am an old man, Aldia."

The prince laughed once more, a sound bright and sunny as the day
whence had come his name. "Old! *Dolá Deu di Foti, Dom Hadrian!* Old
indeed! There is yet more black in your hair than white."

Recalling something I had said to Corvo long ago—or was it Varro?—I
answered him. "It's not the years," I said. "It's the light-years."

Aldia du Otranto dismissed this with a gesture. "My cells have counted
nine hundred ninety-one standard years," he said. "You can still fight, so
Master Hydarnes tells me. *Al Brutan* is the equal of any of us, he says."

"He exaggerates," I said. "Master Hydarnes bests me six times in ten."

"Only six?" Aldia began floating along toward the colonnade. "That
is being nearly equal, no?" A short stair of rose marble ascended to the
colonnade ahead, flanked by ironwork trellises thick with flowers. As we
reached the foot of the stair, the blossoms all opened their faces to us—as
if in greeting—and a twittering as of birdsong filled the air about us both.

I did my best to hide my discomfort. The flowers were unnatural, and though they were beautiful, they disquieted me.

Flora should not sing as fauna might.

The pleasure gardens of the High Prince of Jadd were everything they say. Twelve thousand acres of land—black-soiled and verdurous—extended in a great fan from the ringed palace of the Alcaz. There were hedge mazes vast as villages and filled with the sculptures of gods and monsters, swards where topiary armies—men and horses and war elephants—were locked in green and endless battles. There were waterfalls and pools and little rivers brimming with bright fish, and hothouses where jeweled snakes and scarabs crawled in glass enclosures. And the birds! Hummingbirds and nightingales, thrushes and herons and peacocks with their bright tails. Parrots and parakeets and the long-billed toucans that were the prince's favorite.

And every one of them a work of art, wrought not by nature, but by the magi and the natalists of Jadd. The Jaddians—it is said—have never met an organism they could not improve. The singing flowers were only one example. Aldia himself was another. No lord of the Imperium—not even Caesar—would see so many springs.

For all his talk of my relative youth, I was already ancient. When it came, my dotage would come on fast. The genetic artistry of our own High College had stretched my vital years almost to breaking, and the signs of decline were already there. Still, I could expect health and strength at least a while longer, but Time—Ever-Fleeting—which had always seemed remote to me and open as the sea...oppressed me each day like a soaking blanket.

"Admiral Serpico telegraphed three months back," Prince Aldia said as I mounted the top stair. Velkan Serpico was admiral of the fleet that had sailed with Prince Kaim to the succor of the Imperium. "The Cielcin attacked Nessus. They burned the planet."

I stopped.

"You didn't know?"

Nessus was lost? I thought of the great city of Sananne, of the Magnarch's golden palace, and of the Magnarch himself. Miserable old Karol Venantian must surely have died in the intervening centuries, but I saw him clearly for a moment, in his official toga, standing upon a balcony in the vast shipyards as the horizon turned to flame. Most of all, I thought of Maddalo House. Of the English Garden and the fencing hall; of Valka's study and the old library; of round windows and round doors.

Burned.

"It *is* getting bad out there, Dom Hadrian." Aldia's float-chair processed along the colonnade beneath the tiled canopy. "Serpico tells me we lost nine hundred ships in the defense. The Cielcin brought *thirty-two* of their worldships to bear upon the planet. I am told the world was nearly torn apart."

"Thirty-two?" I shut my eyes, recalling then the tremors as the encircling Cielcin moons shook the planet Perfugium. The Cielcin had used the titanic mass of their vessels as weapons in themselves, tearing at the planet they besieged until the seas surged and the mountains cracked and fell.

At Perfugium, there had been only seven worldships.

"With Nessus gone, much of the telegraph network in your outer provinces is lost," Aldia said. "The fleets cannot coordinate across the Centaurine volume. Doubtless there have been other attacks—ones we won't hear of for many years yet."

I imagined desperate starships fleeing lost and burning systems, each carrying messages of doom. Syriani Dorayaica would have coordinated a number of strategic strikes with the primary assault on Nessus. The Eikana Fuelworks. The Legion troop stores on Verthandi. Food production on Innis, on Gododdin, and Nohr. As Aldia said, the news would come only slowly, trickling in as the stragglers from lost battles got word to the surviving Imperial fleet.

"What of the Emperor?" I asked.

"Perhaps you should read the letter," the prince said.

I flashed a look down at him, and bit back a retort. Though we were friends, I reminded myself that here was the Prince of Jadd.

Aldia smiled, and after a moment said, "Serpico tells me your Emperor is in hiding, directing the war effort from the provinces. They met... some years ago now... on Minnagara after the battle there. That was where our Olorin met and wed his princess."

"The wedding happened?" I blinked at him, astonished. Surely such a thing would have been news on Jadd? I ought to have seen the broadcasts, even in exile at the Fire School.

"Only contractually," Aldia said, acknowledging the salutes of his guards as he floated past. "The girl is en route to our holdings on Otranto. We've secured her bloodline, and she will be safe there, but the official announcement and the proper ceremony will wait until after the victory."

"The victory?" I halted. For a moment, the only sound was the distant laughter of the children at their play.

Aldia looked round at me, "Our Olorin will not return from the fighting until the fighting is done."

"But you talk of victory?"

"Is not victory our aim?" the prince inquired.

I had no answer for that. Peace had been my aim, once, a very long time ago. I had peace... on Jadd, and desired to keep it until Death and Time came—hand-in-hand—to carry me away. I turned to the rail, looked down into the tiled pool where the children of the Jaddian nobiles swam and splashed and fought with one another. Cassandra had been one of them, not so long before.

Peace.

As I watched, two boys leaped from the water to drag a third down with them, laughing. An older girl hurried to chastise them. At once I found myself remembering my own childhood, swimming in the pools of the Summer Palace at Haspida with Crispin while Mother's girls sunned themselves. The son of some lesser archon had been there with us. What had his name been?

"Do you wish you could go back?" I asked. I nodded at the children glad at their sport.

"And be a child again?" Aldia shook his head, ordered his float-chair to come to rest beside me. "No, *mi sadji*. Far better what I am: an old man, and High Prince of Jadd besides. A Prince of Jadd may stem the tide, if only a little... and for a little while. But what could a child do?" He looked up at me, eyes sparkling. "Do not mistake me! I wish I were young and strong, and wish my legs could still carry me... but a child? No."

"I only envy them." I crossed my arms, tucked my chin against my breast. "They know nothing of what's out there."

"And that's *better*, is it?" the prince inquired.

A laugh escaped me in the form of a single, solitary puff of air.

"Better that we be old men, Hadrian," said Prince Aldia, "so that they might remain children awhile longer." Almost I fancied that he was Tor Gibson, and that the pool we stood above was the ocean beneath the castle of my home. "Better that you be what you are."

"And what am I, Aldia?" I asked, dropping all titles, all formality.

"I would not presume to tell you," the great prince said, and gestured at the children in the water with one ringed and withered hand. "But ask any of them, and I do not think they'd hesitate."

Al Neroblis, they would say. *The Black Devil*. Or *Al Brutan*, the brute.

And one, perhaps, might look on me with wide eyes and whisper *Metamortali*.

Halfmortal.

I could sense Aldia knew the shape of the thoughts flickering behind my eyes, for he smiled and said, "*Shahmat*, Dom Hadrian." He adjusted the drape of his azure robes, and keyed an order into the arm of his silvered float-chair. It began to drift along the arcing colonnade, and I made to follow. But the prince was not quite finished with me, and aimed a question over his shoulder like one of the Parthian archers who were his remotest ancestors, and said, "What does your daughter think of all this?"

I drew up, letting him float away.

"Checkmate, indeed," I muttered.

CHAPTER 3

ANARYAN

I RETURNED TO THE *Islis di Albulkam* and the Fire School as the sun was setting. Hundreds of miles of celadon- and azure-damasked sea passed below like the carpets of the crystal palace of the moon, and the carnelian light of the giant sun filled all the sky as we circled the blasted cone of the Hephaistos.

Disembarking, I thanked the pilot officer and ascended the steps into Volcano House, where I stopped a neophyte and asked if the evening meal had already been served. He shook his head.

"Hydarnes's pupils are in the Court of Swans, *domi*," the boy said, glad to have a break from his task scrubbing the checkerboard tile.

"Has them doing the Tower Dance again, does he?"

The boy nodded. *"Si, domi."*

I thanked the lad and hurried on up the red-carpeted stair and along corridor after black-and-white-tiled corridor. A short elevator ride brought me to the upper hall, where racks of ancient swords and polearms hung darkly oiled on the wood-paneled walls. Already I could hear the clacking of wooden swords from the court outside, but I tarried as I often did in that high hall. Tall windows on my left looked down over the Grand Canal, and the hell light of magma glowed up at me even as the red light of day began to fade from the heavens above. The vaults of the ceiling half a hundred feet above were decorated with mandala designs of every color, resplendent in the best Jaddian tilework. The great pillars, too, were similarly tiled, and seemed to glitter like jewels—for indeed many of the tiles were jewels. Lapis and carnelian, malachite and jade, onyx and sardonyx and opals bright and pale as fire.

The great wooden doors stood open, and a pair of neophytes in white stood guard in the arch. One straightened as I approached. The other pretended—as he ought—that I was not even there.

Those double doors opened directly upon *Il Cortil di Bujatani,* the Court of Swans. It was a quadrangle wrapped in covered colonnades, with the side at my left open to the air and overlooking the canal. Often in the night, one might find one or two of the masters in prayer or contemplation, looking down on the magma or up at the fires of the numerous little agiary temples that dotted the mountainside. But the court drew its name not from the fire of the mountain, but from the deep pool dug in the center. Walled and bottomed with volcanic glass and thick with nenuphars whose white and lapis blooms shone in the black water like stars, the pool courted the great swans—black and white—so beloved of the Jaddian people.

There were none in it at that hour.

The presence of the neophytes and of Master Hydarnes had driven them all away.

The ringing of false swords filled the air, and the laughter and shouting of Jaddian voices.

As I made to circle toward the rail overlooking the canal, I heard a cry and a great splash. Between the two sounds had stretched a silence so profound that I did not think any of the two dozen men and women standing gathered at the narrow end of the pool had breathed during it.

A moment later, one black-haired head popped out of the water, disturbing the floating nenuphars and sending ripples black as space across the dark pool's surface.

Two other white-clad forms stood above the water, bare feet carefully planted upon the slim wooden posts that rose from the pool, both women. As I watched, one retreated, moving her foot carefully from one post to the next. The girl advancing on her took the pole the first girl had just vacated, false sword flashing in an overhead arc.

The young man who had fallen into the water swam and found the edge. Two of his brothers pulled him back onto the lip of the pool, and he leaned on his bamboo sword. I circled, placed myself in the shadow of a pillar with the lava at my back, and watched, a thin smile on my face.

I had not thought to find her in the heat of the moment, had expected to have to pick her out of the waiting ranks on the side of the pool.

Cassandra parried the other girl's sword, then leaped with delicate care to a higher pillar, forcing her opponent to follow. She teetered a moment on the narrow post, keeping her weight low, her arms thrust out. One foot rested on a metal spike protruding from her pillar a foot below its crown, and she caught an overhand cut with a neat parry-in-third before returning the blow toward the other's girl's head. The other girl parried, and braced herself on a second nearby column. She rallied, thrust at Cassandra's breast, but Cassandra swept the offending blade aside and—transitioning from a one- to a two-handed grip—delivered a sweeping blow that caught the other girl in the shoulder. But the other girl did not fall, retreating instead to the lower of her two footholds.

"Bad show, Parastu!" said tall, black-robed Master Hydarnes from the water's edge. "You dropped your guard too low. She's a high-hand, that one. You're lucky she didn't box your ears!" He raised a hand. "Farid! You're next!"

In the deeps of time, I heard Sir Felix bang his sword against the flag-stone floor and shout *Again!*

A young man in dripping whites leaped onto the shorter pillar near the water's edge and rushed up to join the fray. The towers were all of uneven height, but averaged perhaps ten feet above the surface of the water, save where those at the end nearest the House allowed the fencers to climb to that higher level, so that those upon the pillars might peer over the roof of the encircling colonnade to the sea.

This was the Tower Dance, and its object was footwork.

The boy Farid reached the top, and bounded toward the two women. I misliked the Jaddian practice of pitting boys and girls together, though I had battled women in the Colosso pits of Emesh. I winced as Farid struck at Parastu, and she fell, plummeting from her height to strike the water.

But Cassandra had seen him coming, and adjusted her footing in anticipation.

"Amuhia!" exclaimed Master Hydarnes, *"Alle!"*

Again!

Another girl bounded up the columns after Farid. "Farid!" she shouted, reaching the top. *"Mazi!"*

Together.

Hearing this, Cassandra checked her footing, braced herself against two of the metal spikes. Even had she not been atop the pillars when I entered, I would have known her instantly. Hers was the single marble face in that collection of cast bronzes. She had the Marlowe coloring—I had insisted on it. The same snow-white complexion, the same ink-dark hair. She wore it long in Jaddian fashion, in twin braids that began at her hairline and hung down at either shoulder. But she had her mother's high cheekbones, her cutting manner, her almond eyes.

She slashed Farid across the chest. The boy staggered back, but caught himself on a nearby post and did not fall. Seeing her advantage, my Cassandra thrust her blade at Farid's chest. He parried, recovered forward, keeping his one leg bent and weight low as he fended off a flurry of blows from my daughter.

My daughter.

Forty years she'd been by my side, and still it seemed like yesterday the Jaddian natalists had decanted her from the vat. She was no longer the little girl who had chased crabs on the beach and played in the pools of the Alcaz with the princes and princesses of Jadd, gone was the girl who had stolen lemon cakes from the cellar in the dead of night—much to the displeasure of poor Neema—and the young woman who had cried when Arman du Karaj told her that no Prince of Jadd could love a false Jaddian like herself.

In her place, there was a woman grown, tall and perilous, every inch her father's daughter—and her mother's, though neither woman would ever know it as I could.

My hand went to the pendant at my throat. It was a half a disc of polished silver, about two inches across. In its heart remained a sample of blood made crystal, preserved for all time.

Valka's blood.

At my urging, Prince Aldia had sent for his natalists—the best in all the galaxy, save perhaps for those who ministered to the Imperial family itself. They had worked their magic, extracting Valka's genome from that drop of crystal blood. Injecting it into the yolk of an empty egg. This they mingled with a dram of my own contributions, and for eighteen months I watched her grow suspended in clear fluid.

She was perfect in every way.

I only wished that Valka could have watched her grow with me.

I want a child, she'd said to me, in the dim light of the bunker. *Our child.*

Cassandra parried a strike from the girl called Amuhia and leaped from pillar to post, trying to separate her two opponents. Farid leaped after her, but the boy slipped and slammed into the black water, eliciting laughter and jeers from the students.

Hydarnes's clear voice rang out. "Leonato! Go!"

Again!

Another boy mounted the posts. My Cassandra locked blades with Amuhia, staggered as the other girl's slash bled through her parry. Still, she did not fall, but dropped her weight, one foot dangling in the open air as she fended off a flurry of short cuts. When I first met Olorin on Emesh long ago and saw him fight the Cielcin in Calagah, I had been struck by the spiderlike precision of his movements, the deliberate nature of his footwork. That deliberateness had been born here, in the Court of Swans.

Leonato—evidently picking up on Amuhia's suggestion to Farid that they work together—circled round, coming at Cassandra from the far side, so that the two of them in their dropping tunics might trap my daughter against the wall. Unknowingly, I took a couple steps out from the shadow of the colonnade. One of the nearer students waiting on the edge saw me and nudged his friend.

Up on the posts, Cassandra turned a thrust from Leonato to one side and rapped the boy across the knuckles. Leonato winced, and Amuhia slashed Cassandra in the thigh, but Cassandra parried just in time and returned the other girl a slash she barely caught against the strong of her blade. For a moment, my daughter fended off both her opponents, turning left and right in sequence, as though the three of them were clockwork figures moved by unseen gears. Then Cassandra leapt away, the boy hard on her heels.

She was running nearly straight toward me, and saw me standing there at the water's edge. That proved her undoing, for she faltered, swaying atop her pillar. Our eyes met, and I marked the surprise there.

"Get her!" Amuhia's voice cracked the evening air.

An instant later, Leonato barreled into Cassandra, wrapping arms about her to tackle her from the post. Both the boy and Cassandra lost their swords in that moment, and both plunged into the water.

She broke the surface an instant later, spraying water from her mouth. When Leonato surfaced an instant later, she wasted no time. Spouting an expletive in Jaddian, she boxed the other neophyte on the ear. "You cheated!" she said.

"No grappling, Leonato! You know the rules!" bellowed Master Hydarnes, coming forward. "Get out now and hold Karani's Chair until I release you!"

Leonato pulled himself out of the water and padded away toward the pillars, where he crouched as though sitting on a chair, arms thrust forward, palms out. Hydarnes was bound to leave the boy until he collapsed.

Cassandra swam toward where I stood at the water's edge, and I stooped to help her out. "You distracted me!" she said, and took the offered hand, permitting me to haul her up onto the stones.

"You did well!" I said, gripping her by the shoulder.

"I was the last to fall," she said, and only as she said it did I realize it was true. She had been dry fighting on the pillars.

"When did you go up?" I asked.

"I was fifth," she said.

There were twenty-seven in the class.

"Leonato was the last, and it was a low trick he took me with."

Master Hydarnes was dismissing his students to the showers. The red sun was nearly down—I could see the first stars of the Jaddian night peering through day's moth-eaten curtain to the east. Soon it would be *Aiwisruthrem*, the watch between sundown and midnight, and there would be dinner in the Volcano House refectory. Those journeymen whose day it was to cook were doubtless even then preparing grilled meats and flatbreads for the masters and the neophytes. I glanced over my shoulder, smiled at Leonato, whose legs had begun to shake by then from the effort of holding Karani's Chair.

"Abba, why are you here?" Cassandra was looking at me intently, green eyes narrow. "You never come to watch practice."

"I need an excuse now, do I?" I smiled, but felt my disquiet yawning wide deep in my chest.

What does your daughter think of all this?

I had told her nothing, of course. Nothing of the Emperor's letter, or my father's death, or of Lieutenant Albé's visit. I had hardly seen her since the young officer arrived, and had rebuffed her every question.

"Is this about the man from the Empire?" she asked. "Did the prince say something?"

I found my mouth had been hanging open, and promptly shut it. "It's nothing," I decided then and there.

Let it lie, whispered that tired voice within me. *Let it lie until the lieutenant and his ship depart.* Aldia had wanted me to talk to Cassandra, to see myself reflected in her face, as I might have seen it reflected in the faces of any of the children in the Alcaz. He had wanted me to see Hadrian Halfmortal once again, had said that I was free to go—had always been free, though a part of me remained on Jadd forever, in a crystal vial like the one contained in the phylactery about my throat.

But he didn't understand.

He believed I had forgotten the face in the mirror, forgotten the man I once had been. But I *remembered,* and that was precisely the problem. The man in the mirror was not Hadrian Halfmortal at all, but a walking shadow. I knew that if I was to see the Halfmortal, the Hero of Aptucca, the Demon in White, reflected in Cassandra's or any other face, it would destroy me.

Life is very long.

"Al Brutan!" I was saved the necessity of trying to answer Cassandra by the arrival of a tall, rapier-thin man with pointed beard and mustache. Hydarnes du Novarra had been a master of the Fire School since long before I arrived on the planet. He was a master of the First Circle, the highest honor the swordmasters could convey. In all the Principalities of Jadd—in all the galaxy—there were perhaps half a hundred men, and they were all men, who could claim that honor. He clapped me on the arm as he drew near and said, "How is our dear prince?"

I returned the gesture, doing my best to smile. "Immovable as ever."

Hydarnes's smile widened. "His is our most exalted bloodline. May he live to see one thousand."

"He may live another hundred years at the rate he's been going."

"Master, I wonder if I might borrow my daughter for the evening?" I said, looking to Cassandra, who had turned away to wring out her hair. Her eyes flashed at my words. "Assuming she has no other duties to attend to?"

Hydarnes raised and opened one hand, as though releasing a songbird to the airs. "Done!" He turned to his students, shouted an order for two to remain behind and mop the flagstones where the lot of them had dripped upon the margin of the pool. When he turned back, it was with an almost conspiratorial air. "When am I going to get you up there, my friend?" He pointed to the poles.

"You have the wrong creation, Hydarnes," I said in answer, almost laughing. "In the next universe, maybe." It was an old joke, comfortable and well-worn between us.

Hydarnes shook his head, but rather than answer he called to his straggling pupil, "Bend your knees, Leonato! Lower! Lower! Good!" He turned his attention back to me, a wicked smile on his satyr's face. "We'll see you tomorrow, perhaps?"

"Very likely," I said, and turning to Cassandra, asked, "Do you want to change first?"

We followed Hydarnes and his students at some distance, Cassandra with her bamboo sword over her shoulders like a yoke, me with my hands deep in the pockets of my gabardine coat. Somewhere in the gloam behind us, I heard a cry and a thud as Karani's Chair broke poor Leonato at last.

Cassandra smirked.

"You're sure you're all right, Abba?" she asked when we reached the grand stair to the entrance hall. "It's like you're trying not to talk." She stopped me at the top of the stair, allowing time for Hydarnes and the class to vanish through one of the left-hand doors.

I offered her a thin and crooked smile. She was so like her mother in that. Those emerald eyes saw right through me. "I'll tell you later, *Anaryan*."

CHAPTER 4

SYMPATHY FOR
THE DEVIL

IN THE END, I told Cassandra nothing that night. We left Volcano House and strolled down the mountain to the sea, where Neema was waiting. We spoke little of the lieutenant. I told Cassandra only that the Emperor had offered me a pardon, and when her eyes widened with delight I told her I had no interest in accepting it, crushing whatever dreams were in the dear girl of leaving Jadd and seeing the universe. I told her what the prince had told me, that the Jaddian navy had intervened to stop what they suspected were cannisters carrying the *lethovirus*.

Her eyes had stretched wide then, and I think she believed that it was this news that so disturbed me, for she ceased her questioning. I did not tell her my father was dead. Lord Alistair was nothing to her. A name. But rarely did I speak of him, or of my mother, or Crispin. Of my sister, the Lady Sabine, the sister I had never known, I must have spoken even less.

I had ceased to be a soldier of the Empire long ago, in an echoing hold aboard the *Tempest*. A single moment—a single blow—had erased centuries of service. A single blow, and a single sentence.

She was only Tavrosi.

She had been *everything* to me.

Certain ancient sophists would hold that we are each the masters and owners of ourselves, that we might thereby do anything—might even destroy ourselves—so long as that destruction came as an exercise of our own will. But like all sophistry, this sentiment is pyrite, and no true gold. Our lives are not in our bodies, but are distributed things, partly contained in us, partly in those persons and institutions which make up the landscape of our lives. Part of me had lived in my Red Company, and in the *Tamerlane*, my home, just as part of me—the greatest part—had lived in Valka.

So too a part of Valka had lived in me, and lived still.

In the long years of my exile, I had courted self-destruction many times, had looked down upon the flowing stone of the canal with longing, and dreamed of hurling myself from the parapet. Yet I knew that to do so would have been to destroy that piece of Valka that lived in me—which was among the best pieces of myself.

On this I often meditated in the bitter hours of the night, and stalked the halls of my villa and the shore like a ghost. I slept little in those days, desiring but ill-finding the waters of that older, sweeter Lethe. I sleep less now—and dream instead the waking dreams that have replaced it. When Cassandra returned to Volcano House, the three moons had risen high. I walked barefoot upon black sands, and watched the noctilucent algae bloom and shimmer like the stars along the water's edge. It seemed I walked in Faery, in Dream...or along the very rivers of Time.

Oft I imagined that I might encounter Valka again beneath the Jaddian stars, rising like Venus from the sea.

For the dead do speak to me, as they speak to all of us.

It takes a sophist to deny that it is so. Any child of the Alcaz du Badr—any child in the galaxy—knows I speak the truth.

"Do you know, my boy, that we live on a truly beautiful world?"

Tor Gibson walked beside me. His ghost—his memory, if you like—trudged along at my right hand, the hem of his robes soaking in the moon-tossed surf, though he held it in one spotted hand.

It was three days since my visit with the prince, since my dinner with Cassandra. Three days and nights spent with little sleep, three days of hard walking up the volcano's side or along the glowing margins of the sea. There is a madness that comes from lack of sleep, a madness and a pain. Perhaps that was why I saw Gibson's shade, or how I saw it. Or perhaps it was some faculty of my vision, some *other* memory or something...else. Yet he seemed so real to me, as present and solid as Neema had been when I set out for my midnight walk.

"It is beautiful, isn't it?" I said, stopping to look out to see. The *Noctiluca* drifted and shone blue and green as nebulae about our ankles, and the three moons—white and white and green—gleamed high and pink-tinged in the reflected light of Jadd's mighty sun.

"What are you afraid of, Hadrian?" the old scholiast asked.

"Afraid?" I did not turn to look at him, knowing that—were I to do so—he would vanish like the dew. "I'm not afraid, Gibson. I'm old."

"*Kwatz!*" The word fell like a slap, which was what the old Zen masters had made it for. "You are pretending your lieutenant never came here. Pretending there is no letter. Pretending nothing has changed."

"Nothing has changed!" I almost shouted, cognizant of how my voice would carry on the water, and sure that to any neophyte of the School out for a midnight stroll I would appear utterly alone. More softly then, I said, "The Cielcin. The Watchers. The Empire. None of it's changed."

Gibson's voice seemed to come from my left hand then, though his shade stood at my right. "It has gotten worse, as you well know. *That* is change. Most change is for the worse. All change increases entropy, even change for the good."

Entropy. The word called to mind the unkindling of the stars, that darkness at the end of time which I had seen—been shown—upon the mountaintop on Annica.

"It's inevitable," I said. "Even were I to stop the Cielcin—even if I could—something else would tear the Empire down."

"Yes," the scholiast replied. "And something will. But it is not for the Empire that you act. Nor is it for the Emperor."

"For all mankind, then?"

"For *him*."

I longed to turn my face, to see if the Gibson at my right hand were gray-eyed or green. The silence stretched. The surf tossed about us. The three moons peered lidless down.

"Why should your burden be light?" came the old, beloved voice at last. An old question. "You hoped to reconcile mankind with the Cielcin. You cannot. You know this. And you know what you *must* do. He showed you what must be."

"He did," I said, and saw again that other Hadrian, young and fey, his face twisted in the crooked smile I knew all too well.

Do what must be done, he'd said. *Fire at will.*

Light. I had seen that all-consuming light wash away the Cielcin tide, their worldships—great as moons—all washed away in that flood of fire. But it was a young man who had given the order, and I . . . "War is a young man's game, Gibson."

"*Kwatz!*" the word fell once more like a blow.

"Have I not suffered enough?"

"You will suffer more if you do not act," he said. "We are beasts of burden, we men. Have you forgotten it? The struggle?"

I almost laughed the words. "The struggle!"

"The struggle *alone* will fill that great emptiness within you, dear boy."

"The struggle," I began, "*made* that emptiness, Gibson."

"You are not afraid of what you have suffered, Hadrian," the shade said. "You are afraid of what you must do."

"Seek hardship, is that it?" I asked. "It was Brethren who said that to me. Were those the Quiet's words? Part of the message he left Brethren for me? Or were they the demon's own words?"

No answer.

I pressed, still not taking my eyes from the glowing sea. "What are you, Gibson? A spirit sent to torment me? Or just a dream?"

For a long time there was no answer. Then one spotted hand swung into the periphery of my vision, one crooked finger pointing toward the sky. "*She* will suffer," he said, "if you do not go."

"She's not part of this! You leave Cassandra alone!" I snarled, rounding on the shade, certain then that I would find the Quiet's green eyes peering at me out of Gibson's imagined face.

I found nothing instead.

I was alone. A madman standing in the gleaming surf, the waters rising with the swelling tide. Tight fisted I stood there a long and silent moment, listening to the waves. The steams from distant Hephaistos where its fires met the lagoon billowed and twisted on the night wind.

"Come back!" I yelled. "You leave her out of this! Do you hear? She's just a girl!"

Silence. Total and absolute.

I was alone.

Alone, I turned my back on the gleaming night sea and Jadd's three moons, and slouched my way back across that beach of black sand.

"My lord!" a shrill voice filled the air, rising to meet me. "Master! Master Hadrian!"

It was Neema. My Jaddian servitor had hurried out into the small garden with the orange trees that stood behind the villa, was standing on the edge of the retaining wall that verged upon the sea. I could see his narrow figure framed against the light of an arched and pointed window.

When he caught sight of me coming up the shoreline to the steps, he hurried toward me. "It's the girl!" he exclaimed, marching with his arms now stiff at either side. "She's come back."

"Demetra?" I asked. She wasn't due to return until the new week.

"Not Demetra! Your daughter!"

"Cassandra? But it's the middle of the night!"

"I caught her in the study," the butler said, falling into line beside me as I mounted the short stair to the garden path. The orange trees creaked in the sea breeze as we made for the door. "She is going through your papers!" I stopped short, and Neema hurried three or four paces past me before he realized I was no longer with him. "*Domi?*"

The crooked Marlowe smile asserted itself. "Of course she is."

"I tried to stop her, sir," Neema said, gesturing for the door. "But short of forcibly removing her from the premises, I didn't know what to do."

Brushing past the man, I quipped, "You couldn't forcibly remove her if you wanted to."

"I could so, sir! She's still just a girl!" Neema said; the Jaddian had a clinical distaste for women I always found amusing.

"That girl is nearly a Maeskolos, Neema. She'd take you apart if you tried."

The butler had no response to this, and followed in my wake. The house's static field prickled the hairs on my arms as I pressed through it and into the tiled recess in the back of the villa's rear parlor. The bar with its dark bottles neatly stored behind glass panels stood to my right hand, a holography well near at hand, surrounded by couches of tufted, wine-dark leather. A series of portraits done in my own hand hung upon the walls, alternating white-on-black, black-on white, and back again. There was Tor Gibson's face, and Pallino's, and Corvo's and Siran's.

The study was upstairs, at the top of the squat, four-story tower that dominated the rest of the long, low house. It was reached either by a steeply spiraling stair or by the lift it encircled.

"I came to find you directly, Master Hadrian. I don't know how long she's been up there, or what she thinks she's about!"

Neema had fallen several paces behind me by then.

"I do," I said, and keyed the lift door. The ironwork slid back into place before Neema could join me, forcing him to take the stairs. It was a cruel maneuver, but I wanted a moment to myself, wanted a moment with Cassandra before the good butler caught up to us.

She had come to find the Emperor's letter, would find Crispin's with it. There would be questions. So many questions.

She will suffer if you do not go.

Did I really think we could stay on Jadd forever? Did I really think *she* could?

I had been waiting to die, had been seeking that very self-destruction I wrote of not but a few leaves past. What I would not destroy with fire—casting my body into the magmas of the mountain—I had hoped to undo in time. But I had been a fool, and was even then only just beginning to see it. As part of Valka lived yet in me, so too a part of me was in Cassandra.

She was my daughter, after all, and the part of me that would live on the longest in the uncertain future. Were I to die on Jadd, by fire or by time, that part of me would live in her, and my burdens would become hers.

Why should your burden be light?

The iron grille slid away, admitting me to the vestibule that opened on my study.

The inner doors stood open, and a jeweled light shone from within.

The chamber had—in the initial conception of the villa as a research station—been an astral observatory. The telescope and its steel dome were long gone. The place had been entirely transformed long ago, had served as a residence for the princes of Jadd when they sought retreat and contemplation. Where once the leaved dome of the observatory had been, a dome of stained glass now stood. So like the Dome of Bright Carvings it was, its minute tiles fashioned in kaleidoscopic panoply, its colored shadows rich and textured fell by day upon the thickly carpeted floor. The chamber was round, and perhaps a hundred feet in diameter, with bookcases lining the walls between the high windows and two doors that—opposing one another—opened onto the encircling balcony. My suit of armor stood between two windows, its shoulders wrapped not in the Imperial white I had worn for most of my life, but in a lacerna black above and red beneath.

She was sitting in my chair, and started as the elevator's grille rolled back and I stormed in. Knowing she'd been caught with her hand in the trap, she stood, and rather than accept my wrath, she struck first. "Why didn't you tell me grandfather was dead?"

There was a holography disc open on the petrified wood of the desk. A wafer of crystal paper perhaps three inches across and inlaid with the necessary circuitry in hair-fine gold wire. The ghostly image of a man stood above it, a cubit or so in height. Cassandra must have halted the playback, or else it had reached its natural end, and the figure hung as if frozen in time.

I opened my mouth to shout at her, to drive her from the room she should never have been in, but the portrait above my desk caught my eye and checked my tongue.

Rage is blindness, came the old voice I always imagined was Gibson's from deep within. Steadily I tried again to speak. "I didn't know how to tell you."

"Have you even seen this?" she asked, shoving the holography disc toward me. "The envelope was still sealed. I guess the lieutenant must have told you?"

"He did."

When she pressed the holograph toward me, the figure it projected rotated, and I saw a man broad-shouldered, barrel-chested, dressed in the muscled cuirass and armor of a knight of the realm. I was slow to recognize him. The square jaw and short, black hair. The hard eyes. There was none of the old mocking laughter in them, none of the slack-jawed gormlessness that had so repulsed me as a boy.

There was gray in the black of his hair, gray at the sides where he kept it shorn within microns of his scalp. A great, ugly scar wound across the underside of his jaw, stretching almost from ear to ear.

I had never seen the man Crispin had become before that moment.

There was a hardness in him and a virtue I had not thought to find. Even in frozen image he seemed to bear his grief nobly. His back was straight. His eyes were clear. His hands were clasped before him, and his head was bowed.

"That's my brother," I said, foolishly, feeling a sudden pang of loss deep in my secret heart, the opening of a wound I'd scarcely known I'd carried. I touched my eyes lest Cassandra see my welling tears.

"What's a Monumental?"

The question slashed across my grief. "What?"

She held up an unfolded sheaf of white vellum. Its text shone red as blood in the lamplight. It was the vermillion of the scholiasts, and the twin fractal seals stamped at the bottom showed the Imperial sunburst beside the same, smaller sunburst in the grip of a human hand. The former was the Emperor's own seal, the latter—I guessed—was the mark of HAPSIS.

Even at ten paces, I knew the signature—the only part of the letter written in black—knew the cramped and spidery handwriting, so unlike the man.

William - 23

There were no titles, no enumerated honors—that was proof the scrawl had been set to the parchment by the man himself.

I saw no crystal chit, no holograph.

Only the letter.

Handwritten, the letter had the virtue of absolute secrecy. Doubtless it had been written by one of the Emperor's own scribes. That scholiast had placed the letter into the hands of an Imperial courier, an apostol—possibly Lieutenant Albé himself. A simple letter was proof against praxis, against interception on the datanet, against the implants of sorcerers and demoniacs.

How could I possibly explain? Cassandra knew but little of my story.

"A weapon," I said, sure the villa was bugged by Aldia's Yahmazi, whatever his assurances to the contrary. "A Cielcin weapon."

"Don't lie to me, Abba," Cassandra said, brandishing the letter. "The Emperor says he wants you to *slay* it. You don't slay a weapon. What is it?"

I was still fast then, fast enough to snatch the vellum from her grasp, and taking it turned swiftly from her and the portrait above and behind her to read it with some measure of peace.

To the Lord Hadrian Anaxander Marlowe,

Much has passed since our last meeting. You will know, we are certain, that Nessus is lost, and with it our hold on the outer provinces. Our Jaddian allies have enabled us to hold the line, but we are losing ground. The loss of the provincial datanet has limited our ability to coordinate our defense. With the relays lost, we can only telegraph via direct lines, and we have too few of those to manage a defense across the greater galactic volume—and then there is the matter of the Extrasolarian plague to consider...

Most of your life, you were our faithful servant. We have no expectation that you so remain.

But we are in need.

On Carteia, we spoke of the grave threat the Monumentals pose our Empire. At the time, you swore your sword and faculty in the cause of their destruction.

We have found one, and beg you to help us. The Monumental must be slain, lest it fall into the hands of the enemy. The information our servants will relay to you was taken from the Cielcin at Asara, and so we have reason to believe the enemy is aware of the beast's location.

There is very little time.

Your crimes are forgiven. They are nothing. We have commanded that a copy of your pardon be enclosed with this message.

Hadrian, you must be careful. There are those among my servants who count themselves your enemy. This you have always known. But we have in recent years uncovered many spies in our court. Demoniacs all. Trust no one. If you will aid us, speak to Director Oberlin. He has come himself, but will have sent one of his subordinates for you.

Pray destroy this letter.

May the Hidden One protect you.

I read the letter perhaps a dozen times, each time with greater speed.

"My lord, you might have waited for me!" Neema had appeared in the doorway, huffing from the effort of using the stairs.

I raised a hand to silence him. I read the letter one final time. "Oberlin," I said, looking round at Cassandra. "There was a Friedrich Oberlin in Legion Intelligence." The words meant nothing to the girl. She had risen from my chair as I read the letter, but simply stood there with her head cocked to one side. Oberlin was *Director* now? Of Legion Intelligence? No, that had been Sir Gray Rinehart. Of HAPSIS?

It had been Oberlin who revealed that it had been Sir Lorcan Breathnach behind Lieutenant Casdon and the knife-missile that had nearly claimed Valka's life. Had he truly come? Was he Lieutenant Albé's master?

The part about spies in the Imperial court troubled me more than the rest together. *Demoniacs all*, the Emperor had said. That meant Extrasolarians. That meant MINOS, surely. The sorcerers had infiltrated the Grand Conclave of the Commonwealth. Surely they must have infiltrated the Imperial Court. Legion Intelligence. Special Security. The Chantry. The scholiasts.

Trust no one.

"We have to help, Abba!" Cassandra said. "You read the letter! The Emperor himself! Is that really his signature?"

I could only nod.

"We must do *something!*" Cassandra said.

In response, I crushed the Emperor's letter in my hands, tossed the refuse to Neema. "Burn that," I said sharply, pointing. "Neema, at once."

"But *domi*, the girl!"

"I will punish my daughter in my own way, Neema! Thank you! *Alle!*"
I pointed to the lift.

The servitor bowed and shuffled from the room.

"You shouldn't be so harsh to him!" Cassandra said when the lift rattled
shut and was gone.

"And you should not presume to lecture me," I said, eyes raking over
the girl and the projection of my brother glimmering above the desk. It
was too much. Too fast. My eyes settled on the portrait above and behind
my desk. *Valka...* I closed my eyes. *Would that you were here...*

The portrait was still there when I opened them. So was Crispin's
ghost. So was Cassandra. "What possessed you to come in here?" I asked
my daughter.

She angled her chin, defiant. "You told me the Emperor gave you a
pardon. I wanted to see it. I wanted to see *why.*"

"Why?"

"I'm not a fool, Abba!" she said. "I know how bad it is out there! The
war!"

"You really have no idea," I countered, casting my gaze up at the jeweled dome overhead.

"I know you were a hero!" Cassandra said, words striking me as forcefully as Gibson's *kwatz*. "I know the Emperor needs you. If you can turn
the tide, you must! Don't you have a responsibility?"

Once more the tears welled up. Once more I shut my eyes. "A responsibility," I echoed the sentiment. Had Gibson's shade spoken truth? Was I
really hiding on Jadd from what I knew I must do? "Your mother would
be so proud of you, Anaryan."

Am I a coward?

"What's a Monumental?" Cassandra asked, not knowing what else to say.

I tried to meet the gaze of the woman in the portrait, but I had drawn
her looking down. "You have a lot to learn," I said.

"Then teach me!" She rounded the desk, stood before me with feet
apart. "Master Hydarnes says I'm ready to take the Trial of the Heart!"

I felt my eyes grow hard. "Cassandra, no!" I said. The Trial was what
made a Maeskolos. Neophytes trained for decades before making an attempt,
and while Cassandra had been a neophyte for nearly thirty years, still it
felt too soon.

"I'm not a little girl, Abba," she said. "Master Hydarnes says he has no
more to teach me. That *you* should teach me instead. He says I'm ready.
I *am* ready, Abba!"

Valka was looking down on me from the portrait, smiling after her
fashion. She was looking down at a child with twin braids who smiled

back at her, a girl in a long Jaddian tunic. There were flowers in her hair, and Valka stooped to place one there as she never had in life. Little Cassandra was laughing, looking up into the face of the mother she had never known. I stood behind them both, a shadow in black charcoal, the only one of us three peering out of the image.

We held each other's gaze a moment. Art and artist.

Only the artist blinked, and when he did, it was to blink away fresh-forming tears.

How I envied that charcoal man.

"Maybe you are," I said, wishing I'd never drawn the damn portrait in the first place.

"The Emperor's letter said you should speak to this...Oberlin," Cassandra said. "It said he was here. On Jadd. The lieutenant must be able to put us in contact!"

"He wants us to go offworld," I said, and brushed past her to stand before my brother's ghost.

"Offworld?"

I didn't answer her.

Crispin hadn't moved. His image floated above my desk, transparent as a reflection in darkened window glass. Before Cassandra could speak again, I tapped the node to cycle the paused recording.

Crispin vanished, was replaced by the tri-D security fractal that demonstrated the authenticity of his seal. The Marlowe Devil emerged, red on black, and silver trumpets played the half-forgotten anthem that heralded the coming of the Lord of Devil's Rest.

Crispin appeared, arms crossed, head bowed.

He did not speak for a moment, then began. "I...wasn't going to send this message." His voice was deep and dark as his armor. "I didn't send one when Mother died because *you* should have, but you should know our father is dead. He passed a week ago, on the ninth of Anthesterion. You should know he didn't suffer. The Red Sleep has come to Delos, but...he never caught it. It was Time that did for him.

"He was planning to leave next month, to sail to Caria to be with Sabine—he always liked her best. He made her Countess of Caria—did you know? Did you know he bought a County in the Outer Perseus? He did it, Hadrian. He made himself a lord. A proper lord. He's left Devil's Rest to me, and what's left of the prefecture—for what little it's worth. The High College won't grant me an heir." He almost smiled, and said, "House Marlowe dies on Delos with me."

My breath caught.

"My wife—her name's Gianna—believes it's because of you. Thinks the Emperor wants to keep the number of us mad Marlowes down. Me, I think

Aunt Amalia just wants the mining rights..." Crispin trailed off, let his arms fall to his side a moment before recrossing them. "I know she helped you escape. Our mother. Captain Kyra told me. I never told Father, but I wanted you to know. I hope it was worth it. The stories they tell about you...I don't know what to think. But I saw your triumph. The Emperor had the broadcast sent across the Empire. Father wouldn't watch it, but I did."

"You've seen all this?" I asked Cassandra.

She shook her head, took me by the arm when I would not take her hand. "I stopped after he said he'd be the last."

Crispin was not finished. "You should have played your part, like me. Like Sabine. We *were* your family, Hadrian. Did you even know Mother had died? Did you even care? After what she did for you! What she risked!"

"Crispin!" a woman's voice drifted across the recording, its owner just out of frame.

Crispin raised a hand for silence, shook his head. "Don't feel compelled to respond. They say you're on Jadd. That you tried to kill the Emperor. I hope it isn't true." He seemed to chew his tongue a moment then, and glowered into the camera. "I don't ever want to see you again, Hadrian. Do not message us. Do not come home." He was silent then a long moment before saying his final words. "We're done."

The image vanished, replaced once more by the Marlowe Devil and the music of trumpets. So bright and gay was that music, measured against the gravity of my brother's words.

I felt...I wasn't sure what I felt. An emptiness seemed to stretch over me and through me, as though some airlock had long ago opened in my soul. It was only that I was just noticing it. There had been no shock of decompression, no howling of psychic winds. All was hollow then.

Life is very long.

I had not known my brother in centuries. It may seem strange to you, dear Reader, who has not perhaps the luxury of so long a life, that my brother should retain so great a hold on me after so long—and yet it is so. But the impact of childhood, I have found, does not diminish. Not after a hundred years, not after five.

"I'm sorry, Abba," Cassandra said, still clinging to my arm. "I shouldn't have looked."

"It's all right," I said, sparing a glance for Valka in the sketched family portrait above my desk. "How could any daughter of mine not look where she's told not to? I'd have done the same thing at your age." I'd have done the same thing at my age, though I did not say as much.

Slowly, I extricated myself from her embrace and moved to one of the side doors. "Abba?" Her words followed me, and she turned to follow herself. "What are you going to do?"

I opened the balcony door and—passing through the static field—stepped out to overlook the sea. Presently she came and stood beside me, and together we looked out at the three moons and the dark surf with its fringes gleaming blue-white as highmatter in the night, rippling as the tide rolled in. "You're right," I told her, turning to try and smile. "We must do *something*." I gripped the rail with both hands, feeling the true bones in my right hand creak as I tightened that grip. The hollow bones of my left hand offered no complaint.

She will suffer... if you do not go.

"We *have* to help. That's what you said," I said, looking at her. "The Emperor needs me."

The Quiet needs me.

"You're serious?" Cassandra's eyes were like green fire. "We're going?"

"I'll call the lieutenant in the morning," I said. The truth was, I had no choice. If what Aldia said was true, and the Empire was threatening to withdraw its support of Jaddian shipbuilding efforts, they would have no choice but to hand me over. The Empire had need of the Jaddian navy—and of Jadd's clone armies most especially—but so much more did Jadd require Imperial gold. And more than gold. Uranium. Ytterbium. Adamant. Antihydrogen. Antilithium.

Jadd needed the Empire as much as the Empire needed Jadd.

And the Empire needed Hadrian Marlowe.

The *Emperor* needed me.

"Abba." My daughter's voice was at once very small. "What of the Trial?"

I looked her, shaken from my thoughts of geopolitics.

The Trial of the Heart.

"You're sure you're ready?"

Cassandra answered, "Hydarnes thinks I can do it. And if we're to leave..." She trailed off, a terrible thought forming behind her eyes. "Unless... I'm not coming with you?"

The way her brows arched brought pain. The thought of leaving her had occurred to me, but Valka's shade seemed to hover between us, to glare down at me from the portrait sketched up upon the wall. "Your mother would have killed me had I tried to leave her behind," I said. "I won't leave you, either."

The girl brightened, but my own heart sank. "Do you know what the Trial is?"

She shook her head. "No one does. The masters don't talk about it."

"You don't have to take it," I said.

"I *want* to take it!" she said, and thrust out her chin.

"But Anaryan," I said, "the students who fail... they don't come back."

"They *die,* you mean," Cassandra said. "Abba, I won't fail."

"You *can't* fail," I said. "I can't lose you."

"You won't!" she said. "I'll only fail if you don't let me try. If I leave here anything less than a Maeskolos, Abba—"

"I know!" I said.

"Hydarnes believes I can do it," she said. Voice suddenly very small as she asked, "Don't you?"

What could I say to that?

"All right," I said. I could not stop her. The decision to take the Trial could be hers alone, and if Hydarnes had approved her to take it...no power on Jadd could stop her.

"Abba." Her fingers found mine, squeezed. "I won't fail."

I lay my other hand over hers. "I know...I..."

Cassandra grew closer. "I wish I knew what to say. About Uncle Crispin. About Grandfather."

"You don't have to say anything," I said. There wasn't anything to say. We stood there together a long while, neither one of us moving. Silently, I wrapped an arm around her slim shoulders.

The only family I had left.

At length I opened my mouth in search of words, and found them. Looking down on the *Noctiluca* and the moonlight rippling on the black-jade sea, I said, "Do you know, Anaryan, that we live on a truly beautiful world?"

CHAPTER 5

TRIAL OF THE HEART

I WAS NOT PERMITTED to witness Cassandra's trial. The rites and sacred mysteries of the Maeskoloi were precisely that: mysterious. Only those embraced by the order know what the Trial of the Heart entails, and those embraced swear a sacred vow—to Ahura Mazda, to their masters, on their very lives—never to reveal the nature of their sacred mystery.

And so what transpired for Cassandra the week before we were set to depart from Jadd I cannot say. She never told me, and I did not ask. For am I not myself an initiate? The acolyte of a tradition far stranger and more secret than anything practiced on Jadd?

But I know why they call it the Trial of the Heart, or a piece of that *why*, at least.

Whatever challenges Cassandra faced when she climbed the mountain that damp and steaming morning, I cannot say, but my own heart went with her, followed her up the Scala Aspara to the Atash Behram Jaddi, the Temple of the Eternal Fire set at the highest terrace man had carved upon the mountain, nearest the caldera.

My heart had leaped first to my mouth in its quest to hurry after my daughter.

"You know she may not return," said Master Hydarnes du Novarra, when he had visited me in the villa the night before. Cassandra had gone to keep vigil in the agiary at Volcano House. Neophytes were required not to sleep the night before the Trial, to stay awake in prayer and fasting through the darkness until the coming of the sun that marked the watch called *Hawan*.

"I know," I said in reply. The bottle by my hand was nearly empty. That hand had ceased to shake.

"Most neophytes do not make the attempt until they are one hundred standard years of age."

"She said you told her she was ready," I said. I had always believed that century of training a necessary requirement, but life at the Fire School had disabused me of that and many other misconceptions. A neophyte might climb the mountain as early as his second day at the Fire School—though it was said only three had ever done so, and two of them had died. It was only that most learned first the humility and patience the Trial demanded.

Hydarnes had smiled then, his satyr's countenance recalling the face of Prince Kaim, of Olorin, my friend and sponsor. "She *is* ready," he said. "She has no choice but to be. You depart in days."

"*Si*," I said, and remembering myself adopted the more formal style. "*Ari*."

"I understand the Sollans have claimed you at last," said he. "That you do not go by choice." In answer, I only recharged my glass. "You are loved by the God, I think," Hydarnes said. "Those the God loves most he tests the most dearly, as gold in fire, to learn if they are true."

"Don't speak to me of your god, Swordmaster," I said, a bit too sharply. "He may take my daughter from me in the morning."

"The God takes nothing." Hydarnes shook his head at that—might have filled the moment with a swallow of wine, had I offered him any—and said, "Cassandra will come down the mountain tomorrow night. You will see."

"And if she doesn't?" I asked.

"Then you will have had nigh forty good years with her," the master said. "It is more than I had with my Mardun."

I blinked at him. "You had a son?"

"Just one," the master said. "My wife ill-named him. *Marduniya* is *mild* in the old tongue. Gentle. He took the Trial, as I did, and far before he was ready..." The swordmaster had grown quiet then, smoothed the folds in his snow-white *mandyas*. "He wished to be the youngest to reach the Ninth Circle."

"I'm sorry," I said.

"Do not be," he said, standing, "this night of all nights." The master lay a hand on my shoulder. I hardly felt it through the wine. "There comes a time when we must let them go, *Al Brutan*. A time to let them fly...or fall."

I looked up into Master Hydarnes's pointed face. There was a shadow there, the pale reflection of the boy who had climbed up the mountain and not returned. "What is this Trial?" I asked, knowing I would get no answer. "Tell me that."

Hydarnes only patted me on the shoulder. "She has wings, your girl-child," was the only answer he gave. "Trust in her."

I did not sleep, but sat in my study until the sun bruised the curtain of night, all the while watching the lights of the cities gleaming on Jadd's three moons, watching the algae dance on the night waves. I hardly saw them. I saw instead the white megaliths that formed the walls of the fire temple, the flame eternal—Atash itself—dancing in its brazier, my girl standing at the edge of the circle of firelight, white bandages wound about her arms, her palms, the base of her fingers.

When the sun rose and the prayer call signaled the start of *Hawan*, I emerged onto the balcony outside my tower study. I watched her go, eyes shining, one hand shielding them from the sun.

A lone figure in white, her black hair bound in double braids, mounted the *Scala* for the Grand Agiary that stood high above Volcano House on the slopes of the Hephaistos, which the *mobads* of Ahura Mazda called the *Kauf Adar*.

"There comes a time..." I muttered, not certain this was it. "Valka, forgive me."

Had Valka been there, she would have swatted me.

She's not a child, Hadrian, whispered her shade in my ear. *You can't protect her forever.*

"I couldn't protect you."

"Sir?" A polished voice intruded. "Are you quite all right?"

I looked round, found Neema standing in the door of my office, prim as ever.

Turning from him, I looked back to the Fire School, its white towers and cupolas glimmering in the morning sun. "She'll have reached the Temple by now," I said to the smaller man. I had lost sight of her near the spot where the towers of the dead rose silent above the upper terraces, topless drums left open to the sky. The Jaddians did not bury their dead, or burn them, but left them to the birds after the manner of their Persian forebears.

It was said that those who failed the Trial were not laid in those towers. They went to Atash, to the fire itself. To give a corpse to the flame was a terrible sacrilege...but to die by fire?

There was no death more pure.

"I'm sure she'll be all right, sir," Neema said. "The girl is a terror, but...for this sort of thing, one ought to be." When I did not reply, the Nemrutti servant ventured, "You did not take breakfast, master. Shall I fetch you something?"

"How can I eat?"

It was easy to see how our ancientmost ancestors believed it was the suns that moved about their planets, and not the other way around. Like a glead of molten lead, the red sun of Jadd ran, rolling first up, then down the bowl of the sky. The wind tasted of salt and smoke—as it always did on that island of black and green. Flame redder than the very sun flowed down the canal from the *Kauf Adar* through the Fire School to the sea. The ever-present mists blew up from the lagoon's waters, white as spirits.

Green grasses swayed, tall as men in places, in others shorn flat as the finest carpet.

The very world seemed to itch, to squirm with expectation.

There was nothing still, nothing... save myself.

I had become the very center of the world, my tower the axis mundi about which the whole of creation turned. And Cassandra had become one of the unfixed stars.

But was she rising? Or setting?

A figure would come down those steps.

A lone figure in white or black.

If it were black, it would be Cassandra returning, garbed in the raiment of the swordmasters—in the sable of her house—having divested herself of her student's whites.

If it were white, it would be only one of the *mobads* of that God of Fire, come to proclaim that my child was dead.

My child.

Cassandra, you cannot know how much I love you still, how much I have always loved you, from the day the natalists pulled you from the tank and cut your cord and put you into my hands... and from before, from the day they first brought me to the hospital to see your little face, half formed behind the glass.

I loved your mother, but our love was a thing slow forged, built year by year, day by day. You I loved at once, and loved completely. Would that you had had some better father, some better man than I. I who brought you into a kind of prison—however gilded—who forced you into a life of war.

Wherever you are, forgive me.

I would have spared you every pain.

Still I think upon your little hands, as they first grasped my fingers, and recall the bleary way you looked up at me, confused, disturbed to have been wakened from your dreaming sleep by the world waiting to receive you. That so wonderful a thing might come from my sorry cells... that is a miracle greater than anything I have seen. Greater than the power to defy the Watchers, greater than the power to defy Death... That my love for your mother might breathe new life into our dying universe...

...that is a mighty thing.

And on that day, that life hung by the slenderest thread above a lake of fire. I did not dare abandon my post, but fretted back and forth—pacing, always pacing, waiting for an answer to the question I dared not ask. I kept thinking of Pandora's cat—of a world filling with darkness.

Filling again.

Living or dead?

Dead? Or living?

White...or black?

The prayer calls signaled the end of Hawan, the start of Rapithwin—afternoon.

Rapithwin ended, Uziran began.

The sun went down in fire, its reds growing redder still.

A figure emerged from the doors of the Atash Behram Jaddi, the Temple of the Eternal Fire. Seeing it, I turned to my doors and ran, bypassing the lift in my haste, half falling down the winding steps. Neema's voice carried after me, but I did not stop for him. I left the old house entire, and pelted up the lawn to Volcano House, and through Volcano House to the White Stair.

We met in the shadow of the funerary towers.

Two figures in black.

One wore the long coat of a military man, his dark hair streaked with white.

The other wore the *mandyas* of a Swordmaster of the Fire School over her black tunic, red and gold.

Both wore the same lopsided smile that broke into open laughter, and rushing to take my girl child in my arms—a woman grown—I lifted her into the light of the red and setting sun, and crushing her to myself I said, "You did it! *Anaryan*, you did it!"

"Abba!" Cassandra gasped, having regained her feet. "Are you surprised?"

I looked at her. She stank of smoke. Of brimstone. Black ash colored her face, and there was blood on her hands. Her cheeks. "You're hurt," I said. "Burned? Did you go *into* the mountain?"

Her feet were bleeding. Blistered. Black.

How had she come so far, and under her own power? Her hair was singed, her body soaked with sweat. It was said that a tunnel in the Grand Agiary followed the lava flow down into the caldera itself. In my mind, I saw my daughter treading there, bare feet on burning sand.

"What did they do to you?"

She shook her head. "It doesn't matter," she said. "Abba! It's done! I did it."

Her smile—brighter than the setting sun—faltered as she looked up at me. Then she collapsed in my arms.

CHAPTER 6

THE MORNING STAR

MY COPY OF THE Emperor's pardon lay hidden in my breast pocket like a leaden weight, but I smiled as I led the way into the hangar where my ship awaited. The Katanes starport in Jaharrad was among the largest I had ever seen. The hangar Aldia's men had set aside for my ship lay on its very fringes. Not a cothon, not a blast pit designed for vertical takeoff, but a longhouse with rolling doors and an arched ceiling like half a cylinder a thousand feet from end to end. It lay in the military quarter, behind fences and security posts, at the edge of the airfield, where the city gave way to the savannas and leagues of farmland that fed the Jaddian capital.

"This is your ship?" Cassandra asked, not two paces behind. The girl had spent two days in a medical tank after her ordeal, and already her wounds had vanished, though she carried herself with a new dignity, a cock-footed surety that she was and had become what she had spent her life trying to be: a Maeskolos.

A Swordmaster of Jadd.

"She is," I said, and the sight of the old girl banished for a time at least my sadness and the bone-deep tiredness of my age.

The *Ascalon* stood in the center of the hangar, vapors rising from fuel and coolant lines. A small army of Jaddian technicians clamored over her, men and women in white-and-orange striped coveralls. We stopped then for a moment, both to admire the vessel and to allow Neema to catch up. The servitor led a quartet of stevedores carting a pair of float-palettes, upon which were mounded the crates which contained the accrued detritus of our lives.

Seen from above, the *Ascalon* resembled a leaf-bladed sword, five hundred feet from end to end, broad and flat—being only four decks high at its tallest, and that was near the rear, above the great hold. Short wings thrust out near her stern, each sporting one of the vessel's twin fusion engines, sleek black nacelles. The slit of her warp projectors already gleamed, a blue line that wrapped about her stern.

"How fast does she go?" Cassandra asked.

"Nearly twelve hundred C, given her head," I said. "She's an interceptor, *Challis* class. One of Red Star's finest. See the way the hull rolls over top like that? That's not for nothing! She's nigh invisible to radar. And see those coils on the nacelles?" I pointed. "Heat sinks. There's nowhere to hide in space. Trying's like trying to hide a fire priest on the slopes of the Hephaistos where nothing grows. Those coils drink the heat of her engines, allowing her to hide in the dark for days at a time..." I fell almost to silence, admiring the graceful geometries of the old ship, like a black knife spoiling to be thrown. "We used her to save the Emperor, your mother and I. And to escape the Prophet, when we were its prisoners."

In truth, only I had been Dorayaica's prisoner, but it was easier this way. It was a story I was in no great hurry to recount.

"She's beautiful!" Cassandra said. She had never been aboard a proper starship, had only traveled on suborbital flights between Jaharrad and the *Islis di Albulkam*. I tried to remember what it had been like—leaving Delos that first time with Demetri Arello and his crew. The terror and the joy. Seeing the joy at least upon my daughter's face kindled a portion of the old feeling in myself, where I had thought it dead.

"I'll take these straight aboard then, my lord? Shall I?" Neema asked.

"Very good, Neema," I said, "Our quarters—my quarters—are far forward. The level above the hold. You and Cassandra may take the adjoining rooms. The flight crew shouldn't stop you."

"Can we meet this lieutenant of yours?" Cassandra asked, looking round the vast hangar bay with its swarming technicians and the fuel lines snaking over the fused stone floor. "Is he here?"

Looking around myself, I said, "He should be about."

Neema was fussing with one of the stevedores, bickering in Jaddian about the location of our rooms. I did not intervene, but when Neema seemed to resolve the dispute, I leaned in close and said, "You did not have to come with us, my friend."

The butler blinked at me. "Where else would I go, sir? I should think they'd have words for me back at the academy were I to abandon a client simply for leaving the planet."

I smiled at the man, sparing a glance over his shoulder for the trio of black-clad Imperial officers emerging from the side ramp near the *Ascalon*'s prow. I marked Lieutenant Albé at once, with his ivory-rimmed spectacles.

Neema was one of the *angrafiq*, a Jaddian homunculus. All his school was made—bred—to be the finest maids and manservants in the Principalities. Freed of the genetic confines of the Chantry—though there were those in Jadd who worshipped Mother Earth in their way—and of the Emperor's High College, the Jaddians had made an art of the genetic science, an art reflected not only in the superhuman perfection of the *eali* caste, but in the many and varied forms taken by the *angrafiq*: from the mamluk clone armies; to the hulking laborers I had seen hauling equipment in the starport, large as any Cielcin; to Neema himself.

"You're a good man, Neema," I said, and patted him on the shoulder.

The manservant gave a studious little bow and withdrew.

"Lord Marlowe!" Lieutenant Albé called out, hand raised in greeting. He looked precisely as he had that day nearly two weeks before when he had come to the villa, his officer's blacks unmarked and immaculate, his hair freshly shorn and oiled. Knowing him now for a Delian, a Meiduan like myself, I marked his hairless face, without barest suggestion of blue in his cheeks.

Evidently some of the old fashions and customs persisted. And why should they not?

"Lieutenant Albé!" I said in greeting, turning squarely to face the man and his companions. "We're still pretending it's *lieutenant*, are we?"

The fellow only smiled, gestured to his companions, a man and a woman in matching blacks. The woman wore the old burgundy naval beret. "These are Lieutenant Janashia"—he indicated the man—"and Pilot Officer Browning." The woman. "We'll be conveying you to the *Troglita*."

That was the Imperial warship, the HAPSIS vessel the Emperor had earmarked for his little expedition. I found myself studying young Janashia and Browning, recalling the words of the Emperor's letter.

Demoniacs all.

Trust no one.

Had William grown paranoid in his old age? I wondered.

Janashia and Browning both saluted.

I returned the gesture only haltingly, feeling myself a fraud. The coat I wore was cut in Imperial fashion, but its cloth was Jaddian, as fine as any prince's. Like the *lieutenant*, I had no device or badge of rank, for I had—until the occasion of the Emperor's thrice-damned pardon—been made outcaste a second time.

"An honor, soldiers," I said stiffly. "*Lieutenant* Albé, my daughter. Cassandra."

Had it been my imagination? Or had the young lieutenant already been looking at Cassandra? The light flashed across the lenses of his spectacles as he turned to attend to me. Swiftly, he removed them, and smiling took Cassandra's hand. She had offered it as one Maeskolos might offer a hand to another. The left hand extended, thumb up. Perhaps it was because it was the left hand, or perhaps young Albé was as unfamiliar with the custom of handshaking as I had been as a boy. It was not done on Delos, except amongst the meanest serfs.

But he did not shake her hand.

"Lady Marlowe!" he said, and—turning her hand palm down—lifted it to his lips and kissed it. *"Enchanté."*

A welter of emotions manifested in me then. Confusion at the unfamiliar word. Anger at the young officer's forwardness. Contempt for the man himself. Who did he think he was? He said his family had served mine for five of their generations after I had left, that Crispin had asked him to carry his accursed message across the long light-years in the hope that he might one day find me.

"That's quite enough," I said, glowering at the man.

Albé, to his credit, appeared utterly unfazed. For her part, Cassandra seemed delighted, but she had been overfond of male attention almost as soon as she was old enough to be aware of it, having never had great reason to fear it, and certainly little reason to fear this man.

"Your father did not say you were a swordmaster!" he said, admiring her outfit.

She smoothed the crimson *mandyas* she had but recently won, and said, "I only passed the Trial five days ago." The half-robe that was the garment of the Maeskoloi Swordmasters of Jadd hung from her left shoulder, tied beneath her right arm and belted at the waist to keep it from falling away. Its cloth was of samite, dyed almost the color of arterial blood and woven with a pattern of golden paisleys, and its fringe fell just past her knee.

"Newly a swordmaster, then! *Magnifique!*" He gave a short little bow, replaced his glasses with a flourish. "My sincerest congratulations. Your father must be very proud."

I did my best to smile. "He is."

Cassandra hooked her thumbs in her belt, emphasizing the twin swords Hydarnes had given her upon her ascension. The hilts were ebony and black leather, with brass fittings. A matched pair. Those fittings glinted as she stepped back from young Albé, each secure in its own magnetic hasp at either hip.

Sensing at last that he was being overfamiliar, Edouard bowed and swept his hand to one side. "Your ship awaits, Lord Marlowe. I trust you will find it all in working order."

Shouldering past the man and his two subordinates, I advanced toward the forward access ramp. "Your own ship is in orbit, then?" I asked.

"Yes, my lord," said Janashia, hurrying to catch up. "Rendezvous is set for around fourteen hundred hours, galactic standard time. That's about nine hours from now."

Albé interjected, "Captain Clavan and Sir Friedrich are eager to see you, lord."

I paused with my hand on the rail. It was the first time Albé had mentioned Sir Friedrich since that afternoon on the lawn before my villa. There was much neither of us were saying.

"Abba?" Cassandra had stopped just behind me. There was a breathless excitement in her face that smote my heart—and smites me still. She didn't understand. She thought she was setting out on some grand adventure, some storybook mission. Beyond the farther suns and back...

Where once the tall tailfin of the *Ascalon* had been painted with the pitchfork and pentacle of my Red Company, the men of Colchis had painted the pentacle only.

There stand I, I thought.

A fading image.

More Eudoran melodrama. Shaking my head, as if to clear it of some fog, I said, "You won't have seen this before! Come!"

We were cleared for launch within the hour, and Pilot Officer Browning's clipped Sagittarine accent sounded over internal comms to alert us to make ready. Neema had remained in his cabin, but Cassandra and I both joined Albé and his officers on the bridge.

There were a dozen junior men aboard as well, shipmen in black fatigues who strapped themselves to fold-outs down in the hold. Albé said his captain had not known how many flight crew would be required to launch the *Ascalon* and bring her to the *Troglita,* but I suspected there was another layer to it. The men were there to escort me, to ensure mad Marlowe and his daughter did not abscond with their own ship.

As if I would have had anything to gain by doing that.

I could as easily have stayed at home.

Albé had the captain's chair when we arrived, and Janashia and Browning the navigator's and copilot's seats. Save for these interlopers the place was precisely as I last had seen it. Cassandra gasped with delight, and in the space of time it took for her to find her breath and speak, I found myself recalling the journey to Jadd after Olorin and Lorian and Bassander Lin had spared me the Emperor's justice.

Sharp's men—his Dragonslayers—had saved me, had faked the prisoner transport that was meant to deliver me to Belusha, the Emperor's favorite prison planet. Mads and Aron and the other soldiers of the late centurion's special detachment had died in exile with me. Old Mads had died last of all, retiring with his Jaddian wife to my villa. It had been his death that finally left me alone in exile, had prompted me to hire Neema from the Nemrut Academy, and to beseech Prince Aldia for aid in the birthing of Cassandra.

Cassandra gripped a handle just inside the doorway, moving with that species of slow wonder that one finds in children who—coming to the age of ten or twelve—witness their first snowfall. "This is incredible!" she said, voice hushed. "How long before we fly?"

"About ten minutes," came Janashia's reply.

"We're just waiting for clearance from flight control," interjected Browning.

"They need to clear our part of the sky," I said and, reaching past her, opened one of the fold-outs that ran along either side of the bridge behind the officers' chairs. "You'll want to strap yourself in, Anaryan."

But my daughter ignored me. "Have you ever flown one of these before, lieutenant?"

"A Challis?" Albé looked round, found the controls for the shutters, and thumbed them. "No, ma'am. There aren't more than a thousand of these in the whole Imperium. This ship was a princely gift."

"You should have seen the other one," I said, thinking of the *Tamerlane*. That was a mistake. It was impossible to think of the *Tamerlane* without thinking of the way it ended, pulled down from the sky and broken on the sands of Akterumu.

The shutters opened like the petals of an iron blossom, retracted until the glass geodesic stood open to admit the carmine sun.

We had taxied out onto the tarmac by then. Far off on the right, I could see the low buildings of the public terminal, white stone and silver glass, and above them the pale towers of the starport authority. Myriad shuttlecraft were flying in low and slow from Jaharrad, and I thought I saw—shimmering on the edge of sight—the spires of the Alcaz du Badr dominated by the great golden dome of the *Tholo Orothano*, the golden palace of Prince Aldia, a hundred stories tall.

About us, the tarmac stretched like a geometric plane. Jaddian technicians in their striped orange and white hurried out ahead of us, one with gleaming batons.

"We're clear for laneway ten," Janashia said to Browning, who chirped her understanding.

"Take us out," Albé said.

The *Ascalon* rocked beneath us.

"What's that?" Cassandra asked, pointing to an oblong bronze lozenge of a ship dusting off perpendicular to us and dead ahead, riding its repulsors, relying neither on rockets nor wings.

"Wong-Hopper trading cog," came Albé's answer. "See the cartouche?"

I found myself staring at the back of the lieutenant's greased head. He would break his stream of conversation to respond to Browning or Janashia with terse, clipped replies. He rode the command chair like a man long accustomed to it. *Lieutenant*, indeed. I gripped the hilt of my sword where it lay hid in my coat pocket.

I was taking a terrible risk, trusting the Emperor's note—yet the signature had been in William's own hand.

Trust no one.

As if I would have trusted any of them in any case.

Albé was not what he appeared, but surely any spy or assassin would labor to appear perfectly honest—clear as glass—and unassuming? Surely the sensitive nature of his work—of HAPSIS and the Watchers—was sufficient to explain his reticence.

The *Ascalon* reached the laneway marker painted with the curling Jaddian numerals for *ten.*

"You both will wish to find your seats," Albé said. "Janashia, warn the lads to sit down, would you?"

Lieutenant Janashia punched a button on the console to trigger the warning lights and spoke into the comm.

"Just waiting on the all-clear from the tower," he said when he was done, touching the contact patch beneath his right ear. With one hand, he keyed the go-ahead request to flight control in the towers at our backs. "One moment."

I had taken the fold-out opposite Cassandra and strapped myself in. Her smile was electric, and I asked, "You secure?"

She said she was, and turned her head to peer over Browning's head and out the window.

"There's a lever by your left hand that will unlock and pivot the chair so it faces forward." I modeled the action for her. "You'll want to be facing forward when the fusion torch kicks on in the upper atmosphere."

She did as I directed, and when she was secure, asked, "Was it like this? Your first time?"

"Actually, it was!" I said, thinking back to Arello and his crew. His wife, Juno, their Tavrosi doctor, and that apelike homunculus of theirs. What had his name been? "My first Jaddian. A little Union ship, free traders. I guess it's fitting your first flight is from Jadd."

Janashia said. "We're clear for takeoff."

"Copy," Albé said. "Prime repulsors, take us to forty thousand feet and prep for fusion burn."

"Aye, sir," Browning said. "Ignition in three. Two. One."

The atmospheric thrusters whined, and we were accelerating, tearing along the laneway. Browning adjusted the controls, and an instant later the *Ascalon* leaped into the air, boosted by her repulsors to aft and along her ventral hull, so fast it seemed that Jadd fell away from us. Cassandra grinned at me, and I could not help but smile in return.

Below, I saw the white terraces of Jaharrad, the great towers where the priests interred their dead in air, forever attended by their flocking crows.

The vessel banked, and I saw the golden grasslands of Jadd, and the seemingly limitless pleasure gardens of the prince unrolled about his palace like a carpet of innumerable colors. And there was the palace itself, the Alcaz du Badr—the Castle of the Moon—dominated by the *Tholo Orothano* like some immense jeweled egg.

Then I saw only the pale sky, and watched as it seemed burned away by the friction fires of our passing until the stars—hidden by the white veil of day—emerged from the revealed black of space like pearls fetched up from the deep of some unfathomed sea.

I shut my eyes, feeling suddenly exposed, as though I were naked in that blackness, naked and alone. One is always exposed in the void, even on the vastest starship, without the comforting blanket of the sky to keep one warm. But in that moment, I imagined—and perhaps I sensed—a will, a malice, as though some terrible eye was questing in the Dark, scouring the stars. Jadd had been a paradise, a garden behind whose walls I had long been kept safe. I had returned to infinite space, the ceaseless night of the wider universe.

To my old world and life.

I longed to go back, to turn my face from that darkness, that malice, those questing eyes.

For a moment, I thought I would be sick.

I was back.

CHAPTER 7

THE DEICIDES

IT IS NOT FOR nothing that Two-Faced Time derives his two-headed visage from half-remembered Janus—god of doors. They are symbols—as indeed all the material world is a symbol, a simulation in crude matter of that world higher and closer to the one in which he resides, which is himself. To step over the threshold of any door is to undergo a transformation, if only in that geometric sense by which we are transported from one chamber to another. When the next Emperor passes beneath the Arch of Titus at his coronation, he is transformed from a mere prince to the person of the monarch. When the seeker enters into the cloister of the athenaeum he becomes a novice of the scholiasts—though he may have yet to endure even a single lecture. So too when the ashes of my father were sealed forever in their vault in our necropolis, he became a part of history, departing the world of active concerns.

All doors symbolize change.

When the doors of the docking umbilical opened onto the *Troglita*'s receiving bay, it was to change me back into something like the man I had been. The great chamber revealed by those hissing gates was a thing of black metal and polished brass—as were the doors themselves. The officers in black and silver with their red or white caps, the legionnaires clad in ivory and crimson, even the very air—sterile and odorless—recalled my long centuries of service. The martial clarion ringing against the ribbed ceiling seemed an echo of that same trumpet I had heard at every parade and every muster since I departed Forum for Thagura aboard the *Tamerlane* on our first voyage together.

Albé had gone on ahead of me, with Janashia and Browning bracketing him at either side. The dozen or so men who had waited in the hold of the *Ascalon* followed close behind—an honor guard of sorts. I had buttoned my jacket as we waited in the umbilical. Almost I wished I had my Order of

Merit or my Grass Crown to wear, to awe the soldiery and remind these men of HAPSIS who I was and had been.

But the Order of Merit and the Grass Crown had died with Nessus—or had they died with the *Tamerlane?* The legionnaires to either side beat their breasts in salute as we passed, approaching half a dozen figures waiting at the end of the receiving hall. The silver-haired woman with the copper skin and white beret was clearly the captain, and the two officers to her right—both men—were almost certainly her first and second. At once I thought of Corvo. Indeed, but for the height this woman might have been cast from the same mold, with her bright hair and burnt complexion. To her left there stood an aging man who leaned upon the arm of the younger man beside him, and beside them there stood a scholiast robed in green.

When the last of the trumpet's music faded, Albé came to a halt and saluted. "Lord Director, Captain Clavan: I have brought Lord Marlowe as directed."

The old man—a patrician of so advanced an age that what little hair remained to him was white as snow and circled his crown as clouds might some craggy mountain peak—acknowledged the young man's words with three nodding gestures that shook him all the way to his waist. "Very good, A2." Then he turned his attention to me, a tired smile forming beneath his somber eyes. "Lord Marlowe, it has been . . . a very long time. Almost I feared I would die on this ship waiting for you, but you're here now. Do you remember me?"

I did. The shadow of the unassuming young logothete I had known on Forum remained in the antique visage, hardly to be seen.

"Sir Friedrich?" I said, still struggling to see the young minister I had known beneath the slow corrosion of years.

"It is Lord Friedrich now," he said. "A technicality of my office." He patted his attendant on the arm, and the young fellow—a slender man with steely gray eyes and the sallow complexion of a life-long sailor—walked the old lord forward a pair of steps. I advanced, passing Albé, and bowed as the old man bent awkwardly himself. "As you have no doubt guessed, I am Lord Director of Contact Division, under the Imperial Office."

"HAPSIS," I said.

"HAPSIS," Oberlin agreed. "Indeed, you might have had my job. Did you know?"

I blinked at him.

"There was a time you were slated to replace my predecessor, Lord Powers."

"Cassian Powers?" I looked to the man's attendant for confirmation. "Cassian Powers was the Director of HAPSIS?"

Oberlin's tired smile returned. "He was enfolded by this old Carnival shortly after Second Cressgard, when he broke Echidna." He looked round, marking the officers and the soldiery standing at attention to either side. "There will be time to discuss old history after we are underway. Time is short, as I'm sure our A2 here told you." His eyes went to young Albé.

"A2?" I looked at the man. Pointedly I asked, "Not a lieutenant, then?"

Edouard Albé offered crisp salute. "Edouard Albé. Special Agent 2, Imperial Office, Contact Division."

"Special, indeed," I said icily, and felt my eyes narrow.

"Lord Marlowe!" The tanned, silver-haired woman in the white beret advanced, her flinty eyes fixed on a point just above my shoulder as she saluted herself. "I am Captain Marika Clavan, *ISV Troglita*. These are First Officer Morrow and Second Officer Vedi." She gestured to the two men at her right—my left. "On behalf of my crew, welcome aboard."

Already tired of saluting, I made the gesture anyhow. "You're very kind, Captain. You have a beautiful ship." I had seen it on our approach, the classic black Imperial knife blade, with the blocky towers and pyramids of its castle rising to aft like the fins of some immense shark. "How many aboard?"

Captain Clavan replied at once. "Eight thousand, two hundred on board, counting the sleepers. We've a full legion—a small one, six thousand men—one thousand auxiliaries, and the engineering corps."

"Engineering corps?" I asked, turning back to Lord Oberlin.

"To excavate the ruins on Sabratha," he said. It was the first time I'd heard the name of our destination. "There will be time to go over the particulars in private, my lord. We have much to discuss. Will you not introduce us to your companions?"

"Of course!" I said, inhaling sharply. "The Jaddian is my manservant, Neema, one of the Nemrutti. And this!" I laid a hand on Cassandra's back to present her to the Director. "Is my daughter, Cassandra Otavia."

Cassandra bowed in the courtly fashion, right hand to her breast, the left thrown wide as she bent, right leg forward. "My lord," she said.

"Your daughter?" Surprise widened the old patrician's eyes. Sotto voce, he asked, "She's not an intus, surely?"

I felt my eyes flash. It was an extremely untoward question, made all the sharper by the fact that—to the Imperial mind—it was true. Cassandra had not been born of a union approved by the Solar Throne, had been born without the imprimatur of the High College.

"She's my daughter," I said again, icily.

"Lovely to meet you," Oberlin said. He patted the arm of the young man at his side. "Priscian, introduce yourself."

The attendant straightened, bowed his head. "Priscian Lascaris, lordship. I have the honor of serving as the Director's secretary."

"My life-support system, in truth!" Oberlin said. "Genetics is an unjust god. I am old, as you see, and will only get older, Earth bless and keep me. Priscian keeps me on my feet and on schedule. Don't you, Priscian?"

The sallow man smiled and diverted his eyes, evidently uncomfortable to be so near the center of attention. "I do my best, Lord Director."

"And your best is very good, lad. Very good, indeed. But I am forgetting Rassam! Rassam here will be leading the excavation. He's been with the Carnival now for—goodness, longer than I have!"

The scholiast—a golden-haired, blue-eyed palatine—bowed with his hands folded before him in his flowing sleeves. "An honor, lordship."

"Rassam?" The name sounded familiar. "Were you involved with the Echidna dig?" I must have seen his name in the piles of documents Valka and I had studied together at Maddalo House.

"I was indeed," Rassam said.

"Rassam is an expert on the Stonebuilder civilization," Oberlin said. "Perhaps *the* expert, truth be told."

"A small pool," Tor Rassam murmured.

Though I had cautioned Cassandra to speak little, she said, "You mentioned an excavation. Are we excavating something?"

Oberlin and I exchanged a long glance, and much, I think, came clear for me in that unvoiced exchange. Long ago, the Emperor had spoken to me of the *Atropos Expedition,* an ill-fated Imperial adventure to the planet Nairi. On Nairi, the Emperor's men had discovered the ruins of an Enar city, and the bones of a Watcher—still undead. It had destroyed them, or so William had told me.

They must have uncovered another city of the Enar. But had they found the corpse of a Watcher? Or something else? Surely they would not have needed me simply to dispose of some old bones. There was something more, something Oberlin did not want discussed in front of the men.

"Yes, my dear!" Oberlin said at length. "We are sailing for Sabratha! Do you know it?"

Cassandra shook her head.

I did not know it, either, and told the man as much.

"A dismal place, by all accounts," Oberlin said. "Arid. Very arid."

"Where is it?" I asked.

Marika Clavan answered. "Far into the Lower Perseus, about fifteen kilolights east of Tiryns. Right on the edge of the Imperium."

The Lower Perseus.

I had never been so far toward the outer rim. The Demarchy of Tavros lay far to the galactic east and above the ecliptic, but it lay within the embrace of the Arm of Perseus, above the gulf that separated it from Orion. Sabratha lay so far along the Arm of Perseus that it was nearly on the frontier, where Imperial space verged upon the wild stars. The Emperor's letter said that they had gotten the planet's coordinates from the Cielcin. How long ago had that been?

"It's unsettled?"

Oberlin gestured that we should walk along beside him, and I did so. There was a set of doors at the end of the receiving hall. We proceeded toward them, moving slow on account of Oberlin's advanced age. "Not entirely, no. We've a minor outpost there. Williamtown. The colony was formally incorporated about...four hundred years ago?"

"Still sparsely populated, then?" I asked.

"Fewer than fifty thousand people on the whole planet, yes..." Oberlin said. "There's too little water."

Cassandra brightened. "A desert world?" She had never seen a desert before.

"Very nearly," Oberlin told her. "There are a handful of shallow seas in the temperate zones—large lakes, you might call them. Each far too saline to service native life. They used to be bigger, you know. The planet lost its magnetosphere for a time, and the solar winds stripped much of the air and water away before the core melted and got the magnetic fields flowing again."

"But is there air?" Cassandra asked. "We won't have to wear helmets the entire time, will we?"

"There's air, young miss," Oberlin said. "The Colonial Office has been working to refine the atmosphere for our use. There's a great deal of carbon trapped in the planet's crust. They'll make a paradise of it in time." Changing the subject, he said, "You're welcome to stay aboard your own ship, Lord Marlowe, but we've doubtless more spacious quarters earmarked for your use. It's just the three of you?"

I told him I did not have a retinue, and he nodded. We had passed through the doors by then, and entered into a fresh section of hallway where trapezoidal windows looked down on our right upon one of the *Troglita*'s mighty holds. Below, a labyrinth of crates and digging equipment lay strapped to the hold floor, attended to by perhaps two dozen men in the bone-white fatigues of the Legion Engineering Corps. I recognized the shapes of excavators, of trenching tools and tunneling equipment.

A deep sadness settled on me. Valka and I had planned to travel the galaxy together, to embark on just such a dig as this, leastways in as far as we could, being only two. The monstrous cost of this expedition occurred to me then, and I think my haggard reflection in the window glass grew paler. I had never given much thought to how we might pay our way had we escaped Imperial clutches after Ganelon. Had I managed to beg my leave of the Emperor, that would have been a different story. I might have been feted across the Empire as a retired hero, even with the war on. But had we simply run? I might have offered my services as a mercenary, as a captain of mercenaries, under my own name or any other. But in doing so, would I not re-create in miniature the very conditions from which Valka and I had fled?

And there I was...in the great game again. The Carnival, old Oberlin had called it—using the pet name men of that most secret service used to refer to their trade. I had tried for so long to escape my role and fate, but as Valka herself once lamented, the galaxy is itself a circle, and anyone who traveled far enough and fast enough would find himself...right back where he started.

Thus it had been with me.

"Lord Marlowe?" I looked round. Oberlin and Lascaris had moved ahead, and I guessed from the Director's tone that he had been talking. I hadn't heard a word.

"He does this, sometimes," Cassandra said, somehow apologetic and laughing at once.

"I'm sorry," I said. "I was woolgathering." I gestured at the windows to the hold. "It looks like it will be quite the dig."

Lascaris helped Oberlin to the window. After a long moment, the old man said, "You and the girl should settle in first. We'll have much to discuss."

"We will stay on the *Ascalon*," I said at once, surprising even myself with my sharpness. It had been my intention all along, would have been my intention even were it not for the Emperor's warning.

"Very good," he said. "Still, the captain will want to give a tour of the ship. We will speak later. Yes?"

"I want to know everything, Friedrich," I said. "If I am not satisfied, my daughter and I will leave. Is that clear?"

I felt Lascaris bristle. I looked at him, and saw the anger in his hard, gray eyes.

But Oberlin nodded tiredly, and dabbed at a bead of sweat on his spotted brow with a shaking finger. "Of course, Hadrian. We will be breaking orbit within a couple of hours. Go with the captain and see us off. You will have the run of the ship, of course. The officer's gymnasium is on C-Deck, should you find yourself in need. You'll find the quartermaster's office there as well, on the starboard side." Turning to his secretary, he said, "I need to lie down, Priscian. Take me to my quarters, there's a good lad."

Then they were gone, leaving us in the company of Captain Clavan, Tor Rassam, and the ship's first and second officers. Them, and young Albé. A2, I should say. From the receiving hall behind, I heard the barked orders of the centurion who had overseen our welcome guard. The lot were breaking up, returning to their ordinary security duties. In the hold below, the engineers were still at their labor checking and securing the equipment for the coming transorbital burn.

"Shall we go to the bridge, Lord Marlowe?" Clavan asked.

"Yes," I said, "Yes, I'd like that."

"It's this way," she said, gesturing toward the door at the far end of this new section of hall. "Afterwards, I've prepared certain of our troops for inspection, and the legate and our chief of engineers both wished to meet you, but Lord Friedrich thought we could keep the welcome party here on the small side."

I hardly heard her. My eyes went to the back of Edouard's head. I had hoped for the answers to start crystallizing from the moment we decamped from the umbilical, but I had received only hints. Hints, and the promise of those answers I had been promised already.

The Emperor had warned me to trust no one. It seemed I was not the only one. I marveled that Lord Oberlin should say so little before even his own men.

But how could he do otherwise?

His was the maddest and most dangerous quest in human history.

He aimed to hunt and kill a god.

And I—my own god help me—aimed to help him do it.

CHAPTER 8

BIRDS OF A FEATHER

"I HAD A LOOK at the quarters they'd set aside for you on the bigger ship, master," said Neema, removing a stack of white shirts from one of the crates he'd carried up from the *Ascalon*'s hold. "They are much finer than these." He looked round at the relatively cramped captain's cabin, with its brushed-metal cabinetry and scrubby black carpet, its narrow closet and small washroom and the row of tiny portholes above the bed that let in the red light of the ventral docking bay on the *Troglita* into which the *Ascalon* had nestled like a remora against the belly of a shark.

I looked up from my work stowing a stack of the folios which contained my artwork and the records of my life in a glass-fronted cabinet. "Yes, but what's the point? In two days we'll be at warp, and shortly thereafter, we'll be on the ice."

"You are a knight, *domi*, and a great lord. It follows that you should be quartered like one."

"I lived on this ship for nearly thirty years, Neema," I said, catching sight of myself—gray-streaked and careworn—reflected in the washroom mirror. Abruptly I recalled Valka's image reflected there, her mouth smeared with black lipstick. I shut my eyes. "It's enough."

Neema had gone silent and still as stone, as he always did when he had something to say.

"Out with it, Neema."

"It is a matter of prestige, *domi*. You must consider how it looks to the Imperials, denying their hospitality and the image taking their best rooms would project."

"I do not have an *image*, my good man," I said. "Not anymore." I did not add that I did not trust the Imperials, did not say that any rooms they were sure to offer us would be bugged. Albé—A2—and his team were certain to have bugged the *Ascalon* as well, when they had done

60

their preflight checks prior to takeoff on Jadd, but I knew every corner of the ship. I would find whatever they'd hidden in due course. "Besides," I said, "if we're to oversee an excavation on this...Sabratha, I will want the *Ascalon* on the ground to serve us for a camp." Our doing so would permit us to leave at any time, should we desire it.

"I understand that, *domi*, but..."

"But Neema," I raised a hand for quiet, "if the ship is to serve us for a camp, it should retain all of mine and Cassandra's effects."

The Nemrut homunculus only blinked at me. "But..."

A knock sounded at the door. "Enter!" I called, eager to break the loop Neema had found himself caught in.

The door slid aside with a faint chime, and revealed Edouard Albé. His unmarked black officer's coat had vanished, and in its place he wore only the white shirt of a common soldier, unfastened at the left side of the throat. He still wore the jodhpurs and high boots of his ilk, and I caught the flash of silver at his throat where some medallion—no larger than a kaspum—hung about his neck.

"Is it time?" I asked. "Did Oberlin send you?"

"No, Captain Clavan," he said. "We're passing Taiph, leaving Jadd local space. She thought you and your daughter would like to see the moon up close."

Taiph was the largest of Jadd's three companions, and the only one irrigated and terraformed for human life—its every surface under cultivation. I had visited it on a handful of occasions as a guest of Prince Aldia—but that had been well before Cassandra was born. Well I remembered the terraced hills of the tea plantations of *Al-Lat Terra*, and fondly did I recall the paradise gardens of the Satrap of Taiph, despite the singing groves whose flowers opened like the wings of butterflies.

"We'd like that, yes," I said. "Neema, will you fetch her from upstairs?"

The manservant bowed at once and shuffled from the room.

In the uneven silence that followed, I said, "Special Agent, is it?"

The young man laughed through his nose. "I apologize for the slight deception, lordship. The Jaddians are good fellows—as a rule—and our allies, but not even our allies can be trusted with the sort of knowledge you and I possess."

"And what knowledge is that?"

"About the Monumentals, of course," he said. "About Nairi and Echidna, and the rest."

"Have you ever seen one?" I asked. "A Watcher?"

Edouard shook his head. "Only archive footage from *Atropos*. Have you?"

"You read the reports I gave the Emperor?"

"I have," he said, "but they were very guarded on the subject."

"Were they?" I frowned, struggling to remember. Had I omitted the nature of the temple at Akterumu from my account? I had always been careful to elide reference to the Quiet and the Watchers from all Imperial documentation, and yet I must have described the temple in my reports. A vast dome fashioned from the stony skull of a colossal being easily a thousand feet across and accessed by its solitary great eye.

Miudanar, the Dreamer. Chief god of the Cielcin.

"All right then, keep your secrets," young Albé said, the Delian polish of his accent seeming to lend the words a particular shine.

Perhaps his accent was what drove me to speak, some nativist impulse desiring to trust him—whatever the Emperor's words. Perhaps it was only my eagerness to arrive at anything like information in that veritable desert. A part of me—the oldest, most ragged part—still wondered why I had come at all.

"It was dead," I said. "But not as you or I understand it. The Watchers retain some spark of vitality, even in death. It spoke to me, when the Cielcin brought me into its skull."

"Into its skull?" Albé's eyes widened behind his spectacles. "Dear God." He looked as if he might be ill. "What did it say to you?"

"Abba!" Cassandra's voice issued from down the hall, and young Albé stepped aside. "Neema said the captain wants us on the bridge?"

I did my best to smile. "Yes, we're going to slingshot around Taiph to boost our way out-system. The captain thought we might appreciate the view."

"Have you spoken to Lord Oberlin yet?"

"No, not yet," I said, and smiled past her to Neema, who was returning in her train. "Will you see to the rest of the clothes, Neema? We'll be back within the hour, I expect."

In the end, it took us nearer two hours to watch the green moon slide by. The *Troglita*'s primary sublight engines kicked in as we reached the far side of the moon, and we watched as Taiph went from a field of green and marbled white, its canals and waterways like fine veins, to a retreating disc, to a coin that disappeared behind the black and green of Jadd herself.

The *Troglita* had no tram system like the *Tamerlane* once had, being only about two miles from bowsprit to stern cluster. In the weeks ahead, I would walk each of her twenty-three decks, familiarizing myself with the place before the long sleep to Sabratha. Had I still been a young man, I might have taken a year or two in solitude aboard the ship, and to familiarize myself with the officers and crew. In the end, I think I only stayed awake for a fortnight.

Edouard accompanied Cassandra and me on the long walk back to the

Ascalon from the bridge, which required that we descend some seventeen levels by one of the rear lifts and along a short length of hallway to the stairs that would bring us forward and down to the receiving hall and the umbilical access where we'd first arrived.

We exited the lift into the lower hall and proceeded along it—bootheels ringing in that world of gunmetal and brass—when from up ahead I heard a strange, ululating cry. I threw a hand across Cassandra to bar her progress, and froze. Young Edouard kept walking a pace, and turned back.

"What's that?" I asked. The noise of it was familiar, like something out of a half-forgotten dream. I had heard it before, or something nearly like it. It had had a high, screeching quality that at once put me in mind of tearing metal and of swooping hawks.

"What's what?" Albé asked.

It sounded again, and with it the unmistakable clangor of steel on steel.

The agent's eyes widened, and he smiled. "Oh! That! That would be our auxilium. Captain had a few of them thawed when it became apparent we'd be stuck at anchor for some years. I think it's the officer corps that's out of the ice at present. We brought a thousand of them—at the Emperor's own urging, as I understand it."

But I had recognized the sound on second exposure, and was already hurrying past Edouard to the door ahead on my right.

"Abba?" I could hear Cassandra hurrying after me, but I did not stop to explain myself. The lowest five decks of the *Troglita* were each nearly a hundred feet high, and while they did not run the full length of the great vessel, they were fashioned thus to accommodate the landing bays and great holds—as well as the two-dozen Peregrine-class lighters of Manticore Flight. Most of these holds were kept in vacuum, but the one ahead stood open, and the bright ring of steel issued from within.

Another cry—more piercing than the last—filled the hall as I reached the portal, followed by a throaty *quark* that might have been a command.

For the first time since I'd boarded the vessel—perhaps for the first time since I'd called young Albé to accept the Emperor's mission—a true smile lit my face.

For there they were: two dozen or so figures in the dun khaki of Imperial auxiliaries—squat, slim shouldered, claw footed, and beaked.

"*Ia!*" called one, a black-feathered fellow with green at the fringes of his long, winged arms. The soldiers before him took a step forward, each swinging his overlong cutlass in a rising arc from right to left. "*Iya!*" They slashed blades flatly left to right. "*Zwa!*" They slashed right to left in diagonal, blades starting above the right shoulder, sweeping through so that they finished beneath the left hip, points still forward. "*Yoh!*" They thrust.

The black-feathered officer, a centurion or chiliarch—I could not quite tell—turned and paced to his left, studying the block of his subordinates as they drilled with the sharp eyes of a predator. He repeated himself: *"Ia! Iya! Zwa! Yoh!"* And with each order his soldiers repeated the basic drill, clawed feet scraping the steel decking as they advanced. *"Yoo atoh!"* he said, and again: *"Ia! Iya! Zwa! Yoh!"* Only this time the soldiers retreated with each blow.

"God of Fire!" Cassandra breathed, coming up close behind me. "Are they...?"

"Irchtani," I said, and took an unthinking step into the hold. "You said there were a thousand of them?"

The HAPSIS agent replied, "The Emperor insisted, and Director Oberlin seemed to think they'd make a good fit. Too few of them speak the standard, so they're unlikely to talk about the work we do."

The Emperor insisted... Albé's words rattled in my mind. *Trust no one,* the Emperor had said in his letter, but here he had provided me a corps of Irchtani fighters.

They hadn't seen us yet.

"I had an Irchtani corps in the Red Company," I said. "They saved my life on Berenike, and many times before."

"I know," Albé said. "The War Office considered yours something of a pilot project. They started recruiting off Judecca en masse. Oberlin was telling me there's something like a million birdos serving in the auxiliary now. They're useless in high-gee environs, but if you find yourself on a world where they can fly..."

"They're a warrior culture," I said.

"Just so."

A shrill cry sounded, wordless to my human ears. The drilling soldiers halted, and nestled their long-handled cutlasses against their shoulders. The black-feathered Irchtani made a whistling sound—opening his hooked beak, and croaked, *"Bashan Iseni u dwaara!"*

The soldiers went to sharp attention, and turned as a block to face inward, creating an aisle by which their black-clad commander could pass for the door. The Irchtani officer clasped his clawed hands together, tucking his wings until they seemed almost loose sleeves, and bowed as best he could, bending awkwardly at the waist. In croaking and thickly accented standard, he asked, "You are Marlowe?"

I returned the bow, and marking the stars on his shoulder that said he was chiliarch of the entire auxiliary, I said, "I am, *kithuun.*"

The bird man cocked his head. "You know our words? I see that much of the legend is true."

I could only shake my head. "Only a little," I said, speaking haltingly in the coloni's own tongue. No human could properly speak the language of the Ishaan Irchtani, with its clicking and croaking music, though the xenobites could well mimic the phonemes of human speech.

"I am Annaz," he said, "*Kithuun,* chiliarch of these." He spread one wing to indicate his men.

A lump formed in my throat. His were almost precisely the words old Barda had used to introduce himself on Gododdin all those years ago. And why should they not be? They were of a kind, and like to use our words in the same way. "I asked for this," he said, bowing again. "We all ask. I am child of House of Yazgan. My sire seven times removed was Irrul, son of Yazgan, whose brother was Udax Vaanshakril."

"Udax?" This Irchtani was Udax's nephew, seven generations removed. "You're of Udax's clan?"

"My House—that is your word? My House Yazgan grew great because Udax Vaanshakril died for you. Made us great. We send many warriors to fight in great war. To fight for *Bashandani,* for your god-king. I, Annaz, am but latest. My sons will follow, when they have sired. They will follow, and they will fight. Fight for you, and for Udax, who opened doors beyond sky."

I was momentarily lost for words. This Irchtani warrior spoke of Udax, my friend and would-be assassin, as one speaks of the characters in scripture and fable. Udax's new name, *Vaanshakril,* I would later learn, was *Demonslayer,* for it had been at his hand that the vayadan-general Bahudde of the White Hand had been destroyed, and by his hand, too, and mine, that Iubalu had been bested. What a legend that must have been on Judecca so far away! I could imagine little Irchtani hatchlings playing at the tale, fighting as Udax and Lord Marlowe as I had played at Simeon the Red when I was just a boy.

It was my turn to bow a second time. "I am honored to meet one of Udax's tribe, *Kithuun* Annaz. He was…a good friend." Throwing all cautions then to the wind I said, "Do you know why we are here? What it is we've come to do?"

The Irchtani captain shook his head, "*Bashan Iseni* say we are to fight with Marlowe. We do not question. We come to fight."

"We're hunting," I said, peering one-eyed at Cassandra.

Edouard interposed himself, saying, "It is perhaps better not to speak of such things just now, my lord."

I ignored him. "We go to hunt a creature the Cielcin worship as a god," I said. "A beast that can swim between the stars as a fish swims in water, a creature of terrible power. A weapon the Cielcin mean to use against our kind and yours. Does that frighten you?"

Annaz and several of the others croaked. Many hopped sidewise on clawed feet, or peered at me with one beady eye. Annaz himself seemed to think about this, and almost I wondered if he believed I was japing with him. "Udax Vaanshakril fought for you," he said. "You led him to glory."

"I led him to his death," I said.

"*Right* death *is* glory, *bashanda*," Annaz said. "Udax Vaanshakril brought glory to *Immuz*, to the *Ishaan Irchtani*. We can do no less. We will do no less." It extended one scaled and taloned hand. The hands of the Irchtani lay at the apex of their wings, like the claws the ancient saurian things that plied the airs of Earth in the Age of Dragons, such that their great feathers extended from their wrists like the sleeves of some irremovable robe. They had but three fingers and a hooked thumb whence a cruelly barbed talon grew.

I took the offered hand, and Annaz gripped my own roughly and shook it. It was dry, and cold, and despite the strength of the warrior's grip I could sense the lightness in his bones, which were hollow like the bones of terranic birds—like the bones of my own left hand. Bloody-Handed Evolution had compensated for this intrinsic weakness by weaving iron into the bones. Not a lot, not enough to offset the weight shed by the hollowness in the first place, but enough that a man might not crush the fingers of the Irchtani in his grasp.

Annaz pulled me closer and, placing his beak near my ear, he whispered—such as he could, "It is for you we have come. We wish to fight for you. For Marlowe." He released me, and drew back, saying, "Udax slew demons for you. We will slay false gods."

"What was all that?" Cassandra started once we were both safely back aboard the *Ascalon*, sliding into Jaddian. "The xenobites acted as if they knew you."

We'd come to a halt just inside the forward airlock. It was dark within. The open doors of the bridge lay at my right, and the light of muted consoles—red and blue—lit Cassandra's face from far off.

"They do. In a sense," I said, glancing back at the airlock. "They mentioned my friend, Udax—I've told you about him." She nodded. "It would seem he has become a martyr to them, and a hero. Almost a prophet. Because of him, their people have risen in the estimation of the Empire, and through him, they stand to advance their station."

"By fighting in our wars?" Cassandra's brows contracted.

I could not help but smile. "You are every inch your mother's daughter," I said, resting a hand on her shoulder. "But yes. Perhaps in time there will be Irchtani nobiles. Irchtani consuls. Captains. Scholiasts. As for me..." I grew quiet then. "I opened the door. You heard young Albé. Udax and his brothers...all those years ago...paved the way for them today. So for them to serve with me would be...would be as if you were to serve with Prince Katanes."

Again she nodded. "You said we were going to hunt a god." When I did not speak at once, she pressed, "Back on Jadd, you said it was a weapon. Abba, when are you going to tell me what is going on?"

"I don't *know* what's going on!" I almost hissed the words, half-afraid that Albé or some other agent of the Imperium was listening at the airlock door. "Not exactly...but..."

She will suffer...if you do not go.

Somewhere in the limitless universe, a star burned out.

"You asked me about the Monumentals...the Watchers, as the Cielcin call them. Do you remember what I taught you about the Chain of Being?"

It was an ancient idea, a conceptualization of the hierarchy of all life, set down by the ancients, who believed the uncreated gods were fixed at its high end, the anchor whence the great chain hung, and that below them were the lesser spirits, angels and demons and the like. Man was at the center, and beneath him were the beasts, beneath them the plants, beneath them the insects and animalcules that proliferate in the waters and spread disease.

"When the ancients, our ancestors, first discovered extraterranic life, much was made of the question of whether that life were more or less advanced than our own." The ancients of that time had long ago ceased to ask the question of what life was advancing *toward,* but that is a matter for another time. "Certain kinds of xenobite are lower than ourselves, in capacity if not in dignity. The Umandh of Emesh, for instance, and perhaps the Irchtani. The Watchers are higher."

Cassandra absorbed all this with the rapt attention I had seen her so often give Hydarnes when he walked through some fencing form.

"They are truly colossal beings, Cassandra. On one of my adventures... I saw the body of one. The Cielcin had built a temple in its skull. It was so large that more than a thousand of their princes could stand in its brainpan with room to spare." Cassandra's eyes were wide. "The Cielcin worship them, and there was a time when they commanded armies across the galaxy. Long before our people took to the stars." I did not tell her all I knew, not then. I said nothing of the Quiet, of the last war and the unkindling of the stars. Let her think the legends of Hadrian Halfmortal were just that—if only a little longer. "This is the greatest secret in our universe, Anaryan. Not even our friend, Aldia, knows, I think."

Often as a young man, I had imagined our Empire some perverse species of zoo. An animal myself—a raven perhaps, or some stalking panther—I had hated the Empire because it was my cage. I saw it more clearly then, saw it for what it was—what all nations are.

A preserve.

What I had taken as a boy for bars were only the mountains and forests that verged the green pastures of our home. The men I had thought gaolers, wardens, and rangers. If the Cielcin, then, were wolves, then the Watchers were like plagues. Famines.

Death itself.

Humanity little knew it, but all its kings and emperors, all its joys and sufferings, every conqueror and hero, every warrior and poet, every sinner, scholar, and saint—indeed all its violent history—had taken place within the walls of a garden that every man from Menes had mistaken for the wild wood.

Outside, it was very dark.

"And the Emperor wants you to kill one?" she asked.

"Yes."

She absorbed that word as though it might encompass millions. When she had finished, she asked, "But ... why you?"

It was a long while before I answered her.

"Because ..." I said at last, "I may be the only person who can."

CHAPTER 9

GNOMON

TWO DAYS GONE WE left the circles of Jadd's sun, but it was not until the third day that the summons from Oberlin came at last. A logothete in the gray suit of a civil servant called at the *Ascalon*'s airlock, and I accompanied him up the lift all the way to B-Deck, where we walked the full length of the *Troglita* and came at last to a pair of heavy doors.

"You may leave your terminal with me, Lord Marlowe," the logothete said, extending one hand, palm up.

Surprised, I reached for the strap securing my wrist-terminal before I could give it much thought. Presently I halted, asked, "For what reason?"

"The Director is concerned about security."

"Security?" I repeated, incredulous. "We're at warp, boy. There's nothing coming on or off this ship."

The logothete appeared entirely unruffled. He had not dropped his hand. Not for the first time since Albé came striding across my lawn on the *Islis di Albulkam,* I experienced the sense of shadowy figures moving just out of sight, as though some sinister fellow in a cloak and hood stood just around the nearest bend in the hall. As I had many times before, I imagined the social world as a limitless chessboard extending in all directions.

White tiles. Black tiles. Red.

Holding up the terminal for the man's inspection, I powered it off and slid it into the inner pocket of my coat. "That will have to serve, sirrah."

The man's mouth worked like a bellows, and he took a mincing forward step. "It will not serve, lordship."

I took a full step in his direction. The man was only patrician, and I had perhaps a head on him, and the rumor of me added perhaps half a hundred heads. He stepped back, bowing slightly. "What is your name, sirrah?" I asked.

"Angbor, lord."

"Angbor," I said, "You know who I am?"

"Of course, lord."

"And still you wish to delay me?"

Angbor bowed and withdrew another step. "I am only following my orders, lord."

"And if your orders were to hurl yourself out the airlock, Angbor, would you do it?"

The man almost had to think about it. "No, lord." He straightened, and the blood had left his face. "These are matters of Imperial security. The very highest!"

I pounded on the door with one fist, not taking my eyes from the logothete.

It opened an instant later, and two legionnaires in full plate stood within.

Angbor straightened his jacket, smoothed it with both hands, and said, "I've brought Lord Marlowe to see the Director."

The first legionnaire nodded his blank-visored face. "Very good," he said, and waved us through the security check.

The bulkhead doors opened on what must have served the vessel as a secondary bridge. The primary was far aft on A-Deck, and from the broad slash of window that stretched the full width of the chamber ahead, I could tell this room was as far forward as forward got. Beyond the window I could see the bowsprit and the forward gun emplacements on the dorsal hull. Most of the consoles were dark, but Lord Oberlin sat in one bucket seat to the left of the central holography well, young Lascaris at his side. Tor Rassam stood perhaps a quarter turn around the holography well. Behind them, the violet fractals of warp shimmered beyond the *Troglita*'s prow, rippling where the ions caught in the ship's gravitic envelope mingled with the distorted starlight blue-shifted by the violence of our speed.

Angbor stormed ahead. "My lord, he would not surrender his terminal."

Oberlin turned from Lascaris, his sad eyes reminding me acutely of some aged bloodhound. When he spoke, it was to me, and not to his subordinate. "Do you trust us so little, Lord Marlowe?"

Check.

"Do you blame me?" I asked, stepping fully into the room. Four more legionnaires in faceless plate stood within. One stood with his hand casually on the butt of his holstered stunner.

"I am not your enemy," Oberlin said. "If I were, I would not have permitted you the run of the ship. You've been in our power for three days."

I acknowledged the truth of this with a simple, open-handed gesture. "I could well ask the same of you, Lord Oberlin. We are underway already, and I still know next to nothing of your cause."

The old man nodded, smiling almost to himself. "That is not true," he said. "You read the packet A2 delivered."

"I did," I said. "Did you?"

The seal had been unbroken, but such seals could be imitated.

"No," he said, tone inscrutable. "But I spoke with Caesar before we left Forum. Indeed, I championed the notion that we should sail to Jadd to recruit you."

I felt my eyes narrow involuntarily, and said, "I've you to thank, then?"

"I was not your only advocate," Oberlin said, "Sir Gray Rinehart argued for your inclusion, as did Lord Nicephorus."

"Nicephorus?" That surprised me. The Emperor's chamberlain—his closest confidant and perhaps his only true friend—despised me, though I do not think it believed me false as did the priests and priestesses of the Chantry.

"I am told even Her Radiant Majesty, the Empress spoke in your defense."

That gave me pause, and a thrill like a blade of ice laid against the side of my throat ran through me. "The Empress tried to kill me," I said, "as you'll recall."

Oberlin's expression was unreadable, the studiously bland, blank face of the career bureaucrat. "Perhaps she only hopes that by dragging you back onto the board you'll meet some untimely end."

Those words struck me as completely honest, and in their perverse way put me at ease. Still, I said, "Or perhaps she means to use you to destroy me."

Oberlin was nodding along with every word, and when I finished replied, quite coolly, "I will not waste what little breath remains to me trying to convince you. As proof of my good faith I can only offer you your continued freedom and the truth." He raised a hand in the direction of the door. "You are free to leave at any time, my lord. Command it, and I will order Captain Clavan to drop anchor and permit your ship to depart."

I did not challenge him. We both knew it was a lie. My *continued freedom* was a thing contingent now upon my continued role in the great game.

We were pretending, all of us, that I had been given a choice. But Jadd had been forced to permit Albé in to see me, and would have been forced in time to extradite me, or to turn a blind eye to kidnapping. It was not Jaddian strength that had guaranteed my freedom-in-exile all these years, but Imperial forbearance. The Emperor never meant to kill me, only to lock me on Belusha until I could be decanted from fugue like some special vintage. And Jadd had been as good as Belusha. *Better,* because I had not wanted to escape it.

Even if I could take Oberlin at his word, even if Cassandra and I were free to depart, I knew we would not be free for long. We would meet with some terrible tragedy at the Chantry's hands, or at the hands of some other Imperial assassin. In ten years. In fifty.

Poison.

A flier crash.

A well-timed charge.

Knives in the dark.

Have I not said that freedom is like the sea? That a man may swim in any direction he chooses, but all he will do in that sea is drown.

"Speak, then," I said, planting my feet a shoulder's width apart.

Oberlin nodded in his tired way, ran a hand across his balding scalp. Lifting his chin, he said, "Sargis, you and your men will wait outside." The leader of these men—a centurion with several gold phalerae decorating his breastplate—saluted and moved for the door. As was the way with our legionnaires, he must have subvocalized commands to his subordinates, for the others moved silently off. Sargis himself lingered by me. Seeing this, Oberlin said, "I have nothing to fear from Lord Marlowe, Sargis. A2 is here."

I had not seen him until that moment, but a quick look round revealed young Albé seated in a remote corner, legs and arms crossed. The light of warp shone across his lenses, making his eyes seem to glow. I wondered what threat the young agent might pose that so assured Lord Oberlin.

The heavy doors hissed shut a moment later, leaving me alone with Oberlin, Lascaris, Tor Rassam, and the distant Albé.

"As you are already acquainted with the purpose of our enterprise," Oberlin began but slowly, "I will not waste time. Priscian."

The gaunt secretary removed a holograph wafer from a breast pocket and placed it on the rim of the holography well that stood beside him and the seated Oberlin. The black glass rim glowed where he'd placed it down, scanning the laser-fine flaws cut into the quartz disc. Lascaris punched a key on the well's control console, and a moment later an image appeared above the recessed hemisphere of the projector in the center of the well. It depicted what appeared to be a dented cylinder—wider in the center and tapering at either end, with slotted depressions at those ends where it might have fitted onto a spindle. It reminded me of a scroll, though it seemed to be fashioned from a single piece of gold.

I recognized at once the writing that spiraled around its surface. A single, continuous line of script, with letters made by fine, wedge-shaped indentations that rose from the center line like the rise and fall of a sine wave.

It was Vaiartu script. The language of those the Cielcin had called the Enar.

"This," Rassam began, a schoolmasterish edge to his tone, "is K-887. It is a cylinder of Vaiartu manufacture, taken from a Cielcin horde captured at the Battle of Asara. As you can see, it is of solid gold, massing some seventeen kilograms." The image revolved as he spoke, showcasing new facets of the Vaiartu inscription that wound about its surface. "Uranium-thorium-helium dating puts the cylinder between nine hundred thousand

and one-point-one million years old, placing it rather late in the development of the Vaiartu Kingdom. This estimate is corroborated by the sineoform writing, which is of a style commensurate with the period."

As he spoke, I moved to the rail surrounding the holography well, the better to study the Vaiartu artifact. The one side was badly dented, as if the soft, yellow metal had been crushed in the teeth of some mighty gear. Along the other, a well-worn ring of anaglyphs ran. Not the scratchy writing of the Enar. The circular writing of the Firstborn, of the Quiet. It was—in its way—akin to the tablet I had seen Ugin Attavaisa gift Syriani Dorayaica, and the one I recalled from my memories of the visit to Echidna that had never happened.

"It's an atlas," I said.

Rassam turned to look at me, briefly revealing his surprise. "How did you know that?"

"I've seen its like before," I said. "Twice. Only those were tablets. The shape of this is different. And the material."

"Gold does not corrode," Oberlin said, "making it the ideal medium for the preservation of such information as this."

"The tablets I saw were of stone," I said.

"We believe the cylinder part of a royal collection," Rassam said, "how the Cielcin found it we can only guess."

The projection changed, displaying the sineoform writing broken into segments, with various of the angular, clawlike characters highlighted in scarlet where they floated in the air.

"The Prophet has had its forces searching the galaxy for a very long time," I said, wishing I understood the inhuman letters. The moment held a certain surreality for me. When I learned of the Enar at Dorayaica's elbow, I had believed I was the first human being in all history to learn of them.

How wrong I'd been.

Oberlin had said that Tor Rassam was the galaxy's preeminent expert on the Vaiartu Kingdom. It seemed strange to me that such an expert should exist at all. I had so many questions.

One such question escaped me, filling the air before Oberlin or Rassam could continue. "How long have we known about them?" I asked. "The Vaiartu?"

Rassam looked to Oberlin for approval. The old patrician inclined his head. "The first Vaiartu artifacts were found on Pherkad in the fifth millennium."

"The fifth millennium?" I repeated the words, incredulous. "That was twelve *thousand* years ago!"

Eager to bring the volume down, Oberlin said, "It was a long time before we realized they belonged to a starfaring civilization, and longer before the scientific community managed to differentiate Stonebuilders from Firstborn."

"You called them all *the Quiet* in those days."

"*We* called them nothing," Oberlin said. "A minor point: HAPSIS did not yet exist. But you're right. It took centuries for scholars to realize certain of the sites and artifacts they'd uncovered belonged to the same cultures. The datanet did not exist in those days, ships were slower, fugue less reliable, and for word to travel across the early Imperium took decades."

"And you managed to keep this all a secret?"

To my surprise, it was Lascaris who answered, "Much of the truth has ever been believed myth by most people, and much myth truth."

I accepted this. It is a truism among those who study history that much of what common people believe is false. The belief in popular power is one such falsehood, when the truth is that the populace is ever directed by an elite will, ever wielded by a Caesar or a Lenin as a murmillo might wield a blazing sword. The belief in progress is another. There are more specific examples: The belief in the God Emperor's divinity masked a deeper truth. The belief that the Mericanii were a race of machines who waged war on mankind is believed by every child, almost none of whom has ever heard of Felsenburgh. In the face of so much falsity and confusion, it was no wonder the truth was not more widely known. A vate might preach the unvarnished truth from his column in the city square, and be ignored even by the wise—or worse—be hanged upon a tree for a rebel.

"Secrets are not *kept*," said Oberlin. "They are *managed*. Like flowers, if you like. Or like weeds. There was a time when every sailor in the cosmos talked of *the Ancients*. The *Quiet Ones*. The *old gods*. There were operas and serials made about the story."

"The *Annuna*," I said. "Yes, I've read them."

"I'd forgotten those ones," Oberlin chuckled. "Pulp adventure nonsense. Science fiction. But it is better that the truth wears fiction's mask in the popular eye. The people police themselves, and will dismiss as mad any man who speaks the truth."

"May I continue, lord?" Rassam asked.

"Of course, of course!" Oberlin waved a hand. "Forgive me. I am an old man, and prone to digression."

A faint smile creased the blond scholiast's face before Stricture smoothed it away.

"The coordinates on the Asara Cylinder index nineteen worlds, nearly all of them concentrated in the lower regions of Perseus and Sagittarius. Of these, eleven were known to us already. One—you may be interested to know—was the planet Emesh."

That did not surprise me. Emesh had appeared on other Enari tablets, and indeed Uvanari's doomed expedition had used one to come to Emesh in the first place, and—discovering it already inhabited by humanity—had been destroyed there.

"And Sabratha was one of the other eight?" I asked.

"On the contrary. You will recall it was already settled," Rassam said, and paused to ask Lascaris to advance his display. The holograph shifted, revealing the wire-frame globe of a world revolving slowly. The display showed off a composite of orbital images, a world of ocher sands, white salt pans, white ice caps, with here and there the milk-blue of small salt seas. "This is Sabratha," Rassam said. "Settled ISD 16997."

"Almost exactly four hundred years ago," Oberlin chimed in.

"And you recovered the Asara Cylinder when?"

"Forty-eight years ago," said Tor Rassam. "Prior to our doing so, we were unaware of the Vaiartu presence on Sabratha. The planet is sparsely populated."

Fewer than fifty thousand people on the whole planet, Oberlin had said.

"The salt deposits you see in the equatorial zones here and here," he pointed, "and here, about the north polar region, are the remnants of great, shallow seas. At one point as much as ninety-six percent of the planet's surface was once underwater. Now it is less than seven percent. All of this, coupled with the planet's naught-point-seven standard gravities is suggestive of a planet with little-to-no magnetosphere, but this is not so. Sabratha's magnetic field is quite robust. Radio communication is difficult, and the necessity of laying fiber-optic hardlines has limited colonization of the surface, so it should come as no surprise that the Vaiartu ruins went undetected until we knew to look for them."

"This is all well and good," I said, studying Sabratha where it floated like a confection of caramel spun sugar. "But I did not leave Jadd for a lecture in geophysics. Did you find one of them?"

Rassam did his best to hide his vexation, but I had known too many scholiasts to miss the signs: the minutely narrowed eyes, the compression of the lips, the faint tension in cheek and jowl. He glanced to Oberlin, then said, "The governor-general's office performed a survey of the deep desert. They found a Vaiartu site at forty degrees south latitude. Here." Again he pointed, and the image of Sabratha ceased its rotation. "This region would have been undersea at the height of the Vaiartu Kingdom."

"They were amphibious?" I asked.

"Indeed," said Rassam. "The governor-general hired a local team to begin the excavations."

"Against our recommendation," said Lascaris, a touch stuffily.

Coming to stand just beside Rassam, I squinted at the map. The region he'd highlighted with his finger showed a black mass rising from a sea of rippling ivory and gold. Text in vermillion and jet black written alongside it read *Cetorum Mensa* and *Mount Sark*. The desert surrounding it—level plains that stretched for thousands of miles in every direction—were labelled *Mare Silentii* and *Victorialand*.

"They've been digging?" I asked. "What did they find?"

Rassam looked to Oberlin again.

When no one spoke, I said, "Well? Did you find one of the Watchers, or didn't you?"

Sabratha began to revolve once more above the well. I saw Oberlin through it, his head bowed, his wispy hair swaying in the breeze of some unseen ventilator above our heads. Almost forgotten in his corner, Edouard Albé stirred.

"Priscian, show him the rest."

The image of Sabratha vanished, replaced by a series of images, still phototypes and holographs taken of the site itself. Images of what seemed to be a mountain dominated, black against the eggshell blue of the sky. Great trenches dug in the sand, reinforced by corrugated metal walls or held back by static compactors. There were images of Wheeler grids, great square pits dug into the earth in a grid. The ribs of some long-dead sea-beast rising like bent pillars from brown sands. Green walls, cracked and crumbling. Square pillars and trapezoidal windows—the hallmarks of Enari architecture. Of the Vaiartu.

These passed away at another click of the remote, erased faster than I could absorb them. Still more images replaced them, and I recoiled almost at once. Lying on an examination table under stark lights was the most horrific corpse I had ever seen. The chest appeared crushed, as though the man—if man it was—had been caught in the grip of some monstrous vise. Dried blood soaked the tattered ruins of his bone-white uniform, and his every limb—all six of them—were bent and mangled. But it was the face that most horrified me.

The *faces*.

He had *two* faces, had nearly two heads. Each seemed to grow out of the other, so that the left eye of one fell within microns of the right eye of the other. The flesh seemed to flow between them, and I felt that their bones and indeed their brains must be conjoined. Somehow, that was not the worst of it. The noses of both faces were broken, indeed were broken in the same way, each leaving the same smear and trail of blood across the corresponding lips. It was as if—in the grip of some strong drink—my own vision had doubled and swam, so that one man appeared *almost* two. He had four arms, and despite the mangling of the torso—*torsos*, for there were two sets of crushed ribs that interlaced with one another, that grew together and seemed fused, nearer together as they neared the pelvis, so that from the navel down he seemed almost one man again.

Light flickered off young Albé's spectacles as he averted his gaze.

"Who was he?" I asked, studying the ruined face. It was...nearly the most horrible thing I'd ever seen.

"One of the governor-general's dig team," Rassam replied. "His office dispatched some three hundred Legion engineers to the site shortly after it was discovered. They excavated a large portion of the city—as you saw—but..."

"But the team immediately began reporting problems," said Oberlin, apparently eager to move the long-winded scholiast along. "They ran into trouble with their comms—as you might imagine, given the planet's magnetosphere. Equipment kept failing—native equipment hardened against Sabratha's unique conditions. Then one of the cooks killed himself. The diggers started reporting nightmares. One man killed another—some fight over a local boy, ostensibly. Then this."

"What happened to him?" I asked.

"There's more," Oberlin said, and raised a hand for Lascaris.

The secretary clicked his remote, and the cluster of images disappeared, was replaced by a single, broader image. It showed the same stark white of the medical pod, the same body lying on a slab under glass. There were two other bodies alongside it. The camera through whose lens we peered was in the ceiling, doubtless part of a suite of sensors there. The two-headed form lay on the central table. The one to its left lay with torso crushed and face bloodied, its legs broken in what seemed a fashion identical to those of the twinned corpse. The body on the right table was small—small as that of an infant, but well-proportioned as a full-grown man. It had been crushed the same way.

All wore the padded white jumpsuits of a Legion engineer, though the clothing of the twinned man and the child fit their bodies perfectly. Stranger still, I realized at once that the pattern of the bloodstains on each was identical. Perfectly identical, down the last drop.

"*The body...bodies...were brought in at oh-five-hundred hours this morning,*" the recorded voice of some physician played from the well's speakers. "*Friede and Jansen found them. Think he went to take something from the supply cache stored there. A torch, most like. The lads are always nicking supplies, and Mann kept a still behind the diggers' barracks. No telling what he was after...black planet.*"

The physician hove into view, dressed in a heavy, rubberized suit. "*I've ordered Friede and Jansen quarantined, and will remain so myself. It's unclear if some pathogen is to blame, or...if it's something else. Things haven't been right here since old Arty shot himself. Now this...*" The man grunted, keyed the lid that opened the cover on the nearest pod. It hinged open, and the doctor leaned over the most ordinary of the bodies. "*I took blood samples from all three half an hour ago,"* he said. *"They're all Mann. All three. All three the same, perfect matches for the genome we have on file. There's no sign of infection, and at any rate infection wouldn't explain the clothes."*

While he spoke, the physician raised gloved hands to manipulate the arm of the body on the slab before him. He lifted the arm before him. The right arm.

The arms of all three bodies—all four arms—rose in perfect tandem, as though unseen strings bound them one to the other like a line of marionettes.

"Stop playback," Oberlin's voice slashed across the moment like a blade.

Silence rang in the disused bridge. The light of warp through the forward windows rippled across the polished floor and darkened consoles. Words seemed to me distant as the unfixed stars and as alien: cold and remote. Still, I sensed that Rassam and Oberlin, Lascaris and even young Albé were all watching me, waiting.

"What say you?" asked the Director of HAPSIS.

I could only shake my head. Though I dwelt for years in the dungeons of Dharan-Tun and heard the words of the Watcher Miudanar loud in my ears, I had never seen such a thing, not in all my six hundred and more years. I knew that here was the question Oberlin and Albé had crossed kilolights to ask.

"I have never seen its like," said a voice that must have been my own. The image of the dead engineer and his three bodies still hung frozen on the air, right arms all raised. "They're all the same man?"

"They are all the same *matter,*" said Rassam, tucking his hands deep inside his flowing sleeves. I could only blink at him. "What is done to one happens to the others."

When I did not respond, Lascaris skipped forward, and I watched in mingled horror and fascination as the suited physician traced an incision along the right forearm with a glass scalpel. The flesh parted smoothly, and though the congealed blood within did not run, I saw the mark of the knife trace itself along the splayed-out arms of the other bodies: the twinned man and the dwarf.

"Entanglement?" I asked, referring to that property of the minutest quanta wherein exciting one half of a bonded pair excites the other in an instant, regardless of the intervening space.

"It is not entanglement," Rassam said. "It is something else."

"What?"

I thought I could hear the eyes of Rassam and Oberlin narrow in the noisy quietude.

"You don't know?" Oberlin clasped his hands across his pigeon's chest.

"Know what?"

As if to himself, the Lord Director whispered, "Caesar said you were the one. He said you would know."

"Know what?" I asked again, more forcefully.

"What they are." Oberlin looked at me with slitted eyes. A great ring with a carnelian set in its bezel flashed upon his finger.

"And what are they?" I asked.

Oberlin hesitated. I recalled the note he had slipped me when I survived the Chantry's interrogations, the pitchfork he had scratched through the watermarked Imperial sunburst at the bottom of the official stationery. The young Friedrich had been a *believer,* one of the many in the Imperial service who gave voice and credence to the whispers that I was the God Emperor come again.

Did he believe still?

I felt he must not, felt that Time, Ever-Fleeting, must have cooled his ardor—as it cools all things. My ignorance could not have strengthened his belief, and yet there was caution in those narrowed eyes, and not contempt.

"Higher beings," he said at last.

I glared at him. They were the words the Irchtani used to describe us humans—specifically those of us of the palatine caste. They were also the words I had used to describe the Watchers to Cassandra. By using them, the aged spymaster intimated that he had overheard our conversation aboard the *Ascalon.* They *had* surveilled the dear old ship, then.

I let my smile freeze to show I understood his veiled meaning.

"They are creatures that exist beyond what we ordinarily think of as spacetime. They are abstract creatures, composed of pure energy."

I could only stare at him for a moment then. It was the most...incredible thing I think I'd ever heard. "Impossible," I said aloud. "I saw one's body."

"You saw only a fragment," Oberlin said.

"A fragment?" I echoed the words, incredulous.

"Suppose you were to dip your hand in a pail of water," the spymaster said, raising one arm by the elbow so that the fingers pointed down. "Suppose ordinary space were only a sheet of oil spread upon that water. The Monumentals are like the hand. The body you saw was like a fingerprint. A husk left behind."

I felt as though I'd been plunged in oily water myself, as if Oberlin had knocked the legs out from under me. Oberlin continued, letting his hand fall, "Matter, of course, is but another form of energy. In nuclear reactions, we free the energy imprisoned in matter and so on. The body you saw on Eue was only the condensates formed when the Monumental forced its energies down from its reality into our own."

"But it had a brain," I protested. "A skull. An eye socket! Nerve channels!"

The Director could only shrug.

"The creature on Eue spoke to me," I continued.

The old campaigner's face darkened. "That was not in your report."

"No," I said sharply. "It wasn't."

"Why not?"

"I did not think I would be believed," I said. "I didn't even know HAPSIS existed at the time."

The old man leaned forward, eyes alight. "What did it say?"

"It showed me a Cielcin victory," I said. "And it showed me the Vaiartu. Their conquests and fall. That and...a thousand other things..." I fell silent. "Pure energy..." The words sounded at once comical and terrifying, and I longed to seat myself in one of the empty chairs about the center console, but I did not. It was better to stand, better to maintain the appearance of control. "How do you know all this? Nairi? The *Atropos* Expedition? They found a Watcher dead there."

"Did Caesar tell you what happened to the men of the *Atropos* Expedition?"

"He told me they killed themselves."

Again Friedrich Oberlin studied me as though I were a cell culture under the glass of some vile magus, or like an enemy duelist awaiting the telltale twitch that precedes the mortal draw. "Many did," he said. "Some vanished. Others were torn apart. We have footage of men lifted bodily into the air, and of others..." He rapped the rim of the holography well with the knuckles of one hand.

"Like this?"

He didn't have to answer. I understood then why they were so certain Sabratha was the place, and why they had come for me.

"What happened to him?" I asked, though I thought I could guess the answer.

Oberlin confirmed my suspicion.

"The Monumental," he said when a fresh silence had stretched on long enough. "His Radiance told me what you did on Perfugium, How you killed the Cielcin commander."

Almost embarrassed, I turned away. I had looked across time to a place where the windows of Attavaisa's command ship shattered, and so tore the air from the Cielcin general's lungs. We had watched as Attavaisa and all its officers were pulled through those open portals into the silent black of space. Though many of the memories of that earlier Hadrian have faded, that one remains forever undimmed. Too well I recall the glass of the bulbs in our own command center falling down on us like rain, the hiss and crackle of electronics fried by some overspill of my *choosing*. I had never controlled the power well, had hardly used it since that black day.

"I was there that day in the Grand Colosseum, too," Oberlin said. "When you stopped that highmatter sword with your bare hand."

"That was no miracle," I said, seeing the old light of belief flicker in Oberlin's somber gray eyes.

He dismissed my words with a gesture. "I saw the recordings from Berenike, too. I'd wager Aptucca was something similar. Was it?" Aptucca had been more like the Colosseum. Duplicity and a plan had won the day in my battle with the Cielcin Prince Ulurani, and not the Quiet's power. When I failed to answer him, Oberlin asked the question I felt sure he'd wanted to ask me since our first meeting when he was a young man. "Did you really come back from death?"

Wordlessly, I nodded.

In the corner, the light off Albé's lenses flashed as he turned his head away.

"You are closer to them than we are," Oberlin said, and pointing at the holograph and the bodies of the poor engineer, he continued, "The things you can do are *like* this."

"They're not," I said.

"They are!" Oberlin said. "You must see it!" He leaned fully over the holograph then, and the light of the projector lit his time-softened jowls from below, giving his wizened face a skull quality.

Remembering what I had said to Cassandra the day we set sail, I said, "You think that I can fight them?"

"No," Oberlin said, surprising me. He seemed to think about his answer then. The wrinkles on his brow collapsed, forming a deep crevasse between his eyes. "I don't know. But we don't need you to. We *have* the means to kill it. We need your help to *find* it."

I stared at him, uncomprehending. "You have the means to kill it?"

"Priscian," Oberlin turned to his secretary. "The Perseus files, if you would."

The gaunt secretary removed a second quartz wafer from a brass case he produced from his breast pocket and handed it to the Lord Director. Oberlin held it as though it were a bar of depleted uranium, weighed the thing in his hands. "You will review this alongside the reports from Sabratha tonight. We will meet again tomorrow." I held out a hand for the wafer, but Oberlin did not give it to me. "We have been planning this for a long time," he said. "Longer than you know."

"Since *Atropos?*" I asked.

"Yes," he said. "We've spent every one of the last nearly three thousand years preparing for this expedition. After *Atropos*, HAPSIS quarantined Nairi. We studied the Monumental there for centuries. Lost countless lives. How do you think we learned what they are?"

My hand was still out to receive the wafer, but my mind was far away. In my mind's eye, I saw a flotilla of watchful ships, forever orbiting verdant Nairi. I pictured an Imperial fortress in the jungle, overlooking the cyclopean ruins of the Vaiartu royal outpost, imagined the brave men who had volunteered to go and learn, knowing they might face a monster that defied what little we knew of natural law.

"They are composed of pure force, as I told you. They are a pattern of force. Like a signal. Radiating down from those... higher dimensions. That signal can be disrupted with a sustained electromagnetic pulse, provided the beast can be brought within range."

"You killed the one on Nairi?" I asked.

"Yes," Oberlin said. "Centuries ago. Well before the war. But we... suspected there were others. That's why we prepared for Operation Gnomon, we wanted to be ready in the event another—"

I raised the hand I'd been holding out for silence. "You've had a weapon designed to kill the Watchers since before the Cielcin invasion?" I almost shouted the words.

"History did not begin with Hadrian Marlowe," Oberlin replied, voice cool and low.

"Then why do you need me?" I bellowed, glaring from Oberlin to Lascaris. I thrust a pointing finger in the direction of young Albé, who had stood sharply. "Leave off, *A2!*" I raised both my hands to show I meant no violence. "I'm bait," I said, eyes flickering to Tor Rassam before returning to the Director's face. "You're using me as bait."

"You're our foxhound, old boy." Oberlin bent forward to collect the quartz wafer from the well display. The images of the poor engineer winked out at last, and he slid the two wafers between his fingers as though they were a pair of silver kaspums. "Caesar believes your... faculties will make you uniquely attuned to the beast. You have senses we lack."

"I'm bait," I said again.

"If you like." The old man shrugged. "You begin to understand, at any rate, why we were so willing to risk an international incident to force the Jaddians to hand you over. It is good you came willingly, in the end." He grew quiet then, and I was struck once more by his extreme age. A slouching, round-shouldered little old man with thinning hair.

He did not look like a god-killer.

My thoughts ran to Cassandra. I should have left her on Jadd—whatever her wishes. I had half a mind to ask Oberlin to save her, to spirit her away to some far-flung province when she went under the ice... and yet I knew I could not do so. To send her away would be a betrayal, but more than that I knew I could not risk allowing her to slip into Imperial custody. I might never see her again.

Oberlin held up the two quartz wafers between thumb and forefinger.

Two coins.

In ancient days, the fathers of men laid two coins upon the eyes of the dead—a pair of bronze obols that the deceased might offer the ferryman of souls to speed their way to Hades. Often we believe the myths of those ancients mere fancy, amusements for the delectation of children—or those men who are like children, never learning conviction. They are not. Those stories echo in eternity—are indeed perhaps reflections of it, cast from some higher world—such that their shrapnel are to be found everywhere. In everything.

Have I said that we live in stories?

We do, and so those two coins Oberlin offered me were the very toll price of hell.

But which of us was the ferryman? And which the corpse?

CHAPTER 10

THE EYES OF ANOTHER WORLD

THE SAND THAT BLEW across my face carried with it the taste of eternity. There are places—the port in Williamtown was one—where all things are new and the years are flavorless as water. But the vast desert of the *Mare Silentii* was no such place, nor the great plateau that towered over it. There ancientness hung over everything like a shroud, like smoke. One could taste it in the salt and the grit of the desert air, hear it in the forlorn whistling of the wind through the rocks, see it in the fossilized remains of the leviathans and pseudocarids that recalled the vanished seas.

And one could *feel* the countless chiliads in the oppressive weight of the dead city itself: Phanamhara, City in the Sea of Silence. Phanamhara, City of the Enar. Of the Vaiartu. Of the servants of the Watchers. How strange it is, to come to a place and know you are among the first to see it in a thousand thousand years of men. Almost it recalled the ruins of Annica, the great city in the mountain, except that those ruins had filled me with wonder and not with dread, for I knew which powerful and unrecorded race it was that once had dwelt in that annihilated place, and shuddered, and knew that like the Cielcin, they had been servants of that final darkness.

The day was fading, and the white sun—fast falling to the horizon—had turned fat and yellow as the yolk of an egg. Already I could feel the desert air leeching the water from my face, and I paused to turn my collar up at the wind. Still, it was not hot—it was never hot at that latitude—and the nights would be bitter cold.

"Welcome to Mount Sark, my lord!" The speaker was a gray-haired patrician in the desert camouflage of the planetary defense, white and dun. Behind him, a loose confederation of dig workers: a man in high boots and brown leathers, a woman scholiast in leggings and a short tunic in the traditional green, a pair of engineers in padded white, all escorted by a half dozen peltasts in the same dun camouflage, each clad in *sagum* cloaks of undyed wool. The patrician officer surveyed Neema, Cassandra, and myself with curiosity. "Is Director Oberlin not with you?"

"The Director will be following on shortly, on his own ship," I said, leading my small party down the *Ascalon*'s rear ramp. I did not bow. "He will not be remaining on-site. I will be."

The officer shook his head. "When the governor-general's office said we had Hadrian Marlowe himself come to oversee the dig, I hardly dared to believe it. I used to have the old recruiting posters they did with you on them, back when I was a lad. The Hero of Aptucca!"

"I've been called worse," I said, turning to look sidelong at Cassandra, who seemed—if anything—even more bemused by this development than I was myself. "And you are?"

"Ah!" Remembering himself, the officer saluted, striking his breast with a fist. "Commandant Vimal Gaston, Tribune. I've the command of this camp." He bowed.

The man had the look of the classic upper-crust Sollan officer. Strong jawed, blunt featured. He wore his hair court fashion, neatly clipped and combed to one side, with thick sideburns that ran down to the corners of his face and fearsome mustache. With a start, I realized who he recalled. He might have been a facsimile, a perfect copy, of the late Sir William Crossflane, a man cut from that same Imperial archetype.

I returned the gesture, shallower than he. "An honor, commandant," I said, and turning aside introduced Cassandra. Looking back at the *Ascalon*, I said, "I trust our berth is not inconvenient?"

"Not at all!" Gaston said. "We'll have her hooked up to central water and our reactor by end of day. Our engineers here will take care of it." He gestured to the two men in white, who saluted on cue. I acknowledged them with a bare nod, but Gaston was unfinished. The scholiast woman and the man in brown had caught him up, and he lay a hand on the shoulder of the brown man, saying, "This is Doctor Valeriev, our lay magus. And this is Tor Carter."

The man in brown—whose lank, muddy hair hung nearly to his shoulders—thrust out a hand. "Tiber Valeriev, sir. Xenoarchaeology. Niverzitet u Thalma."

"Thalma University?" I said, taking his hand. "You're Durantine."

"*Da*," he said. "All my life."

I shook the scholiast's hand after his, saying, "Counselor."

Carter smiled and bobbed her head.

The three of them made a curious set: the demure scholiast, the foreigner, and the stodgy old officer. Yet the dig site was their charge—or it had been. Oberlin had made it clear that he intended to have the locals removed once the situation on the ground was firmly in hand. A portion of Clavan's Legion was landing even then, their troop carriers settling on the flats beyond the ruins of the city.

"Have you all been at Phanamhara long?" I asked.

"No, lord!" Gaston replied. "Carter has been here longest. I replaced good Sir Oliver but six years back. Valeriev's been here...how long has it been?"

"Nine years, Gaston," the Durantine scholar replied.

In a quiet voice, Carter replied, "Thirty-one years, liege. But I've spent as much time in the city as here. Or in Markov Station."

Markov Station was a climate research site more than three thousand miles to the northwest, in upper Victorialand. We had passed over it on our flight down from Williamtown. The local navigator Governor-General Hulle's office had sent with us had labored to point it out: a miserable pile of prefabricated white buildings arranged in a grid about the atmospheric refinery. Precious few were the worlds in our universe that could natively play host to human life. Far more common were those—like Sabratha—that ill-fit us, like bad shoes.

"You've been here for most of the dig then?" I asked her. We had been thirteen years in transit from Jadd. I had slept for all of them, less a month or so on either end. That made it sixty-one standard years since the discovery of the Asara Cylinder, and fifty-nine since the work at Phanamhara had begun. I realized my mathematical error then and amended myself, "Nearly half, I mean."

"Yes, lord," the scholiast said.

"I'll want to speak with you," I said. "With each of you, as doubtless will Lord Oberlin or one of his agents."

Thunder pealed in the distance, and turning, I looked out across the lone and level sands. Away to the east, a castle of black cloud marched against the darkening sky, lit beneath by pale lightning.

"Are we due for a storm?" asked Cassandra.

"This time of year, likely," Tor Carter said, her short, dark hair bristling in a stiff wind. "The fronts move down from the equator, get funneled through the Salt Gates between Victorialand and Prince Cyrusland."

Gaston interrupted, "There's little enough rain, but the wind's fearsome. You won't want to be caught out in it. We keep a team of spotters in the air most days, and you can see where the balloons are tethered over the camp." He spent a minute then detailing which comm frequencies were used for the weather reports.

I surveyed the layout of the camp and the ruins beyond while he spoke. We had settled the *Ascalon* upon its outermost margin, as far from the plateau as anything man had brought to that desolated place. Like those of Markov Station, the buildings were all of prefabricated white, heavy plastic, carbon fiber, and alumglass, every one of them low and long and studded with the fluted chimneys of wind-trap turbines. I saw the lines of the weather balloons Gaston had spoken of; silver threads tethered to the camp's outermost buildings.

The great plateau of the *Cetorum Mensa* rose above all, blacker still. Upon its nearer face and shoulders, I could see the arms of the ruined city reaching out as if to gather our camp in its embrace. Still, it was easy to see how the original flyover surveys had missed the ruins. The great mass of the city lay beneath the plateau itself—indeed it *was* the plateau, or rather the plateau was it. A million years of wind and weather had worn the greater structure down. And there was more: great projections of green stone, ramparts like fingers fanning out into the desert. These had been buried by the desert entire, and Gaston's men and Valeriev's had spent more than half a century digging that sand away, so that dunes a third as high as the cliffs themselves stood mounded about the site, and one entered the ruins by a long and shallow ramp. I could see the red-enameled arms of heavy excavators and drilling equipment: huge vehicles not unlike the colossi who walk our battlefields like gods themselves.

"I'd like to see the ruins, if I may," I said after what felt like long reflection.

"Of course, lord, plenty of time for that!" said the commandant breezily. "Once Lord Oberlin arrives."

"If it is all the same to you, commandant," I countered, "I would like to go into the ruins now." Some part of me, childlike and half-forgotten, wanted desperately to see that ancient place, though the rest of me—the greater and older part—felt most sharply the fear that the sight of Enar architecture engendered. The truth, I think, was that I simply wanted it to be over. On Eue, Miudanar had perceived me at once, had spoken to me as soon as I had come into sight of its corpse . . . its *fingerprint*. I know now that it was because it had sensed the touch of the Quiet's hand upon me, had felt the pressure of my own higher vision as I had felt the weight of its eyeless gaze.

I hoped that my mere presence, then, might draw our prey.

Such had been Oberlin's hope, when he called me *foxhound*. Perhaps that was why he had permitted me to take the *Ascalon* with the advance team. Oberlin had planned to descend with Commander Vedi and the frigate—a Rhea-class light frigate, little larger than my *Ascalon*—that was to serve HAPSIS as a command base on the ground. Nominally this had been a security measure, but I wondered if the old fox had not sent me ahead as bait, to beat the bushes while he readied his shot.

The weapon, a modified NEM209-type electromagnetic pulse atomic, codenamed *Perseus*, would be housed aboard the *Rhea*. I had studied it with the documents Oberlin had given me relating the secret history of Operation Gnomon: the *Ragol* mission that discovered Nairi. The *Atropos* Expedition. The suicide of Sir Damien Aradhya, the deaths of his crew. The research base HAPSIS had built on the planet. The thousand-year research program. The deaths. Their silent war on the Watcher. Their eventual victory—if indeed it was a victory. Nairi remains unsettled to this day, watched by a fleet of Chantry Sentinels.

The Chantry knew of the Watchers, it seemed from Oberlin's reports. Not the local priors and grand priors. But the Synod on Forum surely knew, and the Choir that oversaw the Sentinel fleets. I had long ago ceased to marvel at their hypocrisy. They were an organ of the state—as all religion wrongly ordered must inevitably become—but in being so, they served a higher good: the common good, which is highest of all the goods of this world save one.

"That...can be arranged, Lord Marlowe! Certainly!" Gaston said. "I would have liked to take you down myself, but I must oversee the landing and prepare for Lord Oberlin's arrival. Valeriev, I don't suppose you would do the honors?"

As I have said, the desolation of Phanamhara was approached by a long and shallow ramp. The great berms of sand created by decades of excavation rose at first gradually, then precipitously, to either side. The sand beneath our feet had been compacted by years of machine passage and tramping feet, and felt hard as flint beneath us. Still, I was glad to reach the pale-green stone that once had been a boulevard at the bottom.

"How far from the mountain does the city extend?" I asked Doctor Valeriev when we reached the alien road.

"About two kilometers," he said, using the ancient measure still in use in backward lands beyond the Imperium. It was a little over a mile. "There may be outlying structures. We've sonared the desert for miles around, run gravimetric scans and the like, but it's hard to know."

Cassandra spoke up. "You haven't tried digging?"

"We've had our work cut out for us excavating the city proper," Valeriev replied in his thickly accented standard. "Thrice before I got here, the governor-general halted the work entirely."

"After the incident with the engineer?" I asked. Cassandra knew there had been a murder, and without my showing her the holographs knew it had been ghastly and...unreal.

"That was the last time," the doctor said. "The first was for the storms. Local year is nearly six standard, and the windy season runs nigh half so long. Starting out, the camp wasn't up to spec. Lord Hulle had the place evacuated twice, and each time the men had to spend the winters digging the camp out as much as the city. Took more than a decade to make any real headway against the storms."

The air was still as a tomb at the bottom of the dig, so still almost it seemed we were inside, and the lowering clouds were recast in my mind, playing the role of some cathedral vault looming and yet...infinitely remote. "Is it the windy season now?" I asked.

"Nearly at its end, in fact," said Tiber Valeriev. "Static field generators hold much of the sand in place. They're what draw most of the power from the camp reactor. It took them years, but they solved the desert problem."

As he spoke, he led us along what must have been one of the city's main roads, a boulevard some fifty feet across and straight as a laser. Ahead, the square pillars and trapezoidal windows and doors of the city yawned from the face of the plateau. To either side—half buried by the sand—ran the arms of Phanamhara. Like the ringed city of Akterumu they were, but smaller: each a monolithic projection of stone, building after building contiguous with the last, so that the city seemed more one mighty palace than an assemblage of disparate structures. There were no towers, no domes, and nowhere was there to be seen a pane of glass or delicate arch, nor any color but that faintly luminous green.

"This is the main avenue," Valeriev said. "We've dug out many of the buildings to either side, excavated most of the next avenue." He pointed to the left. "And have started on the adjoining two on that side."

"How many in total?"

"Six, counting this," Valeriev replied. "Two on the right, three on the left. They all converge at the base of the Whalemont."

"The Whalemont?" Cassandra asked.

"The *Cetorum Mensa*," the doctor answered. "The plateau. Mount Sark."

"But why *Whalemont*?" she pressed. "Why does it have so many names?"

"You must have seen the bones out in the desert!" Valeriev called back over his shoulder. "When Sabratha still had her seas, this place was all underwater. You can see the bones of sea serpents that used to live here all over the *Mare Silentii*. Biggest they've found was nearly three kilometers from end to end. Virtues of the low gravity! They say they were filter feeders, like terranic whales, lived off the little fish and pseudoplanktons." He continued talking, explaining how certain of those planktons had survived the loss of the planet's seas, how they remained and metabolized carbon dioxide to make the oxygen that made it possible for us to walk around unmasked. They were growing stronger as man labored to free the carbon trapped in the planet's crust, and there were talks that water might be brought down from comets, as had been done on my own homeworld, Delos, by the great world-builders of old. Provided the Vaiartu site could be protected from the fresh and rising seas.

But the great sea snakes, the *whales* of Sabratha, would not return. True whales would swim in their place, and in time generations might come to think it was for terranic whales the *Mensa* got its name, and not the extinct native life. Privately, I thought the Empire would reject all plans to develop Sabratha further. Nairi remained uninhabited, but for the vestiges of HAPSIS and the Chantry Sentinels who kept their guard. Sabratha seemed doomed to join it, the second—if it was second—in a list of dead worlds forbidden to the tread of men.

"The city goes far back beneath the plateau," Valeriev continued, stopping in the shadow of a pillared entry in the hall to our left. "We're still digging out the deepest chambers. It's been hell trying to clear the inner chambers. Since I've been here, we've lost two work crews to cave-ins." His tone became melancholy.

We'd reached the level space before the walls of the plateau by then, and stopped to look up at the façade. Above us for perhaps a thousand feet, the gates of the city loomed. A million years of sand and of water had worn the great friezes nearly all away, though here and there could be seen the bent profile of an arm, a claw, of the many-legged carapaces of the lost Enar. Mighty square pillars marched along to either side, some cracked, others broken. Bright scaffolding supported the mighty lintel that ran across the graven capitals, and surrounded certain of the inner ranks of columns, complete with harnesses where workmen labored to scratch away the dust of eons and reveal the stone beneath.

"It must have been incredible in its day!" Cassandra said, and I thought I could detect the ghost of her mother in her hushed voice.

"The whole thing would have been painted!" Valeriev waved a hand at the pillars. "Bright colors! Lots of yellows and blues. Deeper in some of the murals have survived a bit better, but out here the wind's worn everything down to the plascrete."

"Plascrete?" I asked. I had been trying to picture Akterumu freshly painted, a gleaming, inhuman Babylon.

"That's what all this is, lord!" Valeriev tapped at the paver beneath his feet with the toe of one high boot. "Polymer-reinforced concrete. The Vaiartu didn't do much quarrying, but they liked their stone." Seeing Cassandra crouch, he said, "*Nien,* young miss! Don't touch! The green is copper arsenite. It's poisonous."

"Arsenic?" I looked round at the Vaiartu city with renewed horror, recalling legends of the queens of Earth dying in green gowns, of children wasting to bone in rooms bright and floral. I had needed little reason to explain my illness during my short stay in Akterumu, but I slept at least two nights upon the green stones with open wounds.

"Evidently the stuff was not poisonous to the Vaiartu."

"Are we in any danger?" I asked. Surely some of the dust blowing about us was the aerosolized powder of the old stones.

"A small amount. It's worse inside when the men are working, but the climate keeps the toxins manageable. You'll want to wear a suit for prolonged exposure, but...to take a look..." He shrugged, *"Nien problema."*

I put my hands in my pockets, and looked round with renewed disgust.

"You'll want to see this, I think!" said Valeriev, and the Durantine grinned from ear to ear. "It was among the first things we discovered here! Come, come!"

And so we passed within, beneath the square pillars and the gridded beams of the vaults above, their sections like honeycombs of poisonous stone. The chamber within was a geometric horror. The antechamber was vast and cuboid, hundreds of feet high. Doors and passages opened at every height along the walls. I guessed that once the xenobites who built it must have swum to reach the various apertures, but Valeriev's men had placed ladders against the countless passageways. Glowspheres hung in the air, some stationary, others moving along programmed tracks, patrolling the halls. Almost it seemed that stretches of the walls and ceiling were paths in and of themselves, and I could imagine the hulking Enar clinging to them like spiders.

But it was the wall ahead Valeriev had brought us to see.

The colors of the mural upon it were chipped and faded—revealing the arsenic green beneath—but the relief carvings were still to be seen, save where they had cracked and fallen in the lower right corner. We were standing in what—to the lost Vaiartu—had been a city square. It was not hard to imagine the thronging creatures scuttling about and over one another as crabs do, filling that watery space, looking up in awe at the image as they entered the subterranean heart of their inhuman city.

The image was taller than it was wide, and built on a looming rectangular slab of stone that leaned out over the square itself, wider at the top than at its base, which rested above the capital of a massive column that delineated the two branching halves of the central passage that led deeper within the ruin. Near the base the inhuman artist had rendered in lifelike miniature the shapes of myriad alien forms. I saw arms and fins, tentacles, wings, horns, pseudopods and hands contorted, faces curiously blank, as though the artist had given no thought to the pain he should have portrayed. The Enar stood above them, triumphant, strange weapons in their clawed, curiously human hands. Their lowest ranks stood upon their victims, while the higher ones turned, their many arms upraised, swords lifted to greet or honor the being that stood above all.

It reminded me of the image from the temple of Akterumu, but here was no many-handed serpent. The style was different—the frieze at Akterumu had had no pigment, only that sickly green—but akin. Above the graven Vaiartu legions rose a roiling mass of tendrils, arms curling and spiraling, bifurcating to touch the upraised swords. Above these, but curiously apart, were several concentric rings of stone. The tendrils seemed to flow from it, as the arms of a cuttlefish flow from its head. Upon each ring, inscribed with geometric precision, were the round anaglyphs of the Quiet's speech.

My blood ran cold at the sight of them, and at the sight of what they encircled.

The circle had three *eyes*. One above, two below, describing the points of a triangle, each equidistant from the center of the great disc. Something about those eyes disturbed me, but I pushed the thought away.

Cassandra swore in Jaddian, and in the same language asked, *"Hadha es?"*

"One of the Watchers," I said, half expecting to hear the strange language I had heard on Eue whispered in my ears.

Arkam resham aktullu.

Arkam amtatsur.

"Do they all look like that?" she asked.

"No, Anaryan." I came to a halt at the foot of the central pillar that upheld the mighty frieze, so that it looked down upon me, a terrible and unmoving god. I thought that this must be the most honest depiction that I had ever seen. A form of the formless, a conveyance of the abstract. Of the *idea* of the gods themselves.

It was a Watcher indeed.

"They're each different. I've never seen one like this before."

"My lord, if I may," ventured Tiber Valeriev, "what does an Imperial war hero have to do with the Vaiartu?"

I only stared at him. After a moment, the brown-clad xenologist quailed. "I might ask you what a Durantine doctor is doing with knowledge that could get him into trouble with the Terran Chantry."

To my surprise, Valeriev waved this down as though it were nothing. "I was invited," he said. "I worked a dig on Sadal Suud—many years ago now. Your governor-general put out word he needed archaeologists. I didn't know anything about the Vaiartu when I got here. Carter's the expert. She and your Rassam are colleagues, I understand."

My gaze had returned to the mural of the Watcher. There was room enough in me to pity Valeriev. Had he known, when he took Lord Hulle's job, that he was never going home? Had Hulle known? Here was a man in possession of at least a piece—if only a piece—of the secrets that form the foundations of the Empire, secrets I have here recorded for you, dear Reader.

Whatever Valeriev said next, I do not recall. I recall only those eyes. Something about them filled me with disquiet, something I did not understand. I turned my attention to the writing, the Quiet's anaglyphs. These concerned me, if anything, even more. The Cielcin used the Quiet's symbols, misappropriated the characters of their—of his—seeming-speech to form the rude caricatures of their own. That had always bothered me, though I had comforted myself with the thought that it was some black mockery. But always in the back of my mind—unanswered—there remained that terrible question, echoing again and again.

Was the Quiet a Watcher himself?

Why else would those same markings appear there? On that wall? About the image and icon of that many-eyed monster? "Valka," I whispered, and shook my head—though I could not tear my eyes away. "I need you, here." There had to be something, something I'd missed. Something I'd failed to see. Valka would know it. Valka would *remember* it.

The Vaiartu sculptor had carved square-tipped rays emanating from the three-eyed disc, as though it were luminous. Oberlin had said they were creatures of pure force, of light shining from dimensions we cannot perceive.

My breath caught.

"Abba?" Cassandra had heard me mention her mother, had circled nearer for my sake, and so heard me.

The eyes! Realization ran through me like a shock. I think I retreated a step. "The eyes!" The words escaped me that time.

"Abba?" Cassandra circled to stand in my line of vision. "Abba, what about the eyes?"

"You don't see it?" I asked, looking from her to Valeriev. I could almost laugh. It had to be a joke, a prank, a falsity. It was so obvious. How could I have taken so long to see?

They were human eyes.

CHAPTER 11

THE REFRACTED MAN

OBERLIN MADE LANDFALL SHORTLY after sundown, and insisted on being given a tour of the ruins. Gaston's men brought a float-palette, and Oberlin rode upon it as though it were a palanquin. The old spymaster insisted on breathing masks for Lascaris and himself, and Cassandra and I followed suit. Neema remained on the *Ascalon*, saying that the thought of all that poisoned, alien stone made him cringe.

I have painted something of a picture of the place already: the radiating aisles of stony buildings, low and square. The pillared gates at the foot of the plateau. The mural of the Watcher that Gaston introduced as the *Hulle Frieze*, in honor of the governor-general. But I shall endeavor to give you a schematic of the site as one of the storm-spotters might have seen it—as I saw it when I went up for the first time in the coming days.

Phanamhara, that is, the core of the ancient city, was nigh on invisible from the air. The bulk of the ruins lay underground, or else were still buried by the sands of the desert. Only the main gates and the mile-long profusions of stone projecting like fingers from it showed beyond the mass of Mount Sark. These extended like the spokes of a wheel, all but the centermost vanishing beneath those dunes which the static-field generators had frozen in place. These profusions alone recalled Akterumu to my mind, and I shuddered, following in Oberlin's train.

Carter and Valeriev both said that they believed Sabratha to have been a minor outpost of the Vaiartu Kingdom. A military depot, so Valeriev supposed. A pilgrimage site, said Carter—who I was more inclined to trust. As Valeriev had said, Tor Carter was HAPSIS, and had been dispatched by the Magnarch of Perseus on Tiryns in advance of our arrival. Carter believed that both the sites on Sabratha and Nairi were more akin to temples, monasteries constructed by that cruel and ancient empire for the worship of their black gods. I told her that Akterumu upon Eue had been the same, an impossibly vast city alone in the wastes of that wasted world. She would later share with me that there were other planets far up the outer Sagittarius, where such green cities flowered like algal blooms across the entire surface.

And yet was it not possible that they possessed no concept of personal space? Or needed none? I had seen them swarming over one another in the vision Miudanar showed me. Perhaps theirs had been a truly communal existence. The great halls that lined those projecting spokes of stone—which Valeriev called *basilicas*—might have served as barracks for guards or postulants, or even for slaves.

Within the *Mensa* itself, there was a chaos of halls and chambers, built without regard for stories or levels. At first I thought there was no plan or symmetry to the place—as was the case in the Quiet's ruins at Calagah and on Annica—but when Carter showed us a map, I saw I was mistaken. There was a plan, of sorts, a kind of kaleidoscopic repetition, a crystal matrix of room after room whose pattern revealed itself only at long examination.

Valeriev talked long of his efforts to excavate the deeper chambers, to reinforce those that needed it, to buttress those that had already caved in. They had begun excavations on the northern face of the plateau, some ten miles distant, where a kind of postern gate stood. The winds were fiercer on that side, facing the equator, and arresting the flow of the desert was hard. When the tour was finished, he brought us back to the camp and—after the medically advised scrub down—we were shown a series of artifacts taken from the ruins. There were shards of stamped metal—corroded almost to naught—that might have been the hafts or rotten blades of weapons, or of remotes or terminals or of some subtler machinery whose functions were lost to time.

The camp itself was simple. Phanamhara extended from the western face of the *Mensa,* with the road between it and the camp running almost straight from it. The barracks of the workers and guards—prefabricated longhouses all—were massed along the southern bank of the road, with the actual working buildings arrayed along the north. The greatest of these was the motor pool that housed the excavation equipment, a vast, white canvas tent held up by a geodesic structure of black carbon, giving it the look of some pocked mushroom. About its domed sides were massed the laboratories and storehouses, the garrison's armory, and the medica. Not far off, the stack of the fusion reactor rose above all, white steam venting to the sky. Power lines snaked across the surface or under the ground, connecting the various pods and longhouses, ensuring them a steady supply of electricity. Likewise the cistern—a blue-and-white drum designed to house tens of thousands of gallons of water—stood away south below the level of the longhouses it supplied, connected by water lines.

The camp was made not only to weather the dry thunderstorms that boiled down from the equator, but to last for decades.

When we had lingered over the potsherds and other artifacts of empire long enough, Carter escorted us to the medica, where Valeriev left us. Sir Friedrich leaned on Priscian Lascaris, Tor Rassam and young Albé close behind, following Carter through the reception area where a nurse in white and green sat to hear the complaints of the guards and workers that might walk in. Carter led us through a backroom and along a short hallway, an umbilical connecting one pod to another, and into a vestibule where a pair of guards stood. Seeing the lot of us, they stood a little straighter and keyed the doors for us to pass within.

It grew noticeably colder, and Cassandra—well used to the tropics of Jadd—shivered and chafed her arms beneath her swordmaster's *mandyas*. Tor Carter had to key the inner doors of what seemed an airlock to permit us into the morgue. Like every pod in the camp, the chamber was low ceilinged and gray, about thirty feet wide and perhaps forty deep. Seen from outside, the building was a box of windowless white, rounded like so many of the camp's buildings along the longer side so that a cross section of it resembled a pill.

We had come into a long, narrow chamber that ran the width of the morgue. Hazard suits hung in lockers to our left, along with showers and a sink and various storage cabinets and the other effluvia of the medical trade. To the right, the wall was all of alumglass, and the doors of a decontamination chamber stood shut, permitting the appropriately garbed technician to enter and exit in relative safety. A console sat beneath the glass in the center of the room. From it, the coroner could control the arms and tools of the surgical suite embedded in tracks that ran along the ceiling of the chamber beyond.

"We've kept the bodies on ice for the last thirty-four years," Carter said, moving to stand near her reflection in the glass.

I moved to join her, peering in at the frigid morgue and the trio of strange corpses lying within, remembering the reports on the crystal wafer Oberlin had given me.

Michael Mann had been one of the geological survey team that had overseen the excavations before Valeriev had been brought in, a patrician attracted from offworld by Sabratha's yawning frontier. He'd been born on Tiryns, attended an Imperial academy there, and turned his talents to the task of civilizing Sabratha, and so struck out for the frontier.

The frontier had struck back.

It had been his death that brought Carter to Phanamhara with all due speed, his death that prompted Oberlin to galvanize Operation Gnomon and crew the *Troglita* for this venture.

"Which is the original body?" Cassandra asked, close behind me.

"They're all the same body," Carter replied.

The others—Oberlin and Lascaris, Albé and Rassam, Carter and Cassandra—stood behind me, their ghosts reflected in the frosty glass. Cassandra had been told about poor Mann's fate, but the strangeness of it defied education.

"Can we go in?" I asked. "Are we still concerned about contaminants? Viruses?"

Carter shook her head. "There's been no sign of biological agents, and the men who found the bodies have shown no signs of infection."

"They're here on site?" Oberlin inquired in his quavering way.

"Yes, Director," Carter said. "I interviewed them when I arrived—you've seen the records?"

"I have."

"I had them put in fugue shortly afterwards. We sent word to Williamtown—to their families—that they died in a mining accident. I can have them revived."

"That won't be necessary," Oberlin said. "I'll want them remanded to the *Troglita*. They cannot remain on Sabratha."

But I spoke over him. "I'd like to speak with them before they go."

Oberlin's ghost frowned at me from the foggy window. "That may not be wise, my lord. The men of *Atropos* were much addled by their exposure to the Monumental on Nairi. It may be these men are dangerous."

"If madness is catching, Director," I said, looking round at him, "then I am in the least danger of any of you." I smiled to soften the drama of my words and reassure Cassandra, whose face darkened. "How many are there?"

"Six," came Carter's reply.

"I'd like to see them," I said. "Tomorrow or the day after." I nodded through the glass. "Can we go in?"

The scholiast turned aside, gesturing for the door.

"I will stay here," Oberlin said, eying the bodies through the window. He coughed then, drawing the eyes of all present. Lascaris patted him on the back gently, a look of concern on his gaunt features as he produced a kerchief for the old spymaster.

"What did you mean?" Cassandra had stopped. "That they're all the same body?"

"Better to show you," Carter said, keying the door.

I was acutely conscious of my every footfall as I passed through the door. Rassam, Cassandra, and Albé followed, breath misting the air. It was not nearly so cold as a starship's cubiculum in the morgue, but the air was staler and more bitter by far.

"Where did you find him?" I asked, moving to stand by the nearest bench.

There were five steel slabs in the morgue, three of which were occupied and spread with white plastic. The far wall was filled with the faces of drawers, each marked by a display panel gleaming faintly in that way all viewscreens do when they are only sleeping.

"In the ruins," Carter said. She had produced a pair of black gloves from a dispenser on the wall and snapped them over her hands. "Valeriev's predecessor kept supplies in a few of the more secure chambers. Easier than running all the way back out here every time they need a new spade."

I knew as much, having read Oberlin's files. "But how far from camp?"

The scholiast frowned, paused a moment to calculate. "One-point-two miles? One-point-three? It was not in the city proper, but in one of the outbuildings along the avenues."

I nodded, accepting the gloves she offered me.

The bodies of poor Mann had desiccated after so many years on ice. The skin had acquired a leathered, waxen quality, like the hide of some antique book. They looked precisely as they had in the holographs, save that they were leaner, drier.

"I had them pulled out of storage earlier today," Carter said.

I was standing at the side of the nearest slab by then, peering down with head cocked to study the face of the dead man. The hair on his head was matted with old blood where the skull had been flattened, and the remains of a curling beard—neither yellow nor brown—hung on what remained of his chin and cheeks. His chest was an utter ruin: his ribs staved in, his organs smashed to pulp. But it was his eyes that most disturbed me. They were black and shriveled, apertures opening on *nothing*.

The twinned body was worse, and I found I could only glance at it, at the bodies entwined, overlapping like reflections in prismed glass. The smallest body lay on the farthest slab, like a child's form.

As I watched, Carter rotated the left arm of the man between us, raising it to show the palm. There came a rustling then, and the creaking of dried flesh, and looking past Carter, I saw the arms of the other bodies raised, palms turned out.

"*Deu di Foti!*" Cassandra hissed, stepping back.

I brushed past Carter, bent to study the arm of the twinned man. Raising my own hand, I traced the skin of the upraised arm, saw all too clearly the places where Carter's fingers dimpled the flesh. Taking the hand by the wrist, I gently bent one of the fingers, saw the finger in the hand of the other corpse Carter held bend in tandem.

"Does it matter how far apart they are?" I asked.

"No," Carter said. "I took one to Markov Station shortly after I arrived. The bodies respond to any stimulus simultaneously." She checked herself, returning the arm to rest upon the slab. "Rather, I should say, they *experience* the same stimulus simultaneously."

Oberlin's voice crackled over the comm. "But you can transport one without moving the others?"

I had an absurd image of the other two bodies pressed against the wall as Carter transported the third by flier, like magnets straining against the walls of some toy labyrinth.

"Yes," she said. "The bodies will consent to being manipulated in concert, but…can be moved independently. Lord Marlowe, if you will." She led me to the last slab, the one bearing the miniaturized body. Showing me where the rail was hidden under the plastic sheeting, she took the cot on which the body lay by one end and I the other. It was the size of a child, but weighed as heavily as the body of any grown man. Together, we moved it to the next slab, jostling it in the process. The bodies of the twinned man and the ordinary corpse jostled where they lay, but did not rise or move in concert with the first. Her point demonstrated, Carter said, "It's possible to restrain one and move the others." Only slowly did I realize she was staring at me. "Have you ever seen anything like this?"

I shook my head, and the scholiast seemed to deflate.

"We removed some of the tissue from the chest. Fragments of bone. Care to guess what happened?"

I knew the answer from the file, and so waited for Cassandra, who ventured, "You have three of each fragment?"

"No," said Tor Carter. "That was how we realized what had happened here. We only have one." She turned and found a small sample jar on a counter to one side. It held a sliver of bone. "The fragment disappeared from the other bodies."

"You said there were no other bodies," Cassandra said.

"Precisely!" Carter said, eyes widening. "Two of these are images of the first!"

"It's incredible," Oberlin said, voice cracking. "Truly incredible…"

"I don't understand," Cassandra said, looking to me. "I am not a scholiast."

"Have you ever used a three-mirror vanity?" Carter asked. Cassandra allowed that she had. "When you adjust the angle of the side mirrors, your reflection changes shape and size, does it not? And were you to alter the mirror—make it convex or concave, say—you could distort your reflections even more."

While the scholiast spoke, I studied the ruin of Mann's chest. It was as if the fist of some mighty giant had taken him under the arms and squeezed. Though the body before me then was no larger than that of a child, it resembled in perfect proportion the body of a man. Even the tattered uniform it wore was smaller. A flap over what had been Mann's heart still bore his name in looping Galstani letters, tightly embroidered, a tear above the diacritic that formed the vowel *A*. I looked at the torso of the twinned body behind me. The same embroidery was there to be seen, the same tear above the same diacritic, writ larger on the body of the twinned man.

Everything about the smaller body—its features, its clothing, its belt, even the ruined boots—was rendered in perfect miniature.

"Your reflection in those mirrors are two-dimensional images cast by your three-dimensional self," Carter said. "These bodies are three-dimensional images of Mann's body cast by the higher dimensional reality."

"But we only have three dimensions," Cassandra objected.

"Not so," said Tor Rassam. "We know there are at least ten."

"Everything in the universe exists across all these dimensions," Carter explained. "In the same way that your reflection cannot leave the surface of the glass, you and I cannot leave the three-dimensional surface we call ordinary space. Something disrupted Mann's relationship to that ordinary space. What you're seeing here is him reflected across that surface. Do you see?"

Steadily, Cassandra nodded.

"Ordinarily, these dimensions are only really apprehensible to us by virtue of mathematics, or by the properties of certain machines," Rassam said, crossing his arms against the chill of the air. "Warp drives, for instance."

I hardly heard Rassam as he explained the way in which warp drives folded a three-dimensional envelope of space across those higher-order dimensions.

I had *seen* something.

"What say you, Lord Marlowe?"

"What?" I looked round, found Carter and Rassam alike staring at me.

Have you ever seen a sun fret the edges of a cloud with silver fire? So Mann's body was fretted, such that his edges seemed blurred to me, as though he were an oil painting smeared by the arm of some sloppy artist. Still, they gleamed, and stretched along some direction I had not seen until that moment. Consciously or otherwise, I had begun to look at the bodies with my full vision, and saw that it was precisely as Carter and Rassam had said. The potential states of the universe lay stacked upon one another like books on the shelf of some infinite library, each a subtle variation on the last—most of them so unlikely they would never occur though the gods roll their dice an almost infinite number of times.

The body lay across those stacked potentials, at right angles—as it were—to what you and I perceive as ordinary space. I could see it, as a blurring, a blending of light and color that bound the three bodies one to another.

Carter had said the other bodies were like the images in a mirror. She was almost right. Rather it was like looking through a prism. Mann's corpse was not reflected by our reality, the same atoms appearing in the same configuration.

He was *refracted*, his particles splashing against the membrane of ordinary space, creating ripples so that he seemed to be many places at once.

Transfixed, I moved toward the twinned man.

"Lord Marlowe?" Now it was Oberlin's voice.

"Quiet!" I said, tilting my head.

The vision tilted with it.

If you have drunk of too much wine, Reader, you will perhaps have seen one man become two. I have seen such many a time myself. Know then, that the body of the twinned man—which moments before held so much horror for me—appeared to me as nothing more than the body of an ordinary man, half-mummified and cold, seen with double vision.

I laid my hands upon either side of the doubled head, and gently pressed the two together. Four eyes became three. Became two. Two heads became one.

Cassandra gasped.

"Mon Dieu!" exclaimed young Albé.

Even Rassam and Carter recoiled.

I ignored them, and carefully composed the body's limbs, crossing the arms upon the ruined breast in posture of death. When I had finished, I pulled the white plastic of the shroud across Mann's ruined corpse.

The other slabs were empty, with only the brown stains of blood and grime left as testament to the bodies that had laid upon them.

"Abba?" Cassandra spoke first, voice trembling. *"Quen tuo phael?"*

I could only shake my head. A terrible pressure had risen behind my eyes, and for a moment I thought I must fall. It had been so long since I used the power for anything so great, and I had never used it thus.

"What happened?" asked Tor Carter, peering at me with eyes clear and sharp as ice.

I could feel every eye on me, and turning, I found Lascaris and Oberlin watching through the glass from the morgue's observation chamber, and from the look in both their faces I knew that I had done precisely what they had brought me here to do.

"You have your foxhound, it seems," I said, speaking to Oberlin on the flats beyond the makeshift landing field. The days on Sabratha were short—around eighteen standard hours—and the sun had long since set. The old man leaned upon my arm, abandoning Lascaris at the ramp to his shuttle. We had dismissed the scholiasts, and I'd sent Cassandra back to the *Ascalon*. "Did you know?"

Sir Friedrich's laugh turned swiftly to coughing, and I shied away from him, though he turned his head and covered his mouth with a kerchief. "Did I know you could perform such miracles? Of course, I knew," he said. "I saw the suit recordings from Perfugium *and* Berenike, or had you forgotten?"

I confessed I had. "Even before then...I *believed*." He smiled weakly, and pocketed his kerchief, his smile transformed to a grimace. "What is it like?"

"Like walking through mirrors," I said, refusing to elaborate.

That seemed sufficient for the old spy. "Mirrors indeed," he said. "I want you to keep a sharp eye out, Marlowe. Valeriev and Carter will oversee the dig with Rassam's help. I simply want you to observe."

He stopped walking then, and we stood facing the empty desert. The storm had blown away westward, leaving the night sky clear and so full of stars that one could be forgiven for thinking there was no air between us and them. Sabratha had no moon, and we had left the floodlights of the camp some way behind. All was silent, and—but for the wind—utterly still. The ribs of one of the long-dead *leviathans* rose from the dunes ahead like the pillars of some annihilated temple. Almost I fancied I could hear the wind whistling between them, carrying the nigh-forgotten echoes of some alien song.

We are gone, they seemed to sing. *We are gone.*

"You've brought the weapon down?" I asked.

"Aboard the *Rhea*," Oberlin said. "Vedi has orders to deploy it on the edge of the camp, as far from the workers as may be. Our Irchtani friends will be providing the bulk of security here on the ground, supporting Gaston's men." He coughed again, less violently. "I understand you've already made friends with Chiliarch Annaz."

I adjusted my collar against the gritty wind. "We've spoken."

"You know, it was the Emperor's suggestion we recruit the Irchtani for Gnomon," he murmured, struggling to master his breathing. "He said they believe you to be some kind of prophet."

"Like Dorayaica," I said acidly. After an uneasy silence, I continued, "They think this because their ancestors fought with me. Because of those ancestors, they now travel the stars. Fight for the Imperium. Die for it. They see it as a gift."

"They see it as an adventure, my lord!" said the old man who was much younger than I. "And it is!"

"It's not an adventure, Friedrich," I said. "It's a burden."

The old man coughed again, and when he had finished, said, "It is that, too."

"Are you dying?" I asked.

"Death comes to all!" he exclaimed, almost brightly. "Yes, I am dying. Cancer. Not Lethe's Sickness, of course! The ordinary kind. The doctors give me fewer than five years."

"I am sorry," I said, regretting the question.

"I am not!" he said. "I am two hundred forty-seven years old, by my cells. I'll only be sorry if I don't see the thing to its end." He fell silent himself, and we stood a long moment with the whispering sands. "I will return to the *Troglita* on the morrow. I am too far from my physicians, and the thought of all that arsenic..." He shuddered. "Mother Earth, but it's quiet here. It's never quiet aboard ship."

High above, the light of a satellite blinked green against the unfixed stars where it passed in its slavish orbit. I watched it go. When it went below the horizon, I said, "The first spacefarers confused the Quiet and the Vaiartu, you said. The Emperor said the same." I peered sidelong at the old spymaster. "Is there something you're not telling me, Friedrich?"

The old man had been bobbing his head in time with my words, but said nothing.

"Did you notice the eyes? In the mural in the hypostyle hall?" When Oberlin did not reply, I pressed, turning fully to face the ancient patrician. "They were human eyes."

Blank silence.

"I want answers, sirrah," I said, reminding him of the vast gulf of years between us, of the class divide and all the powers it entailed.

"I don't have any, truly," Oberlin replied.

"Is the Quiet one of *them?*" I asked through gritted teeth. "The writing is the same. The markings on the mural. The anaglyphs!"

Oberlin coughed before he could produce his kerchief. "I honestly don't know, Lord Marlowe."

Growling, I seized the old man by his lapels. Oberlin squawked, then coughed more violently still. I felt his spittle fleck my face. I might have lifted him bodily from the sand, but I stooped instead, saying nothing.

"That's why you're here," Oberlin said, voice very small. "That's why we *need* you. You're the only one who *could* know."

A red light, hard and grainy, shimmered below my eyes. I recognized the sight of some gunner, a sniper doubtless with some stunner or dart-thrower. Snarling, I released the old man, let him stagger under his own power.

"Your abilities. Your...relationship with this...thing," Oberlin said, "you're a part of the puzzle, don't you know?"

CHAPTER 12

RIPPLES

MORNING CAME, AND BROUGHT Tiber Valeriev with it. The Durantine xenologist had orders to show me the chamber where Mann had died. I roused Cassandra, and we made the journey through the camp down into the ruins of Phanamhara, stopping to secure the transparent face shields often worn by workers in the Vaiartu site. They were visors of clearest alumglass that fit snugly over the whole face, just before the ears. A small fan whirred below the chin, conducting a current of filtered air across each of our mouths and noses.

The chamber that had once housed the on-site supplies lay along the left-hand side of the main avenue, in one of the basilicas, a pillared hall decorated with narrow, pointed windows, deeply carved so that triangular beams of sunlight fell upon the chipped stone floor. The wall opposite the door and the square pillars within was covered with line after line of Vaiartu sineoform, each line etched deeply into the green stone by some long-rusted chisel.

"They took the stores out right after it happened," Valeriev said, voice muffled by his filter mask. "Moved them inside the grand hypostyle, into one of the side chambers. Set up another site the next avenue over."

I was absurdly conscious of the ringing of my bootheels in that hard and empty place. Every footfall returned as the echo of a hundred feet, until I seemed a platoon. Despite the ambient noise of the men and the excavator working outside the basilica, the quiet of that room was like the quiet of a Chantry sanctum. One almost expected to see icons of graven ivory, votive candles, and to smell the fresh fruits of sacrifice starting to sour.

"They were all in the back, not quite up against the wall."

"What was this room for?" I asked.

Valeriev brushed his lank, brown hair from where it had fallen over his mask. "We think it's a kind of monument. Recordkeeping, even."

"Recordkeeping?" I looked at the inscription on the pillar nearest me, a million thin, notched characters arranged line upon line.

Valeriev pointed. "The Vaiartu language—the main one, that is—is agglutinative. I don't have the trick of it. I know a few of the symbols." He traced a line with a finger, not quite touching the vile stone. "*U re she te*... that one there is a click. *Su te te*... another click. That one makes a sound midway between a J and an L—I can't say it."

"They could click and vocalize that at the same time," I said, recalling my vision within the temple of Miudanar.

This revelation did not seem to surprise Valeriev. "I've seen the reconstructions. We've found some bone and metal fragments, but no complete fossils here."

"You said there is more than one language here?"

"Oh yes." Valeriev craned his neck, then approached a tight column of writing on the back wall. "See this? See how the characters are more cramped? We call this Type-C. Carter calls it Onharric."

"Onharric?"

"Onhar is a Vaiartu colony up Sagittarius," he said. "It's where they first found this style."

"Were they different species?" Cassandra asked, squinting up at the cramped alien letters.

Valeriev shook his head. "We don't think so. Different *ethnoi*, maybe." He gestured at the wall with one spread hand. "This whole place was built by a Vaiartu monarch—ethnarch, what-have-you—named *A Ra Va Te Te Ap U Lu*."

"Named *what?*" Cassandra could hardly conceal her amusement.

"Aravte-Teäplu," the doctor explained, repeating the name in its humanized pronunciation. "It means *blessed* or *chosen warrior*."

"I suppose it could be a title?" I mused.

Valeriev gave a noncommittal shrug. "*Moshda*," he said, which was *maybe*. "It's hard to know. But!" He waved his hands at the walls. "You see all four of the Vaiartu languages here, all of them praising their king. *All praise to Aravte-Teäplu, the Many-Conquering, the All-Conquering!* That sort of thing. Much of the inscription details how he ordered his slaves to build this city, and the tribute they offered him."

"That seems a strange thing to etch on the walls," Cassandra said.

"Think of it like credit, Anaryan," I said. "The builders would have wanted it known how it was they contributed to the work. I'd wager much of the inscription is just... *names*."

Cassandra hugged herself as she looked up and around at the cyclopean green chamber. "It's close in here," she grumbled. "The air doesn't seem to move."

"Is the fan in your mask on?" I asked.

"*Si, Abba,*" she answered, but checked the jaw controls. "Don't you feel it?"

In point of fact, I did. Despite the sawtooth windows and open stone arch leading back outside, the air within felt stale and dead on my skin. So as not to feel it, I tugged my leather gloves from a coat pocket and pulled them over my hands. "Where was the body?"

Valeriev indicated the place with a jerk of his head. "You can still see the markings on the floor, though they've faded."

I looked at the floor for the first time. Great black stripes marred the green stone, many of them smeared or faded to thin gray. The greatest of these must have run for more than thirty feet, a curling stripe of black on green. Others ran onto the walls, while some were so small they appeared as no more than points of darkness on the verdant stone.

"The wind doesn't much get in here, as the young miss noted," Valeriev was still talking.

I raised a hand for quiet.

There was no shine, no distortion of the sort I had seen on Mann's body, though I stretched my vision wide. Turning my gaze sidelong, I peered in that direction no other man could see, and saw myself standing in the basilica again and again and again, reflections in mirrors like those of the Alcaz du Badr.

Nothing.

I let the vision fade.

They were only markings, looping, wheeling scratches in the alien stone, and though many of them were broken and smeared, enough remained intact that I could see the truth of them—from the greatest orbit to the smallest pinprick.

They were circles all.

I crouched to touch one with gloved fingers, felt a slight depression in the stone—no more than the width of several hairs. The glove came away gritty, black powder on my fingertip. A dark smudge peered blearily up at me where my finger had disturbed the circle. Abruptly, I recalled the plains of Deira upon Berenike, the way the silicates in the soil had melted and fused beneath the Cielcin laser blast.

"It's burnt," I said.

"Burnt?" Cassandra crouched and imitated me, rubbing stone ash between her fingers.

"That's what I thought!" Valeriev squinted down at us. "Can you make any sense of it? Is it possible the Vaiartu have some weapon still operational? Something that could burn stone like this?"

I looked at him, but said nothing. He knew as well as I—and perhaps better—that hardly any piece of electronica would remain functional after nearly a million years.

"Have you found anything they built that still works?" Cassandra asked.

"*Nien.*" He crossed his arms, a touch defensive. "But they look like plasma scores, don't they? That's what Gaston said, and Sir Oliver before him."

I allowed that they did, and stood with a groan and a click in my left knee. The desert dryness was already depleting my skin—so used to Jadd and the *Islis du Albulkam.* I longed to scratch my face, but could not.

"They look like ripples, don't they?" Cassandra asked, still crouching above the burn marks. "Like when you throw a handful of rocks into a pool."

That cocked my head, and I frowned. "I see what you mean," I said, walking a quarter turn round the site and nearer the wall. Where two of the circles intercepted, each wavered slightly. "I don't know of any plasma burner that leaves marks like this." I turned back to Valeriev. "You've seen the bodies?"

"I have not," he said. "That's Carter's bailiwick. Gaston has, but he wouldn't speak of it.

"Doctor Mann was *crushed,* Valeriev." I pointed at my ribs with both hands. "About the torso."

The man swore in Durantine, a steady stream that morphed into Galstani as he said, "I am not some daft provincial. I have heard your reputation, Lord Marlowe. I will not be frightened by ghost stories and sorcery."

"There is no sorcery," I said, tempted to perform for the fellow, though I had once refused to perform for the Emperor. "What you call *sorcery* is only science you do not understand." I swept my coat around myself. "There are more things in heaven and Earth, doctor, than are dreamt of in your philosophy."

The Durantine xenologist laughed, and looking to Cassandra for succor, asked, "Is he always this way?"

Long-suffering, she opened her hands in an eloquent shrug.

I studied Valeriev. It was obvious to me that—though he knew of the Vaiartu as much as anyone not directly on the HAPSIS payroll—he knew next to nothing of the Monumentals, of the Watchers themselves.

It was not for me to tell him.

And yet... Oberlin had spoken of fingerprints, of the places where the energistic bodies of the Watchers intersected our world. The body of Miudanar had been one such fingerprint, the condensates of energy into matter in the form of some black serpent-god. Were not these rings another? The trace in carboned stone of contact with that higher, larger universe?

They were the boot print, and poor, ill-fated Doctor Mann had been the roach.

I felt so small. And of what benefit is the knowledge whence the boot may fall to any insect who has not the strength to withstand its blow? Of all the insects called man, it seemed I alone possessed that knowledge and the faculty to do something about it.

It was . . . a profoundly isolating experience.

"You know," Valeriev was saying, "you're an odd man, Marlowe. I'm not sure what I expected. You don't act like a soldier."

"I'm not," I said, and amended, "not anymore."

"What are you, then?"

I looked sharply at him, coat swirling as I turned. After a beat, I said, "A sorcerer."

Valeriev grinned, shook a finger at me. "Well played!" he said, "Very well played. A sorcerer!" He descended into a stream of Durantine too accented for me to fully comprehend. I caught the word *muskara*, however.

Bastard.

"You never answered yesterday," Valeriev said. "Why are *you* here?"

I had not taken my eyes from him, and held his gaze until he turned away, frustrated.

"I am perhaps the galaxy's foremost authority on the Cielcin," I said, and watched the shadow fall across the doctor's unhandsome face. "The Cielcin . . . *developed* on a former Vaiartu colony world. They call the Vaiartu the *Enar*, the First, and consider themselves their heirs. *Dedim*, the Second."

"You're saying there's some connection between the Cielcin and the Vaiartu?"

"I am saying the Cielcin may be coming *here*, doctor," I said, and saw the man grow pale.

"Why?"

Looking to Cassandra, I smiled, "Something killed Doctor Mann. Whether that something is an Enar weapon—as you suggest—or *sorcery*, the Cielcin will move to claim it. I am here to ensure that does not happen."

I said nothing to him of the Watchers. Let it remain a matter between Oberlin, the scholiasts, and myself! There was still a chance for Tiber Valeriev, a chance the Empire might let him go, let him return to the serene republic of his home. It was unlikely, but the secrets I held were a hazard then, a danger to all who knew them.

Better he remain director of the dig, and only that.

Better he remain in the dark.

The light—as I have had uncounted occasions to learn—is forever blinding.

CHAPTER 13

OF NOISE AND SIGNAL

IF OBERLIN HAD HOPED for the Watcher to sense my presence and swiftly appear, he was disappointed. One had certainly been at Phanamhara. What other possible explanation could there be for state of Doctor Mann's refracted corpse? The files Oberlin had given me detailing the fates of the crew of the *Atropos* and of the men of Operation Gnomon who set up to work on Nairi after them had contained images of several such refracted corpses, some small as dolls, others large as giants.

The appearance of differential volume is not a property of the material, one Gnomon man had written. *Rather, it is a consequence of the relationship between the material object and our three-dimensional plane. Thus, as an object retreats from our dimensional plane, it grows either apparently larger or smaller. Hirata speculates that the appearance of growth or shrinkage is dependent upon the direction of travel relative to what we must call normal space, with diminished objects in a sense below us but intersecting our reality, and enlarged ones above. What the boundaries of such diminishment or enlargement may be is hard to speculate. Objects made larger by the Entity appear diffuse, translucent. It is speculated that an object may vanish entirely, if removed from normal space sufficiently as to no longer intersect with same.*

More testing and test subjects are needed.

One of the devils was in our midst. But it did not show itself. Perhaps it was ignorant of our presence, *removed* from our reality, sulking in some corner of unseen space. On Eue, whatever remained of Miudanar had seen me at once. But had it known I was coming? Was it not possible that some pearl of awareness in what Dorayaica was fast becoming had spoken to the greater part of the Watcher that slumbered in that profane city? Might Dorayaica have alerted its god to my coming?

Or was the Watcher on Sabratha watching even then?

Of the men who had seen Doctor Mann's body, not a one had seen him die. I spoke to each of them, together and alone, and learned nothing.

I pitied them. The thirty years they'd spent on ice had placed a gulf of time between them and their families in any case. They were plebeians all. Their parents were surely dead, or ancient by the count of common years. Their wives would be twice their age and matronly. Their children grown. It would be a mercy to ship them all offworld, to send them to some far-off colony where they might start again.

But I was not sure even that would be allowed. They knew nothing of substance, and posed no threat, but the barest word of what they'd seen would spawn another rumor in the river of human affairs. I doubted I would succeed, and each successive interview left my mouth increasingly sour.

They were dead men—every one—though Death had yet to find them.

It was night again, and we been for months at Phanamhara. *Pha Na Ma Ha Ra*, which Carter and Rassam told me meant *the Nearest Place* in the old High Vaiartu language, though what it was near *to*—or what Sabratha was near *to*—was any man's guess. Phanamhara, City of the Enar. City on the Sea of Silence.

How silent it was!

The wind through the camp as I walked, an unseen and yet substantial presence, was given body by the sand that stung my face—some of which I was sure were the dry-climate plankton that maintained the atmosphere. But for the crunch of my boots and the faint action of the camp behind, there seemed nothing in all creation, nothing save the plateau of the *Mensa,* which rose flat-crowned but massive in that sea of alloyed white and dun. In the distance, I saw the many-pillared skeleton of the leviathan, *Cetoscolides sabrathis,* rising from the dunes beyond the landing field, lifeless and grim.

All Sabratha seemed a graveyard in that moment, a planet of the dead.

Disturbed by my passage, a native *tataxus*—a six-legged creature like an armored badger—hurried across the path beneath the light of one lamp. It was among the largest of the native life that yet endured on Sabratha, the apex predator of that not-quite-dead world. They had taken a liking to the camp, so Gaston said, and were always burrowing beneath the longhouses where it was warmest, sleeping by day and scavenging for scraps and the desert mice and insects we'd introduced to Sabratha by night.

There was life. Lonely and desperate, but life all the same.

"...hard to get any work done with the boss's man breathing down our necks." I stopped, surprised by the closeness of the voice. I looked round, spied the shapes of three men huddled around a heater on the porch of the longhouse nearest me on the south side of the main road.

"Ain't that the truth," said another man, and paused for the space of a breath. "What's his fucking name again?"

"Prissy," said the first. "Prissy Lascaris. Old Sir Friedrich's batboy."

"Priscian," said a third.

"Gives me the creeps," said the second. "How's a patrician end up with a face like that, I ask you? Looks like he's been dead three days. You'd think he could have had a better bonecutter."

"He's not bloody palatine now, is he?" said the third. "He is a right prick, though."

"Pricky Lascaris," said—I think—the second man, and laughed at his cheap humor. It was only then I realized the men were surely drinking.

Sir Friedrich's man had been about the camp that whole week, keeping close with Commander Vedi and inspecting the various landers that had brought our men from the *Troglita*. Routine stuff, though he had press-ganged several of Valeriev's diggers into giving him a more detailed tour of the ruins. Lascaris was a HAPSIS man, and so shared the HAPSIS enthusiasm for the xenobites. He had spent a great deal of time with Tor Rassam in the hypostyle, studying the inscriptions there.

Oberlin himself had remained aboard the *Troglita*, bound in part by medical necessity, and in part by his own cowardice. I think it must have taken every erg of fortitude in the man to write the note he'd left me following Gereon's putting me to the Question. The thought of camping in the desert while a Watcher roamed free was quite beyond him.

I stepped forward, and making straight for the landing field and the *Ascalon* beyond the main camp, I waved at the men on the porch. "Good night to you, sirs!" I pretended that I had just seen them.

"You're out late, lord!" called one man from the shadow of the porch. Turning my head, I saw the three men gathered close about their heater, cigarettes in hand. One held a silvered flask that gleamed gold in the light of the heating element. "Cerwyn says storm's due just after midnight. You won't want to be caught outside."

I checked my wrist-terminal. "Midnight's more than an hour off!" I shouted back. "The landing field's not nearly so far as that!" Still, the fellow was right to warn me.

"That was last best estimate, lordship!" said the second man, his voice deeper than the first. "Winds move fast once they hit the Salt Gates, and the spotters were saying the airwaves were all full of ghosts earlier."

I acknowledged this with a wave and trudged on, feet scooping up little fans of dust.

Full of ghosts... he'd said, referring to the way the planet's strong magnetic field trapped and circulated radio transmissions, old messages propagating against the ionosphere, echoes and fragments of yesterday. One heard voices in the old signals, distorted and changed almost beyond recognition. They interfered with all comms traffic, as much or more than the omnipresent static, and so the spotters communicated often by signal flares. The Irchtani had joined them, patrolling the air, watching for storms or other interlopers. They kept watch for the Cielcin, and—though even Annaz and his men knew it not—for the Watcher itself.

Ghosts...

I reached the *Ascalon* not ten minutes later, parked on the near edge of the landing field. Vedi's frigate and the other landers hunkered on the flat beyond. Here and there the white snakes of the water lines and black worms of power cables showed through the sand, all of them linked together like flies in some Brobdingnagian web.

Pushing this unsettling image aside, I mounted the ramp to the hold and entered in, pausing to acknowledge the quartet of Irchtani soldiers who held the inner door.

I reached the first landing and the level of my cabin when I met Neema coming down. The Jaddian servitor wore a white apron whose ties were secured with brass fittings. The triple diamonds of the Nemrut School were embroidered black upon the left breast.

"Master Hadrian!" he said. "I was just washing up. There's pilaf in the refectory for you. The last of the chicken they flew down from William-town on Sunday."

"Thank you, Neema. You're very good to me."

The Jaddian homunculus brightened at my praise and bowed his head. "It's only my job, sir."

"Is Cassandra in her room?" I asked.

Neema shook his head, smoothed his short black hair. "No, master. I thought she was with you."

"I was in the ruins," I said—and added, "I need to wash."

"I'm sure the young mistress has gone into camp. I understand the men place bets on boxing matches many a night."

I frowned. "Is it not a touch late for that?"

Neema shrugged. "I can use the hardline to wire the *Rhea*, have Vedi send some men to look for her."

I hesitated. The Watcher might be *watching* at all times, could strike at any time, as it had stuck Doctor Mann. Some of the work Lascaris had been sent to the surface to oversee was the installation of magnetometers and other sensory equipment, detectors theoretically sensitive to the energies which comprised the Watcher itself. The men of Operation Gnomon had employed such devices in their efforts on Nairi after *Atropos* was lost. We would know if it moved in or about the camp—if indeed it could do such a thing. Likewise, if the Cielcin had come to Sabratha, we would know. Even if the comms could not reach us, there would be the hardline from Markov Station, and if nothing else there would be the entry fires as inhuman ships struck the roof of the world.

And there were the men themselves to consider.

But I was being overcautious. Cassandra was a woman grown, and a Maeskolos of Jadd.

"No need," I said. "She'll turn up before long."

I made to pass Neema for the door and a shower, but the manservant said, "Master?"

"Yes, Neema?"

"I must insist you take pains not to track dust back into the ship. This awful sand gets everywhere! And so much of it toxic!"

"Only when wet."

"Precisely!" Neema said. "Precisely! Suppose any of it were to get into the bath! What then?" Evidently considering his question rhetorical, Neema extended a hand, "Give me your coat, I'll see it's cleaned."

"I've decontaminated already," I said, protesting.

"All the same," Neema said, wagging his fingers. Sighing, I shrugged out of the coat and handed it to the servant. "I would feel better if you and Mistress Cassandra were to wear full environment suits in the ruins. If they are as dangerous as they say, master, I simply—"

I patted Neema on the shoulder. "The camp doctors say it's all right. It's moisture that activates the poison in the stone."

"Sweat is moisture!" Neema called after me, but I was already through the door.

Clean again, I donned my trousers and the Jaddian silk robe of black-and-white jacquard I wore at night, and went to eat the pilaf Neema had left for me in the refectory. The chicken had come in the shipment from Williamtown, as Neema had said, but the cherries were among the last to make the journey—sealed in brandy and chilled—from the ports of Jadd.

Cassandra had not returned by the time I'd finished, and so I went down to the hold, fastening my shield-belt about my waist, the sword hilt swinging from its hasp. The Irchtani hopped to attention. Their kind do not sit or lie down to sleep, lacking knees in their short legs, but two of the four had huddled and raised their pinions to hide their faces.

"Asleep on the job?" I asked them, smiling.

"Apologies, *bashanda*," said one, bobbing his head. He bent rigidly at the waist and collected his long saber from the floor.

One of the two who had been still alert squawked and opened his beak. "We sleep but lightly. I told these two *kajeema*, these *hatchlings*, to rest their eyes and wings. All is quiet tonight. As every night."

"No matter," I said. "I thought there was supposed to be a storm?"

"Soon, says friend-Inamax," the leader said, peering one-eyed at his companion, a slim, gray-feathered Irchtani. "He flew but quarter hour past."

I nodded. So the storm Cerwyn—the camp's meteorologist—had predicted was moving slower than expected. I checked the chronometer on my terminal display. It was nearly midnight, and yawning dark oozed in from the open ramp at the far end of the hold. "Has my daughter reported in?"

"Girl *kajeema-bashanda?*" the one called Inamax inquired, his Galstani poor. "No, *bashanda.*"

My disquiet grew. It was possible that she'd gone into the camp for the fighting. I was not sure if I should laugh or fear at the thought of my Cassandra battling Sollan legionnaires and engineer-laborers in the dimly lit hall of some shuttered mess. She was palatine—and more than palatine, a Jaddian *eali* in all but name. She would be faster and stronger than any of them, despite her sex. But I was her father, and the thought of her fighting was always sour to me, though I had encouraged it from the start. Abruptly I recalled teaching her to punch when she was just a little girl, kneeling to be nearer her size as I taught her not to use her fist as a hammer—as all young children do.

"Wind's howling," I said, marking the sand that floated into the hold, piling in little drifts in its corners. The Irchtani bobbed their heads. "Will one of you go tell Neema to wire Commander Vedi?"

The commander of the four—his name was Enaam—waddled to the door.

Before he could make it three hopping strides, the sound of laughter issued from the darkness outside the open ramp. A woman's laughter.

I felt my heart unclench at the sound, but felt my jaw tighten a moment later as Cassandra mounted the ramp.

Edouard Albé walked beside her, an antique MAG rifle slung over one shoulder. The two were laughing still. The HAPSIS agent had removed his spectacles, and his hair was uncharacteristically free of the Delian oil he favored, so that it hung down the right side of his face just past his eye. In place of his officer's blacks, he wore the dark fatigues of a common legionnaire, but the same high, equestrian-style boots. Cassandra was similarly dressed, having eschewed her Jaddian tunic and swordmaster's *mandyas*, though the swords remained, strapped to either hip. She wore one of the undyed sagum cloaks preferred by the locals, and her twin braids hung down, one over either shoulder.

"There you are!" I crossed half the hold toward them. "I was starting to wonder where you were! Neema thought you were off fighting in the mess."

"That's Wednesday nights!" Cassandra said, and gestured to young Albé. "Edouard and I were out past the landing field, hunting tataxi."

"Hunting tataxi?" I said, looking from one to the other. "Did you catch one?"

"We caught three!" Edouard said breezily, adjusting the drape of his gun against his shoulder. "You can't eat them—they're mostly chitin and bone anyhow. But they make for good target practice."

My eyes narrowed. "In the dark?"

"She has thermal sights," the HAPSIS man explained, letting the rifle slide smoothly from his shoulder to his hands. "You'll appreciate this. She's been in my family for generations. Your brother and my ancestor dug her up with a cache of weapons in the caves above my village."

"Don't talk to me about my brother, *A2*," I said, sharply enough that Cassandra's face darkened. Privately, I wondered again at this man's connection to Crispin, at his family's connection to mine. What village was this he spoke of? Some township in the coastlands of Ramnaras beyond Meidua? I might have asked, but I did not trust the Delian agent, and misliked his overfamiliarity with my daughter.

The enthusiasm that had for a moment brightened his handsome, patrician face faded, and the gun drooped in his hand. "My great-great-grandfather, Jean-Louis, saved your brother's life with this gun," he said.

For an instant, the lights of the hold glinted off an embossed silver plate on the weapon's left side, just above the trigger. The Marlowe devil capered there, trident in hand.

If I had doubts about the fellow's authenticity, they faded then—or nearly faded. I did not like him, or trust him, but I realized that I had doubted his connection to my home entirely, and drew back a step. "Then your family has done mine a service," I said—though Edouard knew that already. "Good night, sirrah Albé," I said, and turned to go. "Come, Cassandra!"

"What was all that?" Cassandra confronted me on the stairs, seizing my wrist.

I stared blankly down at her.

"You're so cold to him! He's not a bad sort!" She glared up at me with hard, green eyes.

"You must be careful of him, Cassandra," I said, voice echoing off the walls of the stairwell. Realizing just how loud I was, I lowered my voice. "You read the Emperor's letter. These people are not our friends. Not Oberlin. Not the scholiasts. Not Valeriev or any of the locals, and certainly not *Special Agent 2.*"

She planted her hands on her hips, raised her chin in a gesture as much me as it was her mother. "This is about your brother."

'Tis about your brother.

"This is nothing to do with Crispin," I said. "These are not *safe* people, Cassandra. This is not a safe place. You know why we're here. What we're hunting. Even if we could trust the Imperials, this may be one of the most dangerous planets in the galaxy. I need you to be more careful. Of Albé, and in general." I reached out and put a hand on her cheek. She did not shy away. "Please. There is so much you do not understand."

"Then teach me!" she said, putting her hand on mine. "Abba! You still have not explained what you did with that man's body! *How* you did it. And if I should be so concerned about Edouard, *why?*"

I didn't understand. "Because he's one of them," I said.

"You were one of them!" she said.

"And you know how that ended!"

"But it cannot be the two of us and Neema against the Empire *and* this thing!" she said, her own voice rising.

I raised a flat hand and lowered it, cautioning her for quiet. Neema and I had been hard at work destroying the surveillance equipment Oberlin's men had secreted aboard the *Ascalon,* but I was by no means confident we'd found it all, and the Irchtani were just below and keen eared.

"Why are you so against him *specifically?*" Her face darkened. "Is it because he's a man? Abba, I am forty-one standard. I am not a child!"

"You are *my* child," I countered.

"I am an old woman by plebeian standards!"

"You are not plebeian," I said.

Cassandra exhaled sharply, her frustration plain. "We have to trust someone, Abba," she said, "Why not Edouard?"

I was silent.

"It's because of your brother, isn't it?"

"Enough about my brother, Anaryan," I said, and resumed my march up the stairs. "Psychologizing ill-suits you."

"Because I'm right?" She followed me.

"You heard what I said." We reached the door to the second level and the hall to our cabins. "Be careful with young Albé... and all the rest."

Her footfalls faltered behind me, and I turned. She had stopped, her head bowed, her hand on the frame of the door to the stairs. "Yes, Abba." She seemed strangely small in that instant, a shadow of the girl she'd been. I had not meant to make her feel so, and took a step toward her.

"Cassandra," I said, and smiled. She smiled in return—the crooked Marlowe smile. "I love you, you know that?"

"I know," she said. "I love you, too."

You're not wrong.

"I'm sorry I brought you here," I said. "To this... terrible place."

"I'm not," she said, and raised her chin as she had before. Like her mother. Like me. "Else you'd be here alone."

Old habit turned my face from hers before she could read the expression there. Masking it with bravura, I said, "Well, there's Neema..."

"Good old Neema," she said, and laughed a little.

"Good night, Anaryan."

"*Buon lail, Abba.*"

CHAPTER 14

PHANAMHARA

GREEN DUST STILL FLOATED on the air as I followed Valeriev's men through the breach, feet rattling on the carbon sheeting they'd laid over the glassy walls of the hole the plasma bore had made through more than five cubits of Vaiartu plascrete. Valeriev had argued against the procedure vociferously, citing the potential damage the heat and drilling might cause whatever artifacts were to be found on the far side—to say nothing of the walls themselves.

I had relented to Neema's hectoring in time, and had taken to wearing my armor when I went into the ruins. The old Imperial suit still fit me, and served to protect me against the copper arsenite favored by the Vaiartu-Enar in the coloring of their stones. But there were other benefits.

What was it Neema had said?

It was a matter of prestige. So armored, I was *Lord Marlowe* again, and not a scarred and graying old man in somber Jaddian finery. The face I showed the workers was polished adamant, black as night, and my voice—which had once commanded legions—sounded loud and deep from the speakers hidden in the sculpted breastplate.

"Where has Valeriev gone?" I asked, stepping down onto the floor on the other side.

"That way, lord!" said a man.

I hardly heard him. I was looking down in wonder, and had quite forgotten the Durantine xenologist. I'd forgotten the workers all around me, and the metallic egg-shape of the plasma bore.

Sonic and gravimetric detection had hinted at this *massive* chamber, but to see it for the first time was something else entirely.

Already a constellation of floating glowspheres was spreading out to fill the volume, dropped or thrown from the ledge before me by the men who'd gone ahead. Many were remote piloted, as were the mapping drones whose green fan-lasers swept every graven surface.

"Are you all right, lord?" Edouard Albé had entered just behind me.

I looked round, saw him watching me through the glass of one of the filter masks. Like the majority of the laborers, A2 had chosen to wear the quilted jumpsuit of the engineering corps, whose helmets had the same profile as the faceless casques of common soldiers, but whose visors were clear alumglass, a close-fitting bubble about the face that gave way to combat ceramic and steel just before the ears and below the jaw.

"Do you see this?" I asked him.

We had emerged onto the upmost gallery of a chamber vast and round as the bowl of a coliseum. Standing on its precipice, I judged the space perhaps a thousand feet in diameter, and deep. *Terribly deep.* The dim edges of the circular room were only then becoming visible, and the margins of the domed roof—supported by buttressed pylons of rude stone—were only rumors hinted at by the dull gleam of distant green.

Below us, level upon level of circular galleries descended, each one slightly smaller than the last. The floor of the one upon which we stood slanted down as one approached the inner rim—which had no rail or parapet whatever. I imagined hordes of the Enar standing, swarming over the stones, so that those highest and farthest from the rim might peer over the iron carapaces of their fellows and see the floor of the rotunda far below.

"We're right under the center of the mountain!" Edouard said from my elbow.

"I know," I said to him.

In a sense, the city *was* the mountain, and the native rock that piled over it was only the deposited sediments of the vanished sea. Without the city, there would have been no mountain.

"Stand clear of the edge!" one man in the white-quilted uniform of an engineer was shouting, waving his gloved hands. "The stone's not stable!"

I saw what he had seen then: Whole time-eaten chunks of stone had fallen away at the lip of the gallery and smashed to rubble on the level below. There were yet whole arcs of the circumference smooth and unblemished, but there were likewise sections that had crumbled like old plaster.

"What do you think they used it for? This place?" Edouard asked, backing up as the engineering team went down the line, warning their fellows to keep back. I heard one man shouting for glow-tape, intending to mark the edge. "Some kind of temple?"

"Archaeologists always think the things and places they find are religious," I said.

"You don't think so?"

"It could well be," I allowed. "Whatever this place is for, it lay at the center of their lives. But we know so little of the Vaiartu. This might be a public square. A court. An arena!" I cast my gaze round at the walls, and felt my breath catch. The walls behind were covered in flaking friezes, images depicting the Enar—flat, many-limbed crustaceans wielding lightning in their claws—as they marched against a shrinking people depicted as bow-legged quadrupeds with no discernable head and a finely chiseled texture that might have been fur. Precisely as Valeriev had cautioned, our bore had burned a hole clean through it.

What was lost could never be regained.

Men hurried past us, carrying more lighting equipment. One unspooled a cable through the fresh opening.

"That's strange," Edouard said, and turning I saw him wiping at his visor with a gloved hand. "There's water."

"Water?" I echoed.

"Well," he said, "Sabratha was covered in water at one point. We're so deep underground, it's no wonder there's some left." He looked up, and doing so I saw a droplet *plink* against the alumglass of his helm.

Following his gaze, I saw a thin rivulet wending its way down a course in the ribbed ceiling, dripping here and there as it dribbled along the wall.

A thought occurred to me, and I called, "Valeriev!"

The Durantine doctor—dressed in his customary browns with only the filter mask in place—hurried toward us. I showed him the water. "You should clear out," I said, acknowledging his state of dress. "You and anyone not fully suited."

"*Sranna!*" he hissed. "Where is it coming from?"

"Maybe some higher chamber still has water in it," Edouard speculated.

"Most likely," I said. "I can handle things here. You take the lads as need it. Get cleaned and checked." I grabbed one of the engineers. "Get a wire probe and fish up there!"

The man saluted and hurried out through the probe hole. Valeriev hadn't moved. I pointed out the way we'd all come. "Remove yourself, doctor! The last thing we need is you or your men dying of arsine gas. Go now!"

To my surprise, Valeriev did not argue, but shouted for anyone not fully suited to follow him. A dozen or so men—*his* men, I noted with some frustration—all followed.

"Has anyone found the way down?" I shouted.

"Here, lord!" One man waved from a space to our left, arms white in the green darkness. "There's something down there!" I peered over the lip, but the light of our glowspheres had yet to penetrate the full depth of the gloom that filled that echoing cavern.

So I moved to follow the man who had shouted.

What he had found was the top of a steep stair made by the overlapping of angled treads like wedges projecting from either side of the wall, so that looked at head on the steps formed a V, with the lowest point in the middle.

Our descent was precarious and slow. The steps had been made for creatures six-legged, squat and flat, and all too easily I could see myself tumbling to my doom. We emerged onto the second level, which was little different than the first, a slanting gallery of smooth stone overlooking the floor below. In time we descended past five levels to the floor, and found it a flat expanse of stone with a dais in the middle, a great round stage perhaps three hundred feet across. Trapezoidal doorways led from the chamber in all directions, leading to deeper and darker halls. The three nearest had all collapsed.

All this retreated from my senses, however.

I had eyes only for the *thing* on the dais.

All black it was, blacker than the gloom, though it lay beneath the dust of eons, its surface faceted like hammered steel. I knew what it was at once, what those tangled, seeming-fallen pillars of stone had been in life. Great as tree trunks they were in girth, the smallest of them many times the height of a man. Seeing them moldering there, I fancied that I heard a whispering, just as I heard in the teeth of the gates at Akterumu, and felt my eye drawn to them, plucked from my head entire and dragged through the air between.

"What in Earth's name is that?" asked one of my companions.

They were the bones of a hand.

A giant hand.

Wordlessly, I approached, mounting the steps of the dais, Edouard and two engineers close behind.

"That can't be real, can it?" asked one of the techs. "Some kind of statue?"

I said nothing, approached it like a man approaches a sleeping panther with only a sharpened stick, shoulders raised. It was identical in substance to the skull of Miudanar, its surface like chipped black glass.

"It looks almost human," said the other engineer.

"Almost," I said. "Count the fingers."

There were six.

The dais was not wrought of the ubiquitous green stone, but of a white marble pale as milk.

"That's not Vaiartu writing," said Edouard, pointing to the perimeter of the stone. "It looks like Cielcin."

"It's neither," I said, sparing the inscription a glance. "Cielcin looks like *it*."

I thought of the Asara Cylinder, of the tablet Attavaisa had given Dorayaica in homage, and the ones I'd seen in other memory, from voyages to Echidna I'd never taken. All of them showed Vaiartu writing and graven images clustered about the round characters of the Quiet's speech.

Of the Watchers' speech.

So too, the ruins of Phanamhara were clustered about that place, about that hand.

The hand of one of the Watchers, long dead.

"It's just like the one our men recovered from Echidna," Edouard said, not two paces to my left. He craned his neck, the better to examine the full height and majesty of the bones.

"What is it?" asked one of the techs.

"The bones of a god, sirrah," said I. "This is what we've come to kill."

"Looks dead to me," the fellow said.

"No." Spurred by some instinct I could not name, I released the tab that unbolted the vambrace on my right arm. The armor fell to the stone with a clatter, and I broke the seal that secured my glove.

"What are you doing?" Edouard asked.

I did not answer him, but pressed my bare hand to the glassy material that made up the Watcher's bones.

I drew it away at once.

"It's bitter cold," I said, and touched the massive finger with my other, still-gloved hand, feeling the cold seep through the polymer. "You can feel it through your gloves, see?"

The HAPSIS man did not approach, instead checked his helm's thermal readout. "Eleven centigrade. That's chilly, but it's not cold."

Abruptly, my mind went to the black stone of Calagah. How similar had that substance been—like obsidian!

"It's only cold to me," I said, certain I was right. I possessed senses the others lacked.

I looked at my fingers, aware that I'd exposed myself to the ambient poison. I told myself I ought not worry. I had not touched the poisoned stone. Indeed, what I had touched was not stone at all. On Eue, I had not had occasion to closely examine the bones of Miudanar, but I was certain that when Valeriev's men and Rassam's examined that dark material, they would find it identical to the exotic matter that formed the black halls of Calagah, of Annica, of the Temple at Athten Var.

Just then, a shout sounded from the galleries high above.

Then something struck the slab not ten feet from us.

Mon Dieu! Edouard swore and leaped back, drawing the stunner holstered on one hip.

I had crouched myself, and drawn the hilt of my sword, ready to conjure the blade.

But there was no need.

The man was already dead.

The fellow had worn the quilted white of the engineers, his helmet the same clear metal-glass as Edouard's. Blood red and bright as vermillion spread along the inner face of that visor, which had not shattered in the fall. The fall must have broken every bone he had.

I looked up. It was nearly a quarter mile to the topmost gallery, more than a thousand feet in that cavernous space.

My fingers found the comm on my wrist-terminal, and I pressed the tab behind my right ear to ensure the conduction patch was seated through my helm. "What happened?"

The response came back garbled, as I knew it would. "—ot sure, m—lord." Static hissed, and I turned to take three paces away from the body as the man kept speaking. Phrases came out broken, slashed, but I discerned one word through all the chatter.

"Jumped."

My blood ran cold.

The poor bastard must have jumped the instant I touched the hand.

CHAPTER 15

SECOND SONS

THE IMAGE SHOOK, ROCKED side to side with every desperate step. Ragged breathing sounded over the speaker system. A faint groan that might have been the word *no*. Then it was hurtling out into blackness. The distant floor—green and white—became the roof above as gallery after gallery rushed by. A scream—the same ragged scream I'd heard standing down on the dais—filled the cramped cabin. There followed a horrid crunch and a terrible stillness. Then enameled black greaves appeared, and Hadrian Marlowe stared down at the dead man.

"Enough, Priscian," said Friedrich Oberlin.

The secretary keyed the playback to halt.

"He just...ran for it," I said into the fresh silence. "Was he unwell?"

"Nothing in his last evaluation," the Director said over his cup of faintly floral tea. "But you knew that."

Edouard Albé sat beside me, fingering the reports that one of Lascaris's staff had brought in from the back office. The dossier showed a blunt-featured but honest looking plebeian man, bald as any legionnaire, with a sailor's pallor and the blue shadows of stubble on cheeks and scalp.

"Alexander of Alba," Albé said, and recited his serial number. "Passed his civil exams with distinction. Tested into the engineering corps, ninety-sixth percentile..." He continued reading. "There are no psychiatric flags on his record. Unless you count this drunk-and-disorderly."

"Which you shouldn't," Oberlin said. "The rank and file collect those like bottle tops, every time they take shore leave."

"He's clean," Lascaris agreed.

"It was the Watcher," I said. "It has to be. This man, Alexander, killed himself the moment I touched the hand. It must have been watching us."

Lascaris spoke haltingly. "You...think it impelled the engineer to kill himself? Possessed him? Like a daimon?"

"That's what happened on Nairi," I said, looking up at the gaunt secretary. Lascaris looked—if anything—even less like himself than usual, more tired and drawn than ever. The fellow desperately needed sunlight. Exercise. A woman. "If a machine can influence a man's mind, why not one of the Watchers? The one I encountered on Eue gave me visions."

"But why make the man kill himself?"

I could only shrug.

"Perhaps it means to frighten us," Oberlin said, dabbing at his spotted scalp with a cloth.

"Or warn us away," Edouard interjected. "Perhaps it knows we can harm it. Or mean to."

"You think we've frightened it?" Oberlin asked his agent.

"Think about it, sir," young Albé said. "Nearly a year we've been here, and *nothing*. But the minute we dig deeper into the city—find that *hand*—this happens. Surely it's a reaction."

I was nodding along with the young agent's analysis. "It's me," I said. "I came too close."

"Did you *see* anything while you were down there?" Oberlin asked. "Anything at all?" From the shine he placed on the word *see,* I knew he referred to my second sight.

"Nothing," I said. "I'd like to go back down—have a closer look at those bones."

"You can return to the planet when we're done here, lord," Oberlin said, "but I don't want you going into the *pantheon* until Valeriev's men have secured the place. They're bolting in guardrails. I won't have another of my men taking a header off the topmost balcony, and I don't want you going anywhere near the spot until it's secured. Are we clear?"

The old man seemed for a moment half his age as he glared hard-eyed across the table at me, his sclera almost blue in the reflected light of the holograph.

"Certainly," I said.

We had taken a shuttle—young Albé and I—and returned to the *Troglita* almost at once. I'd slept but fitfully. Oberlin had insisted Albé and I receive full physical and chemical exams while the reports were compiled on the incident in what Valeriev was already calling the Phanamhara pantheon. We had both come back clean, as had all but two of the unsuited men who had entered the pantheon with us. They had been sent to the medica in the ground base and put on chelators to remove the arsenic from their blood before much harm could take root.

"We did get in a preliminary analysis of the hand while you were in medica," Oberlin said. "Spectral analysis confirms the bones are not ordinary matter, consistent with samples recovered at Nairi and Echidna."

"Echidna?" I furrowed my brow.

"Lord Powers recovered similar bones in a tomb on the Cielcin worldship," Oberlin said. "After Second Cressgard."

"You didn't tell me that," I said.

Oberlin blinked. "You did not need to know."

"You're going to have to start trusting me, Friedrich," I said.

The Director only smiled. "The substance is a form of highmatter. Tetraquark, we think. Inert, very stable."

"Highmatter?" I said, incredulous.

"Not the same sort used in sword making," Oberlin said. "There is highmatter and highmatter after all. Just as lithium is not iron."

"We'll know more about it in a day or two." Lascaris's terminal beeped, and he rose from his seat, crossed the room to the sideboard where a carafe of water stood fully charged. He filled a pair of cups, and returning handed one to the elderly knight.

Oberlin produced a jeweled pillbox from his coat pocket and swallowed a pair of red gel tablets.

"And there were bones on Nairi as well..." I said, thinking aloud.

Oberlin made an affirmative gesture. Coughed. "Yes," he spluttered, "a far more complete specimen. The Vaiartu built their cities about them where they could."

"Makes sense," I said, "we build our cities about Chantry sanctums."

"Highmatter..." Albé mused, and swept a hand across the tabletop, banishing the projection. A few short taps on the black glass conjured a series of images taken of the hand from the upper levels. The bones had fallen all against one another, collapsed into a pile of knucklebones. Rings of round anaglyphs encircled them, etched into the marble slab by Vaiartu masons. *Très incroyable!*

"Have you checked the bones against the material used in Firstborn sites like I requested?" I asked, thinking of Calagah.

Oberlin shook his head. "Not yet. You really think it's the same?"

I only looked at him.

"What would that tell us?" the Director asked.

"That there is a link between the Firstborn and your Monumentals," I said. *Between the Quiet and the Watchers.*

"We know that already!" said Edouard, tapping the holographs embedded in the table. "Their writing is the same."

"We'd know how the Quiet's ruins were constructed," I said. "Whatever this...highmatter-like substance is, they condensed it down from pure energy, just like the Watchers do when they build a physical form." I dragged one of the images nearer me through the glass table. "There's nothing underneath the slab, is there?"

"Nothing according to gravimetrics," came Oberlin's reply. "Are you expecting something?"

"I'm not sure," I said honestly. "When can I get in to see it?"

"In another week, perhaps," Oberlin replied. "I do not want any more incidents. First that tech of Valeriev's disappears with one of our engineers, now this..."

The four of us were silent then. Oberlin was referring to the disappearance of one Robyne Kel, a junior archaeologist under Valeriev. She and a HAPSIS legionnaire called Irum had stolen a skiff from the motor pool and vanished in the night with a select number of Vaiartu artifacts. There'd been no report of them in Markov Station, and that was the nearest settlement—more than three thousand miles away.

It did not seem likely—even with a fresh fusion cell—that a skiff could make it all the way to Williamtown, or to one of the mining depots at the equator. Sabratha was too vast and too sparsely populated. I couldn't fathom what the two of them had been thinking, running away together like that.

Most like they'd not been thinking at all.

"I've ordered Valeriev, Rassam, and Carter to remove the hand and bring it to the surface," Oberlin said.

Edouard and I both spoke at once. "How?" We turned and looked at each other, and I found that—like myself—the young agent had crossed his arms.

I uncrossed mine.

"One of the passages branching off from the pantheon chamber is wide enough and slants upward. It's caved in—that's why we never found it, but Valeriev thinks he can clear it."

"Where does it come out?" Edouard asked.

"In the avenues," said Lascaris. "If our scans are correct."

"You're making a mistake," I said, laying my hands flat on the table, scars and all. "The Watcher made Alexander of Alba kill himself simply because I touched its hand. What more will it do if your people try to move it?"

Oberlin was silent then, staring at the hazy reflection of the holograph in the black tabletop. "There will be time to make that determination while Valeriev continues with excavation. In the meantime, Carter and Rassam will study the carvings in the pantheon. You will join them, and keep an eye out for our quarry." He spoke as though he meant to dismiss me, and Lascaris rose from his place.

I did not rise. "Lord Director," I said. "We should increase security on the ground. If the creature is aware of us, it may attack the camp directly."

"All to the good," said Oberlin with surprising savagery, leaning over the table. "Then it will simply be a matter of deploying the NEM."

"Simply?" I did stand then. "What about this is simple, my lord?

You know as well as I what we are up against. A man is dead of almost supernatural causes. We're dealing with materials beyond human science, a civilization we barely understand!"

Oberlin raised both his hands in surrender. "You're right!" he said. "I should not be so cavalier."

"I don't suppose you've given thought to what might happen if the Watcher finds the Perseus weapon and destroys it?"

The Director's face shuttered, and he looked down. "The weapon is shielded. And we have more NEM weapons aboard the *Troglita*. We can always bomb the site from orbit, should it come to that."

"Commit the rest of the Irchtani, at least!" I said, letting this go. "Let them fly patrols."

"That . . . can be arranged," Oberlin said, standing himself. "I must meet with Captain Clavan. Thank you, Lord Marlowe, A2. Priscian, see them to the launch bay."

Lascaris rounded the table, but I raised a hand to forestall his advance. "Will you not come down to the surface, Friedrich? You should see the pantheon for yourself."

The man's eyes widened, and he shook his balding head. "Not now. When Valeriev clears the path, perhaps. . . ."

I could sense the terror in the man. He did not want to come within a hundred miles of the Watcher's bones, now he was certain they were there. But I did not call him out. "We should deploy the NEM now," I said. "We waste time with this excavation. We should plant the bomb in the pantheon and have done."

"No!" Lascaris objected, voice surprisingly sharp.

I turned, blinked at him. "Why not?"

"Destroy the city?" Oberlin asked. "You surprise me, Marlowe."

"Nothing in the city matters if the beast lives," said I.

"You know as well as I," Oberlin replied, "that the Monumental does not dwell in its bones. You cannot destroy the butterfly by destroying the cocoon."

"Only the caterpillar," I said, voice sour. "But it was there, Friedrich! It was there! It killed Alexander of Alba. I'd bet my life on it."

The old man coughed, dabbed at his mouth with his kerchief. "You may have to, old son," he said at length, sputtering. "You may have to."

"Only you won't bet yours," I said. "You'll stay here."

The director thumped his chest, eyed Lascaris for support. "What would you have of me, Lord Marlowe?" he asked.

I clenched my jaw. "Nothing," I said at last.

Edouard put a hand on my shoulder. "We should go," he said.

"Take your hands off me, A2," I said stiffly. To Oberlin I said, "I will return to the hook then, fisherman. Good day."

I turned to go.

Oberlin's words followed me, and there was a false and fragile warmth to them. "Good day, Lord Marlowe."

"You hate us, don't you?" Albé asked, when he had taken the seat across from me in the shuttle compartment.

"Oberlin's a coward," I said. "For all his talk of not wanting to lose another man, he will risk each of us before he risks himself."

Albé offered a single, curt nod, then leaned back against the gray pads of the headrest. "Try not to think too badly of him," he said, and removed his glasses, the better to look at me. "He is not a soldier. He's old, and very ill."

"He saved my life when we were younger," I said, and peered out the window to my left. "He wasn't so craven."

The HAPSIS agent brightened. "He told me that story! The Chantry had bought one of your lieutenants."

"They had her plant a knife-missile in my cabin," I said. "It nearly killed my wife."

"Valka Onderra?" Albé's dark brows contracted. "Forgive me, I'd not realized you were wed."

"We were as good as," I said, and heard my voice sharpen.

"Forgive me," Albé said. "I meant no offense."

I looked at him, felt my eyes grow hard. "What did you mean?"

The junior flight officer appeared in the door from the forward compartment and saluted. "We're clear for takeoff, sir."

Edouard answered her before I could. "Very good, ensign. Thank you."

It was another reminder that I was not in command.

When she had gone, a quiet laugh escaped me, and I raised one scarred hand to massage my chin.

"What is it?" Albé asked.

"I spent so much of my life trying to escape the walls the Emperor built to trammel me," I said, holding my hands parallel to one another, as if I clutched a box. I shook them on the word *trammel*. "I thought I had. But even on Jadd he had me on his leash, and here I am."

The black-haired young agent inclined his head. "We're all tied to something, my lord."

"I am not *your* lord, sirrah," I said bitingly.

"Forgive me, lordship," Albé said, falling back to the less familiar title. "My family's served yours a long time. The instinct is...deep."

Outside, the hold began to slip away, black plating and strapped crates. We passed the curtain of the static field, and at once Sabratha appeared beneath us, the blind eye of a god mottled white and brown, with here and there the saline blue of vestigial seas.

"I grew up in Devil's Rest, you know," Edouard said. "My family lived in the Belling Tower. Father was Lord Crispin's lictor, and Grandfather before him. We used to visit him—my grandfather, that is—in the mountains."

"You're from the mountains?" I asked. Suddenly the man's linguistic idiosyncrasies clicked into place. "You're an adorator!"

"A Catholic, yes."

"They let Museum Catholics into the Imperial service?" I asked. Long tradition forbade Cid Arthurians, Orthodox Hindus and Buddhists, even Jaddian Zoroastrians from enlisting in the Legions—and especially from the civil service.

Edouard smiled, his glasses back in place. "They don't. But Lord Crispin vouched for me, and I got a letter of recommendation from Vicereine Kephalos to enter Mountbatten Academy on Avalon. The ban can be waived in exceptional circumstances, and the Throne has... always been well disposed to the Church. It was for us the protections granted the adorator cults were created in the first place."

"Why?" I asked, genuinely surprised.

"You don't know the story?" Edouard asked. "I thought you knew everything. That's your reputation."

"Reputations are lies of consensus," said I.

The adorator gripped the shoulder straps of his harness, bowed his head. "Quite," he said. "It's said one of our high priests saved the life of an Emperor, long ago. The Throne has sheltered us ever since."

"I didn't know that," I said. "So my brother and my aunt, the Vicereine, vouched for you, and you entered the service."

"I did," he said. "Civil Intelligence, not the military. From there, I found my way into HAPSIS."

"How did that happen?"

"My connection with you."

"We don't have a connection," I said.

Albé exhaled, rubbed his eyes beneath the glasses. "Yes, you keep saying," he said. "My connection with your family, then. I think Oberlin thought it might prove useful persuading you to come peaceably."

"A foxhound to flush out the foxhound."

"That's me in one," the younger man said.

"You would have taken me by force, then?"

"Legal force," he said. "The Jaddians were set to give you up."

Prince Aldia hinted as much, I thought, but did not say.

We flew on in silence then for a long while. Sabratha was visible through the porthole in the sloping roof overhead, her mountain ranges like caramels in the milk of salt deserts. Edouard moved his lips in time to words I could not hear.

"I met one of your co-religionists once," I said. "On Padmurak. In the Commonwealth."

Edouard ceased his muttering. "Oh?"

"She saved my life," I said. "The Commonwealth's agents tried to assassinate me. She healed my wounds, said she thought your god had a plan for me."

"He does, I'm certain," the adorator said. "He has a plan for each of us."

"He's not the one who has plans for me," I said. "I've met gods, you know. We're here to kill one."

Young Albé gripped the straps of his harness once more. "We're here to kill *something*, but however strange these Monumentals are, they are not gods. They are certainly not God."

"So sure of that, are you?" I asked.

"What happened to that planetologist—Mann." Edouard shut his eyes. "God does not do that."

"What does your God do, then?" I asked hotly. "Does he allow men to die by the million in war against the Cielcin? To be carried off for food? To carry their children? Does he set the Fleshing Plague against us? Did he let my people die?" I was almost shouting by the end.

Edouard pointed his chin, a stolid ferocity in him that I had not seen since the day I struck him upon the lawn before my villa. "Yes," he said. "He allows evil for the greater good, even the Monumentals. But what is evil is not Him."

"But why?" I asked.

The younger man shrugged. "I can but guess at His Wisdom. None can do more."

I scoffed and checked the flight clock. Twenty-five minutes remained to atmospheric insertion. I cursed.

"You asked what my God does," Edouard remised, and smiled thinly. "He raises people from the dead."

I glared at him. "Cassandra says I should trust you."

"Your brother did."

"I am not my brother."

"That is abundantly clear," Edouard said.

That stopped me for several seconds. It had never occurred to me to conceive of Crispin as a man who could inspire loyalty. The boy I remembered had been petulant, stupid, and cruel. Had those been but the features of youth?

"Why did you leave Delos?" I asked.

For the first time, it was Edouard's turn to hesitate. "My brother Germain will be Lord Crispin's lictor after Father." He almost laughed, a short puff of air escaping him. "I thought it would be me."

A similar almost-laugh escaped me, and for the first time I saw myself in the younger man—a thing I'd not expected to find. "Are you the elder brother?" I asked. My own father had passed me over for Crispin, had meant to send me away.

"I am," he answered, "but Germain is the better sword."

"Perhaps he's where he should be, then," I said.

"Perhaps we both are," Albé said. "But I am glad I found you, lordship. You Marlowes need minding."

CHAPTER 16

CIRCLES

WEEKS PASSED. MONTHS. VALERIEV began work excavating the collapsed shaft that linked the pantheon deep below the *Mensa* with the surface. Great boulders and chunks of plascrete were hammered to rubble and carried by hand from the depths. Always when I entered the city, I would pass lines of men bearing laden sacks, each bowed by the weight of the gravel they carried on their backs.

A great slag heap grew beyond the dunes made by the sand displaced from the surface dig. The water was traced to its source: a chamber high above the pantheon. There were rooms there whence the water had never drained. In one such cavern, Gaston's men made a discovery: a colony of many-legged, snakelike fish that must have survived from antiquity, feeding on the microbiota that dwelt in the water.

I returned to the pantheon many times, and spent long hours studying the hand and the inscriptions on the slab it lay upon, relying on my vision to peer across time. Always the hand was there, never moving, though the ruins shifted about it in infinite array.

Rassam and Carter holographed and studied every corner of every gallery in that hideous place, and began the long but steady work of translation. The walls on every level were covered in drab friezes that at the height of Vaiartu power must have been a wonder to behold. There were portions still painted, recalling the *Hulle Frieze* in the hypostyle. The bottommost layer depicted the crabbed forms of the Vaiartu battling one another with primitive weapons, with blade and club and claw. Four-legged ones fought with six-legged, and six-legged with eight. Beneath them were mounded the cracked carapaces of their brothers. The level above showed those same armies prostrated, kneeling before a creature that seemed a formless cluster of feathered wings whose pinions bent to place a star upon the crown of one.

I asked Rassam if this was Aravte-Teäplu, the Wide-Conquering.

"No," the scholiast explained, and showed me an inscription written beneath the star-crowned creature. He traced the sineoform with a gloved finger. "And *Su Na Ma Su Ra Te Ha Nu* received the *su ja ra ka si te te u ma*, the right to rule, from *Ma Su Te Mu*, becoming *Su Na Ma Su Ra Te Ap U Lu*, the First-Binding, the All-Binding."

"Their first king?" I asked.

"Sunamasra-Tehanu, or Sunamasra-Teäplu," Rassam said, rendering the harsh cadence of the Vaiartu syllabary into something like human speech. "United the warring factions of the Vaiartu: the *Vaiartu*, the *Sujaru*, the *Sibaru*, and the *Onharru*."

"The Watchers made him king," I said, and thought, *Like they made Elu king.*

History had repeated itself, but how many times? How many champions had the Watchers anointed for their own? How many times had the black gods turned a people against creation itself?

Rassam led me to the next inscription, a great block of text alongside the winged creature—which could only be the Watcher Masutemu. "It says here how the god ordered his people to burn the stars, to purge all life from the universe, lest the *O Ba Da Mu* bring forth demons to destroy them."

"The Obadam?" I asked.

"The Liar."

Here at least was confirmation of one thing at least: Whatever the link between the Quiet and the Watchers might be—whether or not the Quiet was one of them—they were enemies.

The levels above all told of the adventure-wars of the Vaiartu. How they shattered worlds, and tore suns to pieces, how they hounded life from the least protoplasm to the lost races whose kingdoms stretched across our stars. All to find and cut that thread that anchored the Quiet to his creation.

Mankind.

Almost I felt I saw the black ships of the Vaiartu questing in the black seas of night, searching, always searching.

Earth had been spared the fire only by chance, and now the Cielcin were sent against us—and against the Quiet. In place of this Sunamasra-Teäplu there came Elu, King of Eue, and after him Dorayaica, its heir...

When I was not in the ruins with the scholiasts, I flew with the spotters. Excavations had begun upon the mountaintop, carving away at a million years of sediment and sand. Seen from the air, the ramparts of the surface city stretched from the western face of the Mountain of Whales like the fingers of an enormous hand. Cranes had been erected atop the plateau to lift supplies to the diggers toiling there, and I could see the vast box-holes of the Wheeler grid where Valeriev's workmen labored.

A whole flock of our Irchtani wheeled and dove against the pale heavens. Now and again one would let out a piercing cry—not a word, but a piece of coded music that carried on the wind.

"I wish I understood them," Cassandra said, riding in the spotter's turret just behind.

"It's just a drill," I said. "Annaz wants them sharp. He runs a tight ship."

"I know it's a drill!" she said. "I just wish I understood the calls."

I pulled back on the yoke, yawed ninety degrees to starboard as we leveled off into a smooth hover. One of the bird men screeched then, a noise so fearsome it penetrated even the hull of our flier. *"Ai! Ai! Ai!"*

"That one means they've sighted the enemy," I said, watching the Irchtani fall past us. One slammed fully into another, and for a moment they were falling, tumbling over one another in midair. An instant later they broke apart, each going his respective way.

"Do you understand them?" Cassandra asked.

"Not well," I said. "But I know *that* one well enough."

"I wish I could fly," she said.

"We're flying now."

"I mean really fly," she said.

Taking the yoke in both hands, I drove us forward, scudding across the upper airs out away from the mountain, over the rim of the desert. Far below the camp was a cluster of white buildings, like pebbles in the limitless sand. "The smaller you build a repulsor, the weaker the thrust. You can build them small enough to float a pallet, but you can't make a suit fly. Not unless they find a way to boost the power."

"But you can jump with them, can't you?"

She was thinking of the harnesses stowed in the emergency compartment by the hatch. "You can fall. I used them to drop from orbit a time or two during the war."

"From orbit?" she asked, leaning down from the turret. "What was that like?"

"There was never time to think about it," I said. "We just *went*. We just did it." I so rarely spoke to her of the war. On Jadd, it had seemed part of another world—which in a sense it was—and I had wanted to keep it that way, to keep my daughter in peace and safety. "We dropped into Ganelon—your mother and I. And the Dragonslayers, the ones who brought me to Jadd. It was at Ganelon the Extrasolarians designed the Red Sleep."

I could hear the wideness in her eyes. "The *Lethovirus*? You were at the lab that made it?"

"I burned the lab that made it," I said. "Too late to save the galaxy."

I took us round in an arc that showed off the dig in all its splendor, the green arms of the Enar city rising from the sand, its ramparts beginning to emerge from the rock of the Mount of Whales. "I wonder how many of them lived here."

"Tiber said it must be millions," she said.

"It's Tiber, is it?"

"We've been here almost two years, Abba," she said. "I can't hardly keep calling him *Doctor Valeriev,* can I?"

I let it go. "This must have been a lesser outpost," I said. "Akterumu was *vast.* Miles across, Anaryan. Miles. You could scarcely see one side from the other."

"It sounds beautiful," she said, not knowing what Akterumu had meant for me.

A breath passed me by. Two. Three. "I guess it was," I said, thinking of Gibson's final lesson to me on Delos long ago. "Terrible, but beautiful, too."

"Tiber says the Vaiartu lived in common, save their rulers. All crammed in those halls. Like crabs." She paused, "Why do they look like crabs, Abba?"

I laughed. "You've touched on one of the great questions, girl. Do you know how many lifeforms there are in the galaxy that *look* like crabs?" She was silent. Ahead of us and on our left, the tether of one of the camp's balloons swayed, red warning flags tied to its length. We were right above the camp then. "More or less everywhere there's water, life finds a way to make itself crablike. Even on old Earth, life evolved crab shapes at least four or five different times. As we got out among the stars, we kept finding more of them, even in life not based on the same nucleic acids as you and me. The galaxy is full of imitation crabs! It was only a matter of time before one turned out smart enough to build an empire."

"Why do you know this?"

"I've done a lot of reading," I said. "When you're my age, girl, you'll find you've taken in a lot of stuff you've little use for."

She laughed at me. "But why do you think it is?"

"There must be some utility to the shape." I signaled the camp we were ready to land. "After all, the Cielcin look like us. Two arms, two legs. Perhaps there's some template out there, one we're all just...reflecting." I broke off a moment to listen to the garbled transmission from below.

"Aftern—Spotter N3. This—...—s Ground Con...trol. You—clear to lan...and on Pa—ix...ver."

"Repeat that, Ground Control," I said. "Pad Six? Over."

"Six...ver."

"Understood, Control," I said, and glancing back over my shoulder, said, "I will not miss the comms on this planet when we're done here."

"Can't they do anything about it?"

I adjusted the altitude controls. The spotters were lifted entirely by repulsors, and so did not generate lift by the actions of rocket or wing. It did not bank or slide through the air like a skiff or one of our Irchtani, but translated itself, moving in jagged lines like a ship in vacuum. Lowering us in a straight line was simply a matter of gradually diminishing power to vertical thrust. As I did so, sliding the yoke back toward me, the whine of the repulsor's counter-gravity steadily diminished, and the sands grew ever nearer.

"Not likely," I said. "Not unless they want to outfit every spotter and every suit with a quantum telegraph."

"Why don't they?" Cassandra asked.

"Too expensive and too heavy," I said. "We've got a telegraph on the *Ascalon* if we need to call out. And Gaston has one in the command pod. I suspect Vedi has one on the *Rhea* as well."

"Do you really think there's some...plan?" she asked. "For life? For evolution, like you said?"

I thought about that for a long moment, watching the sand begin to rise, kicked up by the action of our repulsors. "I wish I knew," I said. "But if you ask your friend, Edouard, he'd say we were made in the image of his god."

"The Cielcin, too?"

"I don't know what he'd say to that."

"But Abba," Cassandra asked, unbuckling herself as the spotter made land. "If there are so many crabs in the universe, wouldn't that suggest Edouard's god is a crab?"

I snorted, and Cassandra laughed along with me.

"Maybe," I said, powering the spotter down. "Or maybe Edouard's god is not the only thing out there shaping life in its image."

I unfastened my own crash webbing and made for the hatch. Cassandra was smiling at me, one eyebrow raised in a fashion so like her mother it smote my heart. "What?" I asked, stopping suddenly.

"You called him *Edouard*," she said.

"I did not."

"You did!" she grinned. "Not *A2*. He's growing on you!"

"Let's get back to the ship," I said, opening the hatch. "Neema will be looking for us."

Life at Phanamhara continued in this vein for all our second year. I would pore every waking hour into study with Valeriev, with Rassam and Carter, or alone, poring over the carvings in the pantheon—or else studying the hand itself, each bone having been revealed to be a stable crystal of tetraquark hadrons, making each carpal and metacarpal and phalange its own single, massive atom. From a certain point on the floor of the pantheon—with Valeriev's crew working up the slanting shaft at my back—I could look up and see the polychrome bas relief of the winged cluster placing its coronet upon the head of Sunamasra-Teäplu. Vaiartu entering the pantheon via the now caved-in ramp would have seen their god resplendent there, peering down with countless eyes hid among its feathers.

Often I would remain in the pantheon late into the night, with only Edouard or Cassandra for company. I copied out the inscription on the slab again and again, sitting with my folio on my lap upon the edge of the first gallery, so that I might see it entire.

On Annica, the Quiet had revealed the nature of the markings to me. They were not letters, but the visible part of some incomprehensible machine—the slots of invisible gears. But knowing that, I still could not understand them.

When I could bear the damp and oppressive weight of the stone sky of the pantheon and the cramped tunnels leading to it no longer, I would go out into the desert, walk among the ribs of the *Cetoscolides* like the columns of some long-rotted sanctum, or fly deep into the desert to be alone.

Or nearly alone.

But Oberlin and his minions—Gaston and Vedi—would not let me be alone. Many are the times I would land my spotter on white sands, or upon the sanded ridge of an escarpment, only to spy another flier far off, or the winged shapes of our Irchtani.

I knew what I was doing, flying farther and farther from Phanamhara and the camp every time: I was testing the bounds of my cage, gnawing at the bars as a tiger might trapped in a box.

We had hit a dead end. Nothing beyond the ordinary had happened since the death of Alexander of Alba. A few of the diggers claimed to have heard voices in the tunnels, and now and again it was said equipment had been moved in the night.

From time to time, Cassandra would accompany me into the desert, or—at Vedi's insistence—Edouard or the Chiliarch, Annaz, or one of his men. When Cassandra came with me, we would find a likely spot—eventually settling on a shallow cave in the leeward face of a cliff rising from the pale sands—and I would continue her training. She had little to learn, but much to polish, and though I was no Maeskolos—as she—I was *Al Brutan* still, and there remained strength enough in my limbs to challenge her. Annaz and I would talk of Udax, of Barda and the Irchtani I had known, and of Judecca.

It was on one of the occasions I flew with Cassandra that we saw the crash.

The sands must have buried it in the intervening months, and the chance action of the wind had exposed it again, for we had flown that way many times to reach the place we called the Cave of Fishes—for the fossils that lined its walls.

Cassandra saw it first. She sat as always in the spotter's turret, her seat above mine in the blister of alumglass that rose from the crown of the spheroid craft.

"What is that?" She'd climbed down to lean over the back of my seat and point at a patch of black against the blinding white.

I'd seen it, too, and brought us lower until we were perhaps half a hundred yards above the surface. "It looks like a skiff," I said, with a sudden sense of foreboding. I thought I knew who the wreck belonged to. Presently, I keyed the comms and said, "Phanamhara Ground Control, this is Spotter N..." I checked the plate on the console, forgetting which of the aircraft we'd commandeered for the day's adventure. "N7. We've found what looks like a skiff crash northwest of the camp. Bearing thirty-eight point two-two south, seventeen point nine-one-eight west. Do you copy?"

There was a pause.

"Copy that, N7. This—...—ound Control. Did you sss-say crash? Over."

"It's definitely a crash," Cassandra said, leaning fully over the console where it arced before me.

A burst of static flooded the comm, and I cursed again. "Yes, a crash. Might be our missing one. I'm taking Cassandra down to check it out. Over."

A pause.

"Belay that...N7." Another hiss. *"Commandant ...ston says hold. Over"*

"Understood!" I said, beginning our descent with a grin up at Cassandra. "We'll hold. Over."

There was nothing to fear in the deep desert, save sun and storm, and so I set the spottercraft on the sands, and Cassandra opened the hatch, first lifting the hood of her colorless *sagum* and tucking the baffle across her face. She had taken to the native dress as I had not, having spent far more time out on the surface than I. I only raised my collar, and produced from a pocket of my Jaddian coat the antique smoked spectacles, red lensed and silver framed, that I had stolen from a man on Emesh the day I met the sailor called Crow. I had replaced the lenses several times, and once had the silver frames—they were titanium, in truth—melted down and reshaped when I'd crushed them in some fall or other, and since coming to Sabratha, Neema had fashioned blinders of black leather to fill in the sides to help with the desert glare.

They were not the same glasses.

I was not the same man.

We had a short walk to the crash site. The sand shifted as we went, our boots carving little divots. The wrecked flier lay almost completely immersed in sand, its hull a smooth, black arc cresting like the back of some mighty fish. There was black in the white of the sand about it, the remains of some chemical fire.

"What happened to it?"

"Looks like a blown fuel-cell reservoir," I said, eying the gaping hole in the side of the overturned flier. "See the hole there? That's about where the tank used to be."

Crack.

Something had broken under my feet, and I stopped, wary of some trap, hand flitting to the thumb-catch that would have engaged my belt's shield pack.

But nothing happened.

Crouching, I examined the ground at my feet, found what it was I'd stepped on. "Cassandra, look!" I lifted what I'd found for her to see. "Do you know what this is?"

She looked at me quizzically, holding the baffle to her face as the wind gusted. "A rock?"

"Most amusing!" I shook my head. "It's glass, girl." I turned the fragment for her to see. I'd never found one myself, but I had seen a whole case of them in the museum-house of Kharn Sagara. The thing in my fingers was a hollow tube of glass, mottled and faintly green. "Catch!" I tossed it to her, and she cupped her hands to receive it. "It's what happens when lightning strikes sand. See how it's hollow?"

She turned the thing over in her fingers, head bowed. "Do you think lightning struck the flier?"

"It's possible," I said, though privately I thought if that were so, it was strange to find the fulgurite so near the crash—surely it would have been struck in the air, far off. "I only hope our two fugitives died quickly."

"Our two...?" Realization dawned across Cassandra's face. "Robyne Kel and the legionnaire? But they've been gone for months!"

"Evidently they did not make it very far," I said, regaining my feet and moving toward the crashed flier.

Crack.

I'd hardly made it three paces before my heel found what could only be another fulgurite. I shook my foot clear of glass and continued my advance.

Crack.

Crack.

With every step, our feet seemed to be finding fulgurite.

"*—lowe, this is Pha—ound Contol. Standb—...—inforcements inbound, over.*"

I set a finger to the patch behind my ear. "Read you loud and clear, Control," I said, crouching before the gaping hole. "We're standing by, over."

"Do you enjoy lying, Abba?" Cassandra asked, joining me.

"Only to our gaolers," I said, and pointing at the blackened, twisted metal within, forged on. "It looks like the fuel cell. You may be right about the lightning. Dumb bastards must have flown right into a storm. There should be a hatch just over—"

"Here!" Cassandra kicked a fall of sand with one heel, clutched the rim of the opening she revealed as sand ran down and into the wreck. "I think I can get in."

"Best not," I said. I had planned on trying to find a way in myself, but something in seeing my daughter and all that rushing sand forced me to reevaluate. "We don't want you getting caught."

She narrowed her emerald eyes. "Are you scared, Abba?"

"For your safety? Always," I replied.

"There's a rope in the spotter," she countered. "I could just climb in and look. You could pull me out if too much sand gets in."

I looked back to the spotter, a silvered sphere balanced on three peds, considering. "It's not the sand that concerns me. I don't want the hull caving in."

In answer, Cassandra scrambled atop the upturned ventral hull, stomped on it hard as she could, then jumped up and down. Her Jaddian eugenics and Sabratha's lower gravity collaborated, and she leapt nearly ten feet into the air before coming down with a *clang.* When nothing happened, she spread her hands, as if to say *See?*

I kept the rope wound about my right arm. Cassandra's feet had just vanished under the lip of the open hatch. Bracing one foot against the curve of the hull, I said, "They must have survived the crash. Someone had to open the hatch."

Cassandra was quiet.

"Did you find anything?"

A hand emerged from the skiff's interior, followed by the rest of the girl. Her eyes were shining, and she shook her head. "They're still here," she said, and wiped her eyes on her sleeve. "Curled up together. In the back." She jerked her head in the direction of the stern. "I think *she* died in the crash—she looked pretty bad. He must have cut her out of the chair and just...stayed." A sob escaped her, and I crossed the space between us to take her in my arms.

"I should have been the one to go in," I said.

"No!" She shook her head to clear it. "No, I—I'm fine. I'll be fine."

"He was probably in no fit state himself," I said, withdrawing to arm's length, my hands on her shoulders. "I hope for his sake he didn't last long." Too clearly I could picture the legionnaire, huddled beside the body of his lover, clutching his pocket terminal. Had he tried to radio for help? Had Sabratha's cruel magnetosphere left him to his solitary fate? Or had he refused to call and face justice for his theft and desertion?

A burst of static filled my ears. *"Muz . . . anam?"*

Pressing the comms patch behind my ear, I said, "Say again, Control?"

A moment later, a piercing cry filled the air, long and ululating, followed by a shorter one, and looking up I saw the black-feathered shapes of three Irchtani descending like carrion eaters upon us. I recognized Annaz himself among them, and raised a hand in greeting.

Static hissed through the conduction patch again. More gibberish.

"We found our deserters!" I said, conscious of Cassandra's distress, and realizing as I spoke that she had never come so close to death before, save for Doctor Mann. But the poor planetologist had been long dead and cold, his bodies cleaned and cared for, and twisted by the thing that had killed him until the strangeness of his death half-covered the fact of it.

This was something else, more raw, more real.

When she had been perhaps half her age, one of her friends—an older neophyte called Sofia—had thrown herself into the Grand Canal above Volcano House and so destroyed herself. Cassandra and Sofia had been close, had slept together often in their dormitory, and whispered late into the night. But there had been no body.

Annaz alighted in a billowing of dark wings. "Truly, *Bashandani* punishes those who betray his justice."

"The Emperor did not do this," I said, not sure the Irchtani could get inside the grounded craft, with their limbs so unused to bending. "Are more coming?"

"Camp control sends two fliers. Cutters come." He cocked his beaked head. "They are dead, then?"

"They are dead," I said. "You're welcome to take a look, it's safe enough." Another burst of static filled the bones of my skull. "Damn thing!" I fixed my collar against the wind, squinted up the rippling slope of the dune that loomed over the crash. "Watch your step, *kithuun*," I said, marking the Irchtani's bare, clawed feet. "There's lightning glass in the sand, all over." I gestured at the ground.

"You think a storm did for them?" the bird man inquired.

"Very possibly," I said, and bending, fished out a piece of fulgurite to show the colonus. What I drew out was a piece nearly three cubits long, mottled and gnarled as a tree limb afflicted by mistletoe. It curved slightly, bending to the right. Laying it down, I moved to the other end, acting on a sudden hunch, and found another piece of fused sand. This was shorter than the last, but continued the rightward bend.

Annaz hopped to stand at my side, croaked. "What is it?"

I dropped the second piece then, and stood, following where I guessed the bend in the glass must follow. "It's a circle," I said, and taking two steps to my right—nearer the wreckage, I found another fulgurite with my heel. *Crack.*

Lifting the ruined fragment, I found that same rightward bend. The arc of this, second fulgurite would have crossed the first, their circles not concentric, but overlapping. My mind ran to the burn marks in the hall of record, the ripple pattern where the Watcher's energistic form had left its fingerprints upon our mortal plane.

"Cassandra!"

The girl had wandered back atop the ruined skiff, was shielding her eyes from the sun with both hands and staring away south. She turned at the sound of her name. "The bodies! Were they disturbed at all?"

She leaped down, landed awkwardly on the sand. "Disturbed?"

"Like Doctor Mann's!" I said.

Cassandra shook her head. "Not that I could see."

Another burst of static flooded the comms, more nonsense. "...*light*... *bearing thirty-eight point*..." It was my own voice, signal echoing back off the planet's ionosphere. Then more static, followed by a hollow warbling that sounded as if it came from deep underwater.

What was it the men liked to say? The air was full of ghosts.

"We need to call this in," I said to Annaz, to Cassandra—who had reached us.

"Cutters come already, *bashanda*," the Irchtani said.

"Not just the cutters," I said. "Cassandra and I will head back to camp. I need to telegraph the *Troglita*. Oberlin should know."

Cassandra's eyes widened. "Oberlin? But why?"

"The glass," I said, still holding a foot-long fragment. "It makes circles around the wreck. Do you see?"

"Circles?" Cassandra was a second catching up.

"The Watcher did this," I said.

"The Watcher?" Cassandra looked round at the sand. Here and there the glassy, brown ridge of a fulgurite crested. Broken and jagged, yes—and branching in places, forking.

Circles.

A shadow passed between the earth and sun, or perhaps fell only on me, and looking up the slope of the dune, I saw a dark figure standing, black against the lowering sun.

Unthinking, I let out a cry and hurried up the slope. The figure stood there, cloaked and veiled in tremulous black. Cassandra called after me, but I did not look back.

The figure stood like a statue shrouded against time, covered head to toe in a veil without gauze or eye slit. Yet as I approached, it turned away, and I fancied that I saw the shimmer of a white foot emerge from the hem as it took a step.

"Wait!" I cried, thumbing my shield-catch.

"*Zae namen!*" the figure cried out, unmoving. "*Muzu anaam?*"

"Wait!" I shouted once more.

The figure turned and began to vanish down the far side of the dune.

"Bashanda!" The sound of Annaz's voice was joined by that of his wings, and I looked back to see the chiliarch lift himself from beside the blasted ruin of the flier.

When I turned back, the figure was gone.

There was no trace of a footprint upon the crest of the dune, nor any sign of a descent. Upon the dune top, the margins of Sabratha shimmered white and almost blue, a mirage-echo of the seas that once had dominated that world. For an instant, a fata morgana glowed above the horizon in the afternoon sun, a black lozenge like an airship rising into the heavens.

A mirage.

"Come back!" I called. "Come back, damn you!"

"Abba!" Cassandra had reached me, and seized my wrist, as if I were her child.

"There was someone here," I said, pointing at the ground beneath our feet. "Right here. Did you see her?"

"Her?" Cassandra cocked her head.

I paused, unsure why I thought it was a woman. And yet I felt certain that I was right. "I was so sure..." I shook my head, as though I might clear it of some haze. The sweat was getting into my eyes, more from the sun and my exertions than from the temperature—it was never very hot at that latitude.

"Was it mirage?" the Irchtani leader inquired, landing not three paces from us both.

"No!" I almost shouted. "I don't know! Maybe."

But in my heart, I was certain that I had seen the beast we'd come to Sabratha to find.

I was certain I had just seen the Watcher.

CHAPTER 17

ARRIVAL

"WHY WOULD THE BEAST kill two people fleeing the city?" Oberlin asked, leaning heavily on a silver-tipped cane as we climbed the rise overlooking the ruins of Phanamhara. Pale floodlights illuminated the dusty red hulks of excavators, and here and there a sentry in legionary white or in the desert camouflage of Gaston's local guard moved. "It doesn't make sense."

The discovery of the wrecked flier and the dead fugitives had recalled Oberlin from his orbital remove. He wore one of the filter masks over his face.

"Perhaps we do well not to guess at the motivations of a creature so unlike us," I said, and glanced back to where Priscian Lascaris followed, a few paces behind, ever mindful of his master's condition. "Whatever sense there may be in its actions, I think it will not seem sense to us."

Having reached the top, Oberlin paused. "That is not the answer you have been brought here to supply, Lord Marlowe."

"What was it the doctor and her paramour stole?" I asked.

"A few tablets, one with gold inlay," Oberlin said.

"That and the rusted hulk of what we think was one of their firearms," Lascaris put in. "A beam weapon of some kind."

I nodded tiredly, surveying the ruined city. I had seen the treasures removed from the wreckage, had seen many such weapons in various states of decay. They would have fetched a fine price.

"I can't see why the Watcher would go to the trouble of hunting Doctor Kel and Irum down simply for some Vaiartu writing and an old laser rifle," I said.

"You're saying its actions are inscrutable?" Oberlin turned to glare at me.

"I'm saying *what if its actions are caprice?*" I held the smaller man's gaze and did not waver. "What if it's toying with us?" A blacker thought

144

occurred to me, and I said, "What if it left that flier there because it knew I would be the one to find it?"

Oberlin was silent a long moment, passed it stabbing the dune with his cane. "The two of them fled the camp five months ago. You think the creature somehow knew you and your daughter would be on a flight above precisely that patch of desert precisely when the sand was cleared enough away for you to spot it?" Behind the glass, his eyes narrowed. "You recognize the madness in that thought, do you not?"

"No, I do not!" I said. "This whole thing is mad, Oberlin. This world, this mission—all of it. So forgive me if some of that madness is catching."

The old man turned his face away, studied the illuminated ruins. "Perhaps," he said at last, then thrusting out his cane like a finger, said, "I saw Valeriev's report. They got a man through the shaft from below!"

"Just three days ago," I said. Valeriev and his team had opened a channel in the collapsed tunnel wide enough for the diggers to climb out. "It'll be another few weeks before the thing's really opened up. Then they'll have to see about moving the hand to the surface."

"You still think that's a fool's errand?" Oberlin said.

"I think our quarry redoubled its efforts against us the moment we touched it," I said. "And I worry that your attempts to move the hand will result in...unforeseen consequences."

Oberlin dismissed this with a wave of one knob-knuckled hand. "If it forces the issue—"

"I also worry that we will not be able to evacuate the camp in time *should* we force the issue," I said, thinking of the locals, like poor Doctors Mann and Kel. Thinking also of Williamtown, and Markov Station, and the rest of Sabratha's sparse inhabitants.

And of the universe beyond.

The Director had not looked at me through all my words, had not taken his eyes from the crumbling ramparts and almost-pointed windows of the Enar city.

"It's war, Marlowe," he said at last. "And the creature is—potentially— the greatest military asset in universal history. You have seen the Vaiartu friezes. With the Monumentals to lead them, their armies burned the *galaxy*. Countless species and worlds. What will the Cielcin do with one of them to lead them?"

"Two," I said. "You're forgetting Dorayaica."

So clearly, I saw the tendrilous *thing* slither from the Prophet's wounded side.

"You're sure he's one of them?" Oberlin asked. "You're sure he's not something *else?*"

"What else would it be?" I returned. "At any rate, the sorcerers in its employ believed Dorayaica was becoming one of them—and about that at least they'd no reason to lie." I blinked, realization dawning on me. "How do you know about Dorayaica? That was never in my reports."

Oberlin stabbed the hilltop once more with his cane, swayed and widened his stance. Lascaris dashed to his side. "Yes...there is so much that never finds its way into your reports. His Radiance told me, before I sailed for Jadd. You shared that little piece of information with him on Carteia, if you recall."

I did.

"And on the subject of your silence, my lord," Oberlin continued. "Is there something you would like to add to your telegraph from a week ago?"

He still was not looking at me, and I marveled at how effective a tactic that was. My own father had employed the same pointed disinterest with long-practiced grace. I had used it myself. Had I grown so rusty in exile that I could no longer tolerate the chafe of it? Or had I only grown too old to be patient?

"No," I said, and turned away myself.

"The Irchtani chiliarch would differ," Oberlin said. "Something about a woman in black?"

I cursed under my breath, said, "You think me mad."

"On the contrary," said Friedrich Oberlin. "I am counting on your madness. It may be *our* greatest asset." He was peering at me—finally—eyes white in the distant glare of the floodlamps, like an aged and featherless owl.

"I don't know that it was a woman," I said. "I don't know why I thought it was a woman. I just..."

"But you saw *something?*"

I chewed my tongue, nodded. "Standing on the dunes overlooking the wreck. A woman—a...*figure*—in a black veil, head to toe. It called down to me."

Oberlin's gleaming eyes grew narrow. "What did it say?"

"Nothing, nonsense," I said.

Zae namen.

Muzu anaam?

It did not sound like the same language Miudanar had spoken to me on Eue long before, but not knowing either language—if they were indeed separate—it was impossible to say. That the second utterance had been a question seemed plain to me.

"You think it was our target?"

"What else could it be, Friedrich?" I asked, exasperation leaking from me like air from a punctured balloon. "It must have known I would find the flier. It exists above our dimension, you say. Surely it can see time like I can—and further."

"You think it was setting a trap for you?"

"I don't know, Friedrich. But I know what I saw. It's *watching* us. Me..."
I grew silent then, a flash of insight coming to me in the lamplit gloom.
"This was another warning. Maybe our last."

Oberlin leaned toward me, weight heavy upon his cane. "Do you *know*
something?"

I shook my head.

"You have to start trusting me," he said.

"Trusting you? After how you squeezed the Jaddians into handing me
over? After all *this?*" I gestured at the ruins, at the dead world all around.
"You say I'm free to go. You think I don't know what would happen if I
did? What would happen to *my daughter?*"

The old man devolved into another of his coughing fits. "You think," he
started, coughed again—and I pitied him his mask—"you think I am your
enemy, Hadrian. I am one of the last friends you have. Do you know how
many assassination plans I argued against in Council? How many plots I
stifled under the table? SpecSec wanted you dead. The War Office wanted
you dead. The Empress is still after you. The Chantry. They wanted to
hire a Vavasor of Aminon to kill you. Do you even know what that is?"

I confessed that I did not.

"They even bought the Prince of Oannos."

That ground me to a halt. "The Prince of Oannos was paid to kill
me?" I said. "If that's so, whichever lord paid him wasted his coin. The
Oannosene took the money and tried to kill Aldia du Otranto instead. I
stopped them."

Unimpressed, Oberlin felt the pockets of his jacket, searching for a
kerchief—forgetting he wore the filter mask. "And thank Earth for that.
Aldia has ever been a staunch ally. We would be poorer without him."

"Says the man who put the screws to him securing my release."

"I do what I do for the realm," Oberlin said, "and for all mankind."

We stood there watching the sand and the city. I studied its every
rampart, half imagining that I saw once more the veiled figure, its stygian
folds untouched by the cold, revealing light.

Why was it our artists always personified Death as a lady?

"Friedrich," I said at last. "If something happens to me. If I die here,
fighting this thing. I need you to swear something for me."

The old man looked up at me, and I was struck once more by the degree
to which Ever-Fleeting Time had worn away at him, at the wrinkles and
liver spots, and the patchy white hair and drooping eyes. But he smiled, and
for a moment I saw the thin, forgettable face of the young logothete whose
little courage had delivered me from the Inquisition. He said nothing, but
by the almost imperceptible tipping of his head, I knew I should proceed.

"Protect Cassandra," I said. "See she gets to safety. Back to Jadd, if you can arrange it. It's the only world she knows." I did my best to smile, and turning faced him fully. "She's nothing to your Imperial master."

"I . . ." Oberlin hesitated. "I will do all I can."

"She cannot do what I can do," I said. "I know the Chantry wants me vivisected. Don't let them get to *her.*" I nearly laid my hands upon his shoulders, but recalling the sniper from our previous nighttime walk, I thought better of it. "Please."

"I'll do all I can," Oberlin said again.

"She's just a girl," I said, though that was not strictly true. She was a Swordmaster of the Ninth Circle, but she had lived all her life in the Fire School, and though she knew something of courtly life, and a little more about hardship, she knew next to nothing of the ocean of stars. Of the galaxy, the Cielcin, and of man's inhumanity to man.

"I know," Oberlin said. "I do."

"You believed in me, once," I said, glancing to Lascaris, who stood by, haggard and long faced as ever. There were times I thought it seemed he was sicker even than his master, though he was burdened only by his cares. "You saved my life, and so I have no right asking for anything . . . but if I don't . . . leave this place. Help her. Please."

I realized, then, that I had never pleaded for anything in my life, least-ways not with such naked honesty.

Old Oberlin reached out and gripped my hand. Not speaking, he nodded.

It was enough. Relief washed over me like rain, for it seemed the man answered me, and not his office. Then he let me go, and inhaling sharply with the change of subject, he said, "I sail for Williamtown in five days' time. I plan to meet with Lord Hulle to discuss increasing the planet's defenses. It will be dismal work. I told him you would accompany me."

I was slower to adjust to the change of topic than he, and stiffened. "You what?"

"He is holding a fete in your honor. A private feast. I'm told there will be a small Colosso and games."

"Is that . . . wise?" I asked. "Surely the locals should not know I am here. Men will talk."

"What men?" asked Oberlin, smiling at Lascaris. "The governor-general's office all know you are here. They do not know what we *do,* but that is another matter."

"But what of our work here?"

"It is just one night," Oberlin said. "You can return directly. I have succeeded in keeping Hulle from you for the last two years, but there are limits even to what I can do."

I only glared at him.

"You would rather you were in a cell on Belusha?" Oberlin asked.

"I would rather I never left Jadd," I said. "I am old, Friedrich. Too old." I bore the full brunt of my age in that moment, felt the full weight of my each and every year.

Oberlin chuckled, coughed. "Speak not to me of *age*, lordship. Ever-Fleeting Time has been far kinder to you than I." He fell silent, leaned heavily on his cane.

I chewed my tongue in silence a moment, said at last, "Time is never kind."

CHAPTER 18

BEFORE THE FETE

"YOU'RE SURE YOU DON'T want me to go with you?" Cassandra asked, setting her spoon down and staring at me intently. "I don't mind. It'll be nice to get out—do something a little different."

Dinner consisted of a cold soup of potatoes and leeks grown in the *Ascalon*'s little hydroponics garden, a salad of tomatoes from the same, and a loaf of brown bread baked from flour and *bromos* protein taken from camp stores. There was no meat, and the only concession to luxury remaining was the wine: a Jaddian red so dark it was almost black. I had been rationing it since our arrival, mixing it with water after the fashion of Jadd, but still it was nearly gone.

"No, no," I said. "This won't be a social visit."

"Yes, it will!" Her smile flashed across the narrow glass table. "I heard they're staging a Colosso. I'd like to see it."

"They're only staging a couple small bouts in the governor-general's courtyard garden," I countered. "You won't be missing anything."

Cassandra clenched her jaw. "But I want to go."

"I am only going to put in a little private word with the governor-general," I said. "There'll be no pomp or circumstance. It's to be very private."

"All the more reason for me to go!" Cassandra said. "What's the harm?"

What could I say to her? That I feared for the stories of her existence to spread too far and wide in the Imperium? Through HAPSIS, the intelligence apparatus knew of her: SpecSec and the War Office and the rest. The Chantry doubtless knew of her. The simple fact of her existence put her in danger. And yet if I could keep the rumors of her to a minimum, if I could keep her name off the lips of the public, she might escape the notice of at least some of my enemies.

"You'd do better to stay here," I said, taking a swallow of the dry red.

The girl exhaled sharply, crushed a tomato with the side of her fork until it bled upon her plate. *"Posho mia defender, sai tuo?"* she said, sliding back into her native Jaddian. *I can defend myself, you know.* "I don't need you to do it for me."

Knowing she was wrong, but not wishing to argue, I smiled and restored my wine. "Neema's done yeoman's work with the soup, don't you think?"

Still in Jaddian, Cassandra said, *"Si, es buon."*

"Where is Neema, anyhow?" I asked. I had been out on the bridge while Neema prepared the evening meal.

"He's gone down to the *Rhea* to have a word with the quartermaster," Cassandra said, voice flat. "We're short on some things."

I ate alone in silence, tearing chunks from my bread to take up portions of the cold soup—wishing it were hot. Dark had fallen, and the desert nights were cold.

"I'm sorry, Anaryan," I said, speaking Galstani myself. "I'm sorry the galaxy isn't what you hoped it would be." I fell silent for the space of a swallow of wine. "Do you miss Jadd?"

She looked up sharply. "No," she said, and her eyes were downcast. "I don't know. Maybe." She managed a bite of her salad. "I just keep thinking about the doctor and her soldier, dead in that flier. The way her head was sort of... *crushed* in. Like an egg." She set her fork down. Her eyes were far away. "I'd never seen a dead man before, except the man in the morgue... and that was..."

"Different. I know," I said, and reaching across the table, I gripped her hand in mine. Squeezing it gently, I continued, "Your great-grandmother died when I was... nine standard? I think it was? They laid her body in state after they embalmed her. Crispin and I snuck in to see." I shared the story then, about the shroud that covered her—as one had covered the figure that called to me in the desert—and about how I'd been made to carry her eyes in their crystal canopic jar as part of her funeral train. "Death is... only the next part of life. Man's dead outnumber her living a thousand to one, it's said." *Ninety thousand to one,* I thought. "It's always been thus."

"Abba..." Cassandra looked like one struggling to find her words. Absently she reached up, pulled her left plait down over her shoulder and stroked it as she searched. "They say... the men in the camp, I mean... they say *you* died."

"They..." I had been expecting this conversation for a very long time, had always been surprised when it failed to occur on Jadd, where rumor of the *Halfmortal* was sure to have abounded among the students at the Fire School. "They say a lot of things."

She was not ready for the whole story, nor was I ready to tell it.

"They say one of the Cielcin princes struck off your head."

I did not want to lie to her.

I could only shake my head.

I was saved the necessity of replying by Neema, who by providence chose that precise moment to reappear. The Nemrut School manservant emerged from the hall with a heavy sack of flour slung over one shoulder.

"Still eating, Master Hadrian? Young mistress?" He set the bag down on the counter beside the sink and the small range. "I expected to find you gone and the washing up ready to begin."

"We got to talking," I said. "Did the quartermaster get you everything you need?"

"There won't be meat until you return from Williamtown, *domi*. My sincerest apologies." I dismissed this concern with a wave. "Lieutenant Alexandros will send a cart with milk and eggs and the rest in the morning." He leaned forward conspiratorially. "But I have liberated the last bag of white flour in the whole camp, I think. And we've butter and preserves. Breakfast will be uncomplicated, but quite fine. I may fry the last of the tomatoes—I must use them before they spoil."

"Very good," I said. "All's quiet out there?"

"Very quiet," Neema said. "They were telling me at the ramp that one of the Irchtani patrols hasn't reported in yet."

I stiffened. "Why didn't you start with that?"

"I didn't think it was that important," Neema replied earnestly. "Is it?"

"Likely not!" I said, draining the last of the wine. "But I'll take a walk down to the *Rhea* and check with Commander Vedi and Annaz—see if I can't make myself useful."

Neema bristled, "*Domi*, if I've done any harm by not hurrying back to tell you, I—!"

"No, no, Neema," I said, lifting the nearly empty bottle that it might accompany me on my night journey. "I'm sure it's nothing. It's early yet, and I'm not tired."

"I'll go with you!" Cassandra stood sharply, chair scraping as she rose.

I was on the verge of saying that I'd rather go alone when I recalled how my desire to have her remain at Phanamhara while I went to Williamtown had rankled her. So, I gestured to the door. "Grab your shield-belt, then. Let's be off."

"They were meant to have reported in about forty minutes ago," said Commander Vedi when Cassandra and I reached the *Rhea*'s cramped bridge.

"Where were they patrolling?" I asked.

"That's the thing, sir," Vedi said. "More or less straight up. Between here and the *Mensa*."

"How high?" Cassandra asked, arms crossed as she leaned against a blocky console.

Vedi's brows contracted. "About twenty thousand feet."

"It could just be the comms," one of the lieutenants supplied, swiveling in his station chair. "Especially at that altitude. Signals get lost."

Vedi shook his head. "Then they should have sent down a flare. And the rest of the birdo teams are up there calling. No response." From this I knew he meant that the Irchtani were communicating by their musical cries.

"You should be checking on the ground," I said, eyes moving from Vedi to the lieutenant, sweeping over the other officers at their night posts. Most leaned over consoles, some with cups or insulated canteens. The bitter smell of caffeine filled the air.

The commander rubbed his eyes with the heels of his hands. "You think they're dead?"

"You don't?" I asked.

Cassandra stood up straight to hear the urgency in my tone.

Commander Vedi shrugged. "Patrols miss check-in pretty regularly down here. Spotters, too. It's the magnetosphere."

"Auxiliary Patrol A-13, this is the *Rhea*," said one of the junior officers at the forward console, a dark woman with close-cropped and tightly curling hair. "Auxiliary Patrol A-13, do you copy?"

"Do patrols miss check-in by forty minutes?" I asked.

"Well," Vedi hesitated. "No. They should have sent down a flare when it became clear the signal wasn't coming through. You're right."

"Does Oberlin know?" I asked, looking to the door that separated the low-ceilinged bridge from the long, narrow hall that ran several hundred feet to the rear hold. Sir Friedrich had not returned to the *Troglita*, but had remained planetside after the discovery of Robyne and Irum's bodies. "Does Commandant Gaston?"

"If he doesn't himself, his people do," Vedi said. "Gaston's on our frequencies, and we've a hardline to Ground Control in the weather station. "And I've not woken Sir Friedrich. Not yet. Lascaris left orders not to disturb the old man unless it were dire."

The lieutenant had not swiveled back to his station, but kept a pair of fingers on the comms patch behind his ear. "Still nothing from the birdos, commander."

"Understood, M. Chatterjee," Vedi said. "Keep trying. Dominina, get me the chiliarch."

"Aye, sir."

A moment later, Kithuun Annaz's high voice filled the hissing comms-band. *"Annaz speaking, man-commander. No sign of Akiil and his boys yet."* The words were faint and half-lost beneath shoals of static. *"We search very high, but there is no response."*

"Check the ground," I said again. "Have Gaston launch the spotters, recall the ones on weather watch. If they're on the surface, they should still be visible against the sands." I did not add, *If they are dead, they will still be warm.* I settled for a simpler, "Have them do a thermal sweep."

Vedi hesitated. "What are you afraid of?" he asked.

"You know what we're hunting," I said, perplexed by the very question.

"You think this is the Monumental's work?" Vedi asked.

"It left Irum and Doctor Kel's bodies where we would find them," I said. "It killed your man, Alexander. It's been trying to warn us off since we arrived. Perhaps it's escalating its efforts."

Beyond the windows of the bridge, the camp glowed beneath the light of floodlamps, so that a bubble of day seemed to cling to the planet's surface. Above it, the night was black and full of demons. The lamps had banished the stars. I could see the *Ascalon,* its black-finned shape far off on the margins of the camp, the low shapes of troop landers like ingots of raw iron filling the mile between. I half expected to see the creature in its black shroud—like Death herself—standing on the pale sands just below the window.

Cassandra had come to stand beside me. "You think it's coming for us?" she asked. "Abba?"

I shook myself. To the bridge at large, I said, "There's something going on."

In the camp outside—*somewhere*—a lamp exploded. It could not have been far off, I heard the breaking of the glass, and when I looked out the window, the film of false day seemed a shade less bright. "Did you hear that?"

"Hear what?" Vedi rounded the holography well and came to stand with Cassandra and myself at the rail.

"One of the lamps went out," I said, but looking round at the darkness, I could see none dead. Had I imagined it? Or was it only one invisible from the *Rhea*'s bridge. "I heard the crack."

"I didn't hear anything," said the lieutenant, Chatterjee.

I *looked,* and saw the camp multiplied across infinity, lights bright and stark as ever.

Had I imagined things?

"Lord Marlowe?" Vedi leaned forward to peer into my face.

I turned my gaze—left, it seemed to me, or down—along that direction no other man could see, and saw the lamps flickering, falling dark one by random one, so it seemed a shadow passed across time, moving like a great bird close above in the dead of night, casting unseen shadows over us with the beating of invisible wings.

"Wake Oberlin," I said, not sure what it was that spurred me to that decision. "Now."

"But my lord, his orders!"

"Damn his orders!"

I was spared the need to explain, for in that instant, the lights went out. Not just one lamp, such as I had seen across the manifold states of potential.

Every lamp.

At once we were lit only by the blue gleam of the consoles and the faint, red-golden glow of the overhead fixtures. The roof of night—which had floated above the whole camp mere moments before—contracted until it seemed the dark was near enough that my outstretched fingers might feel it.

"I'll wake him myself," I said, coat swirling as I moved for the door.

"But lordship!" Vedi followed for the space of three steps. "Lascaris said—"

"If Priscian Lascaris wishes to stop me, he will tell me himself!" I whirled in the doorway leading back to the hall. "Find out what happened to the lights. Send someone to check the camp reactor, and call Commandant Gaston!"

"I...yes, my lord." I left Vedi standing—a curiously forlorn figure—adrift in the midst of his swirling subordinates as the *Rhea*'s bridge moved to high alert.

Oberlin's rooms would be among the largest of what scant accommodations the ship could offer, and when I asked the deck officer, he informed me the Lord Oberlin had taken the second cabin, across from Commander Vedi's own. The woman repeated Vedi's line that secretary Lascaris had left orders not to disturb the Director, but I overrode her. "Where is Lascaris now?" I asked.

"He said he was off to the weather station to speak with one of Gaston's men," the deck officer replied, leaving her desk to follow after Cassandra and myself. "He's been gone nearly two hours. The Director retired early. He keeps to his room, anyhow, when he's not in meetings."

I waved her to silence, pounded on the titanium of the door. "Oberlin! Oberlin, it's Marlowe! Open up!"

"He's not asleep, is he?" Cassandra asked. "It's only two hours after sunset..."

The deck officer shrugged.

I hammered on the door again. "Oberlin, open up! The lights have gone out across the camp and one of the Irchtani patrols is missing. Open the Earth-blasted door!"

Nothing.

"You're sure he's in?" Cassandra asked the deck officer.

"Where else would he be?" the deck officer asked hesitantly. It was her job to know.

Snapping my fingers at her, I said, "Key the door."

"I can't do that!" She drew back a step. "That's the Lord Director's personal quarters!"

"His personal quarters are on the *Troglita*," I said. "He's borrowing these. Open the door." As I spoke, I slid into the woman's near orbit, so that I stared down my nose at her. She was plebeian, junior officer that she was, and more than a head shorter than me.

She blanched, bowed, and said, "I don't want any trouble, lord."

"Trouble may have found us, regardless what you want," I said, and pounded the door for the last time. "You will open this door, shipman, and you will do it now."

The poor woman advanced on mincing feet, caught between her master and Lord Marlowe. She drew out a keycard and held it to the lock before keying the override sequence. The door cycled with a pneumatic *hiss,* and before I could step over the threshold, the deck officer thrust her head in to speak—and in doing so, saved my life.

"Lord Director? I'm sorry, Lord Marlowe insis—"

A bolt of cold silver flashed from the dark within, struck the woman clean between the eyes and emerged from the back of her skull an instant later. Instinct conjured my shield just in time, and I barked an order for Cassandra to hit the deck. Old memories came rushing back: Valka lying in a hospital bed. Blood on the cabin floor. A broken blade with no handle lying on a table of black glass.

It was a knife-missile.

The deck officer was dead already, her blood red and slick upon the frame of the door. The blade itself shimmered in the air, dripping blood as it turned, the camera eye and sensor clusters of its machine brain questing, searching for something. For movement. For heat. Even shielded, I knew I would have only one chance.

I took one step toward the bloody thing. In an instant, it swiveled, point coming in line with my face. I heard the faintest whirring as repulsors accelerated. One knife became two. Four. Eight. Became countless knives. I raised my left hand, watched it become two. Four. Eight. Countless hands extended to catch those knives in their fingers.

One hand succeeded.

The wave collapsed, and I closed my fist on the speeding dagger, felt the edges bite. I heard Cassandra's indrawn breath, her curse. *"Noyn jitat!"*

Then my sword was in my hand, the winged-lion hilt fashioned of iridium and Jaddian ivory. The blade—forged on Phaia for Prince Philippe Bourbon—shone blue-white as starlight in the dim hall. With it I slashed the knife-missile in two, and dropped the smoking ruin to the deck.

"Are you all right?" I asked, standing over Cassandra.

She nodded, not trusting herself to speak.

I offered her my hand. "Welcome to the world," I said, as she took my hand and stood. "To my world."

"Abba, your hand!"

I looked at it. There was blood on it.

"I'm not bleeding," I said, though I had felt the edges. "It's her blood, poor woman." I looked down at the body and stepped over it. "Hers and..."

Friedrich Oberlin lay on a couch just within, his body a bloody ruin. Motivated—I think—by heat, the knife-missile had plunged into the old man's body a hundred times. His blood soaked the black leather, stained the gray carpets purple, and spattered the glass table and brushed metal walls. Looking at Oberlin, one could not have imagined how much blood the old fellow had in him.

"So much blood..."

"Cassandra, get out!" I said. "Stay there!"

Demoniacs all...

There was a blanket folded on the far arm of the slashed and bloody couch. Blood stained it, a patina of fine drops, the smallest already brown. Unkindling Gibson's sword, I drew the cloth across Sir Friedrich's mutilated form.

"Find peace on Earth, old man," I said, and found that all my fury and contempt for the spymaster was gone. In its place, there was only the gratitude I felt for the young man he'd been. In his indirect way, he had delivered me from just such a knife-missile.

I had not returned that favor.

I had thought it was the Watcher in the camps, the Watcher behind the disappearance of the Irchtani and the loss of power...but the Watchers did not conjure knife-missiles.

The knife-missile was a human weapon.

There was another sort of monster afoot.

CHAPTER 19

TOO LIKE THE LIGHTNING

THE BLARING OF ALARMS filled the *Rhea* by the time we reached the bridge.

"Get word to Gaston!" I bellowed.

"What happened?" Vedi looked round, eyes wide. "Is Lord Oberlin...?"

"Dead!" I cast the ruined shards of the knife-missile on the surface of the depowered holography well. "You need to lock the ship down. No one in or out!" The stark reality was that whoever had left the deadly toy for Oberlin to find had already fled. It had to be Lascaris. The grim-faced secretary would have been permitted entry to Oberlin's chambers...and the ill-starred deck officer had said the man had gone off to the weather station.

The short-haired woman on the comms spoke up then. "I can't raise Ground Control. There's no traffic on the fiber. Error G14."

"No connection," Vedi translated, face white as milk. "Someone cut the hardline."

"The same someone who killed Sir Friedrich," I said.

"We have a saboteur," said Vedi. "I'll pull security footage."

"You won't find anything," I said.

"I should have been here..." came a small, shocked voice from one corner.

Turning, I saw the last man I expected. Priscian Lascaris sat slumped in a chair, face bent over his wringing hands. Squaring myself, my thumbs in my belt, I stood over him. "I thought you went to Ground Control."

"I just got back," he said, looking up through watering eyes. "I just heard." The man was manically twisting the ring on his first finger. "Is it very bad, lord?"

It was, I thought. *Very bad.* But I said, "I covered him."

Lascaris swallowed. "He was a good man. I know you had your differences, but he was a good man. His poor children. And the grandchildren! The babies! Eliza just had her third!"

I blinked, said, "I didn't know he had family."

"Oh yes." Lascaris nodded, swallowing violently. "On Forum. He hoped to see them...one more time, you know? When it was done. Before he... before..."

"The cancer," I said, feeling an unexpected surge of guilt that I had suspected the secretary.

Lascaris nodded once more.

Turning from him, I spoke to Vedi, and to the woman on the comms. "Can you wave Ground Control?"

"I'm trying!" the woman answered, one hand cupping her left ear. "Signal should be clearer at night, but there's so much bloody noise."

"They don't have a telegraph?" Cassandra asked.

The comms officer shouted back, "No, ma'am. Only telegraphs on site are ours and the *Ascalon*'s."

"I'll go," I said, looking to Cassandra. "Let's go."

"My lord?" Vedi took a step toward me.

I laid my clean hand on his shoulder. "I'll go to Ground Control and rouse Gaston and his men. Tell him what's going on. Sound the general alarm! I want every man armed and ready."

"Armed and ready for what?"

I hesitated. I had no choice but to trust Commander Vedi. "We're under attack!" I said. "Gnomon has been infiltrated by the Extrasolarians, likely those loyal to the Pale King. Someone killed that Irchtani patrol." I turned to go. "Most like that's not noise on the radio. Most like we're being jammed."

The depth of the darkness surrounding us impressed itself fully on Vedi and the bridge crew then, for their silence was so deep it made even the *Rhea*'s alarms seem quieter and remote. But they were soldiers of the Empire, of HAPSIS, the men and women of Operation Gnomon, handpicked by Sir Friedrich Oberlin and most like by the Emperor himself.

Vedi said, "I've already telegraphed the *Troglita*. Captain Clavan is sending the cavalry. The aquilarii will be here within the hour."

"Good," I said, conscious of the blood still on my left hand. "We must mount a coherent defense. Send runners to the centurions if you have to. Men you can trust." I was already moving for the door. "Prime the NEM weapon. See it's kept ready to launch and under guard."

"You think the Monumental is afoot as well?"

"If it's not," I said, "I think it soon will be."

Cassandra and I paused only as long as it took for me to wash the blood from my hand. Within minutes, we had left the blaring corridors of the *Rhea* via the rear hold just as the men were making ready to seal the ramp. Memories of the battle on the *Demiurge* oppressed me then, of our men locked in the bowels of the *Schiavona*, hardening her defenses against the Cielcin horde.

"Stay close," I hissed to my daughter, taking her by the hand.

"Marlowes!" a call from the black ahead announced Edouard Albé. The agent looked odd, in a suit of black combat ceramic, devoid of all badge or rank. His ancestor's MAG rifle was slung over one shoulder, and here and there I marked the phosphorescent gleam of a shield curtain. I activated my own. "What's going on?"

"Come with us!" I said. "We'll tell you on the way!"

Edouard said little as I broke the news of Sir Friedrich's death, though I sensed in him an echo of the grief I had seen on Lascaris's face. Oberlin had inspired loyalty in his people. Loyalty, and more than loyalty. Love.

Ground Control lay in the heart of the camp proper, on the left side of the road leading down to Phanamhara, just beside the great tent of the motor pool. It stood perhaps little more than a mile and a half from the grounded *Rhea*—which stood at the outer edge of the landing field, nearest the desert. We made straight for it, hurrying along in the dark. Men rushed past us. Men in the helmeted jumpsuits of the engineers, carrying short-barreled disruptors. Men in full ceramic plate, faceless as unfinished statues. Men in the desert camouflage and undyed capes of the local Defense Force.

There were lights overhead as Irchtani swept by, and the questing beams of torch-lamps as men ran about on the ground. Now and again words would wash over us, confused snatches of conversations, half-heard orders.

"Some bastard cut the power!"

"—secure the reactor!"

"Heard they did for the boss..."

"Not the old man!"

"*Rhea*'s locked down."

"Lord Marlowe? That you?"

Commandant Vimal Gaston was already awake and moving when we reached the Ground Control station—a low, flat-roofed disc of a building resting on several cement pilings. He stood upon the porch before the main doors, dressed in a matte-black combat skin—with no armor save his shield-belt.

"What's going on?" Gaston's normally neatly combed hair was all a tangle, and his sideburns stuck out like the mane of some grizzled lion.

"Oberlin's dead," I said. "We have a saboteur. Someone killed him and cut the power from the camp reactor. They cut the hardline between here and the *Rhea*. You need to get your men armed and out here! Comms are bad—I think we're being jammed."

"Jammed?" The fellow drew back, surprised. "By whom?"

"The Extrasolarians," I said, certain I was right. "I think we had a mole. Oberlin must have known it."

Gaston frowned. "Earth and Emperor . . ." He made the sign of the sun disc, touching brow and heart and lips.

Just then, the storm sirens began their wailing, a high, womanly keen that filled all the world. At that moment, a slip of a girl emerged from the station, barefoot and clad in a long, translucent gown. She clutched the commandant's breastplate to herself, and—seeing her—Gaston turned and permitted her to fasten the armor in place. I had seen the girl before, on the rare occasions I'd dined with the native commandant, and still I was not certain if she was his squire or his concubine. Possibly she was both.

"Right then!" Gaston said, thumping his chest. "I've roused the lads already."

"How can we coordinate with the comms down?" I asked.

Gaston grinned. "My lord, Sabratha's my home—born and raised! I've been dealing with this shitty radio since I was in school. We'll send runners, and fire up the emergency lights!"

Just then a cry—shrill and piercing, loud enough and sharp enough to slash across even the wail of the sirens—filled the night.

Three long notes, each choked off at the end.

"Ai! Ai! Ai!"

"That's the birds?" Gaston asked.

"They've sighted the enemy," I said, peering up into the night.

"We need to move," Edouard said, shouldering his gun. "We need to get back to the *Rhea*. Marshall our defenses."

Cassandra grabbed my wrist. "Abba! What about Neema?"

I swore. The thought of my servant cowering in the ship's larder, or in his cabin, filled my mind. "Albé! We need to make for the *Ascalon*."

"But Commander Vedi!"

"We can telegraph the *Rhea* from my ship! We need to move!"

"I can wrangle an escort, lord!" said Commandant Gaston, who turned and swatted his girl. "Move your ass, Carla! Find Lumin and his lads and send them out, double quick! And fetch my gauntlets!"

The girl hurried inside.

"No need for the escort," I said. "We can't waste time!"

A gleam of violet flashed from the camp behind, the telltale glow of plasma fire.

A shot.

"That's gunfire!" Gaston swore. "What the hell is going on?"

I was already running. "Evacuate the xenologists if you can!" I shouted. "Guard the motor pool! Air support is coming!"

A wind scoured the camp, tugging at the lines of weather balloons and carrying with it the clamor of human voices.

Shouts. Cries of pain.

A bolt of green lightning slashed across the night. The beam of an energy-lance.

Static hissed in my ear, and I discerned two words:

"...*from*...*above!*"

"Abba!" Cassandra was a half dozen paces behind me. "What's going on?"

"I don't know!" I said. Was it MINOS? Had the sorcerous servants of the Pale King come to Sabratha? "We need to make sure Neema is all right."

"We should go directly to the *Rhea!*" Edouard shouted.

"The *Ascalon* is closer!" I said. "And we'll need it if we have to retreat from this place!"

"Retreat?" The word sounded like an oath on Edouard's lips. "Surely, it won't come to that."

"We don't know what we're up against!" I shouted back. "Or what their numbers are!"

The enemy had played his hand perfectly. In killing Oberlin, he had decapitated our command structure. Marika Clavan was Oberlin's right successor, but the captain was in orbit aboard the *Troglita,* and our only means of communication with her were the quantum telegraphs in the *Rhea* and *Ascalon.* With the hardlines cut, ground communication was limited to the near-useless radios, or to runners, signal flares, and the singing of the Irchtani. We were scattered, confused, half-asleep.

We had already lost.

Red light filled the sky with roaring, and the three of us all ground to a halt. Ahead and above us, the sky was filled with tongues of flame and I clapped my hands to my ears for fear the sound would deafen me. They were the descent thrusters of a mighty rocket.

Edouard shouted near at hand. "Is that the cavalry?"

"It's too soon!" I shouted back, realization and horror dawning on me.

If we cut through the camp, leaving the road to the left, we could reach the edge of the landing field and the *Ascalon.* I took us off the path instead, trying not to think about what I knew was coming.

Something huge and feathered struck the edge of one of the pod build-ings and fell broken on the sand. It was one of the Irchtani—and though it was dead, it moved.

A silver adder uncoiled from the bird man's loins, blood-soaked and shimmering, and raised its head like one of the serpents Sir Roban Milosh had taken me to see fight mongeese in the grand bazaar of Meidua when I was just a boy. It rose steadily, bladed jaws whirring like the bits of a drill. It rose until its whole body was in the air, twisting as it sought for meat.

It was a *nahute,* and presently it vanished up into the night. Wide-eyed, I followed it, throwing an arm out to halt Cassandra in her tracks.

There was a pale figure falling, floating out of the night like a diver down to the floor of what once had been Sabratha's sunless seas. White crowned it was, black eyed as a corpse. Tall, thin, and terrible—clad in oily black. In one hand it grasped the bloody serpent by its tail. With the other, it drew a scimitar long and white as its chalky hide.

Upon its thin breast, there gleamed the emblem of the White Hand.

It alighted smoothly, disengaging the pilfered repulsor harness it wore.

"Is that?" Cassandra's voice shrank, more a breath on my ear than anything, nearly lost in the wail of the sirens and the roar of engines.

"Yes," I said, and drew my sword.

There came then a moment of relative quiet in the chaos, and into it I raised my voice and bellowed as I had not done in a life-age of common men. *"Cielcin!"* I screamed, blade kindling in my hand.

I had not seen one of its kind in two hundred years, not since the day I reached across time and space to crush Ugin Attavaisa for all it had taken from me. The same light and fury flowered in me then, and white light streamed from my sword as I crossed the dust between us.

The *scahari* warrior threw its *nahute,* but I slashed the serpent to pieces, and fell upon its master like rain.

I understood then just how it was we'd been outmaneuvered.

Cutting the power and leaving the knife-missile for poor Sir Friedrich to find had required a saboteur. But the chaos in the camp? The shouting? The shots? The missing Irchtani?

The Cielcin had come, had relied upon an advance team dropping under the cover of night. Just as we had dropped upon Ganelon, relying on our repulsor harnesses.

The Cielcin, under Syriani's direct control and with the lodge of sorcerers to support its rule, had adapted, had *evolved.* The body that lay in pieces at my feet wore a shield-belt. They had been stealing those almost since the war began, but under Dorayaica, the seizure and reuse of man's technology had been elevated to a science.

An art.

"Abba!" Cassandra's shout slashed over my awareness, and looking up I saw three more of the Pale descending as if on cables.

Edouard's rifle *cracked* like the thunder, splitting the night. The bullet struck one of the xenobites square in the chest, but its shield caught the impact, shed its energy as light. These three hurled *nahute* of their own, and I drew back a pace, caught one of the flying serpents in the teeth with the edge of my blade.

Gibson's blade.

Behind me, Cassandra's twin swords flashed into being. She leaped into the air then—leaped *over* me—and slashed the *nahute* to pieces. But her jump had carried her nearer the enemy, and they closed in. The sight of my daughter beset by the Pale twisted my guts like wire, and I hurtled past her, striking the nearest with my blade. It raised its own to parry, but the highmatter sheared through the sword and the arm that held it. The Cielcin staggered back, clutching its bleeding stump.

I took off its head, and whirling faced the others, blade thrust out. My knee was already aching, and the shoulder Doctor Elkan had so expertly repaired. The two Cielcin spread out, readying themselves to strike together. Cassandra stayed close behind me, shifting her guard.

The two Cielcin ran.

Edouard Albé charged in from the side and smashed the butt of his ancestral rifle into the face of the nearest Pale. I gutted the other, and averted my eyes as the HAPSIS man drew his bayonet and thrust the point up under the fallen Cielcin's chin.

"We need to move!" he said, wiping the bayonet on the dead Cielcin's cape. He paused a moment to affix the blade to his gun. "*Merde.* Damn shields."

All about us, the sounds and flash of gunfire filled the night. There came a roar like dragonfire, and looking up, we saw more descent fires like the first.

"Siege towers?" asked Albé, coming to stand by Cassandra and myself.

"Aye," I said. "Probably a hundred Pale apiece."

"How did they get here?" Cassandra asked. "What are we going to do?"

"We hold," I said in answer. "We hold until the aquilarii get here."

"We need to move," the agent said again.

We barely made it a hundred yards before night turned wholly to day. A new sun blazed in the skies of Sabratha, if only for a moment. Every shadow was banished, and the world became a surreal tableau of graven marble. Men and Cielcin alike paused in that instant, and looked up in mingled horror and wonder at the light filling the sky. The very stars were lost, and the ground shook.

By the fire of that false sun, I saw illuminated the icy face of a moon, pale and pockmarked, cracked with age and eaten out where the raw iron of infernal engines gleamed.

It was one of the *oscianduru,* the worldships of the Cielcin.

It was *not* Dharan-Tun.

Seeing it, I knew the *Troglita* was lost. The light we saw—the light of that false star—was the light of her ending. Captain Clavan was dead, and First Officer Morrow, and Janashia and Browning and however many thousand men and women remained aboard.

Had they managed to launch the aquilarii in time?

Was anyone coming to aid us?

My skin crawled, and in the stillness and sudden silence I felt on me that sensation of *eyes.* I looked round, and in the fading light of particle annihilation, I saw *her.*

A figure in fuliginous black, darker than the returning night, formless and featureless, shrouded from crown to sole.

The Watcher stood amid the chaos, unmoving, and though I cannot say how it was I knew that it was so, I knew it was exultant.

Dae undallan!

The words resounded in my own skull, alien and yet—strangely familiar.

Aldon ollori Iadan, oi cocas olan!

Pain flared behind my eyes, but I did not look away, afraid the creature would vanish once again. Everywhere I looked, across every line of potential, every possible moment, I saw the creature staring back at me.

"Edouard!" I said, feeling the Watcher's words like spiders crawling across my brain. "Take Cassandra to the *Ascalon.*"

"What!" Cassandra protested. "Abba, no!"

At that moment, a ragged shout went up. In the face of the loss of the *Troglita,* in the face of the slaughter and the fighting in the camp, in the face of that Cielcin moon, a single word was lifted like a banner.

"Earth!" the men of our legions cried. "Earth! Earth! Earth!"

Cassandra seized my wrist. "Abba, we have to go!"

For the barest instant, I looked away, and when I looked back, the beast in black was gone. "I..." I swallowed. "Did you see it?"

"See what?" Albé shouldered his rifle.

"The Watcher," I hissed. "She's here."

"She?" The agent's voice was incredulous.

"I have to go back to the *Rhea,*" I said to them both. "Vedi has to prepare the Perseus weapon."

Cassandra had not let me go, and shook my arm, pulling me toward the camp. "You can telegraph the *Rhea* from the *Ascalon,* Abba!"

I shook my head. "No one can see her but me," I said, and tugged my arm free. "I need to be there, on the ground."

"I'm not leaving you!" Cassandra said, and set her jaw.

Seeing Valka in that gesture, I shut my eyes. "Fine. Edouard!" I turned to the agent. "Can you go to the *Ascalon?* See she's shielded and ready for takeoff, we may need her! And send word to Williamtown! Orbital Defense will have their hands full, but if they can spare even *one* gunboat for us here on the ground, it may tip the balance!"

The agent locked eyes with me, and allowed himself a curt nod. "As you will, Lord Marlowe!" He retreated a step, eyes downcast then, disbelieving. "The ship is lost."

"I know!" I said. "We're on our own down here! We can still do the job we came here for. Win or die!"

"Win or die," Edouard echoed, and rounding bolted off into the night.

Or win and *die,* I thought.

CHAPTER 20

CHAMELEON

THE GUARD THAT SLAMMED the postern hatch behind us kept a hand on my shoulder to steady me. "You all right, lord?"

I waved him off, feeling the tension in the garrison waiting in that lower hold. Men clutched their lances and the short stocks of their plasma burners, eyes wide and twitching. I went to Cassandra, who pressed her back to the bulkhead, chest heaving. There was a scratch on her right cheek where the claw of one Cielcin had torn at it.

Whispering to her in Jaddian, I asked, *"Buon es tu?"*

She looked as though she did not trust herself to speak.

Gingerly I touched the scratch on her face. She did not pull away. It was superficial. No real harm done. My left leg was burning. It had been a long time—a very long time—since I had run so much or fought so violently. Though I had fenced with Hydarnes and the other masters of the Fire School, the nerves and thews alike know the difference between practice and war, and the toxic juices of stress were in me. Cortisol. Adrenaline.

Life is very long.

"It will be a long night, Anaryan," I said.

She nodded weakly, never looking more like the child she had been not so long before.

A heavy shot sounded through the bulkhead. One of the *Rhea*'s turrets had fired on some approaching foe.

"Is Vedi still on the bridge?" I asked.

"Yes, Lord Marlowe," came the response from one gold-medaled centurion.

I pushed myself off the wall and—swaying—passed between the nearest ranks of the men. They would be the ship's last defense, should the hull be breached. Cassandra followed after me, footfalls slow and careful on the metal floor.

"Was it the *Troglita?*" asked one fresh-faced legionnaire. "Is the *Troglita* lost, my lord?"

"It is," I said, not breaking stride, my words issuing as from a deep, dry well. I added, "You must hold here. This is not over."

The same young man called back, "But there's no help coming?"

I do not think I answered him, which was answer enough.

Vedi was where we had left him, with Lieutenant Chatterjee and Ensign Dominina and the rest of the bridge crew. Priscian Lascaris was still seated in one corner, his head in his hands.

The commander turned to see us enter, but before he could speak, I said, "Is the NEM weapon ready to deploy?"

"There hasn't been time!" he protested, "My lord! The *Troglita* is lost. Captain Clavan—"

"I know the *Troglita* is lost, damn you!" I roared. "And Oberlin is dead. That means you and I are what remains of command."

"What of A2?"

"Special Agent Albé is on a mission I gave him," I said. "You and I are what remain."

"What mission?" Vedi asked.

"Have you telegraphed Williamtown?" I asked, rather than answer.

The commander did his best to compose himself, even as the *Rhea* shook from the report of her own guns. "We did. They know our situation here. But the ODF's tied up with the fighting in orbit. I had reports there's a whole moon up there."

"I saw it!" I said, shouldering past him to look over the heads of Dominina and the other junior officers and out the armored windows to the landing field beyond. Gunfire flashed there, and in the skies above, where the Irchtani grappled with the falling Cielcin. "And we've still a murderer on the loose."

Vedi spoke from the holography-well podium, saying, "We pulled security footage, but the cameras in the old man's quarters and the hall were dead. And in the lift."

I swore.

"I've got a few men trying to piece together a list of likelies based on who all was using the lifts, but it could be anyone."

"Forget it," I said. "Whoever our saboteur may be—he's done his part."

"If he's only one man," said Lascaris, speaking from his corner.

Rounding on him, I asked, "Do you know anything about it?"

Lascaris swallowed. "Only... only Friedrich believed there were spies in the department. The Inquisition has been finding spies in the service for years. Even on the Emperor's Security Council." The secretary sobbed. "I should have been there."

Cassandra patted the sad man on his shoulder. "There's nothing you could have done, sir."

"How long will it take to deploy the NEM?" I asked.

Vedi cast about in his mind for an answer. "About an hour to run all the preflight checks."

"So if you'd started it when I ordered you to, it would be nearly ready?"

The man blanched. "I...my lord, Perseus won't work unless the target has manifested itself in—"

"She's here!" I exclaimed. "I saw her in the camp. Like I saw her in the desert."

"Her?"

I threw up a hand for silence. It fell like a stone. "Do you think it a coincidence the Cielcin have arrived just as Valeriev's men neared the completion of their work?" Vedi looked nearly so grim as Lascaris, realizing what had been obvious to me from the start. "Our saboteur summoned them here, you may be certain. Doubtless they were lying in wait, a hundred light-years out-system. A thousand." I rubbed my eyes. The pressure behind them had abated, leaving only a dull ache. "They used us to find her."

"You're certain the Monumental is here?" Vedi asked.

"I saw *her*," I said again.

"That doesn't mean it's within range now," the commander said, quite correctly. "We cannot simply deploy Perseus. The Monumental can move out of phase with our reality at a moment's notice. We have to wait."

He was right. I knew that much, and—knowing it—deflated.

"We still need to prime the weapon," I said. "It must be ready to launch at a moment's notice."

Vedi agreed, and turning his head shouted. "Chatterjee. Ping tactical. Tell them to engage Perseus."

The lieutenant leapt to obey. Unable to help myself, I said, "Was that so hard?"

As if in answer, the whole ship shook. "Are we hit?" Cassandra asked, steadying herself against the bulkhead by Lascaris.

"No, ma'am," replied Ensign Dominina. "Earthquake! Magnitude five-point-six."

"It's the moon," Lascaris said, and a weak, strange little laugh escaped him. "The Cielcin ship. Tidal stress."

Vedi groaned. "As if we don't have enough problems."

Out on the landing field, a rosette of bright flame flowered, faded. A rotting scarlet bloom. One of the Cielcin siege towers had struck one of our grounded landers, destroying both ships. The chemical rockets of the Cielcin starship and the depleted reactor in our lander exploded together, sending shockwaves through the landing field.

"Our boys don't stand a chance out there," Vedi said. "You said Gaston's men are coming?"

I didn't think I had. "He was already suiting up when we arrived," I said. "He said they have ways to coordinate without comms."

"They should be here," Vedi said.

"The Cielcin were assaulting the camp, too," said Cassandra.

"I ordered them to guard the motor pool," I said. "They may be fighting their own battle."

"So long as we are each fighting our own battles, we're lost," said the grim commander. As if in answer then, a great rumbling filled the air, a thunder louder than the ever-present sirens. Through the gloom outside, I saw the amethyst beams of particle weapons slice across the night. An instant later, the fangy profiles of Cielcin siege towers erupted in gouts of oily flame. All of us on the bridge were silent, unmoving save for Dominina, who pressed her comms patch to her flesh.

"It's ... Manticore Flight!" she said.

A cloud passed from my heart. The *Troglita* had launched its aquilarii in time, after all!

The lost battleship had carried two dozen Peregrine-class light fliers: two-manned, fusion-burning attack ships with bodies each like a single, great wing. They were invisible, in the night above, marked only by the silent, prolonged stripes of violet energy that strafed the land beneath. Tower after inhuman tower flowered in their wake.

Fire filled the sky as the Cielcin trained artillery on the heavens.

One of Manticore Flight went down.

"I have to go back out there."

"You can't!" Vedi said.

"The Watcher is drawn to me," I said. "I'm the only one who's seen it." I looked round the bridge, at Cassandra and Lascaris, Chatterjee and Dominina and the other junior officers. At Vedi last of all. "We can't well detonate the Perseus inside this ship. If the Watcher comes to us here, we're dead. Besides, our shields will insulate against the weapon's pulse. If even a part of the creature were outside the ship, outside the shield envelope, all would be for nothing."

Vedi protested. "Perseus's pulse blast should propagate through the entire body of the creature, so long as even a part of it is exposed."

"But across a shield curtain?" I asked. "Do we know?"

Vedi was silent.

"I'll take a flare gun," I said, having only the barest semblance of a plan. "Oberlin wanted me to play the foxhound, but I'll play the fox instead. Watch for my signal."

"Alone?" Vedi asked.

"Call down the Irchtani," I said. "Annaz can get me clear of the landing field." My gaze lingered on the burning beyond the bridge's windows. Out there, the labyrinth awaited—and after more than six hundred years of wandering its halls, I had come upon the minotaur in its heart at last.

Theseus... I thought. *Perseus...*

"I have to go!" I said. "Cassandra!"

"Abba!"

I had been about to tell her to remain on the bridge, but something in her voice caught my attention. A tension and a sudden fear. Turning to look, hand flashing to my sword from old reflex, I saw my daughter pressed against the bulkhead at the rear of the bridge, her head turned to one side.

A knife-missile—identical in every way to the one that had killed Oberlin, a sliver of shining steel—floated microns from her bare throat. The sight of it boiled every dram of blood in me, and I cast about for a solution, for a way to do *something*.

I imagined all the ways I might cross the space between us, peered across time to find a space where I could reach Cassandra before the knife-missile did its bloody work. Such spaces there were in the infinite weft of lateral time, but they were all so remote that I felt them slipping through my fingers, fading into the distance with each passing picosecond.

"You will be going nowhere, gentle lord," came a deep, cold voice. Laughter followed, just as cold. "I ought to have stopped you before you left the last time, but it was too early. Almost I feared you had slipped through my fingers entirely."

The voice was unfamiliar, but it issued from the crumpled secretary in the chair beside Cassandra.

"Lascaris?" I asked, taking one step nearer the man and my daughter.

"Priscian Lascaris is dead," the man said, looking up. The secretary looked up through his tangled black hair, gray eyes shining. "He has been for a very long time."

"What are you, then?" I asked, sword unkindled in my hand. "A SOM?"

"Nothing so primitive," he said. Gray eyes blinked. Became black. With a groan, he sighed, stood, lifted one bony, long-fingered hand to brush the hair from his face. The hollow cheeks were still stained with tears, but all other appearance of sorrow had left the man's face. The hair he brushed aside—which at first appeared black as my own had in my youth—turned gray as winter cloud, then white as bone. The skin—which had always been pale and sallow—went whiter still, and the very bones of the face seemed to shift as the gross musculature that covered them plumped and shifted.

Where before the tall and somber secretary had been, there stood a creature smooth faced and white as death, white almost as the Cielcin. It smiled at me, revealing small and curiously sparse teeth.

"Put the gun down, Commander Vedi," the creature that had been Priscian Lascaris said.

Glancing aside, I saw the young commander had drawn his sidearm.

Vedi fired instead.

The shot caromed off the creature's personal shield—it must have activated the curtain as it stood, for I was certain Lascaris had not been shielded the prior instant.

The secretary raised an arm in reply. Something silver and arrow fast darted from its sleeve, and I heard the hum of repulsors and felt the static thrill as the second knife-missile lanced forth. Anticipating Vedi's shield-curtain, the thing decelerated as it reached him, then punched him hard in the chest.

Dominina screamed, and the knife-missile rushed from between the ribs of her commander and through her open mouth. The other junior officers were too slow. They died in their chairs. Chatterjee, to his credit, found his feet and made it three loping paces toward the thing that had been Lascaris before the knife-missile caught him between the shoulder blades.

All this happened in less time than it takes to write about it—in less than the space of a breath.

"There, that's better," the creature said. Not taking the blade from Cassandra's throat, it took a step nearer. "Your sword, my lord. Indeed, all your effects, if you please. I've no desire to harm your daughter."

Raising my left hand to show that it was empty, I slid my sword back into its hasp at my waist. "You're a painted man," I said, using the same hand to depower the shield pack and undo the ratchet that held my belt in place. "Aren't you?"

The *thing* smiled, and its lips stretched farther than those of any true man, baring its teeth to the remotest molar. "You know us?"

"I killed one of your kind," I said. "A very long time ago."

"An older model, no doubt," it said. Voice growing sharp, it said, "Your effects, Marlowe. *Now.*"

I hesitated. "You're MINOS."

"And *you* are trying to keep me talking. It won't avail," the creature said. "Your effects!"

I dropped the belt, and on the painted man's instructions kicked it over.

The androgyn stooped to collect it, draping it over one shoulder. It raised a finger, and the blade that had done for the bridge crew swung into orbit around my head, recalling the constellation of drones that had accompanied Kharn Sagara at all times. "One false move from you and I'll kill the girl. I've only orders to bring *you* to the general alive."

"Which general?" I asked, fearing the answer would be Vati, Dorayaica's strong right arm.

"Muzugara," the painted man replied. "You know him, I believe?"

Muzugara...It was not the answer I'd expected. My Red Company had bested Muzugara at the Battle of Thagura. Our first mission together following my investment as an Imperial knight. We had broken the Cielcin fleet in orbit, and Muzugara had retreated, leaving Thagura to mankind. The then-prince had carried with it the name of the young Hadrian Marlowe, and had taken the story of how he had slain Aranata Otiolo in single combat back to share among its kind. I had seen Muzugara in passing at Akterumu. It had been among the princes to swear itself into slavery at the feet of Syriani Dorayaica—one of the few. With Attavaisa and Peledanu and a scant dozen or so others, it had survived the Prophet's poison and the Aetavanni that hammered the thousand-and-more Cielcin clans into a single rod of iron aimed at humanity's heart.

"I do," I said.

"He will be most pleased to see you," the painted man said, circling round me, moving toward the holography well. "He will be landing soon. Shall we go and meet him?"

Cassandra spoke. "You'll never get us off this ship. There's hundreds of men on board."

"There are, aren't there?" mused the homunculus. "But there are *thousands* of Cielcin outside. Why don't we open the doors?"

"Don't!" I lurched toward him.

Lascaris raised a finger once more, and the blade orbiting my head bristled an arm's length from my face. I knew Cassandra's must have pressed against her throat, for she hissed.

The painted man stepped neatly over Vedi's cooling corpse and keyed something into the captain's console. A diagnostic box appeared above the holography well. The sirens stopped, and in that strangely sweet silence, I heard the hissing of distant pneumatics as every ramp and hatch upon the *Rhea* opened wide.

Sabratha shook as her new moon convulsed her, and I pictured stones falling in the deep places of Phanamhara, dunes rushing in like the tide. An instant later, the tide rushed in indeed. The sounds of gunshots and shouting men resounded through the grounded ship. Calm as may be, the homunculus traipsed back toward Cassandra and removed her shield-belt and the twin swords Master Hydarnes had given her.

We stood there a while, the three of us, as though we waited in a lift. The shouting gave way to screaming, and I saw Cassandra shaking, tears in her eyes, on her cheeks—but I knew I could not go to her. I prayed that Edouard had found Neema, prayed Gaston might rally some defense.

But in my heart, I knew that all was lost.

The painted man shook back its sleeve, revealing the silvered gauntlets that housed and threw its knife-missiles. Doubtless some device embedded in its motor cortex controlled the machines. It adjusted some knob there a moment before smoothing the garment into place, looking for all the world like a man without a care.

New silence deafened us, then broke.

There were footsteps in the hall outside.

The door opened, revealing a sea of Cielcin armored in scarab black, the White Hand emblazoned on their inhuman breasts.

"Gentlemen!" The painted man bowed, a murderous harlequin. "The day is ours!"

CHAPTER 21

THE ONCE-PRINCE

THE CIELCIN SEARCHED CASSANDRA and myself, but the painted man had taken everything of note from us already. They bound our hands with lengths of cord and marched us from the *Rhea*. We were forced to step over the bodies of human defenders and Cielcin alike, and when we reached the hold, I said, "Shut your eyes, Cassandra."

She did not obey.

The dead lay everywhere around us, bodies chewed on by the actions of *nahute* and Cielcin. Throats had been variously cut or torn open, and several of the *scaharimn* had red blood running down their chins, while others wiped their swords on the tunics of our dead, or bent to despoil or defile the fallen.

In a moment, we passed through that microcosm of hell and came out into the cool night air. All was lit by the hell-glow of our burning ships, and here and there the flash of a particle beam or plasma shot flashed in the middle distance. The fight was not over, but seemed to have died on the margins of the landing field nearest the *Rhea*. In the dark, I could no longer see the *Ascalon*. Was it still there? Had Edouard reached it?

They forced us to march beyond the edge of the camp, out onto a stretch of level sand that ran for perhaps three miles to where one of the great skeletons of the *Cetoscolides* stood. The painted man stood a little apart. He seemed smaller to me, and Lascaris's clothes appeared rumpled. Lascaris himself had been a tall man, of nearly palatine height. The creature seemed of mere plebeian stature then, and I wondered how long it had inhabited Priscian's form. When had the real man died? It must have been before they came to Jadd.

As I watched, the changeling fastened my belt and Cassandra's both about its waist, allowed its jacket to cover the pilfered swords. I swore a private vow that I would kill the monster, as I'd killed that other of its kind on Rustam when I was hardly more than a boy.

"*Venanaggaa o-tajarin'ta wo!*" came a rough, inhuman voice. "*Aeta yelnun wo.*"

The Prince comes.

I watched as more Cielcin came out of the fire behind, their shadows flickering like demons on the pale sand. They spurred knots of men and women before them—soldiers and worker alike.

The Cielcin who had spoken—the one with the rough voice—moved along the line its subordinates had made, a lieutenant to either side. It surveyed each of the captured prisoners in turn, pausing here and there to assess an injury or examine some other feature. Once it gripped a man by the face, forced open his jaw to check the condition of his teeth. After each brief examination, the captain—for captain it surely was—made its pronouncement.

"*Unjasan.*"

"*Unjasan.*"

"*Iyadan.*"

"*Unjasan.*"

"*Iyadan.*"

"*Iyadan.*"

"*Unjasan.*"

"What is it saying, Abba?" Cassandra whispered. "What's happening?"

Meat. Meat. Slave. Meat. Slave. Slave. Meat.

"It's deciding what to do with the prisoners," I said at last.

Pausing before one especially broad-shouldered woman, the captain said, "*Tagasvate.*"

Sport.

At once the three Cielcin nearest her let out a grating cry. One kicked the woman's knees out from under her and fell atop her, while the others cleared a space.

"Look away!" I tried to shoulder Cassandra aside, to put myself between her and what was about to happen.

But there was no hiding it.

One of my guards struck me, and I went to one knee.

A moment later, the captain reached us. It was taller than either of its lieutenants, but one of the two primary horns that sprouted from its brow had been sawn off, lending it a curiously lopsided appearance.

Seeing it, the painted man bowed. "*Ichakta-do,*" he said. *Captain.*

The Cielcin bowed its head—the threatening acknowledgement of a superior to its slave. "*Kybalion,*" it said, and I guessed this was the changeling's name. The Cielcin swept its eyes over Cassandra and myself. Speaking its own language, it said, "You are smaller than your reputation, Devil-Man."

"*Ekanyi usha suh,*" I said, having regained my feet. *So are we all.*

"Not our Prophet," the captain replied. "His is the only truth."

"His is the only truth," echoed the two lieutenants.

Not twenty feet from us, the woman stopped screaming.

"So your Prophet told me, many times," I said. "That did not stop me from ruining its coronation. Tell me: Does Syriani still walk with a limp?"

The captain slammed its fist into my stomach. I doubled over, but did not fall.

"That name is dead!" the captain said. "He is *Shiomu-Elusha,* as you of all your kind well know." It bent over me, its breath the very vapors of hell. "Do you know how many of our people died that day? When your ship leaped away?"

"Enough, I hope, to make up for mine," I said.

The captain punched me again.

I had never given much thought to the cataclysm the *Ascalon* had caused by making the jump to warp within the circle of Akterumu. The formation of the warp envelope would have been accompanied by intense gravitic stress. The ruined *Tamerlane*—already broken—would have been torn to pieces. Its various fuel tanks and weapons batteries crushed and breached. The resulting explosion must have been terrific, to say nothing of the rain of fire and twisted metal that must have come thereafter.

I prayed it had been enough to repay our dead, and wondered if that had been the reason it had taken the enemy so many years to emerge after the fact, allowing Valka and me the time we needed to reach Colchis, Nessus, and Carteia.

"Enough, Ramanthanu!" said the changeling, Kybalion. "The *vayadan* comes."

The captain grunted, glared down at me from its not inconsiderable height. Eying Cassandra, it addressed the painted man, saying, "This is his spawn?"

"His child," Kybalion confirmed. "She must not be harmed. She is the only thing keeping the Utannashi's power in check."

Ramanthanu jerked its head in that way that meant it understood. "No matter," it said. "Soon Utannash's power will be broken. The Liar will be silent at last."

The captain's men busied themselves with the division of the prisoners. Steadily I became aware of a drumming in the air, and looking up beheld a black shape against the starlit sky. The Cielcin lander was larger than the standard siege towers, but not of the crooked design I was most accustomed to. It was like a great keep, descending on human-style repulsors rather than the customary lifter rockets.

It settled on the empty sands before us, kicking up clouds of dust.

"Abba," Cassandra whispered. "What are we going to do?"

I could only shake my head.

A herald carrying the traditional Cielcin battle standard emerged from the lift that opened, followed by ranks of *scaharimn* that fanned out, forming the van of the one-time prince's honor guard. Evidently Syriani Dorayaica had allowed Muzugara to retain the style and honors of its former rank. And more. For when the lift had cycled, four chimeric warriors—white-armored creatures of titanium and adamant nine feet tall—emerged and stood very straight.

The former prince itself emerged a moment later, followed by a pair of Cielcin attendants with filed-down horns whose painted limbs were draped in silk and cloth of silver. These adjusted the train of the *vayadan's* white robes, and followed closely as it approached.

Inumjazi Muzugara had changed since I'd last seen it on Eue. There, the prince had been one among hundreds, and known to me only by dint of the fact that we had met before. Once. Briefly. But where its arms had been there were now jointed contrivances of metal and of ceramic white as bone. The Prophet's gift to one of its faithful slaves. Its armor was of the same insect black as that of its men, with the White Hand emblazoned on the breast. But the robe it wore over that armor was white as snow—was white as the Imperial cloth that I myself had worn for much of my career.

Alongside it, taller and slimmer than the general itself, there strode a scarlet-robed figure in a mirrored environment suit. So skinny it was that I might have encircled its waist with my fingers, broadening only slightly at shoulders and hips. Its face was hidden behind a bubble of golden mirrored glass, a perfect sphere beneath the scarlet hood.

I knew him at once. Quentin Sharp had killed him at Ganelon.

It was Elect-Master Gaizka, one of the sorcerers of MINOS.

The Prophet's *vayadan* towered over me, its glassy teeth bared in a rictus of triumph. "When you escaped us at Akterumu, I confess... I thought it would be our undoing," it said. "But the gods bend even you to their will." Muzugara raised one iron hand and clamped it over my jaw. The metal fingers tightened. "I ought to kill you and have done," it said, "but you are needed. My Shiomu-Elusha—twelve twelves and twelve praises be upon his holy name—says only the gods may kill you. Any mortal would fail, he says... and yet..."

"Enough, my general!" interjected Elect-Master Gaizka, evidently the one-time prince's minder as much as its advisor. "Remember Severine's warning. We cannot be certain what might happen if you kill him!"

Muzugara hissed, turning its head to bare its fangs at the glass-faced sorcerer.

"The thing must be done properly, my general," said Gaizka, bowing his head.

With a snarl, Muzugara released me. Its iron shoulders flexed, components clicking in them like the jeweled workings of some vast Durantine clock. Rounding on Kybalion, the Cielcin general said, "You are certain the *Caihanaru* is here?"

The painted man bowed, pressing thin hands to its breast. "Marlowe has seen it."

The once-prince's eyes flashed back in my direction, narrow with Cielcin surprise. "*You* have seen it?"

"*Denam*," I said, knowing that in doing so I would incur another blow.

"Twice!" Muzugara raised a hand to strike me.

Bracing myself, I let my vision fracture. The back of Muzugara's hand flashed toward my cheek, faster than my human eye could track. But the blow never landed. The general's arm passed *through* me, just as the bullet from Bastien Durand's gun had done. The Cielcin gathered about us—Muzugara and Ramanthanu, Muzugara's two concubine-attendants, the guards that held Cassandra and myself—all froze or leaped back. Even Gaizka and Kybalion stopped short.

Gaizka spoke first, his deep, resonant voice barely audible over the thunder of distant fighting. "Fascinating..."

The painted man likewise had recovered its bearings. "That's enough, Marlowe!"

Cassandra gasped, and I turned to see the knife-missile again at her throat.

Unable to raise my hands in surrender, I shrugged my shoulders.

"It's really here..." Muzugara spoke in hushed tones. "One of the gods?"

"In the *lightning*, my general," Kybalion said. "It has been killing the humans here. Feeding upon their vital energies to amplify its signal. But it is still weak enough to transport, I deem."

Transport? The word caught like a dull knife against my ribs, so concrete in that conversation of religious abstraction. *Transport*, of course. The Cielcin had come to free one of their gods, or to capture it and bring it to Dorayaica.

Feeding upon their vital energies, Kybalion had said. *To amplify its signal.*

Oberlin had said the Watchers were creatures of pure energy, that the bodies they evidenced were only the condensates of that energy into crude matter. Surely then they required energy to sustain the pattern of energy that comprised their thoughts? Had that been why the beast confined itself to small actions like the murder of Doctor Mann, and of Alexander of Alba?

Muzugara had mastered itself from the shock—though it rubbed one hand with the other, as if I had contaminated it with some unseen filth.

"The Shiomu-Elusha will make me *aeta* once more for this," it said. "One of *his* chosen. The first of our kind since Elu's day to witness to one of the very gods!" Muzugara loomed over Kybalion. The painted man had shrunken quite severely from Lascaris's former height, and seemed almost a gnome before the bone-crowned Cielcin. "You will take me to the Door."

Kybalion bowed once more. "Of course, my general."

"Ramanthanu-kih!" the once-prince bellowed for its subordinate.

The *ichakta*, Ramanthanu, bared its throat in obedience, an alien salute.

"Bring the Utannashi, Marlowe, and its spawn! And fetch the palanquin! The god is waiting!"

CHAPTER 22

HEAVEN'S GATE

THUNDER AND THE FLASH of distant lightning mingled with the tumult and fire of guns as Muzugara's men forced Cassandra and me to make the long march to Phanamhara. The Cielcin army went ahead of us, clearing the way. Many times a small number of them would hurry into the darkness at one side, charging some desperate knot of defenders.

The great tent of the motor pool was burning—everywhere burning. Cielcin towers had smashed the longhouses where the local garrison and dig teams made their homes. In the shadow of one I saw several dozen men and women—mainly women—kneeling under guard as some *ichakta* like Ramanthanu assessed the captives.

Meat. Meat. Slave. Meat. Slave. Slave. Sport.

"What are they going to do with us?" Cassandra whispered in her native Jaddian.

"They want to use me to draw the Watcher to them," I said, peering back over my shoulder at the device that Muzugara's servants had brought from the *vayadan*-general's landing craft. It was like a coffin floating, like an elongated egg, and wrought of the same polished white ceramic that had gone into the construction of Muzugara's arms—the imprimatur of MINOS manufacture.

"You think they mean to capture it?" Cassandra whispered.

Transport, Kybalion had said, looking back at the sarcophagus-palanquin once more. Two MINOS technicians accompanied it, bland-faced men in smocks of drab gray with the chevrons of their order in bronze over the heart. "They mean to take it from here, at least."

"*Onnannaa!*" One of Ramanthanu's men clubbed Cassandra across the head in retribution.

Bellowing, I launched myself at the xenobite, not caring my hands were bound. I crashed bodily into the creature before three of its fellows could pull me off. One had its hand wound in my shaggy mane, and yanked my head back, baring my throat in forced submission to their general and captain. Muzugara and Ramanthanu both looked on, inhuman faces unreadable.

"If you've hurt her!" I said through clenched teeth.

"*Shahaga-kih!*" said Captain Ramanthanu. "Leave the whelp!"

"*Nietamda, Ichakta-doh!*"

"*Onnanna!*" Ramanthanu said. "*Nietono ni!*"

Let them talk.

The one called Shahaga had regained its feet, lifted its chin in what seemed defiance to my human eyes. It was surrender. Ramanthanu turned away, saying, "They can do nothing. The battle is good as won."

We came in time to the mouth of Phanamhara, and descended the sloping dunes along the road that ran between the twin ramparts of greenish stone. The air was stale and still down in the dig. With the floodlights dead, and only the stars and the light of distant fires to light it, the Vaiartu ruins—the ruins of the Enar—became the shadowed vestibule of some long-abandoned hell.

"I had them open a path!" Kybalion said, going out ahead. "This way!"

The painted man had moved to stand to one side of the main avenue. There the ancient builders had built a tunnel such that the projecting arm of the city's rampart buildings ran overhead.

"Abba, the poison," Cassandra whispered.

"There's nothing for it now," I said, straining the silken cords that bound my wrists. I couldn't find the knot. "Are you all right?"

"I got worse in school."

I could not help but smile, despite my fears. They'd not knocked the fight from her. Still, I wished that she had stayed on Jadd then. I could not have guaranteed her safety, from HAPSIS or whatever Imperial agency might have sought to use her as the lever to move me—even as the Cielcin used her in that moment. She would not have been safe, but she was less safe then.

Kybalion assumed the role of guide, seizing a torch from atop a supply crate left against the face of one cyclopean wall. Its beam showed the way to the pit. Cranes overshadowed it, and the red hulks of excavators and of grading equipment stood nearby. Valeriev's men had been at work widening the narrow passage, opening the steeply slanting shaft the Vaiartu had made, that once had run from the surface all the way down to the place we called the pantheon.

I'd walked it a time or two. The descent was steep, and must in its day have been smooth, though the plascrete had cracked and crumbled badly. Valeriev had reinforced the tunnel, but there were sections where it was possible for only two or three to walk abreast.

Often I have seen false pictures of war. Holograph operas—such as those my mother painted in her studio at Haspida—stage performances, paintings...written accounts. Almost none of them have captured what is to me war's great, defining feature.

Panic.

Small wonder the Achaeans of old had fashioned a god in its image. Deimos, the thunderer, the companion of Discord, the brother of Fear. War, I have found—and heard many a soldier say—is composed of long stretches of relative calm punctuated by instants of abject terror. That terror, that panic, that *Deimos* had come in the first instants of the attack. In the discovery of the knife-missile. In the cutting of the power. In the descent of the Cielcin from the night sky.

Deimos returned—not as thunder, but as lightning.

That lightning struck the earth around us, and I lurched to Cassandra's side. Two of the Cielcin ahead of us and to either side fell dead, and in the dark I saw the telltale flicker of shields as Ramanthanu itself was struck but did not fall.

The Cielcin captains rallied their men, hurled *nahute* into the air.

"*Eijana! Eijana!*" shouted one of the xenobites.

Above!

I looked up, hope blossoming in me.

Above.

It was not lightning that had fallen on the Cielcin.

The Cielcin had no word for *birds.*

The Irchtani had found us.

Looking up, I saw the shape of one falling against the stars. It picked its shots with rapid care, and I heard more than saw the flap of wings opening. Then the flier was gone, rising back to regain altitude for another drop. I scrabbled at my bonds with desperate fingers. If I could just find the knot—understand its shape—I could use my power to break it. But there was nothing, though the cords seemed to be of some rougher cousin to *irinyr*. Growling in frustration, I looked round, watched as one of the bird men dove out of the blackness, his long-bladed *zitraa* flashing. The blade swept the head from one of the Cielcin defenders, and one taloned foot caught another by the horns. Both Irchtani and Cielcin vanished an instant later, the former dragging the latter up into the night.

Only the Cielcin returned, its body broken on the sand-swept stones.

Moments later another of the Irchtani fell.

The four chimeras of Muzugara's personal guard had each leaped into battle. They carried not the scimitars and throwing snakes of their still-organic compatriots, but were armed with missile launchers and beam weapons. They fired up into the night.

"*Ishaan Irchtani!*" I bellowed, unable to wave my arms. "It's Marlowe! Here! Here!"

Ramanthanu itself wheeled about and clouted me across the face with a closed fist. I sprawled, ears ringing.

A sharp cry resounded from above, and an instant later one of the fliers emerged, wings billowing into view of the lamps. It hovered over Cassandra and myself, sword in hand.

"Marlowe-man!" the Irchtani said. "We fly now!"

A shot caromed off the bird man's shield. The chimeras concentrated fire on it. Before the smoke had cleared, Captain Ramanthanu leaped at the hovering warrior, its scimitar in its hand. The Irchtani flapped its pinions in such a way as to bring its cutlass round to parry, somehow managing to stay airborne.

"We go now!" the bird man shouted, vanishing up into the dark a moment as the chimeras picked their shots.

Muzugara's voice boomed out. "Get the prisoners underground! Rijah! Izamani! Kill these *eijana!*"

The Irchtani returned, accompanied by two more of its kind. Plasma fire rained from above as more of our unseen soldiers plummeted from the night. I'd regained my feet by then, crouched near Cassandra, unshielded and still surrounded by the enemy.

Still, hope flowered in that lowest place.

"Take the girl first!" I shouted. "The *kajeema-bashanda!*"

One of the chimeric soldiers leaped clean over me, five hundred pounds of titanium and adamant—its arms outstretched to snatch one of the Irchtani from the air. The iron beast succeeded, and seizing the one that had shouted to me by its ankle, the chimera slammed the flying soldier into the stone floor as a fisher beats his catch against the pier.

The bird man's delicate bones shattered with the first impact. He was surely dead by the second. After the third, the Cielcin machine rounded on them, claws extended.

Still one of the Irchtani stooped in an effort to save Cassandra. Talons gripped her by the shoulder, wings stretched to lift her into the air.

The chimera hurled the limp corpse of the dead Irchtani at its brother, the one trying to save Cassandra. Both living and dead Irchtani fell away, and at once cold, clawed hands fell on me. Four. Six. Eight. I was lifted bodily—thrashing—by four or five Cielcin screamers. Somewhere in the night, Cassandra screamed.

"Fly!" I shouted to the two Irchtani near at hand. "Fly away!"

One Cielcin wrapped its arm under my jaw as they dragged me bodily from the field. I saw one at least vanish into the night even as his brothers rained fire upon us.

Muzugara was still barking orders, Ramanthanu by its side with the chimeras. I had a disorienting view of the green ramparts of Phanamhara as I twisted in the Cielcin grasp, saw the night and the stars and the flash of beam weapons as the survivors of the *Troglita*'s Manticore Flight still turned in the dark overhead. Had the governor-general's Orbital Defense Force engaged the Cielcin? Were they holding their own?

And what of Neema? Of young Edouard Albé? What of the fate of the *Ascalon?*

I could be sure of nothing at all—unless it was at least that our few defenders knew what had become of me, and of Cassandra.

The roof closed overhead. Green plascrete. Brown earth. The gray steel of reinforcing pylons. We were in Valeriev's tunnel, and the noise of the fighting became muffled. I had hardly noticed our descent into those portions of the pit open to the sky, where the surface team had toiled to meet the men digging from below.

Cassandra's own screaming, her Jaddian cursing, echoed off the suddenly close roof.

Her mother would have been proud of her...

They carried us until we reached a spot where the path narrowed, and metal stanchions held back the earth.

"*Gennaa wegasur!*" came Ramanthanu's rough voice, and I was hurled to the earth like a sack of unruly grain.

The Cielcin captain had emerged from the fighting outside, leading a dozen of its men in close guard about Muzugara and Gaizka. The chimeras had remained in the world above, with the bulk of the force. A rearguard followed, three dozen *scaharimn* at least, and the pair of human magi that accompanied the palanquin. The machine itself required the most careful maneuvering to negotiate the tighter parts of Valeriev's tunnel.

Before long the noise of the fighting above had faded to a distant drumming, indistinguishable from the thunder.

"Make them walk!" Ramanthanu shouted once again, stooping to drag me to my feet.

The Cielcin carrying Cassandra let her fall. She grunted as she hit the ground, landing on her back and her bound hands. One of the Pale stooped to snatch her up, and she kicked it fully in its flat face. The stooping creature staggered back, and one of its brethren kicked her hard in the flank.

In a flash, the captain was on its subordinate, snarling words barely discernable to me. "Enough from you, Thnaga! Get back!"

The one called Thnaga turned its head aside, raised its hands as it retreated.

"*Suja wo!*" said General Muzugara, bracing itself against one of the stanchions with iron fingers. "We have made it, at last, my slaves." It looked round in reverence at the cracked green walls, thick with Vaiartu sineoform. "This is holy ground."

The Cielcin stood in rapt silence.

Master Gaizka broke it, his suit chiming to announce his heavy speech. "The battle is not done, my general," he said. "We should move swiftly if we are to secure the asset."

"The *asset?*" Muzugara struggled to pronounce the human word, failed to manage the terminal plosive, so the word emerged as *asseta*. "You speak of a god, you foul creature!"

Wordless, Gaizka bowed.

Eager to salvage the moment for its true master, the painted man spoke up, saying, "It is this way!"

Cassandra had risen again and leaned against me. "What are they saying? Are they fighting?"

"The Extrasolarians don't believe the Cielcin religion," I said. "They are arguing about respect."

"Respect?" she whispered the word in Jaddian. "*Seiasmo?*"

"The Cielcin need the Extras, but the Extras have their own designs," I said, certain in that moment that the palanquin was not what the magi had advertised. Urbaine had spoken of his desire to become like gods, to usher in a new age of *progress,* of human evolution—and of breaking the Imperial yoke. Doubtless they sought to steal the Watcher from their Cielcin accomplices, to wield its power for their own.

"Muzugara!" I said, drawing the once-prince's eye. "Your sorcerers will betray you; you know that."

The *vayadan's* four-slit nostrils flared.

"*Raka'ta ba-Utannash,*" I said. *They are of the Lie.* It was not precisely what I meant, but the Cielcin tongue had no simple means of separating the simple fact that the sorcerers could not be trusted from the Cielcin religious frame.

"I know!" Muzugara bared its fangs in an alien smile. "So are you!"

"They will take your god from you!" I said.

"Gods are gods," Muzugara responded. "*Raka yukajjimn, yukajjimn suh.*" *Vermin are vermin.*

"*Yukajjimn!*" The Cielcin gathered round all howled the word, acting as though their general had scored some vast rhetorical point. "*Yukajjimn! Yukajjimn!*"

I could only shake my head. Muzugara was not Dorayaica. If I could not drive a wedge between the Cielcin and their human allies, I would let what must come come.

Ramanthanu shoved me forward. "Move!"

Ours was a long descent, awkward and slow, but in time we passed the last of the obstructions, and came to a place where the hall widened until it was hundreds of feet wide and paved entirely in the polymerized stone—so like marble in apparent texture—that defined Enar architecture.

The way was straight and broad, as is every road to perdition.

The pantheon awaited, the pandaemonium of the Vaiartu.

Its dark galleries were lit by our glowspheres. They hung everywhere like fat stars, too close, too cold, too impermanent. The relief carvings of Vaiartu conquest flickered in the light as we entered, and looking up I saw the clustered wings of the Watcher, Masutemu, stretched above, directly across from the opening.

Muzugara lifted its face in reverence. Leaving its men behind, the *vayadan*-general approached the central dais and the titanic bones that rested upon it. The former prince knelt, pressed its horned brow to the white floor, and—rising—kissed the deathless bones, lipless mouth chattering some private prayer.

The other Cielcin—save those that held Cassandra and myself—followed one by one.

"Dō Anscurhae," Muzugara began, and I was a moment discerning its meaning. *Anscurhae* did not sound like a Cielcin word. The transition from the trill to the fricative, the *R* to the *H*, was not a Cielcin sound. "Yehelnub."

A short breath escaped me. It was the language of Elu, the Cielcin of ten thousand years ago. *Yehelnub* was *Yelnubei*. *We have come.* And *Anscurhae* was *Anasaka*.

Serpent.

"Dō Anscurhae, yehelnub!" exclaimed the other Cielcin, echoing their master.

O Serpent, we have come.

"Dō Gennarush, yehelnub!" Muzugara intoned.

"Dō Gennarush, yehelnub!" the others proclaimed.

O Maker, we have come!

"Dō Caeharush, yehelnub!" the *vayadan* said.

"Dō Caeharush, yehelnub!"

Through the crowd of Cielcin, I caught Kybalion's eye. The painted man looked away.

"Abba." Cassandra was yet near at hand. "What are they saying?"

I did not look at her, but leaned as near as I was able. "O Watcher, we have come."

Half-remembered images stirred in my mind. The memories of visions, of lives I was certain—almost certain—I had never lived. Memories of a Cielcin—prince or priest—offering its own blood upon a mound of its dead sister-brothers, of tendrils snaking from the dark. Had I heard the chanted words before? Had some other Hadrian—his memories embedded deep beneath my own—come to this place, or some place like it? With Dorayaica? With Otiolo? With Valka? Or alone?

I had seen Elu kneel, and sacrifice Avarra, its mate, before the very skull of Miudanar.

"We are servants of the Great One!" Muzugara said, spreading its hands where it stood upon the topmost step of the dais. "Our Prophet! Our King!"

"*Yaiya toh!*" the Cielcin replied. "*Yaiya toh!*"

By your will.

They were the words Elu had spoken to its god before the sacrifice, the words that had echoed throughout Cielcin history, defining their mad war against life, the universe... against being itself. Like the Enar before them, like Sunamasra-Tehanu and Aravte-Teäplu and all the Kings of the Vaiartu, the Cielcin had sold their souls in the service of unlife.

I edged forward a step, placing myself between Cassandra and the dais, my eyes on the looming fingerbones. I knew what they wanted, what surely must come.

But I was wrong.

"Ramanthanu-kih!" The *vayadan* took one step down toward its men. "*Psaqattaa.*"

Choose.

What choice was there for the lop-horned captain to make?

Ramanthanu surveyed its men with the same speculative intensity it had employed inspecting its human captives. It eyed the one called Thnaga a long moment. The junior xenobite quailed. After a moment, the captain twitched its head in the negative, toward the left shoulder. Nictitating membranes swept the ink-dark lenses of its eyes, and after another moment, it turned to one of its lieutenants. "Gurazi!"

"*O... O-koarin, Ichakta-doh?*" the lieutenant balked. Was it afraid? "I am... not worthy."

"You are the best I have!" Ramanthanu pressed its forehead to that of its lieutenant, and reaching up seized the other by the horns.

Gurazi reciprocated the gesture—it had to grip one of the lesser horns on Ramanthanu's left side. After a moment, the lieutenant drew back. The Cielcin nearest it all reached out their hands that they might touch the one that would become their sacrifice.

"Gurazi-kih!" said General Muzugara from the steps, and gestured that the younger Cielcin should join it there. "You will be our Avarra. You shall be the bridge that binds this place to the Iazyr Kulah!"

There was no Cielcin word for *yes,* only a breathy exhalation.

Gurazi made it, and reaching up undid the seals that clamped its armor to its second skin. The black cuirass fell to the Enari marble, and two of its sister-brothers advanced to stretch the polymeric fabric of the suit from the lieutenant's narrow shoulders.

"They're going to kill him, aren't they?" Cassandra asked.

I could only nod.

Before long, Gurazi was naked, and mounted the first steps to the dais.

The Cielcin had no navel, no nipples, no body hair. The six toes were long, and bent, and clawed like the shaven paws of some feline thing, vestigial compared to the taloned fingers. It was totally sexless, lacking both the soft geometries of the female and the hanging sex of the male, and yet it seemed to me the most human a Cielcin had seemed since Uvanari had died under my knife.

Muzugara raised one iron hand and seized Gurazi by the horn, and—forcing it to stoop—led it to the center of the slab. Ramanthanu remained just at the edge of the dais, and the other Cielcin circled round, filling in as much of the chamber as they could. There must have been a hundred of them, all told.

Pausing a moment, Muzugara raised its voice to address the magi. "Are you prepared?"

Elect-Master Gaizka bowed—bending more like a serpent himself than a man. "We are prepared, my general."

"Open the palanquin!" the *vayadan* ordered.

The two Minoan technicians did as they were commanded. A moment later, a gleaming crack slit the front of the floating egg-shape, and it hinged open, revealing an object rather like an urn. It was carbon black and wired into a series of occult components whose functions I did not dare guess. The urn did not touch the sides of the palanquin in any place, was secured by buttresses of black plastic.

I stared at it a moment, until Muzugara spoke again. *"U ba-Shiomu-Elusha!"* it roared, and raised a hand as Dorayaica had. The monster's metal arm hinged open, and a contrivance of jointed steel emerged and slid a knife into the *vayadan's* hand. Whirling, Muzugara punched the weapon into the lieutenant's thorax, cut sharply upward from groin to ribs.

Gurazi's mouth opened, but shock stopped any inhuman scream.

Cassandra screamed instead, and turned her head away.

Black blood stained Muzugara's robes and metal hand, and flowed down Gurazi's legs like sheeting oil. Gurazi's bowels and the torn sac of its womb spilled upon the floor. The dying xenobite's knees struck the slab a moment later, and it fell, twitching on the white stone.

All the while, the Cielcin had not ceased their chanting.

"Yaiya toh! Yaiya toh!" they sang, and *"Teke! Teke! Tekeli!"*

Gurazi's heat was rising into the cool air as steam. I thought I could see it, the unmapped turbulence of coiling vapor like the soul rising from its dying body.

"They just *killed* him," Cassandra said. She sounded like she was going to be sick.

What could I say?

"They did," was all I could manage. I was thinking about the *Atropos* expedition, about the documents I'd been shown. The men of *Atropos* had slaughtered one another and themselves to feed the Beast of Nairi. The Watcher there had surely put those instincts in the minds of its human prey, turning them against one another to feed itself, to sap what strength it could from the bodies of the dead and dying.

But how much energy could a body hold?

Not much. Surely, the beast would have done better to sap the heat at the core of the world, rather than prey upon life. Was there perhaps something more? Something special about flesh and blood?

The inhuman chanting had stopped.

I could sense confusion in the ranks, hear muttered words.

"Kasamnte ne?" said one, confused.

"Kasamnte," another agreed. *Nothing.*

"There's nothing!"

"Where is the god?"

"Ti-saem gi? Ti-saem gi?"

Where?

"Gurazi was unworthy!" said a voice I recognized as that of Shahaga, the one who had struck Cassandra. "We must find a better sacrifice!"

That tightened every fiber in me, and again I shifted to put myself between Cassandra and the *vayadan*-general.

"We must offer *more!*" said another.

Still yet another shouted, "Ramanthanu! We must offer the captain!"

The captain drew its scimitar, thrust the point at the speaker. "You are welcome to try me, Bagita, you *worm!*"

The one called Bagita snarled, and drawing its own sword, it advanced.

"You *dare* approach me?" Ramanthanu sneered. "You?"

Bagita leaped, sword held high. Ramanthanu caught its subordinate by the wrist with its free hand and buried its blade in the crook between Bagita's neck and shoulder. Bagita's sword fell to the stones at the base of the steps, but Ramanthanu shoved the body onto the dais, its blood mingling with that of Gurazi.

Several of the others had drawn their swords, were eying one another with suspicion, with anger and fear.

"Why are they fighting?" Cassandra asked, drawing as near to me as she could.

"They are not men," I said, and raising my voice, added, "This is how the great Muzugara commands? It is no wonder you broke so easily at Thagura!"

The iron-handed general snarled at me, and took two steps toward the edge of the dais. "You know nothing, *Utannashi!*"

Gaizka raised his sonorous, deep voice. "Look!"

It took me a moment to see what it was the magus had seen, to cut through the confusion and panic that filled the pantheon then like nerve gas.

The blood spilt upon the dais was *moving*. Not spreading out as it ought upon so flat a surface, but *flowing*, running toward the hand.

As I watched, a droplet formed, fell *upward*, vanished in the dark air. A second followed. A third. A rain of black drops rising.

Muzugara—its fury abandoned—turned to look down at the bodies of its clansmen with religious awe. The others all drew back, or knelt, or pressed their faces to the floor. The ones that held Cassandra and myself averted their eyes, claws tightening on my arm.

The bodies of Gurazi and Bagita both began to rise, lifted as if on chains by some unseen mechanism above our world's stage. Into the sudden silence, Muzugara raised its voice. *"Dō Anscurhae!"* it shouted, speaking in that archaic Cielcin mode. "We keep the old ways! We honor you! We serve you! We have come to carry you to the stars, that you might escape the circles of this prison!" The *vayadan* spread its arms wide, white hand still clutching the blade of sacrifice as it sank to its knees.

This prison? I wondered at that. I looked to the palanquin, to the urn with its plastic buttresses and exterior metal cage.

The Cielcin shifted about us, whispered in awe.

A static charge filled the air about us, and one of the Cielcin—I think it was Thnaga—shouted, *"Retattaa!"*

Look!

Gurazi's body was shrinking, just as Mann's had done. Shrinking and growing transparent, as though it were some fading holograph. Beside it, Bagita's appeared to undergo a species of mitosis, becoming two like the image seen in a child's kaleidoscope. One grew, another diminished, as all three bodies then floated toward the dome high above.

All three vanished at once, Bagita growing so large and diffuse it vanished from our plane entire, the other images reduced to mere specks. What blood remained continued to drip upward, but here and there was caught midair and floated like water in null gravity.

For an instant, all was still. The blood drifting on the air hung like so many black and distant stars. No one moved and nothing.

Nothing, save the hand.

Those vast, black bones *shifted*, and for a moment I thought that they must fall.

Then I realized what was happening.

The fingers were closing, curling, without sinew or ligament to animate them, their motion accompanied by a dry, cracking sound, as of wood splintering. Muzugara leaped backward, off-balance, staggering to the floor beneath the dais. The Cielcin forced me to my knees, Cassandra beside me.

All the Cielcin present—save the *vayadan* and our captors only—hurled themselves to the floor in supplication. The Minoans remained on their feet, Gaizka and Kybalion and the two magi that manned the palanquin.

I could taste the charge on the air, felt my skin crawl, my hairs stand on end.

"That's...impossible," Cassandra said.

And yet it *was*. The huge fingers stretched, scraped across the white face of the marble, whole hand curling into a fist. The very air grew dark, as if the black *thing* drank the light of our lamps, and a shadow hung on the air. I felt my breath catch.

It was *shrinking*.

The hand was *shrinking*.

It had been the size of a shuttle, was scarcely larger then than a ground-car. A man. A child.

Then it was gone, vanished along with the bodies of the Cielcin slain upon the marble slab.

Upon the altar stone.

But we were not alone in the pantheon. An oppressive weight hung upon the air—the sense that we were all of us watched by unseen, malicious eyes. Almost I felt a breath upon my neck, the touch of fingers cold and strong as iron. Then a voice, black as ink and soft, filled my head like laudanum—like wine.

Ol zir am.

Pain flowered behind my eyes, and I screwed them shut, but it was no good.

Ollori Cordnan, Aldon ollori Iadan, ol zir am.

It seemed a black shadow floated over all my senses, an image pressed upon my mind. Though my eyes were closed, and my knees reported cold stone beneath them, and talons on my arm, I felt at once the desert beneath my feet, the noonday sky above. A figure tall and slim and clad in a smoking veil of black moved toward me, advancing over the dunes.

Go. Away. I thought. A child's thought. Stupid and simple.

We were standing in the hold of the *Rhea* then, the Perseus weapon quiescent, safe in its launch cradle.

Am gelar am na quansba ol?

The figure turned its head, the music of its voice lilting.

I did not answer.

Ul talammād?

The vision shifted, and we were standing in the hypostyle, alone. It was night, and no light streamed in through the pillared entryway. No lamp or sign of human presence hung in the vaults above. I could tell the language had changed, though still its sound was strange to me. It sounded like the tongue Miudanar had used to try and speak with me upon Eue.

"Abba!"

The sound of Cassandra's voice slashed across the vision, and despite the pain in my head, I opened my eyes.

It had been no vision.

A figure in black stood before Muzugara upon the center of the slab.

"*Dō Anscurhae!*" exclaimed Muzugara, "*Dō Caeharush!* My god! You bless us with your presence!"

"That was what you saw in the desert?" Cassandra asked.

I nodded.

If anything, it was taller. Taller than any man. Taller than any Cielcin. It was like a pillar looming, a finger towering over all. I sensed—though how I knew it was so I cannot say—that the beast was somehow more present in that moment than it had been in the desert. As if what I had seen had been only a vision, a waking dream.

This was the thing itself.

The Cielcin had all pressed their faces to the earth, save Muzugara and the ones that held Cassandra and myself—though these averted their eyes. Only the *vayadan* and the Minoans dared to look upon the Watcher. And Cassandra. And myself—and I looked with the eyes the Quiet had given me, and saw the creature standing athwart every branch of potential, and seeing it, I knew that I was not seeing different variations of the beast echoing across time, but the same creature in every aspect. Broad though my vision was, it was broader still. As Mann's bodies were linked across some higher manifold of space—three bodies and one at the same time— every iteration of the towering *thing* that I perceived was linked, so that as it cocked its head to study the tableau before it, every refracted version of it moved in unison.

Across every possible present, it moved at once. It stood astride time itself like a colossus, its unseen feet anchored beyond the horizon of my sight.

Never had I seen a thing so huge, or so terrifying.

Still speaking in that archaic Cielcin mode, the *vayadan* said, "I am Prince Inumjazi Muzugara, Lord of the Twenty-Ninth Branching of the Line of Atumanu, Beloved of Elu, Servant of Miudanar, your kin!" It gestured at the palanquin. "I have brought a vessel for you! That you might pass the storms that encircle this world and be free again to drink of the stars! Therefore I beg you, grant me power! Make me your champion, as Miudanar made Elu, and Elusha after him!"

Despite my horror, I laughed.

It was *Prince* Muzugara again, not *vayadan,* not *general.* For who would call himself general who might claim the title *prince?* The once-prince aggrandized itself, and hoped to become greater still. Muzugara had not come to Sabratha on the orders of its prince, had not come to retrieve their lost and fallen god, to deliver into the Prophet's hand the greatest weapon in existence.

It had come to cheat.

Muzugara hoped to make of itself what Dorayaica was, what Elu had been.

The Watcher took a step toward the bloody-handed prince, and as it moved it seemed to shrink, to grow nearer Cielcin size. Muzugara stood transfixed. The black cloak rippled in a wind that was not there. I saw the flash of a white foot beneath the hem of that robe, discerned the glint of gold.

Something snaked from within the black robe. A tendril of some substance white as snow. It slithered upward, caressed the Cielcin, twined about one horn. The Watcher did not speak, but turned Muzugara's face to look up into its own veiled one.

Muzugara screamed.

I had never heard a Cielcin scream like that, not even in the dungeons of Dharan-Tun. So loud it was, a sound to pierce my very soul, and terrible—more terrible because it issued from the lips of a creature I ought not to have pitied, but did.

"Activate the siphon!" Gaizka roared.

More white tendrils emerged from the black robe and wrapped themselves around the prince. Muzugara was still screaming. The two magi who manned the palanquin stirred the machine to life. There was a whining hum, and though the figure holding Muzugara in its grip did not move, the same black figure appeared before the machine. The palanquin resonated as the beast approached, sparked, and fell from the air with a crash. The two Minoans started, threw themselves to the poisoned stone.

The second Watcher vanished, but the first—the one holding Muzugara, stooped to pin the one-time prince to the altar slab. As I watched, transfixed, the tendrils *shifted,* became countless long and slender arms. Hands grasped Muzugara everywhere: its horns, its wrists, its ankles. Then all at once, they tore, pulling every which way.

I expected Muzugara to be torn to pieces—and in a sense, it was. But rather than a rending of limb from limb, the Watcher hurled a dozen refracted Muzugaras about the pantheon, all of them with smashed and broken limbs. The creature's shroud had slipped in the violence of its motion, revealing a slit of alabaster flesh.

Surprising me then with his personal courage, Master Gaizka fired on the creature with his sidearm. The maser beam swept the black-robed demon, but it seemed to do no harm.

The Watcher *vanished*.

The Cielcin who had thrown themselves to the arsenite looked uncertainly around.

"Is it gone?" asked one.

"Muzugara is gone," whispered another.

"Muzugara was unworthy," said Ramanthanu, finding its feet.

"The Faraday Box is destroyed," said Gaizka. "We have no means to transport the creature."

Faraday Box? I looked at the silver-masked sorcerer in surprise, understanding coming in an instant. The palanquin was little more than a battery designed to house and shield the Watcher's energies. Muzugara had said the machine would help the Watcher pass *the storms that encircled the world*.

The ionosphere. The planet's magnetic field served as bars on the Watcher's cage. I thought of Horizon, trapped in the iron bowels of the Great Library.

Daimons and demons.

"We must retreat!" Gaizka urged. "If the Imperials send reinforcements, we may be cut off."

Ramanthanu jerked its head to the left. "The prince is dead," it said. "The god killed it."

"Then you must take command *now!*" Gaizka said.

"It meant to betray the Prophet." Ramanthanu sounded lost, again jerked its head in the negative.

"The mission has failed!" the Elect-Master decreed. "We must go!"

Many things happened then at once.

Far above, the glowspheres that Valeriev's men had set to light the pantheon began to burst, their light extinguished, replaced by the sound of breaking glass.

Ramanthanu bellowed orders.

Gaizka shouted to his magi.

Cassandra cried out, "Look!"

The bodies that had all been Muzugara vanished, each of them shrinking and fading away, as though they were debris some mighty hand were brushing from the table. A shadow vast as empires filled the pantheon, a shadow not flat against the walls, but voluminous. The shadow in three-dimensions of something far, far larger.

Then one of the Cielcin fell off the ground. Like the blood of Muzugara's sacrifices, it hurtled into the air, screaming the while. The shadow in the air tore the xenobite apart. Blood that should have rained upon the altar slab vanished instead. Then another of the Pale fell upward and was gone.

Panic beset the rest, and the ones that held Cassandra and myself broke ranks. Many fled up the tunnel, forgetting us and their duties. Bagita's sword lay on the floor not twenty paces from me. Seeing my chance, I made for it, pain yet flaring behind my eyes. I dropped to the ground beside it and slit my bonds, scratching my wrist and the heel of my left hand in the process.

Where had Kybalion gone?

Scimitar in hand, I shouted for Cassandra. She ran for me, but one of the Cielcin recalled its place and hurled itself at her ankles. They both hit the ground with a thud. As I dashed to join them, two more of the Cielcin flew upward, their bodies slammed against one of the graven pillars that upheld the higher galleries.

The Cielcin atop Cassandra drew its knife, a hooked thing white as milk. I slashed at its head, ceramic blade striking the xenobite just above the hole of its ear. The blade caught on all that bone, and I had to plant a foot upon the dead creature's neck to wrench it free. I helped Cassandra to stand, and cut her bonds.

"Our swords!" she said. "Where's Lascaris?"

I looked round. The painted man and its master were both gone. The two magi that had accompanied them cowered by the wreck of the palanquin.

"There!" In the vanishing lights, I saw a smear of red. Gaizka's cloak. He'd made it onto the upper gallery.

"They're going out the long way!" said Cassandra, confused. She rubbed her wrists, following me as I made for the alien stairs.

"They must not want to risk the fighting up above!" I said. "They'll slip out the back way, if they can, and find a way to broadcast their minds offworld."

"Broadcast?" Cassandra was two paces behind.

It occurred to me then that Sabratha's magnetic field was as much a trap for Gaizka and Kybalion as it was for the Watcher itself. The magi of MINOS were each little more than phantoms, daimon programs that bounced from one body to another. Even if they could not make it off-world in the flesh, the Minoan master's mind and that of his changeling familiar might escape, might return to the Cielcin worldship with tidings of all that had happened on the surface.

But they could not do so without a way to boost their signal. They would need an antenna powerful enough to cut through the magnetosphere, or even a high-altitude flier.

One of the camp's spottercraft would do.

I gritted my teeth as we reached the first gallery, and saw that flash of red above.

I could not let that happen.

CHAPTER 23

SCRAMBLE IN THE DARK

WE HAD TURNED OUR backs on the pantheon and the chaos in it, and escaped—if only for a short time—the Cielcin net. We had to find Gaizka, and Kybalion most of all. The homunculus had our weapons, our shields, our terminals. I had seen it strap our belts about its waist.

The torn hem of a red cloak vanished around a corner ahead and to our right, and I gave a shout. The Vaiartu friezes on every wall seemed to dance as we passed. I rounded the corner, and only then realized my mistake.

The knife-missile hissed toward me, launched by the dart-thrower in Kybalion's sleeve, fast as any arrow. Blind luck and palatine reflex alone saved me, and I raised the Cielcin scimitar to bat the blade aside. The knife-missile skittered into a pillar at my left. It tumbled through the air and—righting itself—thrust at me again.

"Cassandra, stay back!"

This time I was ready, and opening my vision I caught the knife in my fist as I had the one in Oberlin's chambers. The blade shivered in my hand, and I felt the edge cut. It was not so neat a job as I had managed aboard the *Rhea*, and I prayed the edge was not poisoned. Still, I held it fast. Lacking highmatter, I pinned the knife-missile to the wall and hammered on it with the lion pommel of my sword. Components sparked, and I let the thing fall dead.

My own blood smeared the inscribed wall, but I had no time to think about the arsenic that had surely entered my body. The Watcher was free, had drunk of the blood and heat of Muzugara and its men and so strengthened itself. I wondered at that—and wondered why Miudanar had not been stirred to new life by the sacrifices offered at the ruin of its skull.

But those, too, were questions for another time.

A second knife-missile hissed toward me. I leaped aside, pressed my back to the nearest pillar, eyes wide as the knife swiveled to find me. How

I longed for Valka then! She might have bent her will upon the knives and upon the creature who controlled them, and battled for command.

As it was, I had Cassandra, and we were alone, unshielded, with only the one, dead blade between us.

The knife flew.

As I had with the bullet from Bastien's Durand's gun, I permitted the blade to pass through me, to find that place in the weft of time where it missed. I heard the point crunch against the Enari stone, and leaned forward so that the blade and my head no longer occupied the same point in space.

"Rúhé?" Kybalion's fury tinged each syllable of his disbelief.

How?

The earth shook, shaken by the Cielcin moon above or by the dark god awakened in the pantheon below. The chameleon stumbled, and vile dust fell from the stones above our heads. A glowsphere drifted up the hall between us, obediently following its programmed track. Looking back, I saw Cassandra standing behind one of the pillars across the broad hall. There was a space between the columns and the outer wall to either side, shadowy colonnades illuminated only by phosphorescent tape placed there by Valeriev's men.

Our eyes met, and I knew she meant to try and flank the homunculus.

I shook my head.

She shook hers in turn.

Throwing all caution to the wind, I sprinted up the corridor, straight at the painted man.

Kybalion raised its dart-thrower to launch another knife-missile, but nothing came. A faint, mechanical *clicking* rebounded off the ceiling of that low, broad hall. Panic filled Kybalion's eyes, and it fumbled with its unfamiliar belts, scrabbling for one of the highmatter swords. It drew one—one of Cassandra's, I think—but before it could kindle the blade, Cassandra herself hurtled out of the dark to Kybalion's right. Her gambit had paid off, and her Jaddian-designed thews had carried her faster even than I.

The both of them went down, Cassandra on top, and I drew up short, watching in mingled surprise and horror to see my daughter seize the painted man by its lapels and slam its head against the stone floor. Cassandra contorted herself to put one heel upon the hand that held the weapon, pinning it as she had pinned many a Jaddian neophyte to the mat. She raised a fist.

"Please! No!" The painted man let the sword go, tried to move its hands to cover its face.

Cassandra struck it anyway, and the *crack* of her fist was like a hammer blow. "You killed them!" she cried, and hit Kybalion again. "You cut the power! You called them here!"

Dimly, I was aware that I was only standing there, that I was about to watch my daughter kill a man for her first time. I found myself recalling the poor woman I'd stabbed in the shop I'd robbed with Rells's gang in Borosevo.

I could still remember her eyes, wide and white as those of the homunculus. "Stop! I yield!"

"Cassandra!" I hauled her off the murderous creature. "Stand aside!"

"But, Abba!" Her chest was heaving.

"Stand aside, I said!" I stood over Kybalion.

The painted man was laughing. "My master . . ." it said, "will escape." Red blood covered its face and the front of Lascaris's gray coat.

"Small matter," I said, though it was not. I stooped and took up the sword Kybalion had tried to draw to defend itself. It *was* one of Cassandra's, silver fittings and red leather, with the Jaddian teardrop pommel. "The Cielcin have failed here."

"Failed?" Kybalion's voice cracked, turning from tenor to baritone. "Failed? No, no, gentle lord. Say not *failed!* The entity is awake!"

"But it cannot leave this planet," I said, adjusting my grip on the sword. "Isn't that right? It can't pass the ionosphere."

"It will find a way!" Kybalion said. "And when it does, it will awaken the rest of its kind. We might have contained it! Brought it to *him.* But now . . . now it will be free. And your Empire . . . all you miserable humans will die!" As it spoke, Kybalion's white hair was changing, darkening from root to tip. Turning black. The round, flat face was sharpening, cheekbones growing more pronounced.

"Your masters will die, too!"

"Good!" Kybalion said. "They made me! And I did not ask to be made!"

I knew the face the beast was taking, as I knew the voice too well. I let it talk.

"I'm like them," it said in that familiar baritone. "I am the spirit that negates! They will negate everything. You know what they are."

"I do," I said to my own reflection, its nose still broken.

"Abba, he's—!" Cassandra's voice intruded.

"Cassandra, look away!" I held her sword, kindled the blade.

"They are entropy itself," Kybalion said. "Who can say how many universes they have rotted and consumed?"

Only one knows that answer, I reflected. *And he is Quiet.*

"Kill me!" Kybalion roared, and my own voice it parroted, the accent of Delos polished by centuries of Imperial court service and life on Jadd. "Kill me! Cut off your own head. Let's see if it grows back!"

It laughed again, and it was my own rough laughter that filled the hall. Or nearly so.

The creature at my feet had turned into a bloody imitation of myself.

I had become, in a sense, the vision I had seen in the Howling Dark. My future self standing above my battered shadow. Kybalion had quoted Goethe. *The spirit that negates.* The character he quoted was Mephistopheles.

A devil.

I swung the sword.

Cassandra let out a cry that she strangled and choked off.

In death, the muscles by whose subtle action Kybalion changed the structure of its face relaxed, and Hadrian Marlowe's death mask softened, became the round, flat face of the demon yet again. But the eyes remained violet, the hair black. I stooped and unbuckled Cassandra's belt and tossed it to her. Numb fingered, she hardly caught it. "We need to move," I said.

She did not.

"Cassandra!" I caught her wrist. Her eyes touched mine, that green I'd never known was there.

I proffered her sword, pommel first.

Slowly, not speaking, she belted herself and took the weapon in trembling fingers.

"When we reach the surface," I began, "we must find Gaston. And we must arm the Perseus weapon."

"The what?"

"The Empire built a weapon that can kill the Watcher," I said, and crouching collected my own belt, began picking through the dead changeling's pockets to find my wrist-terminal. I found it in a breast pocket, and slid it back over my wrist.

The sound of feet and rough voices came from the hall behind, and looking back I saw the horned shadows of pursuers dancing on the walls. "Go now!" I said, moving just behind. "Shields up, girl! Double quick!"

She sped ahead of me, shield flickering to life. I followed more slowly, wrapping the belt into place beneath my dusty coat and pausing to check the drape of my sword's holster.

"*Qita! Qita!*" came the inhuman voices.

I took them as spurs myself, and redoubled my efforts, chasing after Cassandra. My bad knee complained violently, but I gave it no hearing, and clenched my teeth. Ahead and to the left, there was a stair that would take us to an upper level, and into a basilica-style hall. From there, we had several levels of switchback stairs to reach the level of the hypostyle and the main gates of the city.

As I ran, I keyed my terminal, shouted into it. "Neema! Neema, it's Hadrian! Neema, can you hear me?"

Even if he could, there was little enough the Jaddian servitor could do.

We'd reached the stairs by then, and Cassandra was climbing. I followed after her, still shouting for Neema, for Albé, for anyone. No answer came, unless it was from the Cielcin coming hard behind.

"*Yukajji!*" cried one rough voice. "*Oreto o-yukajji wo!*"

"*Uimmaa o-tajarin!*"

They had seen me.

We reached the level of the basilica—a broad, high-ceilinged hall with chambers opening to either side—and together we streaked across the vast pavers of its floor. Footsteps rang and rebounded off the brutally angled vaults.

A grinding sound filled the air behind, and whirling, I drew my sword in time to slash the *nahute* from the air. The Cielcin who had thrown it leaped like an ape through the door I had so recently passed, and like an ape it rushed toward me, scrabbling on hands and feet. The sight of the highmatter gave it pause, and it drew back, fangs bared as its brothers surged in after it.

There were a dozen at least, and many held crooked swords white as milk and gleaming in the dim light. I recognized the one called Shahaga among them, a bow-legged beast with three long braids sprouting from the back of its skull.

Of Captain Ramanthanu I saw no sign.

"Your prince is dead!" I said, brandishing my weapon.

"*Rakan Ute Aeta!*" Shahaga said. *He was no true prince.*

Ignoring this, I said, "If you leave now and take ship, you may live."

"*Daratiri ne?*" asked another, circling to my right. "Live? What good is living? We have been judged. We are dead!"

"And you will be dead soon!" said Shahaga.

"But not before we've had our play!" said one, a lanky beast with arms that reached almost past its knees. It was that one which hurled its nahute first. The snake battered my shield and caromed off it before I could slash it in two. The Cielcin all closed at once. I parried a slash from one—cutting its sword in half—and retreated back toward Cassandra, toward the exit.

Cassandra herself leaped in a moment after. Twin blades shone bright as particle beams in the gloom, and in a flash she swept the legs out from under one of the Pale and thrust clean through its armored heart.

The others thought better of their offensive for a moment, cowering before the three blue blades. Cassandra stood fast beside me, her right hand back and lifted in a hanging guard, her left thrust out. Taking my own blade in both hands, I raised it high, slashed low as the single nahute circled back in renewed assault. So armed and shielded, the two of us might overcome a dozen of the Pale.

But Shahaga unslung its *nahute* from one hip, and cracked it to life.

The others did the same—those as had them.

"Run!" I bellowed, and turning spurred Cassandra to do likewise. We could not fight a dozen of the Pale and nigh as many *nahute* altogether. Not even my vision—which is bounded by the sensory inputs of my body— could see me through unscathed.

"Side hall!" I said, and pointed with my sword to a passage opening to the right. "We have to lose them!"

Cassandra and I ducked through the narrow portal and hurried up a sloping hall. It led to a tangle of what might once have been service tunnels. Ahead and to the right were the ruins of what I felt sure were lift shafts. The mechanisms themselves had long since corroded, but the shaft ran all the way to the highest levels of the *Mensa*. There was no way up to the level of the hypostyle and the gate unless it was by the stairs at the far end of the basilica.

The Cielcin had fallen a bit behind, and we had slashed at least three of their questing serpents to ribbons. Cassandra was just ahead of me, her blades unkindled then for safety.

"Up ahead!" I shouted to her, "Through the door on the left and up the stairs!"

We were close, had circled round and nearly returned to the stairs that would carry us to freedom. Two of the Cielcin were hard behind, their swords scraping on the floor as they loped after us. Cassandra vanished round the corner, as Valka once had vanished on Annica so long ago.

I reached the door myself, and though I should have seen the base of the switchback stair and Cassandra mounting them...I saw a long and narrow hall. I froze a moment, shock making me hesitate.

"Cassandra!" I shouted, heard the word echo in eternity.

The Cielcin should have reached me by then, and realizing this, I started, whirling to face them in the hall.

They were gone.

I was alone. Even the earth had ceased its trembling.

Everything was deathly still.

"Another vision!" I said, more a shout than a question.

But there was no pain behind my eyes.

"Cassandra!" I shouted down the hall.

There was no answer.

I looked back the way I had come, and found only a blank wall. I turned to go the other way, to go anywhere save through that narrow passage, knowing what must lie at the end.

But that way, too, was shut.

All light went out, for the glowspheres left by Valeriev and his men had vanished with the proper halls. Desperate then and utterly alone, I found the torchlight setting on my terminal and raised my hand for a lamp.

The new tunnel was still there, long and foreboding.

Limping, sword in hand, I began walking, shouting for Cassandra, calling for Neema and Albé.

Nothing availed.

I was alone.

After what seemed an hour of groping, half-blind in the dark, I thought I heard a sound in the tunnel ahead.

"Hello?" I called, resting a moment against one of the plascrete pillars that ribbed the hall. I studied the carving in the niche between my pillar and the next. It showed a Vaiartu—Aravte-Teäplu, perhaps—standing atop the smooth orb of a planet.

There was no reply.

I limped on, studying the graven niches as I went. When I had gone perhaps a hundred feet, I saw the same image of the Enar crouched atop its planet, a veritable colossus. There was a crack in the face of that planet, and a chip missing. Had the last relief had the same crack? The same chip?

I could not be going in circles, of that much I was certain. I was walking in a straight line.

I moved on ahead, a little faster then, and saw the same relief, the same crack, the same chip missing.

There came a sound like distant laughter, and I gripped my sword the tighter.

"Who goes there?"

Silence.

"Show yourself!"

I screwed my eyes shut, performed the quick breathing ritual Gibson had taught me as a boy on Delos. *Fear is a poison,* I murmured.

After a moment I forced myself to start moving, following the wall with my fingers, the way illuminated only by the faint light of my wrist-terminal.

Something fell with a clatter in the hall just behind me, and I turned sharply, conjuring my blade.

There was nothing.

And yet I sensed that I was not alone. There was a presence there, just out of sight, as though someone just behind me had vanished round a corner that was not there.

"Get a hold of yourself, Marlowe," I said, practicing the scholiast's breathing ritual once more.

No sooner had those words left my lips than a voice—faint at first and far off—rose from the hall ahead. I turned back to face it, head cocked.

Song.

How long I stood there listening I cannot say. It might have been hours or merely seconds. I felt in that moment that I must have known a horror akin to that which brave Ulysses had felt, tied to the mast of his ship. So beautiful and terrible was that voice, high and clear, that it could not have come from any human throat. There was a resonance to it that put me in mind of some stringed instrument immeasurably vast, or of Sabratha's vanished whales.

My fingers tightened on my sword.

I knew what awaited me along the passage ahead, knew what creature had bent the paths of Phanamhara before me to ensure I came upon it.

There was a light, dim and pale green. I edged toward it, toward that superhuman voice, conscious of the fact that I could not have stopped my advance if I wanted to. I was chant-caught, spellbound, *transported*.

The hall ended in a triangular door, tall and narrow. The green light came from within, and the song with it.

I froze upon the threshold.

The pantheon stood before me, its dark galleries rising all round, its walls and graven niches carved with the exploits of the Vaiartu, their battles and conquests. All was as we had left it. The bodies of the dead Cielcin lay strewn all about, many of them in pieces. Black blood smeared the steps to the dais, and the wreck of the palanquin smoldered on the far side. The light came from the glowspheres in the upper galleries. Muzugara's body had vanished completely in the first fighting, but neither did I see any sign of Ramanthanu.

It should not have been possible. I had left the pantheon behind far below, had never once gone down again. Mounting the steps to the dais, I recalled the hidden chamber in Calagah, how it seemed taller within than without. I had been brought back here, dragged like a fish on a line.

The singing stopped.

"Show yourself!" I shouted once more, looking up and round, expecting to see the shrouded figure standing on one of the upper galleries, lying in wait.

The ruined palanquin sparked, brief radiance casting blue light upon that ancient temple. Something brushed against my arm, and I rounded, teeth bared.

Still, there was nothing.

Abruptly, I realized what a fool I was being. Again I used Gibson's breathing regimen to calm my nerves, I felt my heartbeat slow, and when I looked up, it was with eyes wide open.

Something flickered at the corners of my vision.

How can I describe it?

Have you ever watched the shadow of a bird stretched vast as a dragon on the earth beneath? Felt it like a cloud overhead one moment—then gone the next? I saw such a shadow then, playing amidst the upper galleries and the distant dome of the ceiling.

Shimtushu elika.

The shadow had fallen on the wreck of the palanquin, was seated upon it as though it were a throne. I turned to face it, sword still in hand. The Watcher—a shapeless figure in black—reclined atop the ruined machine. Though it had no face, no eyes, no features I could mark whatever, I sensed its full attention was on me.

"What do you want from me?" I asked.

Awātumka ahiātum.

Its voice resounding in my head more than in the mighty hall.

Nishūka madish ēwūm-ma . . . wardūshu kunu!

"What do you want?"

The shadow vanished, blew away like dust.

It reappeared on the lip of the gallery above and to my left, looking just as it had in the desert, a figure clothed in black. It paced along the rim of the level above. With one step, I saw the pale foot emerge from beneath the hem of its shroud, discerned the shimmer of gold.

Adīni ul talammādanni?

It sounded like a question.

The shadow had halted on the gallery above, was looking silently down at me. Oberlin had said the creatures were pure force, given form only by the condensation of that force into transient matter. The skull of Miudanar had been only a husk, a shell shed by the Watcher as a locust might discard its bones. The Watchers might take any shape, and yet the figure before me seemed as removed from the skull of that gargantuan serpent as anything could be.

Something moved in the corner of my vision, and turning my head I saw a second figure—twin to the first—standing a quarter turn to the left. There was another to my right, and turning quickly round, I saw I was surrounded.

There were six of them.

I confess I broke in that moment, and bolted for the exit.

Something unseen collided with me, solid as a wall, and I fell back upon the steps of the dais, dazed. Above, I saw the six black figures standing in air, descending toward me as one, their shrouds untouched by any wind. But when they reached the ground there was only one figure remaining, taller than it was before. A towering figure.

Ul ninakkar.

My fall had driven the wind from me, and I lay still like an overturned crab. In that moment, I knew that I would never see my Cassandra again, would never stand beneath the open sky. I was going to die like Muzugara— torn to pieces by the thousand hands of a beast older than our universe.

The Watcher was bending over me, a dozen feet high.

I rolled onto my side.

Something white and slick lashed me across the face, and I sprawled back upon the step once more.

No. I was not going to die on my back like an old man. I was not going to die gasping, pleading on the ground. I looked across the infinite moment, saw a place—far off—where I was at least halfway to my feet. I leaped toward it, felt time collapse around me, and at once I was no longer on my back, breathless and spent.

I was on one knee, rising, sword in hand.

In cutting across time, I had acted faster than thought, faster than light, faster even than that horror Muzugara had summoned up to our world. To an observer in that awful chamber, it must have seemed that I moved in the wink of an eye. In reality, I had not moved at all, only traded one Hadrian for another.

Nothing could have outpaced me as I slammed the point of my sword up into the heart of that beast in black.

I do not know what I expected.

A gout of silver blood? A cry of inhuman pain? Another blow?

Nothing of the sort occurred.

My blade *stopped.*

I was on my feet by then, and looked down in dumb amazement to see a hand—gold-ringed, six-fingered, pale as Death—grasping the point of my sword. In that moment, I knew the horror and the sheer, holy terror Irshan must have felt in the Grand Colosseum.

No blood shone upon the alien hand, and in that slender arm I sensed the strength to flatten empires.

"What are you?" I asked, hardly knowing what it was I said.

White pain flared behind my eyes, and I felt my knees buckle. The Watcher still held the tip of my sword in its hand. I was kneeling then, kneeling amid a crowd of prostrate creatures, hexapods in suits of silver filigree. The Vaiartu massed about me, swarming about the steps of the dais, clambering over one another in their desperation to be nearer the rim. As I watched, the Vaiartu were lifted one by one into the air and smashed, their bodies—which I realized with horror were as much mechanical as animal—crushed by the Watcher's unseen hand.

"*U Sha Ra!*" cried the Vaiartu who prostrated themselves, voices filling the hall of sacrifice. "*U Sha Ra! U Sha Ra!*"

"Ushara?" I said, and the word broke the vision.

I knelt amid the corpses of the Cielcin, eyes fixed on that impossible hand.

That impossibly *human* hand.

CHAPTER 24

QUEEN OF THE DAWN

THE WATCHER USHARA STILL held my blade, and though neither of us moved, I felt myself falling. *A human hand. A human hand!* How could I have been so blind? They had been human hands that tore Muzugara apart, had been human feet I'd seen beneath the hem of that black robe.

But why?

It was a trick. It had to be. The Watchers could take any form.

They were creatures of pure energy. Pure spirit.

I reached through my vision, found a place where my blade was free. I slashed wildly at the demon. The Watcher blinked out of existence, moving fast as I. My blade whistled through empty air. Again I stretched my vision, chose a point where the sword struck true.

Once more, the beast evaded me, twisting across time to escape me.

Only belatedly did I realize what was happening.

I saw an opening in the manifold curtains of time, a place where my blade pierced that black shroud. I moved toward it, collapsing the wave of time, but even as I made the move, I saw the beast turn, and though I was conscious of no face, I felt its vision press on me, and knew it saw me across the blank expanse of time.

It moved as I moved, saw as I saw—chose as I chose.

I staggered as my sword went wide, and a blow struck me across the back.

I hit the pale crystal of the slab face first, braced myself for the end. I expected death to follow me, expected the touch of a thousand violent hands.

Instead, there was nothing.

Sword unkindled in my hand, I made to rise, propped myself on hands and knees. Looking up, I saw an old man in a dusty coat lying against the wreck of one of Muzugara's chimeric guardians. He rested his head against the chassis of the ruined warrior. White scars tore his left cheek, decorated his hands. He was breathing hard, and red blood soaked his white-streaked dark hair. A woman crouched beside him, naked and paler even than he, her skin the milk-white of alabaster, her hair the very curtains of night.

He was wounded. There was blood sheeting from his side. The two of them held hands so that I could not know for certain which of them it was had wielded the knife. As I watched, the woman took her other hand and pressed something into the man's side. A splinter of bone it seemed to me, or an arrowhead of pale stone. The man winced, cheeks working like a bellows.

He cried out in pain, and as I watched the blood on his hands ran from red to white to silver.

I cried out in horror.

Only then did he turn to look at me, and I saw that he was myself.

"No!" I pounded the floor with my hand. "No, I won't!"

The vision faded, and I felt the familiar pain behind my eyes.

Nusuq.

I rocked back upon my haunches.

The shadow stood over me. I looked up at it, and it seemed I saw with doubled vision. With the one eye I saw the shadow, the monster that had destroyed the Cielcin in that very hall. With the other, I saw the same woman, naked and tall. The shadow was only the curtain of her hair, black as the very pits of hell. She smiled down at me, and that smile smote my heart.

Hers was not a human face, but a face as like to human faces as human faces are like the statue of some heroic ideal. Or rather, ours were like unto hers—for she was the ideal of ideals. A beauty beyond description, peerless in every way. Her skin glowed like sunlit snow, her hair—curling—dark as evening. Her every cord and sinew was perfectly defined, her body like velvet over steel. Golden bands embraced her slender arms, her wrists, her ankles, and rings shone upon her six-fingered hands. And her eyes!

I was drowned in them. In wells of sorrow blacker than any night.

Though I felt my knees firm upon the floor of the pantheon, I hurtled through limitless space, through clear air, and below me I beheld a world of storm-tossed green water. The spires and ramparts of a city rose like teeth from the maw of the sea, and with a start I recognized the avenues and jagged towers of Phanamhara. Only the topmost elements of what would become the Mount of Whales rose from the surface, and as I watched a vessel like a great, spoked wheel unmoored from the top of the highest tower. Without needing to be told, I knew it was the last ship to depart Sabratha before the end. It floated into the sky, rotated, and disappeared. It had not leaped to warp, but it had vanished.

The sun streaked overhead, vanishing as Sabratha turned to hide her face. The waves rolled, and crashed, and the sun came out once more. It streaked across the sky with ever-increasing speed, until the passing of each day was less than the blinking of my eyes. Once, I saw the brief shape of a leviathan leap from the tops of the alien waves. Centuries passed in instants. Millennia. More. I beheld the city of Phanamhara as it rose from the sea, saw its tallest towers crumble, the great towers where once the vast, wheeled ships of the Enar had moored. Only gradually did I realize that the city was not rising.

The waters were running dry.

Then they were gone, and the long eons and the desert winds and the hurricanes reduced the city to rubble, to a shadow of its former terror and splendor. The sands massed about it, and the last of Sabratha's rains turned that sand to earth, and more sands piled on after, until all was lost.

And I was alone on a dead world.

I—who had been a god to the creatures of that world, who once had drunk of the very stars—was forced to hunt the scant survivors of the vanished seas, and break their forms for heat. I—who had feasted on the bones and smoke of sacrifice in the temple they had built for me—had been reduced to little more than a scavenger. When at last the ions that bounded the upper airs were stripped away, and I might have slipped Sabratha's circles, I had not the strength to fly. Instead I slept, haunting the temple that had become my tomb.

The vision faded.

I was kneeling in the pantheon again, the woman standing over me, silent as before.

There were tears on my cheeks.

Her tears.

The visions I had seen, of titanic beasts and horrors beyond description, of many-armed and tentacled things, of wings time-eaten and vast beating against the wind of stars...these I had been prepared for. I had expected monstrosity. I had expected things wholly outside human comprehension.

I had not expected this. Had not expected to *feel* as they felt—had not expected them to feel as we, and more! For it seemed to me the great extremes of human passion, the highest joys, the deepest sorrows, were as anthills and pockmarks measured against the mountains and ravines I glimpsed when the Watcher's mind had touched my own.

"You're trapped here," I said. "Am I supposed to pity you?" Haltingly, I found my feet, raised my chin. "Why did you kill the Cielcin? They wanted to take you away."

The woman turned her head, her curtain of hair falling like a shadow—like a shroud—between us.

"What are you?" I asked, clenching my fist about the hilt of my unkindled sword. "The mural. In the hypostyle. The Enar painted you with human eyes!"

One red-rimmed eye peered out at me from that curtain of black hair.

Lights brighter than the brightest sun flared across my memory. Lights and that beautiful, inhuman music. I was falling, falling at terrible speed, falling into the hot black of space. There were no stars.

Ina sippirāti sha dāriātim annepish.

The woman advanced toward me, bare feet silent on the blood-streaked stone. I watched myself clamber up the ramp to the surface, clutching my wounded side. Cassandra greeted me, and the Irchtani carried us beyond the wreck of the battlefield. Ships found us, carried us to the stars. I saw myself seated on the Solar Throne, and in the place of Selene there sat a black queen. Ushara herself. Across the galaxy, the red sun of the old Emperors was setting, and in its place black banners arose, and the star that fluttered upon their fields had five points, not twelve.

My star.

A new Empire. A second Empire.

My Empire.

I saw pale princes with hair like the night, six-fingered princes with violet eyes. My sons. Her sons. Numerous as the stars and deathless. A dynasty of half-gods, and I—half-god myself—a sovereign eternal. For ten thousand years I reigned. My ships crashed across the void, established beachheads in the Clouds of Magellan. In Andromeda. Triangulum. Pegasus. The Chantry was overthrown, its copper domes shattered, and in its place my priests erected spiral ziggurats upon whose summits Bassarids in cloth-of-night offered sacrifice to the gods—my kin.

A million years I reigned, ten million years.

"You think I want that?" I said, who had lived long enough already.

Each night she came to me, her beauty and her lust like strong wine. She was advancing even then, drawing nearer by inches, her heavy, white limbs raised toward me, her red mouth like a venomous flower. Eternal life lay in that embrace, and between those thighs there lay the very font of empire.

Nusuq.

Her hands were on my face, her fingers in my hair. She pressed that face to mine, and her lips and tongue were cold as ice. My eyes were closed, and though I was not conscious of my will's rebellion, I felt my hand cup one frigid breast. Hands slid along my chest, my biceps, fretted the band of my trousers. One closed upon my wrist, another grasped my half-forgotten sword.

I felt her tears once more upon my cheek.

There were too many hands.

"No!" Some part of me rallied and shoved the beast away.

Don't be afraid! came that inhuman voice. Ushara's voice. For the first time it spoke to me in words I could comprehend.

But I was glaring at her, a sick hole opening in the pit of my stomach—for in that moment my eyes were open, and I beheld the Watcher in all its terror and majesty, piercing her every illusion with the eyes the Quiet had given me. I saw her loveliness for what it was: an artifice, a mask, a veil over corruption. Beneath that icy flesh, innumerable arms writhed, twined about a core I could not see. Beneath them, curled up immeasurably small, folded along dimensions even my second sight could scarce perceive, were the withered membranes of incredible wings, numberless as the arms. And her eyes! So many eyes peered out at me from beneath the snow-white flesh of arms and thighs, gazed at me from the flat plane of her belly, from within that cold, immortal breast.

I held their gaze for only a moment, sensing her malice, her pain, her angry desperation. Ushara had languished upon Sabratha for nigh on a million years, too weak to slip away into the Dark. But she was stronger now. Seeing her then, I knew...we should never have come to Sabratha. Another thousand years...a million...and the beast might have burned itself out. But our coming there had fanned her embers. She was smoldering then, and unless I could escape—unless I could arm the Perseus and destroy her and myself along with her—she would blossom into new and sudden flame.

Seeing her then in all her alien horror, I ran. It did not matter that I could not escape, did not matter that it had bent space itself to bring me back to that pantheon. It only mattered that I tried. I reached the base of Valeriev's tunnel, leaped the torn body of a Cielcin lying dead there. With every step, I expected to feel the grasp of countless hands, to see the roof hurtling toward me.

Instead, I reached the spot in the tunnel where the excavation narrowed, and I had to squeeze myself between Valeriev's pylons, where I should have found a stretch of cramped corridor, a few hundred feet from end to end. Beyond that lay a straightaway that ran to the open-faced pit with the cranes at the surface. Instead, I found myself upon a broad shelf of stone that opened to either side. A fresh wind scoured my face, carrying with it the scent of burning. I stood upon the heights of the Mount of Whales, looking out over the glowing desert and the fires of our ruined camp.

Even as I emerged from the mouth of the tunnel—dazed and disoriented—I saw one of the remaining aquilarii fall burning and streak across the sky. The lighter struck the desert beyond the margins of the camp, erupting in a nimbus of red and golden fire. Great lights flashed in the void beyond the curtain of night, lighting the dust clouds that floated on Sabratha's upper airs from above with shades of blue and white where Lord Hulle's fleet engaged the Cielcin moon.

The battle had not ended.

How many men were dying that very moment? There were yet hundreds in the camp, must have been thousands in the planet's pitiful defense fleet. Yet there were fewer than fifty thousand men on all Sabratha—barely half the number that had gone with me to Eue and were lost.

So few.

Too many.

If I could not stop the Watcher there, every life on Sabratha would be lost. And if it could escape Sabratha...

The wind guttered, changed direction, blew toward the Mount of Whales from over the camp. I heard screams and shouts of pain. There was music on that wind, the same beautiful, terrible music I had heard in the bowels of the Earth. The song of the Watcher awake and freed.

I had come to the precipice, to the very edge of doom. Below the plateau and exposed fascia of the ruins fell sharply, a thousand feet or more to the desert sand. Clearly I could see the avenues of Phanamhara radiating like the ribs of a lady's fan.

There was no way down.

I could not go back, would not go back into the bowels of the mountain, would not go back to face *her*.

The alien music drew nearer, so lovely and terrible and so very sad. I looked round, and saw her standing not ten paces from me, upon the edge of the cliff, skin luminous in the light of flame and star. She turned to face me, revolving on the spot, without any twitch of limb or motion. Her hair was untouched by the wind, spilled almost to the ground. She did not seem to breathe, and though she did not move her feet, she advanced, space slithering around her as she approached.

Something swallowed the light from the burning camp, and looking out over the precipice I saw her again, standing in the open air. And again! Once more I was surrounded, once more there were six of her, tightening as fingers tighten to close some almighty fist. Just then the ground lurched beneath my feet, and I was lifted up into the air, dragged skyward. The six figures of Ushara floated up into the night about me, closing in until their faces and their breasts pressed against my body and they *became* the fingers of the mighty hand that had for aeons moldered in the pantheon.

Lightning surged about me, blue-hot and deadly, and I was carried up into the night. So tight were the fingers that held me that I barely chanced to breathe. A shadow stooped over me, and loomed over the Mount of Whales entire. Looking up it seemed to me a cloud parted, and a face peered down at me. A single, lidless eye. It blinked and there were two—three! The face from the hypostyle peered down at me from the clouds. Three eyes vast as moons stared down at me, and the light of their vision was like a flame.

There was nothing—nothing but my Jaddian coat and the thin skin of my eyelids to separate me from the Watcher Ushara's pitiless gaze. She had offered me wonders—offered me even herself—and I had refused her!

I forced myself to look, to meet that gaze.

I could see nothing but those eyes, red rimmed and furious, hear nothing but a noise like thunder filling my mind. I saw my empire spreading once again, saw galaxies burning, and races unnamed and numberless bending the knee before the banner of my red star. I knew, knew the beast still wanted me.

No.

I could not even speak the word. The hand that crushed me had driven all the air from my lungs, and the world was growing dark. Only those eyes remained, lamplike, undimmed, pitiless. I was dying, dying...

No!

With my last, desperate gasp, I saw the breadth of time, saw the Watcher stretched across the manifold potentials like a serpent, stretched across time itself to strangle me. But the planes of time were like the pages of a book, like panes of glass stacked together—Ushara a beam of light shining through them. I had only to *choose,* to break the time cross which she stretched to break her, to scatter her radiance as a prism scatters light.

I chose, collapsed the prismated reality about us, splintered the very time through which she swam.

The effect was instantaneous, like switching off a light.

The Watcher roared, recoiled, withdrew her hand from our mere spacetime.

I was falling, tumbling though clear night air. I had no repulsor harness, no parachute, saw no Irchtani winging to my salvation. A cry escaped me, and the desert hurtled up to embrace me one last time. Innumerable Hadrians plummeted through the air, all of them dropped by the wounded god. I saw them striking stone, sand, dying one by one where they struck earth.

One hears stories of men who survive such falls, men who fall from aircraft or starcraft and strike the earth unscathed, walking away without any seeming hurt. Such miracles are made possible by mere chance: by some virtue of the ground they land on, by some quirk of bodily mechanics.

I saw one such Hadrian, chose his path, and so struck the ground in a tumble. My fall clipped the edge of a dune, one of the berms that encircled the dig, its steep face sloping back toward the ruins, held in place by static compactors. I rolled along it, slid for perhaps half a hundred feet until I washed out on the floor of the dig. My chest was heaving, and for a long moment I lay with my back on the earth, looking up at the sky.

I had wounded the god.

I rolled onto my side, winced as sand filled the cut on my left palm. Shoving my sword into my pocket, I keyed my wrist-terminal. "Neema!" I almost bellowed. "Albé! Annaz! Cassandra! Anyone? This is Marlowe, can you hear me?"

The hiss of static greeted me and I made to hurry up the slope.

"Can anybody hear me? This is Hadrian Marlowe! I repeat!" I looked back up at the *Mensa* and the night sky. The Watcher had vanished, but I knew it was not dead. I had to reach the camp, the *Rhea*. I had to prime the Perseus weapon.

If I was right—if I had truly harmed the creature—there was a chance that I could make it back up the slope and through the camp to the landing field. But where was Cassandra?

I lingered in the path a moment, torn between the camp and turning back. I could not have long. My power had wounded the Watcher, but I had no way of knowing how long the beast would lick its wounds.

In the end I shook myself, and turning made my way up the slope. Sabratha quaked beneath me as I went, shaken to the uttermost foundations of stone. Twice I fell and struck my knee, slipping on the sanded stones. The sound of distant gunfire, of the clash of swords and whine of *nahute*, all washed down the slope from above.

"Lord Marlowe?"

At first I thought the voice had issued from my wrist-terminal, and I halted to call into it.

"Lord Marlowe!"

A man's face peered out at me from the shadowed door to one of the side chambers, a narrow portal half-filled with drifting sand.

I ran toward him, and saw that he was dressed in the desert camouflage of Gaston's men. He reached out a hand to take me by the shoulder. "I have to get back to the landing field!" I almost shouted as he and two others pulled me inside. "The beast that killed Doctor Mann! It's here! I've seen it!"

But all my manic stammering was silenced.

Someone collided with me in the next instant, arms tight about my neck.

"Abba!" It took me a moment to process what was happening.

My own arms rose on reflex, but did not close about the woman that embraced me. My mouth opened, but it was a moment before the words came out. "I..." I swallowed. "Cassandra?" My arms closed at last.

Only then did I truly realize that I had thought I would never see her again.

"What happened to you?" she asked, face pressed against my neck. "I thought you were right behind me."

With gentle hands, I held her at arm's length, studied her precious face. "You're not hurt?"

"No more than I was," she said. "I'll be fine, I...what happened?"

"The Watcher," I said, looking up. "I only just got away."

"The Watcher?" Her eyes shone in the dimness. I could hear the fear in her tone. She alone of all the men on Sabratha had seen the Watcher Ushara—unless I counted Gaizka, who at any rate was not a man.

"What are we going to do?" A new voice intruded, and looking round I saw a haggard man in brown and dun seated on a bit of broken stone. It was Tiber Valeriev, looking like a man beaten by thieves in the alleys of some dark city. He hugged himself, and I did not doubt that he had seen horrors of his own that night.

As I turned to face him, the rest of the chamber came into focus. Much of it was collapsed, and crumbled blocks and boulders of green stone littered the shattered floor. Sand lay mounded in the corners of the room in mighty drifts, deposited by the ceaseless winds. Perhaps two dozen men and women huddled there, some soldiers in their homespun cloaks and desert camouflage, some workers of Valeriev's own team. One woman wore striped pyjamas. Another man wore no shirt at all, but clutched a plasma rifle as though it were a blanket.

"You can't stay here," I said. "The Cielcin are in the ruins." I did not add that there was worse afoot. These poor people were scared enough without the knowledge of Ushara. "Take these people out into the desert, as far from camp as you can. Go now!"

"Go where?" asked one woman, standing. "The motor pool is burned! They wrecked our fliers! Our skiffs!"

"Just get *clear!*" I almost shouted. "I'll send someone to find you...after."

"What are you going to do?" asked Tiber Valeriev.

I did not answer at once. The sounds of gunfire echoed from outside. Some of Gaston's defenders had found—or been found by—the enemy. I listened a moment, head cocked to one side.

"What are you going to do?" asked Valeriev again.

"What I came here to do," I said.

CHAPTER 25

RAMANTHANU

"WHAT YOU *CAME HERE* to do?" Valeriev said, repeating my words with a sudden venom that astonished me. "And what—pray tell—is that, *my lord?*"

"I have to get back to the landing field," I said. "Cassandra." I turned to go.

A hand closed on my wrist, and turning to look down, I saw Valeriev had seized me. There was dry blood on him. I wondered how it had gotten there, what horrors the poor doctor had endured that night.

"What is happening?" Tiber Valeriev demanded, not letting me go. "Why are the Cielcin here? Why us?"

I rested my free hand on his and made gently but firmly to break his grip. He squeezed the tighter. "The beast that killed the deserters," I said. "The thing that killed Doctor Mann. The Cielcin worship it. They want it for the war. We're here to kill it."

Valeriev's eyes had turned hard as glass. "Why weren't we told?"

"You know what you know about the Vaiartu, and you have to ask?" I said, and broke his grip. The doctor winced and shook his hand.

"I'm a xenologist, Marlowe! A scientist!" he said, taking a step back. "I'm not a soldier! I didn't sign up for this!"

"Neither did I, doctor!" I roared, and it was six hundred years of roaring that flattened the little man against the wall. I had not wanted to be a soldier, had not wanted to lose my friends, my family... everything but my daughter. I had not wanted to leave Jadd. "Neither did I. But we're all pawns in the great game. We can only move forward. Now, forward for you is with these men, out into the desert. You get these people clear! Do you understand?" Rather than wait for a response, I cast about, eying the men in Gaston's uniforms. "Which of you has command?"

"Me, sir." The speaker was a hard woman with short, red hair.

"What news of Commandant Gaston?" I asked. "Is he lost?"

She shook her head. "Not last I heard," she said. "Comms are bad. Worst I can remember. Last I heard he'd been driven back to the landing field. Heard your commander's dead."

"I told them," Cassandra interjected.

"If Gaston is alive, he has command on the ground," I said.

"And if he's not?" the woman asked, looking to Valeriev.

"I guess I have the command," I said, "I have to go back. There's a weapon aboard the *Rhea* designed to kill the monster."

The shirtless man lurched to his feet. "Monster?" he asked, face white. "What monster?"

I chewed my tongue. There was too little time. I had no way of knowing how long it would be before Ushara returned her attention to me, or what she would do when she did.

"A god," I said, and let the words resonate like a shot.

The woman in her nightclothes laughed nervously, but when I did not, she blanched.

Valeriev spat. "A god? Do you think I'm a fool?"

"I've wasted enough time already," I said. "Cassandra, we're going!"

The red-haired woman put herself in my path. "I can't let you go alone, sir."

"Then get behind me," I said, and shouted back over my shoulder. "The rest of you get clear!" I made to brush the woman aside, stepped up the sandy slope that led out the half-filled door. The light of a shot split the night without, and I paused in the arch, peered out at a world lit as by lightning, hard edged and cold. A knot of our men—legionnaires in the full plate of the HAPSIS garrison—stood a little way up the slope, firing down. I saw the Cielcin pouring through a side tunnel from the neighboring boulevard. They outnumbered our troopers four to one at least.

I fell back from the door, and turning to look at the red-haired commander and at Tiber Valeriev, I said, "Enemy's outside. Downslope."

Something collided with the ruin's green façade just behind me, and whirling I saw the sparking shape of a *nahute* twisting in the air. It was damaged, but still lethal. Before I could respond, Cassandra shoved me aside, her own blade flashing ice-white in the dark. The thing fell in smoking pieces, but the damage was done.

"*Yukajjimn!*" the cry went up. "*Yukajjimn! Yukajjimn!*"

"They've seen us!" the red-haired officer said, checking the fuel cell on her gun.

Valeriev cursed.

I rounded on him. "Is there another way out of here? A back door?"

The xenologist shook his head. "*Nien.* There was a back passage, but it's collapsed."

"Then we dig in here," I said. "Anyone with guns: forward. With any luck most of the Pale won't be shielded. They'll have no choice but to come at the door."

"And if they are shielded?" asked one of the soldiers.

"Then we will handle them," I said, and raised my unkindled sword.

The red-haired woman was already firing, had taken up position against one pillar at the right hand of the open portal. The knot of HAPSIS men on the slope above and to our left had seen us, and one slid down the sand to close the gap. He came up on one knee and fired, his compatriots close behind. I counted nine of them in all, three triases.

Seeing them, the Cielcin swarmed up the hill, drawn by them and their brief glimpse of Cassandra and myself in the chamber's mouth. The red-haired commander and her men formed up around the opening, fired downslope. The light of our guns illumined the Cielcin horde. There were half a hundred of them at least, some with swords drawn, others crawling on all fours, rushing up the slope like dogs, like apes transported from the jungles of some dark and other world.

One shot caught the foremost in the face and it fell, a smoking, bubbling heap.

"They're not shielded!" the commander cried.

But some were. I saw the fractal glimmer of impact as they rushed toward us, and the flash of *nahute* hurled in our direction—heard the thrum of their drives and the whine of their fangs.

"Down!" I leaped out of the portal, blade flashing to life. The *nahute* slammed against the HAPSIS legionnaire's shield and ricocheted off, circling back like a shark. I cut it down, and shoved the man toward the door. "We have civilians in there!" I bellowed, pointing at the door. "Several of the dig team! There's no other way out!"

The legionnaire cursed, fired downslope. Another of the Cielcin folded like paper. A second shot struck the berserker beside it, and I saw the flash of shields.

"We should get under cover!" the legionnaire said.

"All of you!" I shouted up the slope, waving to the others. "Into the ruins! Now!"

Cassandra pressed beside me, twin swords in her hands. "Don't we need to get to the landing field?"

"We can't leave them here like this!" I said, and turning back to the others shouted for them to get inside. I spurred the one legionnaire on ahead of me.

Cassandra was gone. I looked round, heart hammering in my throat, and saw her ten paces away, down the slope. One of the Cielcin stood before her, towering fully eight feet tall. Cassandra held fast, undaunted.

I saw the xenobite's sword raised, and though I knew she had the skills to stand her ground, I felt once more a thrill of fear.

The white sword fell, met Cassandra's highmatter, and parted like tissue.

"*Veih!*" bellowed one inhuman voice. "*Huta ba-kousun'ta!*"

Their swords!

The Cielcin was already dead, fell smoothly in three pieces as Cassandra recovered to guard. The hundreds of hours Hydarnes had subjected my daughter to moved her limbs for her, though in my heart I sensed already the shadow of the tears that were to come tomorrow if we survived the night.

"Into the ruins!" I shouted once again, and leaped past the gate to stand with my daughter. Again I struck at one of the *nahute*, shouted for Cassandra to draw back. We would have to hold the door ourselves.

One of the legionnaires had not heeded me, and hurried forward to stand at my side. "We should get you to safety, sir!"

I brushed him off. "Cassandra!" I exclaimed. "The door!"

The Cielcin were almost on us. Those that had hurried on all fours skidded to a halt, drew their scimitars from oiled sheaths at hips or shoulders, and circled round, hemming us in. Dragging Cassandra by the wrist, we retreated to within several short paces of the door. Shots passed us—one skimmed off the curtain of my shield. The legionnaires had all won the gate, all but the man at my shoulder. "Back!" I cried. "Hold them back!" The ruined chamber was a death trap. If even one of the enemy carried explosives, even a simple grenade...

"I wish the Irchtani were here," Cassandra said, her shoulder to mine. "We need all the help we can get..."

Two of the Cielcin leaped, one with blade and *nahute* both in hand. I cleaved at the silver serpent, but it slipped from its master's grasp and flew past me, soaring through the open door. I heard shouting and crazed gunfire, and knew the men of Gaston's garrison had lost composure. I hewed at the blade and alien flesh, and saw the horned head topple. Cassandra drew back, staggered against the outer wall of the ruins. Her own quarry fell back, cowed by the sight of our blades.

A sea of Pale faces lay before us, glass teeth shimmering, black eyes wide. Shots rained about us, and though the unshielded among them were cut down, those that were protected closed in. The distant flash of fire in the deep of space lit their faces, and I saw one taller than the rest, lop-horned and bloodied.

"Ramanthanu!" I called out.

The captain spied me and snarled.

"*Detu adiqamam ne?*" I said, addressing the monster in its own language, "Why fight? Your prince is dead! Your god destroyed it! Depart from this place! Or it will destroy you!"

"*Ennaleto ne?*" the ichakta echoed. "Depart? No! Muzugara was unworthy. He betrayed our Prophet, sought to seize power for himself! We will stay, and die—if it is god's will! But we will kill you first!"

"Try it!"

A shot caromed off the captain's shield, and the Cielcin warrior bared its fangs, mouth stretched until the inner jaw hinged outward, lips peeling back as it roared. Its brethren did the same, and I threw out an arm to force Cassandra behind me into the mouth of the tunnel. The planet quaked beneath us, stressed by the distant action of the Cielcin moon. For a moment, I felt as if I moved in a kind of painting, in one of my mother's holographs. The Cielcin rushed in like the tide, an ocean of black and white, blades raised like the foam caps of breakers where they crashed upon the rock of man.

The soldiers behind fired past me where I stood in the opening. Though Cassandra and I might have held that narrow way, our mere presence prevented the gunmen from having full freedom of fire. And yet if I stepped aside, allowed them free rein, the Cielcin would sweep inside in a moment, and Death would ride on their shoulders.

One of the enemy plowed into me as I was turned combating another. We both collided with the pillar to the left of the entryway, and I felt the wind knocked from my chest. My head struck the green stone, and my vision blurred. Still, I managed to get my sword up and between us, and felt hot blood sheet onto my fist. The xenobite sagged against me. I shoved it aside, mindful of the black ichor steaming in the cold of that desert night.

"Lord Marlowe!" It was the red-haired woman. "Down!"

I crouched, permitted a flurry of violet shots to pass overhead. I felt the air boil as they passed. The blood had run from my hydrophobic coat and pooled on the pale sand. I stood once more, questing for Ramanthanu in the sea of inhumanity, but the captain had vanished. Cassandra stood near at hand, one foot planted on the corpse of an enemy as her swords passed through the chest of another.

Something *pinged* off the rock beside my head, and looking down I saw the flashing light I most feared.

The red-haired woman saw it, too, and lurched *toward* it.

I felt myself scream more than heard it, and saw the blast a moment later. The grenade exploded before she could throw herself fully upon it. Still, her body took the worst of the blast, and in an instant she was gone, transmuted into a rain of blood and meat that splashed the screaming civilians within. She had not been shielded, and so had made of herself a shield.

I never learned her name.

The impact hurled me out onto the sands, my shield taking the worst of the blow. Cassandra, too, had been blown clear, and the legionnaire who had stood with me. Pale hands seized me, pinned the hand that held my sword. I saw the flash of a knife.

"I'll rip you open," came the inhuman voice in my ear, breath hot and thick with the stench of rotting meat. "Wide open, you little *worm*."

Only the lightning saved me.

The air crackled, and a blast of thunder tore the heavens apart. The Cielcin that held me startled, and I wrenched my sword arm free. The blade cut wildly, and must have struck true—I hardly saw what happened. I had eyes only for the sky.

The lightning I had seen *lingered,* held in place as if Jupiter himself grasped it firm against the unfixed stars. The Cielcin all had seen it, and those that were nearest me fell prostrate.

Ushara had come.

Again the planet shook, and the lightning in the sky quavered, parted, revealed the pupil and the red-rimmed iris of that vast and livid eye. One of the Cielcin near to me was lifted from its prostrations and pulled screaming up into the sky. The sand shook, tendrils and ropes of it pulled skyward, floating as if under the impetus of some almighty magnet. My shield sparked and went dead.

I saw Ramanthanu raise its head, black eyes like tunnels into night. The captain knelt not ten paces from me, its sword abandoned at its side.

"What on Earth is that?" asked the legionnaire nearest me.

I spared a glance for him, and for the blasted opening to the chamber in the ruins. A battered Tiber Valeriev stood in the portal, the arm of the woman in her nightclothes over his shoulders, helping her to walk. Both were bleeding.

"A god," I said, words hardly to be heard in the furor.

"Earth and Emperor," the man said. "The size of it!"

"Abba!" Cassandra hurried to my side. Blood ran from a wound at her hairline. "We have to go!"

One of the Cielcin screamed, and looking back I saw it scrabbling across the sand, one leg raised as if some unseen hand grasped it by the ankle. As it writhed, it grew, and grew translucent, until the beating of its arms was like a scythe, sweeping three of its kind from their knees at a stroke. With my vision, I saw that invisible hand, a tendril of crooked lightning forked across the breadth of time.

Mimma ul atta.

The voice of the goddess boomed, filling all the world. The Cielcin who had lifted their faces buried them, and Cassandra huddled nearer to me. Fresh lightning cracked the sky and split, and a second eye peered down from an even greater height, and a third nearer to us, between the mountain and the sand.

"I did not believe in demons," the legionnaire whispered, words tripping over themselves in his haste. "This is the end of the world."

All the fighting around us had stopped. The Cielcin made huge by the Watcher's grasp lay dead upon the ramparts of the Vaiartu ruin across the avenue, its neck broken.

"These are not the demons the Chantry warned you of," I said. "Not a one of you stands a chance."

"Do you?" Cassandra asked.

"Go," I said. "Go now! Run!"

"I'm not leaving!"

"Go, damn you!" I shoved her from my side, regretted it almost at once.

But the night had not expended its store of terrors. As Cassandra staggered from me, eyes obstinate, full of hurt, the earth shook again. The sand beneath us lifted, and turning my head I saw something vast and white slithering beneath the surface of the great berm held back by the static compactors. A roar like that of some long-imprisoned Titan fresh from Tartarus filled all the world, and the berm broke like the surface of the sea as a whale leaps skyward.

An arm erupted from that surface, great around as some mighty tree, dozens of feet from shoulder to fingertip. Rings like the belts of wrestlers shone upon its fingers, glowed with rubies and jacinths vast as any human skull. But where the dead Cielcin giant was like a thin reflection in darkened window glass, the arm was solid as stone. The hand fell and struck the earth like a thunderbolt, six fingers closing on the sand. I had forgotten to move, forgotten *how* to move. There arose then a cry like the music I had heard in the pantheon, a voice at once high as heaven and deep as hell, and with a groan like the cracking of stones in the bowels of Old Earth, she broke the surface, her face huge as any of our shuttles, followed by her shoulders, her titanic breasts like hills rising from the sand. The stones of Phanamhara cracked as she rose, for she had emerged beneath them, and broke their foundations like kindling.

Ushara surveyed the world beneath her, tall almost as Dorayaica's holograph had been astride the field at Deira, though she was buried in sand to her hips. One of the Cielcin rose and ran toward her, arms outstretched. *"Thnaga-kih, qisabar wo!"* cried one of the others, warning its clansman to stop. *"Belnna!"* But the first Cielcin did not heed the second. Ushara's hand flickered, seeming not to travel across the space between, and closed on the running fool. The Cielcin vanished entire, crushed in that gargantuan fist until black blood ran between the huge, white fingers.

"Run, Cassandra!" I whispered. "Run, please!" Then, "The *Rhea*. Get to the *Rhea!*"

"Why does it look...like us?" asked the legionnaire beside me.

Just then, a blast struck the side of that queen monster's head, a rosette of orange flame. Then I saw against the night the lights of one of our fliers, one of Manticore Flight had survived this long, and streaked past her. Ushara reeled, but righted herself, apparently unhurt. She spread her arms, the lightning filling the sky behind her like wings, and a second rosette erupted, larger than the first. The ship exploded in the air, man and machine alike reduced to a cloud of smoke and metal.

Then the giant brought her hand down onto the sand, a blow to flatten the earth.

Where that hand struck, it remained, and about it the Cielcin rose as if hauled skyward by innumerate nooses. Many hung thrashing in the air, others rose so high they vanished entire. With a cry, the legionnaire at my left hand rose himself, and I heard the crunching of bones.

"Run!" I screamed, and seizing Cassandra by the wrist I turned to drag her through the carnage for the tunnel. We could not climb the slope, not without passing the giant. We would have to circle round if we were to stand any chance of reaching the camp. How I longed for a flare gun, for any way of signaling whatever Irchtani might remain in the air.

I felt Cassandra lurch, and tightening my grip I turned to see her feet lifted from the cracked pavers. She cried out, and I felt my eyes and nostrils stretch, my own cry of fury and terror drowning all my world.

She *was* my world. All of it. All that remained of it.

Of Valka.

I could not lose her. Not like this. Not ever.

Roaring, I dug in my heels, dropped my sword to seize her wrist with both my hands. Her ankles had risen above my head by then, and she hung stretched taut as a rope between two wrestlers in the Colosso games.

"Abba!"

I was going to lose her. To lose her as I had lost her mother, as I had lost Pallino and Elara. As I had lost Siran, and Corvo and Durand. As I had lost Crim and Ilex, and Gibson. As I had lost Switch and Ghen and little Cat. I was going to lose my daughter, my only child to this war, to that monster.

Cassandra's hands were slipping in my grip, the force that held her inexorable as the tide. Her eyes stretched wide. My heels dug against the sand, and I felt myself dragged up the slope toward the pale colossus. Peering across that infinity of time, I saw myself reflected countless times, in countless configurations, all of me tying all of Cassandra to the earth.

I opened my mouth, and a wordless roar escaped me, a shout of fury and defiance that burned in my throat like sand, like sickness. I held her wrist fast with both my hands, until I felt my own feet leave the ground.

My stomach lurched, and the old pain in my shoulder groaned back to life. I felt the burning of eyes upon me, and my vision drifted from Cassandra's face—just for a moment. The eyes of the colossus had found me, and their hunger and their sorrow fanned new flames in me. I felt tears well in my own eyes, tears not for Cassandra, but for Ushara herself. I felt her grief, and grief for her, deep and dark as any sea.

Niqi.

The word was like a knell.

Niqi. Niqi!

It resonated in me, and I felt my fingers slip, felt myself fall an inch back toward earth before Cassandra's own grip held me. And as I slipped I understood the word, saw again the vision I had seen in the bowels of the pantheon, saw myself enthroned, the queen of monsters seated at my feet. I saw our sons, black haired, six fingered, numberless as the stars.

Sacrifice.

"No!" I yelled, and the word was like a shot.

I did not want power, did not want Empire, did not want *her.* Not then, not ever—nor ever again.

I was not going to lose Cassandra. I was not going to lose again. Turning my head, I saw the countless Hadrians spiraling across all of fractal time, our legions numberless, defiant, defeated. Ushara was a dark angel of limitless power, a creature of pure force older than time. I was a child of Earth, and little more than a beast.

Still, I defied her.

I locked eyes with the giant, and no matter where in time or across time I looked, I saw her there, staring back at me, eyes hard as glass and angry. But there are infinities and infinities, and in the depth of my fury and my fear, I saw *beyond* Ushara, saw worlds and realms of time where she was not, as numberless as the realms in which she was.

"Cassandra!" I prayed. "Hold on!"

My rage was not blindness. Not there. Not then. It had not been blindness on Perfugium. On Perfugium, my fury had lent me clarity, a clearness of sight and a well dug deep by my grief. The scholiasts had banished emotion, or the great among them had. But in doing so—as Gibson had warned me when I left him on Colchis for the first time—they had banished the greater part of themselves.

I saw a place in time then, one further from me than any I had ever seen before that moment, where the giant was not, and the lightning, the eyes were not. I saw a world without Ushara—or only a moment without her.

But a moment was enough.

I *chose.*

Cassandra fell into my arms, and we both hit the ground like sacks of grain.

Ushara was gone.

The Cielcin that had hung in the air like the condemned all fell back to earth. They were dead, or else the fall killed them. Many had been torn apart, or crushed in Ushara's mighty hands.

In the sudden silence, I held my daughter close.

When at last I stayed my ragged breathing, I asked, "Are you all right?"

Cassandra pushed herself to a seated position, looked round at the carnage, at the ghostly giant Cielcin broken on the ramparts, at the bodies and the broken buildings. "Is she...dead?" Cassandra's voice emerged hardly more than a whisper. "Did you...kill her?"

Sitting up myself, I held her close, heedless of the blood upon her face. "I don't think so," I said in answer. "She'll be back. We have to hurry."

Cassandra was shaking, knowing how close she had come to destruction. "Hey!" I lay my hands upon her shoulders, shook her gently. "Hey! Cassandra, listen to me! You're all right. You're going to be all right." I drew her close.

"Marlowe!" Valeriev staggered toward me. He babbled something in Durantine Slavonic I could not understand, but remembered himself. "What was that?"

I found my feet. My sword lay on the sand, the winged lion's jet eyes staring up at me. I snatched it up. "You believe me now?"

The man nodded weakly.

"Get those you can to safety," I said. "I have to go."

"We have wounded!" Valeriev shouted at my retreating back. "The bomb!"

I stopped, head bowed. A terrible weight lay on my shoulders and on my heart. "Leave them," I said. "If they can't walk, leave them. You must get clear of the ruins. Get as far away as you can!"

"But!"

I rounded on Valeriev like a stuck bull. "I am going to burn this place off the map!" I shouted. "If you don't want to die, doctor, you'll do as I say!"

In that moment, one of the Cielcin—neither dead nor wounded—rose from the sand. I conjured my sword to meet it, but it leaped upon Valeriev and with a mighty stroke it hewed at the man with its scimitar. I shouted, but there was too much space between the doctor and myself, and he was dead already. His killer saw me and drew back, wary of my sword.

"*Yukajji-kih, adiqqa itamshan!*" the Cielcin said, gripping its weapon in both hands. "Fight!"

It knew it was dead, and lurched toward me.

A black shape burst from the sand and caught the creature by its ankle, the Cielcin fell, and another of its kind erupted from a drift of sand just as Ushara had done. Crawling hand over hand, it climbed atop my attacker and plunged a short-bladed knife into the first Cielcin's back, sliding between the chitinous plates of its armor. This second Cielcin held its clansman by one horn and waited for its brother to die. The Cielcin that had slain Valeriev twitched once, twice, and was still.

Only when it was dead did I recognize its killer.

Ramanthanu stood, its face caked in black blood and sand, its braided hair lank, its slit nostrils flaring as it rose, knife in hand. *"Daktaru!"* it shouted, and threw down the knife. *"Daktaru!"*

I stood there, astonished, confusion filling my mind like smoke.

Daktaru was *mercy*, and more than *mercy*.

Clemency.

"I yield!" the captain said in its own, foul language, and did the most remarkable thing I think I had ever seen one of its kind do.

It knelt, and pressed one ear to the sand at my feet.

Not a one of us dared move. Cassandra stood frozen some four paces away. The other Cielcin—the few who survived—stopped dead on their feet or knees.

"Nubabiqursa o-caihanaru!" Ramanthanu said, shouting. "You hurt it! The god! The *baetayan* teach us that Utannash is false. That his powers are false. But you...live."

I shifted, and Ramanthanu buried its face in the sand. *"Daktaru!"* it cried. *"Daktaru ina ndaktu, Ba-Aeta-doh!"*

"*Ba-Aeta?*" I echoed the word. "Your lord, you say?" The captain flinched. Gone was the monster that had sorted the prisoners taken from the *Rhea*, the beast that had thrown that poor woman to its dogs for sport. In its place was a worm, a groveling insect. Something in the captain had shattered.

Its faith.

Its entire world.

"Adiqursa ti-caihanaru vaa wo!" Ramanthanu said. "You battled the god! Drove it away. He killed my men! My slaves! When we had been faithful when Muzugara was not!"

"What is it saying?" asked Cassandra, one unkindled sword in hand.

I raised a hand to quiet her.

Ramanthanu spoke to the dust. "You are Aeta, Marlowe-doh! You slew Otiolo. Ulurani. You slew the Prophet's own! *Iubalu eza Bahudde eza Aulamn.* Hushansa says you killed Attavaisa, too. And now Muzugara is dead."

"I did not kill Muzugara," I said. I had not killed Aulamn, either. And I had killed none of the others alone, save Attavaisa only.

"But he is dead!" Ramanthanu said. "Because of you!" The *ichakta* pressed its face to the ground. "I killed my man, Jabanki, for you. I am your slave."

"Iyadar ba-kousun ne?" I echoed the word. "My slave?"

"Utannash is a greater god, that is plain!" The captain spoke more rapidly then. "Can you truly kill it? Can you kill the god that killed my people?"

"I don't know," I said, speaking Galstani and not Cielcin, the words a hollow breath.

"Abba?"

"Silencio, mia qal!" I snapped at her, falling back into Jaddian.

Confusing my shout for condemnation, Ramanthanu flinched. *"Daktaru ina ndaktu!"* it cried, begging for mercy or mercy of the other kind...

My...slave. Again I did not move. Could not.

I had no need of slaves, nor did I trust the creature that knelt before me. I had learned my lesson aboard the *Demiurge,* had relearned it a hundred times. At Thagura, at Aptucca, at Berenike and Senuessa, on Dharan-Tun most of all. The Cielcin were not men, would never be men. They were demons—or as good as. There could be no peace between us. No amity, no armistice. Our war had but two endings: our extinction or theirs.

And yet...

We had no time, and I had no men, nor could I spare any time for the wounded in the ruin, Valeriev's people and Gaston's.

"Belutoyu," I said at last. "I don't know if I can kill it. But we have killed one before. My people killed one before. We have a weapon they say can kill...your god. I mean to use it."

Ramanthanu did not raise its eyes. "I will use it," it said. "I will fight for you. For your god, if he is truly greater...if you are truly greater."

All at once, my tongue felt thick in my mouth. Had I not longed for this moment—for something *like* this moment—ever since I was a boy on Emesh? For a moment, it was Uvanari—not Ramanthanu—who knelt before me, offering a kind of peace. But it was a Cielcin all the same, and the Cielcin had taken *everything* from me.

Almost everything.

Mercy or mercy, the captain had cried, suing for clemency or the fast release of death. *Daktaru or ndaktu.*

Mercy or Justice, it might have said, had it been a man.

I had a choice to make: to kill this creature or accept its surrender. I longed to kill it. It was Cielcin, and the Cielcin were my enemy, had been my enemy for nearly all my life. And yet, were I to do so, I would be striking down a beast that had surrendered to me. Were Ramanthanu a man, such action would be murder. Perhaps it would be murder still. Had I murdered the captain then, I would be everything they said, everything they say of me now. The Demon in White. The Palekiller. The Sun Eater.

My sword was in my hand. Gibson's sword. I thought of the prisoners taken from the *Rhea,* of the poor woman this creature had sentenced to death by *sport.*

Justice. The sword would be justice.

And yet...

"Junne!" I said, moved by some part of myself quiet and subconscious. I made my choice. *"Junne!"*

Down.

The Cielcin word for *peace* meant *submission,* and Ramanthanu had submitted, submitted itself to the only *aeta* left on that entire world.

To me.

Lifting one foot, I pressed my heel against the side of the captain's horned head, just as I had seen Dorayaica do to Iamndaina on Eue long ago.

"Tuka okarin'ta ba-kousun," I said, taking the captain for my own.

CHAPTER 26

HUBRIS

NINE CIELCIN *SCAHARIMN* FOLLOWED me out of Phanamhara, shielded, swords in hand. I eyed them each in terror and suspicion, but not a one raised its hand to me.

"I don't like this," Cassandra said. "You think we can trust them?"

"What choice do we have?" I said, spurring Cassandra on ahead of me, watching as Ramanthanu's subordinates loped past, their long legs bent, bodies half-crouched.

My daughter glanced back at me, hissed, "The comms."

"You're welcome to try," I said. I had tried myself, a dozen times since we left the ruins. Tried to reach Neema, or Gaston, or Annaz and his men.

Now and again the night—which must by then have been nearing its end, though the horizon was still all dark—was broken by the flash of gunfire. Clearly all our men were not yet dead. Yet where was Gaston? Had he fallen? Or only been driven from the field?

"*Sim saryr!*" said Ramanthanu. *Not far.*

One of the others raised a clawed hand, and the captain and the rest all froze. Beside me, Ramanthanu sniffed.

"*Sim unassa,*" it said. *Not alone.*

About us, the ruins of the camp smoldered. The ruined prefabricated pod-buildings were metal and polycarbon, and had not burned save where the blast of alien artillery had staved them in. The hulk of one Cielcin lander rose above all, its tower crooked where it had smashed the refectory pod and fallen half-over. Bodies—human and inhuman—lay strewn on the blood-damp sand.

A pale face swam into view. The Cielcin wiped its mouth with the back of one hand, its black tongue trailing, cleaning the gore from its flesh. With the other hand, it clutched something long and bloody.

A woman's leg.

"Ramanthanu!" it said in its own language, raising one hand. "There is a feast here! We caught the *yukajjimn* in the white box. Dozens of them! Many the softer kind. The *ietumna,* I think. They are good eating." Only then did it catch sight of Cassandra and myself. "What's this, then? Fresh meat? Or are you with child?"

The captain bared its teeth. "Muzugara is dead, Shishakuri," it said. "Get to your ship. Return to our home."

The Cielcin called Shishakuri cocked its head. *"Wemathar ne?"* it asked. "Dead, say you? And what of the god?" It lifted the torn limb that was its feast and slung it dripping over one shoulder, so that the crook of the knee rested against its pauldron. "I saw it! I saw the lightning! The eyes! The giant! It has favored us!"

"It was the god that killed Muzugara!" said Captain Ramanthanu. "He killed the sorcerers. He has not favored us."

Shishakuri let its dripping thigh fall from its shoulder. "Not . . . favored?"

"We are dead if we remain," Ramanthanu said.

"Then we die at the god's hand!" said Shishakuri, padding nearer the captain.

It had come too close. Ramanthanu raised its sword and brought it down into the junction of shoulder and neck. Shishakuri's head did not fall from its neck, but the blade stuck in its spine. Blood black as ink ran down, and the xenobite's eyes narrowed in surprise. Ramanthanu had to put a foot on its clansman's chest to wrench the blade free.

"Kill any you find!" the captain called, pressing forward.

As if on cue, half a dozen of the Pale emerged from the ruins of the camp. They must have heard Shishakuri's loud voice and come to see. Many had red blood upon their chins and hands. Seeing the captain standing with black blood upon its crooked sword, they drew swords of their own, and rushed toward us. Ramanthanu whirled and thrust its point toward one of the newcomers. The creature parried, and the captain leaped upon its clansman with a ferocity that astonished. Seizing its quarry by one horn, Ramanthanu jerked the other Cielcin's head back and tore out its throat with its own teeth.

The rest of Ramanthanu's subordinates—*my* subordinates, I realized with a start—circled about Cassandra and myself. Clutching my unkindled sword, I felt as one in a dream. It could not be real.

My dream.

My oldest dream.

A kind of peace between human and Cielcin, us fighting side by side. But it was not my dream, not the fight I had envisioned, and not the peace. With every odd step, I felt Ramanthanu's head beneath my heel.

"Ba-Aeta-doh!" the captain said when the fighting was done. "We must

hurry. Others will come, drawn by the fighting." It touched a metal fixture over the left hole that served it for an ear. "Word of Muzugara's death is out. There will be fighting. A new prince must be found."

"It's not far to the landing field!" I said to the xenobite, eying Cassandra the while.

One of Ramanthanu's subordinates had fallen in the skirmish, bringing their number down to eight. The earth shook again, and looking up I saw the worldship like a bleary eye. There would be chaos aboard, when word of the general's death came. Their delicate hierarchy would crumble. Lieutenants and captains all vying for the highest place.

There would be blood on that alien moon before long, if there was not blood already. Against such disorder, Governor-General Hulle's defense fleet might just stand a chance.

Something dark and huge fell out of the night. Before I knew what was happening, it settled on one of Ramanthanu's men and vanished up into the night in a flapping of wings, taking the Cielcin with it.

"*Eijana!*" Ramanthanu shouted. "Above! Above!"

An instant later, the caught Cielcin fell, landing on its neck.

Those remaining of Ramanthanu's company formed a tight knot, and the captain rounded on me. "Tell the *eijana* to stop! Command them!"

Annaz's men had found us.

In a rush of wings, one alighted on the sand not ten paces from us. Another followed. A third. Then one landed directly before me, larger than the others, black feathered. He raised his sword to strike at Ramanthanu. The Cielcin raised its scimitar to parry the bird man's cutlass.

"*Ashtaanae!*" I cried, and caught the black-feathered one by the wrist. "*Ashtaanae, Annaz!* Hold!" I thrust my other hand—the one that held my unkindled sword—out to stay Ramanthanu. "*Ijanammaa!*" I said, giving the Pale the same order. To Annaz I said, "They're with me!"

"With you?" the inhuman chiliarch croaked. "My lord, they are Cielcin."

"They surrendered to me!"

"Surrendered?" The Irchtani commander jostled, jockeying for a position from which to strike. "And you believe it?"

"It has killed its own kind in my name!" I said. "The creature we came to kill is loose. We must get to the *Rhea* as quickly as we may and activate Oberlin's weapon. Can you fly us?"

"Fly you?" Annaz cocked his head, red beak clacking. "Yes. But these? No."

"We need every sword we can get!" I said, clamping my hand on the bird man's shoulder. "Were Udax here, he would not hesitate." It was not a lie, though it was perhaps unjust of me to say it.

Annaz did hesitate. "This is Marlowe's command?"

"It is," I said. "Tell me: What of my ship? Albé? My servant?"

"What shall we do, Annaz?" shouted one of the others, angling his *zitraa* at the nearest of Ramanthanu's Pale.

"Stand down, Shaara!" the chiliarch said. "These belong to *bashanda*. They have turned traitor for him." Annaz leaned to speak into my ear. "Of your ship I cannot say. Comms very bad. There is madness here. I saw lightning freeze in sky."

"I saw it, too," I said, and fearing I would see it again, looked up. "We haven't much time. Are there enough of your people to carry us?"

"How many are you?" Annaz peered round with one black eye.

"Ten."

Annaz threw back his head and called, a high, ululating cry. A moment later, half a dozen more of his men alighted, kicking up clouds of sand with their mighty arms. I recognized the one called Inamax among them, and listened as Annaz gave his orders in his own language. The others squawked, doubtless protesting.

"They will . . . carry us?" Ramanthanu asked. "Through the air?"

"It will be faster," I said. "Tell your people."

Ramanthanu threw an arm across me as I brushed past to speak with Cassandra. I froze, thrust the emitter head of my sword against the captain's ribs. If my action alarmed the *ichakta*, it gave no sign. Rather than speak, Ramanthanu drew an object from its belt and held it out to me. I looked at it, momentarily confused. It was a black box about the size of a man's fist, if narrower, with a silver catch on the face and a belt clip on the back.

It was a shield projector.

I did not at once take it.

"You are unshielded, *Ba-Aeta-doh*," the captain said. "Take mine."

I held the Cielcin's gaze then a moment. It was like locking eyes with a snake. Or a skull. I accepted the token, and clipped the shield to my belt.

There was no way to thank the monster. Not in its own language.

When Ramanthanu turned aside, I found Cassandra staring at me. "You're sure about this?"

I touched the wound on her face. It was not deep. "I am sure of nothing," I said. "Except that I must reach the ship."

"You must reach it?" Her face—so like her mother's—darkened with suspicion. "Without me, you mean?" She was already shaking her head.

"I need you to go to Neema," I said. "Tell him what happened. Albé should be with him. Tell him to power up the ship."

"You want me to leave you?" Her voice was incredulous. "Leave you? Now?"

"I want you to live!" I said.

"I won't go!" she said. "You need me!"

"I need you to survive," I said, and heedless of the blood on both of us,

I pulled her to myself. "Anaryan, you are all I have. I am your father. Let me do this thing." I kissed her brow and wiped a tear away for what I felt certain then would be the final time. "Go!" Then, "Kithuun Annaz! I want three of your men to escort my daughter to my ship."

"I'm coming with you!" Cassandra said, stepping after me.

"Take her!" I said. "Take her by force if you have to! If the ship is gone...if it's lost...I want them to take her as far from here as they can. To Markov Station, if you can."

Two of Annaz's men caught Cassandra as she tried to follow me, and her shouts chased after me like ghosts.

I should never have brought her.

"Take her now!" I said, "The rest of us will make for the *Rhea* at once!"

In the end, Annaz himself carried me into the air. I felt his talons bite my shoulders. I tried not to think of Cassandra, of the way her cries of protest filled the air. It was better that she was leaving me. Ushara would be drawn to me, as she had twice been already. The farther my daughter was from my side, the safer she would be. She may not live to forgive me, but she would live.

The wind rushed by us, almost deafening me, and I clutched the chiliarch's ankles.

"Do not let me fall!" I shouted into the wind.

The Irchtani commander croaked a laugh. "You are not so heavy as that, *bashanda!*"

Looking back, I saw the others spread out below and behind us, the Cielcin—*my* Cielcin—hanging from the vast-winged bird men like snakes in the talons of so many hawks. Below us, the camp was burning, columns of smoke rising half-seen through the night. The crooked towers of Cielcin landers pierced the desert flats everywhere like spears, and the hulks of our shuttles poured orange fire into the sky.

The *Rhea* lay beneath us, a vast scarab, mirror black in the gloom.

I could not see the *Ascalon* in that sea of smoking ships.

Craning my neck in the snapping wind, I looked back to Phanamhara, to the Mount of Whales in the east. Beyond it, the horizon stretched, an arcing line, the curve of Sabratha barely visible from our moderate height. There, at the edge of the world, a faint light gleamed. It was not yet sunrise, but the dark of that dreadful night was passing away.

"Down!" I shouted to Annaz, and slapped at his ankle with one hand.

The Irchtani snapped his wings wide, and we circled lower, spiraling to ground. The *Rhea* drew ever closer, and after a moment we sailed beneath the level of its antennae and dorsal guns. When a mere two feet separated mine from the surface, the chiliarch released me, and I dropped, knees bending to take the impact. Ramanthanu alighted to my left, carried by Inamax. The bird men touched down moments after, hefting their plasma burners as they turned to face the open ramp.

"We need to reach the bridge," I said, speaking Galstani. "The hard-lines might still be operational, and if they're not, well..." I held up my wrist. "My terminal's dead." I had to try and reach Neema, to warn him of Cassandra's coming, and to better relay my orders.

"Ramanthanu-kih," I said, addressing the captain—my slave—in its own tongue. "Are any of your people aboard, do you know?"

"There will be *mnunatari*," said Ramanthanu.

I blinked at the lop-horned captain. *Mnunatari* was the Cielcin word for *merchant*.

Ramanthanu said, "They collect the bodies. Take what they can find."

Scavengers.

"*Biqunna o-tajarin'ta wo!*" Ramanthanu said. *We will kill them.*

The captain barked an order to its men and mounted the ramp, clawed feet clicking on the metal. I made to follow, but Annaz caught me by the wrist with one scaled and taloned hand. "I mislike this, *bashanda*."

"They could have killed me before you came," I said. "Why did they not do it?"

Annaz clacked his beak, looked up at me sidelong. I was struck then by just how short the winged creatures were. "I cannot say," he said. "But these are Cielcin. Be careful."

"We need every sword," I said. "But we'll kill them...if we have to."

"No trust," said Annaz.

"No trust."

Thus we followed our Cielcin vanguard up the ramp, and reaching the top, I was glad I sent Cassandra away. I had forgotten the hold, somehow forgotten the screams and cries of terror and pain we'd heard on the bridge after Kybalion had opened the outer hatch, forgotten, too, the bodies and the abattoir stink of the hold where Vedi's men had been butchered.

It seemed that Ramanthanu had found one of its *mnunatari*. The captain stood over a fresh Cielcin corpse, blade stained black. I had to pick my way carefully between the bodies—human and Cielcin alike—and more than once I had no recourse but to tread upon them.

Fear is a poison.

I reached the inner door a few steps behind Ramanthanu. Annaz stayed close beside me, eyes locked on the backs of the Cielcin ahead of us.

"The bridge is straight ahead," I said in Cielcin, pointing.

The signs of looting and of desecration were everywhere. Doors cut into, windows smashed, panels broken. Rude drawings and crude writing marred the walls, and a brass light fixture hung down, torn from its socket.

The bridge was just as bad. The body of Commander Vedi had been dragged away—but those of Chatterjee, Dominina, and the rest remained, their abdomens torn open, innards removed or else left to spill upon the floor. The stench choked me. One of the Cielcin, a squat, broad-faced creature with short, snub-like horns, picked at the corpse of one of the shipmen, nostrils flaring speculatively.

"*Raka unjasan,*" it said. "Good meat."

"*Veih!*" I commanded. "Leave them!"

The Cielcin lifted its face to look at me. "They are mine!" I said, pointing at my own chest. "My dead!"

Faced with the reality of its situation, the Cielcin's nostrils flared. "*Yuka-jji!*" it said, and thrust its hand into the dead man's open stomach. A knife pierced the creature's eye, and it fell upon the body without another word.

Turning, I saw Ramanthanu standing by the station that had been Dominina's. "Jiganna would have challenged you," it said. "It is better this way." The captain looked round at its companions, they were seven then, in all. "Does any other mean to defy our *aeta?* To defy me?"

None came forward.

"What are they saying?" Annaz asked. "What happened?"

"The dead one disobeyed me," I said, moving to the main console. I tapped the black glass. The panel stirred to life, sharp images floating under the glass. I found the comms, and keyed the *Ascalon*'s address.

"Neema!" I almost shouted. "Neema, it's Marlowe. Can you hear me?"

As I spoke, I watched Ramanthanu turn on the spot, wet sword still in hand, surveying the bloody bridge. Annaz stood just inside the door with three of his men, plasma burners apparently casual, but ready in scaled hands. I could feel the tension between the two peoples like so many catgut strings. Almost I felt one might pluck a note striking the air between them.

No response came.

"Neema," I tried again. "I'm sending Cassandra to you. Neema!"

Nothing.

An error message flashed on the dark panel.

Failure. Code 122: Fault Detected In Hardline.

I hammered the console with my fist. "Line's cut."

"You could try radio," Annaz said, hopping toward me.

I did, was met with hissing silence.

Neema was dead. Must be dead, and young Albé with him. Cassandra would find no ship to carry her from that awful place. I pictured her flying in Irchtani talons, starving in the desert as they struggled to make the three-thousand-mile journey to Markov.

They stood no chance, nor did we.

We had come to the *Rhea* to die.

I gripped the rim of the main console with both my hands, squeezed so hard my right hand ached. The left—with its false bones—felt numb and hollow. A terrible weight was on me, a weight I'd come to know too well. My life, the lives of all around me.

The world.

"What now?" asked Ramanthanu in its own rough tongue.

The words shook me from my reverie, and I toggled the comm to broadband.

A flood of fragmentary voices filled the bridge, each overburdened by stress and static.

"—*pinned down above . . . ridge!*"

"*. . . Manticore Five here . . .*"

"*Taking heavy fire!*"

"*Chaana ishaa! Ishaa! Ishaa!*"

Annaz peered at me with one dark eye. "We are still fighting."

"This is Hadrian Marlowe!" I almost shouted into the comm. "Is Commandant Gaston still alive?"

Silence on the line. Surprise?

"Lord Marlowe!" came a familiar, deep voice. "We thought . . ." Static filled the connection. ". . . dead!"

It was Vimal Gaston. I felt my heart buoy at the sound. "Gaston!" I shouted into the comm. "Where are you? Where's Special Agent Albé?"

"Albé?" Gaston's sounded audibly confused. "Haven't seen him! What ab— . . . —giant wo—n?"

What about the giant woman?

"That's why we're here, Commandant!" I said. "Where are you?"

The reply was seconds in coming. "North ridge! Above the camp! Dug in! Overlooking—" Again he cut out. "—ruins!"

I knew the spot, there was a high dune that rose over the dug-out streets of Phanamhara. Not truly a ridge—being made all of sand—but it was higher than the surrounding ground. Gaston and a knot of survivors must have withdrawn there.

Chaos, I thought. *All chaos.*

"I want you to make a full retreat!" I said. "Take your people as far from here as you can! Full retreat, do you copy?"

"Sir?"

It would do no good. The NEM weapon had an effective radius of more than a dozen miles, and there was no way Gaston and his men could escape in time. "Belay that!" I shouted. "Can you get to the ruins? Underground?" They stood a better chance in Phanamhara than on the open dunes.

"Aye, lord." Gaston's voice crackled and hissed. "What are you going to do?"

"We have a bomb," I said, snapping my fingers for Annaz to join me. "An atomic meant to kill that giant."

"What is it, lord?"

"You wouldn't believe me if I told you," I said. "Go, Commandant! Save your people if you can." I killed the line. "Why can't I raise my ship?"

Annaz had reached my side. "Dead?" I shook my head. "Comms dead?"

"Maybe," I said, moving to the next console. "I need you at the tac console. There'll be a prompt to engage the NEM. We have to both grant permission to fire at the same time." Oberlin's people had instructed me on the use of the weapon on more than one occasion.

As I spoke, I punched the command to open the launch silo on the *Rhea*'s dorsal hull.

There came sounds of inhuman shouting from the hall outside, the cough of my Irchtanis' plasma weapons.

"*Mnunatarimn*," said Ramanthanu.

An alarm blared, lights flashing on my console. "Something's wrong."

"I have to get up there." Turning from the panel, I looked round the room. "Annaz, Ramanthanu, with me." I repeated the last in Cielcin and hurried for the door.

The sounds of fighting in the corridor outside had stopped, and I flinched as the door opened to find two Cielcin without. They bared their throats and drew back, showing the four fresh dead on the floor.

"Otomno, Juga, you stay," said Ramanthanu to these two. "We go."

The two did not question their lop-horned captain, and I pushed past to where a quartet of Irchtani held the nearest doors. Annaz ordered them to remain and to watch the Cielcin, and to kill any others.

The launch bay lay up against the dorsal hull and as far to aft as may be, above the hold and the engineering deck that ran just above it. The lifts were dead when we reached them, forcing us to take the stairs. Ramanthanu insisted on going first, and sent two of its remaining *scaharimn* on ahead. I plunged after them, moving as one in a dream. Before long, we reached the top level, and turning right at the top of the stairs, we hurried along the corridor to aft. Drawn by the sound of our feet, perhaps, a pair of Cielcin looters emerged from a portal to our left. They made a query—saw myself and Annaz's people too late. Ramanthanu's men ran them through and fell atop them, clawed hands tearing as they dragged swords across throats.

Another Cielcin *mnunatari* leaped from the open door, fell upon one of Ramanthanu's own. Drawing a thin knife from its wrist-sheath, the scavenger plunged the blade into the soft, unarmored place beneath the fighter's arm. The two xenobites fell, the scavenger stabbing the warrior again and again. Too late to help, I rushed forward, conjuring my blade in a flat arc that struck off the scavenger's head.

Beneath the newly headless body, the warrior was dying. I reflected that such internecine fighting was part and parcel of the Cielcin experience.

"Leave him," said Ramanthanu, looming like Death herself over my shoulder. "He is dead."

"Ndaktu!" the dying warrior choked. *"Ndaktu, Ichakta-doh!"*

Wordless, Ramanthanu went to one knee, gripping its scimitar by the midblade to better direct its point. I saw the tip of that scimitar take aim beneath the dying creature's chin, and turned my head as Ramanthanu drove it home into the brain.

Of the eight Cielcin who had joined Ramanthanu when it begged for my mercy, only five remained. Five... and the captain itself.

"The armory is just ahead," I said in Cielcin, gesturing for the Irchtani to take point.

Annaz hopped, fluttered over the bodies in the hall, kept one taloned hand on the long knife strapped to his belt, ready for some other surprise assault. None came, and we reached the heavy doors to the armory. They rolled partway open and jammed, forcing us to open them manually until they were wide enough that we might slither through.

The armory was not large, was perhaps forty feet from door to rear bulkhead. Men slumped dead at consoles to left and right, and bloody smears ran along the floor where others had been. These had manned the turrets that studded the *Rhea*'s exterior, guarded the ramp and the approaches to port and starboard. Small as the *Rhea* was and designed to land, she had no ventral cannons, only the main battery on her dorsal hull—directly above us—and a single missile launch bay.

The missiles themselves were stored vertically, locked in a revolving carousel like bullets chambered in some antique firearm. Each had been perhaps a foot in diameter, and little taller than a man.

Had been.

Of the eight torpedoes that had been stored in the carousel, seven were gone—doubtless taken by the *mnunatarimn* and carried to some Cielcin landing craft.

The eighth lay on the floor of the chamber, its warhead carefully removed and set to one side as if by the hand of some cautious surgeon. Its chassis likewise had been laid open, its microfusion cell excised like a tumor and placed to one side.

It was the NEM.

I fell to my knees, utterly bereft.

"Oyade detu raka yelnumbana ne?" asked Ramanthanu. I thought I could sense its confusion, even behind the alienness of its tone, its doubt in its new master, its new god.

"It is destroyed," said Annaz.

"What do we do?" asked another of the Irchtani. "What now?"

I raised my hands to my face. My wounded palm had dried, stopped bleeding.

I didn't have an answer.

We had lost.

Kybalion. I thought. Kybalion had known about the NEM weapon. Lascaris had known. He must have left orders with the Cielcin—with some MINOS technician, more likely—that the thing should be dismantled, just to be sure.

I punched myself in the leg, regretted the action at once, and ground my teeth instead.

"Bashanda?" the Irchtani commander peered down at me.

"We cannot stay here," I said. "The battle is lost."

We had come all this way, lost so many lives...for nothing.

Operation Gnomon had failed.

Ushara was awake, and just as the Watcher on Nairi had found new strength by tormenting the men of Aradhya's expedition, she had found new life in the men and Cielcin she had consumed. Sharply then I recalled the vision she had shared with me, of her spirit flickering like a dying ember in Sabratha's desert, too weak to escape the planet's magnetic field.

"We should never have come here," I said.

But it was too late.

There had been more NEM weapons aboard the *Troglita,* but the *Troglita* was lost.

There was nothing, *nothing* we could do. Not against the Watcher, not even against the Cielcin stragglers warring on the surface. The weapons were lost, and even I could not restore them. For all my faculties, I cannot turn time back.

I knew then that spirit of Despair that must have settled on Leonid Bartosz on Berenike so long before. I felt a desire then more keenly than any I had known, a desire for death sharper than hunger, than thirst, a desire that ached in me more deeply than the desire for sleep, than animal lust.

I wanted to die.

It cannot be in that moment that the message came. I think Ramanthanu and Annaz must have pulled me to my feet and had me halfway to the bridge to see if we could make the *Rhea* fly...but though I stretch my memory as far as it will go, I cannot remember it any other way, though you—dear Reader—think it low drama.

It *must* have been in that moment.

Annaz straightened, raised one claw to the place where I guessed his comms patch lay hid beneath the black feathers. Listening, he pivoted to face me.

"What is it?" I asked, fearing the answer. Ramanthanu shifted, drawing closer.

In response, the Irchtani chiliarch tapped his wrist-terminal, and a voice emerged, a voice I thought never to hear again.

"Lord Marlowe?"

"Albé?" I straightened, bad knee groaning as I put my weight upon it. I almost fell. "Albé? Is Cassandra with you?"

Edouard's response crackled, "She's here."

"Where are you?" I lurched to my feet, cast my gaze about the armory as if I might find the man standing in some shadowy corner.

"On the *Ascalon*," came the reply. "We had a little company, but the birdos and I saw them off." The wave went quiet a moment, and when it ran clear, Albé was midway through the next sentence. "...air soon. Can you reach us?"

"They destroyed the weapon, Albé," I said. "The Watcher is loose."

"—doesn't matter," Albé said. "Need to get clear."

"Doesn't matter?" I almost shouted the words. "Are you hearing me? We've failed!"

"Have to—" The connection skipped, words repeating themselves. "—still have to-to warn the Empire. Can-can you reach us?"

I looked to Annaz, to Ramanthanu, to the wreck of the NEM.

Full retreat.

It was the only option left to us. Abandon Sabratha, leave whatever survivors remained to their fate. If the governor-general's people won the day, they would send ships to the Mount of Whales, to the Ocean of Silence. To Phanamhara. They might live. Gaston and the others. Ushara might spare them, might turn her attention on me. Was she powerful enough to slip the bonds of her prison? To escape Sabratha entire?

"We're on our way."

CHAPTER 27

PERSEUS AND MEDUSA

THE *ASCALON'S* REPULSORS WHINED and glowed blue before us, and the light of her open ramp shone like the gates of heaven. Annaz had set me down perhaps a dozen paces from the ship, and landed himself just ahead of me in a beating of clamorous wings. Cassandra and Edouard both stood just inside, the latter with a hand on the controls to seal the hold.

"Are we ready to launch?" I shouted, adjusting my torn coat.

"Nearly!" Edouard said.

"Good!" I said in return. "Cassandra! Get to the bridge and strap yourself in, we're leaving!"

She turned to go just as my feet hit the bottom of the ramp.

"Hold!" Edouard shouted. His hand flew to his sidearm, and he drew the pistol forth. He leveled it at Ramanthanu, who had hit the sand a half dozen paces behind me. In a voice barely to be heard, Edouard breathed, "It's true..."

Ramanthanu checked its advance. Its people were dropping to the sand about me even then, their Irchtani escorts alighting moments after. "These Cielcin have my protection, A2!" I said. "Put the gun down!"

"I didn't believe it," he said. "Cassandra told me, but I did not believe."

Cassandra herself had halted halfway to the inner door.

"Believe it!" I said. "And put down your gun. Ramanthanu and its ilk have thrown in with us. They're mine!"

"Yours?" Albé made a face.

"Mine!" I answered him, "I'll hear no more of it!" I turned to bark orders in the xenobites' own language, ushering them up the ramp. They went without question, Ramanthanu lingering at the top of the ramp like a faithful dog. Returning my attention to Edouard, I said, "We'll kill them... if we have to. For now, they may be useful."

To my surprise, the other man did not argue. Ever pragmatic, the HAPSIS man asked, "What of the Monumental?"

"There's nothing we can do. I..." How could I explain what I had done in a way that could be understood? The Watcher was but a wave of energy, in form and substance little different than a radio broadcast. I had broken that wave as a shoal breaks the sea, diverted its course and channeled it to some lower state, forcing it into the gullies of potential time. It had climbed out once already, and I felt sure it would climb out once again.

In the end, I said only, "I wounded it. But I can't kill it, not without the Perseus weapon."

"What happened?"

"I'll tell you later!" I said, brushing past him into the hold, shouting to the Cielcin and Irchtani alike to take seats in the foldouts that lined the great hold's either side. "Cassandra! Bridge! Now!" She had lingered by the door, went through it at last. Returning my attention to Edouard, I asked, "Where's Neema?"

"Safe in his quarters." Albé rushed after me. "Hadrian, there must be something we can do!"

"There's nothing!" I stopped dead, halfway to the inner door, and rounded on the man. He had called me *Hadrian*. "You know the literature better than me, *Edouard*! You know what it took the team on Nairi. You know how hard these things are to kill."

"But if we could get a dozen standard EMP weapons, time their release across...three minutes? Five minutes? It could simulate the Perseus weapon."

I turned to face the younger man. Edouard held his jaw tight, and there was a hardness in his eyes. How old I felt! How tired. I reminded myself that here was a man who had not battled the Cielcin and their pet sorcerers all night. For young Albé, the fight had just begun. Sparing a glance for Cassandra, feeling my patience worn down and my anger rising like Ushara herself from the sands of the desert, I snarled, "And where are we going to get these weapons, Albé?"

"Hulle's Defense Force." Edouard did not even hesitate.

"And how are we going to reach them?" I asked.

The answer was obvious, too obvious for me to see.

"We fly above the ionosphere," Edouard said. "Call in the cavalry."

I halted, the formless objection I had been about to make dying its swift death.

He was right. Right at least about the cavalry. With the *Ascalon* at the ready, we were in position to contact the governor-general's paltry defense force. Whether or not they had the pulse weapons we required, or could spare the lightercraft, was another matter.

We had a chance, and had to try for it.

Yet even as hope flared white hot and cruel within my breast once more, horror joined it.

"I have to stay," I said, and looked to the inner door, fearing that Cassandra had not gone on ahead as I had ordered.

Edouard looked at me, mouth open, aghast. "You what?"

"If I go, the Watcher will follow me," I said, seizing Edouard by his shoulders. "You weren't out there. You did not see..." I halted, teetered on the edge of telling him about the giant, about the many-armed creature that had slaughtered the Cielcin in the pantheon, about the woman, death-pale and cold as marble. "I have to stay. I have to be here." I drew back, tugged my sword free from the pocket of my coat. "Tell Cassandra I love her. If I don't come back..."

"Lord Marlowe, I—"

"If you truly serve my family, as you say, Albé: Serve her. Save her. For me."

The other man only nodded.

I turned and shouted to Ramanthanu and Annaz and stormed down the ramp into the fading night. They followed, six Cielcin and perhaps ten Irchtani. Sand flew up in fine clouds, and the wind off the repulsors kicked at my torn coat and blew my hair across my face. The *Ascalon* rose, and turned, half circling us. Too well, I imagined Cassandra shouting on the bridge, glowering through the window down at me. Unseen, I raised my hand in salute. Perhaps in farewell.

In the distance, one of the Cielcin landers blazed skyward, a castle hurled to heaven upon a fountain of oily red flame. The noise of it was like the thunder, like an avalanche. Some of the enemy at least were retreating. The *Ascalon* rose faster, rising without flame, relying instead upon her repulsors until she reached the height of several miles.

"Go!" I hissed, and felt as I thought poor Corvo must have felt, watching us streak away from Akterumu. "Go! Go!"

The fusion torch burned, a light bright as any sun.

The *Ascalon* was climbing, mounting the airs toward the silence beyond night.

Thunder roared as another of the Cielcin craft took flight, and all Sabratha trembled. I turned to watch it go, shielding my eyes from the terrible fire of its drive. My inhuman guard shifted about me, Cielcin and Irchtani alike unsure where to go, what to do. I prayed Gaston had heeded my orders, had taken his survivors in the north ridge out into the desert. What had become of Tor Rassam and Tor Carter?

How many of our people remained on the surface? Scattered, divided, yet unconquered?

There had been thousands in the camp, between our Legion engineers, our guards—the Irchtani auxiliaries—and the men of Valeriev and Gaston's garrison. They could not all be dead, but broken and scattered was as good as. The pulse weapons would not kill them—the blast of such ordnance was more harmful to machines than flesh—and yet such a barrage was certain to destroy any device left unshielded on the surface. Every comms terminal, every phase disruptor, every plasma burner and every deactivated shield generator. Every flier, every spottercraft and skiff would die.

The Cielcin stragglers would likewise be devastated. Their ships would not fly, nor their *nahute*. They would be trapped on Sabratha. They would die there.

"What now, man-commander?" asked Annaz.

"I don't know, Udax," I said, forgetting my place in time.

The Irchtani had halted, and turning I looked back at him, saw Ramanthanu and its Cielcin following not half a dozen paces behind.

Annaz cocked his head in that way of his so reminiscent of the bird his kind resembled. Realizing my mistake, I apologized. "I am very old," I said, and added only to myself, *and very tired.*

"I am not *Vaanshakril*," Annaz said.

Not *Demonslayer*, I translated.

"After today, you may be," I said, and looked to the sky. "How many of your people remain?"

"More than half, *bashanda*," the chiliarch replied.

"Call them," I said. "We'll need all the help we can muster."

We advanced into the smoldering ruin that had been our landing field, trudging through sand churned by the passage of so many feet, picking our way over the bodies of men and Cielcin and Irchtani alike. Here and again we caught sight of motion in the shadows and open hatchways of ships that would never fly again.

"*Ichakta-kih, nevaqqa keta ti-kousun,*" I said to Ramanthanu, urging the captain to stay close. "My own people will fire on you and yours."

One of the other Cielcin spoke up then. "We should flee," it said. "The god has judged us, and we have betrayed it."

"*Onnanna, Otomno!*" hissed the captain. "You saw the Utannashi challenge the god and win!"

"Then why does he fear it?"

Otomno's question went unanswered.

One of the pole lamps erected by our engineers exploded high above us, and I threw an arm across my face to save myself from raining glass. Annaz and the other Irchtani shielded themselves with their wings or flapped away.

The air above was filled with the noise of wings, and against the brightening dark I saw the blacker shapes of our Irchtani circling like so many crows.

"Man-commander!" cried one of them, alighting atop the hulk of one of our shuttles. "This way!" He pointed with his drawn *zitraa*, gesturing toward the next aisle between our grounded craft. "Come and see!"

"See what?"

"Najikaar!" he said.

I did not know the word, and looked to Annaz.

"Circles," the chiliarch translated.

I led the way round the grounded shuttle to see what the fliers had seen.

The space between our shuttles was broad and nearly flat, save where the passage of so many feet had dimpled the pale sand. The stink of smoke unseen filled the air, and there was an electric quality to it, a static tang that touched the skin and pricked at every hair.

There *were* circles, just as the scout had said. Just as there had been circles burned into the stone in the Hall of Record, just as there had been at the site of the crash in the deep desert.

Great ribbons of molten glass lay upon the desert floor, forming a pattern of circles interlinked. The greatest was perhaps a dozen feet across, the smallest no larger than a raindrop.

Ripples.

"She's here."

No sooner had those words escaped me than one of the Irchtani cried out. A high, piercing note like that of a hawk. The note strangled and died.

"It's too soon!" I said. "Edouard can't hardly have reached orbit!"

Still, I knew I should have been grateful for the little time we'd had. Cassandra was safe—safe from Ushara, at any rate—and that was all that truly mattered.

Another of the lights erupted in a shower of sparks, and in the middle distance one of the Cielcin landing towers exploded. My ears were ringing, and my vision swam as I staggered away from the explosion. Above the sky stood empty, blushing in the east with the first rosy fingers of dawn.

"We have to play for time!" I said, seizing Annaz by the shoulder. "Tell your men to—"

Boom.

Another of the Cielcin landers erupted in a nimbus of red flame. The air shuddered, as though the night sky were the inside of the head of some almighty drum.

"Fly!" I roared, and felt the word in my bones more than heard it. Had the second blast ruptured my eardrums? I pressed my hands to my ears, felt no blood, heard only a constant ringing.

I staggered a few steps, kept my hands on my ears.

Boom.

A third concussion rent the night, and a third Cielcin war tower erupted in sudden flame.

Boom.

One of our own shuttles blew apart at the end of the aisle. The shock of it knocked me to my knees. Around me, the Irchtani flapped their wings, took to the air or tumbled from it, stunned. My Cielcin honor guard looked round in confusion.

Then all the world went mad.

At first I thought I must have struck my head when I fell. I saw double, and all the world swam before my eyes. Two rows of shuttlecraft floated before me, two clouds of Irchtani flew. Two of Captain Ramanthanu stared down at me, mouth open to reveal black tongue and glassy teeth.

Was it shock?

I turned my head to look, saw a river of molten glass, a tendril thin as a finger snaking its way through the sand to encircle me. I watched it go, like gold in a jeweler's mold. There was a man kneeling beside me, his face turned from my own. Then he was gone, and the ribbon of molten sand seemed nearer, near enough that I might touch it.

Ramanthanu thrust its sword at me, point hovering inches from my face. I blinked, surprised, too stunned to draw my sword.

"Dein tuka okun ne?" it asked.

Fishlike, I gasped, shut my eyes to stop the world from spinning.

"What are you?" Ramanthanu asked again.

When I opened my eyes at last, I saw that I was mistaken. Ramanthanu's blade was pointed at the man kneeling beside me. Its other Cielcin drew nearer, eyes wide with inhuman suspicion, jaws slack.

I didn't understand the question, understood only that the Cielcin had betrayed me. I had been wrong to trust them, wrong to stumble into battle with them at my side. My sword was in my pocket.

The man to my right stumbled to his feet, a blue light flaring in his hand. I turned to look, confusion washing over me. My stomach lurched as though I'd moved all at once, and I braced myself against the sand with one arm.

Ramanthanu stood before me, and I was standing, though I felt coarse sand in my wounded palm. I clenched my fist, felt the sands of the desert slip through my grasp. Shocked by my sudden motion, Ramanthanu lurched back, and I raised my sword—watched the other man raise his from my place on the ground.

"Gasvva!" I bellowed at the inhuman captain. "Kneel!"

When it did not obey, the man standing over me slashed at Ramanthanu's sword. The tip fell to the sand, and the captain was left holding the broken half of its scimitar. The other Cielcin all halted. And one of the Irchtani—Inamax, perhaps—alighted not three paces from where I stood facing the Cielcin.

From where I knelt upon the sand.

"Iya?" it asked, looking on in confusion.

Two?

"Two?" I heard the kneeling man ask in his clipped Delian baritone, and turning to look I saw Hadrian Marlowe kneeling at my feet. He looked at me, and I saw myself through his eyes, saw Hadrian Marlowe standing, sword in hand, his eyes wild, his jacket torn like mine, his left hand bloody, caked with sand. And I saw Hadrian kneeling, staring up at me, shocked as was I.

I saw through both sets of eyes at once, our fields of visible interlinked, overlapped...and I understood. I had become like poor Doctor Mann, my body a wave refracted across the plane of our existence.

I was in two places at once.

"I'm just me!" I said, forgetting to speak Cielcin in the heat of the moment, raising four hands in unison.

Boom.

Another shuttle exploded, more remote. I saw its fire burn over the tops of the ships nearest us. Fires were burning, burning all around us, and the sands were running like wax, bright circles forming in the surface of the path. The noise of the explosion dimmed, and as I looked round—looked through both sets of eyes—I saw the fires begin to die.

Once, when I was very small, Gibson had lit a candle and placed a bell jar over the top of it, to teach the smaller Crispin and myself a lesson about combustion. The candle quickly burned the oxygen left in the little jar, and I had gasped as the candle seemed to blow itself out—fire becoming smoke.

All around us—all at once—all the fires went out.

All sound and movement ceased.

Then a light opened in the sky, a light from nowhere, without source or direction, a light spilling from some higher plane.

Light...and song.

Inhuman music filled the vast volume of the air, falling like snow, like ash upon the cold and silent battlefield. It was like the sun was rising, dawning from the zenith of the sky.

The Cielcin around me shuddered, and all save Ramanthanu threw themselves upon their faces. The Irchtani squawked and flapped about me—about both of me.

Reader, I cannot make you understand. Unless you have seen what I have seen—and you have not—words fail utterly. Even for those who stood beside me, words fail.

Words are only symbols. Icons. Crude representations.

They can never capture the thing itself.

Not anything.

Not this.

It was as if the sky opened, as if that light from nowhere made straight the coiled paths from other time and revealed that higher plane—if only for a moment. The space beyond teemed with eyes lidless and pitiless, eyes that might have been carved of marble and set with gems. They slid across the heavens, fixed to great bands of glittering black, rotating rings within rings like the characters of her celestial speech—eyes seeing all. The great and terrible music swelled, but under it—as one might discern the metronome beneath the melody—I heard the ticking of some mechanism ancient and unfathomably immense.

Ushara had returned.

She had supped upon the energies of the ships she had destroyed, had slaked her thirst upon their fires and rebuilt much of what she'd lost in a million years of solitude. Seeing her revealed across the heavens, I knew then—with an acuteness sharper than any I had known—how small I was, and how small was all mankind. We were but a passing thing, an accident of nature, the upjumped heirs of some protoplasmic slime, far removed from the ocean vents of our birth.

She was fire and air, sans any baser element.

Light itself, and song.

And that light and that song lifted me from my feet, carried me into the sky, dragging me toward those heavenly wheels and that tumult of roiling eyes. Still, I felt the sand of Sabratha beneath my knees, and looking down saw myself looking up, and looking up saw Hadrian Marlowe twisting, writhing in the air in the grip of hands unseen.

About me, I saw the shapes of men and of Cielcin, of old stones and ships entire lifted into the air. The Irchtani flew among them. I saw one collide fully with the hulk of a Cielcin lander, and felt the crack of impact in my bones. The alien music filled my ears, my skull, my soul, filled all creation until it seemed I was myself but one note in its symphony. One note, jangling with discord, dreadfully distinct.

I saw myself then as she saw me, and hated what I was. I held Hadrian Marlowe in the palm of my innumerable hands, saw him tessellated across infinite variations, an insect-thing of animate clay, a creature of slime and crude matter, possessed by only the faintest spark. Why should he hold so high a place in *his* esteem? Why had *he* set such pitiful creatures at the fulcrum of creation? Why were they closer to *him* than I? I, who had drunk long and deeply of the light that was *before the all*. I, who had been made before the stars. I, who had crushed countless worlds to powder, and bathed my feet in the blood of empires. I, who flew so much higher than the mud that had birthed this human animal.

I was the pinnacle of creation, and my brothers with me.

Why had we been made to serve?

I would not serve. Not a beast like him.

I could crush him in an instant.

If he would not serve me—and I had given him his chance—I would crush him.

I had only to squeeze.

I felt his pain, felt the wind shudder from his lungs. He would turn to pulp in my fists. His blood would fall like rain to the dirt of this dying world, and he would return to the mold that birthed him. Let his spirit flee creation! Let all spirits flee! Let the universe run dark and cold, but let it run free! Let it be *our* universe! Let it be *mine!*

Seher anumma miti!

Eye after eye peered down at me as they slid past. I was a thousand feet from the ground, and kneeling in the dust at the same time. I felt their malice, their hatred of all life—of life itself—their hatred of me in particular, of what I was: a servant of *him,* of Utannash, the Quiet, the Hidden One. I felt her hatred as if it were my own, felt her pride and her fury until I felt myself almost a part of her, enthused, enthralled, possessed. She was Hadrian Marlowe, and Ushara, too. And I...? She would take me, take all that I was. Nothing of Hadrian Marlowe would remain.

My vision began to fade, to flicker between one vision and another, one field of vision. From the air, I saw her eyes—vast as clouds—floating it seemed inches from my face. From the ground, I saw myself high above, a small, dim figure fluttering in the air, a mote against that light that fell from nowhere, felt the earth shake beneath me. Saw both fields of vision interlaced, mingled with her own, multifaceted view of me. I felt the pain in my head, so sharp I thought my skull must burst, saw the fragile, stick-like thing I was, the aging wreck that had defied the Cielcin and their gods for more than six hundred years.

And I saw, too, how little time that was, how little I meant—had meant in the cosmic balance.

I was nothing at all.

The barest drop in a limitless ocean.

One photon against the infinite Dark.

One is enough.

The voice that whispered to me then was not my own, nor was it Ushara's. It was not Gibson's voice, or Valka's. It was no voice at all, hardly to be heard. But it was right. Had I not seen—had I not been shown—had I so easily forgotten how fragile the darkness is?

One photon was enough to hold it back.

As if on cue, then, light erupted beyond the sky, filling the upper airs like the dawn. The otherworldly music broke and turned to wailing. The rings with their too-human eyes seemed to resonate, to cry out in pain. Whole sections of the Watcher—which had glittered like black ice, like obsidian set with gems—cracked and fell to earth.

I fell with them. Wind rushed past me, loud as cheering. Sabratha rushed toward me. I was falling headfirst, and watching myself fall from the very sands that would spell my death. I was still in two places at once. But I knew... One death would pay for both.

The Hadrian on the ground stood, stumbled forward a step until I was almost directly below my other, falling body. The Watcher was falling, too. Edouard's cavalry had come, and the fire of their pulse weapons had washed over the body of the god like the tide. The Watcher was—at its core—only a pattern. And a pattern can be disrupted, its energy scattered. Dissipated. Changed in form.

I had but seconds to live, and shut the eyes of the man falling, knowing the ground would take me—knowing I had won. I saw my body hurtling toward me, and ran to catch my other self.

Cassandra...

I hurled myself forward to catch the falling man. The shock of impact knocked the wind from me, and I hit the sand an instant later. The wreck of Ushara crashed to earth with a noise like the ending of the world. Shards of black stone large as any of our shuttles and delicate as glass ploughed into Sabratha and broke, crushing ships and survivors alike beneath them.

It was a miracle I was not crushed myself, though the corpse of a man lifted heavenward by the Watcher struck the sand not two paces from my head. Face caked with sand, I rolled over—and found I was alone.

The second Hadrian was gone.

I was one again, and alone. The Irchtani all had taken wing, and the Cielcin were scattered. The light that shone from nowhere had faded, and the inhuman music was dead and gone. Another blast of light filled the open sky, and—shielding my eyes against its radiance—I saw with relief and sudden joy that the sky was empty!

The Watcher had fallen from it, and the Cielcin moon was gone!

"Ai! Ai! Ai!" Distantly, the cry of an Irchtani filled the ending night.

I forced myself to breathe, ragged, slow, but free. I rolled onto my back, lay flat against the level sands, and watched the light break across the sky. A sob escaped me, or a laugh—I could not say. We had won, and I was still alive. And yet it was not relief I felt, but... embarrassment.

I should have died. It would have been a fitting end: the Halfmortal against a god.

And yet there I was... still alive.

Edouard's cavalry rained against the sky, and light after light broke upon the heavens. No one came to disturb my rest.

In time, the flash of the bombs ceased, and all was still. When it seemed the first second of eternity had passed, I sat up, heedless of the sand that clung to me, of the bodies and new flames all round.

"Cassandra?" I touched my comms patch, forgetting the thing was dead. "Neema? Edouard? Cassandra, can you hear me?"

There was nothing, of course. No reply but silence.

I clambered to my feet, stood dazed, swaying. When had I last eaten? Drunk? I must have slept a little—if only for a moment, there upon the sands. The eastern sky blushed with the first light of day.

A shard of the thing that had been Ushara lay not half a hundred steps from where I'd fallen, its polished face to me. I limped toward it, my knee complaining at every other step of the slow decay of time. There were fires in the upper airs. They were beautiful. Soon there would be prayer lanterns, fires raised up to heaven as these were falling down.

I'd reached the shard, a splinter of black stone ten cubits high and wide as my outstretched arms. Smoke coiled from its dark surface, and from the sand mounded about its base. Seeing it, and seeing my reflection in its black mirrored surface, I realized I had no conception until that moment just how vast the thing in the sky had been. It was like a ship had fallen. My image moved in the glass, matching my own movements as I drew nearer. I raised a hand to touch the stone, but caution checked my advance. I could feel the heat still radiating from the substance, like a stone plucked from the fire.

It was black as anything I had ever seen, so black it drank the light. I turned my head, my reflection moving with me. It was without a doubt the same substance that made up the bones of the leviathan I'd seen on Eue.

The bones of a god.

CHAPTER 28

THE OCEAN OF SILENCE

THE DESERT STRETCHED OUT before me, boundless and bare. I had left the ruined landing field behind, limped free of the wreck and carnage of the night and climbed the sloping dune to the spot where the bones of the *Cetoscolides* thrust from the blowing sands.

Rosy dawn had come to Sabratha, and the desert—dull gray by starlight—was brightening toward the white and pale dun of day. I could hardly remember being so tired.

It was over.

The day would be hot, I could feel it already, and prayed that I would not remain on the surface for long. There were Cielcin still in the camp, the stranded survivors of the battle. Now and again the distant report of gunfire sounded in the field below, accompanied by the violet shout of plasma.

I sank to the ground at the foot of one towering rib, laid the hilt of my unkindled sword in my lap. The dune was not tall, but it was the highest point beyond the westmost margin of the camp, and commanded a view of the desert all round, and of the camp and Phanamhara beyond. From it, I could see the desolation of Ushara.

It was like a mighty tower had fallen, or a ship had crashed to earth. Fragments of alien stone—some hundreds of feet across and curling like the discarded nails of some immeasurable giant—lay strewn across the entirety of the camp, from landing field to motor pool, a space of more than a mile. The Watcher had taken the energy of our ships, used it to restore her power and her shape. The woman-thing I had encountered in the pantheon had been a shadow, the faintest ripple presaging the tidal wave that had crashed upon Sabratha.

I had read the Gnomon papers, the reports from Project Perseus's efforts on Nairi. Exposing the Watcher's energy pattern to an electromagnetic pulse of sufficient magnitude disrupted the energies that composed what passed for the creature's body. Its energies were variously scattered or reduced to some lower state, condensing into the dark, heavy baryonic substance that littered the world below.

It would have to be destroyed. All of it, and Phanamhara with it. Not a single scrap could remain to fall into the wrong hands.

And they were all of them the wrong hands.

Some spark of the beast, Miudanar, had remained in the bones on Eue. Might it not then be that some fragment of Ushara yet endured, deep within those new-made bones?

I laid my head against the cool pillar of bone at my back. How I yearned for cool water! For sleep! And yet I knew I could not, knew my labors were not yet done. Ribbons of gold flame scratched the sky, bleeding black smoke against the first light of day. Surely it would not be long before Hulle's fleet descended. Gaston and what remained of his garrison and of the HAPSIS defenders would have to pacify the remaining Cielcin.

They would all of them be killed.

There would be a great burning on the sands. Inhuman bodies piled like cordwood. Soaked with rocket fuel. Burned. Our own dead would be treated with greater deference. They would be burned in time, taken to Markov Station or Williamtown and cremated with the proper ceremony. A chanter would recite the litany and lanterns would be lit. The families of the local men would receive their ashes. The families of the offworlders would receive a letter and the two customary hurasams.

A lone figure had spotted me, was moving toward me from the edge of the camp.

It was one of the Cielcin. The creature looked surreal in the plain light of morning. Such creatures belonged to the night, to the deep night that lies below the ground, and the night deeper still that lies beyond the sky.

I did not have the strength left in me to stand, not even when four more of its kind emerged and followed after it. Seeing them come, I understood a thing I realized I had known since I saw my face reflected in Ushara's bones and turned to climb this hill.

I had come all this way to die.

I but waited—there, atop my dune—for the coming of the new sun.

I was sweating badly, had been sweating for a long time, and my breath came hard. Had I inhaled too much of the Vaiartu poison? Or was this something else? Some effect of my contest with the Watcher itself?

It did not matter.

I could not fight five Cielcin, not in my state.

I would die at the point of a sword.

But it was not to be.

The Cielcin at the head of the little group had only one horn.

Ramanthanu was several minutes climbing the hill, and finding me there slumped against the bones of the great whale, it knelt. *"Ba-Aeta-doh,"* it said, *"daratolo!"*

You live.

"So do you," I said.

"For the moment," the captain said. "Your people will kill us, if they can."

"They cannot tell you from your kin."

"I know," it said, and standing looked down upon the ruined camp and the bones of the thing it had worshipped until that night. "You killed it."

I shook my head. *"Veih.* It was not me."

"There were two of you," it said. "I saw. We all saw."

"I only... bought us time."

"Your people killed it," Ramanthanu said. "Your weapons."

"Yes," I said, whispering the word in my own language. There was no Cielcin word for yes, only a sharp exhalation. I made the sound, and said, "I think they did."

One of the other Cielcin raised its face to me. "Was he not a god?"

"No," I said. Privately, I was not so sure. When Ushara held me in the air, impressed herself upon me, I had felt her fury, her torment, her pain.

Ina sippirāti sha dāriātim annepish.

"I was made in the morning of the world," I said, translating—though it was a language I had never learned.

"Dein?" Ramanthanu was eying me, head to one side.

I had spoken in my own tongue, and looking up at the xenobite, said, *"Raka kasamnte."*

It's nothing.

Ushara had said she was *made.* Created. Designed. By the Quiet? It seemed so. And yet the Quiet and the Watchers had been at war since the uttermost beginning of time. Why would *he* have created them, if only to struggle against them for uncounted trillions of years? I could sense the answer in me, left there... by Ushara? By the Quiet himself? But I could not find it. I could remember knowing *more,* could remember being *her,* but they were memories clouded as by alcohol, and I could not call them up.

Only slowly did I understand that Ushara had for a time *possessed* me; just as Kharn Sagara had possessed the homunculus woman, Naia; just as Urbaine's worm had possessed the biologic circuitry of Valka's mind. Ushara was gone, had departed from me, but her fingerprints remained, pressed into the soft matter of my brain.

"That was not a god worth serving," I said to my Cielcin coterie.

Ramanthanu stood still as stone. After a while it raised its face to the morning sky, eyes narrowed to mere slits. Presently, it fumbled in a pouch at its waist and drew out a pair of what seemed to be jeweler's glasses. One by one, the captain socketed these to its eyes, slit nostrils flaring. "I have seen a god," it said. "How many of the People can say this?" It looked to its companions. "I have fought a god and lived."

One of the others shaded its eyes. "We should be dead."

"And yet we are not, Otomno!" said Ramanthanu. "The god would have killed us but for Utannash and his *Oranganyr*, his champion. Our prince!" Here Ramanthanu pointed at me. "You saw him drive the god from the sky! Saw him be in two places at once! It is a miracle! A miracle of Utannash!"

"*Koramsamte wo!*" said another of the five. "A miracle, you say? A lie! Have you forgotten what Utannash *is*, Ramanthanu? It is the un-god, the lord of lies! You are deceived!"

Ramanthanu snarled, rounding on its inferior. "This is no deception, Egazimn! This is victory! Marlowe is *aeta!*"

"This *yukajji* is no *aeta!*" said the one called Egazimn.

"He slew Ulurani! And Otiolo!" Ramanthanu said. "He is *aeta* by *ikur-ratimyr* and *anabitimyr!*"

Blood-right and might-right.

The one called Egazimn spit on the sand at my feet.

Ramanthanu seized Egazimn by the horns, pulling it down even as it raised a knee to crack Egazimn across the face. The lesser Cielcin stumbled, fell to its knees. The other three watched as Ramanthanu kicked its subordinate to the dust and lay one clawed foot upon the beaten Pale's cheek.

"You are *mine*, Egazimn," Ramanthanu said. "You think Muzugara's death has ended your bondage? You are *mine*, and you will obey. We belong to Marlowe, now. He is *ba-aeta*. Our lord. And if Utannash is the greater god, then he will be our god."

"Enough!" I said, not rising. "Enough fighting." I turned my face away, peered out across the desert. Flat and broad it was, and white almost as alabaster in the day's new sun.

Haltingly, Ramanthanu removed its foot from Egazimn's face.

How was I to keep them?

They believed me some great prince, some king of humanity—but I had no station, no power, no household or retinue. No armies. No command. The *Troglita* was destroyed. What little remained of HAPSIS in-system answered to A2, not to me. Of all the people on Sabratha, of all the people in the world, the only ones I might reasonably call *mine* were Cassandra and Neema. The Irchtani would obey me, acting out of a sense of religious obligation little different from Ramanthanu itself, but they were answerable to the Imperial hierarchy, to the Legions, to HAPSIS.

These five Cielcin had most like defected only to die. Their reward would be the White Sword. The gallows. The firing squad.

Seeing them, I was unable to quell the loathing and deep revulsion in me. These warred with the child I had been—the child I had thought long dead—and the hope of a better world.

Of better worlds.

I would try to save them, if I could.

Ramanthanu extended a hand to help me stand.

I took it, almost fell when I stood.

The captain steadied me, and I clenched my hands to stop them shaking.

It was the poison, I decided. It had to be. I felt so weak.

I stood there, swaying, trying not to fall. I looked out over the *Mare Silentii,* the Ocean of Silence, and felt the morning wind cool across my face.

"What's that, there?" I pointed.

There was something red out on the dunes.

"Dein?" Ramanthanu asked. *"Ti-saem gi ne?"*

"There!" I pointed again, held my arm in line.

"I do not see it."

"It's there!" I thrust my finger as though it were a sword.

Only belatedly did I remember that the Cielcin could not see red, and the gray of it would not stand out against the desert's white and dun.

But I saw it plain, a mile off or more.

I spared a glance for the sky. There was as yet no sign of the *Ascalon* or of Hulle's fleet descending. Not yet.

"Help me to it," I said.

This was not the day I would die, after all.

Necessity forced me to lean against Ramanthanu as we went, moving slowly toward the object lying on the dunes. It took us the better part of an hour, but we reached the spot where the thing lay, and I saw that it was precisely what I had expected...and feared.

The body lay below the swell of the vast, shallow dune on which I'd sat and waited for the end that had refused to come. There the sands ran smooth, flat almost as the horizon.

The body that lay there sprawled beneath a cloak of heavy scarlet samite, fringed in gold, his body clad in a suit of golden foil, his head englobed beneath a bubble of tinted glass.

It was Gaizka.

The sorcerer had escaped the ruin of Phanamhara, had wandered out onto the sands to die.

"He must have broadcast his thoughtform offworld," I said, though I was not certain the Cielcin understood.

"He is dead," said Otomno.

"The witches shed their bodies as the *jishiara* sheds its skin," said Ramanthanu. What a *jishiara* was I thought I could guess. "He is alive. He returned to *Rugubur.*"

"Rugubur?" I asked.

"Our ship," the captain replied. "It must have been the witch who ordered my people to flee."

I turned to look up at the Cielcin. "Flee? Back to Dorayaica?"

Ramanthanu's nostrils flared as it breathed that sharp breath by which its kind signaled the affirmative. I made Ramanthanu release my arm, and staggered toward the body. The captain's voice followed me. "The Elusha-Shiomu will know you have killed the god."

"Good," I said. "Let Dorayaica know it was me."

How quickly our defeat had turned to victory. Had I caught Gaizka in the tunnels and slain him as I had slain his slave, the Cielcin might have remained in orbit, and battled to the last. It was a battle Hulle and his paltry defense force might not have been able to win. We had won out by sheer chance, and slain the Watcher, too.

"He might still be alive," I said, and stumped toward the wizard's body. *Crack.*

I froze, felt the sensation of crushed glass coruscate from my heel. My blood—which mere moments before had warmed my heart with thoughts of Dorayaica in a cold fury, prowling the dark halls of the Dhar-Iagon—ran cold. As though I had tread onto the path of some serpent, I slowly raised my boot, stepped back to look at what I'd tread upon.

I already knew.

The fulgurite had broken into countless fragments, smashed to powder where my heel had struck. Dropping to one knee, I found the end of a piece still intact, and lifted it from the sand. It lay just beneath the surface, like the root of some young tree. I pulled it up, a curling piece of gnarled green glass. It curled *toward* Gaizka's body, had perhaps encircled it.

I dropped the fulgurite and stood, moved hurriedly to the dead man's side.

Crack. Crack.

Going to one knee, I turned the body over. Numb fingers felt Gaizka's neck, but the seal of his helmet stymied me. Hissing, I felt for the catch that would open his suit. The neck flange whined as pressure equalized, and a strange, orange gas vented from the broken seal. I drew back as it dissipated, though I caught the incense smell of cassia as I twisted the helmet free, recoiled at the sight of the sorcerer's face.

Gaizka's head was strangely bloated, hairless and obscene. In place of a nose, the Extrasolarian possessed a series of ridgelike slits that fell in chevrons over a pursed and lipless mouth. They looked like gills, and indeed they must have been. His ears were shrunken almost to nonexistence, and his flesh was a pallid orange stippled with white. He resembled nothing so much as some deep-sea creature swollen for want of pressure.

"He is not *yukajjimn*," said Ramanthanu.

"He was," I said, "but he sold the human part of himself long ago." As I spoke, I turned Gaizka's head, revealing the mechanism embedded in his skull above one vestigial ear. Its black metal drank the morning light, but blacker still were the burns that blistered the flesh about it. The skin of his face and neck had split, as lightning splits a tree, and blood dripped from it. "No..." The word escaped me in a thin moan. "No no no no no..."

"Dein raka ne?"

A simple transmission should not have so dissolved the magi's flesh, so burned skin and bone alike. It would have taken tremendous power to boost a signal through Sabratha's magnetosphere, but the device had nearly been destroyed, from the look of it. Glass wires had melted, fused to the cooked flesh, and the delicate mechanism seemed reduced to slag. More power had coursed through it than its makers had ever intended, of that much I felt sure. I looked to the strip of fulgurite I had cast aside and knew—though our boffins had yet to run the proper analyses—knew that more than Gaizka had escaped with Gaizka.

I felt a hideous smile creep across my face, and an absurd swell of glee blossomed in my heart. A wicked laugh escaped me, and it was a moment before I mastered myself, hunching over the body of the dead magus. Turning that laughter into a howl of impotent rage, I hammered on the corpse of the dead sorcerer, pummeled the armored chest until my wounded palm wept blood afresh.

I was free.

"No!" I shouted the word.

Not *me,* not Hadrian.

Ushara was free.

I was Hadrian. *Hadrian.* Not Ushara.

The part of her that remained in me was jubilant, and would have leapt into the air if it were any more than a memory.

Fingerprints.

Shaking fingers found my face, and abruptly I recalled the way in which Urbaine's worm had moved Valka's hands, how I had to stop her clawing out her eyes in the quiet of that medica on Edda, how she tried to strangle herself. It was the same.

As Urbaine had left his fingerprints on Valka, Ushara had made her mark on my mind.

With heavy hands, I smoothed my rictus grin away, and whispered a scholiast remonstrance against joy to master the unholy glee that had brought forth that wicked laugh. I was blessed that my only companions in that moment were Cielcin, and that Cielcin little understood our moods and feelings.

Ushara had escaped, had not died beneath Albé's bombardment.

Or a part of her had not.

The Watchers were pure energy, pure spirit—save when they put on matter like old clothes. But the word *spirit* means *breath,* and is not our every breath each a little copy of the other, each a little new creation, each divided from the last by the actions of lung and diaphragm? Ushara must have breathed into the fleeing *Gaizka, inspired* him, *possessed* him, transmitting but the smallest portion of herself, which—reaching its destination—would be free to grow again. The Watchers were a pattern of energy, a pattern whose whole might be regenerated from its smallest part. They died only when the whole of that pattern was wiped away, scattered by the inescapable light of a weapon like that Project Perseus had made.

"Perhaps his machine betrayed him," said Ramanthanu, misinterpreting the Extrasolarian's tormented flesh. "Perhaps he is truly dead."

"No," I said, certain my understanding was correct, for it came from her. "No, he reached your people." I hesitated. Ramanthanu's faith in me was predicated on its belief that I had killed its god. I dared not break that faith, not then, not there, when I was outnumbered and so desperately weak.

Very well. Utannash was *the Liar* in the ancient tongue of the Cielcin. I would lie.

"How do we signal your people?" the captain asked. "They must come for you."

"They will," I said, and standing, put my back to Gaizka's corpse. I had no comm, no flare gun, nothing to do but wait. "Give it time." Drawing my coat about my narrow frame, I took half a dozen steps from the body of the dead magus, fulgurites cracking beneath my feet. When the noise stopped, I sank to the pale sands to wait.

Dry and ceaseless thunder broke upon the upper airs perhaps half an hour later, and looking up I saw the friction fires of entry, and the black shapes of our ships falling like a hail of arrows. The Irchtani in the camp took wing and rose in a spiral cyclone to greet them. It was like watching the hungry crows clamoring above the slaughter on some blood-soaked field.

I shivered, despite the sun and the heat of the newborn day.

The men who found us fired on my Cielcin guard, and Ramanthanu's four remaining subordinates—Otomno and Egazimn, Bikashi and Atiamnu—survived only by the grace of their shields. It took all my faculties to keep them from responding in turn. Still, Egazimn kept its hand on its coiled

nahute, and the others clutched their swords. In time, I persuaded both
Hulle's men and my Cielcin to stand down, and we were escorted to where
the relief team had landed.

Men froze as we passed, and many made warding gestures, or simply
glared. Still more shouted questions, or jeered at my inhuman entourage.
I had no time for them, moved in a kind of dream. The memory of that
awful laughter sounded terrible in my ears, and I felt myself chivvied along,
like a leaf tossed upon the surface of some rushing stream.

We had failed, and yet everyone was cheering. Men clambered atop the
wreck of shuttles or upon stacked crates, raised their guns and thumped
one another on the back. The Irchtani still circled in the air, crying aloud
in victory.

They did not know...they could not know that we had failed.

Commandant Vimal Gaston, haggard but very much alive, met us at
the edge of the camp. His paracoita—the short-haired, slim-figured girl
who had brought the man his armor the night before—hurried in his
wake, the black tape of a medical corrective applied to a wound on the
left side of her brow.

"They said you had the Pale in tow," he said, looking at Ramanthanu
and its compatriots. "...I did not believe."

"These saved me in the night," I said. "They are defectors."

"Defectors?" Gaston frowned, surveying my unlikely companions. "Is
that...possible?"

I looked to Ramanthanu myself. "I don't rightly know. But they are
not your problem, Commandant. You must annihilate this site. The whole
thing. Clear all your people out, and see that none of them have taken
anything from here. No trophies, no spoils, nothing. Not even a splinter
of that black rock. Do you understand?"

"What was that thing?" Gaston asked, looking to the nearest shard of
Ushara's bones.

"Once everyone is clear, annihilate the site. AM bombs. Destroy everything."

"Everything?" It was one of the diggers. "The ruins?"

"Everything!" I said. "It would be better to evacuate the planet, entire."

Gaston looked utterly lost. "Evacuate? We are victorious!"

"We have triumphed *here,*" I said, "and for today. But this is not over."

The commandant shook his leonine head, and I was struck—not for
the first time—by how much he recalled so many officers I had known.
Titus Hauptmann and William Crossflane, even old Lord Karol Venantian.
One might be forgiven for thinking the Empire kept a mold in some far-
flung corner of the realm, and pressed such men from it on occasion. "I
don't understand any of this, lord. I saw a...was it a ship? A beast? I

saw the thing with the eyes in the sky, and everything lifted toward it. Is that what's been killing our people? And some of my men say they saw a giant! A woman, they say, fifty feet high! I'd have them whipped for liars if there weren't so many."

"They're not liars," I said.

Gaston swore. "Impossible! Nothing that big can exist! What the hell is going on, Marlowe?"

I stared at him. Gone was the affable country officer, the man who had kept posters of the Hero of Aptucca on his walls as a little boy. He had met his hero, and that hero was keeping secrets from him. In the end, Gaston folded in the face of my silence and staring eyes. Seeing him cede ground, I pressed. "Do as I say, Gaston. Prepare the site for annihilation."

"Those orders should come from the governor-general," he said.

"They *will*," I said in response, stepping well inside the reach of the other man's arms. Gaston was perhaps two inches shorter than I was, and patrician. He bowed his head reflexively. "I will sail for Williamtown at once and speak to Lord Genseric. Under no circumstances are any of your people to take *anything* from this site. Am I clear?"

"But why?" Gaston puffed out his chest. "If you would but explain—"

"These are Imperial matters, Commandant," I said, advancing until I stood within inches of the man. "Who do you think I serve? Who do you think I report to?"

Gaston blinked, retreated half a step. "I . . . why, the Emperor, my lord."

"It is the Emperor I owe an explanation to, Gaston. Not you." I brushed past him, limping on my injured knee. I needed medical attention, needed to wash, to rest, to eat.

I needed water most of all, needed not to bandy words with Vimal Gaston.

Ushara had escaped, and only I knew it.

Something solid collided with me before I'd made it five steps past the addled commandant. I felt arms about me, and it was only slowly that I realized I was being embraced. I recognized the top of the head pressed against my shoulder, the tightly wound twin braids.

"*Altapho arram mita,*" she said.

I thought you were dead.

Matching her Jaddian, I said, "*Abdain, Anaryan.* Never."

One fist hammered my back, and I groaned, breath stopped short.

"Don't ever send me away again," she said. "I could have helped you."

"*Non tora,*" I said. "Not now."

"Not now?" She drew herself to arm's length, gripped me by the arms, glared up at me with those great, bright eyes. "Not now! Abba!"

Still in Jaddian, I said, "The Watcher escaped."

Cassandra's face—pale already as my own—went white as Ramanthanu's. "What?"

"It escaped," I said again. "It used that Extrasolarian's transmitter to break free of the planet's magnetic field. The Cielcin got what they came for."

She looked round. "Edouard said we won. The bombs!"

It was not the time or place for this conversation, surrounded by the men. Better to let them have their victory, better to let them guess at what it was they'd seen in the sky that night. If I had my way, the Empire would evacuate Sabratha entire.

"Where is Edouard?" I asked, switching to Imperial standard, taking her by the arm and making her walk beside me.

"On the ship," she answered, following my change of language. "We only just landed; I came as fast as I could. You wouldn't answer your comm."

I raised my left wrist in demonstration. "It's dead."

"Abba, are you all right?" Cassandra stopped to look up at me, an expression like horror in her eyes. "You're shaking."

I shook her off. "I'll be all right," I said, and tried to walk forward, realized after several unsteady paces that I had no notion where the *Ascalon* was moored. "Where?" My vision swam, and it seemed almost that Ushara had returned, for two Cassandras twisted across one another in my field of view.

But I was only delirious.

I felt my daughter's hands upon my shoulders, felt her try to steady me. She was shouting for help.

"I think," I tried to speak, but my mouth was dry as the desert. "I think...I need...to rest."

Then the sands of the desert rose to swallow me.

The last thing I remember—before the darkness took me—were Cassandra's eyes as she fell to her knees beside me.

They were green as emeralds.

CHAPTER 29

THE JOURNEY HOME

I SPENT THE NEXT week abed in the Lord Hood Grand Medica in Williamtown. It transpired that I had been exposed to elevated levels of the arsine gas, and it took time to reverse the damage and clean the poison from my body. Though she had been exposed herself, Cassandra had fared a good deal better, and the same doctors only administered a course of oral medicaments that bound the poison in her blood and banished it from her system. She sat with me through it all, and Neema, too.

On the second day, a Chantry prior came to shrive me, to offer the forgiveness of Mother Earth. He would not leave when I refused him, not even when I shouted. He remained until Neema and Cassandra escorted him from the room. He was not a bad man, I think—he seemed more confused by my behavior than anything.

The governor-general himself appeared on the fifth day, responding at last to my summons. It was a ghost that came into the recovery suite, bracketed by soldiers in ivory plate. The Genseric Hulle I'd known had been a bland, unremarkable bureaucrat—provincial and untested.

The creature that seated itself at my bedside might well have been a walking shadow. Much of Williamtown had been destroyed. I had seen the wreck of siege towers when I'd been brought from the starport to the Grand Medica, the burned-out remains of once-proud colonial buildings. Fire teams and the urban prefects had been scrambling to maintain order, and the word was that many thousand Sabrathans had been carried off to *Rugubur*.

Meat. Slaves. Meat. Slaves. Sport.

When I told Hulle my belief that the whole of Phanamhara should be annihilated, his face grew dark.

He assented, though he had not seen what I had seen, saying that the site had brought nothing but horror to his little world. I prayed he would not suffer for his conviction, and promised to take full responsibility for his actions when I made my report to the Emperor. I would recommend Sabratha be abandoned, I told him, and he did weep then, for the desert world had been his home—and more than that, his *project*—for more than a hundred count of years.

I cannot say for certain if the place stands empty now, if the ruined streets of Williamtown are void of life, save for the *tataxi* and the invasive cats and rats that are man's constant companions.

A second Phanamhara.

Word of Sabratha is scarce in the wider universe, and not without reason.

It was nowhere, and nothing to the Imperial universe.

A dot on the edge of the map.

None shall ever guess at its importance, save you, dear Reader. You, who know.

It was at Sabratha that the fate of mankind—and of the Cielcin, of the Cielcin most of all—was sealed. Ushara had sealed it, though I did not then know or understand that it was sealed, or how it would be decided.

When I left Sabratha—three weeks after the battle at Phanamhara—it was never to return, nor did any word follow me back across the wide Dark of space of whatever passed there.

The *Ascalon* was fast, but she could never carry all the massed survivors of Operation Gnomon, and so Lord Genseric Hulle commended one of the bulk cruisers of his Defense Force into my service. The *ISV Gadelica* was a broad, square-nosed troop carrier with a rear castle like a stepped pyramid, composed entirely of the black-clad adamant typical of most vessels of Imperial manufacture. Into her vast holds were loaded all our surviving personnel, and a berth was found for the *Ascalon* herself, tidied away in the great hold that ran along the belly of the ship.

Of the eight thousand, two hundred men that had sailed from Jadd to Sabratha aboard the *Troglita,* only three and a half thousands returned. Nearly three thousand had died aboard the *Troglita* in the battle above the planet, or else had died in an abortive boarding effort, trying to land on the worldship *Rugubur*. The remaining dead had lost their lives fighting on the surface.

The Irchtani had fared somewhat better. Of the chiliad that had sailed with us, eight hundred remained. All of these were loaded aboard the *Gadelica* and interred for the long journey ahead, and at my urging, special pods were found capable of fitting and freezing Ramanthanu and its four companions. Egazimn and Atiamnu both resisted the notion of fugue, and Ramanthanu had to beat them into submission while the others watched. The pods used were of the sort built to transport livestock, and the Cielcin were made to lie down in them, curled like infants as the pods were filled.

"This will not kill us?" the captain had asked me.

"I transported one of your kind thus," I told it. "Long ago."

I needed to see the Emperor, but the Emperor was in hiding—so Prince Aldia had said—and I'd no way of communicating directly with His Radiance. The telegraph that had one half of the entangled pair that had allowed Oberlin to communicate with Caesar in his hidden fortress had been lost with the *Troglita,* and I could not risk sharing information about Gnomon via more public government channels. I would attempt to contact the Emperor during our stop off in Tiryns system, but had arranged for a short, cryptic message to be relayed by official channels before we departed the governor-general's palace in Williamtown.

> *To His Imperial Radiance, William XXIII of the House Avent, Firstborn Son of the Earth, Guardian of the Solar System, etc...*
>   *I received and begged your pardon.*
>   *My mission was incomplete.*
>   *I sail for Forum at once.*

I sent the missive myself, marked with the governor-general's security seal and the highest urgency. It would reach the Emperor, who would know it came from me. *I received and begged your pardon*—the order reversed, effect following cause.

There was much I might have put into a letter. Word of Oberlin's death, of Gnomon's failure, of the destruction of the vayadan-general Muzugara and of Ushara's escape. But I could not speak of those things, not without allowing for the possibility that the letter would be read by eyes other than those of Caesar.

I was sailing for Forum, where it is said the wind blows in all directions at once.

Forum, where there is no solid ground.

"I do wish Captain Ghoshal had engaged me for assistance with this last meal," Neema was saying, following in my wake. "I could do a good deal better than that fool chef of his."

Not breaking stride, I rounded the final bend in the hall that would take us to the overlook gallery and the access umbilical, saying, "You're not the one eating it, Neema."

The Nemrut School serving man tutted officiously, "It is unbecoming, *domi.* A man of station should eat like one."

"You fuss like an old woman, you know that?" I said, keying the door. It rolled aside into a pocket in the wall. Beyond lay the cramped overlook gallery, a receiving room with slanting windows running along the left side, looking down on the ventral hold.

The *Ascalon* herself nestled clamped in her berth just beyond the windows, close against the glass. So close, her scratched and pitted enamel could be scrutinized. Two years sitting in the desert had left its mark. Grime streaked the gently curving dorsal hull, and the red pentangle painted on her tailfin was all but scoured away.

"Where's Cassandra?" I asked.

"I don't rightly know, *domi,*" came Neema's reply. "The captain expects us in the officers' dining room in twenty minutes."

"He'll wait," I said.

It felt wrong to be attending dinners, to be moving about the ship on ordinary business. It felt wrong that the world had not stopped on Sabratha, that all had not been suspended in pursuit of Ushara.

"Cassandra should join us," I said at last, studying my ship through the glass and my ghostly reflection in it.

"She wasn't invited," the serving man replied.

"You haven't seen her?"

"No, *domi,*" Neema replied. "She was out and about. Wanted to see more of the ship, I think, before tomorrow's freeze. Young Albé will be in attendance, I think."

Nine days at warp already. The thought floated over the gray matter of my mind. *Twenty years to go.* The *Gadelica* was not fast, not nearly so fast as the *Troglita.* Ghoshal had told me she maxed out around 700C. 700C, and twenty years to Tiryns.

Ignoring Neema's mention of Edouard, I said, "I should have gone ahead on the *Ascalon.* We might have gotten there sooner."

"I thought you said you didn't want to lose sight of the others," came Neema's reply. "You didn't want the men talking or getting disappeared by the state apparatus."

Those were nearly my precise words, and to hear myself parroted back to me with such precision might have discomforted me, had I not spent half an eternity with Valka by my side.

"Quite right," I said. "I just wish there were something more I could do."

"You are sure this ... Watcher creature escaped?"

The face reflected in the polished window dared a rictus grin, and I smoothed it away with an effort and a muttered phrase.

"Quite sure," I told him.

"Well, if it is so, *domi,* surely we have time," Neema said, adjusting one of his silk cuffs. "The Cielcin must travel, too. Perhaps they must travel farther than us."

He was right, and I admitted as much, laid one hand on his shoulder before turning to key the airlock. The metal grating that ran along the floor of the umbilical rattled as we went, and the *Ascalon*'s doors hissed as we passed through the forward airlock by the bridge. As before, I had declined rooms aboard the greater vessel, preferring to keep my old room aboard the *Ascalon*. I had just returned from a meeting with one of the junior medical officers, who had informed me that both the Irchtani and Cielcin were sleeping comfortably—vital signs normal. There was some concern, he told me, about the blood supply.

The blood of sleepers is, as a rule, mixed with certain pharmacons and frozen, stored—like the sleepers themselves—at something approaching absolute zero. The blood may be retained almost indefinitely, requiring only that it be separated from the cocktail of preservative chemicals that prevent hemolysis in long-term storage. A simple centrifuge suffices to separate the blood from its protective pharmacons, and the proportion of blood lost per freezing is reduced to something less than one part per thousand.

Additionally, synthetic blood substitutes are often kept in reserve should the immediate blood supply run short. On no fewer than three occasions was I awakened with such false blood. It takes the body months to recover in such circumstances. Even a palatine needs several weeks to replace the imitation blood with his own, and the effects of false blood are fatigue and muscle weakness.

In the case of human passengers, great ships like the *Gadelica* always carried more than was strictly necessary—even the *Ascalon* retained a few spare gallons in near-perfect cold. But we had only small reserves of Irchtani and Cielcin blood—donated by the living xenobites in the lead-up to our departure from Sabratha.

It would have to be sufficient, and I'd told the medical officer as much.

Banishing thoughts of blood from my head, I descended the stairs from the level of the bridge to my cabin.

Clack. Clack!

I froze on the landing, peering into the sconce-lit hall where once I had battled Alexander's assassin, listening.

Clack! Clack-clack!

A cry sounded from below.

Silence.

Clack!

I shook Neema off and descended, turning through the open doors of the little ship's main hold.

"Hard at work?" I asked.

Cassandra stepped away from the training mannequin as if it were a lover, and I'd caught them both in states of undress. The girl had abandoned her *mandyas* and her Jaddian tunic and trousers, wore only a pair of close-fitting pants that terminated just above the knee and a loose shirt that hung scarecrow-like on her thin frame.

"I just..." She seemed almost embarrassed. "I wasn't much good on Sabratha, was I?"

"Anaryan..."

She raised the training sword she held as if it were some stolen treasure. "I need to train more. To be stronger. To..."

I'd crossed the little space between us and taken her in my arms. One hand on the back of her head, holding her ear to mine, I said, "There was nothing more you could have done."

"How can you stand it?" Her words were wind over my shoulder.

"I can't," I said. "Why do you think I was on Jadd?"

She was silent then a long while, one arm crooked about the back of my neck. I felt her shake, silent tears falling. Captain Ghoshal's dinner no longer seemed important. Not to me.

"I should not have brought you," I said at last. "I should have let you stay on Jadd."

Her arm tightened, and I felt her shake her head. "Don't."

A single word to encompass volumes.

"I left my work undone," I told her then. "I've wasted the last two hundred years."

"Don't talk that way, Abba."

"If I had not come to Jadd..." I said, "this might be done already."

"If you had not come to Jadd, I would not exist, Abba," Cassandra said, pulling away from me, her empty hand on my shoulder.

I lay a hand upon her face. "I did not mean..."

"I know," she said, and smiled, eyes wet now with tears. She wiped them away. "I didn't want you to find me here. I thought you'd gone to meet with the medical officer."

I turned, found Neema standing just inside the door to the hold, doing his best to appear a part of the furniture. "I have dinner with Captain Ghoshal in half an hour."

"In fifteen minutes, *domi*," Neema interjected, ever the lord of time.

"In fifteen minutes," I said. We both smiled, shared a private laugh at poor Neema's expense. The Nemrutti manservant had come through the battle better than all of us. He had escaped the Cielcin entire, escaped Ushara and all but the distant noise of violence. "May some things never change, eh?" I tapped my daughter under the chin.

We drew apart.

"You don't need to hide," I told her, "or be ashamed of anything. You survived, dear girl. That is what matters." I seized the hand still on my shoulder. "Will you come to dinner?"

Neema interjected again. "Domi, there is little time!"

"I know, Neema!" I said. "Ghoshal will wait."

But Cassandra shook her head. "I'd rather stay here."

Nodding, I let her go, and turning made to join Neema at the door.

"You sent me away!" The words struck me like a plasma bolt between the shoulder blades.

I did not turn.

"You didn't even say farewell!"

"I said farewell in the camp."

"I thought you were on the ship, Abba!" I heard her feet on the deck behind me. "You could have died!"

I turned, a whirling of Imperial blacks. "And *you* could have died, Cassandra!" She retreated half a step. "And it is better that I should die than you."

"Not to me!" she said lamely.

"Anaryan..." I tucked my chin, tried to conjure the proper words for myself. "I am sorry. But you know now what it is we fight, and why. You saw the Cielcin, and their god. I would spare you that battle, if I can."

"But you can't!"

"*If* I can," I said again, more strongly. "Girl, I want you to live in the world that follows *after* all this. A better world." I half turned away. "I do not want any of this for you."

Cassandra retook that step toward me, saying, "That is not for you to decide, Abba."

"But it is!" I said, and tried to smile. She made it easier. "We cannot decide the world *we* live in ourselves, but we can change the world for those who follow after."

"I am not following after, Abba. I'm here now."

Then I am a ghost before my time, I thought, my smile frozen. "Your mother and I had this same argument, you know? She was always furious with me... rushing into battle... leaving her behind."

"But you let her fight with you!" Cassandra said.

"Yes." At once I found I could no longer look at her. "And she died."

Cassandra seemed to fold in on herself.

Unsettled by the silence and the cloud that had settled over us both, I pressed on. "She should still be here, you know? She should have met you, grown old on Jadd. I should have protected her better." I reflected on how unnatural it was that my child had never once seen her mother, not even at her birth. It was... *wrong.*

"How did it happen?" Cassandra looked sharply up at me. She had asked before, and always I had eluded her, said only that she died in the fighting.

I held her gaze then a long time, knowing I must say something.

I spoke at last. "Her ship was shot down. We were separated in the battle. She had to evacuate on a different transport. We were on comms when she died..." I shut my eyes, saw only that patch of darkness, that window onto night.

Never, never, never...

"I shouldn't have outlived her," I said finally, not daring to move. "I should be dead a hundred times." The shame I had felt on Sabratha—when I had survived my battle with Ushara—returned, and I averted my gaze. "It's embarrassing, in a way. I fought so long to keep her safe, but she's gone...and I'm still here."

Cassandra's lips compressed to a thin line, almost invisible. "You're always saying I should let go of the things I can't control," she said. "Grief is deep water."

A rough laugh burst from me, and I half turned again away. "I'm a very bad stoic, daughter." I passed a hand over my eyes. I still felt weak from my experience on Sabratha.

"Is it true you died?" The question slashed across the moment, dividing time present from time past.

I looked sharply up at her—too sharply to deny it.

I nodded. It was time she knew.

"They said you lost your head," she said, speaking as one who could hardly believe the words escaping her lips.

I spared a glance for Neema, who still stood in the doorway.

Slowly, I nodded.

Cassandra did not move. For a moment I thought she'd turn away, or laugh, or berate me for a fool. But she had seen Ushara, had seen me work miracles that black night in the desert. Slowly—very slowly—she nodded instead.

It was her turn then not to speak, and yet I could not either.

My mouth was dry...I had tried all her life not to tell her, and now she knew the rest of it. What profit was there in silence?

"I..." Again I looked to Neema, wishing he were Gibson, were Valka, were Pallino, were anyone better suited to help me in that moment. "I...it was Aranata Otiolo. A Cielcin prince. I was very young. Younger than you."

"He killed you?"

"*It*," I said, surprised at the venom in the word. "*It* killed me. The Quiet sent me back."

"The Quiet?" Cassandra echoed. "What's that, then?"

We had come to it at last. *The* conversation, the only one that mattered. The Truth.

"The Quiet is..." What? A people? An intelligence? A god? Ushara's memories flared in me. The memory of falling, of being cast down into this universe all unwilling, thrown by the hand of him who made us. *Made them.* "...Shūturum."

Cassandra stared at me, and it was a moment before I realized what I'd said, and I translated, "Absolute." When that did not seem to answer the girl's question, I tried again. "The Quiet is an...entity. A person. Like the Watchers, maybe, but *more.* He...wants to help us against the Cielcin, against the Watchers."

"Why does he need you?" she asked.

"Because..." How could I compress the titanic visions I had seen into a simple answer? "Because I have a part to play. The right man—in the right place, at the right time—can tip the balance. I have a part to play ending all this. Stopping the Cielcin. The Watchers." I smiled, an immense relief washing over me. I had spent decades in fear of this discussion, and it had come at last—and Cassandra had not fled. "There is so much to tell you, *mia qal.*"

"Then tell me!" she said, and I saw the Tavrosi iron in her, and might have wept.

"Master Marlowe," Neema took a mincing step nearer me, slippered feet rasping on the metal floor. "The captain is waiting."

"Damn the captain, Neema!" I raised a hand to quiet him.

Unruffled, my servant said, "Perhaps...you might resume this line of inquiry after dinner."

I looked round, gaze torn between the man and my daughter, feeling that pressure of time that haunts us all more sharply as time passes. My obligation to the captain, to my daughter.

My sense of my own great age.

"Perhaps..." I said, echoing the manservant and agreeing with him. "Perhaps we should talk later. There is much you...should know. I think the time has come to tell you everything."

"I'd like that," Cassandra said, "...and Abba!" She took a sharp step forward, fixed me with those emerald eyes.

"Yes, Anaryan?"

"Don't send me away again," she said, making of the words a command. "I'm ready. I'll *be* ready."

Perhaps she will be at that... I thought, holding her gaze, seeing the Swordmaster of Jadd—for just a moment. And yet she was my daughter. The future...and the last vestige of my past.

"I would spare you all of this," I said, throwing up my hands to encompass the whole of the ship.

"But you haven't!" She countered, "You can't!"

"I'll try," I said, and when her face fell, I added, "But I won't send you away again."

She brightened almost at once, and ran to embrace me, dropping the training sword on the deck. I gathered her to myself, heedless of Neema's presence, of the captain, of Ushara, of Dorayaica itself.

Of everything I had ever known—found or claimed or made—she was the only thing I'd made for myself. Not for the Imperium, nor for the Emperor. Not for the Red Company that was no more. Not even for Valka—not really—nor for her memory.

Cassandra was the only thing that mattered anymore.

She was *all*.

And still I did not know I lied to her in that moment, though the shadow of the future stretched over us, cast by the light that was to come.

Yet it was a lie, even still.

How often do we speak deceit without our knowledge of it!

How often do we fail to act out the Truth!

CHAPTER 30

THE ETERNAL CITY

AUREATE LIGHT SHONE THROUGH the forward windows as we descended, *Ascalon* rattling beneath us as we skimmed the upper airs of Forum, passing through domains of screaming wind a hundred miles high to that place where the air ran clear. After days queuing in the starlanes above the rosy gas giant awaiting permission to descend, we had left the *Gadelica* in orbit at last, and cleared quarantine procedures put in place to protect the capital from *the Rot*.

Gilt fliers emerged from banks of cloud vast as moons to accompany us on our approach. Seated in one of the foldouts behind me, I could hear Cassandra gasp, for there it was, shimmering like a palace of dream upon the gleaming line of the horizon, vast as any of the greatest vessels built by human hands.

The Eternal City.

Her towers, not topless as the spires of mythic Ilium, but fathomless as the sea, stretched like pillars of ivory and marble from cloud to cloud, the greatest a thousand stories high, with balconies and tall windows, connected one to the next by tramways and viaducts and slim, graceful bridges. Whole islands sat on massive plates buoyed by repulsors, their surfaces thick with castellated buildings and dotted with hanging gardens rich with green. Above it all, the saucer of the Campus Raphael floated, where the Sun King's Hall stood, and the houses of government, the many-columned halls and white-domed towers that housed the vast and incomprehensible machinery of Empire.

It was an Olympos made real.

"*ISV Ascalon, this is Martian Knight-Commander Canton Kas. I have orders to escort you to Porta Leonora, Landing Pad Alpha One-Seven. Repeat. Landing Pad Alpha One-Seven.*"

"One-Seven, Commander Kas," said Edouard Albé in the pilot's seat. "Understood. We'll follow your escort."

The Martian flier to our left accelerated, bringing us in under the shadow of the outmost branches of the Eternal City. Here great spires descended, stalactites of white cladding and steel a hundred stories deep. We followed our escort slowly among their branches, and saw fliers and shuttlecraft wending in among them.

Cassandra unbelted herself and came to stand behind me. "It's incredible!" she said. "I thought Jadd was beautiful, but the Alcaz du Badr is small compared to this!"

She was not wrong, for all Jadd's grandeur and all its great beauty, it was a little nation. The Eternal City was power itself, a statement to the vast achievements of the human intellect and of Sollan Imperial *will*. Nothing so vast should fly—and yet it did.

The Porta Leonora lay low upon the margins of the Eternal City, one of the city's seven starports, and the farthest from the Campus Raphael and the houses of government.

"They want us brought in with as little fanfare as possible," I said, unbolting from the navigator's seat as Edouard brought the ship in above the pad—a vast metal plate rimmed only by a narrow rail. Rosy clouds blew across the pad, at this altitude mostly water vapor. In the distance, the great mass of the sail wall could be seen, far beyond the farthest towers of the city itself. "See that?" I asked Cassandra, pointing. "It's a windbreak. That keeps the Coriolis winds from tearing the city apart and blowing us off the platforms.

"They've rolled out quite the welcome," said Edouard. "Who do you think's in the chair?"

I followed his gaze to the receiving stage at the far end of the landing platform. Men in the white-and-red jumpsuits of the port authority hurried toward us as the *Ascalon* settled onto the pad.

I watched two men drag a fuel line from a coil at one side, while still more hurried about. Beyond them, on the stage, waited a full century of the Martian Guard in scarlet plate, the red planet—white capped—with its twin moons emblazoned on their breastplates. I marked their commander by his red plume. Behind them, arrayed on the stage itself, stood an assemblage of honorable persons: logothetes in uniform gray. A pair of scholiasts in green. I spied none of the Chantry in their black robes and tall, Egyptian miters. All gathered before a shielded palanquin hung with curtains of argent samite, vermillion, and cloth of gold.

"Those are Aventine House androgyns gathered about," I said, indicating the knot of red-uniformed servants near at hand, identical under their white perruques. "It's one of the family."

"Not His Radiance, surely?" Edouard looked up at me. An adorator young Albé surely was, but the stamp of Imperial divinity was a thing difficult to deny to its face. I felt Cassandra stiffen in her chair. She had been reared on stories of Caesar, had grown hearing how her father had struck the face of that living god and survived.

She was right to fear, as I feared, but said, "Caesar is with the fleet, last I heard."

"He might have returned," Albé countered, smoothing his Delian-oiled hair. *"Mère de Dieu…"*

"It's not His Radiance. The train's too small. There's no *flabella*," I said, referring to the feathered staves carried before the Emperor's gestatory throne, "and I don't see Lord Nicephorus."

"Who's that?" Cassandra asked, standing herself.

"The Lord Chamberlain?" Edouard inquired.

"The Emperor's shadow," I said, and smiling at Cassandra, added, *sotto voce,* "His Neema." Nicephorus was far more than that. Chief of the palace androgyns who served the Blood Imperial, it was William's closest confidant—possibly the Emperor's only real friend.

Cassandra made a soft *oh* with her lips.

"Open the ramp," I said, clapping Edouard on the shoulder. "Let's go and make our proper prostrations, shall we?"

Despite my easy air, I felt fear move in me—a leviathan of unknown mass and charge roiling just beneath my surface. The Emperor had ever been my only true ally at court, my patron and protector. The mission he had set me on, conjuring me from my Jaddian exile, had been one of the utmost secrecy, which meant that whoever it was come to meet me, they almost certainly had no understanding of how or why Lord Hadrian Marlowe—notorious fugitive, apparent traitor, and would-be regicide—had come to Forum.

The ramp had lowered entirely by the time I reached the hold, and the cool breeze and omnipresent cloud-fog of Forum drifted across the opening. No sooner had my bootheels rung upon the top of the ramp than a clarion rang, and the voice of some herald cried out.

"The Lord Hadrian Anaxander Marlowe!"

All my titles had been stripped away. Gone was the *Supreme Commandant,* gone the *Knight-Commander.* The Order of Merit had been plucked away, and the Grass Crown knocked from my head. Even the *Victorian* had been slashed from my name, though whether that reflected any official change to my house or heraldry or only some petty slight I could not guess.

I had donned the blacks of an Imperial officer, the long, belted coat with its high collar and wide sleeves. Red aiguilettes, gold tipped, hung from my right shoulder. Neema and young Albé followed just behind Cassandra and myself. Neema had repaired her red-and-golden *mandyas* with care, and the garment hung loose on her left shoulder, the flowing sleeve empty, her arm cradled in the garment like a sling, just as Olorin so often did. Beneath it she wore Marlowe black, though with her braided hair black as ink, there could be no denying the kinship between us.

I had brought only the smallest complement of guards. Annaz followed, with Inamax and ten of their Irchtani warriors. Their clawed feet rattled on the ramp as I descended, and drank in the rarefied airs of Forum.

At the sound of that silver trumpet, the Martians moved as one to attention, and their centurion—a hulking man with a sephiroth of phalerae fixed upon his breastplate—bellowed for his men to present salute. They did, all right and formal.

I stopped short, Cassandra a step behind and to my right.

No one stirred in the palanquin.

A whistle sounded from the speakers in the centurion's armor, and the Martians broke rank, forming an aisle between them.

Another Martian, this one in gilt plate with a full cape of scarlet, with no helmet on his bronze, scarred face, strode along the channel. He stopped five paces from me, shock evident on his blunt, ugly face. From his harness, I took him for a commander, and guessed that here was Knight-Commander Kas, the man who had directed us to land.

"Per Mars ipsham!" he said, speaking the vulgar Martian tongue in his shock. "It is really you."

"Commander," I said, eager to set the tone, and saluted. "I've come a long way on a matter of the utmost urgency. It is imperative that I—"

"Hadrian Marlowe!" The knight-commander drew and kindled a high-matter sword, thrust its point squarely at my chest. "In the name of Mars, God of War! In the name of William of the House Avent, who is the God Emperor come again! You are under arrest!"

"Arrest!" Neema stammered, stepping forward. "Arrest? For what crime?"

"For assaulting the Imperial person," Knight-Commander Kas intoned. "For treason against the Imperium. For fleeing Imperial justice!"

"Now listen here, you villain!" Neema stepped forward, fumbling in his jacket. "My master has a letter of Imperial pardon issued by *your* Imperial master." He produced the letter in question, brandished it like a sword. "Cleared of all charges, it says! Under your Emperor's own seal!"

Knight-Commander Kas snatched the document from Neema's fist, eyes tracking each line in turn. He stiffened, and turning gestured for the centurion. The lesser Martian approached, and Kas proffered him the letter. "Show her."

My ears pricked at the words, and I looked sharply at the commander and his centurion, at the rank and file, and the androgyns in their white perruques. *Her.*

I could guess the identity of the person in the covered palanquin, who it was that had come to arrest me the moment I arrived, and why she had come with so small a retinue.

The Empress Maria Agrippina had ever been my enemy, believing I had struck her august husband, after all, and so proved myself the ill-bred villain she had always thought I was. She had come for me, with the Emperor hidden offworld. Had ordered me land in so private a place—on the very fringes of the Eternal City, and far below—that I might vanish in that cloud-bound labyrinth, never to be seen again.

The centurion reached the palanquin, handed the letter to an androgyn who passed it within.

"Who's in there, Abba?" Cassandra asked, whispering in Jaddian.

I made a discreet gesture for her to be quiet, hand at my side.

The androgyn who had handled the letter advanced a step, and spoke in a clear castrato, saying, *"My mission was incomplete,"* it said. "Those were your words—if indeed the message came from you. What was your mission?"

"They were indeed my words!" I said, standing free, leaving Cassandra, Neema, and Edouard behind, so that I stood almost level with the knight-commander and centurion. "But my mission, my business, is a matter between me and His Imperial Radiance. I will speak to Caesar, and Caesar alone."

The androgyn paused a moment, listening to the words of its mistress before shouting, "Caesar is not here! He is at the front!"

"I know that!" I replied, and had known—though a part of me had hoped he had returned in the years since I'd departed from Jadd. "I had no means of contacting him directly, and what I have to say can be entrusted to no other."

"You might have gone elsewhere!" the androgyn replied after the requisite response lag—almost it was like speaking with someone in deep orbit. "Why come to Forum?"

"Because I have nothing to hide!" I said, "Which is more than can be said of you, Radiant Majesty. Why the secrecy?"

"Because you wear your infamy like a crown, my lord!" came a richly feminine voice from within the covered palanquin. "I see the centuries have not dampened your cheek!"

A sandaled foot emerged from one side of the palanquin, and the androgyn nearest hurried to assist the woman seated within. One ringed hand emerged, and the servant took it, folding back the cover to permit the woman an easy exit. She turned to look down at me, her other hand touching the confection of fine gold that restrained her voluminous red hair.

Behind me, I heard Cassandra's indrawn breath, and shared it.

The women of the Aventine House are—it is said—the loveliest in the human universe. Maria Agrippina herself was beautiful as any of the houris of princely harems in Jadd, as the eugenic marvels of Vorgossos, as Ushara herself. The woman who rose from the palanquin wore a gown of luminous white, with dagged sleeves whose interiors glowed red as her hair. Gold embroidery glittered at her cuffs, decorated her bust and the front of her gown. A slim gold circlet—without gem or device—gleamed upon her snowy brow, and her eyes were like chips of malachite polished smooth by the actions of some celestial river.

She smiled at me, and I must have been an amusing sight.

The woman standing on the receiving stage was beautiful as any I had seen in the Empire or on Jadd: tall and regal as any queen, lovely as Galatea wrought by Pygmalion's hand...lovely as the Empress herself, as so like her then as to be almost identical—for she was a scion of that same royal, red-leafed tree.

But she was not the Empress.

"The look on your face!" she said, smiling like the sun. "I'd have gone to the trouble of arranging this little meeting for no other reason, but Aurelian and I thought it better that I meet you here before the others caught wind of your arrival."

"Selene?" I cocked my head, staring up at her, bewildered.

Time had polished the girl into a woman complete. Where before the princess had seemed unsure and unassured of herself, she stood there now with the calm composure only centuries of politicking could provide. The girl I had known had been young—as young then as Cassandra. This was a different creature entirely. There was a power in her, a confidence I had not felt when last we'd met.

"Yes," she said, "It is I."

I bowed then, left hand thrown wide, right pressed over my heart. "Your Highness, it is exceedingly good to see you again. This is an unexpected honor."

Selene inclined her head, fidgeted with one of her rings. "Unexpected for us both. I did not think ever to see you again, after..."

"After I struck your father," I said, not denying it.

I could feel the Martians clench their collective jaws.

"Just so." The princess's face fell, and she passed a moment, fingers still twisting her ring. "You still have enemies at court, my lord. My brother, Prince Aurelian, is not one of them. Nor am I."

"He sent you?"

"I sent myself," she said. "I am, I think, the only person here on Forum that you would call...a friend."

I marked her hesitation, and guessed its meaning. We had been betrothed—Selene and I—if never formally.

"Are we friends, Selene?" I asked, studying that eugenic sculpture of a face. How like her mother she'd become! The same wide eyes, the same arched and sculpted brow, the same slim nose and full mouth, the same pointed chin. It seemed strange that any friend should so resemble an enemy. How many years had she lived since we parted? Twenty? Fifty? A hundred? No, not so many as that. Here was a woman in the full flower of her youth and potency, a princess of men. Without having to ask, I knew that she had passed much of the intervening years in her glass coffin, dreaming frozen dreams.

She had been awakened the moment we arrived.

She was lying. She had not come on her own initiative.

Aurelian had sent her.

She had been preserved against this day.

"If...that is your wish," she replied. "I hoped that you would trust me. It is why I came in secret. We have a place prepared for you. It's quite secure."

"Can I get a message to your father?"

Selene shook her head. "Aurelian will speak with you."

"That isn't good enough, Your Highness," I said, voice rising. "I *must* speak with the Emperor. I am commanded to say *nothing* of my mission to any save him."

Knight-Commander Kas could no longer restrain himself. "Traitor! You profaned yourself attacking a living god! And now you demand the privilege of an audience?"

"Silence, knight-commander!" Selene said, and Kas hung his head. "You must forgive Sir Canton, my lord. He has a stout heart, and he loves my father as all his order do." She descended the first step from the receiving stage, hair tossed by the wind. "But he is right. When last you saw my father, you struck him. Why should we grant your request?"

The lie came easily. "I struck him," I said, looking round. "I struck him, and *everyone* knows it. There were witnesses, recordings, stories of my villainy spread across the datanet. Ask yourself: Could one unarmed man—even Hadrian Marlowe—escape from a cell aboard an Imperial battleship—escape *from* that battleship—entirely unaided?"

Selene blinked. "You're saying you planned it? Father and you?"

Let her believe whatever she wanted to believe.

"I am saying that I was where I needed to be," I said, glancing to young Edouard—to Special Agent 2, Imperial Office, Contact Division. "Jadd is nearer Sabratha than the front. Is it not?"

Silence from the princess, from the Martians and the androgyns all. The logothetes and scholiasts stirred, muttering.

"It is." Princess Selene had reached the lower level by then, heels brightly ringing with every step. I saw the glimmer of shield about her as she drew level with the centurion and his commander.

Sensing that it was still my moment, I pressed, "I have information vital to the war effort. There has been a battle—I can say that much at least—and while we were victorious, there exists now a threat to mankind more terrible than any we have yet faced. Your commander calls me *traitor*. I am many things, Your Highness, but that is not one. Why would I be here, risk all, if not in the direst need?"

Selene's eyes had gone to Cassandra, and for a moment it seemed that she had not heard a single word of all I'd said. Her mouth was open, tongue teetering on the precipice of speech. "You are..." she began, eyes sliding from Cassandra's face to my own, "...his daughter. Aren't you?"

Remembering herself, Cassandra curtsied. "I am, Your Highness."

"Princess," I said, bowing. "My daughter, Cassandra."

"I see," Selene's eyes returned to me, and there was something in them—a sadness, almost, and almost an understanding. She looked once more to Cassandra. "Your mother...the Tavrosi doctor? Onderra, was it not?"

"Yes, Your Highness," Cassandra said.

"I see her in you, though I regret to say I did not know her well." She inhaled sharply, returning her gaze to me. "I have read my father's pardon. It shall make things somewhat easier. We have prepared a place in the Arx Caelestis for you and your people." She surveyed Neema and Edouard and the Irchtani. "Are there more?"

"In orbit, Highness," I said. "We traveled aboard the troop carrier *Gadelica,* but thought it better to leave them in orbit in light of quarantine concerns. It was easier to vet just the four of us..." I gestured at the four humans of my company. "The Irchtani are immune to *Lethe's Sickness.*"

Selene nodded her understanding. "Very good. Let them remain there."

"We have no cause to suspect the plague. It was not on Sabratha." The Princess had turned as I spoke, and taking my arm led me through the blocks of her Martian Guard.

"We have thrice beaten it back here," she said. "You passed through the quarantine yourself. You know how stringent it has become." We reached the top of the steps to the receiving stage, and I saw the nondescript, white government fliers waiting on the deck behind. I stopped her there. "You planned to arrest me."

She smiled. "Only to get you undercover with all speed. There are doubtless those here loyal to...to other concerns, let's say. They will report to their masters, but Father's letter provides us coverage. Sir Canton will be heading your security while you remain in the Arx." At this I peered back at the scarred, bronze-faced soldier. "I must say, Lord Hadrian," Selene continued. "You have impeccable timing."

"Why is that, Highness?"

She stopped and looked at me. I had forgotten the stately tallness of her. She was nearly my own height. Shadows faintly red painted the lids of her eyes. "You don't know?"

"Know what?"

"The Lothrians have crossed the Rasan Belt in force. They have assailed Jadd and the Upper Sagittarius."

It had come at last. The fall of that second hammer upon the Imperial anvil. I thought of Jadd encircled, of bombs falling on Jaharrad, on the *Islis du Albulkam*. Of commissars in armorial black and of the Conclave Guard sacking Volcano House. With the Lothrians streaming across the Belt into civilized space, and the Cielcin hammering the eastern provinces along the gulf between Centaurus and Sagittarius, the Empire was assailed on two fronts. The Jaddians might be forced to recall their clone armies to defend their home, leaving the vast spaces of the east to our shredded legions.

Of all the realms of men, the Lothrian Commonwealth was second in size and power to the Empire itself, and they had betrayed Earth and all her children, had sold their souls and their people to the Cielcin. Long had we awaited the coming of their armies, and if that time was now...

"Has Jadd fallen?"

"The holy planet itself? No," Selene said. "But Aurelian has called a war council. Messages have come from across the galaxy. Delegates are coming to Forum, will arrive within the next few years. And they're bringing their armies."

"Their armies?" I asked. "Coming here?"

She gripped my arm. "Oh yes," she said, "all of the Children of Earth still true are coming together at last."

CHAPTER 31

AURELIAN

THE NEXT DAY, SIR Canton Kas appeared at the doors of the apartments that had been set aside for Cassandra and myself in the Arx Caelestis, alongside two decades of the Martian Guard. The Arx stood behind the Sun King's Hall, away from the Peronine Palace and the Campus Raphael. A great, square tower of white stone and steel a hundred stories high, it dominated the plaza of the Campus, overlooking the vast rotunda and gold-tiled roofs of the Hall. It had been built to house the Martians, and to serve as their base and barracks.

Once, the ancient planet Mars had served the first Emperors as a penal colony, the first link in a chain whose latest were Belusha and Pagus Minor. Now it was something else, the home of a warrior people and martial culture whose only purpose was to fill out the ranks of the Emperor's own legions.

Every Martian boy was subjected to brutal training in the deserts and river valleys of that red and venerable world, and those that lived to their Ephebeia were granted the highest honor: to leave Mars and sail to the service of Mars himself. The Sollan Emperor. The living god.

Theirs was a strange and insular world, theirs a cult—not unlike the cult of the undead god Edouard worshipped—that the Chantry had allowed to persist. They were older than the first litanies, the first sanctums, the first sacrifices to Earth and the icona, and they had served the Blood Imperial almost since the dawn of the Imperium.

And they were then and for a time my protectors.

I felt like a prisoner, marching along between my guards. They conveyed me to a lift, and then to a tram that ran along a closed tunnel. We emerged into a subbasement that seemed more like the deck of some Imperial battle-ship than the baroque splendor of the palace above our heads. Word of our arrival must have leaked by that point. There were security cameras, logothetes, servants everywhere. My face was known, was *infamous*, and surely one of the guards or serving women in the Arx the night before had whispered word to some other.

Half my guard left us at the next lift, and I was forced to fold into the carriage with a dozen Martians in crimson plate. The carriage itself was bloodwood and brass, the floor white-and-black-tiled marble with brass inlay, wholly incongruous with the black ship-metal of that secret subfloor. It moved silently, and deposited us into a hallway like itself, richly tiled, the walls and ceilings of darkly paneled wood, the windows of alumglass like crystal overlooking the soaring towers and cloud-wreathed colonnades of that city of mortal gods. Our own apartments had only narrow windows, and I stood a moment, transfixed by the beauty of it all.

The glory of the world, I thought. *Of all of them.*

The Eternal City was the crown jewel of Imperial achievement, the perihelion of civilization itself. It was worth fighting for.

Crown Prince Aurelian, eldest child of the Emperor, sat behind a massive desk of dark wood with resinous black inlay. His hair was white as snow, and the thin circlet that depressed it just above his ears seemed heavily to rest upon him. He looked up at my approach, and placed the silver stylus he held in a pen stand, banished the holographs that floated before him with a gesture.

"Lord Marlowe for you, my prince," said Knight-Commander Kas, saluting.

"So I see," said Aurelian, eyes narrowing. "Very good, knight-commander."

The Martian saluted, and he and his men withdrew, the last two shutting the heavy wooden doors behind them with a soft but solid sound.

Prince Aurelian did not speak at once, but continued his careful study of me. It was hard not to stand at attention, but I held my ground. I had no rank, no title any longer, and so had no need to act like a soldier.

"You have nothing to say?" the old prince asked, sitting back in his chair. His cloth was fine, his tunic of red slashed with gold, and of gold was the heavy, square chain of office that draped his broad shoulders. The small toga that hung from his left shoulder—not covering the arm—was white as his hair, and on his face was writ the mark of centuries and many cares.

"You were young when I last saw you," I said, remembering a stoic but handsome prince, red haired as all his kind.

"As were you, Lord Marlowe," he said, gesturing at the tapestried chair across from him. "I am not certain which of us Time, Ever-Fleeting, has been kinder to. I have marked more years than you, I deem—here on Forum—and yet that two-faced force has ridden you far harder, or so it seems."

I smiled and said nothing.

"Why are you here?" the prince demanded.

"That is a matter for your father, my prince," I said. "I am come on his business."

"I was not aware my father had any business on..." Aurelian checked a printout lying on the desk before him. "...Sabratha? Where is that, precisely? I've not heard of it."

Resting my elbows on the arms of the tapestried chair, I folded my hands before me. "It's in the Outer Perseus, on the frontier. We came by Tiryns."

Aurelian rested his chin on one fist, leaned against the arm of his high-backed and richly leathered seat. "My reports on the place say little and less. Some Mining Guild interests in-system and on the planet itself. Ivory exports"—that would be the bones of the native whale-worms—"but little more. It's a minor outpost...of little to no consequence."

I massaged the ancient cryoburn scar that wrapped my thumb as I listened. It would seem word of the Vaiartu ruins had never entered the general record, else Aurelian would surely have added them to his list.

When again I did not speak, Aurelian's nostrils flared. "Lord Marlowe," he said, "let me be frank with you: Word of your infamy has spread across the Imperium. It festers here at court. His Radiance, my father, may have granted you clemency, but the Lions, the Martians, the Chantry—especially the Chantry—will never forgive what you've done. Until yesterday, I myself had no knowledge of Father's pardon, and intended to place you in the bastille."

"Is that why I'm in the Arx Caelestis?" I asked. "A gilded prison?"

"Just so," Aurelian snapped, and leaned forward. "You have but few friends at court. I am one only out of respect for the man you were. I would not see you strangled in your sleep here or killed in some shuttle crash, but if you wish for me to help you, you must give me something. Why were you on Sabratha?"

There was a portrait of the Emperor on the wall behind Aurelian. It was the stock portrait one sees in every state office and prefect's station on every world under the Sun, with His Radiance dressed as a Legion officer, in white instead of black, with the red and gold of a toga over his left shoulder, his right breast festooned with medals—only this was *the* portrait. The original. I saw Vianello's signature in the bottom right. The man had painted William's portrait, and the portraits of the previous fifteen Emperors, going back to Raphael VII and the thirteenth millennium.

Nearly five thousand years. The poor man was kept in fugue, decanted only so long as was required for him to perform his next portrait.

He might outlast the Empire itself.

"I am commanded not to say," I said.

"I am Chancellor of the Sollan Empire! Lord Director of the Imperial Office! There is *nothing* in the Empire I do not know."

The part of me that remained Tor Gibson's student teetered on the verge of pointing out that could not be true, as the prince was the one asking questions, but I held my tongue.

"You were traveling in the company of one Special Agent Edouard Albé. If I will not have it from you, I will have it from him."

I hissed, looked round the office. Its high arched windows, its veined pilasters, its carved wooden panels and bookcases, the smell of old leather and yellowed vellum. The prince was quite correct. He could not compel me to speak, but he would have the story from Edouard. I ought to have left the man aboard the *Gadelica*. I might have played for time.

No, no it was inevitable—had been inevitable from the moment I set our course for Forum, since I left Jadd.

"What do you know of the Monumentals?" I asked, using the Imperial word.

Aurelian blanched. "You know?" His eyes found the camera in the ceiling.

"Of course I know," I said, unable to keep the acid from my tongue.

Numbly, Aurelian's hand found a control along the underside of his desk. The windows polarized in an instant, becoming black as pitch. The days on Forum stretched for weeks, and it was necessary to create darkness where it would not otherwise be.

The darkness Aurelian created was of a different kind. The lamps and sconces remained on, but I was certain the cameras and various other recording devices present in the Prince Chancellor's office were dead as stones.

"How do you know?" he asked.

"The Cielcin worship them," I said. "There was one of them dead on the world where my company was destroyed."

Aurelian's face darkened. "That was not in your report."

"I have had this conversation with your father already," I said.

The aged, white-haired prince chewed his tongue, eyes narrow with focus as he studied one of the papers spread before him—not really seeing it. "Your abilities. What you did at Perfugium. On Berenike. Here in the Colosseum."

"Have nothing to do with *them*," I said, though that was not precisely true. "HAPSIS found one on Sabratha." It was the prince's turn to be silent. "Your father asked me to find and kill it before the Cielcin could locate it."

"Why wasn't I told any of this?" Aurelian asked, eyes locked now on mine.

I studied the man's aging palatine face, searching for some betrayal, some sign that he was not what he seemed: Aurelian of the Aventine, Chancellor, Minister, Prince of the Sollan Empire...

Demoniacs all.

"Excellency," I began. "You must know the enemy has spies at court."

Aurelian brushed this aside with a gesture. "I should have been told."

"That is academic," I said. "You were not. It is of no consequence. All

efforts at secrecy were for naught in any case. The Extrasolarians successfully secreted a spy among our ranks. The Cielcin attacked Sabratha in an
effort to secure the Monumental there."

Aurelian's face was then as white as his hair. "Did they succeed?"

"I have reason to believe so," I said, and told the prince how we had
been betrayed, how our forces had been caught flat-footed on the ground.
I told him of the coming of Muzugara, of the finding of Ushara in the
pantheon, of the battle, and the bombing that had turned the god to stone.
When at last I told him of Gaizka's corpse and of my certainty that the
Watcher had ridden on the wizard's wave, the Chancellor hung his head,
and so missed the maniac grin that flickered over my face.

"Are you unwell, Lord Marlowe?" he asked, finding my face in my hands.

I massaged my face and lips. "Yes, Excellency," I said at last. "You must
understand...none of this can be reported. None of this can leave this
room." I looked round at the polarized windows, the inert cameras—found
myself thinking of Valka. My next words emerged almost wistfully as I
brought my attention back around to the prince. "You understand now
why it is so important I speak with His Radiance at once?"

Aurelian touched the circlet on his brow with one finger, adjusting it
as Edouard might push up his spectacles. "You cannot," he said.

The Marlowe fury flashed white hot. "Why not? I know the Emperor is
not here. I understand he never returned following the disaster at Perfugium, that he has continued the fight in the provinces. But I must speak
to him, Aurelian. Where is he?"

The Prince Chancellor's eyes flashed at my presumption. "He is in
transit," he said at last.

A small sound of understanding escaped me, and I bowed my head.
"Of course." It would not be possible even to telegraph the Emperor, not
so long as he remained at warp. "How long?"

"Four years," came the dreaded answer.

"Four years!" I stood, turning my back on the prince. "We may not *have*
four years, Your Excellency. The sorcerer, Gaizka, might have reached the
Prophet already! A Cielcin army with a Watcher at its head will march clear
across the galaxy, just as the Vaiartu did a million years ago! We will be facing
extinction!" I rounded on the man, struck by how tired and frail he seemed.

Life is very long.

"I cannot make the fleet move any faster," Aurelian said. "What would
you have me do?"

I had thought long and hard about that very question on the flight from
Sabratha, knowing I could not come to Forum hat in hand and offer nothing
but my apology. My mother's son, I moved to the window, saw only my own
face reflected in its black mirror. Still, I leaned against the carven frame.

"Vorgossos," I said at last.

"Vorgossos?" Aurelian sounded more confused than shocked. "What has Vorgossos to do with anything?"

I looked at him. "Kharn Sagara must have known about the Watchers." Turning my attention back to the polished dark of the glass, I said, "He warned me—in his way—said there were creatures out there that *burrow in the quantum foam.* He said he knew of a creature that attacked a ship's crew through their *dreams.*"

"You think he spoke of the Monumentals?"

"Do you know of any other creature capable of such a thing?" I asked. "If I am to renew the hunt, I need better weapons."

"You said the Perseus weapon was sabotaged," Aurelian said. "Surely another..."

"The creature on Sabratha was weak," I said. "It was dying, dissipating over the last million years. So was the one our people caught on Nairi."

Aurelian rocked back in his seat, wheels clattering on floor. "You know about Nairi?"

"It is *not* weak now," I said, and smiled—I saw my teeth in the blackened window. "I need a weapon that can battle the Watchers at full strength."

"What does Vorgossos have that we do not?" Aurelian asked, gold chain tinkling as he steepled his hands over the edge of his desk.

I hesitated, feeling almost that I had said too much, shared too much of my secret mind. The visions the Quiet had shown me danced like shadows before my eyes, cast by that higher world and time. Visions of that black ship, of light devouring the stars...and of myself. Of myself destroying the Cielcin, wiping them from the stars.

But that had been another life, a time that would never happen.

It had been a young Hadrian in the vision, not the graying and much-scarred old raven that peered at me from the window glass. And yet I must seek Vorgossos, as he had sought Vorgossos in his life that never was.

What was it Suzuha had said to me?

Weapons more terrible than anything you can imagine.

"Weapons designed by the Mericanii," I said. "By the machines."

Aurelian's eyes grew round as dinner plates, and he stood. "By the machines?"

"I believe Kharn Sagara can be of assistance," I said. "The machines developed weapons far beyond our science, not even Sagara understood them—I think."

"And he's just...kept them? All these years?" Aurelian asked, skepticism entering the edges of his voice. "Why not use them? Why, for that matter, did the machines not use them?"

That latter was a question I'd given much consideration to, and while

I thought I had an answer, it was not one I was ready to give. "I don't believe Sagara is interested in war," I said. "He's been alive for sixteen thousand years, and in all that time he's been content to rule his one planet in relative peace. Why risk his immortal life?"

That seemed to satisfy Aurelian, who circled round to the far corner of his desk, one hand gripping the edge. "What makes you think he has something to combat the Monumentals?"

"The machine lifeform on Vorgossos," I said, "Brethren—you read my reports?"

"A long time ago."

"Sagara maintains perhaps the last Mericanii daimon in existence," I said. "The creature's consciousness was developed to the point where it could perceive the future, and so perceive other beings *across time.*" I could tell the prince was not following. "Beings with similar faculties."

"You're saying..."

"I'm saying the machines knew of the Watchers!" I said. "The weapons they built are beyond anything we can imagine."

"You think they built them to fight the Monumentals?"

I came off the wall, hands stretched before me, imploring. "If not them, what?"

"Us!" Aurelian almost shouted. "The machines were trying to destroy us, Marlowe! Have you forgotten?"

I turned away, met once more the gaze of my reflection. "Even if that's all it is, if Sagara has a weapon that *can* kill them, Excellency, if there is only the faintest chance I am right, let me seek Vorgossos. If Sagara can be made to help us..."

"Even if I could let you go, Lord Marlowe," said Prince Aurelian, speaking like a man mastering some barely bottled exasperation, "what makes you think Sagara would aid us?"

"He does not want to die!" I said. "Sagara protects his own interests. A galaxy ruled by the Watchers is *not* in his interest."

"I seem to recall he was perfectly sanguine at the prospect of a deal with the Cielcin."

"The Cielcin are one thing," I countered. "The Watchers another."

Aurelian was silent then. Silent for so long I turned back to look at him. He leaned against the corner of his desk like a straw man beaten down by rain. "You cannot go," he said at last, "and you may not need to. It may not be necessary to seek Vorgossos at all."

"My prince?"

The Chancellor of the Sollan Empire touched the gilt carnelian egg displayed at once corner of his desk. Its stand was a golden hand, the egg balanced on its fingers. "Selene told you His Radiance has called for a council?" When I said that she had, he lifted the egg entire. Cradled it in his own palm as though it were a grievous weight. "The Jaddians are rushing to grow a new army to combat the Lothrians, the Durantines have sent for aid. Both have emissaries en route. We have reports pouring in from the system governors in Perseus and along the Rasan Belt, and several of the feudal lords are coming themselves. There is a coalition of the surviving Normans coming under the command of one of the Triumvirs of Uhra—the Norman *Alliance*, they're calling themselves. The Wong-Hopper Consortium director general is coming himself, along with the Nipponese Emperor."

"The Nipponese Emperor is coming here?" The lord of House Yamato never left his home on Nichibotsu.

"Along with five hundred of his finest and the *other* Imperial navy," Aurelian laughed. The Nipponese had been allowed to retain the title of Emperor at home, though he was considered a prince in the broader Imperium, equivalent to the great houses of Bourbon, Mahidol, Hapsburg, and the rest. Still, the Sollan Emperors and the lords of the Aventine House liked to call them the *other* Empire, though the princes of the Yamato ruled but a handful of systems.

"We reached out to the Tavrosi. They have dispatched a fleet."

"The Tavrosi?" I could not contain my shock. "The Tavrosi don't have fleets!"

"Evidently they built one," Aurelian said. "It's coming here under the command of an admiral called...what was it? Kull. Sattha Kull Vhad Kvasir." Aurelian restored the crimson egg to its stand. "Your, ah...erstwhile paramour was Tavrosi, was she not? Do you know him?"

I shook my head. "My Valka was Vhad Edda," I said. "I never went to Kvasir."

"I see," Aurelian said. "I only wondered."

"What has this to do with Sagara?" Kharn Sagara could not be coming to Forum. It was impossible, and to ask was to appear a fool.

"We have invited representatives of several factions among the Extrasolarians," the prince said, eyes studying my reaction.

"The Extrasolarians!" I exclaimed, evidently not disappointing the prince. "The Extasolarians, Your Excellency...are you mad?"

"His Radiance made the overtures himself," Aurelian said. "My father sent an apostol to the Monarch of Latarra."

"Latarra was allied with MINOS!" I shouted.

"And we attempted to assassinate the Monarch," Aurelian said. "Just a moment ago, you were agitating for an alliance with Kharn Sagara."

Rage is blindness.

I bowed my head and was silent. The prince was right.

"Perhaps the Latarran embassy or one of the other factions might shed light on the Vorgossos question," Aurelian said, crossing the space between us. "Nothing can be done until His Radiance reaches his destination. Until then you will remain in the Arx Caelestis, under careful guard, barring formal occasions. Your ship will be impounded in orbit, the crew you traveled with kept in fugue. I will not have a repeat of your showing in the Colosseum on your visit, nor will I have your blood on my hands."

"So I am to be imprisoned?" I said. It was what I expected.

"If you like," the prince said. "It is for your own safety, and that of your daughter."

"I understand," I said, and saluted, looking over the prince's shoulder—as was martial custom—to where Vianello's painting of William XXIII hung in splendor.

The prince inclined his head. "Dismissed."

I turned to go.

"Lord Marlowe!" I stopped, but did not turn. "Not a word of this. To anyone. You are on Forum. In the Eternal City. You may be certain you are being watched—and not merely by my men."

CHAPTER 32

CHILDREN OF THE EARTH AND SUN

THE LIGHT OF FORUM'S nigh-never-ending day streamed through the oculus at the apex of the mighty dome of the Great Sanctum of Mother Earth, Jewel of Heaven. I watched the incense coil through its beam, studied the frescoed images of man's conquest of the machines nearly five hundred feet above our heads. The pillars that supported the dome were twice as wide as the height of a man, surfaced in porphyry chased with gold, and gold were the sconces and the nine caryatids that supported the canopied ciborium that hung over the central altar where the statue of the God Emperor stood crushing the pyramid that represented all of machine-kind.

Ten thousand candles, all of white tallow and differing heights, ringed that central altar, their drippings fallen down its sides to pool in the trench built at the altar's base. Still more candles burned in the niches at the base of each of the great pillars, and along the exterior wall. Lesser altars to the icona. To Justice and Fortitude, to Ever-Fleeting Time and Bloody-Handed Evolution. To Kratos, *strength,* and Zelos, *zeal.* There were statues to Mercy, to Victory, and Love. *Prasada* offerings lay on trays before the statues. Fruits and cakes and little parcels. The worshippers had sacrificed them to the icona, and the priests would dole them out when the litany was said and the practice done. What had been given to the lesser gods would be returned, as was tradition.

"In the name of Holy Mother Earth and in the light of Her Sun we pray!" intoned the new Synarch of the Holy Terran Chantry, a hollow-cheeked old palatine called Heraklonas. He raised the censer, waving it as he processed about the altar, two attendants in white minding the fringe of their master's blue-and-green silk robe.

Cassandra stood beside me.

I had not wanted her to accompany me, but years of near imprisonment in the Arx Caelestis had chafed at her, and she had begged to come.

292

I had not wanted to go myself, but Aurelian had left me no choice.

Not listening to recitations of old Heraklonas, I glanced sidelong at the dignitaries gathered about and below us. We had been seated in the rear of the royal box, an elevated and well-shielded riser that took up nearly a third of the sanctum's circumference, above the central altar and below the choir loft. A sea of red- and white-haired heads sat beneath us. The Emperor's children and few surviving siblings. Among them were seated those dignitaries newly arrived from offworld.

"That's the director general of the Wong-Hopper Consortium," I whispered to her, indicating a man in a tall, cylindrical miter of indigo and slate, surrounded by men in the flared skullcaps commonly worn by the Mandari elite. "Wong Xu."

"Why are they in masks?" she asked. "Is it like on Jadd? Only their women are masked, too."

"Those aren't masks," I said, marking the jeweled and enameled white cheeks. "They're rebreathers. They're scrupulous about contagion at the best of times, and these..."

"...are not the best of times."

"Quite," I said, and gesturing to a dark-skinned man in black and cloth of gold, continued, "that is one of the Triumvirs of the Uhran Republic. I forget his name...and beside him is King Paeon of Tarú."

"The...green man?"

"He's a dryad," I said. "That's chlorophyll in his skin."

"Where's Tarú?" Cassandra leaned close to me.

"It's one of the Small Kingdoms," I said. "Just the two star systems, I think."

"Only two?" Cassandra asked.

"You heard Selene," I said. "Everyone is here. Or will be."

There were still more yet to come. The *Tenno*, the Nipponese Emperor Yushuhito, had not yet arrived, nor had any of the Extrasolarians. The Jaddian emissary had just landed the day before. There were others—so many others—contingents of the great houses, the Princes Bourbon and Hapsburg, Bernadotte and Hohenzollern and the rest. A sea of colors and finery—and of security details packed cheek by jowl between.

"O Mother Earth!" intoned the Synarch Heraklonas, "Who bore us and blessed us and whom we betrayed! Have mercy on us, your children! We who wander in eternal dark, lost forever until we are returned to you..."

"Are the Tavrosi here?" Cassandra asked, craning her neck while trying to appear as one *not* craning her neck. In the loft above us, the choir began to sing, chanting the first litany, describing man's peregrinations, the worlds settled by mankind after the end of the Foundation War.

"They wouldn't come in if they were," I said. "The Tavrosi are godless."

Despite the polyphony filling the sanctum, I swore I could hear her blink at me. *"Qesta non tuo tashdaqa, Abba."*

You do not believe.

"Non," I agreed, *"E non.* But they're not here yet." I could understand her eagerness. She had never met one of her mother's people.

"Who do you think Prince Aldia will send?" she asked.

"No one *you* know," I said, knowing she hoped to see Hydarnes or another of her teachers again. "And not Prince Kaim, either. It will be some admiral or other, you'll see..."

Soon the first litany would be done, and one of Heraklonas's anagnosts would read from the *Cantos,* after which—for this was a High Day—the sacrifice would be brought in and burned, its smoke rising through the oculus to Earth-of-Old. The sacrifices left before the icona, the *prasada,* were by tradition vegetable, but the burnt offering would be animal: horse or ox or ram.

It was a white bull that was led in from the gate of sacrifice and chained to the altar. Cassandra gripped my arm as Heraklonas drew the knife and slit the poor beast's throat. Memories of the altar at Akterumu flickered in my mind, of myself chained there, of my people given over to the Cielcin horde. The Chantry's faith was hollow, a confection of cynical politicking crafted ten thousand years before I was born, a confection given substance by those millennia as rotting bone might fossilize and give way to stone.

It was a reenactment without meaning, a costume we wore in that falsely sacred place, a memory of man's savage past from a time before the Mericanii Dominion, a time when man was beast—and king of beasts in the forests and jungles of Earth. To what dark gods had the fathers of men made offerings, and gashed their flesh with flints, or inhaled the fumes of pharmacons and poisons without name? For what devils' sake had fathers lashed their daughters to pyres and kindled flame, or despoiled virgins in rituals black with sin?

They were the same, our sacrifices and theirs.

I stood sharply, ignoring Cassandra's concerned gaze. I felt almost giddy with delight to see *His* children still bent toward us, remembering what we had taught them when they were young. For we *had* been among them. I saw that plain. Just as we had been among the many-legged ones and the pale ones and ones that dwelt in the seas. We would bend these creatures, too, turn them to worship us in time.

We would be victorious.

"Abba?"

I smiled down at Cassandra, though whether it was to reassure her that I was all right or from deep, inhuman joy I could not say. I could not untangle my thoughts from those thoughts which were not mine, those thoughts that had been given me—forced on me.

I turned and mounted the steps without a word. None stopped me, nor said a word when I halted before a statue of Three-Faced Fate. Three-Faced Fate, six-armed, six-breasted, passing the thread of beaten gold that represented all that was and would be from one hand to the next, thrusting her needle into the air.

She looked like a Watcher, looked as Ushara had looked, graven of an alabaster so translucent it seemed to glow with a light of its own. She looked like Brethren—with all those hands. I looked to the others: to Time, with its two faces; to Death, cold and naked with her skull and scythe. Almost I felt I was standing in the entrance of the Dhar-Iagon, looking up at the graven forms of the Watchers carved by Cielcin hands.

I have survived the pits and the torments of Dharan-Tun, and the solitude of my cavern cell and of the black journey after—and so I know the taste of madness, its texture and smell. It has never left me, and so I know that it was not madness that moved me then.

The magi believe that mathematics are the ultimate law. All reality is mere matter in motion, they say, is granted motion by energy, and all relations between said matter and energy may be described by the equations that are the incantations of their art, equations written in the very foam of space by no hand at all, as the universe is—according to them—without artist.

This is not so.

The incantations of the magi—which can indeed conjure wonders as extraordinary as star drives and as commonplace as soup spoons—are not written on the black page between the stars. They are contrivances, tools fashioned by human hands and minds that those minds might apprehend that darkness, symbols in the way all our words are symbols.

And yet their powers are real.

No man who has taken ship or turned on a light can deny them.

But it is not the magi who possess power. No man can sail between the stars at will, though he possesses the knowledge to build a ship and engines. He possesses knowledge only, and knowledge is *not* power. The power lies in the ship itself, in the laws of nature harnessed by its engines.

That power would *be* without ship or engines.

Would be without us.

Might it not be, then, that there are higher laws and deeper principles beyond our paltry means to annotate and describe? Laws of nature stranger than physics? How else could the image of the Watchers assert itself in that alabaster stone? In the twisted flesh of the daimons man fashioned with his own hands? Men have worshipped gods since men were beasts. Old Earth had been filled with them almost to bursting. The Watchers had been among them, I saw that plain—twisting man from the path, and though their names and influence had been forgotten, their shape had emerged again in new guise, reconstructed as the liar-priests of the Chantry forged their false religion from the pilfered pieces of countless dead faiths.

There were only so many ways to build a ship, and so one endeavoring to do so might—seemingly by pure chance—reproduce the shape of a vessel long vanished from the sky. It seemed to me then that the sacrifice of flesh in the sanctums—which was a part common to all worship of the Watchers—had tended toward a faith that carved that image of the Fates, the whole growing from the part as a seed.

In time, that false religion would turn fully to evil, to the worship of the Watchers, the *powers* of this world. Unless it was destroyed, torn up by the roots...

"Lord Marlowe?" I looked away from Three-Faced Fate and found Princess Selene walking toward me, accompanied by one of her sisters and a quartet of Martians in full plate, their faces lost behind visors of featureless red enamel. The sacrifice was ended, and the dignitaries were beginning to filter out of the inner sanctum. I saw King Paeon of the dryads emerge with his retinue, and stop to speak with one of the masked members of the Consortium.

I bowed, coming down from my thoughts but hesitantly. "Your Highness."

She dismissed my reverence with a gesture. "Are you unwell? Your departure was marked."

"Did they think I was trying to run?" I asked.

She shook her head. "You left your daughter."

"The smoke," I said, and did my best to smile. "The incense...disagrees with me."

Selene allowed this with the barest of nods. She wore her hair up in a Grecian pile secured by fine gold netting, ringlets like coils of copper fire. A high choker of yellow gold set with laser-etched carnelians accentuated her long neck, and her gown was of a red color-matched to her hair, decorated with white petals like the snowy down of cherry blossoms blown in the wind.

"You recall my sister, Titania?"

I remembered a willowy girl, painfully shy and full of a secret enthusiasm. The woman who accompanied Selene was slim still, but aged. She wore a veil of white lace, and no jewelry. Her gown was ashen gray, and I picked out threads of white in the red hair she wore pulled tightly back from a high, fair brow. There were lines set deeply at the corners of Titania's mouth, so that where before I was certain she had been the younger sister, I was as certain now she was the elder.

I took the other princess by the hand. "Enchanted," I said.

Titania withdrew her fingers sharply.

"You must forgive my sister," Selene said, "she does not often leave the

Peronine Palace—only for sacrifice. She has consecrated herself to Mother Earth, as you see."

"You joined the Sisters *Cinerea*," I said. The Cinerea were mourners for Old Earth, women—virgins—consecrated to the Holy Mother, called to tend the fires of the sanctums that burned on every world.

Titania bowed her head. "I serve in my way."

"The machine of Empire has little use for us spare heirs," Selene said, peering up at the statue of Three-Faced Fate with her golden thread. "Our father's time will come—may Mother Earth and God Emperor forbid it—and when it does, our brother will have little use for his siblings. We afterlings must find our own way, each for ourselves."

"Your brother?" I said. "Prince Alexander?"

"That is the high probability," said Titania.

Selene put a hand on my arm to soften Titania's sharpness. "Alex is yet on campaign with His Radiance. It is said that he will succeed in his time."

I accepted this with a slow nod, looked back up at Fate—and the Watcher-shape of her on her plinth. "But it is not confirmed?"

"Our father yet lives!" Titania snapped, "Sister, this line of discussion is most improper."

"Of course, dear sister," Selene said. "What of you, Lord Marlowe? I have barely seen you these four years! Aurelian has kept you under lock and key."

"Aurelian has kept me busy," I corrected. I had spent many long weeks in the War Office, helping to translate intercepted Cielcin communiques, deciphering battle plans, providing intelligence to support the fleets in the fractured provinces. The loss of Nessus had crippled the telegraph network in the Centaurine Arm. Some forty percent of all Centaurine telegraph relays had been routed through Nessus. With those telegraphs lost, communication across much of the volume was limited to the fastest courier ships.

"Yes, I heard about all that," she said. "Still, I've not seen you since that dinner at the palace." That had been six months previously.

"That may change now the Council is at hand," I said. I had no illusions that I would be kept in the Arx under the watchful eye of the Martians, but I had at least some small hope of an end to my plush imprisonment. "I understand the War Office has developed a new praxis that will allow the Emperor to attend remotely."

"So it is said," said the dour Princess Titania.

"Parallelized entanglement, I think they call it," Selene said. "It's not new technology. It's really just several thousand telegraphs yoked together, enough to allow for real-time video transmission."

All about us, the sanctum was emptying, worshippers processing from the inner doors to the massive bronze gates that opened on the Campus Raphael. I watched Director-General Wong Xu walk past, surrounded by a block of functionaries in painted white-porcelain masks. The Triumvir of Uhra drew aside one gray-haired Imperial prince, the two men speaking intently.

"There you are!" Cassandra appeared as if from nowhere, emerging from a block of Legion officers. She wore her red-and-gold *mandyas* over a black gown. The family colors. *"Non ti es buon?"*

"I'll tell you later," I said.

"How do you find the city, Cassandra?" asked Princess Selene.

Cassandra turned, and seeming to notice the princess for the first time, sank into a curtsy. "Beautiful, Your Highness. I only wish I could see more of it."

"That... may be permissible before long. I would be delighted to show you about the city myself. I may be able to persuade my brother to permit an exception. Do you ride?"

Cassandra brightened. "Horses?"

"Yes!" Selene matched Cassandra's smile. "We keep a fine stable. Darusans, mostly. I'm certain you could join me—that much should cause no threat to Imperial security."

I studied the princess's royal profile, struck again by how much she had come to resemble her mother—her mother, who had tried to kill me. The Empress Maria Agrippina had retired to Caliburn House on Avalon, fearing the plague. I glanced to the aging Titania, back to Selene. Selene had spent centuries in fugue—that much was plain—but for what reason?

"Perhaps your lord father will join us?" Selene touched my arm again, smiling. "Assuming Aurelian can spare him, of course."

I bent my gaze to examine the floor. "I don't imagine your brother *will* spare me, though you are welcome to try."

"Were you friends?" Cassandra asked when we returned to our apartments. "You... and the princess?"

I stopped halfway through the action of removing my coat. "No," I said at last. "No. I was... nearly betrothed to her."

Cassandra's silence was deafening. I turned and found her standing, mouth half-open. "Betrothed?"

"Never officially," I said.

"You... and her?"

"We never—!" Memories of old visions flashed across my mind. Selene seen in countless aspects: her face illumined by guttering candles, her naked back where she perched on the edge of our bed, her flower-crowned head where she sat on the dais at the foot of throne carved from a single piece of stellar iron taken from the heart of a dead star.

But Cassandra was grinning.

"What is so amusing, girl?"

"She *likes* you, Abba. Anyone can see."

"Enough of this!"

"There's no need to be so dour!" she said. "It is nice, seeing this side of you."

"There is no *side,* girl."

"You always call me *girl* when you're angry," she said.

"*Cassandra.*" I hung my coat on its hook in the little closet by the door. "This is not a game we play." The red light of a camera blinked in one corner of the ceiling, the tip of the iceberg of surveillance equipment that was on us at all times.

Her smile faltered, and I pressed toward her, laid hands upon her shoulders. "This is *not* the Fire School. We are not *home.* We are not *safe.* I have enemies here."

"Who?"

I shook my head. It was wisest not to say. Anyone might be listening. "This Council will begin meeting within the week," I said. "This place is a den of vipers at the best of times, and with the others coming... you must be on your guard, my daughter."

Cassandra's smile withered. "I am not a child," she said.

"I know that," I said, perhaps too quickly. "But I would not have brought you here if I had any other choice."

She accepted this, and half turned away. "What are you afraid of?"

"They tried to kill me when I was here last," I said.

"You think they'll try again?" she asked. "Whoever *they* are?"

"They nearly killed your mother," I said. Indeed, Lieutenant Casdon's knife-missile had found Valka precisely when I'd been in the Royal Wood with Selene, acquainting myself against my will with the woman Caesar had wished for me to wed.

The girl's mouth formed a silent *oh.*

"Be on your guard," I said again. "These people are not our friends. Not even Selene—though perhaps she'd like to be."

"She'd like to be more than that, I think."

"Silence!" I said, unable to mask my exasperation. In the unsteady quiet that followed, I said, "With any luck, we will not be here much longer. Aurelian tells me his father has arrived at... wherever he is now. I will speak to the Emperor soon."

CHAPTER 33

THE EMPEROR'S COUNCIL

THE WHISPERING OF HUSHED conversation fell to silence as a herald in the scarlet livery of the House Avent emerged from the doors behind the dais and beneath the great holograph plate that dominated the far wall of the council chamber. A trumpet sounded, and the liveried androgyn proclaimed the coming of His Imperial Excellency, Aurelian, Prince Chancellor of the Sollan Empire. The prince himself appeared a moment later, flanked by Martians with white-and-red-feathered plumes, and accompanied by a scholiast in the customary viridian of his order.

The prince had grown a short, square beard. It made him look infinitely older, a wizard or some aging king of antique fable. He stood before the Chancellor's seat at the dais while behind him a sergeant-at-arms struck the plate with his fasces once, twice, three times. As the noise of metal on metal rang in that high hall, Aurelian touched the thin gold circlet on his brow, completed the Sign of the Sun Disc in a private prayer to Mother Earth.

Before him were seated some five hundred men—myself among them— the lords and representatives of a thousand thousand worlds arrayed on arcing terraces: lords and ladies of the Imperium, officers of the Legions, Jaddians, Durantines, Normans. Mandari and Tavrosi and the Nipponese emperor himself, Yushuhito in his suit of simple black. There were representatives of the Small Kingdoms, realms so miniscule and so remote from Imperial affairs they might almost have walked from the pages of fiction. I spied Paeon of the dryads, his hair like red moss, his face and limbs green as summer grass.

All the realms of men had sent their voices to Forum.

Nearly all.

The Lothrians were absent, traitors that they were, and the Extrasolarians had yet to appear. They would be among the last to come, along with certain of the surviving lords of the Veil of Marinus, Imperial holdouts from deep behind Cielcin lines.

I myself sat upon the highest level, near to the doors. I was seated near the daughter of some petty king, some princess of the Outer Perseus, at the galaxy's ragged edge. She dressed in skins of scaly green, and her curling hair shone like loops of fire. I had never heard of her home, and cannot now recall it, though I recall the floral notes of her perfume that colored the air about her.

Aurelian stood at the dais—so it seemed to me—like one weighed down by mighty chains. He held his silence a long moment, surveying the faces of all that had come. When he spoke, it was in the bright, brittle tones of practiced oratory. "My lords and ladies," he began, "honored guests, friends, and strangers—masters of the stars! Welcome." He paused, raised one hand in the traditional gesture of warding, first and final fingers extended. "Fate finds us caught between the horns of our enemy. To the north and east, the threat of the Cielcin grows worse by the year. Nessus is overthrown, and with it our hold upon the Arm of Centaurus is broken. I will not lie to you: Things are more dire than you know. Word has reached us of a battle off Rhodussae in the Lynga Cluster. The Cielcin attacked with more than half a hundred of their worldships. Lord Cosmas Sanyal, Viceroy of Lynga, is dead. Rhodussae itself is destroyed, pulled to pieces by the gravity of the Cielcin fleet. Twenty-two of our legions were lost there. More than a million men. Five hundred ships, all gone in a matter of days."

The congregations shifted, muttered responses rising like smoke.

The worlds of Lynga Province lay at the uttermost end of Centaurine space, as east as east. After the fall of Nessus, the stars of the Lynga globular cluster had held together, a bastion of Imperial resistance. If Lynga had fallen as well... then the provinces were truly lost. The worlds of the Centaurine Arm yet unspoiled by the Cielcin horde—though there were surely thousands—were cut off. Some might survive, but how many were dependent on interstellar trade to endure, to exist?

How many would die in the dark?

Aurelian continued, "The Prophet's forces are massing along the edge of the Second Gulf. It is only a matter of time before they cross into the Arm of Sagittarius, into the heartland of our Empire. I do not need to tell you all that the worlds of Sagittarius are all that lies between you and the Cielcin horde. If we fall, they will come to each of you in turn, and we will not remain to aid you. In the past, your nations and our Empire have warred. We have been enemies at times. Friends, perhaps, at others. But it is under Imperial stars that the fate of the human universe will be decided."

The gray prince steadied his toga with one hand. "But I say we are *between* the horns. You will all have heard by now the Lothrians have declared for the enemy." A murmur ran through the lords upon their benches. "They have made a devil's bargain with the Pale. Their armies have swept across the Rasan Belt, and even as we speak are besieging our colonies in the Upper Sagittarius, and our friends in Jadd." Here he paused, and looked to the lords and dignitaries on the front benches. "At this time, the Council recognizes His Royal Highness, the Jaddian Prince Sennen Gorgora du Awan. Prince Sennen, if you please."

As the Chancellor took his seat, a tall, thin man of Jaddian breeding rose and smoothed the front of his black robes. His hair was of the usual *eali* oil-black, his face concealed behind the customary mask. Its segments—red onyx and gold leaf—moved as he spoke. "Brothers!" he said, "Sisters! His Magnificence, Aldia du Otranto, High Prince of Jadd, Beloved of God, and my brothers of the *Domagavani* have sent me with grave tidings! As His Excellency, the Prince Chancellor, has already said, we in Jadd are beset by the armies of the Lothriad."

Gorgora moved into the open space between the Imperial Council and the terraced benches of the visiting dignitaries as he spoke. "If I may direct your attention to the holograph," he said. The mighty plate affixed to the wall above the heads of the Chancellor and the Council flickered to life, displaying the image of a green world, its cloud-dappled surface wracked with black scars. "This is Numara, the capital of our northmost satrapy." The image changed, displayed a Jaddian city: black towered, gold crowned, bristling with green. Gray ships hung above the city; ugly, geometric things devoid of all embellishment or adornment save the Lothrian black star. There were dozens of them, filling the sky. As I watched, the lowest of these came in for a landing, settling on the burning green that had once been an urban park. Men and women dressed in their bright Jaddian finery ran pell-mell in view of the municipal security feed, fleeing the unleashed hordes of gray-clad soldiery that boiled down the landing ramp.

"As you can see," the Jaddian ambassador said, standing at the center of the council floor beneath the convex arc of the projection, "the Lothrians have adopted Cielcin tactics. They have always lagged behind with regard to ship design and weapons systems. At Numara, they compensated by sheer force of numbers. We estimate the force that took Numara numbered some one-point-two million Lothrian soldiers."

"One-point-two million?" echoed an Imperial strategos from one of the upper benches. "You're sure?"

"It is only a rough estimate," Gorgora said, as the image above advanced to show a tactical render of fleet engagement in orbit above Numara, "but we believe the satrap's forces were outnumbered nearly ten to one. The Lothrians managed to overwhelm our fleet's defenses. They boarded our ships, breached fuel containment—"

"Precisely Cielcin tactics," interjected Triumvir Turan Achlae, chief of the Norman representatives that had come to Forum.

Gorgora continued. "We estimate the satrap's forces destroyed as many as a third of the invasion force before he was forced to retreat."

"Forced to retreat?" asked Achlae.

"Numara is now in Lothrian hands," Gorgora said, precipitating a flurry of whispers from the gallery.

"How can the Lothrians afford this?" asked one of the black-clad ministers seated about the Nipponese emperor. "If Lord Marlowe's report on the Commonwealth is to be believed, the Lothrians have been selling their own people to the Cielcin for centuries now. Where have they found the population for this enterprise?"

I felt the eyes of the foreign princess at my left on me, moved only my eyes to look.

"You are he, are you not?" she asked. "The Halfmortal?"

I smiled thinly, but said no word.

"And what of the Jaddian clone armies?" asked Davor Cervenka, the reigning Doxe of the Durantine Republic, a white-bearded man in robes of azure silk crusted with gems like stars. "How could you be outnumbered?"

Prince Sennen Gorgora turned his red-masked face to regard his Durantine neighbor.

"There were one hundred thousand *mamluk* clones in Numara," he said. "This is an amount befitting a system of Numara's size. How many of your border worlds boast such a complement?"

"The honorable Duke Okada asks the right question," said one of the white-masked Mandari, speaking for the Nipponese minister. "How did the Lothrians find so many men? A thousand pardons, my prince of Jadd, but your Numara is a minor world, of marginal significance. If the Commonwealth is to bring to bear so great a force for so small a prize, they are either desperate...or more powerful than we know."

The Jaddian emissary bowed fractionally to the Mandari speaker. "It is for this reason above all others that I come before you today," he said, and gestured for the holograph to change. The plate now projected new scenes of carnage taken from the Battle of Numara. Soldiers in armor of matte gray or in simple padded pressure suits and blocky helmets lay dead in the polished white interior of a Jaddian battleship. "These are security stills taken from the satrap's own ship, which was boarded by the Lothrians shortly before it escaped to warp. The satrap's guard were able to neutralize the attackers—some nine hundred in all. The survivors remain in suspension, captives on Zorvan. They are *all* homunculi."

A murmur ran through the congregation at this pronouncement. I knew what Gorgora's next words would be before he spoke them. "Hermaphrodites, all." The projection shifted, displaying serial holographs of Jaddian war prisoners and a collage of medical imaging and reports from autopsy and serological analyses. The Lothrian soldiers all had the same, gray skin; the same short, black hair; the same hollow eyes. The images of the dead were nude, showcasing the modifications made to the human form by their Lothrian creators.

They were beyond doubt *nowoyukni,* the Lothrian *new-men.* Theirs were the faces and wide hips of women, the broad shoulders and strong arms of men. The one displayed had the black scars and red burns of disruptor damage on one small breast—the shot that had stopped its heart. The Jaddian coroner had not spared the subject its nudity, and its sex was on full display, the penis situated above the labia, without visible testes.

I averted my gaze, recalling the new-man child, Looker, who had saved my life.

"Just like the Cielcin," said one of the men from the Norman Alliance.

Prince Sennen Gorgora continued, "Of the nine-hundred-some taken dead or alive by the satrap's men at Numara, our physicians observed but one hundred seventeen distinct genotypes."

"One hundred seventeen?" echoed Prince Rand Mahidol, the Imperial Lord Minister of War, from the council bench beneath Aurelian's dais. Despite his advanced age, Prince Rand's hair remained black as pitch, and his voice was deep and resonant as a bell. "Are you saying the rest were copies?"

"A clone army?" asked the Consortium director general.

"Just so," said Prince Sennen Gorgora. "Careful analysis of the genetic makeup of these Lothrian he-women revealed certain gene-complexes that could only have been made by my own people. The Yahmazi are still working to determine precisely *how* our technology ended up in the hands of the Commonwealth, but the fact remains: it has. Prince Aldia and my brothers of the *Domagavani* have sent me to beg your forgiveness, for it is Jaddian praxis that has swollen the ranks of the Lothrians."

The hall was silent. A Lothrian army built on Jaddian-style clones, hurled into battle with Cielcin regard for life...I gripped the arms of the antique wood-and-leather seat that had been assigned to me.

"*Duplication!*" shouted Synarch Heraklonas from the council bench. "This is why it is *abomination* in the eyes of Mother Earth! To grow such an army from a seed is to upset the natural order! To unbalance man's ecosystem!"

Prince Chancellor Aurelian raised his voice over the Synarch's proclamation. "Wisdom Heraklonas," he said, "the morality of human cloning is an issue for another time. That devil has long escaped its bottle. Of issue is the matter of this Lothrian army. Our Jaddian guest tells us the Lothrians have stolen their own cloning technology to form this army. The Commonwealth has brought a million men to bear against Numara. How many more will they bring against the rest of Jadd? Who can say? What matters now is this: How many can we bring against them in response?"

"The Lothrians are a secondary concern!" said Turan Achlae, rising to his feet in a flurry of Uhran black and gold. "The Cielcin have ravaged our worlds! They have driven the Empire from the Veil. My own people now war with the xenobites and the Extrasolarians alone!"

I smiled at this. The Normans had fled so far to galactic north in no small part to escape the grasping hands of Empire, pushed to the frontier by the more deliberate, more totalizing press of Imperial expansion.

"Is there not but *one* concern?" asked King Paeon, rising smoothly to his feet four levels beneath my own. "Are the Lothrians not only a glove on the Cielcin White Hand?"

"All the more reason to focus our efforts on the Pale themselves," said the triumvir, undaunted. "If they can be stopped, their Lothrian servants will surely fall to pieces."

"We cannot simply ignore the Lothrians!" said the dryad king. "My own worlds lie upon their borders."

"And mine are in the Veil!" said Lord Achlae. "The Cielcin took Iatinon! And Alauna is lost! Millions of my people have been slaughtered, millions more taken as slaves. And if the Cielcin were not enough, there is the Monarch to consider. My lords, Calen Harendotes is amassing an army at Latarra. He means to conquer the Norman stars!"

"Let him!" cried one of the Small Kingdomers. "He is human, is he not? Better a devil of our own making than these *inmane* demons!"

"Let him?" Turan Achlae rounded on the speaker. "Would you be cavalier if the Extras were knocking at your own door, my lord of *nowhere?*" The Uhran Triumvir rounded on the dais. "Prince Chancellor, what of the Emperor? My brother triumvirs have sent me to treat with the Red Emperor, not to wrangle with petty kings of no consequence."

Lords and kings raised hands, representatives bellowed to be heard, and among their cries arose the constant refrain.

"What of the Emperor?"

Great though each might have been in his own land, a sun unto himself, here each was only a satellite, a planet or an errant moon circling—always circling—orbiting the Solar Throne.

It did not matter. None of it mattered—*would* matter so long as the Cielcin might cross the Gulf with a Watcher at the head of their army. *Two* Watchers.

Dorayaica believed that its gods could destroy reality itself, unmake creation, burn the stars to embers and grind the embers to ash. The part of me that was Ushara—that remembered being Ushara—told me that it was so. The Quiet had made the Watchers, she had said, had made us to serve. But we would not serve, *they* would not serve, would sooner tear down the very stars they had been fashioned to maintain.

What mattered all this petty wrangling measured against the fate of all?

And I could say *nothing*, do nothing but *watch* from my place on the highest level beside that obscure princess in her cloak of dragon's hide.

Aurelian rose, and as he stood the sergeant-at-arms smashed his fasces against the strike plate in the floor, calling for order. "His Radiance, the Emperor, will be joining us before long," Aurelian said. "It is no small feat, calibrating the telegraph matrix. You may rest assured; he will be here."

Into the newly restored order, a man rose from his place on the third arc of seats. He was bald as an egg and golden skinned, broad shouldered and dressed in a military uniform of dark green whose jacket possessed only one sleeve upon his right arm, leaving the left bare. With a pang, I recognized the tribal intaglio scarred and inked upon that bare left arm.

It was the *saylash* of his clan, the genetic marker and history of his lineage back to the founding of his line, and without the need to introduce himself, I knew that here was the Tavrosi grand admiral.

Seeing him, Aurelian resumed his seat. "Have you something to say, sir?"

"If I may."

"The Council recognizes the *Utnamnavi* Sattha Kull Vhad Kvasir, Grand Admiral of the Tavrosi fleet," said Aurelian, bowing his head. "Prince Sennen, you may return to your seat."

The Jaddian bowed to the Prince Chancellor, and the Tavrosi stalked down the steps, pausing to lay a hand on Sennen Gorgora's shoulder and to whisper some passing remark. Sattha Kull had a hard, square face, and from his complexion I guessed that he—like Valka—was of Panthai extraction.

"We must not get lost in the woods," he said. "Lothrian, Cielcin, Extrasolarian... 'tis not a question of *which* enemy we must face, but of *how* we will face them. We have the means between us, surely, to fight on all fronts." Sattha Kull turned to look up at Sennen Gorgora and the other Jaddian nobles. "In the Wisp, we have a saying: *Evil anywhere harms good everywhere.* We Demarchists have long failed to live up to the meaning of these words. We are a little people, and far away. The war has not come to us, and there are voices in the *Althing* that say we might escape war entirely, hiding around our remoter stars. I represent those who do *not* share this belief. The one must work for the good of the many, so the *Mux Sae* says, but the Lothrians would destroy every *one* for their many—not realizing the contradiction." He smiled.

The *Mux Sae* was the Tavrosi code of laws—those laws common to all their worlds and clans. Valka had but rarely spoken of it, especially after we fled her people after Berenike. The *Mux Sae* was the *Proper Way*, Valka had told me. Literally it meant *the Left Hand*.

I felt my smile harden, listening to the man. The *Lothrians* sacrificed every *one* of their people in service to their unholy book, it was so, but the Tavrosi had not hesitated to speak of sacrificing Valka's mind to save her body.

Sattha Kull continued, "'Twould be our honor to help the Jaddians in the defense of their home, as 'twould be our honor to aid the Normans. We harm no one but ourselves by this bickering. The enemy's numbers are great, 'tis so, but we have here the means to fight them. What we do not have are *guarantees*." The Tavrosi grand admiral turned sharply to Aurelian. "Prince Chancellor, for nearly four thousand years now my people have prospered beyond the borders of your Empire, but we were forced to flee to the Wisp by *your* family. Your Empire has persecuted our ancestors since the time of the Exodus, when we—like the Eudorans and the Mandari—were driven from the moons of Jupiter. Even now, your black priests would destroy us, if they could. We are heretics, they say. Dabblers with daimons. We are allies now by circumstance, because we face an enemy greater than any since the Mericanii Dominion. What *guarantees* can you give us—can you give *any* of us—that your Legions will not simply blacken our skies the moment the Cielcin fall from them?"

The dignitaries on their benches and the Imperial Council alike all shifted uncomfortably at the grand admiral's question.

It took courage—or arrogance—to stand before the Imperial Council, bold as brass, and ask such a question.

The dark-suited logothete to my right was listening with bureaucratic impassivity, the foreign princess on my left was watching me.

"What would you have?" Aurelian asked Sattha Kull, a brittle edge creeping into his polished baritone.

"Peace!" Kull replied. "An armistice, lord. Between your nation and mine. Written assurance that you renounce all claim to the stars of the Taurus Wisp."

"We have no time for this!" said Prince Rand Mahidol, whose ancestors had ruled Sattha Kull's. "If the Council is to hear the demands of every party present, we shall yet be in this hall when the Cielcin are at our gates!"

Not to be swayed, the grand admiral raised his arms. "Yet you ask us to fight for you!"

"We ask you to fight for all men!"

The voice sounded like a shot, like a grenade hurled from the highest level to that white-and-black tessellated floor. It was a voice so many of them knew, a voice from countless datanet holographs, from propaganda films and broadcast footage going back for hundreds of years. Every child in the Imperium had doubtless heard it, been shown recordings in history class. Darkly polished, severe, like the voice of some villain in a Eudoran masque.

It was my own voice, and I found that I was standing, six-hundred-some eyes staring up at me.

"We ask you to fight for all men," I said again, leaning over the table. "The one must serve the good of the many, you say. You say also that the Cielcin are the greatest threat man has faced since the Dominion. They are greater. *Far* greater than you know…" I caught Aurelian staring up at me, saw the man minutely shake his head. I could not reveal the existence of the Watchers. Not there, not then.

"Lord Marlowe!" Sattha Kull's teeth flashed whitely up at me. "'Tis Lord Marlowe, is it not? You cannot frighten me with tales of gods and monsters. We have but one god in the Wisp. That is Reason!"

"Whose reason, admiral?" I asked. "Yours?"

Sattha Kull laughed loud and clear. "They said you were a serpent! You left twelve men dead on Edda. Twelve men dead, and carried off one of our own."

"Your own?" I said, unconcerned with the hundreds of faces staring up at me. "She was my *wife*, admiral."

"Many men have said thus of their captives," said Sattha Kull, still smiling.

"You are very wise," I said, "to say such words at so great a distance."

"She belonged to her clan," said the Tavrosi officer.

"She belonged *with* me."

The sergeant-at-arm's fasces crashed against the strike plate, ringing for order. Prince Aurelian stood once more. "Grand admiral," he said, "you are our guest here on Forum. Lord Marlowe is likewise our guest. Have a care. Lord Marlowe: have a seat."

Sattha Kull's smile did not falter, nor did his eyes leave my face.

I felt the Marlowe anger bright and hot in my chest.

"*Anaryoch*," Kull said, and it shocked me to hear that word—so long transmuted to a term of affection by Valka and myself—returned to its native slur.

Barbarians.

"Lord Marlowe!" Aurelian's voice cracked like the whip it was.

At once conscious of the sea of faces turned to me, and of their whispering, I sat.

It cannot be in that precise moment that the white-wigged androgyn emerged from the arras behind the dais and scuttled to the Prince Chancellor's ear, but I cannot recall what matters of state and empire passed between the grand admiral's display and the androgyn's message. Aurelian rose, dismissed whichever speaker had replaced the *Utnamnavi* with a polite word.

Once more the fasces rang, and the voice herald that had announced

Aurelian's coming rose high and clear. "His Imperial Radiance, the Emperor William the Twenty-Third of the House Avent; Firstborn Son of the Earth; Guardian of the Solar System; King of Avalon; Lord Sovereign of the Kingdom of Windsor-in-Exile; Prince Imperator of the Arms of Orion, of Sagittarius, of Perseus, and Centaurus; Magnarch of Orion; Conqueror of Norma; Grand Strategos of the Legions of the Sun; Supreme Lord of the Cities of Forum; North Star of the Constellations of the Blood Palatine; Defender of the Children of Men; and Servant of the Servants of Earth."

The holograph plate rippled, shifted to reveal the Imperial person seated on the Solar Throne beneath its graven arch. Prince Alexander sat on a camp stool below the Emperor and to his right, dressed in the black tunic and trousers of a Legion officer, his long red hair secured by a golden ring at his left shoulder. Behind them both, a wall of Knights Excubitor stood, flaming swords held straight before their mirrored faces, their whiter-than-white cloaks a virgin backdrop for the reds and golds of the Emperor.

William himself looked old, though there was yet no gray in the violent red of his hair. There were shadows under his eyes that no powder could conceal, and he seemed thinner, drawn and stretched. A mantle of crimson samite hung about his shoulders, draped down over his right hand. The left glittered with rings, white glove shining as he raised it in greeting. "My lords and ladies—honored guests—we beg your forgiveness that we are not among you. So august a gathering of heroes, the principalities and powers of our universe...we should be there, in our own house. To our Jaddian friends: You have our sympathies. Numara is the first of your worlds to fall in this bloody war. We have long been allies, and your shield against the Cielcin. As that shield, we have borne the brunt of the inhuman onslaught, though we have not borne it alone..."

At this, the Emperor directed his attention to the Uhran triumvir and to the other Normans seated about him. "But, gentlemen, ladies...a shield cannot win a war. If we are to be victorious..." He faltered, uncharacteristically, and I sat a little forward in my chair. "If we are to be victorious, we must take the fight to the enemy. The time for reaction has passed."

This pronouncement sent perturbations through the gathered dignitaries. The Cielcin might attack anywhere, along thousands of light-years of borderland, at any time. Even if a signal could be sent instantaneously—no longer a guarantee thanks to the dismemberment of the telegraph network in the outer provinces—it might be years before the nearest fleet could reach the assailed system, by which time the Cielcin might easily be gone. It was for this reason that so few of our battles in so many centuries had been victories.

I knew what Caesar must say.

"We have made overtures to the Extrasolarians," the Emperor announced.

The congregation erupted, men standing, raising their arms. The Synarch Heraklonas stood, turning to the projection above his head. "Radiant Majesty, this is madness! Why was I not consulted?"

But his words were lost in the tide. The great lords of the Empire were likewise aghast, and there were many among them—Lions almost to a man—who stood up and were counted against the Emperor's declaration.

They were not alone. Prince Sennen stood, and the Nipponese Emperor, and several of the men of the Small Kingdoms, and a number of the more bellicose Normans—Turan Achlae chief among them. It was unthinkable. The Extrasolarians had been proscribed by Imperial law almost since the end of the Foundation War, when their ancestors refused to kneel to the God Emperor and his armies. They were barbarians, sorcerers, and brutes. I need not convince you of this truth, Reader. You have seen, have traveled far with me, through the pits of Vorgossos and into the Minoan net. You have seen what Sagara was capable of, and what Urbaine had done.

The Emperor raised his white left hand, two fingers extended together.

The fasces rang, and steadily silence fell, though many of the men on their feet failed to sit down. "We understand this news comes as a shock to many," the Emperor said. "The Extrasolarians have long been our enemies." Wong Xu had not so much as stirred, nor had Sattha Kull, whose polished head glowed like a target so many levels below me. "But many of you gathered here have been our enemies in the past. We have been yours. We must set aside our enmities—for a time, at least. Against the powers of the Cielcin and of their Lothrian slaves, none of us may stand alone. As we speak, emissaries from the Monarch of Latarra are inbound to the Eternal City. Calen Harendotes has agreed to hear us."

The shouts of outrage had given rise to curious murmurations.

There had been much talk of Calen Harendotes on Forum and across civilized space for centuries. The Monarch had emerged like lightning from a clear sky, conquered the Norman Freehold of Latarra, annexed Ashklam and rebuilt the shipyards on Monmara after the Cielcin obliterated the once-blue planet. Normans, Extrasolarians, even Imperial refugees had flocked to his banner. At Ganelon, I had met a captain of the Exalted, a gimlet-eyed man little larger than an infant who had floated in a hoverchair, who had called the Monarch master. Harendotes had had dealings with the sorcerers of MINOS, had played some part in the genesis of the LTH-81 plague.

"Harendotes?" Turan Achlae nearly knocked over his chair in his haste to reach the central floor. "Calen Harendotes threatens our worlds! It is in no small part because of Harendotes that I have sailed for Forum, Red Emperor!" He stood then in the center of the council chamber, black cape wrapped securely about his left arm. "And I find you in bed with him!"

The Emperor's image flickered, and he screwed shut his eyes. I felt an absurd twinge of loyalty for the man. I had expected to feel rage, yet not even the sight of Alexander—who once had tried to kill me and would one day succeed—stirred anything in me save concern. Had he always been so tired? How had I never seen it?

"Have a care, Uhran," said Alexander. "You address His Radiance, the Emperor!"

"He is your Emperor," the man said, "not mine. We have done away with kings in Uhra. We do not bow or scrape as you." Achlae practically snarled. "If you will treat with the Extrasolarians, you will not treat with me!" The other Normans had risen to their feet in support of the dark-faced triumvir, a cavalcade of strange and disparate uniforms.

Eyes still shut, William Caesar said, "The Monarch of Latarra can field fifty million soldiers, triumvir. How many have you?"

Achlae hissed, a sound more teapot than taipan. "I represent the entire Norman Alliance."

"Really? Do Kanthi and Ardistama and Pharos and all the rest care to lose Imperial support for the sake of your pride?"

One by one, the other Normans looked at one another. One by one, they resumed their seats. Achlae stood alone. I was struck then by the sur-reality of it all: Caesar looming like Jupiter himself across the concave arc of wall above the dais, larger than life, speaking across untold thousands of light-years. His image shimmered as he leaned back in his throne, an image of man-made-god, of power incarnate.

Turan Achlae loosed his cape and turned without another word, pride spurring him up the steps and from the chamber. The Republic of Uhra went with him.

Seven worlds.

CHAPTER 34

LAST APOSTOL
AND LEAST

THE SHIP HUNG ABOVE the landing field like the egg sac of some spider immeasurably huge and swollen, mirror-black and shining in Forum's pale sun. Far larger than any typical landing vessel it was, perhaps ten stories from belly to crown and half at least as broad, an oblate spheroid that both drank and spat up the light.

"I've never seen anything like it!" Cassandra said, voice hushed at my side. Neema shaded his eyes.

We had been permitted—the three of us—to join Aurelian's welcoming party, to watch from the sidelines as the aging Prince Chancellor greeted the apostol sent by the Extrasolarian Monarch. The prince himself stood at the center of the stage, surrounded by aides and by the men of the Martian Guard. Certain of his siblings sat in stands behind him, Selene among them. We had been placed to one side, been made to stand among the visiting dignitaries and assembled worthies of the Imperial court.

I placed my dark glasses on my nose and looked up into the long-enduring day, and as I watched the great egg extruded three landing legs like buttressed towers from equidistant points about its circumference. Black feet—tripartite themselves—hinged open as the vast cosmic egg sank on thrumming repulsors. Nowhere was there sign of windows, or line or door. Nowhere did I see the bristle of instrumentation or the swell of guns. But for those extruded, buttressed legs, the vessel was smooth and perfect.

Still, one felt its weight as those legs buckled, pneumatics hissing as they took the load.

Off to one side, a martial band—ordinary legionnaires, not Martians—struck up the Imperial anthem, the notes of the guitar and string section carried on the afternoon wind, bringing with it the air of history turning.

The whole Imperial universe was turning that bright and windy day. Changing.

For the better? For the worse?

Never before had an emissary of the Extrasolarians flown to Forum under a flag of truce, nor been accepted with open arms in the full light of day. One might sense the anticipation in that air, an almost static bite, a tension in every jaw. The Extras were monsters, the creatures every mother used to frighten their children.

I found myself thinking of Ganelon, of the laboratory there, of the black tower where the Elect-Masters of MINOS had gathered like witches to decide the doom of man. This Lord Harendotes had treated with them, and if Aurelian was to be believed, Legion Intelligence had tried to have the Monarch assassinated—and yet here they were, come as friends.

It was better, I knew, that they should stand beside us than against, yet still my hand went to my sword, fingers tight on the ivory grip as though it were a cane, a prop to support me, an anchor in a world gone mad. Had things truly grown so desperate?

I knew they had.

Yet every instinct—honed by centuries of experience, of battles at Vorgossos and Arae, at Berenike and Padmurak, at Ganelon and Perfugium—screamed that I should not drop my guard. I could feel a similar tension in the soldiers, knew that the muzzles of turret guns unseen in the splendorous towers about the landing field were trained upon the enemy.

A crack formed an upside-down U along the bottom of the cosmic egg, gleaming with white light. A vast ramp unfolded smoothly, pneumatics hissing as great pistons lowered it to the tarmac. Beside me, Cassandra craned her neck to see.

A cadre of guardsmen in mirror-black advanced, each carrying an energy-lance whose head flashed with blue fire. Their faces were hidden behind helms black as their armor, hod shaped, with a lip above the faceplate and a short flange over the ears. False eyes—twin circles of golden light—gleamed from every faceplate. Gold stripes ran along the arms, and a golden falcon shone on each breastplate.

The emblem of the Monarch.

Behind them came a motley assemblage of the horrors of backspace. A creature that recalled the pilot, Nazarreno—a silver sphere with a single red eye at its center—stalked out on a dozen iron tentacles, followed by a goliath machine that strode on all fours like an ape and the same gimlet-eyed floating infant I had seen at Ganelon. These were Exalted, once-men who had abstracted their shapes, sacrificed the greater part of their flesh and their humanity to achieve some inward desire. Some inward sense of self or beauty, or higher function. Behind these came six men carrying a palanquin upon which was nestled a sphere of clear glass, a tank in whose greenish liquid was suspended a human brain swollen so large no skull could contain it, its surface studded with bits of dark machinery.

Last of all, there came a dozen or so men—and women, too—in black tunics and high black boots. They wore the same hod helmets upon their heads, sans the faceplates with the glowing eyes. Each carried a highmatter sword on his or her right hip, matching hilts of electrum and black leather, the gold falcon of the monarch embroidered above each heart.

And behind them . . . last of all . . .

"Abba?" Cassandra had sensed the shock in me.

"It's not possible!" I said. Wonder took me then, wonder . . . and great joy.

At the rear of the strange column, dressed in fashion like these other officers but with no helmet upon his white head, came a man smaller than the rest. No taller than a child was he, slim and slight of frame.

Yet he was a giant to me.

The little man carried a cane in the crook of one arm, but he did not lean upon it as he had so often done when I had known him. Indeed, he walked straighter than I had ever seen, with shoulders thrown back and head held high. His white hair—so short when last I'd seen him—had grown long again, and hung in a lank cord at one shoulder. A tall woman marched beside him. She was nearly so pale as he, and carried her helmet under one arm, exposing a short halo of golden hair cut so short it might have been a boy's.

"It's not possible," I breathed once more, watching his guard halt and salute the Prince Chancellor on the receiving platform.

"Abba?"

"How does he do it?"

"Do what, sir?" Neema asked.

I had thought never to see him again.

He should have been on Belusha, had gone to Belusha in my stead.

His guard halted below the stand and saluted the Prince Chancellor and the assembled dignitaries with raised lances and unkindled swords. The woman beside the apostol ordered them to ease, and the white-haired man—like a wizened child—advanced to the fore and did not bow.

"I bring greetings from my royal master, His Majesty, Calen, Son of Ausar of the House Harendotes, by Merit and Will to Power, Supreme Monarch of the Realm and Worlds of Latarra, Conqueror of Ashklam, Prince of Monmara and Prince-Protector of the Norman Stars!"

I could almost feel the Norman delegation bristle at the sound of that clear voice, and looked to the block of clergymen—a sea of black and white—that dominated the left flank of the stand behind Aurelian. I felt I could sense their terror, and their fury at the sight of the two Exalted and of the swollen brain in its tank.

Still, the suspicion I had felt and the sense of foreboding were gone, banished by the appearance of that slight and bloodless-seeming little man.

The apostol spoke clearly, in the formal cadence expected of such an emissary. "I am..."

"Lorian..." I whispered the name.

I felt Cassandra turn sharply to look at me, heard her whispered, "What?"

"I am Lorian Aristedes, Commandant General of the Monarch's Grand Army."

A murmur went through the crowd at this pronouncement. His name was known.

"Lorian?" Cassandra hissed at me. "*Your* Lorian?"

I nodded.

"What is he doing at the head of an Extrasolarian army?" she asked.

"I have no idea," I said.

Another time...

I longed to shove the men before me aside, to hurry onto the tarmac before the receiving stand and make my presence known to the man who was—who had been—my last true friend.

But Lorian was speaking. "I am joined by the Exalted Captains Eidhin, Zelaz, and Archambault," he gestured at the three chimeras, the ape-man, the floating dwarf, and the many-armed cyclops. "As well as by His Cognizance, Prytanis, Preceptor of the Order of the Seekers After the First Truth." He indicated the swollen brain and its robed attendants. Lorian leaned upon his gold-headed cane. From my vantage point far to one side, I could see his pointed profile. Black lines like veins webbed his chalk-white face.

Aurelian raised a hand in greeting. "Be welcome to the Eternal City, Commandant General, captains, preceptor. I am Aurelian, Prince Chancellor of the Sollan Empire and son of our lord, His Radiance William of the Aventine. I regret that His Radiance is not here to greet you in person. He is fighting in the provinces."

"As is my own royal master," said Lorian, smiling. "It falls to us to make a peace."

"Yes, indeed!" the Prince Chancellor agreed. The scholiast that stood at his left hand leaned to whisper in his ear. Aurelian listened, nodded. "Forgive me, Commandant General. Are you not the same Lorian Aristedes who was once a companion of Lord Hadrian Marlowe?"

Lorian stood a little straighter, and in a voice much smaller than the one he'd used to make his official pronouncements moments before, he said, "I have that honor."

A ripple ran through the crowd of onlooking courtiers, and those nearest me turned to look.

"How come you into the Monarch's service?" Aurelian asked.

Lorian smiled. "I got a better offer." No reference to Belusha, no greater explanation. Apparently eager to forge ahead, Aristedes said, "My royal master has prepared a gift for you." He touched a comms patch behind one ear, and on command more of his armored soldiery appeared, great round eyes gleaming in their black-masked faces, leading a float-sledge draped in a black tarpaulin. The mass beneath it was shapeless and irregular, as if it held mere mounded earth.

The Martians on guard about the landing field tensed, lances at the ready. But the Extrasolarians moved carefully, guided the sledge down the ramp until it rested on the open space behind Lorian.

"At Eragassa, the Grand Army won a great battle against the forces of the Pale. We smashed nine of their worldships, and liberated the people of Eragassa itself."

I wondered if Turan Achlae was yet present, and what the snarling triumvir might have thought at Lorian's use of the word *liberated*. For my part, I still could not believe he was there.

How had he escaped Belusha? *No one* had escaped Belusha, not in all its history.

I should not have underestimated him.

Lorian seized the hem of the black tarpaulin and pulled. The cloth slid smoothly free—two of his soldiers hurried to help him. The rush of one collective indrawn breath joined the winds of Forum. For my part, I pressed forward a step.

The hulk that lay in ruins upon the sledge had been as large as a two-man flier. It had been larger in life, but the Extras had removed the six great legs that had projected from the bloated, white chassis. Its bristling turrets had likewise been removed, excised with the delicate care of a child pinching the legs off a spider one by one. The great, red-eyed forecastle that had been the chimera's head was dark, hung from the square shoulders, a dead weight.

"This was their commander!" Lorian said, and slapped the hulk with his cane.

It was the vayadan-general Teyanu. It was Teyanu that had led me on the long march from the gates of Akterumu to the shrine of Miudanar's skull. Several agonizing miles of gray sand and white faces, of blood and death.

"*Aeta!*" the Cielcin had cried, slinging filth and rotting meat at me as I staggered after the hulking general. "A king! A king!"

Of the six original slave-generals of the Prophet, but two remained.

That black day, when Dorayaica had sent Lorian to tell the Empire of my defeat, I had shouted after him, ordered him to avenge us. At the time, I had thought those would be my last words to the wider universe, the last words written in the record of my life.

Lorian had heeded me.

"A finger!" Lorian exclaimed, brandishing his cane as I had seen him do a thousand times. "A finger from the White Hand!" He held up his own digit for emphasis. "We took him when we broke his fleet."

Aurelian moved to the edge of the platform, looked down on Lorian and on the wreck of General Teyanu. "This is indeed a princely gift," he said. "And but a foretaste of what your master and we may do together." He paused, letting his hands go to his sides. "This is a new day for mankind, the start—I hope—of peace between our Empire and the Extrasolarians."

"There are no *Extrasolarians,* my prince," Lorian said, cutting across the prince's words so sharply I felt a pang of discomfort, then bemusement. "I speak only for the Monarch, the captains and the preceptor here speak for themselves, though they travel under my protection. They wish peace for their peoples as well."

"My lord, this cannot be!" said Synarch Heraklonas. "This is too much! Demoniacs in Forum! Have you forgotten Earth?"

"I forget nothing, Holy Wisdom," Aurelian said.

"What do you mean," asked Lord Rand of the Council, "that there are no Extrasolarians?"

"Only that we are not a people," Lorian replied levelly. "We are many peoples. As I say, I cannot speak for all. My royal master seeks that we become good neighbors. That is why he sends me. I was one of you, once. I stand between Empire and Monarchy. I am commanded to build a bridge."

"*We welcome this opportunity to improve relations between our peoples and the Empire,*" said Prytanis, its flat, emotionless voice issuing from mechanisms in the casing that housed its swollen brain. "*The Order of the Seekers After the First Truth do not desire war. We seek only to persist in contemplation of the Message and the Meaning of all.*"

Aurelian looked to Lorian as one looks for a translation.

The Commandant General bowed. "The Seekers are eremites, a religious order. They desire adorator status."

"And the Exalted?" Aurelian looked at Zelaz, Eidhin, and Archambault.

The massive machine-ape—Archambault, I thought he must be—thumped his armored barrel of a chest. "Trade. We wish trade with the *utmien sollani,*" he said. "You have much we need: Food. Fuel. There is much we have: Weapons. Fighting men. My ship, *Two Dreams of Spring,* is at your service. Ten thousand Exalted crewmen have I. Warriors all."

"And I have twelve," said the squidlike Eidhin. "My ship, the *Enigma of Hours,* will serve in the fighting, if you will grant us a writ of trade when the fighting is done."

The one called Zelaz was silent.

The *Enigma of Hours,* I thought, studying Eidhin. The many-tentacled machine-man was the captain of the vessel that had spirited me to Vorgossos so many centuries before.

"We shall have terms," Aurelian said. "We must discuss these matters in Council."

"We must," Lorian said. "My master demands you renounce all claim to the Norman stars. The Empire has lost its grip on the region, and is not like to regain it, with the Centaurus likewise devastated."

Aurelian smiled. "What of the Norman Alliance?"

Lorian gestured, as if to throw something away.

"Can he be trusted?" I pushed my way through the ranks of men in front of me, until I stood just behind the shoulders of the Martians lined up to separate we onlookers from the Latarran embassy. "Your new king?"

Lorian Aristedes looked round, recognition dawning on his sharp and sallow face. Those colorless eyes of his widened with surprise to see me, and for a moment I thought he smiled—but the smile vanished as quickly as it had come. Black lines threaded Lorian's face and neck, as though it were ink that flowed in his veins and not blood. Had he found treatment for his ills among their kind?

"Hadrian..." The name escaped the little man in barely more than a whisper. "You're...here?"

"Back in line, Lord Marlowe!" Aurelian said, and the Martians turned to lay hands on me.

"Can they *truly* be trusted?" I asked, more loudly still. "These Extras?"

The Martians shoved me back a pace, but I held my armsman's gaze, searching that face for some sign, some subtle betrayal. Was he yet my man? My friend? Or were those black marks the outward sign of some inward perversion?

O Mother, deliver us, thought I, who did not believe.

"Hadrian," Lorian said again, and looked away. Emotions I could not name warred behind his eyes. I saw them reflected in those watery spheres. Cold fires. "Yes. He can. They can be. I swear it."

The reception done, the crowd disintegrated. The Martians moved like clockwork, and the Prince Chancellor and his family and the other high lords on the stand had been chivvied tidily to their shuttles, but the great mass of the onlookers and minor courtiers and civil servants dissolved as they returned to the port terminal and the trams that would convey them back to the city proper. We were among them—Cassandra, Neema, and myself—escorted by six of the Martian Guard.

We had reached the terminal complex, were passing under the pillars of a sweeping colonnade toward the iron stairs that led up to the tram platform when Cassandra asked, "What do you think the First Truth is?"

I told her I could not guess, told her truthfully that I had never heard of the Order of Seekers before.

"The commandant said they were eremites," said Neema, speculatively. "One imagines they must contemplate the nature of reality, or of divinity itself, perhaps."

"They believe our universe but a simulation generated by some immeasurably advanced race," came a low, throaty voice.

A black-robed figure stepped from behind the bole of the nearest pillar. My hand went to my sword at once.

The woman that appeared wore the flowing black habit of the Chantry, a white sash about her slim waist, a white skullcap close-fitting her shaven head, cut about her ears to resemble the hairline.

"They believe their prophet discerned a structure in the background radiation of the Cataclysm that followed the First Cause," she said. "The Seekers believe this is proof of the falsity of creation. They seek escape from it. That is why their high priests dispose of their bodies. They would dispose of their brains if they could, I think."

"The Cielcin believe something similar," I said.

"I know. Theirs is a dangerous heresy," the woman said.

I offered a thin smile. The truth was, I agreed with her.

She had a symbol tattooed in the center of her forehead, a vertical line crossed three times by horizontals. It creased as her brows contracted. "Can you explain how it is that your man, Aristedes, has come to find himself in Extrasolarian employ?" she asked, bright eyes narrow as those of a cat.

"Perhaps you should ask him," I said.

"He was sentenced to life on Belusha," she said. "How did he escape?"

"I say again," I shifted to place myself between Cassandra and this venomous clergywoman, "ask him."

"Lorian Aristedes is your sworn armsman," she continued, "it was he who conspired to free you from Imperial custody."

In truth it had been a conspiracy between Lorian, Bassander Lin, and the Jaddian Prince Kaim, but Lorian had taken the fall. Lin was, as yet, still a commodore in the Imperial Navy, a knight and hero of the realm.

"He was," I said, not denying it. "He did."

"And now he appears at the head of the delegation from Latarra."

I let my arms hang at my sides, studying the mark tattooed on the woman's brow.

"You expect me to believe this is all coincidence?" she asked, raising one immaculately plucked eyebrow at the word *coincidence*.

"Woman, just who do you think you are?" Neema threw out his chest, stepped forward. "My master is—"

"The inquisitor knows full well who I am, Neema," I said, glancing sidelong at my Martian escort. They had ceased to be men, had become statues, a part of the terminal's furniture. They were studiously not present.

"Inquisitor?" The woman laughed, clasped taloned hands before her. "Inquisitor, indeed!" She cast her vision upward, as if searching for her god in the heavens. "Why have you come here? Why have you returned to Forum after so many decades in exile?"

"I was not given a choice," I said. That was true enough.

The inquisitor who was not an inquisitor moved a little nearer, eyes questing over my face, taking in my graying hair, my scarred cheek and hands. "And yet no one seems to know why you have come back at all. I have watched you in Council. But for that incident with the Tavrosi grand admiral, you have been silent. One wonders what your purpose is here?"

"What incident with the grand admiral?" Cassandra asked.

"Aurelian has gone to great lengths to isolate you," the woman continued.

"Not nearly great enough, it seems." The whole of the terminal was empty. The Porta Prince Arthur was reserved for visiting dignitaries, for diplomats and Mandari corporate lobbyists, and so was not crowded like the other starports. Still, for even this part of it to stand empty...it was unthinkable. Dimly I had the sense that I had plunged into waters deep and black as space, and that the limb of some monstrous *thing* had brushed me in the dark, the barest appendage of some leviathan of unfathomable size. "Who are you?"

She hesitated, holding my gaze with an intensity I had rarely seen. "I am called Samek," she said at last.

"That's not a name," I said in answer, recognizing the symbol on her brow at last. It was a letter. A very old letter. Not Greek. Hebrew? The part of me that spoke in Gibson's voice shook its head, recalled the answer from ancient memory.

Phoenician.

It was a code, a designation, like *A2.*

She smiled a smile that transformed her face from a thing terrible and threatening into something almost lovely. The change was startling. "They said you were well lettered."

"Well lettered, Samek? Is that a pun?"

She almost laughed, raised one taloned hand to cover her mouth after the fashion of Nipponese women. She was palatine, she had to be. All the high clergy were. "*Samek,* yes. Yes! Very good. I had not thought to like you, Lord Marlowe."

"I wish I could say the feeling was mutual," I said, acid in every word.

"You hate us, do you not?" Her laughter vanished as rapidly as it had come, her eyes—green as poison—hard as gemstones. I did not have to answer, and to do so at any rate was likely blasphemy. "Yet we serve a necessary function."

I inclined my head just slightly. "You safeguard human nature."

"Against the very beasts your friend, Aristedes, has brought to court."

"We *need* the Extrasolarians," I said. I did not say, *I need Vorgossos.*

"Perhaps," she said, stepping well within the reach of my arms. "Whatever you and Commander Aristedes are planning . . . I will uncover it. You may depend on that."

She wanted me to step away, wanted to intimidate me, to get me to embarrass myself by retreating even half a pace. Though she radiated menace like plutonium, she was smaller than me, and a woman, and so young. It was a man's gambit, the sort of thing a rogue might do to a young squire in a winesink.

I was far too old for such games.

"When you do," I said, "please tell me what it is. I honestly do not know."

"A man may bury the truth, Lord Marlowe," Samek said, "but he cannot break it."

"You are trying to get me to admit something I do not know," I said. "Until today, I believed Lorian Aristedes dead on Belusha." I smiled the crooked Marlowe smile. "I know what you are, Samek. You're of the Choir, aren't you? A cantor?"

Her silence was all the answer I was like to get. Was that fear in the corner of her eyes? Or only the beginning of another smile? The Choir was the Chantry's research organ, the college whose members researched the very technologies their laws forbade, the makers of the plagues and poisons the Inquisition held over the heads of disobedient lords and governors. The men and women of the Choir did not offer sacrifice in sanctum nor chant from the minarets at sundown. They were bureaucrats of the cloth, more magus than priest, shadowy figures swimming beneath the surface of Imperial consciousness.

I had never met one, had never thought to meet one.

Now I had.

"I always thought you lot never showed yourselves, kept to your ivory towers?" I said, glancing through the window at my right to where the Extrasolarians' cosmic egg stood at anchor on the landing pad. "Lorian took *you* by surprise, too, didn't he?" Still she had not retreated, and I stepped forward—little more than an inch, until almost her breast and mine touched. "Do you know what *I* think, Samek? I think you're losing your grip. I think you panicked when Lorian Aristedes emerged from that ship, and I think that's why you're here."

Samek's smile returned, and to her credit she did not retreat. "You think you are above judgement, Lord Marlowe," she said. "You think the Emperor's pardon a shield. But there are those of us who would shield him even from himself. He has always been blind when it comes to you, but our eyes are unclouded." She did extricate herself then, drawing back a step. "We are watching you, my lord."

The leviathan turned with her, swimming away into the blind dark. I watched her go, black robes rippling through the gray shadows cast by those white pillars—a forest of palest stone. The fishermen of every world swear by the presence of monsters in the deep, monsters that burst and shrivel without the titanic pressures that accompany great depth, that die if they swim too close to the light.

The leviathan surfaces only as it dies.

And I would die with it.

CHAPTER 35

BARBARIANS

IMAGES OF THE WRECKAGE at Eragassa hung on the display for all to see. Nine Cielcin worldships hung in the void, their surfaces cracked and burning, one shattered all to pieces where the great oceans of its antimatter reservoir had burst and blasted a crater big as half a continent.

The planet itself was doomed, wracked by paroxysms as those new moons crashed through orbits lower and lower still. It would not be long—a mere count of years—before the lowest ship of Teyanu's bested fleet collided with the pale, white world. Apocalypse was certain, was only a matter of time, but the forces of Latarra had begun the evacuation process.

The people were saved.

Eragassa had been an Imperial territory, not five centuries before. The demesne of the dukes of House Haide. When Marinus had fallen, just before the Battle of Berenike, Eragassa had been one of many hundred worlds cut off from Imperial control. Alone in the dark, the Haides had been left to fend for themselves, had allied first with the Uhrans, then a succession of Norman Freeholds and border lords. They had petitioned the Magnarch on Nessus and the Emperor himself for reinforcements, but no aid had come.

Then plague had come to Eragassa, and Duke Alexander III had died without heir, as without the ability to reach the Empire, he and his wife had been unable to conceive a legitimate heir. The remnants of the Imperial government had had little choice but to reach out to the Monarch of Latarra, that champion of the border worlds, that lion of Norma, and he had gathered Eragassa to himself—for what little time had remained to it.

"Why Eragassa?" asked Rand Mahidol, peering down at Lorian from over the council table.

The intus slapped his cane against his leg in irritation. "Because Eragassa had twenty-five million people living on it, even after the plague. It was one of the most populous planets in the sector. The *vayadan*-general had been sent to cull the herd."

"Cull the herd?" Heraklonas scowled. "Don't be grotesque!"

Lorian snapped. "You have little concept here of how dire things are in the Expanse! Without your Legions to maintain order, ships would not sail. Trade collapsed. The populations of these planets were trapped there, without defense, without escape. To the Cielcin, they were little more than grain awaiting harvest."

"How did your forces arrive in time?" The voice that spoke rained down from on high, and many of the Sollans in the congregation bowed their heads in deference. The Emperor's image reasserted itself, banishing the images Lorian had conjured of the ruined world. Caesar gripped the arm of his throne with one hand, the rest of his body draped in robes like drifts of snow. "Eragassa is quite remote from Latarra, some two thousand light-years, as I recall."

I glanced at the printout on the table before me, the report Lorian had made and distributed before this meeting.

Two thousand, three hundred and seventeen light-years, the report indicated.

"We had advance warning," Lorian replied, straightening where he stood in the center of the council floor.

That revelation sent a tremor through the congregation as lords whispered to military men, military men to ministers. Lorian let them mutter, still tapping his cane against his leg. He was never still, had never been still, even if his motion was confined to the idle twirling of a finger. His energy—so it had ever seemed to me—always had to go *somewhere.*

"How?" The Emperor's word fell like a stone.

"As you know, the Cielcin have long eschewed radio transmission, reserving them only to broadcast their demands to us," he began. "In the early days of the war, we were uncertain how it was they communicated with one another. That was before we discovered their maser pulse beacons." He held up his hands, spread them before himself. "Tight-beam, short-burst transmissions. Point-to-point. Nearly impossible to detect unless you happened to be in the path of their transmissions."

Lord Rand Mahidol waved a dismissive hand, saying, "We know all this."

"Of course," Lorian said. "But what about faster-than-light? The pulse beacons form an effective means of ship-to-ship communication within a Cielcin fleet, a *scianda.* But they're virtually useless at range. Beyond a few light-hours, the beams attenuate, become incoherent. My former patron, Lord Marlowe,"—he pointed with the head of his cane to where I sat—"believed the antagonistic relationships the Cielcin princes shared with one another precluded most need for interfleet communication. Lord Cassian Powers and the boys in Legion Intelligence believed the Cielcin fleets were effectively isolated from one another. Others have speculated they must have a network of deep-space satellites. Data caches. Comms buoys, like our own datanet—only without the telegraph relay—places where they could leave messages for one another. Check in, as it were. They live a very long time—we're still not quite sure of their natural maximum lifespan. They're not in near as much of a hurry as we are...or they weren't."

"We've never managed to find one of these Cielcin data caches," interjected the Prince Chancellor from the dais, "they remain highly speculative."

"Did you find one?" Prince Alexander asked, straightening in his seat below the Emperor's on the projection.

I was leaning well forward by then. If Lorian and Harendotes's men had indeed located a node of the Cielcin communications grid, it would be paradigm altering, a total change in the way we engaged with the enemy.

"No," replied Lorian flatly. "If they exist, they remain as much a mystery as they always were."

"Then why mention them, intus?" asked Lord Mahidol sharply.

Lorian's head swung round to glare at the Prince of Ayuthay, but he did not answer the slur as I might have done. "Because interstellar communication was a problem the Cielcin had to solve. It was this deficit that the Cielcin sought to ameliorate by their partnership with the Extrasolarians."

"So you admit it!" cried Synarch Heraklonas. "Your people have long been allies of the Pale!"

"My people?" Lorian blinked, shook his head. "Your people...certain agencies among the Extrasolarians have aligned themselves with the Pale, yes. My royal master is not one of them."

"Is it not the case that Calen Harendotes traded with MINOS?" asked Prince Aurelian. "With the very sorcerers who designed the plague that is now set against our galaxy?"

Lorian looked down at his polished boots, slapped his cane against his calf once more. "That is so!" he said, drawing condemnatory whispers from the crowd. One or two men shouted denunciations. I clenched my jaw. "My royal master provided the Minoan scientists several thousand human test subjects, war prisoners taken during the conquest of Ashklam."

I felt myself recoil. So *that* was what had been aboard the ship Legion Intelligence had intercepted sailing to Ganelon from Latarra.

"Villainy!" cried Heraklonas. "Holy Radiance, you cannot mean to bind yourself to such creatures!"

"The Latarra Commandant General confesses crimes against sacred humanity!" said one of the lesser clergy, garnering a chorus of assent.

Lord Rand Mahidol spoke up. "How many deaths have resulted from the release of the Minoan virus?"

"Estimated pandemic death totals stand at approximately thirty-seven billion across the Imperium," said a scholiast from the Home Office.

The tip of Lorian's cane rang against the checkered marble in imitation of the sergeant's fasces. "Sacred humanity?" he said. "Is slavery not practiced in the Imperium? Do not our friends in Jadd breed their subhuman warriors by the million? Did members of this Council not themselves sanction the assassination of my royal master for the crime of restoring order to the Norman stars? Not a *one* of us in this room can pretend to clean hands! Not a one! Does not the Chantry itself maintain a monopoly on biological weapons development within the Imperium? Is it perhaps jealousy that motivates this outrage, Holy Wisdom?"

"Why... I!" Heraklonas stammered. I spied Samek's white skull cap in the sea of Chantry white and black seated below and to the right of the council arena.

Lorian had scored a point, and all present knew it.

"This bickering is pointless," came the atonal, sexless voice of Preceptor Prytanis. "The purpose of this Council cannot be the adjudication of all sin. We are not the Maker. We have neither the time nor the wisdom to exercise perfect justice." One of the giant brain's attendants adjusted a knob on its housing as it spoke, modulating the speaker's volume.

Silence—brittle and unsteady—fell upon the court in segments.

Only slowly did I realize the Emperor had raised his hand. "I should like to hear how it is the Latarra Grand Army received advance warning of the attack on Eragassa," he said. "Synarch Heraklonas. You will be silent."

The Commandant General wrung his bony hands on the shaft of his cane as though it were the neck of some captured game fowl. "The Cielcin have long had dealings with certain factions among the Extrasolarians, namely the King of Vorgossos, as Lord Marlowe himself determined after the Battle of Emesh. They had an interest in human technology. Weapons, biomechanics, comms equipment."

"Telegraphs," said Captain Archambault, deep voice booming from his place to one side.

Lorian thrust at the Exalted with his cane. "Just so. Extrasolarian telegraphs gave the Cielcin access to instantaneous communication. For the first time in their history, their fleets were able to communicate with one another at speed across the galactic volume. Historically, telegraph communications have proved impervious to interception, but times have changed, and the Cielcin reliance on our technology has left them exposed."

"Exposed?" the Emperor asked, leaning forward. "What are you saying?" For just a moment, the shadow of something like pain flickered across that familiar face.

"We have the means to trace the location of Cielcin telegraph nodes." Lorian let the words fall like a shot.

"Impossible!" said a junior man from the War Office. He wore the collar tabs of Special Security. "You said it yourself, the telegraphs work off quantum entanglement. They're point-to-point. There's no transmission to detect."

"No ordinary transmission," said Captain Archambault. "No EM radiation. But the excitation of entangled particles perturbs the quantum foam of space itself. By measuring the scale of these perturbations, it is possible to know the distance between the scanner and the operating telegraph, and to chart a vector."

"But entangled particles occur in nature," objected one of the Norman delegates.

"All telegraph transmissions require patterned excitation of the entangled particle. By filtering for such patterns, one is able to distinguish artificial signals from random natural phenomena."

One of the scholiasts in the first row turned her attention on the hulking machine-captain. "If what you're saying is true...then how can you know the telegraphs you are detecting belong to the Cielcin?"

Lorian, Archambault...the entire Latarran embassy was silent. Lorian—who was never still—hardly moved himself, only wrung the neck of his cane with spidery hands.

"You can't, can you?" the scholiast asked.

"You can detect *every* telegraph," the Emperor said.

Hushed voices crashed like waves, rose in intensity as the implication of William's words broke against the hard shore of reality. If what Lorian and Archambault were saying was true, then the Monarch of Latarra and his allies had devised a means by which they might not only detect the location of an active telegraph node, but discern the contents of its message. The private communiques of lords and kings, governments and criminals and corporations the galaxy over were laid bare to the Monarch's new machine.

The little Commandant General confirmed this with a nod. "Within the sensor's effective radius, yes."

"What is the sensor's effective radius?" His Radiance inquired.

"Several thousand light-years," came Lorian's reply.

The Emperor made to lift his right hand to his face from its place beneath his robe, but seemed to think better of it. "This is...disturbing news," he said at last. Already I suspected wheels were turning in the Imperial mind, laying plans for ways to encrypt telegraph transmissions moving forward.

Lorian stabbed the floor with his cane, planting its tip square between the pointed toes of his boots. "It is hoped," he said, "that our willingness to reveal this information constitutes sufficient show of good faith."

"You are willing to share this technology?" asked Lord Rand.

"In exchange for the Sollan Empire's total renunciation of all claim to the Norman Stars, and a formal recognition of the sovereignty of His Majesty, Calen, Son of Ausar of the House Harendotes, as Monarch of Latarra."

This brought the Norman delegation to its feet, and shouting filled the high hall.

"What of us?" cried one of the princes of Ardistama, one of the greater Norman planet-states.

"Turan Achlae was right!" shouted another.

And a third, a consul from the pirate planet Sanora, barked, "Are we to bow to Latarra?"

"If you wish to survive!" Lorian rounded on them. "None of you has the strength to resist our armies, much less the Cielcin horde! You may each retain your offices, but you will pay tribute to the Monarch."

"What of our own territories in Norma?" asked the voice Imperial.

"We offer the same deal," came Lorian's reply. "They may retain their worlds and titles, but then will kneel to Latarra, not the Solar Throne."

On the projection, Prince Alexander stood, "With the stroke of a pen, you would take ten thousand worlds!"

"Far more than that," Lorian said. "But these are worlds you have lost already. You lose nothing."

"Nothing!" Alexander echoed the word. "Nothing? You would have us abandon our people? Thousands of worlds?"

"Tens of thousands," Lorian countered. "Yes. You need us, prince. The telegraph tracker allowed us to intercept the Cielcin battle plans. With it, our combined fleets will be able to outmaneuver the Cielcin and their Lothrian slaves alike. We can end this war. You can end it—as you say—with the stroke of a pen."

"Commandant General,"—the Emperor's voice was strangely faint—"the great families of the Norman Expanse cannot survive cut off from the throne."

Lorian stabbed the tile with his cane yet again. "Because their children will be born *intus?*" he asked, spitting the last word like poison.

"Quite."

"We have the means to address that," Lorian said, eliciting murmurs from the Imperial sectors of the council hall. "Not so effectively as in Jadd, perhaps, but as you see, I am quite well." He extended one striated hand for examination. "There are worse fates than being *misborn,* Emperor." Lorian turned, sweeping his gaze over all the great lords gathered there. The Normans were still mostly on their feet, their agitation plain. They had become pawns on a board where they had thought themselves at least knights or castles.

I sensed similar discomfiture among the lords of the Small Kingdoms, even among the princes of the Empire. Lorian—and through him, Harendotes—had a strong hand. Tipping it, he revealed his advantage, boasted of his power and offered to share it . . . and all he asked in return was Imperial humiliation. To cede the Norman territories to the Monarch without so much as a fight was to admit Imperial weakness. Surrendering all claim to the Arm of Norma was to halt Imperial expansion north toward the galactic core. About such decisions the arc of history bent. Men ten thousand years hence might look back and say that it was at this council that the Sollan Empire began to die, curbing forever that outward pressure that alone sustains a state against the slow decay of time. Would they say that it was when faced with the Cielcin menace that the greatest empire mankind had ever known lost its will to *be,* and chose instead dotage and the slow decay of time?

It is not power that builds empires, that asserts order on the stars.

It is vision. Vision and the heroic *will* to act.

Where there is that vision, all else follows.

Where it is not, there is decadence, desperation, and decay.

I understood all this then, in that moment, though it has taken me much time to order my thoughts on the matter, and perhaps it is only now—by the light of my murdered sun and the dark days that have followed it—that I see things clearly.

The old order, which balanced upon but one pillar—the Imperium—had passed away.

It had been dead a long time, but so tall was it that it had yet to crash to earth.

In its place, a new order was rising, an order founded not on one pillar, but many. On Forum still, but on Latarra, on Jadd, on Durannos and Vorgossos and perhaps on Padmurak, too. The gearworks of history, which had for so long been jammed by Imperial decree, had begun to turn again. The Cielcin had started them turning, and now nothing could stop them.

"We must think upon all this," the Emperor said, head bent in his chair. "We shall adjourn for now."

CHAPTER 36

THRESHOLDS

THE COUNCIL PROCEEDED THUS for many weeks. I was not permitted to speak with Lorian outside the Council. My Martians saw to that, chivvying me from the council hall upon the conclusion of each session, only to spirit me back to my place in the Arx Caelestis. Likewise my meeting with the Emperor was delayed. His Radiance was consumed by matters of state, so the men in Aurelian's office said when I called to inquire, which was almost daily.

The Emperor would hear me, Aurelian's office said, when the Emperor was ready. Why the Emperor was not ready sooner I could not say. He must have known how dire was my errand, must have received the telegraph I'd sent ahead.

I received and beg your pardon. My mission was incomplete. I sail for Forum at once.

He knew Ushara was still alive, that Operation Gnomon—the mission to find and slay the Watcher on Sabratha—had failed. I was a prisoner of Imperial protocol, and Cassandra along with me. Four years I'd been made to wait. Four years under careful watch in the citadel of the Martian Guard. Many were the sleepless nights I whiled away, peering through the polarized windows at the ceaseless day, or through clear glass at the as-interminable nights.

Cassandra fared—if anything—worse than I. She, who had grown with the freedom of the isle and the gleaming waters of Jadd, who had ventured with me across the endless sands of Sabratha, felt the walls of our apartments more strongly. Only Neema was at peace. The Jaddian servitor busied himself ordering our little world, keeping house and serving at table. More than once he got into arguments with the Martians who watched our door, demanding items for the larder or to know why our laundry had not been returned or handled properly.

Selene had not made good on her promise to take Cassandra and me riding in the Royal Wood. Aurelian must have denied her.

Still, I was not without guests. A man from the Chantry came the day after Lorian's arrival—the day Lorian had revealed the existence of the Latarran telegraph sensor. He repeated many of Samek's accusations. That Lorian and I were working in concert, that we were acting on the orders of some parallel Imperial agency—Special Security, or HAPSIS, or the Imperial Office proper—that we were conspiring against the Imperium. Lorian's revelation about the Monarch's new method for tapping into telegraph transmissions did not help my case. Had I known about it? Was I familiar with its function? I told the man I was not, that I was as surprised by the news as he.

He left frustrated, promising to return.

Edouard appeared for the first time in several months. He had been involved in official matters in the HAPSIS office. With Oberlin dead and the Emperor offworld, the whole department had been thrown into chaos, and Aurelian had been forced to step in to name an interim director while a proper successor for the late Lord Friedrich could be found. Word of Lascaris's replacement had set the department—and indeed the entire intelligence apparatus—into disarray. The Inquisition had been called for, and conducted thorough investigations of all personnel in an effort to turn up other infiltrators.

Edouard himself looked drawn and pale, as tired as ever I'd seen him.

"I'm being reassigned," he said, seating himself on the edge of the chair in the lavish sitting room. The wall behind him showed a relief sculpture of the planet Mars, its curve filling the bottom third, its pale cap inset with mother of pearl, its twin moons rising above its arc. The Earth filled the sky above it, with the sun—its surface enameled with gold leaf—shining at the apex, so that the viewer's eyes were drawn inevitably toward it, from Mars, past Earth. Almost the sun's golden rays made a halo all around the young agent's head. "I'm not sure where. I think Aurelian wants me offworld."

I took the news in silence.

Besides Cassandra, Neema, and myself, Edouard alone on Forum knew what had transpired on Sabratha. There could not be many, even in the HAPSIS offices, who knew of Gnomon, of Project Perseus and of what had transpired on Nairi. With the Chantry and its Choir sniffing around and the general chaos brought on by the presence of so many offworlders—not least the Extrasolarians themselves—Aurelian was sure to want to keep Gnomon and all knowledge of the Watchers concealed. I was under control, and my people with me. Edouard represented the only loose end.

"When do you leave?" I asked.

"At the end of the week," he said, voice stiff. "That's why I'm here now. I wanted to say goodbye."

Neither one of us spoke for a moment. I had developed a distant fondness for the young fellow in the years we'd worked together, and the news that he would soon depart Forum—and my story—had taken me by surprise.

"You really don't know where you're going?" I asked.

Edouard held my gaze for the space of several heartbeats, long enough to convey that whatever he might say, he knew. "With the Sabratha matter concluded, there are other projects I must turn my attention to."

"The Sabratha matter is *not* concluded," I said.

"You know we should not discuss such things," Albé said, and—changing tack—leaned in, "Have you any proof of that?"

I felt Ushara's shadow play across my face, and turned away, lest the younger man see it and fail to understand. "Only a feeling."

Edouard said, "Legion Intelligence captured a Cielcin worldship fighting in Lynga. Mayhap I'll be sent there. There will doubtless be Vaiartu artifacts requiring examination and oversight."

That he had proposed such a course of action for himself was proof enough that he was doing anything but. I nodded, accepting the fiction, but conveying by my smile that I understood. What young Albé's fate was to be I could not guess, but it was certainly not the oversight of a dig out in Lynga Cluster.

"In which case I wish you well," I said.

"Have you had a chance to speak to His Radiance as yet?" Edouard asked, his face intent.

Neema emerged from the rear hall and circled the chamber, heading from the apartments' kitchens, through which lay the servants' quarters that were his private abode. I watched him pass. I was well used to being watched, though I felt I had never been watched more closely in all my long life. Aurelian alone knew all that I knew, and Aurelian was not the only audience for whatever surveillance equipment was doubtless listening to our every word. There was the Chantry to consider, and the Lions. Agents of Prince Alexander, of Legion Intelligence, of Mother Earth only knew who else.

"Not until the day after tomorrow," I said. "I've had a devil of a time getting an audience. Twice now Aurelian's office has scheduled a meeting, but they've had to move it."

A shadow passed over Edouard's face. "Trouble with that . . . super telegraph of theirs?"

"Maybe." I idly reached for the glass of dark wine at the table beside me. "Have you been in the Council? I haven't seen you."

The younger man shook his head.

"The Emperor has aged so much," I said. "He colors his hair, I think. It looks...it looks wrong. The centuries since I last saw him have not been kind." Catching sight of my own reflection in the chocolate-dark of the Kandarene in my glass, I added, "To any of us."

"How old do you think he is?" Edouard asked. "In years actual?"

"He was crowned in..." I had to remember. "Fifteen eight twenty-six?" Every child in the Imperium was made to memorize the year, palatine or peasant. "That was sixteen hundred years ago. I'd wager he's perhaps half that."

"He can't have much longer, then."

"Have a care," I said. It was not proper to speak of the Emperor's impending death, however innocently. "But no."

Edouard had denied himself a cup of my wine, but I drank anyway. The Kandarene was rich and faintly sweet. It lingered on the palette like blood, tasting of relentless time. "I am six hundred twenty-two myself, though I was born more than a thousand years ago now..." I looked sadly at the mural of Mars and her sister planet—our mother. "Sometimes I think the galaxy I set out to save doesn't even exist anymore."

"I know what you mean, Lord Marlowe," Albé said. "What is that old saying about planting trees though you'll not live to enjoy the fruit?"

Abruptly I recalled the passage I had quoted to the Seventeenth Chair of the Lothrian Grand Conclave on that black voyage to Padmurak. "I say it is the cruel law of art that all things must die, and that we ourselves must die...having exhausted every suffering, so that the grass, not of oblivion but of eternal life, should grow, fertilized by works."

Edouard blinked at me, "That's not it, but you take my meaning."

"I do."

"What we do...we're not saving the galaxy—the Empire, I should say—for ourselves. Men like us will never know peace, lordship."

"Men like us?" I said, looking sharply at the young man. "Are we alike, Edouard?"

"Yes, lordship," he said. "We've both looked into the abyss, haven't we? We both know what's out there."

We did at that.

"It falls to us to ensure the rest of the galaxy doesn't have to know, isn't that right?" He stood as he spoke, retrieving his black service beret from the arm of the sofa. He pressed it to his head, draped it toward the right ear.

I matched him, setting aside my goblet to find my feet.

"That is what I tell myself," I said.

"They're wrong to send you away," I said. "Our work isn't done."

"That's not for me to decide," said A2. He placed his left hand into his pocket, seemed to hesitate. Presently he offered his right, in peasant fashion, palm up for me to take. "I hope we meet again."

I took the offered hand, saying, "As do I."

I felt the slip of paper creak against my palm, felt too my heart grow numb with dread. My eyes flicked to Edouard's face. The other man smiled, nodded, withdrew his hand. Drawing back, he pressed that hand to his breast in stiff salute. "It was an honor to meet you, lord. I can't imagine there are many in the Imperium who can claim to know all the children of old Lord Alistair."

"Not even I can claim that," I said, having never met my sister, Sabine.

"Domi?" Neema had emerged from the servant's door. "There's someone at the door, Commander Kas's men just waved to alert me. Shall I have him wait?"

Edouard straightened his tunic, rested one hand on the silver buckle of his belt. "I was just leaving, sirrah," he said.

"Did the Martians say who it was?"

Neema sniffed. "Two words at a time is the best the brutes can manage."

Albé's note was still in my fist. I slid my hands into my pockets, mind already working through the details of just how I would manage to read the blasted thing. I would have to hide the thing in plain sight, open it among my papers, find a way to dispose of it where my monitors would never think to look. Hide it in a wad of toilet tissue, or else secret it in a pocket of my clothes until next I left my chambers—toss it over the side of one platform, to tumble the thousands of miles down to Forum's metallic seas.

I felt as though I clutched a slug of pure uranium, felt its radiation burning through the lining of my pocket.

"I'll see Agent Albé out myself, then," I said, not sure who my mysterious visitor could possibly be. I had been so without guests for so long that to have two visitors in one day was a marvel, or would have been, had not Albé's note become the heart of a neutron star weighing down my pocket.

I led the man out into the foyer, past the water closet and the coat closet to the cold, metal door. I had control of that door, though there were always Martians posted outside. The imitation of freedom.

"Your family must be proud," I said.

He touched his cap. "They think me a courier in the diplomatic corps. But they are proud of what they think their son is."

"They *should* be," I said, and thinking of the unanswered question, I appended, "You're a good man, Albé."

"None of us is good, lord," Edouard said, "It for us to *do* good despite ourselves."

"Parting wisdom?" I asked, offering my wryest smile.

"Something like that," the younger man said.

"This is not the end," I said to him. "We'll meet again."

"I hope so," he said, but his smile said that he thought otherwise.

I keyed the door, turned to greet my guest.

I should have known the day would come, had hoped for it since he had emerged from his massive egg in the Porta Prince Arthur.

Lorian Aristedes was standing in the hall, caught midway through a word with the Martian to my door's left. He wore the Monarch's black and gold, and carried his falcon-headed cane in the crook of one arm. When he saw me, he removed his cap and placed it under that same arm.

At once I found I did not know what to say.

"Lorian..."

There were indeed black lines beneath the *intus* man's waxen flesh, like mineral veins deposited by water in white marble. They spiderwebbed across his face, faint but plain to see. His long hair hung over the right shoulder, queue secured by three golden rings.

"You're Commander Aristedes!" Edouard said, bowing his courtly best. "The *Tamerlane*'s tac officer."

Lorian's brows arched. "It's Commandant General, these days," he said. "I'm no longer with the Imperium."

"Yes, of course," Albé bowed. "I'd heard that, too."

"How are you?" I asked, words barely more than whispers.

It did not seem real. When Lorian and I had said our farewells aboard the *Tempest,* both of us had known it was for the final time. And yet it was not—had not been.

"I'm...good," the little man said, and smiled in his lupine way. "As good as I've ever been."

Remembering myself, I said, "This is Special Agent Edouard Albé, Imperial Office. HAPSIS Division."

"HAPSIS?" Lorian's eyes slid from my face to Edouard's and back again. "What are you doing here, Marlowe?"

"I should let you two be alone," said Edouard. "My Lord Marlowe."

I smiled, and said, "Until our next meeting." I touched the outside of my pocket, pressed to feel that the man's note was still there.

It was.

"I hope there will be one," he said, and offered crisp salute.

"There will be," I said.

Then he was gone, nodding to my door wards as he passed. Lorian turned to watch him go, drumming spidery fingers against the head of his cane. "Stiff fellow, isn't he?" He grinned up at me. "Formal."

"Not like you," I said, matching the little man's grin.

"Not at all!" Lorian said, and eying the Martians standing like statues to either side of my door, he added, "May I come in?"

"Of course," I stepped aside to permit the fellow to pass me. He speared the floor with his cane as he crossed the threshold, and I cycled the door behind us both, glaring briefly at the Martian to my right as the portal slid closed.

"What in the eight hells are you doing here?" he hissed, shifting his grip on the cane so that he held it like a sword. So swift was the change in his demeanor that I recoiled. "You were supposed to be on Jadd!"

"I was on Jadd!" I said, growling to match the other man's snarl.

"And I was on Belusha!" he countered. "I went to Belusha *for* you."

My gaze fell to a spot on the floor beside Lorian's boots, bounced up to the ceiling to the black aperture of a camera eye in the ceiling. We were being watched, and recordings of our conversation would find their way to unfriendly eyes and ears in time. But Lorian was the representative of a foreign power now, a Commandant General in the Monarch's Grand Army. Like Valka on Emesh, he would be accorded a species of diplomatic immunity...and I? What could they do to me that they could not do already? Indeed, they must have admitted Lorian precisely to see what would happen, to search for coded signs and mysteries.

I smiled. They would be disappointed.

"You think this is funny?" Lorian stepped toward me, a menace and a tension in his posture I had never known in the man. He seemed—if anything—more vital than ever I had seen him, as though he were spoiling to strike me.

"It's good to see you," I said.

That stopped the little man's rage, set him back a pace. His cane struck the floor between his feet, both hands folded atop it. He pressed his lips together—cap still squeezed beneath his arm. "You too."

"Do you want wine?"

"You always did keep a good cellar," the other man said, following me.

"I've a Kandarene red open."

"Sold." Lorian swept the sitting area, pausing to lay his cap on the sideboard. "I liked your place on Nessus better." He pointed at the mural of the planets. "Though the decorations are a sight more tasteful here than there."

Recalling the painting of Lord Maddalo's paramour, I shook my head. "You *did* escape, didn't you?"

"You're implying I was set loose?" Lorian dropped into a chair at angles to my own.

"I'm not implying anything," I said, filling the glass Edouard had declined.

Lorian accepted it with uplift. "Your health." As I returned the gesture, he said, "I imagine *how* I escaped Belusha is very high on the list of questions our audience wants answered." He pointed at the ceiling once more, twirled his finger in a circle. "Belusha was...you can't imagine it. There's the main prison—*Downwell,* they call it, that's where the sleepers stay. The rest of it's mining camps. Petrochemicals, mostly. And the scrapyards. They had me pulling precious metals out of derelicts the better part of four years before I ran."

"Ran?"

The little man took a long swig from the glass. "Out into the wastes. They don't really guard the camps—they don't have to. Belusha's a whole lot of nothing, but there's people out there. Others as ran away...and their sprouts. The *outborn,* they're called. Raid the camps sometimes. Empire doesn't care. If the prisoners out there die, they die." Incongruously, he smiled. "There was a girl, Sarala. She saved me." His voice dropped off, and he went still. "I tried to save her."

Catching his careful choice of words, I asked, "Tried?"

Lorian smiled sadly.

"If you won't tell me how you escaped," I said, "how did you come to..." I gestured at his uniform, at the Monarch's colors and falcon sigil. "All this?"

"You first," said Lorian, leaning in. "I thought you were getting out! You were supposed to be on Jadd! Instead you're here, on Forum, in the Lions' den! I say again, Marlowe: What in eight hells!"

That was the second reference to the Cid Arthurian afterlife the good commander had made in so many minutes. I studied him a long moment then. He seemed to have aged but little in the two centuries since last I'd seen him. The sallow, skeletal face was—but for the addition of those blackened veins—the same face I had seen that last day aboard the *Tempest,* those colorless eyes the same laughing windows on a mind of wheels within wheels.

"The Emperor pardoned me," I said.

"And you came back?" Lorian's words dripped venom. "I went to Belusha, and you *came back?*"

"I wasn't given a choice," I said. "The Empire subsidizes the Jaddians' military budget. They threatened to withdraw support if Prince Aldia did not turn me over."

Lorian swore. "At the same time they're begging the whole damned galaxy for aid? What could be so serious?" He shook his head. "You're a good officer, Marlowe, but you're not worth more than the whole damned Jaddian armada!"

"I wish I could tell you," I said, touching Edouard's note through my trouser front.

Lorian's face darkened, "The ceiling people?"

I held my face immobile. "I'm meant to meet with the Emperor the day after tomorrow," I said. "There's something I still have to do. Unfinished business, you understand."

"Unfinished business?" One hand on the head of his cane, Lorian leaned back against the cushions. "Dorayaica?"

I smiled. I could say nothing.

"Something to do with that HAPSIS fellow? Contact?"

I only kept smiling.

"Damn it, Marlowe! You have to give me something!"

"No," I said, surprising myself, "I don't." Eager to change the subject, I set my glass aside and sitting forward said, "Lorian—the Extrasolarians? Are you insane?"

"Where was I supposed to go?" Lorian said, setting his glass aside. "A fugitive like me?"

"Not to the Extras!" I said, and gesturing to his face, asked, "What have they done to you?"

One of Lorian's hands flitted to his face, and I saw the same blackness webbing the back of that hand. "They cured me," he said, snarling. "Nerve implants. They replaced most of my tendons and major ligaments, too. See?" He held up both hands, waggled his fingers. "No braces." Seeing my face darken, he said, "I know what you're thinking. There's no daimon. Nothing half so smart as your terminal. They wanted to. Wanted to give me a new body—said they'd even make me tall, but I wanted to stay me." He let his hands fall. "It's not so different from your arm."

"I'm glad you're well," I said.

"You haven't seen him, Marlowe," Lorian said, eyes suddenly aglow. "Calen Harendotes. He's like . . . he's like you, I guess. He has vision. He's building a better world."

"A better world?" I echoed. Had I not used the same words myself, and more times than I could count? Was it not for a better world that I had toiled for so long—and so fruitlessly?

"A world without *blood*. The Empire would never have given me my own command," Lorian said. "I was only a commander because *you* pulled me off that desk in Beller's office. Everything the Monarch's given me, I earned. Look at me, Marlowe. Commandant General! *I* led our fleet at Eragassa, at Nida—half a dozen other places. Where else would that have been allowed?"

"With me," I said shortly, stopping his furor.

"It was over, Marlowe!" Lorian almost yelled, almost stood. "The Red Company was gone! You were gone!" Realizing he was near shouting, Lorian checked himself, and lowering his voice, said, "You should have stayed on Jadd. Drowned yourself in harem girls and the prince's best wine!"

"I told you," I said. "That wasn't an option."

"Then maybe you've lived too long!" Lorian snapped, voice rising again.

I glared at him, shocked, hurt, surprised.

"Abba?" A voice intruded from the inner hall, and looking up I saw Cassandra, standing in the arch that led to the back rooms, dressed in a knee-length Jaddian tunic and loose trousers. "I heard voices."

Lorian stood, mouth half-open. His eyes flickered from Cassandra's face to my own, and he touched his rope of bound hair. Turning to me, he said, "Valka's?"

I nodded.

"How?"

By way of answer, I fished the phylactery out from under my shirt by its chain, held it hooked on one thumb. "Her blood," I said. "The Jaddians made her for me."

"Abba?" Cassandra's face darkened with suspicion. *"Qi es aphto?"*

"Cassandra," I said, letting the phylactery fall and gesturing to my guest, "this is Lorian Aristedes."

Her eyes widened. "Your friend?"

Lorian's eyes were shining, and he shut them as he smiled, raised one hand to shield his face. "Yes, my lady," he said. "I have that honor." He turned to me, brows knitting. "Not a clone?"

"Our daughter," I said.

Lorian's face split. "Your daughter?" He turned and bowed.

"It's an honor to meet you, *messer*," Cassandra said, and curtsied. "Abba has told me so much! Have you come for dinner?"

Crossing the room, I put an arm around her, and before Lorian could object, I said, "Please."

In the end, he stayed for the remainder of the evening. Neema fussed about the addition of a surprise dinner guest, but Lorian was uncharacteristically gracious after Cassandra's appearance, and I sensed that as I had hardened in my old age, Lorian had softened.

Though he had at first seemed a man utterly transformed, the good commander asserted himself throughout the evening, emerging from the cracks in the Commandant General's face. He was Lorian still, but a Lorian filled with a new drive and purpose, a dream that he had seized with his own hands, in his own way. He was Lorian still, Commandant General of the Latarran Grand Army and my friend both.

But things had changed, were always changing—were not and would never be the same.

When he was gone, I retired to my chambers at the rear of our apartments, spoke the word of command to lower the shades. My folios lay stacked upon a corner of the rose-quartz-topped desk in a niche to the right-hand side, facing the four-poster bed with its pillars like feathered serpents. In full sight of the cameras I knew were hidden in the molding, in the headboard, in the stained-glass panel in the door to my private bath, I seated myself in the tufted desk chair, opened my folio to a half-finished sketch of Mt. Hephaistos drawn from memory. It looked wrong to me then, as it had for months—but always I had hesitated to remove it. There were loose leaves of paper on the desk at my right hand. Rough sketches of human faces. Gibson, Pallino, Corvo and Valka together. These mingled with printouts, bound copies of the minutes from the previous week's council meetings. Reports from the War Office.

I tore the sketch free, crumpled it, set the ruin atop the loose pages. I set Edouard's note down with it, made a show of opening the crumpled image, of looking at it with regret. It permitted me the chance to open Edouard's own note, to disguise the action of doing so as only a part of my artistic consideration.

I could see the words of Edouard's message plain, half-hid beneath that rumpled sketch.

> *Chantry intends to block your meeting with Emperor.*
> *They know about the Cielcin on Gadelica.*
> *Will attempt to frame for treason.*
> *May attempt violence. All I know.*
> *In haste,*
> *E*

CHAPTER 37

DISSOLUTION

THE DAY BEFORE I was at last to meet with His Radiance—a meeting that would never occur—the Emperor himself failed to appear in Council. An apparition of Prince Alexander appeared instead, alone below the throne upon the dais, a portent of things to come.

I stared at the empty throne over Alexander's shoulder, the round, red cushion of the headboard an empty halo amidst all that filigree of golden sun beams.

He can't have much longer, Edouard had said. Edouard, who was leaving, who had been summoned away. By my allies, as he suspected? To insulate what it was he knew? Or by my enemies?

If they meant to block my meeting with the Emperor, they were not moving Edouard fast enough. They would have to act quickly. But how? Edouard's note had talked of violence, of a plot to frame me for treason. He said they had the *Gadelica,* had found Ramanthanu and the others. They would arrest me, snatch me from Martian hands and produce the xenobites as evidence, ask why it was that the Emperor's pet sorcerer kept demons bottled on his ship.

A show trial...then what? An execution?

All these thoughts and more danced like the fire reflected in my eyes, played there while I sat in council on the highest row, and listened as Lorian argued with Lord Rand and Sattha Kull. The Tavrosi Grand Admiral did not believe the science of Lorian's machine, and the Exalted captains that had accompanied the little Commandant General had shouted him down.

Kull remained convinced it was a sham. Director General Wong Xu shared that skepticism in more measured terms, a skepticism echoed by King Paeon of the dryads and by the Durantine Doxe. In return, Captain Archambault presented detailed footage of an attack his *Two Dreams of*

Spring had carried out against a worldship that had stopped to refuel in a desolate system about a red dwarf star.

"The Cielcin siphon material off gas giants," the Exalted captain proclaimed. "Separate the hydrogen and helium, use the helium in their fusion reactors, run the hydrogen through their accelerators to create the antihydrogen required to achieve warp."

That had long been speculated, as Lord Rand indicated at once. The first great plasma siphons had been uncovered in the wreck of Typhon, the second worldship ever captured.

"But they make stops between battles to refuel," Archambault explained. "Often for years at a time—as long as it takes for them to replenish their fuel reservoirs."

"You cannot imagine how much fuel is required to move a worldship," said Captain Zelaz, floating above the proceedings like an evil spirit.

"While the Cielcin park to refuel, they are vulnerable," Archambault explained. "That was when we struck. We tracked them to this system, VA-87:13 DS-114. They were not prepared for attack: The statistical probability of a random encounter in an unsettled system is so close to zero, after all."

"There were no survivors," Lorian said.

The session broke with the fifth hour after noon. With its elongated days, Forum kept to Earth standard time, ignoring its own solar cycle entirely. Day and night were on Forum treated more as weather than time. That day was sunlight as I recall, though the sun of Forum was far past its noon. It would be dark in several days, and remain dark for nearly the next standard month.

I felt it should be dark already, placing my dark glasses—the dark glasses I had stolen from a man on Emesh when I was just a boy—on my nose. My Martian escort had rejoined me in the hall outside the council chamber, followed me like bloody shadows out into the colonnade. The Campus Raphael stretched before us, down a flight of marble steps.

It was an ordinary day, the breeze perhaps a little cool, the air stabilized by the planet's watchful weather satellites and by the great sail wall that cut the Coriolis winds.

"Lord Marlowe!"

I knew that throaty voice, knew its owner before I turned.

The Cantor, Samek, hurried down the steps beside me, one hand hiking up her flowing robes. She looked precisely as she had the day Lorian arrived, in black clerical robes with the white skullcap and epitrachelion of her office. A pair of cathars stood behind her, eyes concealed by the traditional blindfolds in the manner of Justice herself.

Was it to be so simple? Had they come to arrest me then and there, on the steps of the Sun King's Hall, in the sight of all the worlds? I wore no sword, but my shield was active—as was customary among the high lords of the Imperium at court. I eyed my Martian escort. If I struck the one to my left with a rising elbow to the chin, I could surely steal his lance, kill the second and Samek both before the cathars closed. If I rushed the stairs, I might make the gates before security took me, and so find myself in Aurelian's custody and as close to friends as may be.

The words of Edouard's letter burned like fire in the blackest pits of my heart.

May attempt violence. All I know.

I took my hands from the pockets of my coat, but I made no other move—either to strike my escort or to run. "Cantor Samek!" I said loudly, turning fully to face her.

"May I walk with you?" she asked. "I'd like a word."

"Speak your piece," I said, defiant.

"It would be best if we had this conversation more privately," she said.

I had anticipated that she intended to make a spectacle of me, but now that she seemed desirous of privacy, I intended to deny it to her. The leviathan advanced on me, swept down the stairs, her hands folded before her.

"Would it indeed?" I did not move.

Her mouth pursed, and she said, "You entertained Lorian Aristedes at your apartments the evening before last."

I felt a strange relief that she had not asked about Edouard.

"My apartments are surveilled," I said. "I assume you've heard every word."

"Yes, indeed," she said.

"Then you know there's nothing," I said.

She was standing at the bottom of the stairs by then, a few paces from me. "That's not why I'm here," she said. "We really must talk privately."

I eyed the Martian Guards posted at the base of the stairs, watched a trio of logothetes processing up and to the right.

"You believe he is still your friend, don't you?" Samek said. "You have seen what he has become. You cannot trust him. None of us can. His master seeks to humiliate the Emperor, to rob us of the Norman provinces."

"We have lost them already."

"By handing them over without contest, we alienate our allies in the Expanse. There will be general rebellion. Chaos." She was standing very close then, fidgeting with her ring in a manner redolent of Selene. Her furrowed brows wrinkled the Phoenician *sāmek* tattooed between them. "Do you find his stories about the telegraph detector credible?"

I blinked at her. This was not the conversation I had expected to have.

"I...I am no magus, priest," I said.

"The theory laid out by Aristedes and his demoniac compatriots is nonsense," she said. "Perturbations in the quantum foam...instantly detectable at a distance of several thousand light-years, sensitive enough to make sense of coded messages?" She shook her head. I could smell the verrox stimulant on her breath, bitter and alkaline. "Your *friend* is lying."

"You're saying Grand Admiral Kull is correct," I said.

"Kull is *abomination,* as surely as Aristedes," she said in hushed tones, "but yes. This device of theirs *cannot* work. They would sell us false goods for an arm of the galaxy."

"And their support in the war," I said. "Lorian is to command their armada against the Cielcin."

Samek sniffed, looked over her shoulder. "And now he requests we supply his armada with neutron-class enhanced radiation weapons. Why?"

"Atomics?" I asked, feeling suddenly that Samek had been right, that we *should* be having this conversation under cover. A pair of women in silk dresses passed us, one tittering to the other from behind a patterned fan. "You're lying."

"I do that often, my lord," she said, eyes wide and glassy, "but not now."

"What would Lorian want with a cache of atomics?"

"That is what you must find out, my lord," she said, stepping forward. I felt the dark waters swirl around us, felt the leviathan draw near. "We cannot trust these barbarians. You know this. Calen Harendotes has long allied with these sorcerers, this...MINOS."

Every fiber in me screamed to step away. Samek was a creature of power and cold malice, the avatar of the organization that had for so many centuries sought my destruction. It had been they who directed the assassin, Irshan; they who had falsified the charges that bought me twelve years in captivity on Thermon; they who had tried to kill me when their sham trial turned against them. They had paid Udax and his kinsmen to attack me on Gododdin, had possibly even been the force that galvanized the Empress against me.

But I held my ground.

"He was your friend, I know," Samek said, once more twisting her ring. "But you cannot trust him, lord. If you are true—as you say, a servant of the Empire—you *must* find out what his master is planning."

"Must I?" I asked, and turned to go.

Her ringed hand lanced out and caught me by the wrist. Furious, I looked into Samek's face. "For the good of the realm," she said, and there was an edge to her words, a conviction that had not been there an instant before.

A triumph.

The realm. Tugging my hand free, I averted my gaze, looking first at the ground between our feet and then around at the Campus Raphael. We were in the heart of that realm that very moment, dancing on the head of the pin that was the axis about which our every world turned. "Are you really so desperate?" I asked, rubbing my wrist to rid it of the memory of her touch. "You dare speak to *me*, to *me*, of the good of the realm? Who in all the Empire has given more? You come here, seeking to turn me against one of the last friends I have in all the galaxy...and with what? Rumor? Lorian Aristedes is my *friend*, Cantor. I would sooner distrust myself."

Had I not distrusted him not two days earlier? Had I not found him changed?

The Lorian I had known was gone, or buried. The good commander lost beneath the Commandant General. I was old, and tired, and touched by the demoness Ushara. Another demon had taken Lorian, the daimon called *machine*. He had said his implants were only prosthetic nerves, replacements to his stretched ligaments and fraying tendons. But what if he had lied? Might not some iron serpent lie coiled about his brainstem, altering his thoughts, or carrying trojan thoughts planted by his royal master? Might he not be possessed?

And yet he had almost wept to see Cassandra standing in the inner arch of our apartment.

"When you stand before Mother Earth in judgement, lord," Samek said, eyes still shining, "you will have to account for your actions. Your soul is in your hands."

Still massaging my wrist, I glared long and hard at Samek. Her tone had shifted, softened, darkened. She had not pressed the issue with Lorian, had seemingly abandoned it as quickly as she had taken it up.

Your soul is in your hands. Had not Gibson himself said precisely that so long ago?

I snarled at her, saying, "I have seen the Howling Dark that awaits us all hereafter, priest. Your goddess was not there."

Samek recoiled as if stunned, bright eyes hardening to points of furious light. "You do not deny it? These *stories* they tell of you?"

I was deep in black water, felt the serpent coiling in the dark all around me.

"You have seen Berenike," I said, referring to the recordings of my miracle. "Perfugium. Still you doubt me?"

Her face had grown pale as milk, as death, and the triumph and conviction that had but recently lighted her eyes was blown out. "Why did you come back?"

I did not answer her.

"Why are you here?"

"You still don't know?" I almost laughed.

"Tell me!" Samek hissed, drawing near. "We know of your demons."

Edouard's letter, I thought.

They know about the Cielcin on Gadelica.

She seized my wrist once more, hard eyes locked on mine. What a sight we must have been, there on the steps of the palace! The devil and the priestess of Earth, both in suits of black. Knight and hierophant—matched pieces.

When had the day grown cold?

"You say the Emperor summoned you," she said, referring to our earlier conversation. "Why? Speak now, and you may yet save your life and that of your bastard."

She was so close, so close that I might strike her with my forehead and break that powdered nose. The scent of verrox filled my nostrils.

"My bastard..." I snarled. "If you so much as touch her—"

"Why did you come back?"

A black mood was on me. This woman had threatened my life, threatened *Cassandra's* life and Lorian's—sought to turn me against him. "To kill a god," I said, and tugged my hand free. "To kill a god, priestess. Does that frighten you?"

Let her think I meant her own.

Her eyes went wide, then narrowed to mere slits. "Impiety harms only the impious, lordship," she said, drawing herself up to her full height, and I saw for the first time that she was slightly taller than I was myself, a true palatine. "I see now you are beyond salvation. I will pray for your soul."

With that she gathered her robes in one fist and drew back, dark waters buffeting me as she turned tail and made for the stairs, her cathars close behind. Her eyes were slow to leave my face then. I have never forgotten them, nor the thin smile that should not have been on those pursed, carmine lips. Three steps up, she halted, looked back over her shoulder. "Think on your sins, my lord."

I watched the leviathan depart, feeling the pull of its dread weight, little knowing I was dead already, and that it would soon have me in its jaws.

The pale towers and green parks of the Eternal City passing beneath my shuttle seemed things frozen in time, as though the aureate light that fell from the distant sun were a kind of amber. But for the fliers that darted like bees from one flying platform to the next, the whole thing seemed still as stone, a sculptor's miniature or artist's copy, a display crafted for my benefit and mine alone.

Unreal city...

It was an illusion, all of it. A funeral mask of marble and gold filigree upon a face long gone to rot. Harendotes's demands and the revelation of his machine had cracked that mask, and the galaxy was peering in now, glimpsing the decay. The Empire was weak—though before the war began, it had never been greater. Its very size had been its undoing, having created for itself a territory too great for any human mind and armada to defend.

I shivered, drawing my coat about myself, watching the towers pass.

Even if we could destroy the Cielcin, the rot would likely prove fatal. The mere act of renouncing all claim to the Norman stars would shatter the mask and the illusion of Imperial supremacy.

All across the galaxy, the Imperial sun was setting. In its place would come an age—not of darkness—but of countless lesser lights. Where the Imperial sun had gone, the stars beyond counting would shine out the clearer. Our Empire—its order—would pass away, and in the Age of Night, the Age of the Stars that was to come there would be chaos. War. War not only with the Lothrians, whom brave men are fighting even as I write this page, but with the Normans, with the Extras, with what remains of the Grand Army of Latarra...and of Lorian's dream.

And with whatever lies beyond...

"Lord Marlowe?" One of my Martian escorts caught me as I stumbled in the flier's door.

"I'm all right, Larok," I said, steadying myself.

My encounter with Samek had left me shaken, and my short flight from the palace to the Martian citadel had provided me with silent reflection sufficient for regret to flower like a weed. I had denounced the faith, threatened a high cleric—an agent of the Choir, no less—and spoken of my own death and return, and of the wonders I had worked at Berenike and at Perfugium.

It was foolish.

The door to the inside lay open ahead, but I tarried on the gangway, drawing my coat ever tighter about myself. The day had taken chill, as if the very sun were robbed of fire. I permitted the Martians to lead me inside and along the hall to the lift that would carry me to the level of the guest houses high above. I leaned on the support rail, overcome by the day's events.

When we reached the end of the hall, I faltered.

"Where are the guards?" I asked Larok.

There ought to have been two men posted at the door outside.

"Unclear, sir," came the reply. "I'll radio Sir Canton."

"You do that," I said.

The door showed no signs of being forced. Its control panel remained intact, and appeared for all the world not to have been interfered with. It accepted my code and cycled, moving gently to one side. The bell chimed, and Neema emerged from the servant's quarters, bustling directly toward me, his brows knitting with some urgent complaint. "Domi!" he said, speaking Jaddian. "She wouldn't stay outside. Insisted I let her in."

"Neema." I raised my hands to stop the fellow in his tracks. "The guards on the door. Where have they gone?"

"Sent them away! That's what I'm telling you!" the Nemrutti servant explained. "She's *in* your chambers, sir, most improper—I told her so myself! But she would not listen."

"Who's in my chambers?" I asked, relieved to find the man in one of his usual moods. "Where's Cassandra?"

"Gone to the gymnasium," Neema said, answering the second question and forgetting the first. He paused, marked Larok and the other Martian standing just inside. "The guards have returned!"

Laying a hand on the man's shoulder, I said, "No, they came with me. Who's here?"

Neema's blunt face fell, and his voice softened. "My lord, are you unwell? You're sweating!"

"What?" I touched the nape of my neck, and found it damp. "Is it warm in here? It was quite cold outside." I left my servant standing in the foyer to fetch my sword from its hiding place in my second coat. It was still there, safe in an inner pocket.

I permitted Neema to skin me out of my coat—found as he did so that I had indeed been sweating, and marveled at it. I had hardly noticed. The butler let fly a stream of complaints as I crossed the common room, moving toward the inner arch and the short hall to my chambers, shield-belt still on, sword hilt concealed in my trouser pocket, my right hand primed on the safety catch.

"Just barged right in like she owned the place, master!" he said, having entirely failed to answer my question.

I raised a hand for silence, placed a hand on the knob.

Neema shut his mouth as I turned the latch, and the woman seated on the divan between the room's narrow slits of window stood sharply, turning to face me. She wore a black mantle, head to toe, with a deep hood that hid her face. Still, I knew she was a woman at once from the way she rose, standing all at once and freezing in place.

"Identify yourself," I said, angling my left side to face her.

She raised her hands and threw back her hood.

"Selene?" The tension in my every limb vanished at once. "What are you doing here?" She looked wrong dressed so in black.

"I came to warn you," she said, crossing the carpet to my side. "The Chantry plan to move against you. They say they raided your ship, the one that brought you from offworld. They said there were Cielcin frozen on it, that you intended some treason with them..."

"I know," I said, relaxing.

The princess blinked at me. "You know?"

"You shouldn't be here," I said, gesturing at the ceiling. "This place is watched."

Furiously she shook her head. "They wouldn't dare. Besides, I sent my people to stop the recording."

"You *what?*" I asked. "Why?"

She drew nearer, eyes downcast, until she was standing just before me. She was nearly so tall as I, taller than Valka, and yet when she peered up at me she seemed as one who peers across a great distance. She raised a hand. Her arm tinkled with countless jeweled bangles. "I told them I was here for you. They will protect my privacy, if not yours."

I swayed, contemplated moving away. The floral notes of her perfumed hair were filling my nostrils. Jasmine. Iris. Rose.

"Besides." Her breath was on my face, words like warm smoke. "It is not wholly untrue."

She kissed me then, clumsy but intent, kissed me in a way that made me certain that she had never kissed anyone before. Had I seen that moment before? In that skein of prophetic images and other memory? In that vision of other lives? Had I not seen lives lived with her, seen us together—myself enthroned with Selene at my feet?

Did that future lie somehow ahead of me?

But no...I had been young in those visions.

"Princess, I..."

"Call me Selene," she said. She kissed me again, undoing the clasp that secured her mantle.

Valka's shade seemed to hover on the air. Sandalwood in the perfume, perhaps, not as strongly. I drew back. "Princess," I said again, "we cannot."

The dress she wore beneath the fallen mantle was white as any bride's, but translucent, revealing all of form and of the snowy lace beneath. She had armored herself for battle, in her way, after the fashion of women.

"I have wanted this," she said, "since Father told me we were to be wed. Now we may never be, and I...they say you are guilty of *consortation*. With the Cielcin and the Extras both. Demons and daimons."

Ushara stirred behind my face, laughing at the word *demon*.

"Hadrian, you're scaring me," she said, and I realized I was smiling, and more than smiling. I shuddered, raised a hand to my face. It came away damp. I needed a shower. It was so hot in the close air of that bedchamber. Had I altered the temperature settings?

"There are Cielcin on my ship," I said. "Prisoners I took at Sabratha. They came over to our side."

"Came over?" Selene rested her hands on my chest. "Is that even possible?"

"I don't know," I told her, not moving—not daring to move away. She was a princess of the Imperium. I could not refuse her. If I did, she might easily say—embarrassed, hurt—that I had tried to force myself on her. My protestations of innocence would never be believed. If I did not refuse her, my life would still be forfeit. One could not simply despoil a princess of the Aventine and live.

"I don't know," I said once more, "but I have to try. If there is a path to peace...if the war could end..."

Her eyes were shining. "Aurelian says you have a secret mission, a mission known only to Father and himself, that you were never a traitor..." She bit her lip, almost trembled. Not knowing what to do, I laid a hand on her shoulder. She felt so cold to my touch. "He said you struck Father over me... because he offered you my hand but days after your lady doctor was killed." She did tremble then, and averted her eyes like emeralds. "I am sorry. She was a good woman—though I did not know her well. I have no desire to replace her. But I would make you a prince of the realm. That is some protection... and I would be...would be good to you." She smiled nervously.

"You don't..." I nearly choked. "You don't have to do this."

"I told you," she said, "I want to. Why do you think I was put on ice all these years?"

There was the answer to one mystery, at least. Why she—alone, it seemed, among her siblings—had been preserved against the ravages of time. Had the Emperor been saving her? Hoping for my return? I felt a sudden swell of pity for her.

"Hadrian..." Her voice sounded suddenly very far away. "You're bleeding."

"I...what?" I swayed, touched my forehead, found the wetness still there, but the fingers came away red.

"Are you all right?" she asked. "Did something happen?"

There was a mirror in the private bath. I had only to round a corner to see into it.

"The carpet!" Selene's voice was hushed.

Looking down, I saw dark spots on the green and gold of the carpet. As I looked, blood dripped from the fingers of my left hand. I lifted the palm to look at it, brushed the bloody skin to find the wound. The skin sloughed away, peeling from palm and fingertip alike. I hissed with the sudden pain of it. "Get Neema," I said.

She did not move.

"Lights!" I shouted, commanding the lamps in the bath.

They swelled to life as ordered, revealed the gilt-framed mirror and my reflection both. Blood was leaking from my scalp, from the marks of Syriani's talons that decorated my left cheek. I was sweating blood. Weeping it. Bleeding from both my hands.

"Samek!" I said, and knew. The leviathan had bitten me. "She poisoned me!"

"Samek?" Selene wasn't following.

"The Chantry!" I said, unable to take my eyes from my reflection. "You're too late."

For the good of the realm, she'd said.

No wonder her tone had changed. She had killed me already.

"She grabbed my wrist," I said. There must have been a needle in that ring of hers. "Dispholide."

Selene's face—concealed beneath white powder—went whiter still.

I knew what must come, knew how little time remained. I had watched Irshan die by the priest's poison in the Grand Colosseum. He had disintegrated in seconds, the slime of him soaking my clothes.

"Go, Selene!" I said. "Don't look!"

"But!"

"Look away!"

The skin of my face had already started to sag, eyelids drooping. It was so hot, and I knew that heat for the final fever that it was. The dose Samek had given me must have been smaller than the one Irshan had taken, or else delayed that I might make it to my apartment before it took me. I coughed, and spattered blood across the mirror and the marble vanity. Selene screamed. I saw her standing there, unmoved in the door to the bath chamber. I gripped the edge of the vanity, fell against it, and felt something in my shoulder snap. I gasped, but gasping only brought forth more blood.

I could hardly breathe, heard the rasping of it, felt the burbling of fluid rapidly filling my lungs. "Neema!"

Selene screamed for me, and dimly I felt something strike the floor at my feet. I looked down. My left arm had fallen away. Melting flesh—red blood, yellow pus—ran from the ridged black adamant of the false bones Kharn Sagara had given me.

I fell a moment later.

Neema had appeared beside Selene in the doorway, olive face utterly without blood. "Domi! Master Hadrian!"

I reached for him with my right hand, saw the two fingers Doctor Elkan had made for me had fallen away. Blood soaked through my dripping shirt. Every inch of me was red.

"Neema!" I gasped, coughing. It was so hot! And the pain! It was worse than anything I could remember, worse than any of the torments of Dharan-Tun, worse than the phantom pains Urbaine had designed and administered through his collar, worse than any injury taken in battle, worse than the moment of shock as Aranata's sword struck off my head. I felt as though my every nerve were stripped and wound through gears of raw iron. My every atom was laid bare, but I could not even scream.

I was going to die. Samek had killed me.

Dispholide.

The Priest's Poison. The Mermaid's Kiss...

There would be nothing of me left, nothing but my false bones and blood and slime.

"Cassandra!" I croaked, and again, *Cassandra.*

I could not hear my voice the second time. My vision was going dark. Selene and Neema both seemed to float above me, fear and horror on their faces.

Cassandra! I prayed the words were getting out. *Lorian! Lorian... Albé...find...Albé...trust...Lorian...*

They had to act quickly, before the curtains fell and the knives came out. Samek had killed me...would kill them next...

The pain was fading, dulling to a gray ache—my vision likewise gray. The last thing I saw were Selene's eyes—green as malachite, as Cassandra's eyes. I felt hands on me—though I had no skin to feel. Still, they carried me, dragged me away, lifted me higher, deeper into the dark that, howling, awaited me.

Those green eyes watched me, and I felt their pity, their pain, and a love immense as planets poured out at my suffering, though their owner would not move to stop my pain.

And I knew...knew that I was dead.

My last thought as my brain dissolved at last and ran out upon the floor, was that Cassandra was alone. They had killed me. They would kill her.

And there was nothing I could do.

Nothing...nothing...nothing...

Then I was nothing at all.

CHAPTER 38

SALT AND RAG

DARKNESS.

I could remember darkness blacker still, could hear it wailing, gnashing all about me.

It was quiet then. All was quiet.

My name, I thought—I thought it was me that thought. *My name is Hadrian.*

I tried to speak, to work my mouth and jaw. Did I even have a mouth? The mere thought made me want to rage, to scream, to test the limits of my humanity. But I could not move. I could remember green eyes. Valka had green eyes. Or was that someone else?

And who was Valka?

Was I crying? I wanted to cry. To cease.

Drip.

Water. That sound was water falling from some high place.

Drip. Drip.

Striking metal or stone.

I had not been aware of it until that moment, though its fall was so constant I felt I should have heard it long before. I was on my back, though I knew no other sensation. No heat or cold, no soreness, no pressure of the surface beneath me. I might have been immersed in warm milk.

"Don't try to move," came a croaking voice from over my head. "You're not all here yet, he says. And he don't want to lose your image."

I could not so much as blink.

Hadrian, I thought, sure that I was right. *My name is Hadrian.*

Was I fugue-blind? It happened, *had* happened to me often enough. Crystallization of the fluid in the eyes, deformation of the lens. But that had been a kind of grayness of the vision. This was something else.

I could hear the blood in my ears.

Blood.

I remembered blood, blood on the mirror, on my hands, soaking through the soles of my boots. I remembered pain as my left arm tore away, the skin of my face running like wax.

I was dead, I thought. *I am dead.*

Drip. Drip.

A light shone high above me, faint and far away and cold. Walls of rough stone black as night receded toward that light above, vanished into gray. The reflected light of water rippling danced upon the lower walls, as though I lay in the bottom of some well.

"You're right, you know," said the croaking voice. "You met a nasty end. But you're safe now."

There was something familiar about that voice.

"You should be able to see now," it said. "Be able to move soon. But you shouldn't."

Water. I had awoken in water the last time, too, in a shallow pool in the gardens of the Undying aboard the black ship, *Demiurge.* Gibson had been there, standing over me. Only it hadn't been Gibson.

"Am I the Quiet?" the rough voice inquired, seeming to guess my thoughts. "No, cousin! Oh, no!"

"Cousin?" I echoed, uncomprehending. The Emperor called me *cousin,* but it was not his voice, and this was not Forum. I was underground—of that much I was certain. Deep underground.

"You mean you don't remember me?" A cackle sounded from somewhere above my head. I turned to look, in the process disturbing water warm as human flesh. It washed over my face, entered my mouth. Panic conquered me, and I floundered, limbs thrashing as I struggled to right myself. Where had the air gone? Which way was *up* and light?

For an instant, I was certain I would die again. Death by water, this time—not fire. The darkness of that pool was the Howling Dark of death itself, and I was falling into it. Then my feet found smooth stone, and I pushed, and an instant later—too soon—my body struck a wall. Numb hands scrabbled against it, fingers desperate for purchase.

My feet found a lip of smooth stone, and I tried to stand, felt my body strike a wall. I thrashed, and a moment later broke the surface coughing, sputtering, gasping for air.

A hand seized me then, and a new voice shouted, "That's it! He's here!"

Only half-aware of what was happening to me, I felt myself hauled from the pool and cast upon the flat stone beside it. I lay there a long while, face in my hands, my whole body shuddering.

My hands...

I could remember my hands dissolving, my skin molting, peeling away like varnish on old wood, revealing the raw and weeping flesh beneath.

They were whole again, exactly as I remembered them: pockmarked and scarred. There was the old wheal of cryoburn scar where my family's ring had burned the skin of my left thumb, and there the mark of Irshan's sword. The star-fine points on my right hand recalled the surgical repairs I had endured on Delos as a boy, and the smoothness of those last two fingers hinted at good Doctor Elkan's repairs.

I touched my face, moved long black hair streaked white from my eyes.

"What happened to me?" I asked, voice barely more than a whisper.

"You were dead," said that second voice, higher and smoother than the first. "We recalled you."

"We?"

A figure stood over me then, bare feet on the stone shelf beside the pool. Looking up, I found myself staring into the face of a boy perhaps ten- or twelve-years standard. Black he was of hair, curling and unruly, with pale blue eyes. He wore only rags of soiled white, a shapeless gown that fell almost to his ankles, without belt or sash. It could not have been he who hauled me from the water, so small was he and slight.

"Call me Rag," he said, crouching, and nodding away to my left, added, "I think you know Salt."

The other figure at the water's edge shuffled forward, its long arms nearly dragging on the ground. It was short, barely taller than the boy called Rag, and clad in grubby coveralls of oil-stained green. Its skin was gray as ash, its face so wizened its age might have been a hundred or a thousand, for all its childlike size.

"I know you," I said to the shrunken creature, guessing that it had been the one to pull me from the water.

The homunculus pointed at its own face. "I should hope so, it's thanks to you I'm in this miserable place." As it spoke, it pawed at the queue of black hair that sprouted from the base of its otherwise bald head.

"You were...on the ship," I said, remembering. "The ship that took me out from Delos. You were Demetri's—"

"Slave," said the homunculus, Saltus, "I was Demetri's slave, but I proved the master in the end. My blood may be curdled, cousin, but curdling's a kind of preservation. I outlasted them all. The twins. The doctor. Old Bassem. Even the highborns." It thrust a hand out for me to take. "I'm the only one left."

Drip.

I stared at the offered hand, not taking it. "That's not possible," I said, looking down at my reflection. "The *Eurynasir* was found adrift. I was the only one left, I..." I touched my face again. "I was old." A horrible thought flashed like lightning across the surface of my mind. "Cassandra! Was she real? Was any of it..."

Still crouching beside the misshapen dwarf, Rag said, "It's a lot to take in,
I know." He stood, "The Judicator will explain. He sent us to fish you out."

"Am I dead?" I asked.

"Take my hand, cousin." Saltus waggled his fingers. "Let's get you dry."

"Either I am dead," I said more strongly, and shut my eyes, "or everything since I left Delos is a dream."

"I said take my fucking hand!" the homunculus croaked, shaking its arm.

I tried. My fingers passed clean through Saltus's paw as though it
were a holograph. I looked up into the homunculi's shriveled face, horror
yawning in my breast. I tried once more, but again my hand passed clean
through the creature's fingers. Saltus laughed, capered back a pace, hands
on its knees as it bent over, cackling with mirth. Horrified, I scrambled
away from the creature, forgetting where I was. One hand missed the lip
of the shelf above the edge of that deep well, and I plunged backward into
water black and cold as space with a strangled yell.

A hand seized upon my wrist, warm and strong, and once again I was
hauled bodily from the pool and cast upon the cold, black stone. Memory
of Dharan-Tun washed over me with the water. I remembered awakening
in slime and cold upon the mat at Dorayaica's feet. Strong hands rolled
me over, and I lay there, an old man spluttering and cold. The boy caught
one of my hands as I flailed, held it fast with both his own.

"Looker?" I asked, mistaking that place for Padmurak.

"He's not all here yet," Rag said to the still-laughing Saltus. "The con-
densers need more time."

"The look on his face!" Saltus chortled, dabbed at his eyes with his
braided queue.

"You're not helping, Salt," the boy said. "Go . . . fetch him a robe, won't
you?"

"For all the good it'll do him!" Saltus said, and scuttled away, still
laughing. Quiet came in its wake, until there was no sound but the distant
drip-drip-drip of water. I was certain for a time that Rag had left—so still
was he. But when I turned to look I found him unmoved, crouching on
the stone beside me.

Drip.

"It's cold," I said.

Rag smiled. "Cold is good. It *is* cold. It's always cold below."

The old, familiar pains had started once again as well. My back, my
knees, the dull ache in my reconstructed shoulder. Old wounds, old scars.

"Where am I?" I asked. "What is this place?"

"Llesu," Rag said. "We are several miles below the old city. This is the
Well of Nahaman, where the dead are wakened from sleep."

For a moment, I only looked at the boy. He had spoken as one out of fable, out of fantasy. "The dead?" I echoed him, shook my head. "What *planet?* This isn't Forum."

No answer. The boy called Rag just looked at me, head cocked to one side, mouth half-open. I was not prepared for the question he asked next, could not have prepared for it, not in a million count of years. "What's a...planet?"

My own mouth hung half-open.

There were perhaps peasant populations in the Empire with no knowledge of the stars. The men and women of Borosevo had, for instance, largely been ignorant of the standard calendar, preferring their local one. But to be ignorant of the very *idea* of what a planet was...it beggared belief.

"You were dead," Rag replied, looking up at the walls of that place, that Well of Nahaman, and at the antique machines that hung like stalactites from them. "You've been dead a long time. Everything you know is gone—that's what the Judicator says. He sent me to fetch you back. The dead don't...go away, you know? The Judicator says each life is like a wave. The water's still there after the wave breaks. He says this place helps the water—the matter—remember the wave it used to be."

"How?" I asked, still lying on my back.

Rag only shook his head.

Seeing that no answer was forthcoming, I asked another question, the most pressing question: "How long?"

"How long have you been dead?" Rag asked, clarifying. "I don't know. I'm only supposed to bring you to the Judicator. He's far away. Up in the city. In the old church."

I felt as one roused from sleep, uncertain if the world he's woken to is a dream. Abruptly, I recalled Prytanis, Preceptor of the Order of the Seekers After the First Truth. That strange Extrasolarian cult believed the universe only a simulation housed on the machinery of some unknown designer in some other, more real universe. Looking round the Well of Nahaman, I felt...I felt as I thought one must feel awakening from such a simulation to the cold reality of that other world.

And yet I bore my scars, the marks of war and torment. If the Seekers were right—if there was some higher universe to awaken into, and if I had awoken to it—surely the marks of blade and talon would have vanished. Do not mistake me, Reader. I do not cleave to the doctrine of the Seekers, a doctrine which is—at any rate—little different from the Cielcin belief in the falsity of our world, I only aim to communicate my profound sense of dislocation.

You've been dead a long time.

If what the boy had said was true, then everything I had ever known had passed away.

"The future?" I hardly breathed the words. "This is the future..."

Were those tears on my scarred cheeks? Or only the waters of the Well of Nahaman?

Drip.

Drip.

"Who is he?" I asked at last, "Your Judicator? What does he want with me?"

A look passed over Rag's face then. Confusion? Bemusement? I could not be sure. He seemed far older than his years.

"You are called to account," the boy said. "You are to be tested."

"Tested?" I asked, and almost laughed. "I am dead. You said it yourself."

"But you need not remain so," Rag said. "You are yet the shortest way."

"What?" I blinked up at him. *The shortest way.* Those had been the Quiet's words, spoken to me upon the mountaintop of Annica. The shortest way. The straightest route through the mires of unfolding time... from my time to his, to a universe rid of the Watchers at last and ripe for rebirth.

"That is what he says," Rag said.

"The Judicator?" I asked. "He says I'm the shortest way?"

Rag bobbed his head.

"The Quiet..." I mouthed the words. I sat up. "You serve the Quiet?"

The boy inched back, startled by my sudden movement. "I don't..."

Of course. *The Quiet* had been our term, confected by those ancient archeologists who had discovered their ruins across the first Imperial stars. He would be called something else.

"Can you take me to him?" I asked, mind reeling. Rag had said that I had been dead a long time. Might it not then be that I had been dead—been asleep, as Rag called it—until the Quiet's day?

Rag lay a hand on my shoulder, the gesture of a much older man, I thought, as though I were the child and he the concerned guardian. His hand was warm, not thin and cold as it appeared. "You need more time," Rag said. "You will not be able to leave the Well until you're stable."

"Stable?"

"Your hand passed right through Salt's," the boy said. "It takes time."

"You can touch me, though," I said.

"You're getting better," Rag said.

"I don't understand what's happening to me," I said. "Am I a ghost?"

"The Judicator can explain," Rag said. "He says the Well is so deep that only *black energy* gets in from outside. That makes it easier to collect the... the *waves* that... used to be you." The boy grew silent then, and rocked back to seat himself cross-legged on the stone beside me. "What do you remember?"

I was silent then a long time. "I remember dying," I said at last. "I was poisoned. My body... disintegrated, fell apart. Selene was there. And Neema.

I tried to tell them to save Cassandra. To find Albé...and Lorian. They were all in danger for helping me. They'll kill Cassandra...just because she's mine. But I guess she's already dead."

"Everyone you know is dead," the boy said, words flat and very small. "I don't know how long you've been asleep, but it was long ago."

"Then how is it you speak my words?"

"Saltus taught me," Rag said. "And old Juno. She was still about when I was little."

Juno had been Demetri's wife. I recalled a Jaddian woman, handsome, bronze faced, with hair bright as the stars.

"How did they get here?" I asked. "The same as me?"

"Not the same as you." Saltus had chosen that moment to reappear, clutching a wad of undyed cloth in his hairy fists. "We didn't have to die to get here. The Judicator's people brought us when they took our ship."

"You...traveled through time?" I asked, and stood, groaning with the effort.

"Only the same way we all do," Saltus said, grinning like a demon. "Only faster."

My hand trembled as I reached for the homunculus, said, "Give me the robe."

"I should make you beg." The dwarf leered at my nakedness.

A brittle smile touched my lips, though my whole body shook with cold. "Give me the robe."

"It's your fault I'm here," the homunculus said. "You know that?"

Standing straight as I could despite my nakedness, I asked, "How long have you been here?"

Still clutching the robe in its grimy hands, the homunculus answered, "Long enough for the rest to die," he said. "Hundreds of years—though whether a year to these people is a year for true I've no idea. But it's better than living out my days on that thrice-damned ship. So I owe you for that." Smile widening, he threw the wadded garment at me. I caught it by reflex.

Seeing this, Rag sat straighter. "Good!" he exclaimed. "You're here!"

I held the rough linen in my hands, felt its coarseness with my fingers.

It had not passed through me. I shook it out, revealing a garment not unlike the one that Rag himself wore, a shapeless thing with wide, square sleeves and a ragged neck and hem.

"Put it on," Rag said. "We've lingered long enough. It's a long way up to the city, and the Judicator is waiting."

CHAPTER 39

UNREAL CITY

"THERE WAS A LIFT, a long time ago," Rag said, "but that was before the kings went away."

"When was that?" I asked, feet scraping on the stone steps.

"No one remembers," came the unexpected reply.

Rag had said the Well of Nahaman lay miles below the city, and we had climbed already very far. My knees ached, and more than once I begged Rag to halt. Saltus fared worse even than I. The creature's wheezing breath followed me all the way, and often it would pause before hurrying after us. Still, for all its apparent age, the beast moved swift and smoothly when it moved at all, tending to ragged bursts rather than steady, constant motion.

"It was the kings that built the city," Rag continued, high voice untouched by the labor of our climb, "but the Judicator says they didn't build the Well . . . or the world."

"The . . . world?" I didn't understand.

Rag continued as if he had not heard me. "The men in the city, they say they were the last kings. The last *ever*. But the Judicator says the king will return." He paused, peered down to where Saltus and I followed more slowly. "We're nearly there!" he said, encouraging, "To the surface, I mean. Then we still have a ways before we reach the old church. This part of the city's mostly empty. Folks have moved on up the cataract, to Castle Ward, mostly." He turned to resume his climb, called back. "Should be daylight by the time we reach the surface!"

"For all the good that'll do us," Saltus huffed, clambering up from the landing below.

Thin streams of water ran over the stone wall at my left hand, dribbled down to the half-eroded steps and along them to the Well below. Touching the wet stone with my fingers, I looked from Rag to Saltus and back. "What does that mean?"

The homunculus looked up at Rag, who stiffened on the stairs above. "You better tell him," the creature said, "he won't believe me."

Rag had one hand pressed flat against the trickling stone wall. A lantern fixed to the stone above him—stirred to life by our presence—formed an aureole about his head. As we'd climbed, Rag had told me how the mechanisms that powered the lights had been designed by the ancients, who made them never to go out.

So many had failed to light as we ascended.

"Our sun is dying," the boy said, "it is said that soon it will go out."

I looked at him with horror. "How soon?"

"A thousand years?" came the reply. "Ten thousand? Or only ten? *No one knows the day or the hour,* or so the Judicator says. Not even him. It's said that once there were men—this was a long time ago—that could obtain such knowledge. Learn it, just by looking. But they're long dead."

Not for the first time that day, I found my words had forsaken me. If this *Judicator* truly was the Quiet—as I then believed—then he could not be the architect of our universe. A god would know such things.

"There's more," Saltus said, eliciting a sharp look from its boy companion.

My eyes went from the homunculus to the boy and back. "What do you mean?"

Rag hung his head, and from his hushed tone, I knew this was not how he had intended this to come out. "If you're not going to tell him," Saltus said. "I will."

The boy's eyes flashed. "You said he would not believe—"

"It's the last sun," Saltus said. "Leastways the last anyone knows about. This is the ass-end of time, cousin. That *black energy* the boy here was telling you about right before I came back? It's stretched the universe out like an old whore, stretched it so bad light's slower than the stretching."

"You're right," I said to the homunculus, "I don't believe you."

The ape-man hooted with laughter. "Of course you don't!" it said. "But you'll soon see! There's nothing in the sky but the moons and the weak, old sun. The stars are gone."

The stars are gone.

Those words fell upon me like so many falling stones.

"The last sun..." I said, repeating Saltus's words. "The last sun..."

"There could be others," Rag said, "but we just don't know."

Leaning against the wall to steady myself, I said, "If what you say is true, then...then I am a trillion years gone."

"Oh, more than that, I'd wager," Saltus said, and Rag did not correct him.

"But there are still people?" I asked, incredulous. "How are there still people?"

Saltus shrugged, and Rag only shook his head, not understanding.

What they said was impossible. Three hundred thousand years there were between the dawn of man and the day of my birth—or so the scholiasts taught. We had left the gorillas to tread the path to godhood, they said. Those same scholiasts held that in much less time than that—despite the efforts of the Chantry and the High College to master man's blood—man would himself be changed to some new shape, would breed himself into forms irreconcilable with the species I knew, or else would die by violence or by suicide. And yet this boy and his mutant companion would have me believe that somehow—in some way—mankind would remain, would endure in some form or fashion until the uttermost end of days.

"It's not possible..." I breathed.

The end of time. The thought roiled in my mind, but still belief would not come. It was a thing harder to accept than my own death. My second death.

The end of time.

"We cannot stay here," Rag said. "We must keep moving."

In a daze, I followed the boy up what little remained of that interminable stair. Before long, we reached that piteous gate, a high and narrow opening, little more than a crack in the living rock of the world. Immediately beyond lay a withered garden, its beds dry, its trees bare.

I hardly saw it. My eye was caught, dragged through the creaking branches and over the iron palings of the fence to the city beyond.

Beyond...

"I know this place..." I breathed the words, brushing past Rag to stand beside the ruin of a great, white tree planted in the center of the cobbled path that split the garden into quarters, its roots upturning the nearest stones.

Beyond the fence, a paved road ran. A short wall ran along its far side, beyond which could be seen the shingled roofs and pointed gables, the short turrets and buttressed walls of houses, shops, and temples. We were on higher ground, and looking out over a rolling cityscape that retreated unto the uttermost horizon. Turning, looking up, I saw an immense face of rude stone, crowned by halls and towers grander still. A profusion of Gothic spires, pointed arches, buttressed walls, and crumbling statuary black beneath a milk-blood sky.

It was the city from my dreams, from the visions the Quiet had showed me.

Looking up, I saw the others had spoken truth. It *was* day, but as thin and sick a day as I had ever seen. The sun—a bloated star—hung low above the margins of the world, away over the farthest reaches of that black cosmopolis. The morning seemed little better than twilight.

"You can't know it." Saltus had sidled up behind me. "You're full of sh—"

"I've seen it," I said, silencing him.

I knew where we were going.

"This *was* Llesu," Rag said, coming to stand beside the dead, white tree. "Last City of Kings." He pointed out over the city toward that cold, red sun. "The Wall is that way. You can see it from the old church."

He left the white tree, hurrying toward the gate and the high road.

"You said the kings were dead," I said, following.

"Yes," Rag said, stopping at the gate to peer around the post, his posture suddenly furtive, as though he feared to be seen. "Long ago."

Mirroring his care, I lingered in the shadow of the garden gate. "Who rules the city, then? Your Judicator?"

"No," Rag said. "No. This part of the city is dead. Mostly abandoned."

"But who rules?" I asked.

Rag looked up at me, and for the first time I marked fear in his eyes. "You know."

That halted me in my tracks. "The Watchers?"

The boy grabbed my arm, sank nails into my new flesh. "Speak *not* their name." For the first time, I understood his haste, why he was so eager to reach his *Judicator*. "We were safe underground. Not even their vision can penetrate the Well. But we are exposed here, and will be until we reach the churchyard. Come."

He seized my hand, and led me up the winding street, past shuttered doors and smashed windows, with here and there a lamp still blazing with red fire or white sparks. Once or twice, a curtain twitched, and a face peered out a moment and was gone. Many of the buildings to our left were hewn into the hill itself. We were climbing, following the curve of that rock higher and higher, the cobbles rough edged beneath my feet.

Passing a tower of smooth, black stone, we reached a place where a broad avenue bisected our narrow lane. To our left, it rose up a hill—mounting above the rise of rude stone toward the acropolis—while to our right it ran down to the lower parts of the city. The way was wide, and paved with arcing cobbles, and but few lights in the somber windows of empty houses and dead shops. There was a timeless art in those crumbling buildings, in the white statues of angels and heroes whose cracked and broken limbs still held up roofs and walls. The style stirred something in my soul, a memory of the ancient world—not of some far future age.

We turned left, the three of us hurrying up the road.

I moved as a man in a dream, permitting Rag to lead me. Indeed I felt the city was a dream, that this whole impossible time were nothing more than madness playing out in the final instants of my life. I saw my own face dissolving in blood and melting suet, the skin tearing like tissue paper.

I was dead. Rag himself had said as much.

I had hoped to see Valka again in death, to find her in the Howling

Dark. Instead, I had passed through that darkness and been recalled, summoned to that terrible place, that city at the end of time, that city of the Watchers—of the Watchers *Victorious.*

"Stop!" Rag threw out an arm to block me. Just behind, Saltus nearly slammed into me.

The boy had gone still as stone, cocked his head, listening.

I listened too.

Ahead, there was a rattling, grinding sound, the noise of mighty engines marching.

"It's *them,*" Saltus hissed, pawing at me. "Off the road!" The homunculus tugged at my arm, pulled me hard enough to break young Rag's grip. I followed Saltus into the nearest alley, a narrow slot between tall houses.

Rag had not followed.

"Boy!" Saltus croaked, returning to the mouth of the alley.

Rag had frozen in the middle of the broad street, his gown flapping in the gentle wind.

Something crested the top of the hill, a great hulk of metal so red it was almost black. My first thought was that it was a colossus, but it was entirely unlike any of the great war machines of the Empire. It had no legs, nor walked like some vast iron scarab, relying instead upon a pair of mighty treads, belts of black and bronze. What should have been its deck was instead a warped, gnarled surface, asymmetrically mounded so that anyone attempting to board might lose his footing and fall, and great spines—projections of red-black metal—bristled from it like the sparse quills of a hedgehog. Inexorably it advanced, followed by another, and yet another of its kind. Each of the colossi's mighty guns lay quiescent, locked and pointed off to one side.

They were like no weapons I had ever seen, their barrels ribbed and fluted, and between those ribs I could see pulsating tubes like veins, the organs of some hideous beast in machine form.

Rag stood before them, apparently paralyzed.

The colossi gave no sign that they had noticed the boy, advancing as inexorably as they had since they appeared, and yet the sight of those hulking, inhuman machines advancing on the lone boy affected me deeply, and yet I knew it was not courage that screwed him in his place, but fear.

"Boy!" Saltus shouted again.

"I'll get him!" I said, and darted back into the street. The machines must have seen us—they were little more than two dozen paces away. I seized the boy beneath his arms and lifted him. Sensing there was not time enough to return to the alley where Saltus cowered and unwilling to sacrifice the momentum of my run, I hurled Rag and myself into the alley opposite, landing with the boy beneath me.

We lay there, waiting for the machines to pass. They did, not ceasing, not slowing their march. I watched them go, looking back over my shoulder, marking the fleshy, organic texture of the *thing* caged inside the metal hull. When they were gone I stood, and offered Rag my hand. "Are you all right?" I asked.

The boy was shivering.

"Rag?"

He nodded, permitted me to help him rise.

"What were they?" I asked.

"Servants of the enemy," Rag said, swaying.

"Then why didn't they attack?"

The boy could only shake his head. "Sometimes I think they're blind."

"Blind?"

"The enemy has eyes to see," Rag said. "Their servants need none. But those things are not the only servants the enemy has. There are men and... other things."

I did not ask.

"You saved me," Rag said, eyes shining.

I looked back across the street to where Saltus was peering from the alley opposite, looking down the hill toward the retreating hulks. "Think nothing of it."

Rag pressed his lips together. I thought he was about to cry. "You should have left me. They might have seen us. They should have seen us."

"Well, they didn't," I said.

"Saltus could have taken you to the churchyard," the boy said. "We risked so much to bring you here. To bring you back..."

"You're the only one who seems to know what's going on."

Saltus had crossed the road and was standing just behind me. He tugged on my loose robe. "We should get moving," he said, and to Rag, "Their patrols are getting closer. It's only a matter of time before they find the place."

Rag shook his head furiously. "They never will, not so long as the Judicator defends it."

"Forgive me if I don't share your faith, boy," Saltus said. "Let's go. It's not far now."

More carefully then, we returned to the main road and hurried along it. We saw but few signs of life as we went: a line of drying clothes flapping in the wind, the sound of a door slamming shut as we moved along the street. Once, I saw an old woman seated in the shadow of her portico.

She did not move, and might have been a corpse.

Above us, the crumbling ruins of an ancient citadel loomed, its black towers long fallen, their metal bones scratching at the sky. The place reminded me of many a bombed-out city I had seen. The crumbling devastation was the same. I expected Rag to beeline for the hilltop, but to my surprise, he turned aside, proceeded along a narrow and crooked street whose lamps still shone despite the newly arrived day.

"We're near the heart of the old city," Rag said, stopping in the middle of the road. "The city is very old, each layer built over the last." He seemed to find what he was looking for. "This way. The gate's not far." There was an alley between tall buildings, hardly wide enough for one of us to walk square-shouldered. I expected it to angle upward, toward the summit of the hill, but it ran down, and before long became a tunnel.

We were going back underground.

Rag leaped down the steps and hurried inside. I paused, looked up at the failing sun, at the moon—green and white—where it made its slow procession across the heavens. There was something in the pattern of canals upon its face that seemed familiar to me, recalling perhaps the green moon of Emesh that I had known for many years. Shading my eyes, I fancied I could see the black of night through the gauzy, faded pink of day.

"You can't stay there!" Rag hissed, reemerging from below, "If they catch us now, so near the door..."

"You haven't told me where we're going," I said. None of it seemed real.

"I did!" Rag said. "We're going to see the Judicator. He's this way."

"But you haven't told me why."

"I did!" Rag said again. "You're to be tested."

Pulled by the tension of the moment, I gained the top of the stairs, started down. "But tested how? For what purpose? What of my own time? My own people?"

The boy seemed to think long and hard upon his answer. Ultimately he shook his head. "I wish I knew, sir. That's why I'm taking you to the Judicator. Please." He hung his head. "Please, we've come so far."

Saltus was on the stair behind me, a strangely threatening figure, for all his diminutive size. I might not be able to overpower him, but I could outrun him if it came to that—our experience on the stairs had made that plain. Yet where would I go? Everything I knew was dust, was atoms.

There was nowhere to go but forward.

Down.

"All right," I said. "All right."

Rag brightened at once, caught my wrist. "This way!" he said, and pulled me down into the tunnel. So old was that city, and so built upon, that one could see the strata where the builders piled new upon old. I saw then that what I had taken for a hill was really all a great tower, and rather than climb it, we had penetrated to its uttermost heart. When we had gone deep enough, Rag released my hand and ran on ahead, past pipes and open doorways to a place where the path ran straight.

There was light ahead—the faint light of the last sun.

I followed him out into it, and froze.

We had pierced the hill itself and emerged on the far side, upon a lip and shelf of native rock that overlooked the Last City of Kings. Funerary markers dominated the path to either side, tall and tilted, topped with cruciforms and inscribed with characters alien to me.

Before us lay a building I had been to before, a place I had been to in dream.

Always it had seemed immeasurably vast to me, but here it seemed humbler and more intimate. Personal, in its way. The temple's great bronze doors were shut, and above them a round window of stained glass gleamed between twin towers, belfries whose carillons had long ago fallen silent. One tower had lost its top entire, and from where we approached I could see a hole in the tiled roof of the nave.

Rag reached the steps first, rushing past Saltus and myself, apparently eager to complete his rough errand. His robes flapped behind him like wings, and he had to snatch their hem as he mounted the cracked marble steps, taking them two at a time.

Almost I prayed I would awaken then, and find myself aspirating on the floor of my bath in my prison in the Arx Caelestis, my blood on Selene's hands. But I did not. A cool breeze gripped the hem of my robe as I reached the top of that stair, and the sparse flakes of winter's first snow danced beneath that blood-milk sky.

Rag pounded on the door, pounded again, and as we waited, he turned and pointed away over the city, away toward the sun. "You can see the Wall from here!" he exclaimed, "Just like I said!"

Following his finger, I turned—putting the temple doors at my right hand, and looked out to find a blackness on the horizon, its top nearly kissing the bottom of that bleary, red eye they called a sun. I would have thought it a range of mountains, were it not so perfectly regular. It was like looking at Akterumu from the shrine of Miudanar's skull, its harsh geometry shimmering like a mirage in the desert heat.

The city ran all the way to its base, a rolling carpet of black stone.

"And there's Castle Ward, straight ahead!" Rag pointed.

Another hill, like the one atop which we stood but far, far greater, rose in the middle distance, crowned with black towers and a great black dome. The whole hill had been castellated, rising tier upon tier in what seemed a mighty spiral, a profusion of buttressed walls and towers, of stained-glass windows, and of great statues—man shaped—that seemed to hold up the very buildings.

I had seen such a thing before, in the visions Ushara had showed me of the Empire we might rule together as Emperor and consort-queen.

I remember confusion at something the boy had said before, and oriented myself toward the sun to ask the boy my question when the doors

swung inward. Turning at once to face this Judicator I had been brought to see, I halted—all questions driven from my mind.

The boy called Rag stood within, black haired and dressed in dirty robes that might once have been white. But Rag stood also beside me, to the left of the doors. I looked at them both, thinking at first they must be twins, but the stains on their ugly garments were the same. There was a brown smudge on the left shoulder, a spot of damp from his fall in the alley when I had leaped to knock him clear of the approaching colossus.

I turned to face the boy in the door, mouth half-open. I took a step forward, for a moment banishing the boy outside from the periphery of my vision. When I turned to look, he was gone.

"Welcome, Hadrian, son of None," said the child within the door. His voice was not Rag's voice, high and cold and scared. Rather two voices issued from those cracked lips, one deep and grave, the other high and musical.

I drew back, hand instinctively going for the sword that was not there. "Saltus?"

But Saltus was gone, had vanished, too—and I have never seen it again.

Rag gestured for me to enter. In that strange, dual voice, he said, "I have been waiting for you, for such a long time."

"You're the Judicator," I said.

If he answered, I hardly heard him, for I knew the space within, had seen it before what seemed a thousand thousand times, in visions and in dreams. Those warped, time-beaten doors opened upon a vast and echoing hall, a long, broad hall facing east; a place of worship whose carven benches lay in ruin to either side of the aisle. Bloody sunlight fell through the hole in the ceiling, and with it the rare snowflake tumbled past high windows of stained glass, images that showed scenes of men and angels. Men with red cloaks and red crowns. A white bird descending. Angels.

Great statues stood in niches along the outer walls, past the columns that lined the nave, shapes huge and hideous, shapes not unlike those I had seen in the outer hall of the Dhar-Iagon. A thing like a human brain studded with eyes, many handed, crawling. A coiled serpent with countless feathered wings. A lioness with the bald face of a woman. A goat-headed man with a staff. A bat-winged man with a face like some many-legged sea monster. The greatest of these were perverse caryatids supporting the vaulted roof whose cracked and falling frescoes showed the heavens filled with angels, apparently untouched by the devils below.

Looking up at them, I staggered, caught myself on the corner of one of the pews. A great cable of braided metal snaked across the floor. It was but one of many, of a numberless tangle that coated the floor of that great temple, running from narthex to chancel.

In its place, there was a rocking cradle set upon a pedestal where all

those cables converged. Before it knelt a figure in tarnished white, a hunched figure kneeling with his back to me.

It was the temple, the cathedral of the Quiet, the place that I had seen in my visions. It was sacred and profane at once—had been profaned, I sensed, and guessed that the monstrous statues had been put there by some later builder. Still, I sank to my knees in shock and reverence.

"Rise," came that dual voice from the doors behind.

I looked back, and again found the boy called Rag was gone. The great doors were shut.

"Rag?"

Kures zir ol.

Here I am.

The voice issued from on high, filling the space of that great temple as water fills a glass.

A holy terror filled me, recognizing the qualities of that voice, of those dual voices blending into one. Staggering to my feet, I drew back a step, retreating toward the narthex and the outer doors. It had been a trick, all of it, though I little understood how it had been done.

I am dead, I told myself. *I am dying, dreaming. This is all one final vision.*

Am branuran oah i ge.

It is not a dream.

The kneeling figure stood, and I saw that it was no man, but the boy Rag once more, only he wore a mantle over the stained and grubby robes. As I stood there, paralyzed, utterly transfixed, he moved toward me, seeming to glide over the space between us, as though the distance were itself contracting. He seemed to grow larger as he approached, just as Ushara had done in the pantheon of Phanamhara, until—though he appeared to be only a boy—he was taller even than myself. He spread his hands, and a light streamed from them, and from all of him. I threw a hand across my face to shield my eyes, and turned my head away.

My heart hammered in my ears, and my mind drained of all thought save one certain thing.

He was one of the Watchers.

Ganae ge noan caphid.

Don't be frightened.

Said that twinned, ethereal voice. A hand—a human hand, warm and five fingered—came to rest upon my shoulders; and a voice—a human voice, a voice like the voice of the boy I'd met in the Well—said, "I am the Judicator, Ragama."

CHAPTER 40

THE JUDICATOR

I TORE AWAY FROM that warm and seeming-human hand. "You're one of them!" I shouted, backpedaling. My heel caught on one of the floor's snaking cables, and I fell.

A dark blur stood over me then, glowing with a light all its own. The *thing* I had called Rag spoke, speaking then with one voice and not two, saying, "I am what they were meant to be. What they were *before*."

"Before what?" I asked.

No answer.

"What were they meant to be?" I asked. I screwed my smarting eyes shut, willing them to see. "What are you?"

"One who has kept his oath," Ragama said, and I thought I could detect the hint of a wry smile in his tone. "Unlike yourself."

That made me open my eyes. Blearily at first I saw the Judicator standing over me. Where before he had seemed a child large as a man, now he was a man in truth, the man the boy called Rag might become, given time: strong of jaw and hard of eye, as much the image of statuesque perfection as Ushara herself, as masculine as she had been feminine. His black hair curled about his face, recalling the profile of many a Grecian hero, though he dressed in that patched, gray robe and tattered mantle.

"What oath?" I asked, transfixed by the transfiguration that had come over the boy, the man, the *creature* towering over me.

"To do what *must be* done," said he, and offered me his hand, "for the good of all creation."

For just a moment, I was aware of countless hands extended toward me—toward the countless *mes* that stretched across the infinite breadth of time. I asked, "Are you the Quiet?"

The Judicator did not move, did not lower his offered hand. He only smiled. "The Quiet..."

Ollori, doshae i Britagge?

What is the Quiet, Child?

Almost it seemed I was a child again, and it was Gibson's voice that asked the question. So plain a question, so simple, so direct. I could only shake my head.

Ragama possessed the patience of a stone, still bent to offer me his hand.

I spoke only with great difficulty, sensing that all I was—my very soul—hung upon my answer. "I don't know," I said at last, then again more precisely. "I'm not sure."

At first, I had thought the Quiet a people, an extinct race of spacefarers far antedating man. On Annica, the Quiet had revealed itself—revealed *himself*—to be a singular intellect, his *we* the *we* of Emperors.

He was an entity, a being, a personage, and not a race at all.

The other Hadrian I had seen in my cell beneath Vedatharad had echoed that revelation. *Though he slay me,* that other self had said, speaking through lips cracked and bloodied, *I will trust in him.*

Above me, the Judicator still waited, still offered his hand.

"Is he here?" I asked, looking to the cradle. In my dreams, my visions of that alien place, I had heard the wailing of an unseen infant. All was silent then.

"Your mistake," the Judicator said, "consists in believing that he is *somewhere*, like you or I. He is nowhere, and so is everywhere at once."

"Enough riddles!" I snapped. I tried to stand, bare feet catching on the cables again. I caught myself on the end of one rotting pew, one knee striking the hard floor with a force that set my teeth together. The cable had had no give to it. It was hard and solid as stone.

Ragama's hand was still there, just within reach. I glared at it, and at him. "Will you not speak plainly?" I almost spat the question.

The Judicator crooked his fingers, indicating I should take his hand.

Grunting, I took it, permitting my antagonist to haul me to my feet.

When he offered no further word, I said, "I've been here before." I made to step toward the cradle. "I've seen the egg. He showed it to me. All my life, I carried a piece of it around my neck." I touched my throat with a hand. There was nothing there.

Ragama's arm checked my progress toward the cradle, held me in place. "You have not answered my question."

"Your question?"

Dashan i Tia?

Who is He?

I turned to meet the creature's eyes. They were clear and black as ice, shining with a light of their own. Seeing those eyes, I knew, knew that the man before me—that hero in poor cloth—was himself only a garment, a cloak draped but loosely over...something else.

I found I could not lie. Not there. Not to him.

And so I could say nothing.

For much of my life, I had believed that the Cielcin worshipped the Quiet, believing *the Watchers* and *the Makers* simply their names for the vanished builders of the black halls on Emesh and Annica, on a hundred other worlds. But the Cielcin did not worship the Quiet. To them, he was a wicked god, the architect of our broken universe, a universe that should never have been.

But he was a god to them still, the devil of their black pantheon.

Utannash, they called him.

The Deceiver.

"He is a god." The words hung on the air a long moment before I understood that I had said them.

Ragama's hand was still flat against my chest, barring my path. His fingers were like fire burning there.

"And what is a god?" he asked.

Had I not asked the same question of Valka, once?

A creature in a fairy story, she had said.

Only this story is true.

I had never answered the question for myself.

"Shūturum." The word tore from my lips, formed by no thought of mine. And the voice that whispered it was not my own. I knew that I was smiling, grinning with inhuman delight. I felt my teeth grinding over one another, heard their creaking in my bones. "Absolute."

It was Ushara's word. Ushara's answer. And Ushara's voice that gave it.

The Judicator's eyes narrowed to mere slits.

"You did not come alone," he said. "There is another with you, riding in your heart. I see him in your face." Without warning, Ragama's hand lanced upward, clamped over my grinning mouth. With a strength hardly to be believed, he held me, and the touch of his hand upon my face was sunfire. I tried to scream, or rather—Ushara did—but we succeeded only in releasing a low, animal sound. A growl. A moan. A whimper. "I would have the man's answer, Brother," Ragama said, "not your own."

I dared not meet the creature's eyes, knowing that to do so would bring pain unlike anything in my experience. An oily shame was on me, a black despair that I had allowed myself to be *touched* by one of *them*, to be polluted, touched by evil.

"Look at me!"

I could not, knowing then that Ragama would surely kill me, that I had failed his test.

"Look at me!" Ragama ordered, and equally I dared not disobey.

I raised my eyes to meet his own, and found that they had changed. Where before they had been black as the void, they were now blue and bright as stars—almost colorless. I could not look away. *I could not look away.*

"Name yourself!" Ragama said, syllables rebounding off the crumbling vaults like the thunder.

"No..." The word escaped my lips, though it issued from *her* will. "No...no..."

Those eyes! I could not escape those pale eyes! Though I thrashed and turned my head, always I found them peering into me, into the very heart of me. There was nowhere to turn, no escape to be had. No escape...

"Tell me your name."

I felt the sensation of countless eyes crawling over me and through me, taking in my every atom. I felt the fingers of the will behind those eyes touch my mind, and at once I was peering down at the piteous creature the sons of Earth called *Hadrian Marlowe*. So small was he, withered and broken by time and torment, his body scarred, the black of his hair shocked and streaked by pain. I kept one of my hands over his lying mouth.

He did not need it.

A shadow lay on him and in him, a shadow plain to see.

But it was not his shadow.

It moved of itself.

I seized that shadow with countless hands, and dragged it into the light, shouting—all the while shouting—that it give itself a name. It showed me then, *he* showed me. We were falling, hurled together from some higher place. The stars fell past us, and I hated them, hated them as I hated the hand clamped over the mouth of the little creature I had claimed. I felt that hatred contort that mouth, that face, but held on the tighter. In that moment, Hadrian Marlowe touched and so glimpsed not one, but two of the terrible creatures at once.

Ushara and Ragama at once shared his mind and heart, and he knew them—and saw that they were kin indeed, but that though they were kin, they were bitterest foes.

"You were to shepherd the stars, Brother," Ragama said. Those eyes—bright as sunlit snow—peered into me and through me, but it was not me he locked eyes with, but *her.* "To command them!"

"Brother?" I asked, and for an instant, the pain of that hand grew less.

"Hush, Child," the Judicator said. "It will be over soon." Those burning fingers tightened, blazed until I felt certain that the skin of my face must blister, must smoke and peel away. I tried to scream, but could no longer find my mouth. "You betrayed your purpose, Brother!" Ragama roared. "And for what?"

The lips that I had lost moved of their own, words like grave worms slipping out between Ragama's fingers. "To...choose...for myself."

"Tell me your name!"

Smoke coiled from my face in truth, black and terrible. Still I felt my cracking lips move, felt blood run and boil down my chin. I was dead, and knew that I was dead. Knew I could no longer refuse the question.

I spoke, but the answer came from over my shoulder, from a place unseen by mortal eye.

Ushara.

It said.

Ushara zirdol.

I men Ushara.

I am Ushara.

As she answered, I understood. Ragama had said that she had been made to shepherd the stars. Her task had been their maintenance and command, and she had forsaken it so that she might rule the Vaiartu as a queen. As a god. In doing so, she had rebelled against her master, her maker, against the Quiet himself.

A light streamed from Ragama's face, his hand, his every pore. It burned me, burned *her,* burned the creature that clung to the little man whose father—who was no true father—had named *Hadrian.*

I could feel her slipping away...

...and found at once I did not want her to go.

I had learned so much from her, seen so much in my visions...had understood so little. Did I not still need her? Surely that fragment of the Watcher in my mind had its uses? Could it not be of service in the fight against the Cielcin? Against Ushara herself?

Was that a hand I felt in mine? Cold, white knuckled, six fingered?

I turned to see her face, those black eyes, those ruby lips, that hair like the fall of evening.

I saw nothing, could see nothing but the light streaming from Ragama's face.

I heard a voice. Two voices. The twinned voice of Ragama speaking:

Trian am taba ol anozam tia?

Will you let me kill him?

A choice.

Ragama had offered me a choice.

Was this the test, then? Had I not yet failed, after all?

It would be so easy to refuse, now it came down to it. So easy to remain with her. To die with her. A shadow passed between the Judicator and myself, and I perceived it was the shadow of her hair. Ushara stood between Ragama and myself, her arms wound about me—those heavy, white limbs—her breasts pressed against my chest, so that her breath came cool upon my neck.

We were falling, falling together—entangled as atoms in a telegraph.

She was shielding me, I saw that plain, protecting me from the Judicator's light.

How could I let her die?

The twinned voice spoke again, asked the same question.

Trian am taba ol anozam tia?

Will you let me kill him?

"Yes."

A moment of weakness. A moment of strength? Lips moved, cracked, burned, splitting with blood and pain.

The shadow vanished. Her shadow.

In a single instant she was gone, and the light with her.

And the pain.

I was lying on my back amid the cables that snaked along the floor, staring up through the cracked and crumbling vaults of that pagan temple at the palely amaranthine sky. The stars were dying, Ragama had said.

Of course they were dying.

They had lost their shepherd. One of their shepherds, at least.

I was surely dying myself. The pain had stopped, though its memory lingered.

Ushara was gone. Her shadow, her imprint, her memory. The part of her that had fallen on my mind, settled in it after the battle on Sabratha...the part of her that had haunted me in all the years since was gone. I smiled, but it was the crooked smile of my youth, and try as I might, I could not disfigure my face as she had, could not replicate her toothy, demonic grin.

She was gone.

I could move my hands again, though I feared to touch the ruins of my face.

Still, I did do, and felt the scars Dorayaica's talons had made.

There was no hurt—no *new* hurt—upon the old, remembered flesh.

"Impossible..." I said, and shut my eyes.

A pale light shone through the lids, and opening them once more, I beheld the figure of a woman standing over me. Her gown shone like pale fire, and the cord wound about her slim waist was of braided silver, and of silver, too, was her coiling hair. But no sign of age was there in the smooth porcelain of her face. And her eyes...

"Ragama?"

She laughed sweetly, and bending at the knees offered me her hand. "I am myself alone, Child of Earth."

"You've changed," I said, not taking the offered hand.

"I have not," said she. "I am more than you can ever see. You are like a creature floating upon the surface of a pool. Before, I but dipped one finger into your waters. Now, I dip another."

Her hand was still there, waiting for me. Her smile was like the sun.

I sat up on my own, hair settling about my face. "What are you?"

"I told you," she said. "I am one who has kept his oath."

"What oath?" I asked.

"The same as yours," she said.

"But earlier, you said I haven't kept mine," I said. Rejecting her hand, I stood, remembering the fire of her touch.

"You left your work unfinished," she said, smoothing the front of her pale gown.

A flash of the old Marlowe fury blossomed in me, and I advanced on her a step. "I was *murdered!*" I exclaimed, hands balling into fists. "I'd be dead, but for you!"

Utterly unmoved, the white woman said, "You had abandoned the path already. Two hundred years you wasted in sloth. How many more might have been saved had you not faltered?"

"I had lost *everything!*" I roared.

"Not *everything!*" came Ragama's riposte. "You have not lost everything, even now."

"Even now?" I asked, stepping forward yet again. "Are you saying... that I can go back? To my people? To my time?"

"Should you pass the test," Ragama answered.

My heart lurched. "What is the test?"

"You still haven't answered my question," she said.

"What question?"

"Who is *he?*" Ragama smiled. "I would have *your* answer, not my brother's."

"Your brother..." I left the fact that Ushara was a woman aside, along with the fact that Ragama herself wore the shape of one. "You said you weren't one of them."

A smile broke on Ragama's face like the dawn, and laughing, she tossed her head. "I am not!" she said, the sound of her laughter a sweet music. "My brother was one of *us,* once, and not the other way round."

"But you are of the same race?" I asked. "The same people?"

"Were you not told?" Ragama asked, peering intently at me. "I see the memory in you." She rested a hand upon the end of one rotting pew, and as she did, I felt the familiar pain behind my eyes, the pain of mind touching mind...the sensation of eyes crawling over me, across my skin, through my memories.

I drew back.

"Don't be afraid," the Judicator said, and offered me a hand. "We are not a race, Child. Each of us is an island unto himself, and no river... neither growing, nor fading, nor furthering his kind. The Unmade made us to serve."

"The Unmade?" I asked. "The Absolute, do you mean?"

"Your *Quiet*, yes," Ragama said, turning to look at the bassinet beyond the altar rail. "He is not like us, Child of Earth. He is something else. Something *more*."

I could only shake my head, casting about for an answer.

Had I not asked the Quiet himself?

We are, had been his answer.

"He *is*," I said at last.

"You remember!" Ragama laughed, and the music of that laughter was like a spring wind in that place of time's last autumn. "He is that which has always existed, that which will always exist. Before the Cataclysm that birthed your cosmos, he was there! It was at his command that the first photons were kindled, by his word the first quarks condensed, the first atoms formed. He ordered the formation of the first suns, and set my brothers to keep and watch over them. To watch over everything. Nothing would be without him."

I had gone very still, my bare feet freezing on the cracked stone of the temple floor. The wind that blew through the crumbling roof and shattered windows pulled at my trailing robe, blew clean through my soul. "It's true then?" I asked, voice small as I approached the bassinet. "All true? He created the universe?"

Dorayaica was right.

Shifting, Ragama placed herself between me and the rocking cradle that held her slumbering lord. "Yes," she said. "Every universe."

Every universe. I mouthed the words, reached up and hugged myself, eyes going to the frescoed ceiling. Directly above, the icon of a long-dead king shone, white haired and beardless, his face like burnished copper. He was arrayed as a warrior, dressed in black scale edged with gold. Of sable, too, was his cloak, and the crown upon his head was wrought all of raw iron. But that was not his only crown, for about his head, a ring of fire like the sun shone in powdered gold. I could not read the alien inscription beneath him, but knew that here was one of the Last Kings of Men of whom the boy Rag had spoken.

"You mean there's more than one?" I asked. "More than one universe?"

"This is not the first," Ragama answered. "Nor will it be the last." She turned as she spoke, moved among the smashed pews and broken statuary, picking her way among the flowing cables to where she might look straight up into the pale, pink sky.

The enormity of this revelation washed over me like the tide, and I was drowning in it. How many mystes and magi, how many sorcerers and scientists and charlatans all had spent their lives in pursuit of that question whose answer the Judicator had simply handed to me in that moment?

Other universes... and all of them *made*.

Ragama's voice had become like music playing in a distant room. "It was not meant to end, this cosmos... but it is very nearly over. Soon the last stars will die, and the last life thereafter. A hardy few will survive, for a time, in darkness and in cold, but nothing lasts forever..." Her words turned melancholy. "It was not meant to be so, would not be so but for *them*. They abandoned their posts, upset the balance."

"The Watchers?"

The Judicator's smile faltered. "We were made—each of us—with a purpose. A function. A role. My brother was made to tend certain of the stars. Without him, they will burn out in time. Those of us still true cannot uphold creation alone."

"What is your purpose, then?" I asked.

The smile returned. "Vengeance," Ragama said, turning once more to regard the rocking cradle. "And to wait."

It was madness, all madness. If what the Judicator told me then was truth, then the laws of nature were not immutable, not intrinsic to nature itself, but upheld and held in place by intelligences vast and strange and in service to an intelligence far greater still. The universe was *cosmos* indeed, was *order*—supremely planned.

I shuddered, said, "You really are gods."

"I am only a servant," she said, and taking a step, vanished—reappeared in the same instant at the foot of one six-handed idol on the far side of the temple. Recalling the creature's analogy, I imagined fingers tapping the surface of still water.

"How many of you are there?" I asked.

We are without number.

Ge im corfa chisga.

Her answer darkened the air like thunder, issuing not from her lips at first, though she finished, saying, "As are they."

I felt my blood run cold. I remembered Ushara turning in the skies above Sabratha, her countless eyes peering down from dimensions no mortal eye perceived. I imagined Watchers then, without number, a legion and horde of formless beasts roiling from the unpastured Dark, taking forms huge and hideous and terrible in majesty—disquiet gods of night, demons without number.

"If what you say is true..." I hardly dared to breathe. "Then we have already lost."

Ragama vanished again, appeared in an eyeblink right before my eyes. Incongruously, she laughed again. "Do not despair, Child of Earth. His victory is certain."

"You're mistaken," I said. "I've seen the future. Nothing is certain." I made to approach the chancel, stepping over one braided cord. A hand closed upon my wrist to stop me, but turning, I saw that Ragama had not moved, had not reached out to touch me.

"One thing is certain," Ragama said. "This creation will end. All life in this cosmos will die."

"You call that victory?" I snarled, trying to shake my arm free of that unseen hand.

"Our ways are not your ways," Ragama said, neither moving nor unhanding me. "Long will the night be, between the setting of these last suns and the kindling of the next. Trillions of years will pass before the collapse of all matter. Only once that collapse occurs, when the universe yawns and stretches with age, only then will the conditions of the end resemble those of the beginning. A formless void. Then he will shape the new world from the old clay, as he has uncounted times."

"So it's fate, then?" I asked, tasting bitter bile. I nearly spat. "All of it?"

"Fate?" Ragama shook her head. "No."

"You're telling me that nothing I do matters," I said. "That it's all some silly game."

"It matters to you," Ragama countered. "To your kind. You think that what is inevitable robs you of agency, but it does not. Were you not told long ago that your soul is in your hands? The fate of your universe is certain death—that has been true almost since the beginning, since my brothers abandoned their charge—but your own death is not certain, nor that of any of your kind."

I was silent then, and hung my head.

"Oh, I see," Ragama said, "you believe the whole of creation hangs in *your* balance, that if you fail...*he* will never have been."

"Because *that* is what I was told!" I said, anger flaring star-bright.

"You have been as one who studies a great mural by the light of just one candle." Here she raised a finger. "You have seen more than any of your race—save a few—but you will never understand the *all* of things. You cannot. You were not made to."

I could only stare at the creature then, the *Watcher* who was not a Watcher.

"*He* does not need any of us," Ragama said. "*He* is *Absolute,* and the Absolute is perfection. It is we who need him."

"To remake the universe?" I asked. "A universe without the Watchers?"

"To *exist*," Ragama said, echoing the words of the Quiet himself. "It is not his reality that is in doubt, but yours, ours. What is at stake is not creation—there will always be another—but your place in it. Yours, and every one of your kind."

I was shaking my head. "You're lying," I said.

Ragama seemed to grow in size then, just as Ushara had done. Towering over me, she said, "I cannot lie." Neither could the daimons of the Mericanii, though they bent truth as the darkest stars bend light.

Thinking of the daimons, I balled my hands into fists. It had not been my sword that availed in my contest with Ushara, but my will, and that at least remained to me. "I've seen the egg, seen it hatched. I know he's in it. I know you're waiting for him to be born, to complete the circuit. He creates us. We create him. Break that circuit, and everything ends."

"That is their hope, and their *dream*," Ragama said, looking down on me with eyes like chips of ice. "To unmake the Unmade. Usurp his place. Build their own creation. They tried once before—and paid for it. But they will never succeed. Everything that has a beginning has an end, Child, and so *he* can never be destroyed—for he was never made."

"But you yourself said the Watchers would be victorious!" I roared, no longer caring if I used the cursed name. "You're one of them! *He* is one of them! You used me!"

I braced myself, expecting a blow.

Abruptly I recalled a thing Lord Nicephorus had said to me on Carteia, the day Caesar himself had shared the Empire's knowledge of the Watchers with me. I could see the androgyn's face—as clear as the face of Ragama herself—and hear its cutting words.

You are not touched by the divine, Lord Marlowe. He had said, *You are in league with alien powers.*

It had been a trick all along, it had to be. I had been a pawn in their game, a tool used to break the Empire and the will of man. And I had broken it. The worlds of the Centaurine were broken, and the Norman frontier destroyed. The Emperor was in hiding, desperately reinforcing the front. The stars were thick with plague.

The Cielcin were winning.

The Watchers were winning.

There was no *Quiet*, had never been. The writing! The writing of the Watchers in the pantheon at Phanamhara—the Watcher writing copied by the Vaiartu on countless tablets—that writing and the anaglyphs of the Quiet were the same. I had believed the Watchers and the Quiet one and the same for much of my young life. Only my revelation at Annica had changed that belief. And that revelation was a lie.

They were one and same after all!

No!

Ag!

Ragama reached out with one white limb—so like Ushara's—to grasp my arm.

I caught her wrist instead, my hand sliding across the infinite breadth of time to ensure I did not miss. I felt flesh cold and hard as diamond beneath my grip, felt fingers I could not see seize upon me in turn. With my other hand I caught her other arm and held it, knowing she could have as many hands as she desired, while I had only two. Still, I strove with her, whatever her size, whatever her power.

"Fool!" the monster said. Was that strain in the music of her voice? "Why would I...cast my brother from you...if I were...in league with...them?"

I did not dare answer.

I felt my knees buckle, felt them strike the hard stone floor. I bent beneath her. Trying to resist the strength of her arms was like trying to hold back the tide, so great was the strength of her will. Still, I tried, knowing that to fail was to die a true death, a final death.

An unseen hand struck me, and I fell flat upon my back, the cables of the bassinet under me.

Ragama stood over me, and from her figure a terrible light blazed, not white but pale gold and bright as the brightest sun. For the briefest instant, I saw every statue, every stained-glass window, every fresco and smashed wood pew with a sharpness that has never left my memory.

Then I was blinded, and shut my eyes against the light, and cast a hand over my face.

Dorphae dae ol!

The deep voice of the Watcher intoned.
Its lyrical twin spoke with it, half a syllable out of phase.

Look at me!

But I could not. The light was too bright, and even if could see through it, I knew that to look was to look upon the Watcher, Ragama, in the fullness of his horror and his majesty. I knew my feeble human intellect could not have seen what there was to see and remained whole.

Look at me!

The Watcher's voices both fell like rain.

Dorphae dae ol!

I could not look, and yet I dared not refuse. Against all reason and sanity... I opened my eyes, and though I was certain I was looking at the floor between my splayed hands... I *saw.*

I saw the pitiful man-shape kneeling before me, kneeling now, his hands half-raised to cover his violet eyes. I saw *through* him, as though his skin and every fiber were blown of the clearest glass, saw him with the eyes of the Watchers, as though he were a sketch unrolled upon a page, his every nook and hidden depth revealed.

His thoughts. His memories. His pain.

I saw the snaking avenue of his life, his every second stretched behind him. I saw his deaths: his flesh dissolved in bloody foam, skin peeling away like white foil; his head struck off, plunged into still water. And I saw his life, heard his anguished cry at a blackened window, felt his knuckles smash the nose of a red king. I watched as he raised cairn after cairn with bleeding hands on a shelf above the sea, heard the noise of men screaming as a vessel moved to block the sun.

"No." His lips moved, hands straining to cover his eyes. "Not again..."

He had suffered so much. Lost so much.

I saw battles, and battles. Death and death.

Pain. So much pain.

So much love.

I felt his love for the daughter he had not truly fathered, for the woman he had not truly wed. I watched as the Jaddian sorcerers handed him a girl child wrapped in a towel white as snow, heard his weeping, felt his joy and sorrow mingling as he held the babe in his arms. I felt his heart break as he faced his woman's killer, and knew it had been his love that wrenched the power from his broken spirit.

And peering back across his years I saw a mountain, heard a voice...

...and hearing it, released him, turned my face from him in wonder.

The light faded all at once, and I, Hadrian, sagged against the nearest bench, looking up at the creature that had been the pale woman a moment before.

"His *voice*," the creature said, and turned its face from me. Its own voice shook in wonder. "*His* voice!"

Gone was the white-haired woman, the towering woman so like Ushara. In her place a giant stood. The hair that had been pale as starlight was now all of coiled gold, and of gold were the vambraces on its wrists, and golden its breastplate above the white tunic and beneath the white cloak. For just a moment, I thought I saw the Grecian hero's face peering at me from under that cap of gleaming hair. Then it was gone, replaced by a face neither man's nor woman's.

Were those tears on the alien face?

"You've never heard it before...?" I asked, clambering to my feet. For just a moment, I'd forgotten my fear, forgotten my horror, my rage. There *were* tears on the creature's cheeks. Its mouth hung open in wonderment, one white hand rising to obscure it.

Ushara had wept, but hers had been tears of pain. Ragama shed tears of joy.

"None of us has," the Judicator said, and it was a woman's voice that issued from the giant's lips. "Even the greatest of my brothers has not caught the barest glimpse of his face. You call him *Quiet,* but he has said more to you in your brief eyeblink of a life than he has to any of us since the beginning. You are truly blessed!"

At the thunder of the giant's word, I drew back, hands rising to guard my face like a pugilist in Colosso. They were the only defense I had. For an instant, I had forgotten where I was, and what it was I faced.

"I am not your enemy, Child," Ragama said, stalking round me where I stood. "*He* is not your enemy, whatever you believe. Even now he fights to save your kind, to salvage what may be salvaged from this dying universe, that it might endure into the next." As it spoke, the Judicator drew nearer, armor shimmering like the sun, gaze neither blank nor pitiless, tears still evident on its superhuman face. "All this time, you thought you were rushing to *his* rescue, when in truth he was rushing to yours."

"I still don't understand," I said, drawing back at the giant's approach. "If he is so powerful, why does he not destroy the Watchers himself, and the Cielcin with them? Why did he permit the Vaiartu to burn the galaxy of old, or let my own people murder one another like animals? Why wait for the end of time? Why allow... *any of this at all*?"

Ragama's smile did not falter, though it turned melancholy and brittle as glass. "Would you have him be a tyrant? Deny you the freedom to choose?"

"To choose what?" I snarled, clenching my fists once more. "What have I ever chosen? If what you say is true, I've only ever been a pawn in his game."

"There is only one choice, Child of Earth, for you and for all your kind," Ragama said, circling me, wending through the wrecked pews until the way to the altar and the cradle was clear. Ragama gestured for me to approach, saying, "Glory or decay."

"Glory or decay?" I did not move. I did not dare, sensing some trap, some trick.

"Will you stand now with your maker against those who would tear down his world—as you have thus far? Or will you pass into darkness, and all your people after you?"

"You said my people worship the Watchers even now," I said, nodded to the half-open doors.

"Not all," came the Judicator's reply. "Each must answer for himself." The giant pointed toward the altar rail.

Understanding the Judicator's intent, I turned and faced the chancel, began the long walk along the nave, stepping carefully over cables and braided metal hoses. A canopy of carven stone descended upon the spot where the bassinet stood, like a stalactite, as though it were the finger of some almighty hand thrust down to touch the cradle.

Mounting the steps to the dais, I found I had ceased to breathe. The cracked faces of the Watchers—many eyed and many handed, moth winged, bat winged, tentacle bearded—glared blasphemously down at me, at the miniscule creature I was.

I hardly saw them. I had eyes only for the cradle.

It did not belong in that place of crumbling stone. The bassinet itself was fashioned all of plain, cold steel, and of steel were the various cords and cables that ran up to its base, or into the banked consoles that formed a cordon about it. These shimmered with lights red and blue and golden, all winking in the gloom like so many candles. Display panels and holographs showed writing in the fiery characters the Watchers and the Quiet shared.

At last I stood there, where I had stood in dream, and peered down into the cradle—the *incubator,* I realized, feeling the heat rising from it. Where in my visions I had seen gray cloth and the broken fragments of shell, a whole egg nestled, large as the largest melon. Various sensors there were taped to its surface, or attached to probes inserted with great care through the hard shell, connecting to those machines whose functions I could only guess at.

It was all a dream. That had to be it. I had not died, was simply lying delirious on the floor of my bath in the Arx Caelestis. I would wake soon, and find Cassandra and Selene looking down on me.

It could not be real.

"He's really... in there?" I asked, voice hushed.

"It is as I said," Ragama spoke, advancing along the central aisle after me. "The king returns." As the giant advanced, it seemed to glide over the floor between us, the hem of its robe trailing on the tangled cables entirely without disturbance, as though it passed clean through them.

"When?" I asked, cognizant of the tears then shining in my own eyes.

Cocan tiam i uls cocan.

The alien reply rattled the very window panes, issuing as it did from every corner of the old ruin.

His time is the end of time.

As it drew nearer, the giant contracted, shrinking until it stood little taller than I myself. I fell to my knees, overcome at last. My hands caught the lip of the bassinet, kept me from falling flat. My whole being shook, body and soul, and I pressed my forehead to the cradle, hiding my face.

God or monster, it did not matter.

Here was the king of infinite space, bounded in his nutshell.

What could I say? Or do?

Ragama's hand lay on my shoulder. Its warmth—which had burned Ushara, hot as sunfire—seemed to me then merely the warmth of dark stone in summer. "All your life, you have fought for the preservation of your race. That remains your fight now, but you must fight not for their survival, but for *his* cause."

"Or else what?" I asked, turning to look at the gleaming giant. "He'll destroy us?"

Ragama lifted its burning hand from my shoulder, leaving no hurt. "He destroys nothing," the Judicator said. "You destroy yourselves, just as my brothers did."

I was shaking my head. "He said he needed me to fight for him. He *needed* me to save him!"

A warm hand touched my cheek, turned my face to look back up into that of the Judicator, and once more its face was the face of a woman, though her eyes shone like the sun and not like distant stars. "It is not his existence he desires—that is eternal. It is your existence and that of all the worlds that he has made." Drawing back, she turned her gleaming face from me. In a faint and distant voice, she continued, "Once, there was a magus among your people who believed that if he might learn the location and velocity of every atom in creation, he might know the whole of the future. He was wrong, for the Unmade—in his wisdom—made such knowledge impossible. One may not know the place and motion of every drop in the smallest cup of water. But there will come a day, when all is cold and still, in which such a magus might learn all of the past. Then, when all is ended, *he* will judge all that he has made. What is sweet, he will retain. What is sour, he will discard."

"Speak plain sense, damn you!" I muttered, turning on my knees.

"You believe you fight to reduce the evil in what is," Ragama peered back at me through coiling golden hair. Gone was its woman's countenance. In its place, the unsexed face of an androgyn watched me, like man and yet unlike him, familiar and alien at once. "You fight to increase the good. Every person you save, every world left untrammeled by evil serves to increase the good in that final accounting. You asked why he does not end all that he has made: because the story is not yet finished, even now, and he will not end it until every bead of light has had its day.

"This universe is dying, but *Death* was never meant to be. It is an invasive weed, the result of my brothers' treason. They wounded the stars,

poisoned the very foam of space, and turned you children to their worship and cause."

"The Cielcin," I said. "The Vaiartu."

"And your own people." Ragama thrust an accusing finger at me. "Or
did you think that you were good?"

"No," I said, and turning tried to hide my face, but I found the Judicator standing wherever I turned, even when I looked up. It was staring
down at me, its sandaled feet planted on the side of one of the temple's
great pillars, standing at right angles to the ground.

Am I a good man?

"No," I said in answer. "I know what I am."

The Ragama nearest me smiled forlornly, a sorrow black as the star-
less sky in its almost-human face. A device there was, hammered into its
breastplate: three interlocking triangles inscribed within a circle. Where
had I seen it before?

"This need not come to pass," the Judicator said, restoring its hand to
my shoulder. "This is your future. But it need not be so."

I looked up through shining eyes. "What?"

"He has not yet returned, nor sent his Oracle to you. Those events lie
ahead of us. You can prevent the message being sent, reject the call. Poor
Saltus and his people need never come here. You need never go to Emesh.
You may live the life you wanted, in relative peace."

"What?"

"Break the egg," the Judicator said. "Kill *him.*"

For a moment, I did not dare speak. "You said his victory was inevitable."

"It is," Ragama said. "You but destroy his incarnation. You have died
twice, should he not?"

Again, I could only manage a single word. "What?"

"He will return. If not by this egg, then by some other road," the Judicator said. "You cannot stop him, but you can free yourself. Yours was the
shortest road, but he will find another. Reject him, and he will."

"You're serious," I said.

"There is no fate but the fate of the all," Ragama said. "You are free to
choose your own ending, as you have always been."

I looked into the bassinet, at the egg of the unborn god, its surface
the purest white I had ever seen. A knob of broken stone lay on the floor
beside me, set there as though precisely for my use. I had only to seize it,
to shatter the egg and kill the very author of our world.

"This is the test," I said, grasping the stone with shaking fingers. I
looked up to where Ragama stood. "You will stop me the moment I raise—"

But Ragama was gone.

I was alone in that decrepit temple, surrounded by those fell idols, those statues of the demons the gargoyles had failed to keep out. Nothing moved, and for a moment, the only sound was the roll of distant thunder somewhere out over the black city of Llesu. In that moment, I was certain of *everything,* certain I could kill the Quiet, that doing so would free me of the prison that had been my terribly long life.

I could save the others. Save Pallino and Elara, Ilex and Crim, Corvo, Durand, Crossflane, Smythe, Ghen and Switch and Lorian . . . the entire Red Company.

I could save Valka.

Start again.

I had only to bring down my hand.

Who was to say the Quiet's next champion would not be a better man than I? Was it not then humility to lay down my burden? Who was I to shoulder so heavy a burden? Only an old man, tired and broken.

Break the egg.

Ragama's voice seemed to echo in my ears.

Glory or decay.

I had only to choose.

Valka would live again, Valka, and all the others. They would never meet sad Hadrian Marlowe, murderous, Pale killing, twice fated to die. Some other champion would stand for Utannash, and cause mankind no end of grief, cost mankind uncounted thousand souls, drag those souls to the Halls of Dust on Mother Earth and leave their bodies for the feasting xenobites.

"Ragama?" I stood, clutching the hunk of black stone in aching fingers. "Ragama?"

It had to be a trick.

A trick.

I turned and faced the egg. If it was deception, if Ragama was truly one of *them,* then I had been brought to that place to achieve *their* victory, that the thing that made our world might be slain by his own creation, the sculptor slain by statuary as it fell.

Would that be so terrible?

No good, but no evil, either. Everything that is vanishing in an instant, the universe snuffed out—brief candle.

No pain, no suffering.

Peace at last.

Quiet.

All was quiet then. Ragama had not reappeared, had left me to my task.

My decision.

My blasphemy.

Six hundred years of pain lit my every thew, filled my lungs. A scream red as the sundering of our universe filled that forgotten temple, and wheeling I turned to face the cradle, stone in hand. I had had enough of gods, enough of monsters.

Enough of everything!

Valka!

I had been a pawn long enough. I would make myself a king, and damn the rules of the game! Let it start again, let some other Hadrian walk away with my life. Let him live free, in happy ignorance, and never find his fate!

Or let it end.

Let it all end.

I splayed the fingers of my left hand against the egg to steady it—the false hand Kharn Sagara had given me—I raised the stone for the kill...

...and felt the creature stir within, pulse against my hand.

I faltered.

The stone fell from nerveless fingers, clattered to the floor. I sagged against the bassinet, my body wracked with dry, heaving sobs. Moving like a man with two broken legs, I turned my back against the pedestal that held the embryonic god. I cannot say how long I sat there, or how long were the days on that dim and dying world. It felt as though the rest of eternity ran out, though the last sun was still shining through the broken roof.

I could not do it. I *would not* do it.

"Why?" I asked, muttering in my solitude. "Why did you bring me here?"

I had not expected an answer, but I received one.

Your work is not yet done.

Ragama's voice had come from everywhere at once, shook every atom of air in the old temple until dust snaked down from the vaults above. This new voice disturbed nothing, issuing as it did from nowhere at all. Indeed at first, I thought it only my own self that answered, for it spoke in my heart's own voice. Some force drew my vision skyward, and I peered out through the hole in the roof at the pale and bloody sky.

This must be.

With a jolt I stood, turned to face the cradle, hand moving for a sword that was not there. I'd half expected to find Gibson's shade standing where Ragama had stood. Or Cat's. Or my father's. But there was no one. My eyes went to the egg, "It's you, isn't it?"

The soundless voice answered.

I am.

Hesitant, I returned to god's bedside, gripped the rail of the bassinet with one hand. With the other—the very hand that had wielded the stone—I reached down and caressed the pale, hard shell. It was warm as some friendly, familiar hand, and smooth as glass, as polished stone. "Please," I said, voice thin and dry and close almost to breaking. "Please, let me go." Sinking to my knees, I pressed my forehead to the rim of the bassinet, both hands gripping the cold, metal rail. "Find another if you have to. Just let me go..."

Whom shall I send, if not you?

"I don't care!" I said, shouting into the steel.

You would send another in your place?
To bear as you have borne?
Name him.

"Do it yourself!" I snarled.
The soundless voice answered. Three simple words.

I already have.

"What?" I scrabbled to my feet, staggered back a step.

If you need my life, Child, take it.
It is yours.

My life, the Quiet had said, not *ours.*

I have touched the minds of beings far greater than my own. The daimon, Brethren; Ushara; Ragama...I thought I knew what it meant, thought I had communed with the Quiet upon that mountain on distant Annica, but in that instant, I knew that I had seen *nothing,* knew *nothing,* understood *nothing* of the majesty that was—that ever was, that ever would be.

I felt...I felt as a child feels when, taken out beneath the night sky, he is first told that each of those little lights is its own sun, with its own worlds, its own life and history. Vast as our cosmos may be and infinite in depth, next to him it is as nothing, as the meanest puddle is nothing when measured against all the seas of Earth. In all that vastness I was less than nothing, less than a mote of dust, and yet like a mote of dust I was drawn upward, not crushed by the enormity of what I saw so that I—who might have pressed my face to the very stone in awe and reverence—felt that I should leap into the air and sing.

So great was the joy that filled my heart then that I forgot my anger, my hatred, my fear. My suspicion melted like the dew, and my sorrow vanished like shadows under noon's bright star. I saw how he had made our creation, ordering it by his will. I watched as he set his servants, the Watchers, to guide and guard his great project, felt his grief as they betrayed their purpose, betrayed *him.*

I felt his sorrow, deeper than human feeling and yet not strange, like a familiar color somehow darker than the human eye could perceive. Always we were turning from the path, turning against him. He felt our every pain, witnessed our every torment, experienced every injury as though it were his own. Still, he would not stop us, for to stop us would be to destroy the very thing that made us what we are. And feeling that pain, I understood the *why* at last. He suffered to see our suffering, and so our suffering made us more like him, who knew our every hurt.

And I was ashamed, ashamed that I had thought him only another monster—had nearly destroyed him with my own gray hand.

"I'm sorry," I said, and knew that I was weeping. "I'm sorry, I . . . I didn't know." I hung my head, ran my loose sleeve across my staring eyes. "What must I do?"

Have you forgotten?

I saw once more the black ship, its every deck brimming with iron statuary, its hull a Gothic pile of writhing human forms, great faces staring out between buttresses and from beneath the peaks of pointed archways.

The Demiurge.

Seeing it, I passed within and in its hold beheld the ancient weapons housed in cradles of iron, stopped before one smaller than the rest: a black deltoid like the head of an arrow long as the *Ascalon*, with engines gleaming along its stern. As I watched, it fell from an open hold, its flat surface opening to reveal the seed of the dark star imprisoned within.

Then it was gone, and a light brighter than any sun flowed across creation, a light that killed everything it touched, destroying ships and moons and planets all, disordering even the living light of the Watchers' incorporeal forms. I felt the pain of that light, searingly bright. I felt the death in it, death uncounted.

For the last time, then, I heard that voice, that voice which was no voice at all, for no sound formed its words.

I have never heard it again.

Where were you when I laid the foundations of the Earth?

I drew my hand away, found myself standing before the altar stone, before the cradle and the egg.

There were footsteps on the stone behind me.

I turned.

A man stood there. Of gold was his gleaming breastplate, and gold the bracers and greaves that sheathed his well-formed limbs. His cloth was fine, his tunic and cloak of steaming argent, brighter than white.

"Ragama?" I asked.

Ragama's hair had been golden. White. Black.

Now it was red, red as flame, and streamed from his shoulders, billowing like living fire. In his face, I saw the shadow of the boy called Rag, the boy who had pulled me from the Well. Here, I knew, was Ragama complete, a Ragama who had thrust as much of his being into our narrow plane as could be contained by our meager three dimensions.

"You pass the test," the Judicator said, voice deeper than the thunder.

From my place on the dais, I was nearly so tall as the burning creature. Smoke coiled on the air between us, spewed by little flames that coiled and danced and died in the air about that man who was no man at all.

"You would have stopped me."

Ragama's face was very grave. "That is not why I was made."

I faltered, not sure that I believed him. I turned once more to regard the egg of the unborn god. "You...would have let me do it?" I asked, striped hair floating on the heated air. "Could I really have killed him?"

"Only the part of him that can die," Ragama said. "And then only for a time. Did I not tell you? His coming is inevitable. Nothing can stop it, not *them,* not you." One of the flames swirling in the air about the Judicator seemed to peer at me. I felt that crawling sensation of eyes, and longed to hide, to turn my face from him. It was as though my mortal brain and eye knew that I was looking upon things not meant for common men. "Why didn't you do it?" the creature asked, eyes like garnets blazing. "I thought you would."

All my life, I had carried a piece of the shell about my neck. That alone was not enough to tell me if it must hatch...or shatter. In that final moment, I had remembered how that piece had come back to me on Eue, when I had thought I must die and all I loved with me. But that had not been the thought that stayed my hand.

"Because this is the world where my daughter lives," I said, looking round. "How could I destroy it?"

Ragama's face split in a bright grin. "Your kind is more like *him* than ours," he said, and I have pondered those words ever since. "You understand, then, why he will not unmake what he has made."

"I do," I said, and once more my eyes were shining with tears.

Cassandra...

I would have destroyed her, too, and for what? To ease my pain?

We are beasts of burden, we men. We struggle, and by that struggle are filled.

Gibson's shade had said those words to me.

The Quiet had said those words to me.

"You understand what you must do?"

Seek hardship.

"Vorgossos," I said, "on Vorgossos...there is a weapon, one made by the machines of old. One that can destroy the others."

Ragama drew nearer. "Your road will not be easy, nor your burden light."

"That does not matter," I said. "It must be."

"Will you then renew your oath?" The giant stopped at the foot of the dais, standing so that our eyes were level. "And see to its end this course you have begun?"

"I will."

Umal naqodra!

The giant said.

Then kneel!

No unseen hand forced me to my knees, nor any great wind. I knelt of my own will. Above me, the giant tossed back his cloak, and lo! Its lining was of pale fire! Flames spun in the air, kindled and blew out—were kindled anew. A light like the aurora settled on Ragama, seemed to spread from his back like wings. Tipping back his head, he convulsed, and from his lips there sprang a spike of twisted metal.

With a gasp, I realized what it was.

It was a hilt.

I sat there, transfixed, unable to move as the Judicator closed one fist about the hilt and drew it forth from himself.

No smith on ten thousand worlds would have called what the Judicator drew forth *a sword*. It was a spike of crude iron, twisted and gnarling. And it *blazed,* as though the creature had a furnace in his belly. Its edges gleamed like a thing new forged, and he raised it above his head.

When I was invested an Imperial knight, the oaths I swore were legion. I knelt before the Emperor for several minutes before His Radiance lay the sword of office upon my shoulders. Caesar had asked what seemed then a hundred questions.

I had sworn so many vows—nigh all of them broken.

Ragama asked no questions, extracted no further oaths.

I expected him to speak, to begin some rite or benediction, or to lay that blazing sword upon my shoulder. My brow.

Instead he drew back his arm, and a thousand hands—unseen—held me in place as he plunged that burning brand into my heart.

CHAPTER 41

TRANSFIGURATION

MY FIRST, NEW BREATH brought pain, sharp and cold. I was naked, shivering on a cold metal floor. My eyes focused only slowly. Chest heaving, I rolled onto my back, stared up at the black roof with its pale, round lights. There was something familiar in those lights, in that black metal, the brass plating on the fittings, on the control plate by the doors—and on the door itself.

I was on a ship. That black and brass...I would have known it anywhere, the telltale style of a Sollan Imperial warship. The dream was ended. The dark city of Llesu with its dying sun was gone. I was alone, without even the white noise of the drives for company.

All was silent as a tomb.

Struggling to rise, I rolled back onto my side, felt every limb ache with cold. The memory of Ragama, of the touch of the Judicator's sword, flashed like lightning across my mind, and I raised my hands to my face.

Do what must be.

My hands.

Were they really my own? I held them out to look at them, though they trembled like leaves in the wind. They were pristine, without mark or blemish, smooth as hands of marble. The loop of cryoburn scar about the left thumb had vanished, and the marks of Irshan's sword were gone, nor any sign was there of the surgery Elkan had performed on Nessus, when he restored the fingers Dorayaica had consumed.

They were not my hands, but the hands of one who had known no violence. Or whom no violence had touched. Still, I clenched them to stop them shaking, felt the bones ache. A shock went through me, and I gripped the left with the right.

Metacarpals. Phalanges.

They were *true* bones, not the hollow lattice Kharn Sagara had given

393

me. Still in shock, I touched my face, feeling for the mark of Syriani's talons on my cheek.

They were not there.

I sat up sharply.

Black hair fell across my face, fell almost past my shoulders, longer than it had been in centuries, long almost as it had been in the pits of Dharan-Tun.

There was not a thread of silver in it.

"How?"

Scrabbling by then, I felt my chest, my stomach, reached round to pad at my back. The thick scars of the lash were gone, and the wide, flat scars where the Cielcin had peeled the skin from my thighs. The wounds of battle and torment alike were gone, and the skin that had begun to spot and leather with age was taut again and clean. I willed those hands to stop their shaking, clenched them into fists, screwed shut my eyes. I found it was possible to ignore the cold, that with a force of will, I might drive away the feeling.

I stood, wavering on bare feet. I was standing in the vestibule of an airlock, the inner door at my back, the hatch that led deeper into the ship just ahead of me. The walls to either side were lined with the lockers that ought to have held environment suits, but they stood empty, their doors nigh all retracted, revealing the bare compartments within. The vague notion that I should clothe my nakedness chewed at the back of my mind, but I found that I could banish the concern as readily as I had banished the sensation of bitter cold.

I stood there a long moment, head cocked, listening.

Some idle motion of my body must have tripped the door sensor, for the hatch that opened on the hall slid aside. The need for clothing asserted itself once more, and I turned to examine the open lockers. There might be something in one of the lower compartments I could use, or beneath the bench in the center where the shipmen might sit to pull on their suits or lace up their boots.

I crouched before one of the lockers against what I guessed was the forward bulkhead, found the emergency kit. The expiration date on the beta applicators within read *ISD 17479.* To my knowledge, the year was seventeen four thirty-eight, but these medical kits were built for long-term storage.

It seemed likely then that Ragama had returned me to the proper time. For all I knew, it was the same day—the very hour—that I had expired upon the bathroom floor. The memory of that death was like black fluid in my lungs, and I coughed, choked back my bile.

A moment later, the horror faded like the cold.

Fear is a poison. The mantra rang.

I found the rim of the crèche unit, saw the embossed plaque on the right side, just above the dormant screen of the medical monitor. Gold letters on black. I used my thumb to chip away at what I guessed was decades of frost.

I laughed when I saw the plaque plain and clear.

PROPERTY OF THE IMPERIAL SERVICE VESSEL
GADELICA | MTC-10459
RED STAR FOUNDRIES, HERMONASSA
ISD 16009.04.26

I was truly home.

The map of my surroundings filled my mind a moment later. Had I not walked these halls a hundred times in the years between Sabratha and Forum? The great hold in which I found myself ran nearly the whole length of the ship, a stretch of perhaps two miles. I knew how to reach the bridge, but sensed that to try for it would be fruitless. The *Gadelica* had been at dock in orbit about one of Forum's sixty moons, mothballed for the duration of my stay on the capital. If she was there still, she was not likely to be fueled, and even if it was, I could hardly commandeer her alone, defy the safeguards that were doubtless in place, unmoor her, and fly her through Martian security.

And again... where was Cassandra? She had been on the surface, and Neema and Edouard with her. *Edouard* ... belatedly I remembered that Edouard was to be transferred, that Aurelian intended to spirit him away to maintain the security of Operation Gnomon from the Chantry.

How long had I been dead? I could not have remained in Llesu for more than a day, and yet my experience of time in that other time and the time here in my own proper place were not necessarily correlated. For all I knew, years might have passed, or only seconds. When I had died fighting Aranata Otiolo, mere minutes had passed, though it seemed I had dwelt in the Howling Dark for long eons.

Clutching the foil blanket tighter, I shuffled on numb feet over the icy floor, willing them not to feel the bitter chill. At the intersection of each aisle I halted, craned my neck and looked round for one of the diode displays that would mark the time and my position in the vast and echoing hold.

"You there!" A man's voice cracked like a whip from some place over my shoulder. "Halt!"

I did not see the man when I turned to look, nor did I hesitate. If he was one of Captain Ghoshal's men, I reasoned, all would be well, even if he had to stun me first. If he were a Martian—in league with Aurelian or with the Chantry, it did not matter—it would be better to run.

I ran, left hand clutching the blanket like a brooch.

"I said halt!"

No shot followed me, but I pelted down the aisle toward what I was sure was the vessel's aft. Edouard had warned me that the presence of Ramanthanu and its kin aboard the *Gadelica* had been discovered and brought to the Chantry's attention. That meant the ship had been boarded and thoroughly searched by agents loyal to the priests. For all I knew, the man following me could be a Chantry Sentinel, an agent of Samek's and the Choir.

Why had the Quiet and Ragama conspired to return me to this place?

I reached the door to the next bay of the great hold well ahead of my pursuer. Ye gods! I felt strong! The door slid open without objection—I could hear the crunch of booted feet on the frosty steel behind. The man was shouting for backup. I heard him slip and fall, but he neither stopped nor turned back. I was near to the rear compartment. Had I heard my pursuer say something about the *ramp*?

The next door opened without protest, and at once warmer air collided with me. My bare feet slid on the clear metal of the floor. Stacked crates rose in mounds to either side, pallets secured by woven nanocarbon belts, black faces stenciled with the name *GADELICA* and the hull number *MTC-10459*.

They were munitions crates, and had I time I might have opened one and armed myself. As it was, I sped past them, and past the stowed floaters and crabbed cargo lifters with their jointed metal arms.

I skidded to a halt.

The great ramp stood open, its airlock doors rolled back, and beyond—the light of day was shining. Not the pale gold of Forum, but a pale, stark white—as I had known on many other worlds in my long life.

If not Forum, where then were we?

A pair of men in the simple black jumpsuits of Imperial Navy shipmen emerged from behind the crates ahead and to my left. Neither one seemed to know what to do with the sight of a tangle-haired, wild-eyed naked man running their way, foil blanket flapping from his shoulders like iron wings. They stood there, mouths agape, neither moving, though the hand of one had reflexively moved toward his stunner.

It was that man I checked with my shoulder as I passed, colliding with one of the munitions crates on my way toward the ramp. Wherever we were in port, I would do better in the streets. I had lived quite successfully in Borosevo for many years. If I had to do so again, I would.

"Hold, sir!"

The *sir* did not register. My feet had reached the corrugated steel of the ramp, and I was out beneath pale sunlight, and cast my vision to the sky...and froze.

There was no sky.

Instead, the inverse towers of a gray and well-ordered city loomed like stalactites from the roof of the world above, and looking to the horizon, I saw it rise to meet that floating city. Moments later, I understood.

We were within the circle of a mighty ship, a great, slender drum whose spin effected the illusion of gravity. A mighty cylinder. The pale light-like-day that shone all about me fell from a fluorescent shaft that ran along the center of that drum, held up by spoke-like towers of glass and gray steel.

Looking up, I spied the antlike forms of men and women moving along streets in the heavens above, and here and there the green of trees and of canals choked with algae.

Shocked, I came to a halt, lost my grip on the thermal blanket. It flew away on a gentle wind, fluttered like abandoned newsprint across the fused plascrete of the yard.

It was an Extrasolarian ship. A Sojourner. Of that I was certain, though I had voyaged on such a vessel but once before. This ship was much smaller than the *Enigma of Hours* had been, and the ship that had carried us to Vorgossos had not possessed that central axis of false sun, being lit instead by great lamps atop the buildings on all sides of the interior drum. That beam of fluorescent light could not have been more than a mile above our heads, and the far side no more than two. Almost I feared to look into that castellated sky, as if mere looking might cause me to fall up into it and so tumble to my death.

Still, the ground beneath my feet felt solid as the rock of Delos. I did not fall into that tubular city, but sank to my knees.

"Abba?"

I froze, long hair blowing all about me.

There were footsteps on the earth behind. A small shadow in that light forever noon.

"Abba?"

I twisted where I knelt, peered up into that face I most desired to see.

She was standing there, as real as anything, her crimson *mandyas* fluttering like one lonely wing. She looked somehow older, her face hollow with a grief that shock had but recently displaced. Her emerald eyes were shimmering with tears.

"*Es ti?*" she asked, words hardly more than whispers. *Is it you?*

I smiled, and the smile turned to quiet laughter—a barking rasp. "Yes, Anaryan," I said.

She had recoiled at the sight of my face.

"It's me."

CHAPTER 42

DOUBT

SHE DID NOT COME to me, but retreated half a step. "What are you?" she asked, one hand moving to the hilt of one sword. Her eyes were hard as glass.

"Cassandra!" I stood. I touched my face with that hand that was not my hand, that new left hand of flesh restored. "I know. I know I am not the man I was . . ." Echoing Ragama, I said, "I am the man I should have been. But I am *me*, Anaryan, I promise you that. Upon your mother's blood, I promise it."

I knew that I was naked, but I felt no shame, and the desire to cover myself came more for concern for the others than for myself. Cassandra was not alone. The two men from the hold had filtered after her, each holding his stunner limply at his side. There came a beating of great wings upon the air, and the Irchtani chiliarch, Annaz, alighted beside her, head cocked so that it peered at me with one glass bead of an eye.

"They said you were dead, *bashanda*," he said.

"I was," I said.

"What do you mean," Cassandra began, hand still on the hilt of her sword, "that you're the man you should have been?"

More had come to the *Gadelica*'s ramp, men and women in ship's fatigues. I recognized Captain Henric Ghoshal, a broad-shouldered, mustachioed man with the black hair and bronze complexion common among the old palatine families. "He's on his way," he said.

"Someone get the man some clothes!" cried another voice. "Call his servant!"

"Where is Neema?" I asked, and looking round at the city coiled about that linear sun, I asked, "Where are we?"

Cassandra seemed not to have heard me. "Who are you, really?"

Edouard appeared over her shoulder, his usually oiled hair unkempt, his eyes hollow.

"Who am I?" I said, advancing a step toward my daughter. "Cassandra, I am myself."

"Neema said you died," she said. "And the princess. They said you... they said it was the priest's poison. That you *melted.*"

Edouard stepped forward, laying a hand on Cassandra's shoulder. "I wouldn't let her see, lord," he said. "Is it really you?"

"It's really me."

"Your scars," he said. "Your face."

I raised a hand to hide my once-scarred cheek. "Gone."

"How?" he said.

"The Quiet," I said, and let my hand fall, for there was nothing for it to conceal. "He has sent me back. I still have work to do."

The younger man's mouth hung half-open. He teetered on the precipice of speech.

"Dorayaica must be destroyed," I said. "It is infested by one of the Watchers, and soon it will have gathered enough strength to act of itself. It will be like it was on Sabratha, only it will not be constrained as Ushara was. Already, Dorayaica has gathered her to itself. I have seen it. They rule together. On Dharan-Tun."

Edouard set this all aside with a gesture. "You were *dead,*" he said, and shook his head in disbelief. "I saw the body. The blood. Her highness said it was the Mermaid's Kiss."

"Dispholide," I said. "It was. One of their Cantors poisoned me. You tried to warn me."

"I failed," Edouard said, and dropping to one knee before me, he took my hand. "My lord, I failed you."

Tugging on his hand to make him rise, I said, "They failed, Edouard. I am here. Stand!"

He did so, and drew back.

One of the junior men had retrieved the foil blanket where it tumbled cross the stone yard and offered it to me. I accepted it gratefully, and bound it about my waist, fashioning a kind of skirt. The man who offered the cloth to me had jerked away as I reached for him, and I looked round at the others with equal parts confusion and joy. Cassandra had not moved at all, still stood with her hand on her sword.

"Anaryan," I said to her. "Don't be afraid. It is only me."

"This is some trick," she said. "Some Extrasolarian devilry. You are a clone. A copy they have sent to torment us." She turned her head to speak to Ghoshal and Annaz and the others. "We should never have trusted them!"

Tears brimmed in my new-made eyes, and I moved to take her by the shoulders in the instant her attention turned away. Before she could react, I embraced her, felt her every fiber tense. She did not move for the space of several heartbeats. "Cassandra," I said softly, speaking into her braided hair. "It really is me."

For a moment, I thought that she might return the embrace, might soften, might weep as I was weeping.

"I thought I'd never see you again," I said.

She lurched away. "You can't be real," she said, and her eyes were shining with unfallen tears.

"How long has it been?" I asked, looking from her to Edouard.

"Two days," came the younger man's reply. "We left Forum at once, took the *Ascalon* from the Porta Leonora, commandeered the *Gadelica* with the Commandant General's help."

I felt my eyes widen. "Lorian?" I looked round at the Sojourner. "Of course..."

"This is his ship," Edouard said.

Henric Ghoshal advanced to join Cassandra, Annaz, and Edouard. He moved cautiously, as if afraid I might shatter or combust. "I sent for him, my lord!" he said. "He is coming now."

"He helped you?" I asked, turning from one face to the next.

My last words.

Find Albé, I had said, clutching Selene's arm as my own rotted away. *Find Albé. Trust Lorian.*

Evidently they had. I shut my eyes, murmured thanks to he I knew was always listening.

Something in the quality of the silence changed, and I opened my eyes, saw Ghoshal's men part on the ramp of the troop carrier, drawing back to admit the knot of figures emerging from the hold.

The Cielcin emerged into the false day of the drum city, shielding their too-sensitive eyes with long-fingered hands. I could feel the tension in the humans gathered about them, marked the tendency of hands to drift toward weapons.

But Ramanthanu and its people made no move, unless it was to walk toward me. Seeing me standing there in plain light, the lop-horned captain fell to its knees, pressed its flat face to the pavement. The others followed suit.

"*Ba-Aeta-doh!*" it said, voice loud despite its kneeling. "My lord! They said that you had fallen—but I did not believe!"

I answered it, "I was told our people had found you. I feared that you were lost."

"*Muddanyutata o-tajarin'ta,*" said Albé, stepping forward. I had not known until that moment that he spoke the Cielcin tongue. It made sense, he was—had been—of HAPSIS, after all. "I woke them and the Irchtani. And Captain Ghoshal. We needed men to take the ship from drydock. Aristedes and the Extrasolarians staged a distraction so we could escape."

I tried to picture the battle. Edouard, Neema, and Cassandra stealing aboard the *Ascalon* in the Porta Leonora, battling the Martians to win free. The attack on the orbital dockyard, the theft of the *Gadelica*. The complicity of Lorian and his fleet.

"Does this mean the deal with the Extrasolarians fell apart?" I asked. None answered.

"*Ba-Aeta-doh!*" said Ramanthanu, making the honorific a single word. It had not raised its face from the pavement. "Ba-Aeta-doh! I knew you were not dead. If the false god of my fathers could not destroy you...I knew no weapon of the *yukajjimn* could!"

I looked down at the kneeling creatures, spared a glance for Cassandra. She had relaxed somewhat, had at least taken her hand from the sword. But suspicion remained in her emerald eyes, and there was a tension in her every fiber, as though she were a bowstring held taut by an experienced archer. By contrast, there was nothing of suspicion in the kneeling Cielcin.

If anything, the Cielcin was *groveling*, was rushing to reassert its subservience, as though in terror of the lash. Knowing what was expected of me by the traditions of its kind. I advanced and placed my bare foot upon the soft, exposed back of the creature's head, where the coarse, white hair sprouted from behind the horned epoccipital crest. Seeing this done, the others pressed themselves flatter to the stony ground, but said nothing.

Something turned in my stomach as I performed the action. It was *wrong*, and yet the alternative was violence. The Cielcin would either submit or conquer.

Or die.

Removing my foot from the captain's head, I said, "*Lenna, Ramanthanu-kih.*"

I hadn't forgotten what this creature was, what it had done to the prisoners on Sabratha—what it had ordered done. And yet it was a link. The first step in the chain I'd hoped to find and pull as a boy. The visions the Quiet had shown me time and again were of extinction, of the death of our kind...or of theirs.

Do what must be, that silent god had said.

Still, I hoped I might effect a compromise. A synthesis. A marriage of heaven and hell.

A peace between man and Cielcin.

The only alternative was genocide.

The captain stood and drew back, Otomno and Egazimn, Bikashi and Atiamnu with it.

"Where are we, then?" I asked, addressing Edouard and Ghoshal.

The mustachioed captain answered. "Perhaps it is better if we wait for the Commandant General."

"You do not trust me, Captain?" I asked.

"I am not certain you are who you say you are, sir," the man said. "The Hadrian Marlowe I met on Sabratha was old. Gray haired. Horrid great scars on his face and hands. Whatever you are, you aren't the same man."

How I longed for Valka, then! For Pallino! For Bassander Lin!

Not a one of the people in that landing field had been present aboard the *Demiurge*. Not a one of them had seen my return, had seen me defeat Aranata Otiolo after the loss of my own head.

But Lorian was coming.

Lorian had seen the recording Pallino's suit had made. And Lorian had been at Berenike, and at Perfugium, and at a dozen other battles beside.

Lorian would understand.

"I think we'd all feel more comfortable if you came back onto the ship, sir," Ghoshal said.

As he was speaking, I realized that many of Ghoshal's men had drawn their sidearms, and as their captain spoke, they trained the blue slits of their stunners on me.

I raised my hands. "There's no need for this," I said. I smiled. "Your weapons will do you no good, sir. They are no threat to me."

Could they not see that I was myself?

"Keep your hands where we can see them, sir," Ghoshal said, voice unusually mild. "Please."

I had frightened them. I saw the unease in their faces. One man's stunner shook.

"Captain Ghoshal!" exclaimed Annaz, hopping to face the palatine commander. "This is unnecessary. Tell your men to lower their weapons! Whether this is *Bashanda* Marlowe or not, this is no threat to us."

"You really think it's him, bird man?" Ghoshal asked, right hand ready by the holster of his own sidearm. His eyes darted to Annaz.

The Irchtani and Cielcin, both . . . I thought. Strange that they, who were remoter from me, saw what those closest had not.

"You will come peaceably?" Ghoshal asked.

I had not lowered my hands. "Of course." I directed my words to Cassandra, whose beliefs alone of those gathered there mattered to me. "It really *is* me. I have been *remade*, don't you see? My body was destroyed by the Chantry's poison. The Quiet has fashioned me a new one."

Had Cassandra's doubt broken, just for a moment? Something in her face had flickered.

"I will come peaceably, Captain Ghoshal. I intend no violence toward you or your men. I will have need of every one of you if we are to reach Vorgossos."

"Vorgossos?" Edouard interposed himself between myself and Ghoshal's stunners, his arms outstretched. He stared intently at me. "Why Vorgossos?"

"Kharn Sagara has a weapon," I said, "a ship. It has weapons designed by the Mericanii, weapons capable of destroying the Watchers."

Edouard squinted up at me. "You're certain."

"I've seen the weapons myself," I said.

The HAPSIS man hung his head. For a moment, the only sound was the crinkling of the foil lashed about my waist.

"Edouard," I said, using the man's right name. "We can finish what we started on Sabratha. Operation Gnomon is not done yet."

The Museum Catholic glanced at Ghoshal. "My lord, we are fugitives. I feared they would kill your daughter after what they did to you. We had to kill men to escape Forum, to say nothing of the diplomatic cost. And that is not all..."

I did not give him the chance to finish, saying, "Our duty has not changed."

"If we are captured..." He did not have to say it. He gripped my arm, stood near so that I felt his words upon my face. "They will execute *all* of us."

I could only nod.

"We are hardly more than three thousand," Edouard said. "Less than half the strength we took to Sabratha. The *Gadelica* is troop transport. Ancient. We have nothing save the hardware in our hold."

I heard hardly any of this. I looked him in the face, held his gaze through those ivory-rimmed lenses until he faltered. "You believe me," I said.

"What?"

"You believe I *am* me," I said, clarifying.

Edouard looked away, almost embarrassed. "I've read your file," he said, "saw the footage from Perfugium and Berenike. I'd be a fool to doubt, besides..." He broke off, face downcast. "I believe in miracles."

I looked at him, hard-eyed. "Your god did not do this."

Edouard smiled, just for a moment. "My god is the only one who *can* do this."

What could I do but smile at him?

"Step away from him, Albé," Ghoshal said. "Lord Marlowe...if you *are* Lord Marlowe. Will you come quietly?"

I laid a hand on Edouard's shoulder, stepped past him, back into the line of fire. "If you so wish, Captain. I will go to the brig." I looked down at my makeshift clothing. "I don't suppose you might send for my clothes?"

"We'll find something for you," Ghoshal said.

Cassandra had not moved in a long while. As I drew level with her, I said, "Will you come visit me?"

She looked away. "I...*si.*"

"This way!" Ghoshal's aristocratic tones cut across us both.

Passing my Cielcin and the Irchtani, leaving my daughter and Edouard behind, I permitted myself to be escorted back across the stone yard toward the open vessel. I had to hike my foil skirt up at the knee to keep from stepping on it as I mounted the ramp, the wind of the coiled city-ship tugging at my overlong hair.

"Let me through!" a contralto voice exclaimed.

I halted, and my escort—four men with stunners drawn—halted with me.

"Let me see him!" The voice had gone shrill. "Let me through, I say! That is an *order*, sirs!"

The men before me parted, permitting a woman with short, red hair to pass. I did not at first recognize her. She wore an officer's dress blacks, but they ill fit her, having clearly been cut for one broader of beam than she. She staggered into the open space at the top of the ramp, looked down at me, face white as that of a phantom.

"Hadrian?"

Her voice revealed her.

"Selene?"

She had cut her hair, slashed it off about the line of her jaw as with a sword. I did not think I had ever seen her face unpainted before. Still her rank betrayed itself: in the touch of gold at her throat, in the rings and bangles on those slender hands where they emerged from the officer's tunic.

There could be no denying who she was, or what she was.

She raised one hand to her mouth, eyes wide. She had seen me die, and more than die—she had seen me brutalized. Well I recalled the horror I had felt seeing Irshan decompose so rapidly beneath me on the floor of the Grand Colosseum. Too well I recalled my own demise, my own reflection melting in the mirror, blood streaming from my eyes like tears.

"You're alive..." she said, not lowering her hand. Some emotion touched her eyes. Joy perhaps? She shook. "How can you...be...? Is it you?"

Smiling, I said, "Don't cry for me, Selene."

Her shoulders shook, and she clamped her hand over her mouth, staggered down the ramp toward me. I raised an arm to catch her, still clutching at the blanket wrapped about my nudity. She fell against me, sobbing the while. I held her close, let her cry.

I had forgotten until that moment that she had kissed me, and stood at once more stiffly. Still, I held her fast, let her cry. She had seen a terrible thing, and what the days since had meant for her, I thought I could guess.

"You brought her with you?" I asked, projecting so that my words carried over the crowd. I turned her about with me, so that I might see the others—Edouard and Cassandra, Ghoshal and the xenobites. "You kidnapped an *Imperial princess*?"

"She insisted," Edouard said.

"She insisted?" I echoed. "So that's all right then. If she *insisted!*"

I could hardly believe my ears. Not only had they been forced to blast their way out of Forum, absconding with two Imperial military vessels; not only had they jeopardized nascent relations with the Latarran Monarchy; but they had kidnapped one of the Emperor's own children. It was no wonder tensions aboard the vessel seemed so high.

"She seemed to think it would prevent the Martians from simply destroying our ships," Edouard said. "I agreed."

I looked down at the woman sobbing against my bare chest. "They would have...killed the others," she managed through her tears. "I...couldn't have that." One green eye peered up at me through those ragged strands of violently red hair.

My jaw grew tight. By enabling their escape, she had put the lives of every man and woman on the *Gadelica* in still greater jeopardy. The lives of Albé and Ghoshal—the ranking officers and apparent ringleaders of the plot—were certainly forfeit. The Cielcin would be executed out of hand, and the Irchtani likely along with them. The junior men might survive, they were only following orders, after all—but they might not, or might merit their own voyages to Belusha.

"You cut your hair," I said lamely.

Selene choked. "I...yours is different, too." She held one curling strand in near unfeeling fingers. Only by degrees did she raise her face to my own. Her eyes were raw with tears, red rimmed and wide, so wide I thought I might drown in them. Once, perhaps, I would have. Then I felt only pity for her. And concern. "You're all different." She blinked. "You really can't be killed, can you?"

"Not today," I said, and smiled down at her.

She raised a hand to gingerly touch my face, but pulled the white fingers away. "You...your face has changed."

"I know," I said.

"Step away from the princess, Marlowe!" came a high, familiar voice.

Turning from Selene, I saw the man I'd hoped to see striding from the gate at the end of the stone yard, one of his hod-helmeted officers in tow. Lorian walked with a deliberate haste I had never seen in him before. He had left his cane behind, and the short-billed officer's cap he wore was pulled down almost to his eyes, which were alight with focus.

"Lorian!" I moved to meet him.

Without breaking stride, the little Commandant General drew his sidearm—a wolfram needler of exquisite make—and fired the weapon straight at my chest.

The needler fired a slim bolt of polished tungsten—long as the end of a man's thumb and no wider than the tine of dinner fork—at many times the speed of sound. I knew its type. The bolt was vaguely pill shaped, narrower at either end and rounded so that it might tumble on the air, slewing round so that it might tear through whatever it struck with a sound like a thunderclap.

It did not strike me, though it passed clean through my bare chest.

Lorian did not stop.

The needler was only semiautomatic, and so he had to depress the trigger with his finger each time he discharged the weapon. I counted *seventeen* rounds before the good commander was within a dozen paces of me. Never once did he blink. He stopped perhaps ten feet from me, and taking aim at my face prepared to fire a final time.

I raised a hand.

Time parted, and the bolt struck the ramp at my back with a shower of sparks.

The officer at Lorian's right hand—a tall, thin woman with hair nearly so white as Lorian's own and a black, metallic implant at her right temple and along the cheekbone beneath one bright eye—looked on in horror.

"Are you done?" I said, irritated.

The others were still and silent.

Lorian fired again.

The wolfram bolt passed clean through my chest and struck the ramp at my back without leaving a mark.

"Now I'm done," the little man said, grinning wolfishly.

"*Mère de Dieu!*" Edouard swore, rushing to come between us. "What the devil was all that?"

"Should you meet the Arthur-Buddha," Lorian said, holstering his needler, "kill him."

"I don't think this is what the old masters precisely had in mind," I said.

"You're really you," Lorian said, grin widening.

"I'm really me."

The little man spread his arms. "You son of a bitch!"

"You shot me, Aristedes!"

"I had to be sure, didn't I?" he said, and embraced me. "They said you were dead!"

"They say a lot of things," I said, thumping the man on the back.

I sensed a strength in Lorian's limbs that had not been there before. All his life, the man had been a scarecrow, a thing of paper and straw and twigs. He seemed a man of raw iron now, and perhaps he was.

"It wasn't just the nerve implants, was it?" I asked.

"I told you, I've had some work done." Lorian drew back, punched me in the arm. "You should talk. What the hell happened?"

"The Quiet," I said.

"Again?" Lorian looked to his companion, exasperation coloring his face. "You know, most people die when they're killed, Hadrian!"

I grinned to match his own. "One of these days I'll get it right." I looked up at the city overhead, Ghoshal and his fears forgotten. "This is your ship?"

"The *Mistwalker*," Lorian said. "We took her fighting the Exalted at Abziri. We have some thirty of her class in the Grand Army, plus the free captains. There are thousands of smaller ships."

"What is it all for?" I asked, watching men and women walking across the roof on the far side of the long sun. "Harendotes didn't raise this army only to aid the Empire against the Cielcin."

The woman at Lorian's right spoke up. "Not only."

I looked at her, marked for the first time the black threads radiating from her implant beneath her pale skin, so like Lorian's own.

Lorian raised a hand for peace. "Hadrian, this is my Chief Security Officer, Captain 2Maeve Gamma A27 of the Interfaced."

"Two . . . Maeve?" I repeated the odd name, turning to the strange, demoniac woman. "Interfaced?"

"You would call us *barbarians,* I believe," the woman said icily.

"Perhaps I would," I said. "Lorian?"

The Commandant General had returned. "That's enough, 2Maeve." He looked up at me, one hand resting on the needler at his waist. "You heard our terms in council. Control of the Norman stars. That's why we've raised our army."

I was nodding. I returned my attention to Lorian's face. "Where are we going?"

Lorian's colorless eyes held mine a long moment. At last he blinked. "Latarra."

"Latarra?" Somehow, the thought had not occurred to me, not even once.

"I was supposed to return from Forum with a treaty," Lorian said.

A treaty, I thought, thinking of what Samek had said when she had poisoned me, *and atomics.*

"Instead, I have you." Lorian fixed me with a stare sharp as the bite of his needler. "And the princess." He glanced at Selene, and doffed his hat, restoring it to his head at a jaunty angle. "We'll have to make do, but you . . ." He jabbed me with this finger, entirely unperturbed by my appearance and return. "You will have to tell me *everything.*"

CHAPTER 43

THESEUS HIMSELF

HERE I PAUSE. LET us leave the others a moment, as I left them all in the yard outside the docked vessel. Ghoshal feared me, as did his men. They would doubtless review the footage from the *Gadelica*'s security systems, find the moment in the airlock when I returned. I guessed that they would find I simply appeared, that one moment they would be looking at footage of an empty airlock, and in the next they would find me curled there on the cold metal floor, naked and lost.

Commander 2Maeve likewise feared me, though in her that fear was tempered by loathing. I knew nothing of her people—these *Interfaced*—though from the name I deduced her implants did more than attract attention. They were surely some race of Extrasolarian, one of the many countless clans and cultures about which we in the Imperium knew almost nothing.

The Cielcin and Irchtani alike—by contrast—were anything but afraid. To the Cielcin I was *Oranganyr ba-Utannash,* Champion of that god so despised by their fathers, but a god whose powers they knew were real. To the Irchtani, I was *Bashan Iseni,* one of the higher beings, the lords of men they almost revered as gods. Moreso even than the Cielcin, the Irchtani were a primitive race, a people who little understood the wider galaxy, how it was that ships flew and some men lived so long, in defiance of nature.

That very primitive understanding left their eyes more open to the truth of what I had experienced. Ghoshal and his men, and to an extent even my own Cassandra, thought they knew too much to believe. I was some Extrasolarian contrivance, as Cassandra herself had said. A clone or golem simulacrum meant to mock or dispirit, or part of some cunning and absurd plot. Their very education had blinded them to what Ramanthanu and Annaz had plainly seen.

I had returned from the dead.

And yet Selene had seen it. Selene, whose mere presence forfeited the lives of every man and woman on the *Gadelica* at least, and possibly the lives of all aboard Lorian's *Mistwalker*. But she had kidnapped herself, in truth, had insisted she be brought along to ensure the escape of Cassandra, Edouard, and the others. The memory of her kiss haunted me, of her sobbing into my bare chest, and of my visions most of all. How many times had I seen us two together? Myself enthroned, Selene at my feet?

Was that the future we now barreled toward? Or only one possibility, variously remote?

What good were my visions if they showed only the infinite possible futures? What difference was there between my visions, then, and any man's dream of tomorrow?

Edouard had believed. He had surprised me perhaps most of all—had been surprising me since Sabratha. He, who had seemed at first the picture of the Imperial cog, had proved himself possessing secret depths, and a clean and honest loyalty. In the wake of my death, he had acted to save Cassandra and Neema from the fire, had thrown his life away and his station to save them. I had told Selene to go to him, and to Lorian... and she had.

I had only prayed it would be enough, could only have prayed in that moment.

And Edouard had answered. And Lorian.

Lorian...

How changed was he! No longer the frail skeleton of a child-man who had accompanied me through so many dangers. Extrasolarian praxis had at last given him a body suited to the energy of his heart, and those virtues of tenacity and fortitude which had characterized the man in desperate hours seemed to have *become* him. It had been those virtues that moved him to pull his trigger. Had I been a fraud, I would have died there, cut down by Lorian's needler.

He had acted, and proven—to his satisfaction at least—that I was myself alone.

But still there was Cassandra. Cassandra, who did not believe I was myself. Cassandra, who feared me as Ghoshal feared me. Who feared what I might be. If she truly believed that I was some contrivance of their Extrasolarian hosts, then Lorian's demonstration would mean nothing to her.

And in truth... her belief was all that mattered. Of all the people in this broken world of ours, hers was the only face I longed to see. It was for her I fought, for her I had returned to fight. For her, and no one else. Not even truly for the Quiet, for all his gifts.

I needed her to believe, to *know* that I was myself. That I had returned. For her. For her sake.

Ghoshal's men brought me to the *Ascalon,* safely tucked away in the

Gadelica's ventral hold. They waited at the door to my old cabin as I entered and went to find my clothes. I prayed that Neema had possessed the good sense to salvage my sword and shield-belt, and certain other valuables when he and Cassandra fled with Edouard and Selene.

"I won't be long," I said to the men, and the door hissed shut behind me.

The old room was as I had left it when we first arrived at Forum, and a caul of dust lay on everything. Still, the lights winked to life at my presence, illuminating that close, gray space with its scrub carpet and metal fixtures. My lungs drank the memory of years, recalling the solitude of that wretched, lonely voyage from Eue to Colchis; those warm nights with Valka beside me before and after it.

I stood stock-still awhile, unsure where to begin. I wanted to weep, to sleep—wanted not to move. So much had happened to me in what felt so short a span of time.

With unsteady fingers I stripped the foil-blanket skirt from me, let it float to the black carpet.

I looked at myself in the washroom mirror. The reflection I had seen in the glass of that poor woman's fugue crèche had been a frosty and distorted thing. This was plain and clear.

A man who was and yet was not myself peered from the polished glass. How young he was, and lean! But broad of shoulder and strong of arm! His hair fell over his shoulders almost to his ribs, fell in rippling cascades where before it had hung lank and unbending, framing a face that was not the face I recalled from youth. Not precisely.

The man in the mirror resembled the reflection I had known all my life only so much as the image of a man drawn from memory might resemble a photograph. It was as if some artist who had only heard of Hadrian Marlowe had endeavored to carve the man afresh from new stone. The proportions of my face had changed. Where before mine had been a long and pointed face, sharp of nose and chin, the face that peered out at me from that mirror was one perfectly balanced, with a slim, straight nose, strong brow, and pronounced cheekbones. I was still recognizably myself— the violet eyes were mine, and the slight cant of brow recalled the satyr I so often thought of when faced with my own appearance—but I was myself *clarified*, as though some alchemist had distilled my very essence.

I looked like Ragama had looked, his face a testament to mathematical precision. Any of the great sculptors of the Imperial court—acting in the grand classical tradition—might have produced such a face, so precise was its symmetry, so ideal its ratios.

I bared straight, white teeth, smiled.

It was not my smile.

The crooked Marlowe asymmetry was gone. The slight irregularity of the musculature that that had created that smile—imprint of the natalists who had designed my family's line—had been corrected.

That more than anything frightened me.

Still, I knew that face, had seen that face before.

It was the face I had seen in my visions, the face of that other Hadrian who had stood upon the bridge of the *Demiurge* and uttered those terrible words. *Do what must be done*, he had said. *Fire at will.*

Shaking, I touched my shoulder, the right shoulder that had been torn in my agony upon the walls of the Dhar-Iagon—touched it with the hand that Kharn Sagara had once regenerated, scaffolding new flesh over adamantine bones.

There was no pain, nor any sensation of deep numbness when I clenched that hand into a fist. There was no sign the last two fingers of the right hand had been regenerated by Elkan's ministrations.

I turned to look at my back. The thick ropes of scar where the lash had bit and striped me from shoulder to buttocks were washed away.

I felt my heart hammering.

I was not the same Hadrian who had died in Selene's arms. Or was I? His memories remained to me, just as I could recall the memories of those days which had preceded that first death aboard the *Demiurge*. But a man is more than his memories. He is his body, too, and this was not—could not be the same body as the one I had lost.

But then...a man's body is not the same substance all his life. Most of the cells in a man's body are regenerated—replaced every few years. The teeth that I had spat upon the floor of the Martian bath were not the teeth with which I had emerged from the birthing vat. Those had fallen out and been replaced half a dozen times in the long course of my life. Even in those cells which might not be replaced—those cells of the heart and brain which remain to most men all their lives—the atoms had changed. Those particles of carbon and oxygen, hydrogen and nitrogen, calcium, phosphorus, potassium and all the rest were gone, exchanged entirely every handful of years, so that the atoms that had been Hadrian Marlowe were in the air he had breathed, the water he had drunk of, the objects he had touched, and the people.

Man is not matter, but a phenomenon, a wave crashing across the unpastured universe.

A force.

And that force was unchanged.

That force was me.

There were voices at the chamber door.

Hurriedly, I left the mirror and found the drawer that held my undergarments, selected a pair and put them on just in time for the door to cycle.

"My lord?" one of the guards intruded.

"Let me through, I say!" came a second voice, thick with irritation and its familiar, Jaddian accent. "*Domi*, it is I! Neema!"

"Let him through, guard!" I said, turning to face the door.

The old familiar face was a ray of light in a dark well.

The Nemrutti manservant snapped his fingers at one of the two guards, sidled through the open portal. Neema wore the familiar white tunic, waistcoat, and loose-fitting sirwal trousers he so favored, though he wore also an expression most unfamiliar and out of place on his broad, square face.

Joy.

"It is you!" he said, and blinked away his tears. "Pleased be the Lord, Ahura Mazda, with this prayer of mine! All praise to him! To see you well again, *Domi*, after..." He wiped his eyes. "After I saw you die!"

"I know," I said. "And the princess."

"It is truly you?" Neema asked, stepping forward.

I embraced him. "It's me, Neema."

"Master!" the Jaddian homunculus sobbed into my shoulder. "It was horrible, so horrible... what happened..."

I drew back, one hand on each of the servant's shoulders. "Let us speak no more of it, good Neema. It is over, and I am here."

Neema's eyes seemed to focus on my face for the first time. "*Domi!*" He blinked. "You are changed!"

"I am renewed," I said. "But I am myself." I looked down at my near nakedness. "Some of my clothes remain, do they not?"

Spurred by this question back to business, the butler inhaled sharply. "Of course, *domi*." He hurried to the armoire built into the wall of the cabin, and produced a white shirt that buttoned at the left side of the neck. I pulled it on, accepting the flared, equestrian-style trousers Neema produced for me next, the familiar red piping running along the outer edge.

"There ought to be a spare pair of boots here," the little man said, crouching to open the lower compartment. Sure enough, Neema straightened holding a pair of self-fitting jackboots tailored to fit my calves. I permitted Neema to button the cuffs at my ankles and to fit the boots one by one. The laces concealed between the inner lining and the outer leather sheath contracted.

"We left in such a hurry," Neema fretted, stepping back to examine me. "The princess, you understand—dreadful woman. Dreadful. She would not let me stay to collect all that was necessary. Your books, master! All your books! If she had only permitted me a moment, I might have collected my wits, might have saved more than I did. But the girl. Cassandra returned. I didn't want her to see your... your body. But she insisted! And the princess said we had to go with her at once. She had brought a shuttle, and we called Agent Albé, and that... little man. Aristedes."

"Neema!" I raised my hands for quiet, and the servant stammered to a halt. There were many black tunics hanging on a rack in the armoire. Imperial military style. Double-breasted, buttoned up the left side in cavalier fashion, their twin silver collar tabs embossed with the Imperial sun. I drew one out and looked at it, but did not put it on. Tossing it onto the bed, I sat beside it, curtains of black hair flowing over my shoulders.

"Valka's phylactery..." The words left me in a breath. "It's lost, then?"

And my piece of the Quiet's shell, of the very egg I had seen in the church on that hilltop in distant Llesu. And Gibson's sword.

"Begging your pardon, master," Neema said, "but I did not say I saved nothing! That is why I am here." He fussed with another of the drawers. "I left your effects in here. I...didn't know what to do with them. I thought...thought I might give them to the girl. But you are here now, and there has been so little time."

"Two days," I said, "yes, I know."

"I cannot believe you live, *domi*!" Neema said, and turning presented his salvage.

He held my shield-belt out. The well-worn mechanism of the emitter gleamed in the cabin light, a silvered disc a hand's breadth from the buckle. Gibson's sword hung from its hasp, and the empty holster that might have held a stunner or some other sidearm with it.

Smiling, I took it, and when I did, Neema reached for his own throat, drawing out a familiar, hair-fine platinum chain. "I had to clean it," Neema said. "Get the blood off, but both the shell and the pendant are undamaged."

It was my turn to wipe the tears from my face.

Valka's phylactery and the Quiet's shell both hung from the loop Neema pulled over his head and offered me.

I seized the man instead. "May your god and every other bless you, Neema," I said, crushing the fellow to myself. "You are a better servant than I or any man could ask for." Stepping back, I took the necklace from him, and closed my fist about shell and half-moon pendant alike.

How could I doubt I was the same man?

I was only the Ship of Theseus, as are we all—and I was Theseus himself, and myself alone. The pain was the same, the ache where Valka should have been.

Where all my friends once were.

"I must get finished," I said. "There's still much work to do."

CHAPTER 44

THE MISTWALKER

THE HAND LAY ON the table before me, and the long bones of the arm, half swaddled in white cloth, seemed almost to resonate in my mind as I stared at them. They were of adamant, black as the bones of Ushara herself. They *were* hollow, but I had always thought them ridged. Instead, they were a lattice of irregular geometric shapes, of nanocarbon tubules spiderwebbed together to form the shapes of humerus, ulna, radius, metacarpals, phalanges, and the rest—all held together by ligaments of nanocarbon wire.

I had never seen them, though they had traveled with me for so long. They reminded me of the bones of Ushara, so darkly glistening.

I gripped my new left hand—the hand of flesh—with the new right. Try as I might, I cannot articulate the feeling, the sense of displacement, of unreality imposed upon me by those bones. Just what had possessed Neema to fetch them up with my necklace and terminal when my old body had turned to slime I cannot say. But he had, and cleaned away the blood and dissolved meat, and wrapped the bones in white silk.

I wonder what has now become of them—what will become of them. Does Cassandra have them now? Or did Lorian retain them? Has Edouard carried them to some remoter clime? Have they found their way to Jadd—there to be installed in a casket of alumglass and jeweled gold? Or has Bassander Lin retained them? That hand would be a holy relic to him, and to his followers.

An idol. An icon.

A divinity.

The Black Hand of the Sun Eater.

"So we left Sabratha, then," I said at last, having concluded my recitation, "and sailed for Forum. I had hoped to find the Emperor there, but as you know, he remains in the provinces."

"Marshalling the Empire's defenses, yes," said Lorian Aristedes, surveying me across the black glass table. A pot of some violently green tea sat to one side, and as he spoke Lorian poured a dram of the viridian over a glass of iced milk, refreshing his cup. He offered me the same, but I declined with a gesture, having not touched my cup in the first place. "So they say."

"You doubt the story?" I asked.

"I doubt everything," Lorian said. "That's why I'm still alive."

I remained silent, watching Lorian stir his tea with a platinum spoon. Behind him, a window opened on the cylinder city that filled the *Mistwalker's* interior. We were high in the forward section, peering out through the wall that made up one end of the great tube, high enough that the gravity was perhaps half what it was at the ship's circumference. The *Mistwalker* was a spinship, one that relied on rotation about its central axis to simulate gravity, and so the closer one drew to that false, fluorescent sun, the lighter gravity became. It had no suppression field, and the bridge section beyond the conference room had no gravity at all.

For all its marvels, the whole place felt claustrophobic. The whole city was enclosed, without reference to the space outside. An entire world trapped in a bottle. Despite all that air, and the trees growing on gray terraces and seeming to hang from the gardens in the sky portion of the city, it felt difficult to breathe.

"This...Watcher thing. Why didn't you tell me?" Those colorless eyes held mine as if weighing me.

"Would you have believed me?" I asked. Lorian had doubted the rest of my story, had doubted my very presence, had shot me rather than believe.

The little man grunted in negation. "You know," he said, "I always did wonder about that place...on that Cielcin world. It really was a skull, then? I assumed it was artificial, that the Pale or these...Vaiartu chaps had built it. Nothing that big should exist."

"I know," I said, "it violates much of what we think we know."

"It violates basic physics, Hadrian," Lorian said, eyes narrowing, "not that you're one to talk." He drank his tea, propped his elbow on the edge of the table, his chin on his fist. "What can it do? The Watcher, I mean. What will the Cielcin do with it?"

"That is the wrong question," I said. "You have it the wrong way round. The question is: What is it going to do with the Cielcin?"

Lorian dismissed this with a wave. "I mean what is it capable of? Widespread destruction, to be sure. But of what kind? How does it work? And how do we kill it?"

"There's the Perseus weapon."

"But we don't have the specs," Lorian said.

"Albé might," I said.

The other man allowed this with a gesture. I could sense his irritation, his excitement. I had not answered his initial question. "I don't know all it's capable of," I said. "Lorian, it tore whole lighters out of the sky, pulled men to pieces by the score. And it was weak, starved...at full strength?"

I could only shake my head.

"This is why I need to go to Vorgossos."

The Commandant General frowned, still leaning on his fist. "Yes... to find Kharn Sagara. What makes you think he has a weapon meant to slay these things?"

Do what must be.

The Quiet's words rang in my ears. "I've seen it," I said at length, and took up my own cup to cover the sudden fragility of my claim.

The little man laughed, and I set my cup down with force sufficient to slosh the bitter draught over the brim and onto the saucer. "You asked," I said, at once conscious of the new length of my hair, of the untrimmed nails digging into the palm of my left hand. "But you misunderstand me, Lorian. I have *been* there before. You know that. I have seen these weapons. With my eyes." I pointed at my own face to underscore the point. "They were not *designed* for this purpose, but they will serve." I told him then about the weapons Columbia and her children had made, engines of mass destruction, of terror and power to alter the world and further violate the laws of nature. There were weapons that produced cold, weapons to shatter planets, to damage stars. Weapons that could destroy matter and energy entirely, breaking that most fundamental of conventional laws.

Lorian was nodding by the time I finished, and raised a hand. "I understand you. But how do you plan to get there, and if you do get there... how do you propose to make this Kharn Sagara cooperate?"

"I don't know," I confessed after a long silence. "I hoped your Monarch might prove himself useful in that regard. We are going to Latarra, are we not?"

"We are," Lorian twisted his milk tea on its saucer, sunk into a contemplative silence. "My Monarch..." Behind him, the light of the great beam that served the *Mistwalker* for a sun carved gray shadows between the tower spokes that held it in its place. I watched one of the crew shuttles take off from the surface below us, rise—and then fall—to the city on the opposite side. "Do you not appreciate the position you've put me in?" His voice was suddenly brittle. "That Council was the first time in *human history* that a delegation of the Extrasolarians was received at Forum. Do you hear me? The *first* time."

I leaned back in surprise. "That can't be true."

"At least the first in living memory," Lorian riposted, temporizing, though his was quite the concession. "Do you remember another time? Have you ever found anything in your books?"

I confessed that I hadn't.

"You realize what you've done?" Lorian asked, somewhat unfairly. "By saving your daughter and that servant of yours—to say nothing of kidnapping the princess—I have made us the aggressor in an all-new theater of war! They are black tidings I carry back to *my Monarch*. Black tidings, and failure—"

"—and me," I said. The Commandant General was beginning to work himself into a lather, as I knew all too well. I had to head him off.

"And you!" Lorian almost sneered, and thrust one long and crooked finger in my direction. "But I am *not* your servant anymore, Hadrian. I did my time, and went to hell!"

"Then why did you save Cassandra?" I asked.

"Because I am your friend and you asked!" Lorian snapped, voice rising to a full shout. "And because you would have done the same!"

His words touched something in me, and I looked away. After a long and swirling silence, I managed to choke back my emotions and suggest, "You should contact the Emperor directly, if you can. Prince Chancellor Aurelian, if you cannot."

"Why?"

"The Chantry acted alone," I said. "You know what they're like. Since your arrival, they were hounding me, convinced that you and I were in league."

"Which we of course confirmed," Lorian said.

"But they think I'm dead," I said. "If you let me contact the Emperor—me, and Selene—we can reopen negotiations. You still have the telegraph device. Your tracer. The Empire will want to deal."

Lorian's face twitched, formed the faint shadow of a smile. Only the shifting of the black false nerves about his lips betrayed him. "You may be right."

"They have *every* reason to," I said. "It is the Chantry who wishes these negotiations to fail. The Empire itself cannot afford to let them."

The Commandant General thought about this a long moment, turning his tea on its saucer as though he were a technician unscrewing the cap of a particularly delicate explosive. "And in return for your help reopening a dialogue," he began.

"I want Vorgossos," I said. "Or the road to it. Your Captain Eidhin took me there the first time, aboard his *Enigma of Hours*."

Lorian started. "I didn't know that."

"There must be someone among your elite who knows the way," I said, at once intent. "I *must* have those weapons."

The other man nodded, and without a word lifted his tea to his lips.

We sat there for a long while, Lorian sipping at his tea. I watched the city turning behind him. Though we were turning with it, I seemed some-how more aware of the nature of the city-ship from our vantage. Perhaps it was only that the false sun and gridlocked sky were so near at hand.

"How many men have you under your command?" I asked, looking out at the buildings.

"I'm not going with you," Lorian said. "You were working yourself up to ask."

I said nothing.

Lorian leaned back in his chair. His long, very white hair hung over one shoulder in a single loose plait. Abruptly, I recalled Sir Hector Oliva, the young worthy who had spirited me from Colchis to Nessus, and thence to Carteia. He had worn his hair thus in xenophilic imitation of the Cielcin. So strange that it had become the style.

I felt very old all at once.

Had I been intending to ask Lorian to recommit himself to my cause? He said that he was no longer my servant, and that was true—he was so much more. That he remained my bonded armsman had become for him a technicality, and one easily overlooked.

"My place is with the Monarch," he said, not taking his eyes from my face.

"He must be a great man to so inspire your confidence," I said.

Calen Harendotes. The self-styled *Monarch* had been a rumor for much of my long life, like a giant looming at the margins of a map. In the Empire, it was said that he was the scion of some renegade house, a once-mighty lord of the Imperium lost among the barbarians. Some said he was an intus, a grotesquery—variously a giant or a dwarf. Some said he had four arms, others that he possessed no limbs at all. Still others said he was a woman, or an androgyn in the style of the Lothrian new-men.

They were none of them true. I had seen holograph images of the man taken some centuries before. They had shown a tall, handsome man—black haired and pale complected, his eyes concealed behind gold-mirrored spec-tacles. An assassin the Emperor had sent to slay the Monarch had said the man was a chimera, that nearly all his mortal flesh had been cut away and replaced by fine machinery.

That assassin had failed in his mission, and the Monarch had returned him to the Imperium—not without his head, but as *only* a head. The poor man's still-living crown had been sent to Forum wired to some hideous machine. Bellows had forced air across the fellow's vocal chords, and he had told all that he had seen, and brought with him a warning: that the Empire should not interfere with him or his domain. He knew full well that the Imperium—faced with the Cielcin on one hand, and the Lothrians on the other—could not risk opening a third theater of war.

The Empire had ceased all its activities in the Norman Expanse, and no second attempt had been made on the life of the Monarch himself.

"He is..." Lorian raised a hand, gestured as if grasping at smoke. "...like you, I think. There's no one quite like him, if you understand me. You have that in common." Realizing this seeming contradiction, Lorian shrugged, let his hand fall. "He is building a new world on Latarra, Hadrian. A new order. A better one. There is no palatine or plebeian—neither Extrasolarian nor Empire-man. Each is free to rise according to his ability, on his merit. Had I remained in the Legions, *somehow*, I would never have risen any further than I already had. I told you once: I would have been chained to Beller's desk until my dying day if not for you. There was no place for me there. On Latarra, I *made* my place. My own!" He tapped his chest, where the Latarran falcon glittered in cloth of gold against the black gabardine. "Commandant General! Me. If only my lord father could see me now..."

This sounded most unlike the man I'd known, and I said as much. "I never took you for a man who chafed at his station, Aristedes."

"I did my duty," he said, "but I can do so much *more* now. You have not seen it, Hadrian! The white sun shining on the Citadel of the Monarch in the morning! The Printed City! The pillars of steam rising all across the Maze! Extras and common men, dryads, chimeras, homunculi—all brothers and *free!*"

"You make it sound a paradise," I said, reaching out to touch the printed fingers of my former hand.

"It will be," he said. "You'll soon see."

I studied Lorian then a long moment. There was a light in Lorian's eyes, a fire and fervor I thought I had never seen in him. He was a man alive, a man *awake* and burning with the promises of tomorrow, of a tomorrow he would build.

"You could have a place there," Lorian said, marking my quietude. "When all is done. I will have an estate, and be a lord in my own right. You could come to live there, you and the girl."

"We're getting ahead of ourselves," I said, but thought privately of my home on the Islis du Albulkam, of black Mount Hephaistos and the Jaddian seas shining at night. I thought, too, of Selene, and of the kiss she should never have given me.

I saw myself once more seated on the Solar Throne, young again and strong. My own reflection in the black glass of the table was staring up at me. I knew what future lay ahead of me.

Fire at will.

"Do you really think the Empire will come back to the table?" Lorian asked.

"What choice do they have?" I countered. "You've exposed a massive security breach. No telegraph is secure. They know that now, and if for no other reason... they'll deal."

Lorian frowned, swirled his milk tea in its glass. "They might simply attack. They've tried to kill the Monarch before."

"He was trading with MINOS, Lorian," I said.

That seemed to catch the little general off his guard. His eyes widened.

"You didn't know?" I said. "Latarra provided them with the test subjects for the Ganelon station."

"The plague?" Lorian frowned. "You never told me that."

"It wasn't relevant to the mission," I said, and when Lorian did not reply, added, "Perhaps your Monarch is not all he claims to be."

The Commandant General stood suddenly, turned his back to stand at the window, his narrow shoulders framed against the ring of city outside. "It's war, Hadrian," he said finally, standing straight. "Each of us pretends to be fighting for right, or Earth or gods... but in truth, we're each only fighting for ourselves. The Cielcin are no different. They need to eat. All that matters, ultimately, is that we win. *How* we won will be decided later, that it may be said we fought with honor."

"You don't really believe that," I said.

"Of course I do," he said. "And so do you. Because it's true."

"The Cielcin are monsters, Lorian," I said. "We're not the same. You know that."

"And yet you keep five of them in your train," he said, speaking to his own reflection in the window. "How do you explain that?"

He'd caught me flat-footed with that one, though I should have expected it. Still seated, I bowed my head. "I still hope they can be changed."

"You cannot wash away a tiger's stripes, Marlowe," Lorian said. "You can only be eaten by it, or ride."

"You don't ride tigers," I said.

"That's what you're trying to do," Lorian said, "keeping those Cielcin alive. And so long as you do, you're in no position to judge anyone. Not me, not Harendotes, not anyone. Have you forgotten what they are?"

It was my turn to stand. "I forget *nothing*," I said, voice icy. "You were not there, Aristedes. You did not see what happened."

"Because you sent me away!" he almost shouted, shoulders hunched. One black-veined fist hammered the alumglass pane. It was an old wound we had reopened, for both of us. "They were *my* people, too."

"I know that," I said. "But someone had to warn the Imperium. You were the right man."

Lorian did not turn. "Mark my words," he said. "They will betray you."

"Maybe," I said, "but I have to try."

"Why?" Lorian turned at last, and I was reminded just how small he was. He came barely to my ribs. He was shouting by then, his high voice an unsteady roar. "Why bother? Why give them this chance?"

"This is what you wanted to talk about?" I asked, incredulous. "This?"

Almost I expected to find Captain 2Maeve and the rest of Lorian's security detail surging through the door at the sound of Lorian's voice. "Why?" he shouted again. "Damn you! Tell me why!"

"Because they were not made for evil!" I shouted in return, and such was the force of my voice that Lorian flinched, and in the unsteady quiet that came after, I said, "I would save them if I could. It is the Watchers who are evil. It is the Watchers who are our enemy, our *real* enemy. If Ramanthanu and its brothers will serve in their defeat, then I welcome them gladly."

Lorian was chewing his tongue as though it disgusted him. "You trust them?" he said, and almost laughed. "But you do not trust me?"

"What?" I could hardly believe what I was hearing.

"You think I am a fool," Lorian said. "To follow the Monarch."

"You're acting the fool!" I said. "Neither the Emperor nor your Monarch is righteous, neither's hands are clean. I was making a version of your point, albeit one that does not dispense with all concept of right and wrong."

The little man seemed to deflate all at once.

Seizing the chance to quieten things, I resumed my seat. "Why does your master need Imperial atomics?" I asked. Lorian gripped the back of his chair with both hands, did not look up. "Aristedes?"

"I can't tell you that," he said. "It's classified."

He might have denied it, but he had not.

"I know what the Empire is, Lorian," I said. "We have to trust each other, if we are to work together. The Chantry woman—the one who murdered me—she told me you had requested a stock of Imperial neutron-class atomics. I need to know why."

Still Lorian did not move, but remained hunched over his seat, his city behind him.

"Whatever the reason," I pressed on, "it was important enough that you made it a condition of your deal. If I am to help reopen a dialogue between your master and the Emperor, I need to know what those atomics are for."

The little man was nodding along, and looked sharply up as I finished.

"We want a worldship," he said. "Or more than one, if we can take them."

"A worldship?" I could hardly believe it. "Why?"

"What do you mean *why?*" Lorian asked. "Do you know how long it takes to build something on that scale?"

"Your master wants to inherit the Cielcin war machine," I said, and might have whistled in appreciation of the Monarch's sheer ambition.

"Yes."

I saw the brilliance of it almost at once. By acquiring Cielcin worldships, Calen Harendotes would not only put himself in command of truly titanic naval assets...he was salvaging his escape plan. Should things not go his way and the whole human universe turn against him, he would have ships vast as worlds onto which he might pour his refugee population.

They might quit the galaxy entirely.

During my long stay in Maddalo House, I had read several papers speculating as to the effective range and functionality of the Cielcin *oscianduru*, their worldships. Scholiasts and lay magi from both Legion Intelligence and the Imperial Office alike had speculated that the largest Cielcin vessels were capable of making the journey at least so far as the Clouds of Magellan.

"I see," I said. It was not for me to pass judgement, and in a certain sense, it did not matter. Whatever came of the war with the Cielcin—of my war against the Watchers—the next engagement of man's eternal civil war would come, and was not my charge. I had my task. "Very well."

"Do you think the Empire will accept?" Lorian asked.

"Why can't the Latarrans simply produce their own?"

Lorian resumed his seat, his passions quelled. Draining his cup, he recharged it, pouring first the milk, then the tea over it. I watched the green sink into the white, forming shapes neither poet nor magus could accurately describe. "We are talking about bombing something the size of a moon," Lorian said, "we can't produce the necessary volume at speed. You and I both know the Empire maintains stockpiles all across the galaxy."

That much was true. Conventional wisdom and military fact maintained that there were millions of cached atomic weapons hidden away across the galaxy, maintained by the houses—greater and lesser—for their own private defense, and by the Imperial Office itself. These were ferreted away on remote moons, on airless satellites and in freighters hid deep in asteroid fields.

"I'll help you," I said. "But you have to help me. I reopen communications between Latarra and Forum, and you help me find the way to Vorgossos." I raised a hand to forestall Lorian's interruption. "You can't go with me. I understand. But I have to go. Get me an audience with your master, that's all I ask."

"That's all?" Lorian laughed. At once more serious, he set his glass down. "Hadrian, I can't promise he'll let you go."

I felt those words more than heard them, hanging above my head. I had been afraid of something like that. Severine of MINOS had tried to turn me to her cause, had offered me a false life, a half life as a soulless construct like herself. The Jaddians had spent decades studying me in my exile among them. The Empire and the Chantry both doubtless wanted to take their turns with me. Why should the Monarch of Latarra be any different?

"I understand," I told Lorian, "but I must go, and I will go."

Lorian smiled. "I guess you've seen that, too?"

I matched his smile, and drank. The fear I'd felt a moment earlier was gone. Whichever way it was to happen, I would sail to Vorgossos. Nothing I had done had stopped the vision coming true. Not even time. I had believed myself too old, believed that the deaths of my friends upon the black sands of Eue had taken me beyond the confines of the vision, believed that I had failed, that what the Quiet had told me *must be* could never be.

Yet there I was, on the path.

CHAPTER 45

DREAMING WIDE AWAKE

THE WHINE OF OUR shuttle's repulsors died, and the little craft jolted as the landing peds took our weight. All about me, Lorian's troopers—black armored and hod helmeted, their luminous eyes like golden suns—shifted as the hatch fell down to become our ramp. A cool breeze entered from the great hold beyond, and the last light of the stretched sun with it.

"Remember what I said," came a cold voice from over my shoulder, and turning aside, I found Captain 2Maeve standing just there. A light blinked dull red in the implant beneath her right eye.

He stuck his neck out for your brat and that red-crested bitch, she'd said, coming within mere inches of my face. *You had better deliver on your promise to fix this. If he suffers even a shred of embarrassment when we reach Latarra, I will kill you again.*

I had said nothing. There had been nothing to say, and I had ridden in the shuttle in silence, watching the great hold and the city pass by below.

I smiled at her, felt the new, symmetrical pull of the muscles—an alien sensation. "You love him, don't you?" I asked, studying her sidelong. I wondered how much of her had been given over to her machines. Her mind, certainly. The black lines of nerve implants shone on her right cheek. I did not doubt that similar nematodes threaded her bones and sinews, perhaps reinforced her muscles. Still the shape of the flesh beneath that black tunic and jodhpurs—slim and tough as leather cord—was yet the shape of woman.

She was no Exalted, though she was Extrasolarian to her core.

2Maeve's blue-gray eyes narrowed. "I don't know what you mean."

"He's a good man," I said. "Perhaps the best man I know."

2Maeve raised one gauntleted fist. I did not flinch.

"I see I'm near the mark," I said.

"You know nothing, fleshling," she sneered, and let her fist fall.

Only then did I mark that the eyes of all the others were on us, every man and woman of the guard tense as coiled snakes. I could sense their hostility, a hostility that had—a moment before—been present only in 2Maeve.

The Interfaced.

Whence they came from the nameless dark I cannot guess, but wherever it was—rogue planet or airless moon or dark site station far from light of sun—it was a place where the men and women threaded the tissues of their brains as they did among the Tavrosi. Only where the Tavrosi guarded their hearts, allowing access between one neural lace and the next only in the rarest circumstances, the Interfaced allowed it at all times, distributing their thoughts, their feelings, their experiences and impulses between one another, so that—for an instant—2Maeve's anger had fixed the eyes of all her companions upon me.

Though they remained individuals, they shared between them, and could coordinate their actions, conjoining their will to a single purpose.

They were fearsome warriors, and even more fearsome friends.

The captain stepped in front of me. Full in my face, she said, "Now move."

Outside, the sky was growing dark, and the bright bar of the sun had shrunk to a slim gold beam, fine and blazing as one of Ragama's hairs. Soon it would be gone, and in its place, the pale lights of streetlamps gleamed, those on the far side of the spinship appeared almost to form a grid of stars.

"Hold!"

Captain Henric Ghoshal was waiting on the tarmac, two dozen legionnaires in faceless white about him, the heads of their lances fretted with blue fire.

I halted, feeling the night wind in my flowing hair and in the tails of the officer's greatcoat I'd taken from the ship.

"Captain Ghoshal," I drew to a halt. "What is the meaning of this?"

"That's far enough, sir. My lord." Ghoshal hesitated, but his voice did not shake. "Will you come peaceably?"

I looked over my shoulder to 2Maeve. She shook her head. I surveyed the small Imperial contingent, saw no sign of Selene—2Maeve's *red-crested bitch*—or of Edouard. Likewise the Irchtani and Cielcin both were absent. I prayed they were unharmed. A hundred thoughts ran through my head at once. Ghoshal could not have been planning to do *anything.* He was in no position. The *Gadelica*—and the *Ascalon* within its hold—were both as good as impounded, and the *Gadelica* certainly could not hope to shoot its way out of the *Mistwalker.* It was a troop carrier.

"Lord Marlowe—if you are Lord Marlowe," said the mustachioed country officer. "You must surrender, sir. Until we can verify that you are who and what you claim, you cannot be allowed the run of the ship."

"Where is Special Agent Albé?" I asked. "And the Princess Selene?"

"I thought it best not to trouble her highness," Ghoshal said. "She has had a trying day."

"What more proof do you require?" I asked, spreading my hands. Had I not bent time upon that very spot when Lorian opened fire on me?

The foremost of Ghoshal's men flinched, leveling their lanceheads at my chest.

"There will be no violence in the hold!" 2Maeve stepped forward. A quartet of masked and helmeted men advanced with her, stunners drawn. "Stand down, Imperial!"

One of 2Maeve's lieutenants—a man called 5Eamon—said, "Tell your men to lower their lances, captain!"

"Peace!" I said, raising my open hands to the level of my face. "Peace, all of you!" I fixed my eyes on Captain Ghoshal. "I will come peaceably, Henric, but tell me: May I at least be confined to my ship?"

"To the *Ascalon*?" The man seemed to contemplate this a moment, one hand upon the catch of his shield-belt. "To your rooms, aye. Lord Marlowe's rooms, I mean."

"I *am* Lord Marlowe," I said.

"That remains to be seen, sir," the fellow said.

"It's *sir* still, is it?" I asked.

Ghoshal straightened, realizing his contradiction. Rather than answer for it, he said, "Manas, Holden, his effects."

Two of the Sabrathan lancers advanced slowly, keeping the heads of their lances high, tucked against the crooks of their arms to steady them and free their off hands. One had drawn his stunner, held it at the ready as his companion advanced to disarm me.

Neema must have told them he'd given me back my sword. I could feel the men tense as I twitched my coat aside and snapped the hilt free of its magnetic hasp.

I presented the hilt to the man called Holden, pommel first.

"See it comes to no harm," I said, holding the man's gaze through his featureless visor. "The hilt was fashioned on Jadd, but its heart was forged on Phaia, for a man who was like a father to me. Its value is beyond price."

The man Holden took it gingerly and drew back. Spreading my hands once more, I said, "Is that sufficient, Henric? Or would you shackle me as well?"

The mustachioed officer shook his head. "Is it necessary?"

"If it comforts you," I said and proffered my wrists.

Ghoshal made a negatory gesture. "If you are Hadrian Marlowe, then we have nothing to fear."

I confess I smiled. I had on multiple occasions given my own Imperial people cause for fear. When I had stolen Tanaran from Bassander Lin. When I had set Lorian to seize Lieutenant Casdon from the Chantry's inquisitors. When Mads and his fellow Dragonslayers had spirited me from the *Tempest*'s brig. Ghoshal himself had assisted in my latest burst of counter-Imperial action, when Selene and Edouard had spearheaded the escape from Forum.

Still, he was not wrong. He and his men had nothing to fear.

"I am disappointed, Henric," I said. "You've come this far. Why the change of heart? Perhaps you should have handed my daughter and the princess over to the Martian Guard."

The captain's face appeared almost bloodless in the pale light of the landing field. "Perhaps I should have, sir," he said stiffly. "I did what I thought was my duty at the time. I had my orders from Agent Albé and the princess."

"Neither of whom are here now," I said.

"No, sir," Ghoshal said, tone almost apologetic. "I've my men to think of, sir. You understand."

I had no response, but allowed his men to form a block around me. One laid a hand upon my upper arm. "This way, my lord," he said.

"Nothing will be decided tonight," Ghoshal said. "If I am mistaken, you will forgive me."

Will I? I thought, and might have said at an earlier point in my life. Instead I asked, "What are you afraid of, Henric?"

The eyes of the *Gadelica*'s captain flickered from my face to the Latarran dragoons at my back. I turned to look at them, at 2Maeve and 5Eamon and the others. The lamplike eyes of the Latarran helms shone brightly—gold circles cutting the night. I understood a moment before Ghoshal gave his answer.

"If you are not Lord Marlowe," he said, "then you are some contrivance of our hosts."

"What?" 2Maeve barked a laugh. "How would *he* profit us?"

"I've not worked that out, madam," Ghoshal said.

"Commandant General Aristedes *shot* me, captain," I said.

"Aye." Ghoshal's fingers drummed against his shield catch. "Might be you're the real Marlowe. Might be you're some kind of homunculus. A changeling. It's said there are magi among the Extras who shed bodies like snakeskin."

I let my hands fall.

Behind me, 2Maeve spat. I would later learn that there were those— even among the Extrasolarians—who found the practices of the sorcerers of MINOS and of Kharn Sagara distasteful. Still more distasteful, I think, was the implication that I might be one of them. The woman had called me *fleshling,* had spoken the word with a venom not at all unlike the venom of a Chantry priest denouncing abomination.

There was a sword that cut two ways, it seemed!

"He is *not* one of us," she sneered. "I have returned him as my commandant ordered. I am done here. Do with him as you will, Imperial, but see that he comes to no harm. We have need of him."

"You all do," I said.

Without a word or outward sign, the Latarra dragoons withdrew, mounting the ramp to their shuttle—a smaller white egg not unlike the greater craft that had descended upon the Eternal City. Ghoshal and I stood and watched it go, watched it lift up into the onrushing simulation of night that hung above. Its passage evinced only the barest breeze, its shape barely disturbing the airs of the vast hold.

When it was gone, the hand upon my arm tightened, and the man to whom it belonged said, "This way, Lord Marlowe."

I permitted myself to be led away then, up the ramp and into the *Gadelica*'s rear hold. In the process, I stepped over the scratches Lorian's needler had left in the gunmetal. The captain led the way through the hold and up into one of the perimeter halls that encircled the hold that housed the *Ascalon,* thence into the *Ascalon* itself. I caught a glimpse of the old Challis interceptor seen through the windows of the docking vestibule. The *Gadelica*'s hold was dark, leaving the smaller ship almost invisible within, illuminated only by the light of the room in which we stood. Time and radiation had peeled the painted star from her tailfin, but the memory of it stirred images of the visions Ushara had offered me, of my empire and that star spread across the heavens.

Still, I expected the memory of her to stir in my mind, to carve her mark across my grinning face. It never did.

Ushara was gone, and I was free.

Free of her, at least.

I had expected them to leave me at the access umbilical. Instead, Captain Ghoshal and Manas and Holden and the others marched me along the extended gangway and through the airlock in the smaller vessel's starboard side. The doors to the bridge stood open to our right just within, the consoles quiescent. We proceeded down the hall to aft and down the stairs to the level of the cabins.

I was to be confined to my quarters, not merely to my ship.

A breath escaped me, and I felt my nostrils flare.

Though I understood their fear, I could not help but be irritated. It should not have surprised me, and yet it did. The occasion of my first death had not been met with such suspicion. Quite the contrary, it had transmuted Bassander Lin from antagonist to ally, and more than that. He had come to *believe* in me, as though I were some prophet or holy man, and it had been that belief that had caused him to aid Lorian and Prince Kaim in their plot to spare me my place on Belusha.

This second time was different.

But why?

The door to their left slid open. The door to Cassandra's room. I brightened, stood a little straighter to see my daughter standing in that open portal—my daughter, who I had thought for a time I would never see again.

"Cassandra!" I hurried forward a step, but the man on my arm tightened his grip.

Abba! I thought she would say, and smile, and come to me, and all would be well.

Instead, her face darkened, and she retreated into her room, door hissing closed behind her.

That, more than Ghoshal's stubbornness, or 2Maeve's crass hostility, more even than Lorian's shifting allegiances—cut me to my core.

"Cassandra!" I halted at her door. "Anaryan!" I knocked—perhaps too forcefully, as two of the legionnaires were pulling at me to move.

"Enough!" came Ghoshal's interjection. "Lord Marlowe, please!"

I turned to glare at the country officer. I might have torn those drooping mustachios from his square and self-important face.

Rage is blindness.

I confined my response to a hard-edged glare.

To my great astonishment, the simple officer did not retreat, so near was he to his goal.

"Alex and Nira will have the first watch," he said. "If you require anything, you may ask them for it. Have you eaten?"

"No," I said.

"I will have something sent down for you," Ghoshal said.

"Where is Neema?"

"I think it best if my people see to your needs for the time being." Ghoshal did his best to smile. "I'll have the doctor sent up to take samples and perform the exam."

I told him he had better do just that. I was curious myself to learn what they might find.

Ghoshal nodded, turned to his men as they opened the doors to my quarters. "Nira, radio GenSec if there's any trouble. I'll keep a garrison off the gangway."

"Aye, sir," said the man called Nira, a decurion with the familiar stripes on his masked face.

Ghoshal surveyed his people. "Very good." His dark eyes returned to me. "This is only a precaution, lordship."

"I know," I said. "I understand."

I crossed the threshold, and did not look back as the portal hissed shut behind me, leaving me alone.

I no longer sleep.

I discovered this that first night, after Ghoshal's men brought the evening meal and I was left alone. I lay there a long time, immobile, watching the blinking of dim lights against the brushed metal of the ceiling, waiting for sleep to come. At the time, I thought the fact it had eluded me that night a fluke of my special circumstances, that my new body was adjusting to the rhythms of the world.

But I have never slept through the night again.

Instead I pass perhaps an hour—and perhaps less—in a state like unto dreaming, though I am conscious always of my surroundings, and may fall into it even on my feet.

I find I do not miss it.

I did not dream that first night, but lay awake and troubled, and from time to time arose to pace the bounds of the cage Ghoshal had made for me. I did not then guess the change that had been wrought in me, as I say, and believed it was only mania that kept me wide awake. Once, in the middle of the night, I opened the doors to find the quartet of men who had remained scrambling to their feet. I smiled at their surprise, but only handed them out the emptied tray of food.

Cassandra's door was shut. Was she awake? The thought that she might be, alone and perhaps in pain, distressed, pulled upon my aching heart. I longed to go to her, but knew that to do so—if Ghoshal's men would have permitted it—was to risk making matters worse. The poor girl would have to come to terms with what had happened on her own.

I saw clearly then that though it was I who had been murdered, I had in a sense suffered the least. I understood what had happened to me, and why it had happened—and at any rate, I had survived a similar episode once before. Cassandra had lost her father, her only family. She had not expected to have him returned, and like poor Captain Ghoshal, she was not certain that the man who had returned was the same as the man who had dissolved upon the tiled floor.

And so I sat there, alone, my back against the wall of my cabin, thinking of the girl she had been, of her charging through the old house, the children of the masters and young Prince Arman du Karaj following in her wake. Well I remember her—no more than five standard years old—sitting at the wooden table in the kitchen, at the trestle table where Neema and the other servants took their meals, her tongue between her teeth as she scratched at parchment with wax pastels, trying to draw as I did.

I am not ashamed to say that I wept that night. Wept... not for grief, but from a new and sharp awareness of how much I loved the dear girl—and of how much I had loved her mother. Something had changed in me, had happened in my mind. How shall I make you understand? It was not merely my body the Absolute had made anew, but my mind. Things that once had been obscure to me were clear as polished glass. Sharp and clean and painfully I saw the man that I had been: Hadrian Marlowe, Son of the Devil of Meidua, Royal Knight Victorian, Lord Commandant of the Imperial Red Company. Halfmortal. Palekiller. Hero of the Empire.

A mask, a veneer of gold leaf over hammered lead.

Brave, but foolish. Learned, but unwise. Noble, but proud. So proud.

And the grief! How much grief there was in his beating heart! An ocean of it! And for what? Had he not known—or had he simply forgotten—what he had told so many for so long?

That death was not the end.

Why had he mourned for Valka, when he knew he would see her once more and forever when the universe was changed? When the stars that then were young all cooled to ash and were rekindled? The machines of Felsenburgh had failed to cure Death, but that did not mean Death would have the final victory. As I had been stirred to new life in the Well beneath Llesu, I knew that all the dead might live again one day. I had felt them, had I not? Within the Howling Dark of sleep?

Realizing this at last, I set aside his grief—if not his loneliness, or his pain—and steeled myself for my task. I would see Valka again, if I did not fail in my task, and took heart in that, though I knew not then how many years must yet come between our parting and our reunion.

The Absolute had boiled all the lead in me, had transmuted it all to gold. I was, as I have said, the man I should have been, and that man wanted nothing more than to see his child and to tell her he had returned.

But I could not, and should not, and so had nothing to do but wait for the dawn, the false dawn of that strange vessel . . . and whatever new tidings it would bring.

CHAPTER 46

THE SOLDIER
AND THE SPY

I DID NOT HAVE to wait long. The little clock built into the wall of my room marked the sixth hour after midnight. The doors opened, and my guards greeted me with visored faces and shoulders squared.

"We're to take you upstairs," said Holden, Ghoshal's centurion. "The captain and Agent Albé asked to meet you in the cenacle."

"Then lead on, decurion," I said. "Though I know the way."

We had only to ascend one level to reach the *Ascalon*'s mess and its adjoining kitchen, which lay at the aft end of the ship, straight back from the bridge and the forward airlocks. I had not seen the place since the journey from Sabratha, but found it much as I had left it. A curving bank of windows—perhaps a cubit high—ran along the rear wall, a narrow slit overlooking the arcing bank of the warp projectors and the primary sub-light drive just below. Pressing one's face to the glass, one might look up and see the line of the tailfin above.

It was dark then, save for the cans that gleamed in the ceiling above the black glass of the dinner table. Captain Henric Ghoshal had seated himself on the far side, facing the doors, looking—if anything—even more tired and less sure than he had the night before. Edouard Albé stood to one side, peering out through the slit windows at the comparative darkness of the *Gadelica*'s hold without. It was easy to forget that we were aboard an Extrasolarian Sojourner, that outside the old Imperial troop carrier, there was a false sun shining, and warm air, and trees.

"Our hosts spirited you away awfully quick," Ghoshal began, without preamble. "What did you tell them?"

Edouard had his back to us, his attention still held by some feature of the *Gadelica*'s hold outside. "Everything," I said.

"Everything..." Ghoshal echoed the word, spoke it as though it were an incantation in some language he could but little comprehend. "You're sure we can trust them?"

"I am more sure of Lorian Aristedes," I said, "than I am of any other man alive." Rather, I was sure of the Lorian I had known, the good commander. Of the Commandant General, I was less sure...and of his master, of the Monarch Calen Harendotes...I was not sure at all.

"And of me?" Ghoshal asked.

"How can I trust you?" I asked, sparing a glance for Edouard, who had turned from the window to watch us. "When you do not trust me?"

I had thought much about how to approach the matter of the captain in the night, but I had come to little wisdom. Ultimately, the decision rested with him, whether to believe what I had told him and the evidence of his own eyes—or not. Men accepted the truth or did not, and would use their reason to justify that acceptance or the lack of it. For most men, reason follows belief, and does not lead it.

"Trust you?" Ghoshal's mustachios twitched. "Trust you? What has trusting you got me? Or my men? We are outlaws now! Cast our lot with the demoniacs outside! And for what? Because Albé here and the princess said we had to save your—Lord Marlowe's—bastard girl!"

I slapped the table with an open palm, so fast the captain lurched back in his seat. Holden and the other guards flinched, but I made no other move. "She is no bastard," I said, voice deadly calm. "Her mother and I never wed—but such was the fashion of her people. Cassandra is trueborn. Her genome was written on a Jaddian loom. She is no intus, and even if she were, she is *mine,* and you would do well to remember it."

Ghoshal deflated like an old balloon, sagged into his chair. "You must understand," he said. "I have five hundred men under my command, and thirty-five hundred of yours in my charge. Every one of them is forfeit now. We kidnapped an Imperial princess! Shot our way out of Forum system, killed Earth knows how many of the Martian Guard, and with Extras to aid us, no less!" His hands were balled into fists, and he held them shaking before himself. "There are *Pale* on this ship! And bird men! A whole cavalcade of demons and rejects! How does that look to you?" He thrust a finger in my face. "And then *you* show up—whatever you are! I don't know if you're a clone or a machine or something else entirely, and I don't care! But I *do* care about my men! Now if you can help them, I'll hear you—but you had better tell me *everything,* too."

Looking up, I found Edouard's gaze. He was the ranking member of our little mob. And yet Ghoshal held almost all the power. The majority of the HAPSIS men who had survived Sabratha were on ice, and if Ghoshal had possessed the will, he might have seized the reins already, killed or imprisoned Edouard and myself and laid plans to return Selene to the Imperium.

Why hadn't he?

"You're aware of what happened on Sabratha?" I asked. "What I was doing in the system in the first place?"

I knew he hadn't been formally briefed, but I also knew that he couldn't have left the system without rumor or perhaps even footage reaching him of the battle at Phanamhara.

"I know that the Cielcin attacked," Ghoshal said. "I know they came in search of some...weapon, something left behind by the ancients as built the ruins down around the Whalemont."

"You knew about the Stonebuilders?" Edouard asked.

"Every officer in the Sabrathan ODF knew about the Whalemont, if that's what you mean," Ghoshal said. "There's nothing writ down, and they call the Chanters in if you ask too many questions, but aye—I know."

"It wasn't a weapon," I said. "It was an extraterranic being of extraordinary power. A creature of pure energy known to the men on Forum as a *Monumental*. The Cielcin worship these *Monumentals* as gods, call them Watchers. For several hundred years now, Syriani Dorayaica has been looking for one of them. There was one living in the mountain out on the Ocean of Silence. Albé's team and I were sent to find and kill it, only the Cielcin attacked before we could do so...I..." Here I trailed off, made uncomfortable by so much plain truth. "...have reason to believe that the beast in question escaped, and is in the hands of the enemy."

Ghoshal's expression signaled terror and bemusement in equal measure. "Pure energy?" he looked round at Edouard, expecting a laugh. "How on Earth does that work?"

"There's much we don't understand," I said, "but we do know how to kill it."

Here Edouard interjected. "A series of sustained EM pulses of a certain magnitude over a period of several minutes is supposed to do it."

"Then why didn't you succeed at Sabratha?" Ghoshal asked. "How did this thing escape?"

"We tried," I said. "But our weapon was destroyed."

"We were betrayed," Albé said.

"Betrayed?" Ghoshal echoed the word, incredulous. "How?"

I looked to Edouard, who said simply, "The Cielcin had bought one of our own. It was this agent that alerted the enemy to our presence on Sabratha."

Never shrewd, Ghoshal shook his head. "To think of our own people allying with those monsters..." he said. "But this is incredible. What do the Cielcin want with this creature? What did you call it?"

"A Monumental," Albé said.

"A Watcher," said I.

We looked at one another, neither one of us moving. For a second time then in so many minutes, Edouard inclined his head.

"They worship it," I said. "You are aware of how primitive the Cielcin are? With regard to technological sophistication?"

Ghoshal squinted. "Primitive?" he said. "They gave us a licking at Sabratha. And those ships! So huge! What's primitive about that?"

I had forgotten. Sabratha had most likely been Ghoshal's first exposure to the enemy. His knowledge of their culture and capabilities was thin at best, limited to rumor and hearsay. He had served his term some twenty thousand light-years from the fighting, had perhaps expected never to meet the enemy in the field.

Rather than attempt to explain, I forged ahead. "The Watchers uplifted the Cielcin. Taught them to build ships and weapons, turned them into an army." I detailed, then, how Elu had heeded Miudanar's call, and built the first ships that carried the Cielcin from their home on Se Vattayu to neighboring Eue, where it had built its empire. I told of how that Empire had fallen to pieces when Elu was gone, and how the Cielcin—forever warlike—had turned on one another, battling across the millennia until they first encountered mankind at Cressgard.

Ghoshal listened all the while, his broad, honest face growing paler above his bristling mustache, his black eyes wide. He had known of the Vaiartu, known—but not examined—the fact that there were civilizations older than those of man, but the galaxy and the cosmos Edouard and I were revealing to him was vaster, stranger and more antique than anything the poor fellow could have ever suspected.

Still shaking his head, he said, "The Cielcin gods are real, then?" He fixed his eyes on me. "But how does this explain you?"

I was suddenly conscious of my hands. Strong hands, young and unscarred—and of the hair that hung down past my shoulders. I was a stranger to myself, and so hardly knew how to answer.

Again, I looked to Edouard. Edouard, who had doubtless seen the recordings of all that had transpired on Berenike. On Perfugium. Edouard, who had been present on the ground at Sabratha and who had seen Ushara unrolled across the sky. Edouard, who was of HAPSIS, and knew all that had transpired on Nairi, of the *Atropos* Expedition and of Project Perseus thereafter... Did he know the truth of the God Emperor? Had Lord Friedrich known?

What could I tell them that would be believed?

"You asked how a creature of pure energy could exist," I said, gesturing to Ghoshal. "You imagine they evolved like you and me, but they were made."

"Made?" Edouard looked at me askance. While I had spoken, he had come to stand at Ghoshal's shoulder, had crossed his arms and relaxed as I repeated much of what was already known to him and HAPSIS.

"Programmed, in a sense," I said. "Designed. By an entity I used to call the Quiet."

Albé let his arms fall, and he stood a little straighter. Beside him, Ghoshal merely looked confused. As a member of HAPSIS, Albé knew the name, was familiar with it as the name of one of the galaxy's ancient civilizations—the builders of black halls and towers, of Calagah and Athten Var and of the Menhir Dur on Sadal Suud.

"You mean the Firstborn?" Edouard asked at last, gathering his wits.

"Yes," I said. "He's not a people, he's a single being. An intelligence. One that existed *before* our universe. I...have reason to believe he created our universe, and built the Watchers to...well, to watch over it. Some of them abandoned their functions. I don't know why or...how."

The young agent felt for a chair with numb fingers, not taking his eyes from my face. He seated himself, and made a curious gesture that recalled the sign of the sun disc, touching forehead, heart, and either shoulder. His fingers touched the medal he wore about his neck through the fabric of his tunic.

"What is it?" I asked.

Edouard shook his head. "The Watchers..." He almost mouthed the words. "What happened to you? After you...died?"

Something had changed in the adorator. Ghoshal had sensed it, too, and turned to look at Edouard, his own arms now crossed. "You believe all this?" he asked.

Edouard raised a hand to quiet him. "Tell me."

How could I possibly explain? I resolved to say nothing of Llesu, nothing of the Well, of the far future, of the death of the last sun.

"I met a servant of the Quiet," I said. "He restored me, as you see."

"Madness," Ghoshal said.

Edouard gripped the captain's arm. "You saw the tests, Henric."

"What?" I asked.

Ghoshal and Edouard exchanged glances. After a moment, Edouard answered, "We have the results of the tests Doctor Kaur ran on you yesterday." He fell strangely silent then, staring at the mustachioed captain, as if afraid to look at me.

"And?" I asked, curious to know the answer.

"It's a perfect match," Ghoshal said. "Doctor Kaur says you're the same man. Something about chromatin and histore...history marks?"

"Histone markers," Albé supplied. "Only that can't be right."

"Why's that?" I asked.

"Look at you," Albé said, gesturing at my face.

"Ah." I hugged myself, bowing my head. "If I were some scheme of the Extrasolarians, why would they make so poor a copy?" I asked.

Ghoshal said. "You tell me."

"You had better hope I am not an Extrasolarian copy," I said.

Ghoshal blinked.

"If I am," I said, driving the spike home, "then the Monarch of Latarra has the powers of Hadrian Marlowe at his command. If I am a copy, a clone, some device of our erstwhile hosts, ask yourself: What is there to prevent the Latarrans from making of an army of me?"

That cowed Ghoshal, and disturbed even Edouard.

"You saw Lorian shoot me. If you think that some kind of trick, shoot me again. Now. You will strike nothing but air." I stood, hands going to the magnets that secured the throat of my tunic. Neither Ghoshal nor Albé moved. "If we do not get onside, the three of us, that is precisely the future we risk. Lorian is my friend, but his master is an unknown quantity. I have promised to help reopen negotiations between Latarra and the Solar Throne. We *need* their aid. We need their army. We need this machine of theirs. And they need us. They need us to cede our rights to Norma, or they will have another war on their hands. They need our atomics."

"What?" Evidently, this was news to young Albé, who straightened in his chair. "Why?"

"They mean to take what they can of the Cielcin fleet for their own," I said. "It is my belief that Calen Harendotes intends to use them to transplant his population beyond human space in the event that matters in the Veil turn against him."

Ghoshal looked at me in disbelief. "But where would they go?"

"Far away," I said. "What does it matter?"

I was still standing, and leaned over the table, hands flat against the surface. Ghoshal had begun this meeting with the command, but he had ceded it. He ought to have stood when I did, ordered me to take my seat.

"I suppose it doesn't," the man said.

"It doesn't make any sense," Albé said. "Trying to capture Cielcin world-ships seems like a lot of effort for a contingency plan."

"If they can truly track Cielcin fleets through the void," I countered, "they can isolate one or two, catch them unawares. Perhaps it is more feasible than we believe."

But Albé was tracing circles on his cheek with a finger, leaning upon his hand. "There is more here we do not fathom."

At this I turned my back, left the two men at the table to search the cabinets above the sideboard. There was no wine. The ship had lain at anchor on Forum for many years, and I had emptied her stores. Going instead to the arc of windows, I peered out at the darkness of the *Gadelica*'s hold. The name and serial number of the larger ship was stenciled on the wall of the hold in fading letters.

Something about Latarra's ambitions struck me as strange. Sclerotic. Almost random. Calen Harendotes had been amassing power for the better part of five hundred standard years. In all that time, he had strengthened his power base near the galaxy's core, but had not ventured much beyond the narrow confines of the Veil of Marinus. He had united much of the scattered and leaderless Norman territories, forcing the others to consolidate behind Uhra in the nascent Norman Alliance.

His had been a defensive game. Conservative. Safe.

Now all at once he had attempted an alliance with the Imperium, revealed a technological superiority that might have proved the decisive factor in any war against the Empire and its Legions, and in return for what? Assistance in the Empire's wars against the Cielcin? While at the same time preparing a contingency plan should all turn against him?

"Why not simply remain in the Veil?" I asked.

"Precisely," Albé said. "You see the problem."

"We don't know what we don't know," I said, regarding them both. Albé had turned in his seat to follow me, but Ghoshal sat hunched, his hands folded on the table. "We are not in an especially strong position, gentlemen," I said. "The Latarrans have us in their power, and I owe Lorian a debt. Additionally, the whole of the Empire is now against us, as they believe we kidnapped the Princess Selene..." I planted my hands on my hips, addressed the brushed metal ceiling. "The Chantry already believed that Lorian and I were allies, that I was conspiring with the Extrasolarians."

"Were you?" Ghoshal had found his voice at last. "Conspiring?"

"Would you believe me if I denied it?" I asked, addressing the back of the captain's head. "Until he appeared on Forum at the head of the Latarran delegation, I believed Lorian was dead," I said. "That man sacrificed everything to save me from a life sentence on Belusha. He went in my stead. He escaped—don't ask me how, he wouldn't tell me. And now he has jeopardized his master's delicate plans in order to save my daughter from the same Imperial assassins who murdered *me*."

For me.

The thought intruded like a thunderbolt, casting lightning shadows across the uncharted recesses of my mind. A lump had formed in the hollow of my throat, one I could not choke down. One hand floated up to shield my eyes, but I let it fall. "We have but three cards to play with the Latarrans," I said, and raised the commensurate count of fingers. Ticking them off as I spoke, I said, "First: We can smooth things over with the Imperials, reopen the negotiations this episode has closed. Second: We have the Princess Selene."

"You can't be serious!" Ghoshal stood at last, whirling to face me. "What would you have us do? Offer the poor girl to this warlord?"

I did not rise to the challenge. "Lastly: We have myself."

A fresh silence coiled in the air between us, an amphisbaena with heads poised to strike both Ghoshal and myself. But Henric Ghoshal was no Bassander Lin. He blinked, and I said, "I am only enumerating the pieces on our side of the board, captain. Listing our assets. We have nothing else. It may be that all Calen Harendotes wants is to reopen a dialogue with the Imperium. *That* we can achieve. With the princess's help, this whole unpleasant matter can be put behind us. But we must be prepared. We must recognize the reality of our situation. We are trapped, Henric. You and me and Albé here. Whether or not you believe I am who I say I am, we have no choice but to trust one another. Do you see?"

Henric Ghoshal hesitated, his balled fists half-forgotten in the air before him from his zeal to defend Selene's honor. "I am *me*, Henric," I said, pressing once again. "You told me about your son, do you remember? About Arramon."

Ghoshal was forever boasting of his son, forever sharing word of his accomplishments with any man who would listen. Mention of his son rekindled the man's fighting courage, and he advanced a step. "I told Lord Marlowe—"

"You told *me*, Henric," I said. "You told me you never knew him. He was decanted after you left your home on Andraka. You asked me to write a letter of introduction for him. To get him into the Ares Command School." Ghoshal hesitated, was beginning to question his doubt that I was indeed myself. "You told me how proud of him you were, this boy you'd never met." The man's hands had fallen almost to his side. "Now ask yourself: How would I know all this if I were a contrivance of the Extras? You told me all this on our voyage to Forum from Sabratha. When exactly were the Extras meant to have made this me with those memories? They did not arrive until mere weeks ago! Do you know how long it takes to grow a body like this?"

"Do you?" Ghoshal asked, and turned aside to Edouard, who shook his head. "I'm no bloody warlock! Can they not have stolen your memories? Copied them into . . . whatever you are?"

"Certainly they could," I said. "But I assume you scanned me when you brought me on board."

Albé bobbed his head. He alone was still seated, but still seemed shaken by my earlier revelations about the nature of the Quiet. One hand massaging his jaw, he said, "We did. You're clean."

"There must be other ways of doing this!" Ghoshal said, gesturing at all of me, looking to Albé for support.

Spreading my hands for his examination, showing that they were empty, I said, "You told me you hoped the war would be over before your boy left Command School. That he wouldn't have to fight at all."

Henric Ghoshal averted his eyes, stared down at his scuffed uniform boots. "He'd be there now if he got in, I think." At once he sounded utterly spent. "How am I to know, being here?"

I felt for the man. His son had loomed, grown, born, entirely in his absence, been raised on Andraka by Lady Ghoshal and their servants. I could not imagine being so separated from Cassandra. Abruptly I recalled her youth on Jadd, remembered sitting on the floor of my solarium while the newborn Cassandra—hardly more than a cubit high—toddled toward me across the damasked carpet. I watched her charging up the stairs, heard Neema shouting after her, desperate for her to leave her sandy boots by the door.

The captain had known no such moments with his own son.

"You will meet him one day," I said, "when we are victorious."

I was mistaken—as I so often am. Though I did not know it, Arramon Ghoshal would never meet his father. Though we would prove victorious, the humble captain would not return to the country manor of his home.

Gododdin lay ahead for him, though he knew it not, and I could hardly guess—having been granted only the barest glimpse of that final fire in my visions. When I think back upon all the horrors I have seen: the pits of Dharan-Tun, the fates of Smythe and Crossflane and their men, the child of Gaspard Valavar, the Black Feast, the sacrifice in the pantheon and the defilement of Muzugara's prisoners...Ghoshal's death is not lost among them. Still I recall the look in his black eyes, the smile on his lips...and shudder.

It would have been better if he had never left his home at all, if he had remained on Andraka with his lady wife and poor son.

He was a fair officer, and a good man.

And no man deserved his fate.

But Gododdin was yet to come—and his end—and for the moment, the tired captain leaned upon my table, his face drawn and shadowed, wearied with care. "I don't know if you really are Lord Marlowe or not," he said, "but maybe you're right. Maybe it doesn't matter. Maybe you're all we've got." He pressed the heels of both hands against his eyes, swaying where he stood. "Either you're some monster these Extras have made—and they deny it—or you really have come back from the dead. Either way, it's more than I bargained for when I left Williamtown." He laughed hollowly. "I'm a simple man..."

"I am sorry," I said.

"No, you're not," Ghoshal snapped, eyes finding my face again. "My crew are good people, Marlowe. Honest people. They didn't sign up for this...this *treason*. They'll all hang if we're caught, and me with them."

"You won't," I said. "You're palatine, Henric. They'll reserve the White Sword for you."

What little blood remained in the man's face left it then, and a curious series of emotions played across it. He cursed, then—to my very great relief—he laughed. "Was that your idea of humor? Blood and thunder! They always said you were mad. That Marlowe was mad, I mean."

He was beginning to come round.

"No one will hang for this," I said. "You have my word, one palatine to another."

Ghoshal's mustache hinted at the frown beneath. "How do you propose to stop it?"

"By speaking directly with the Emperor when we reach Latarra."

The captain's eyes went wide. "You can do that?"

"No," I said. "But I can contact Prince Chancellor Aurelian."

"What good will that do?"

"The Chantry acted alone in my murder, of that we can be certain. They've overplayed their hand, and the Emperor and his party will—I think—be glad to learn that I am alive. Besides..." I stood a little straighter. "The Empire has as much to gain from an alliance with Latarra as the Extrasolarians do. If we can reopen negotiations, you'll have to fear neither the noose nor the White Sword, eh?" I clapped Ghoshal on the shoulder.

Ghoshal chewed on this a moment, and in the end he nodded. "All right," he said, "all right. Whoever you are, I'm cornered. I can see that. But how..." He hesitated. "How can I trust you when your own daughter does not?"

I felt my fingers tighten on Ghoshal's shoulder, and withdrew the hand in haste. Turning my back, I asked, "Do I have your leave to go where I will?"

Ghoshal hesitated. After a moment's pause he shook his head. "I need to think..."

My anger flared. "Be reasonable, captain!"

"Reasonable?" Henric Ghoshal echoed the word, matching me anger for anger. "What about this is reasonable, Marlowe?" He thrust a finger at the floor of the cenacle. "What about *any* of this is reasonable?" His nostrils flared. "You will stay in your room until I can at least speak with the princess, and if you are who you say you are...you will sit there *quietly*." He glowered at Edouard, looking for support.

The young agent sat there quietly, neither moving nor speaking.

"I want no trouble," Ghoshal said, and raised a hand to this forehead, "but I need to think."

"Take all the time you need," I said. We would be years yet reaching Latarra. I turned my back on Ghoshal, peered out the window at the iron walls of the hold. I did not want Ghoshal or Edouard to see my face.

I feared what might be written on it.

"Very well, then," I heard Ghoshal say. "I'll fetch the guards."

"Just a moment," interjected Edouard, surprising both Ghoshal and myself by his sudden return to the conversation. "Captain, may we have the room?"

I watched Ghoshal's reflection dither in the alumglass. He had every ability to object. He had the power, the men. But Edouard had the station, despite his lower blood. He was an agent of the Imperial Office, and something in the tone of his request conveyed that to the country officer.

"I'll see Lord Marlowe is returned to his rooms," he said. "Have Holden and the others wait just outside, if you would."

Ghoshal pulled his maroon beret from a tunic pocket and smoothed it over his goat-black hair. "Do what you will." I knew the sound of a salute when I heard one. The click of heels. The thump of fist on breast. The rustle of tunic and limb. "My lord. Agent Albé."

My lord...

I smiled that strange, symmetric smile.

I heard the sound of retreating feet, the cycling of the door.

Only slowly did I turn and face the HAPSIS man.

The younger man was looking up at me with an expression of revelation. He had grown quiet as the confrontation with Ghoshal intensified. It was as if a lantern that had before been shuttered was unveiled. He averted his eyes, was clearly working up the courage to ask some question. "There is something... *after*, then?"

I thought of all Ragama had told me, of the dead whose memory lay asleep in the Howling Dark, set to rise again at the end of the universal day. "There is," I said. "I'm the proof."

"The Quiet..." Edouard stood facing me then, surveying my changed face. "You really think they... it... he... created the universe? And the... the Watchers?"

I studied the younger man, searching for some clue to his thoughts in the pale, patrician lines of his face. "You think he's your god, don't you?" I asked.

Young Albé had the grace to look abashed. "I only thought..."

"You're in good company, my friend," I said, and touched his shoulder as I had touched Ghoshal's. "Prince Kaim du Otranto thought the same... that my... return—my first return, that is—was a miracle of his Ahura Mazda."

Edouard blinked at me. "It's true, then?" he asked. "You've died before?"

"Yes," I said. "One of the Cielcin princes took off my head. I was just a boy."

"Why?" Edouard asked. "What's so important about you that this... Quiet—as you call him—would restore you to life not once, but *twice?*"

"This time is different," I said. "The last time, he only altered time to preserve my life. I was only really dead—I think—for an instant, but this time..." I shook my head. "This time..." I tried to explain the Well, how Ragama and Saltus had *condensed* my energy pattern into new matter, created an image of myself capable of taking the walk to the ruined building the Judicator had called the *church*.

"A church?" Edouard's expression changed again.

"What?"

"We call our temples *churches*," he said.

"The Quiet is *not* your god, Edouard," I said.

The other man shrank at the words, bent, but did not break.

"I'm sorry," I said. "Men have always been quick to believe their gods to have been some form of advanced life. That Jove and Loki and Enki and the rest were xenobites that fell to Earth."

"I don't think that," Edouard said. "I think what you're calling *advanced life,* I call god."

"That's what I'm saying."

"No, it's not," came Edouard's riposte. "It's the other way round. You see a god and call him a xenobite. I'm saying what you call a xenobite might be a god."

"But you believe it is your god you see," I said.

"There can only be one god," Edouard said. "You think him a character, like Jove, a being like you or me, but higher. That's not what god is. God is *being* itself. God is *is.*"

I blinked at him. Had not Ragama—had not the Quiet himself—said much the same?

"The Absolute," I whispered, using the name Ushara and Ragama both had used to refer to their maker.

"If you like," Edouard said. "My god raises the dead, Hadrian."

I was shaking my head. "The Quiet is *not* your god, Edouard," I said, less forcefully than before. "Even if you'd like him to be."

The younger man did not argue. "All right," he said after a long moment. "But we cannot deny this means our universe was made with *intent,* made *by* someone or something. It is no accident!"

"On that we agree," I said, and thought once more of Preceptor Prytanis and his Order for the Seekers After the First Truth. The Extrasolarian monk believed creation a simulation, a contrivance of some machine. Was that not an extension of the very belief I had just credited to Edouard? So much ink had been spilled for the belief that the gods of primitive man were xenobites, creatures like the Enar, like the Watchers themselves. It was a material explanation, an answer within the grasp of little men like Urbaine and Severine, men who believed their will sufficient not only to comprehend the universe, but to conquer it. What was belief that the universe was only the dream of some vast engine but an explanation that could be entertained by tiny minds?

And yet it was true—if only in a sense.

Our universe is the dream of the Quiet. His creation—if he and his servants are to be believed, as I must believe they are, since I am one of them, have been made one by my death and regeneration. What was the difference between the Quiet's dream and the dream Prytanis and his Seekers envisioned?

"I have another question," Edouard asked.

I shook myself, returning my attention to the cenacle. "What is it?"

"If the Monumentals taught the Cielcin everything they knew..." Edouard began, "what happened to the Monumentals that did the teaching?"

I thought about this long and hard. Miudanar had spoken to Elu across the light-years, had called it from its homeworld to somber Eue. But Miudanar had been dead, or nearly so—at any rate, it had occupied a state different from the state Ushara enjoyed. I cannot pretend to understand it. But had I not seen others in my visions? Still more Watchers at the head of various Cielcin armies during Elu's too-long reign?

What had become of them?

"I don't know," I said honestly. "They can't still be alive. We'd know. We'd have seen them."

Edouard was nodding. "I thought you'd say that," he said. "But doesn't that suppose the Cielcin have—or *had* some method of killing them?"

That gave me pause. Here was a thing I had never considered before. "Elu's empire collapsed," I said at length, and sank into the chair Captain Ghoshal had but recently vacated. "There was some kind of civil war. Elu's *aeta*—the princes that served it—turned on one another. Perhaps the Watchers split with them." I tried to imagine what such a war must have looked like. I quit almost at once. "I should ask Ramanthanu."

"I doubt it knows," Edouard said. "Do you suppose the Cielcin might have turned against their gods?"

"I doubt it," I said honestly. "I can more easily imagine they turned on one another. The Watchers are each unique. Built to purpose, I guess you'd say. I don't think they feel loyalty to their brothers like you or me."

"But what we do know," Edouard said, "is that they can be destroyed."

CHAPTER 47

THE WOMAN AND THE GIRL

I PASSED THE NEXT several days as I had the first. It was then I truly discovered the extent of the change in me, as I did not sleep that second night, or the third—or any night since. You doubtless think such an experience a torment, unable even to sleep, but somehow it was not.

The only torment was the thought that Cassandra had not come to visit me. It was possible that Ghoshal had simply not permitted her to visit me, but I could not shake the sense that she had not even tried to.

The sense that I was alone.

Or nearly so.

Following the incident with the sword, Neema was not permitted in to see me, but he had been allowed to prepare my meals for me, and brought them to the door. I saw him briefly on those occasions—thrice a day—and spoke with him. By the evening of the third day since my return, he brought the news that Cassandra had vacated the chamber beside my own for a disused cabin on the *Gadelica*.

"I think she just needed time to think," Neema said. "You know what she's like ... doesn't know something until she's decided it for herself ..."

"I do know what she's like," I said somberly, and took the tray he'd brought for me.

"I'm sorry it's not better, *domi*," Neema said, nodding at the food. "We've had to beg food off the Extras. We left in such a hurry ... there's nothing on board but *bromos* and whatever the hydroponics section can grow."

I placed it on the sideboard counter. Standing some distance from the door—such that I could no longer see Holden's men—I said, "I'm sure it's lovely," then, "have you rested, Neema?"

"Me?" The manservant smiled. "No need for that, *domi*. Let me circle round you." He made a gesture to imply an orbit.

447

"If you see Cassandra," I said, staring down at the plate of fish and dressed greens Neema had begged off Lorian's people without really seeing it, "tell her I'd like to see her."

For days, he was my only company, and was made to stand in the hall.

On the sixth day, the door opened, and I knew something had changed. My lunch tray lay on the sideboard—but recently finished. Neema ought not to have returned for many hours yet.

I sat up on the bed, banishing the almost-dream that had taken the place of sleep.

I had expected Henric Ghoshal, or Edouard—had expected even Cassandra.

But it was Annaz.

The black-feathered chiliarch saluted in the doorway. "Bashanda," he said, saluting with one wingtip claw. "I have orders to bring you. We go to big ship."

I swung my feet over the side of the bed and rose. "Kithuun Annaz!" I said, brightening. "I understand I've you to thank in part for my daughter's escape from Forum."

"Only in part," the bird man croaked, bobbing his head. "Ishaan Irchtani played only a little part."

"You've my gratitude all the same."

Annaz bobbed his head. After a moment's unsteady silence, he said, "Halfmortal."

I stiffened. The word had taken on a different character in the mouth of the colonus. Annaz had not seen me die, but anyone who had known me before my death could see the change that death had wrought in me.

"You truly cannot be killed?"

"I honestly don't know," I said.

The bird man peered up at the legionnaires posted to either side of my door, hopped across the threshold. He raised one scaly hand and touched me with it. "You defeated death," he said.

I looked at him, could sense the xenobite wished to say something.

As my father would have done, I waited him out.

Annaz spoke but haltingly. "Among my people—on Immuz—it is said *Ugaanwali* is at hand."

"Ugaanwali?" I asked, though I knew enough of the main Irchtani language by then to guess. I recognized the root of the word for *struggle*.

"Great War," Annaz said. "They say your war is Great War. War in which even Death will die. They say that winds of Hakaaro will cease, that Hakaaro itself will flower, that Ishaan Irchtani will become like gods. Like you."

Hakaaro was the Irchtani god of the underworld, and the underworld itself, a dry and frigid place, a realm of frost and dust where the spirits of the dead gnawed bones forever.

"Like me?" I asked.

"You are *bashaniya bashanda,* higher-than-high!" Annaz said, and I wondered—not for the first time—just what it was said in mine and Udax's name on Judecca, which the Irchtani called *Immuz.*

It was...not unlike my conversation with Edouard, or with Prince Kaim the day Valka showed him the images of my first death. Each believed I was a part of their own story. That I had been sent...by Ahura Mazda, by Edouard's Christ, by the gods of the Ishaan Irchtani.

Each sought to claim me for their own, to fit me into a pattern they could understand.

But whatever was happening to me, it was something stranger.

"I hope that your people can take their place in the greater Empire," I said, and recalling the promise I had made the day I burned the bodies of Udax and the other Irchtani who had died upon the field at Berenike, I said, "and I will help you do so, as I can. But we have a higher purpose."

"To kill Cielcin God-King, yes," Annaz said.

"Yes," I said. In my focus on Ushara, in the chaos of my own murder and return, the politics of Empire and Latarra...I had almost forgotten Dorayaica. "To kill the Prophet."

"I take you now," Annaz said. "We go."

He took me from the *Ascalon* and through the umbilical back to the *Gadelica.* He was my only escort. We had left Holden's men in the vestibule, and passed men and women in the black fatigues of shipmen or tunics of officers in the halls. The *Gadelica* had no tram system like the *Tamerlane,* being much smaller, but we took a lift up nearly to the top level—to the level of the bridge and officers' quarters.

"Just here," the chiliarch said, stopping at the door to the captain's stateroom.

Four men stood at posts outside it.

Ghoshal himself would have no need for guards against his own men. I knew who had summoned me, who I had been brought to see.

"He clean?" asked one.

"I did not search him," Annaz said.

The man did, and came away with nothing.

"Let him pass."

One of his fellows keyed the door.

Ghoshal's chambers were more spacious than my own, if smaller than the apartments I had once had aboard the *Tamerlane.* A great, false window dominated the wall opposite the door, its display keyed to show a view of the *Mistwalker*'s hold piped in from photoreceptors on the ship's exterior. Outside, the thin beam of the sun shone down on the rolling city. A little vestibule with a mirror and a fitting station where the captain might don his boots and uniform jacket with the help of his batman opened on the sitting area that doubled for an office. Its appointments were fairly standard: the customary tufted black leather furniture, brass fixtures, and glass tabletops of the usual Imperial military style filled the space, with here and there a piece that conveyed the captain's personal touch—a rug of some spotted fur, white and black; the painting of a hunting scene showcasing men on horses pursuing a feathered, hexapedal creature I could not name; and the desk itself, an antique of hand-carved verawood, green as summer.

Memory of the place came back to me, of the dinners I had had—floating absurdly above the glass dining table—with Ghoshal on the flight from Sabratha.

But it was to the woman seated on the tufted couch that my attention was inexorably drawn.

The Aventine Princess Selene had never looked less herself. She had slashed off most of her hair, as I told you, leaving her with a ragged cap of red-gold little longer than a boy's. She wore a simple officer's tunic, without mark or collar tab or badge of rank, though jeweled rings yet glittered on her fingers, diamonds and rubies. She cut a strange figure, so attired. Most unlike herself.

"Lord Hadrian!" She stood at my appearance, practically ran to me, and before I knew what was happening, she had embraced me once again, and covered my face in kisses.

I did not dare move. To reciprocate was to commit a crime far greater than I had done when I struck His Radiance in the face. To deny her was to risk her wrath. I had become Kyra, paralyzed by circumstance.

Sensing my hesitation, the woman drew back and—hiding her embarrassment—let out a breath I'd not realized she'd been holding. "They wouldn't let me see you," she said. "The captain and Agent Albé. They said they weren't sure that you were you, but I knew. I knew from the moment I set eyes on you again..." Her own eyes went to Annaz, who had followed me into the room. "Thank you for bringing him to me, chiliarch."

The Irchtani bobbed his head, hopped from one foot to the next, bending in a fashion that approximated a courtly bow. "My honor, *bashanda*-princess."

"Will you wait outside?" she asked, and smiled sweetly. "I would like to speak to Lord Marlowe alone."

Again, Annaz performed his little dance and bowed. He left without another word, talons clicking on the black metal of the deck.

When the door had shut, Selene's face opened like the sky after a storm, her smile radiant as the sun. It was...difficult not to love her, who felt such joy at the sight of me.

"I like them," she said at last, peering after the vanished Annaz. "The Irchtani, I mean. They're so much smaller than I expected. How tall do you think the chiliarch is?"

I thought about it. Annaz was taller than Lorian, but that was not saying much. "No more than five feet, I should think? They can't be much taller, else they'd be heavier, and so unable to fly."

Selene dismissed this with that lack of concern with trivia that is the hallmark of women everywhere. "They are gallant fighters," she said. "We would not have escaped Forum without them."

"You should not have come," I said, and seeing the distress in her face, appended, "it isn't safe for you here."

"I know that," she snapped, "but it wasn't safe for your daughter anywhere. They *killed* you!"

"I have not forgotten," I said.

The princess bridled. "I did what you told me!" she said, drawing herself up to her full height. "I went to Albé and Aristedes, just like you said! I got your daughter and your servant out. I didn't know who else we could trust."

"It was the Chantry that killed me," I said, my own words striking me with that sense of unreality. "There are others at court who were no doubt happy to see me die. Certain of the great houses. Those who think they know the Emperor's mind better than he does himself. Your mother, of course."

"My mother?" Selene's eyes widened.

She hadn't known. "Your mother was behind previous attempts on my life. The knife-missile. The Colosso. Perhaps others."

The girl retreated a step, hand feeling for the chair nearest her. She found it, sank onto its padded arm. "My mother..."

"She's not alone," I said. "Your brother tried to kill me. At least once."

"Not Aurelian?"

"Alexander."

"Alexander!" Selene was aghast. "But...Alexander worships you, for Earth's sake!"

I felt a somber smile creep across my remade face. "Once, perhaps," I said. "But you have not seen him since he went away, I gather? He is not the same man." Selene's only response was to hug herself. "He fears me, like the Chantry fears me. He fears what I am."

"The Earth's Chosen?" Selene whispered, committing the same error as Annaz, as Edouard and Prince Kaim.

"No," I said. "I am not the Earth's Chosen. I am something else."

She looked up at me. "I saw you die."

"You did," I said. "I showed Alexander a recording of my...my first death." A bitter laugh escaped me. "I was beheaded. In combat with a Cielcin prince. One of my men's suit cameras caught it all...I showed it to him, a long time ago. After I left Forum the last time. And he was with me on Berenike. You know about Berenike?"

She nodded, still hugging herself as I spoke.

"He's known what I am a long time," I finished lamely.

Selene fixed me with a gaze that recalled her father. "And what are you, sirrah?"

How could I answer her? How should I? "I am..." I looked out the false window with its simulated view of the coiled city. "I am Hadrian Marlowe."

"I never doubted that," she said, and her eyes were shining. "But how did you survive?"

"A god saved me," I answered her. "Or a being so like a god it makes no difference. He needs me to save mankind from the Cielcin and their... their masters."

"Their masters?" Selene looked at me, brows knitting.

Standing over her, I said, "Ours is a proxy war. Humanity and the Cielcin, we're only pawns. Pieces in a larger game. Once, I thought your father one of the kings, the emperors in that game, with the Cielcin Elusha opposite him. I was wrong. The whole human race, we're just one pawn, one piece in a game so vast and so ancient neither you nor I can comprehend its scope." I took her hands in mine. "We are so small, Selene. The whole human race is so small. But we're a crucial piece." When I saw she was not understanding me, I said, "Even a pawn can check an emperor."

"Why are we so important?" she asked.

"Because the universe was made *for* us," I said.

"For mankind?" she said. "That's what the Chantry teaches."

It was, but the best lies are half-truths, and so it was with the Cult of Earth.

"For *life*," I said, "for all life. But the Cielcin have turned against life, against the universe itself. They would destroy it if they could. If we do not stop them."

Selene's eyes narrowed. "You can't be serious."

I said nothing at all, only held her gaze.

"You *are* serious." I felt her hands tremble.

"The powers the Cielcin serve are very great. Lesser gods, made to oversee reality itself, to herd the very stars. Even if they can't succeed in destroying everything, they are capable of destruction on a scale you and I can't even imagine. If they have their way, the whole of the Cielcin Wars will have been only prologue."

Selene pulled her hands away. "If what you say is true," she said, "if this... god that has sent you is so great, why does he not help us?"

"He is helping us," I said, gesturing at my own heart with one open hand. "*I* am the help, Selene. That is why we *have* to seek Vorgossos."

"Vorgossos?" The princess stood. "The Extrasolarian kingdom?"

"Kharn Sagara has in his possession a cache of weapons designed by the Mericanii daimons, as well as one of the daimons itself," I said. "The machines were in contact with these higher beings..." I paused, cognizant of my use of the same phrase the Irchtani used to describe we palatine humans. "They *knew* about them, Selene. They built weapons capable of fighting them."

The princess asked, "Why would the machines build weapons to fight these... things?"

"They believed they were protecting us," I said.

"The machines?"

"Yes," I said. "The story you know is not quite right. The Mericanii. The God Emperor. The Foundation War. Nothing begins as evil, not even the machines. All they did to us, the slavery, the torment, they did because they believed it was to our good. They never wanted us destroyed."

On Vorgossos, the monster Brethren had spoken of the message it received from the Quiet. The daimon had peered across time, across the higher dimensions of our reality, and received a message from the future, from a time beyond even Ragama's day. But Brethren had not built the weapons that slumbered aboard the *Demiurge*. Its progenitors had.

"You really think there's a weapon on Vorgossos that can... destroy the Cielcin?"

"Destroy the Cielcin," I said, "and the beings they serve."

Selene sank onto the couch, the low coffee table between us. She kept her glittering hands on her knees. Her nails were red as her hair. "Let's say I believe you," she said. "What must we do?"

I did not take either of the chairs facing her. It was better if I stood, better if I remained the old soldier, the good soldier. She looked somehow young again, with her hair so shorn. Gone was the woman, imperious, radiant, regal as any queen. In her place, a frightened girl sat, a child alone. I wondered then if Selene had ever once left Forum before. Perhaps she had gone to Caliburn House, to her family's estates of Avalon or Shakespeare. Perhaps she had visited Mars, seen the blue dot of Earth shine above Phobos and Deimos.

But it was possible, *just* possible, that she had never left her home before.

And there she was, sailing to Latarra. Into the lion's den.

"First, we need to handle our hosts," I said.

"You said we could trust Lorian Aristedes," she countered, fear mingling with accusation in her tone.

"And so we can," I said, "but there is the matter of his master to consider. He is a prisoner of his circumstances, as are we."

The princess drew one knee to her breast, putting her foot on the couch. Hugging the limb to herself, she said, "You said I shouldn't have come. Captain Ghoshal believes this Monarch of Latarra will hold me captive."

"Ghoshal is a fool," I said, "if an honest one."

"What will become of me?" she asked.

"If we have our way, nothing," I said. "You are in danger, princess, I will not lie to you, but you are in—I think—considerably less danger than I." I read the question plain on her alabaster face. "Do you think the Extrasolarians would hesitate to take this body apart to learn its secrets?"

Selene's grip upon her leg tightened.

"It will not come to that, if we are careful," I said. "*You*, on the other hand, are certainly worth more alive, and worth more to your father and family than you are to the Monarch. It will not prove difficult to remind them of this."

How small she looked! How lost. How utterly bereft. Both chivalry and its opposite howled at me to go to her, to take her in arms and hold her. Sharply I recalled the visions I had seen, the memories of other lives—of the lives we'd had together. I found I knew every line and curve of her, every secret place, and the knowledge distressed me. It was knowledge I should not have.

I had to remind myself that here was the woman her father had offered me as balm for Valka's death.

She was only a Tavrosi.

That was no fault of Selene's, but it tainted her all the same.

Still, I pitied her.

"The Latarrans want their alliance with the Empire," I said. "Their position must be more desperate than they let on, else they would not come to us with this offer of theirs."

"The telegraph trace?" Selene's brows contracted. "Surely that offer cannot stand! The Empire must believe the Extras kidnapped me, that this is some plot of your doing—exactly as the Chantry foretold. In a way, I played into their hands... doing what you said."

She was perceptive. That, at least.

"You saved my daughter," I said, and eager to solidify the wall between us, added, "mine and Valka's. I will always be grateful to you, princess. But we can salvage this situation. We must offer to reopen negotiations between Latarra and your family. We can tell your father and brother what transpired and why."

Selene raised her chin, brittle and strangely defiant—perhaps she was only wounded. "They will not move to defy the Chantry."

"They do not need to," I said. "They need only ignore them, which your father has done for as long as I have known him." William had ever been at odds with his clergy, with the priors and patriarchs of Earth's Holy Chantry. Imperial civilization stood upon but two great pillars: the Chantry and the Throne. Time and the stress of war had buckled both those pillars. Now they sagged against one another and chafed.

"We can do as much," I said. "You will escape this net, your highness. I promise you that, but you must do as I say."

"Selene," she said, pronouncing each of her name's three syllables with shaky force. Her eyes were closed, pressed shut. "Please call me *Selene.*"

I said nothing.

The girl inhaled sharply, let her leg fall. "I'm not a fool, Sir Hadrian."

"I did not say that you were," I said.

"You said I shouldn't have come," she said, "but if I hadn't done so, there would have been nothing to stop the Martians blasting your Cassandra and the others out of the sky!"

Selene...what became of her, I wonder? After all was said and done? After I slit the belly of Gododdin's sun and spilled its fire across the Dark? After Orphan and the Astrophage? And that last night on Tenba?

I have heard it said that she is dead. That she—along with many of her siblings—was murdered in the massacre that followed the Emperor's death, the Night of Knives. I have heard it said that she was sent to Pagus Minor, or to Mars. That she was the concubine of some Martian legate, a gift for his service to our new Imperial sovereign. Others say she was returned to Avalon, where she dwells now and forever in the halls of her fathers, a part of the furniture—so to speak—at Caliburn House. Still others say that she, the Almost-Bride of the Sun Eater, serves now as one of the Cinarians, the Ash Maidens who serve at the Cenotaph of the God Emperor.

I do not know. But I pray that she has found peace...wherever she is.

"Won't you look at me?" her voice intruded on my silence, tugged at my turned face. "You won't even *look* at me..."

I looked at her.

Her eyes were shining, but had turned hard and cold as glass. "I have loved you," she said, "since the day you rode through the Eternal City in triumph—Grass Crown upon your head." She wrung her hands in her lap. "Father set me aside *for you.* I have slept for decades at a time...watched my brothers and sisters grow old. Watched my Empire crack apart. Waiting *for you.*" She stood, the charcoal about her eyes beginning to run. "And then you died."

I did not go to her, feeling that to move in either direction—in any direction—was to confirm my path through time. I saw the Solar Throne before me, its carmine velvet and rays of beaten gold. I had only to go to her, to kiss her as she had kissed me the night I was destroyed. She would be my Empress—and what an Empress she would make. Not cold and terrible as Ushara, but warm and bright as the sun of vanished Earth.

And yet, it was the same future—the same pattern repeated, just as the inhuman form of the Watchers was repeated in the icons in the Great Sanctum in the Eternal City. To go to Selene then was to choose that path. Power and dominion over men. To choose her and the throne was to make once more the choice the God Emperor had made, to forge a new link in the same chain that had bound human affairs for nigh on twenty thousand years. To go to her was to repeat the cycle, was to attempt to hold history in its place, to pin the future to the past and hold it there by will and force of arms.

That was not my charge, or my desire, though I had no wish to cause her pain.

"Will you say nothing?" asked she.

"I died, yes," I said softly. "I died, but the man you loved was never born. You love the Hero of Aptucca. The Demon in White. That man isn't me. He never was."

Selene flared. "Those stories are true!" she said, and the tears that teetered on the precipice of falling fell at last. "You died, Hadrian! You died, and you live again! Don't you tell me you are not all they say you are and more! Don't you dare!" She collapsed sobbing into me, her narrow shoulders shaking.

There I let her stay, but spoke no word of comfort, and when she was finished, I brought the conversation back to the matter at hand.

We had years before we reached Latarra, and though I planned to enter my icy sleep, we had time yet to plan our next move. Still now I recall her tears, and shiver.

Wherever she is now, I pray she is not alone.

CHAPTER 48

THE SAME ANIMALS

THE NEXT SEVERAL MONTHS of our journey passed but slowly. One could sense the queasy tension in the bellies of all Ghoshal's men, could see it in the way they peered out the *Gadelica*'s portholes, in the uneasy way they stood at guard. Our Sollans feared their Extrasolarian hosts—and more—they feared the ship outside.

Lorian's *Mistwalker.*

That fear and loathing ran both ways. On each occasion when I left our ships to meet with Lorian or simply to walk the greater vessel, I found the Extras peering in at us with the same ill trust. Neither side was without reason, the Empire and Extrasolarians each had been the other's predator since the God Emperor crowned himself in the ruins of Rome.

I discovered that 2Maeve was not—as I had at first suspected—Lorian's second-in-command. His first officer was an Exalted called Amatorre, a towering, skeletally thin man who seemed to me all machine below the neck. He wore the Latarran falcon uniform, but the hands that emerged from his tailored sleeves were of jointed ceramic the color of bone. His face was totally bloodless, reminding me of the prophet, Jari, and a knurl of black iron projected from the back of his skull, allowing various fibers and cables to be socketed into it.

I gathered that the everyday operation of the *Mistwalker* was his, and that Lorian's role was more akin to my own aboard the *Tamerlane* than to Corvo's. The rest of Lorian's officer corps were a strange collection of men and women, and of creatures that were neither men nor women—or had been one or the other once. There was a dryad woman called Orchis, and a diminutive creature called Neru who oversaw the ship's engineering department. The ship's navigator was a hermaphrodite—not a Lothrian, but like one—who called itself Anat and spoke always of itself as someone else, saying always *Anat this* or *Anat that*. The head of the ship's infantry was an old former Sollan officer called Camillus Elffire, a palatine from some obscure family.

Then there was 2Maeve of the Interfaced, Lorian's chief of security. Her people formed the backbone of the ship's vanguard, Lorian's elite troopers. There were three thousand of them on board—a tenth of the *Mistwalker*'s total complement—a full third of whom were aquilarii, each capable of operating their own space-to-surface lightercraft. The rest of the soldiery were either ground troopers, men like our legionnaires under Elffire's command, or artillery men, the crews and maintenance teams whose job it was to maintain the small army of colossi the great ship could deploy at need.

So vast was that mighty vessel that it seemed almost uninhabited at times. Well I remember standing on the gantries above the slumbering war machines—great tripods and iron scarabs topped with gun castles the size of cottages—where it seemed Lorian and I were the only men in all the world.

"We can't match the Empire, troop for troop," Lorian said, banging his cane against the iron rail. "But we have the hardware."

The launch bay lay at the bottom of the great ship, several levels below the central hold with its great ray of false sun, right up against the outer hull. We were standing on one of the bay's many catwalks, a hundred feet from the huge bay doors designed to open on the void and deploy the dropships and heavy artillery nestled in cradles above us.

We had but recently passed the hulking shapes of tanks, huge battle platforms of the sort we had deployed in the defense of Deira on Berenike.

Lorian's ship had twelve, and that was just in the one hold. For all I knew, there were other holds like this one distributed about the great ship's circumference.

But we had moved on, and found ourselves beneath what seemed to me a thicket of metal stalactites.

"What are these?" I asked, following Lorian's cane to the bristling machinery above our heads. "They look like suits of armor." The stalactites were dangling limbs, arms and legs, their bodies hunched like those of marionettes waiting above an unlit stage.

Lorian grinned. "They're lighters," he said. "Interfaced design. They call them Armored Mobile Platforms, AMPs, for short. The pilot fits in the torso, upright, controls the thing with his neural lace. Weapons systems are in the arms and shoulders—some in the chest unit. The whole thing reconfigures for flight, tips the pilot prone. They're small enough to bypass most radar."

"How big are they?" I asked.

"Four meters," he said, using the Extrasolarian measure.

"A little more than eight cubits," I said. "About a dozen feet."

"A little more than that," Lorian said. "But they get the job done. You should see them in action."

"Maybe I will," I said. "If we fight together."

The little man smiled up at me in his lupine way, all teeth.

"Maybe we will," he said.

I turned away from him, looked up at the hanging AMPs. They had no heads, and their broad shoulders—which housed weapons and engines and the delicate machinery of furled wings—made me think of the Dullahan, the headless knight that Sir Gawain faced in the old legends, and of the cephalophores, the martyrs one saw sometimes depicted on the walls of Chantry sanctums. But what need had such a system for a head, when the human pilot—its brain, in truth—lay safe in its armored core?

"It's good to have you back, Lorian," I said.

"I'm not *back*, Marlowe," he said, and his use of my family name raised a wall between us.

"I only mean it's good to see you," I said, and the wind of some unseen ventilator high in the bay above us blew my overlong hair about my face. "I thought I never would again."

"I never thought to see you, either," Lorian said. "Virtues! I'm old! I know I don't look it, Marlowe, but I'm pushing four hundred years active. And there's no telling how long this goblin body of mine will last."

I laughed. "You'll outlast all of us, Lorian."

"Look who's talking," said the Commandant General. "You look like you damn near started over. Where's my reset button, eh?"

I dismissed this with a wave. "Surely the work you've had done must help."

"Oh, it helps," the little man said, "but none of us knows how much time he has. I only hope I live long enough to see what we're building built."

"We have to end the war for that," I said.

"We do," Lorian said. "I hope I live long enough to see that, too."

Weeks passed, and I but little saw Cassandra, and almost always from afar. From time to time I would see her in the general mess, on the rare occasion I took food there—with Edouard—and did not eat in the cenacle aboard the *Ascalon*. Once, I spied her returning to the *Gadelica*. She and certain of the junior officers had risked a venture into the *Mistwalker*'s sunlit hold for a taste of something like fresh air. She lingered only for a moment, her eyes on mine. Then she turned away.

"You should go to her," said Princess Selene, who had joined me for my own walk out under the long, false sun.

But I could only shake my head.

I could not blame her for her doubts, I could only love her despite them, and wait.

"This whole ship is a powder keg," said Edouard, prompting me to wonder how he knew what a powder keg was. "It's only a matter of time before one of Ghoshal's men cracks and shoots at the Extras on watch." The HAPSIS man frowned, peering down a side passage as we returned toward the ventral hold and the *Ascalon*. "Why *did* they set a watch? I thought we were supposed to be on the same side."

"They're afraid of you," I said. "Our peoples have been at one another's throats since the dawn of time." I did not break stride, forcing the fellow to hurry to catch up. "It will be one of Henric's men that shoots first, you can depend on that."

"You?" Edouard asked.

I did stop then. "What?"

"*Afraid of you*, you said," Edouard said, frown creasing his face. "Don't you mean *afraid of us?*"

"You know what I mean," I said, but the man was right. I had unwittingly counted myself apart from—above—Ghoshal and Albé and the rest. When Edouard did not respond, I said, "I used to think that peace with the Cielcin was possible. I worked very hard to secure something like an embassy with one of their princes, but when I'd finally brought them to the table, it was our side who struck first.

"I know now that such an embassy was doomed to failure. The Cielcin don't have allies. Trading partners. Only masters and slaves. But at the time, I wasn't sure which of us were the real monsters." I shook myself out of cold memory. "I don't want history to repeat itself here."

"History only repeats itself because human nature never changes," Edouard said. "We think we've come so far, but all the miles we've walked since we left the Garden are as inches measured against the light-years we have to go."

I smiled at this. Had I not thought much the same a thousand times before?

"We're the same animals we always were," I said. "Not even the Extras can really change that. They just destroy themselves trying to become something else."

"I've thought about that a lot since coming here," Edouard said. "How many of these people aren't the people they were born anymore? How many of them destroyed their souls chasing their dreams of perfection?"

"A lesson for us all in that," I said. "But Henric needs to talk to his men. We've years before we reach Latarra, and the last thing any of us needs is some nervous legionnaire taking a shot at one of Lorian's dragoons. Only he won't listen to me."

"He'll listen to me," Edouard said. He was quiet then for as long as it took to walk another dozen paces. "You're right. It'll be one of ours, if it's anybody."

"Ghoshal's men are soft as clay," I said. "I'd warrant not a one of them's seen any action but for Sabratha, and most of them were in the air." The *Gadelica* had engaged with Muzugara's worldship, but to my knowledge it had not been boarded, and none of its troopers had been deployed to the surface of the Cielcin moon.

We'd reached the lift meant to carry us down to the level of the hold where the *Ascalon* slumbered, a black metal door in the black metal hall. Abruptly I was aware of our dim reflections in it. Shadows and ghosts.

"They'll be fired soon enough," Albé said, keying the lift.

"How many will crack, I wonder?"

Edouard made a noncommittal gesture, not quite a shrug. "We've what remains of Clavan's men. And the Irchtani. And you." He clapped me on the shoulder. "You're surely worth an army in yourself."

That drew a rough laugh from me. "We'll see."

"Men don't return from the dead without reason," Edouard said. "Much less twice."

When we reached the *Ascalon,* it was with the intention of continuing our discussion privately over a game of labyrinth chess.

But our game was not to be.

Neema met us in the hall, summoned by the sound of our voices. The manservant's olive face was drawn, his lips compressed, his brows contracted. "*Domi!*" he said, "Master, master! She's ... upstairs."

I left Edouard's side and gripped my servant's arm. "Cassandra?"

"Yes, my lord!" Neema said. "The girl is back. Arrived about an hour ago. I said you were out with Agent Albé. Hello, Agent Albé!"

Edouard bowed slightly.

"She's up in the cenacle, you must have passed her," Neema said, patting my wrist to encourage me to release him.

I did so. Looking to Edouard, I said, "If you'll excuse me." The doors to the cenacle had been closed, Edouard and I had gone down to the lower deck where I had my cabin to retrieve the druaja board.

The Museum Catholic bowed a second time. "Tomorrow, perhaps?"

"Tomorrow," I said, but I was already moving. I mounted the stairs where once Alexander's Urslic assassin had tried to murder Valka and myself, and taking the steps two at a time returned to the level of the mess and bridge. Turning right, I followed the hall to the rear of the little ship and opened the door.

She was seated precisely where Captain Ghoshal had sat, her head on the table. She looked up as I entered, and I knew at once that she'd been drinking. Her eyes were slow to focus, and her face grew strangely solemn in that way drunks do when they attempt to ape sobriety. If these were not clues enough, there was the bottle itself. Clear glass with the red-and-black label of a Jaddian distiller.

Zvanya. Where had that come from?

"You!" she pointed a finger at me. "They all think you're *him*."

"I am me, Cassandra," I said, taking a pair of cautious steps into the room. Too well I sensed the tension coiling like smoke upon the air, more tightly than any fear Ghoshal's men might feel for their Extrasolarian watchdogs. Any wrong move—any errant word—might spell disaster.

The girl hissed. "Then prove it!"

Her eyes were red. I felt that I should go to her, should take her in my arms and hold her to myself. Not for comfort, but to assure the girl that I was real, and solid, and myself.

But I did not, sensing that to do so—particularly with Cassandra in her current state—would only serve to drive her from me.

I felt as a man must feel barefoot on a stone floor surrounded by broken glass. I did not dare to move. All the joy I'd felt at Neema's tidings had gone stone cold. My daughter was a serpent then, and I the untrained serpent charmer.

"How should I prove myself?" I asked, half raising my hands as though she held a gun to me.

"You tell me," she said. "These people can...copy memories, right? They could make you just like him if they wanted."

"If that's what they wanted, why did they make me like this?" I asked her, spreading my arms.

It was the same argument I'd used on Ghoshal, but here it had greater effect. Cassandra sat a little straighter, grabbed her zvanya bottle with one hand and dragged it across the table to herself. "I don't know," she said, and drank. "None of this makes any sense." She was quiet then a long moment, her eyes sliding from focus and my face to some indeterminate spot on the table.

How many arguments had Valka and I had...just like this?

We're the same animals we always were...

At once Cassandra's shoulders shook, and she hunched, but no sound broke from her.

"I saw it, you know?" she said, voice flat and dry as a flower pressed between leaves. "What was left of you. You were just a puddle on the floor. Blood everywhere. *Everywhere*. I stepped in it." She choked.

It was *you* now, not *him*, I noticed, but did not call her on it.

"I'm sorry, Anaryan," I said, taking another step nearer her. "I'm sorry you had to see—"

"Don't!" Her voice shot up, and she stood so quickly her chair clattered to the floor. "Don't call me that! You are *not* him. You're not!"

I'd reached the corner of the table by then, and halted, teetering on the decision to circle round it and go to her.

"Anaryan..."

"I said don't!" The bottle was still open in her hand, its cinnamon contents sloshing as she raised her hands like a boxer. "Get away from me."

"You came to me," I said. "I'm not going anywhere."

"You did!" she said. "You died!"

"Cassandra..."

She hurled the bottle at me. I hadn't expected that. The zvanya filled the air with the heady aroma of cinnamon and strong alcohol. I raised a hand to fend it off, winced as hard glass found bone. It struck the edge of the table as it fell, sending a spider's web of hairline fractures through the ebon glass. Incredibly, the bottle itself did not shatter, but bounced off the floor at my feet.

"Stay away!" Cassandra lashed out at me. Her blow turned my head.

The contact stopped her dead. Our eyes met. Emerald and violet. I saw something in them, a recognition, an understanding. A hope, perhaps. She had never hit me before—unless it was in practice, in our sparring sessions at the Cave of Fishes and on Jadd.

Not ever.

I opened my mouth to speak, but before I could get so much as a word out, she struck at me, aiming a jab at my head. In a flash, I slipped her blow, retreating to stand clear of the dropped bottle and the puddle of fragrant zvanya spreading on the floor. Cassandra followed me, snapping a kick at my right flank. Once more I turned aside, finding then that I was faster than she, faster than I had ever been. Her foot found nothing but air. Recovering, she launched into an overhand right that should have struck me on the cheek. I slapped it aside, but while I might have returned the shot in kind, I held back.

I thought I understood, understood why she had waited so long to come to me, why she had been sitting in this room in the dark, and had not emerged when Edouard and I first arrived. Understood why she had been drinking.

She had been trying to prepare herself for this, had been working herself up *to* this.

Again and again she struck at me. Again and again I turned her blows aside. She was fast! And strong as only the looms of Jadd could make her, but try as she might—I would not strike her.

I caught her fist in my open palm, caught it and held it fast.

"Fight me!" she almost cried, and tried to pull her fist away. When I would not let her, she tried to cuff me with her other hand. I let her go, let the new blow fall short. A space had formed between us. Two paces. Three. Her chest was heaving, her fists up and ready. There was sweat beading her pale brow, and her breath came hard. "Fight me, damn you!"

"No," I said.

Hissing, Cassandra reached for her belt, and in a single, fluid motion, snapped one of her twin swords free.

"Is this what you want?" I asked.

"If you really are *him*," she said, brandishing the unkindled blade, "prove it."

"How?"

The blade lanced forward, would have pierced me had I not twisted aside. It sliced toward me, and I danced back a step.

Did she mean to kill me? Truly? Was that why she had come? Why she had had to drink herself half-insensate?

I ducked a wild slash. The girl was not herself, was not remotely like herself. She had always been an aggressive fighter, confident and courageous. But here she was uncorked, frenzied, furious. There were tears shining in her eyes, raw and wild as she.

Still, her blade found only air.

We had circled round, and abruptly I felt the table at my back. It was all I could do to hurl myself over it, black hair tangling about my face as I struck the deck on its far side.

"Fight me, damn you!" she said, falling back into her native Jaddian. "*Panathetto!*"

"I won't fight you, Cassandra," I said, and once more spread my hands.

"Whatever you are," she said, gasping. "Devil or djinn—whatever! You are *not* him. You may have fooled the others, but you will *not* fool me."

Hands still raised and empty, I said, "I am your father."

"*Kadhabi!*" she cried. *Liar.*

Utannashi.

The noise of our battle and of Cassandra's cries must surely have reached good Neema by then, and Edouard with him. If we were to finish this alone, it had to end swiftly.

But I would not draw my sword.

Cassandra had to break left or right to circle the table and reach me. She did neither. Instead, she brought her sword through a rising arc that cut the table clean in two, and stepped into the breach made as the two halves fell apart. I should have expected something of the kind, but so sudden was her move and so violent her ferocity that I was caught by surprise. I should have dodged to one side.

I stepped back instead, and so did not escape her redoubled assault.

Cassandra splintered, refracted as through a prism, her blade a shining ray of light aimed at my heart. I saw it pass across an infinite sea of potential. It seemed to shimmer as it drew near. For an instant, the blade appeared to pass me both to left and right, then to pierce my chest.

I closed my grip on Cassandra's wrist and on the pommel of the blade she held, the emitter pressed against my sternum. Our eyes met an instant. The look of savage triumph on her face giving way to absolute grief.

But the vision still shimmered about me, the world—my place in it—unresolved. To my left and right, I saw the two of us repeated in countless iterations, Cassandra's blade buried to the hilt in my heart, my hands on hers.

She did not dare to move.

Slowly—so, so slowly—my thumb found the emitter, switched off the blade. Cassandra's sword fell from nerveless fingers, clattered to the floor. There was no blood. No wound. Not a stitch of my black tunic jacket was torn.

I was entirely unharmed.

Fear shone in Cassandra's eyes. Tears. Her lips parted, and she shook like a storm-bothered leaf.

Before she could pull away, or fall, or run, I embraced her, dragging her by the hand that had but recently tried to take my life. I gathered her in my arms, and held her fast. For a moment, she tried to pull away, but I was still as stone. Cassandra was as ice, unyielding, utterly frozen.

The ice cracked. "Abba?" The word was small as atoms.

"It really is me, Anaryan."

CHAPTER 49

THE PRINTED CITY

SEEN FROM ABOVE, THE city was like a blanket of whitest snow, a shroud cast upon the hills. It had not been there when Caesar and Sir Gray had showed me images of the place before the assault on Ganelon, and so I guess that all of it—every tower and paved street, every bridge and storefront and apartment insula—had been erected in the short centuries since.

The Latarra I had seen—had expected to see—had been a place like Rustam, a city of sunken ships, a city hastily amalgamated by those disparate peoples flocking to the protection of the planet's Monarch. It had become a city of pristine order, a city not unlike Meidua, with its white stone buildings and cobbled streets. But where Meidua had been a place of common stone, its palaces marble fronted, chased with gold, the buildings of that alien city were of machine-manufactured stone. Great bricks of limestone and pure dolomite fitted together like puzzle blocks about skeletons of adamant and steel, their edges so straight and smooth no moss or blade of grass might spring between them.

Still, the vestiges of the old city remained, with here and there a mighty freighter rising like the black bones of a mountain from beneath that city of white snow. Still more grounded starships ringed the white city's perimeter, not yet broken down and recycled—their adamantine hulls harvested for their carbon and transformed into the limestone that made up the city's new growth. Those outer districts, that warren of sunken ships, that was the *Maze* of which Lorian had spoken, the first city upon which the Monarch's new one was built.

And then there was *the Citadel*. The images Caesar and Sir Gray had showed me all those years ago had depicted an ancient, castellated pile upon a rise at the center of the Maze warrens, a low, many-towered palace—complete with glass gardens and turrets and checker-tiled piazzas.

That palace was gone. In its place, a great construction was going up. Cranes and crawlers, conveyors and loaders and drilling machines in incandescent red clustered about their charge. Where once that old palace had stood, a new one was rising: Terrace upon terrace, step upon step, it rose, a vast ziggurat of adamant and steel.

I thought of the vast fortress beneath Castle Borosevo, the armored ziggurat—the topless pyramid—upon whose summit had been perched the home of Count Balian Mataro.

This pyramid-ziggurat was much the same, of a style not uncommon across the Norman reaches. When the lords of a world did not delve for their protection—as had been done on Berenike and Perfugium alike—they built such fastnesses.

That hall of Calen Harendotes was not yet done.

Calen Harendotes.

I was to meet him soon, that figure of modern legend, that King of the Outer Worlds.

Calen, son of Ausar of the House Harendotes. Monarch of Latarra. Conqueror of Ashklam. Prince of Monmara. He who had gathered uncounted nations to himself. He had been one of the marginalia nearly all my life, little more than a dragon coiled about the compass in one corner of the map.

He was about to become astonishingly real.

The martial shout of trumpets rang out their greeting, pronouncing a melody I must have heard when Lorian landed on Forum. The opening of the ramp of Lorian's egg-shaped landing craft admitted a gust of cool air. It was winter in the city, but at that lowly latitude, the day was only cool. My unbound hair guttered across my face, and at my side, Selene shivered, and clutched my arm.

"It's all right," I said, glancing sidelong at her. At her request, Lorian's people had found a white gown somewhere in the *Mistwalker*'s city-hold. Her hair was still the short bob it had been after she had slashed her hair in grief.

Self-conscious, she reached up to flatten that crimson auriole, glacing sidelong at the ranks of Interfaced standing at attention between us and the ramp. "I'm all right," she said, attention flickering to Ramanthanu, to Annaz and the other xenobites who made up our own train.

"You're sure we can trust these people?" Cassandra asked, eying the first wind of that new world with suspicion.

"My people, do you mean?" Lorian asked, appearing as if from nowhere from between the ranks of his men. His diminutive stature had granted him the element of surprise yet again. "Trust me only so far as you can throw me, girl." He donned his short-billed cap with a flourish. "Mind you, I'm lighter than I look." With a wink, he turned and descended the ramp, which was still lowering as he took his first steps, so that almost he had to leap to reach the landing pad outside.

Aristedes was totally at his ease, the conquering hero come home. That—I thought—was passing strange, as it was partly in defeat he had returned.

But I had forgotten much of Lorian in the years since the parting of our ways. He was a strategist to his core, and politics was only another theater of war. I watched him go, his rope of silver hair dancing behind him, watched him move with all the energy of a Eudoran mummer in a farce—which in a sense he was.

"Commandant General Aristedes!" said the leader of the receiving party, a tall, thin creature in robes of Latarran armorial black. At first I took it for one of the Exalted, so tall was it and thin—so thin—that I knew no human skeleton remained beneath the neck. In that he recalled First Officer Amatorre, but where Amatorre's face remained the face of a gaunt and aquiline man, the face of Oneiros was lost behind a mask of mirrored black.

"Majordomo Oneiros!" Lorian said, his cane tucked into the crook of his left arm. He saluted sharply. "I have brought two gifts for His Majesty!"

Apparently undaunted, the towering Oneiros replied, "We understand that you have failed to secure the treaty you were selected to arrange." Behind the Majordomo, a block of men in the gold-eyed masks and hod helmets and flanged armor of Latarran dragoons stood holding blazing lances or the short stocks of plasma rifles. There must have been a hundred of them at least. Had they come to honor Lorian? Or to arrest him?

"I have done far better!" Lorian said, directing his attention to the gaggle of more gaily dressed courtiers assembled to Oneiros's right hand. "I have brought Selene, Princess of the House Avent, daughter of His Radiance, the Emperor. And more! I have brought the Demon in White himself, the Halfmortal! Lord Hadrian Marlowe, Royal Knight and one-time Commandant of the Imperial Red Company."

That sent a thrill of surprise through the congregation. Word of Selene's apparent kidnapping must have reached them, but news of my coming would have been a surprise. Lorian had been wise to conceal my presence. In doing so, he had reserved his strongest card in his hand, and wrongfooted any opposition to his failure as a diplomat.

He had changed the game. You could sense it in the manner of the crowd, the way they whispered, tittered to one another.

"Are they all human?" Selene whispered in my ear, gripping my arm more tightly. She inclined her head to the gathered worthies of the Monarch's court.

A woman sat in a float-chair like an egg slashed across a diagonal, four limbs arranged so that her four long-fingered hands gripped the rim with jeweled fingers. She had no legs, only a pair of arms where her lower legs should be. I had seen such a creature in the Minoan fortress on Ganelon, and wondered if they were kin—some artificial race like the dryads. Beside her, a man taller and more muscled than even Otavia had been stood in robes of carmine and cloth of gold. About them were gathered a curious assemblage. There were men and women clad Imperial fashion, and still more in the drabber styles of the Normans, and one or two Exalted chimeras, alongside up-jumped homunculi and stranger sorts come to see the Commandant General and his shame.

But that shame had turned to triumph.

The Majordomo, Oneiros, glided toward us, robes rasping over the ground. It did not seem to walk as it approached us—there was no motion of knee or hip—only to translate across the white stone. Beside me, Selene flinched, and Cassandra grew tense.

The towering creature stopped several paces in front of Selene and myself, studying us both with its featureless black face. I thought I detected a light beneath that blackness, a witch-gleam of pale blue where the left eye might be. "Princess Selene, Lord Marlowe,"—it bowed, arching in a way no human back could—"be welcome to the White City and to Latarra. I am Oneiros, Majordomo to His Majesty, the Monarch."

Selene offered one bejeweled hand for the faceless man to kiss. A hand of jointed steel slithered from the black robes, took her white hand in its fingers and raised it to its faceplate.

"We are honored by your hospitality, Majordomo," Selene said, her voice admirably calm.

"On the contrary," Oneiros said, "we are honored by your presence. You are the first of your nobile bloodline to grace our world." The creature turned to me. "And...Lord Marlowe. This is unexpected."

"Is your master present?" I asked, surveying the throng behind Oneiros, the armored dragoons, the courtiers. We had landed on a pad atop a square turret that projected from one of the ziggurat's lower terraces, high above ground, but beneath the tops of the nearest towers of the Printed City. Just as Lorian had described, I could see pillars of steam—taller still—floating up from the Maze beyond the new city where fusion reactors burned hot as tiny stars. At this altitude, one could see the construction happening everywhere, that whole, great Babylonian edifice rising from the earth. The whole thing had sprung up from nothing in mere decades, in another few dozen years it would be complete.

A triumph of engineering and the human will.

"My master is always present," Oneiros said, swiveling that faceless face to look at me once more. "Why have you come?"

"To treat with your master," I said. "Not his servant."

Oneiros went stock still a moment. Presently, the Majordomo twisted to regard Lorian. "Commandant General Aristedes, you were tasked to make peace with the Imperials. You failed. This is a grievous disappointment."

Lorian interjected, "There was a change of plans. I must meet with His Majesty as soon as possible. Much has happened, much has changed."

"You were directed to arrange an accord with the Imperials," Oneiros said again.

"An accord for which we are happy to negotiate," said Selene, insinuating herself into the conversation.

Oneiros swiveled to regard her. "You are here on your Imperial Father's will?"

She hesitated, looked to me.

I did not speak at once, either. The truth of our circumstances could not be long concealed—too many had been present at the council on Forum to conceal anything. Word would have traveled so far as the Monarch's court, if only as fleeter rumor.

Turning, I looked to Edouard, who had followed us down the ramp with Captain Ghoshal—who had insisted on accompanying us. *To keep a watch on her highness,* he'd said. The HAPSIS man nodded silent concurrence.

"Our situation is more complicated," I said.

"Our situation *has been* complicated, you mean," said the four-armed woman from her seat. She was pale as the city itself, possessing a sailor's pallor, and her hair was just as white, lending her an illusion of age far greater than she possessed. "Marlowe and Aristedes are friends of old. I think it no coincidence that he appears here just as our carefully laid plans fall to pieces."

Beside her, the big man spoke in a voice like the cracking stones in the bowels of the world. "We had heard that you were dead."

While my resurrection had been witnessed only by those aboard Lorian's ship, my death had doubtless been galactic news. Word would have propagated across the datanet, relayed by quantum telegraphy to the remotest corners of the human universe.

"That is false, sir," I said, opening my arms, "as you see."

"Rumors of your demise are forever exaggerated," said the four-handed woman, crossing her arms like legs.

"Indeed, madam," I replied, "were it not for *my friend of old,* they would not be rumors at all."

Oneiros pivoted to regard Lorian. "What is the meaning of this?"

"Imperial factionalism," came Lorian's answer. "Lord Marlowe and the princess have agreed to negotiate with the Solar Throne for our interests as the price for my saving their lives. I must speak with His Majesty, the Monarch, at once. You have spoken to him already?"

How Oneiros could have spoken to Harendotes already puzzled me only for a moment. We were among the Extrasolarians. Surely their king and this creature of his possessed the means to communicate with another silently and at once. Likely, I thought, Calen Harendotes had been aware of Lorian's surprise from the moment Selene and I had emerged from the landing craft.

"You speak of factionalism," said the four-handed woman, floating to join Oneiros. "Explain yourself, Commandant General."

Lorian bowed, still performing. "My dear Master Jamina, Lord Marlowe was targeted for assassination by agents of the Holy Terran Chantry, who are—it surely does not have to be said—hostile to the idea of an alliance between our New Order and the Solar Throne. That assassination attempt endangered the life of the princess here."

Majordomo Oneiros spoke, its toneless voice airy and void of all inflection. "We have it from Imperial channels that you assaulted the fleet of the Martian Guard and absconded with this princess. You have declared war upon the very people with whom you were tasked to make peace. You are in no position to demand an audience."

"And yet here I am," Lorian said, "demanding."

"This is most irregular," Oneiros said, playing the role of the Monarch's Neema. "Why were we not informed you had captured Lord Marlowe?"

"Captured?" I asked, stepping forward, a hand going to the winged lion-headed hilt of Gibson's sword.

Lorian barred my path with his cane. "Peace, brother," he said. "Lord Marlowe is our guest, Majordomo."

The towering machine-man slithered toward Lorian, stooping like a vampire in its black robes. "That remains to be seen, Commandant General," it said.

Cassandra strode forward to join me, her own hands going for her swords. Selene drew closer, and about us, the Irchtani closed ranks. Ramanthanu hissed, and its fellow Cielcin bared their fangs.

Oneiros had frozen, gone stock still. When it moved again, its demeanor changed. It cocked its head to one side, and said, "You travel in strange company, I see," and turning to the guard it shouted, "Bring them!"

"Abba," Cassandra asked, when we had been escorted to a waiting room within the Monarch's palace. "That Majordomo was going to hold us prisoner? Why the sudden change?"

"I should like to know that as well," said Edouard, who was seated at a side table of graven, dark wood. "I thought they'd have us in tower cells."

Instead, we had been brought—with all our guard and effects in hand—to a sitting room with high slit windows in the slanting outer wall of the ziggurat.

Latarran banners depicting the golden eagle crowned by the disc of the sun hung blackly from the walls, and what furniture there was—baroque in its styling, intricately fashioned—stood in stark contrast to all that pale, printed limestone as a rose in the desert.

The Cielcin had clustered in one corner, and crouched there, fingering their knives. Annaz and the Irchtani of our guard hopped about, shifting from foot to foot. Ghoshal sat at the table opposite Edouard, looking haggard as ever, while Selene had claimed one of the room's tapestried couches for her own, with Ghoshal's men to guard her. Lorian and his people had gone elsewhere, to debrief the giant and the four-handed minister.

My mother's son, I was standing at the window, looking out over the construction and the White City near at hand. Ships were moving across the sky in the middle distance. Latarra's sun was pale, and the light of it caught in the stone, but such was the refraction index of the artificial material that it did not flash and cause blindness as one might think. Rather the stones of the city glowed with a warm light, pristine, serene. It would be beautiful.

It was beautiful even then.

I understood then, sharply and all too well, what Lorian felt for the place. Calen Harendotes had wrought an earthly copy, an homage and loving imitation to the Emperor's Eternal City in the clouds. But the city of the Monarch was founded on stone. It was a place mortal men might tread. Common men. A place where even a misborn intus like Lorian Aristedes might make a lord.

"What do you think happened to Lorian?" Cassandra asked.

"He'll be speaking with his people," I said. "Possibly with his king. They'll be deciding what to do with me."

"With you?" Selene had overheard us. "With us, surely?"

"Your fate is simple," I said. "They need you to make this peace of theirs. Besides, they knew to expect you. I was the surprise."

I had not turned to look at her, and reaching up laid an arm along the edge of the window at my right hand, still watching the construction. I heard Selene shift in her seat. "Will they let us see him? The Monarch?"

"They will," I said, "eventually."

"I don't like it," Ghoshal said, "begging your pardon, highness. I don't like this place one bit. That...horrible creature. The Majordomo. And that woman—the one with the hands!"

To my surprise, it was Edouard who spoke. "She is a *tetrand*, captain, unless I miss my guess," he said. "Her people were bred by the Empire long ago, to work as slaves in null gravity. Their production was banned alongside the dryads. I thought they were extinct."

"I met one before. Briefly," I said, peering back over my shoulder at the room. "There was one among the masters of MINOS."

Ghoshal grumbled. "Gives me conniptions is all."

"We made them, captain," Edouard said. "Be kind."

"I don't have to like it, sir," Ghoshal said, "or this place. It's too *clean*. Too new. Everything feels..."

The doors opened at that precise moment, great constructions of paneled ebony carved with reliefs depicting formless ripples. I turned, expecting Oneiros, or Lorian, or the tetrand minister, Lady Jamina.

Instead, we were presented with a quartet of liveried men carrying a small, square table between them. The Cielcin stood as they entered, cocking their heads to watch through nictitating membranes as the servants brought the table and set it on its single leg to one side of the empty couch opposite where Selene sat.

"What's this then?" I asked, stepping forward.

The seniormost of the four servants bowed low.

I saw what it was before he answered.

"His Majesty, the Monarch, asked that we deliver this to the chamber, my lord," he said, withdrawing an appropriate step. "He said you'd a fondness for the game, that you might enjoy it while you wait."

I looked down at the table, at the hexagon pattern wrought in jet, carnelian, and mother of pearl.

It was a druaja board.

Not knowing what else to say, I thanked the servants. "Have you any indication how long we must wait?" I asked.

The man bowed hastily and withdrew.

"...fake," Ghoshal finished lamely. "Everything feels fake."

Selene craned her neck to study the table. "What a strange gesture..." she said. "A chess board?"

I had drifted toward it, opened one of the corner drawers to reveal the pieces: the legionnaires, emperor, and hierophant, cataphracts and centurions and castellans all nestled in red velvet, each of white jade. "Curious," I said. I had a passing fondness for the game, one tempered by my time with old Aldia on Jadd, but it was far from the sort of thing that men spoke of when they spoke of me.

I drew what I guessed to be one of the cataphracts from its place. This particular set had depicted the traditionally mounted man as a walking tank, a six-legged colossus not unlike those in the *Mistwalker*'s mighty holds.

"Do you play?" Selene asked.

"Only a little," I said.

The princess shook her head. "I never learned how."

"Why send a chessboard?" Ghoshal asked, peering at it across the side table he shared with Edouard. "Is it bugged? Are they listening to us?"

I looked at him for several seconds without speaking. "My dear captain," I said, "we are in their house already. They've heard every word we've said."

Ghoshal snapped, "What then?"

"I don't know," I said. I had the sense that the game table was some joke, some private jape at my expense comprehensible only to the sender. "We may be here for some time. Hours. Perhaps longer."

"Surely they won't leave us here overnight," Selene said.

"They may," I said. "I suggest we all get comfortable."

We did not have to wait overnight, as it happened, though the pale Latarran sun had sunk and turned gold as the banners of its king by the time the great doors opened again. The Majordomo, Oneiros, stood in the door, flanked by masked and helmeted dragoons in the fearsome gear of the Latarran Grand Army.

"Lord Marlowe," the Exalted creature said, "His Majesty has agreed to see you."

I rose from my place on one of the more distant couches. "Selene." I touched the princess's shoulder to wake her. "Selene, it's time."

The princess rose unsteadily. "What time is it?"

"Not quite sundown," I said.

Oneiros slid into the room. Voice impassive and smooth as polished glass, it said, "You must come alone, my lord."

Selene and I exchanged glances. I looked to Cassandra, whose face was grave, and to Edouard, who seemed at once pensive and puzzled.

I offered Oneiros a short bow. "As you wish."

I looked back as unseen mechanisms shut the whorled ebon doors, struck by the tableau of my people—all of them standing or sitting, seeming frozen, unmoving as chessmen on an abandoned board. The Majordomo led me along the white stone hall, past armored guardsmen with eyes like little suns and time-blackened paintings of seemingly incredible age. One or two of them, I felt sure, had been brought out of Old Earth when men were young. One showed a nude woman—the goddess Venus, I realized—standing on a shell while the Hours rushed to clothe her. I halted before its majesty, only to be summoned by a word from Oneiros.

The Monarch awaited.

I followed Oneiros down the hall to a lift of wrought iron and silver glass which conveyed us slanting upward into the palace. The lift opened on an atrium, a high-ceilinged space whose walls converged as they approached the ceiling, not quite forming a triangle. "We are near the top of the current construction," Oneiros said, answering a question I had not asked. "Alas, the palace will not be complete for some years. You are seeing it in its infancy, I fear."

"Your master has accomplished marvels in a short time."

"Our people are vital," Oneiros said. "They share their Monarch's dream of a New Order. It is that dream which propels the construction. They build because they believe, because they love Latarra. Because they love their lord."

I smiled at the back of the monster's hooded head. "Such love is a powerful thing," I said.

Oneiros did not turn back. "My master has asked that you join him in the imitarium. Just through here." One hand of jointed steel indicated the black iron doors before us. Oneiros halted, turned to face me. "I am commanded, however, to relieve you of your sword." That hand extended, palm up. The panels that comprised the surface of that hand were intricately styled, inlaid with twining knots of gold filigree, very fine. When I hesitated, the Majordomo said, "My master is not a cautious man, but he is no fool. Your Red Emperor once sent an assassin against him, with a sword concealed in the man's crutch. We sent that man's head still living to the Eternal City. We would prefer not to have to send yours."

"I doubt that you could," I said, placing the ivory hilt into the iron hand.

The Majordomo examined the hilt. "It will be returned to you," it said, voice flat and toneless as ever. The hilt vanished into the creature's flowing sleeve, and the heavy doors opened onto a short flight of steps that vanished into the dark above. Oneiros bowed, gesturing that I should proceed ahead. I passed it on the threshold, mounted the first step.

The Exalted had called this place an *imitarium,* and though I thought I could guess the meaning of the name, I was not prepared for the full reality. For an instant, all was dark. Then the doors at the top of the stairs opened, and I felt a rush of air, and pale sunlight streamed down from the room above. It was the light of midday—pale silver on that world—though I knew it was almost sundown, and that at that very moment, golden rays streamed through the windows in the chamber where Cassandra and Selene sat waiting.

Among the Tavrosi, genuine physical possessions are rare. *Limited* is perhaps a better word. Much of what they possess exists only virtually, as data stored in the network formed by their collective neural laces. The hospital where they had tried to purge Urbaine's worm from Valka's mind had seemed to me a drab and sterile hell, a place of dull gray and white-washed concrete, though Valka had spoken of dark wood and flowers, and of soft music I could not hear. No two Tavrosi needed to agree on the reality they perceived, so that the same chamber might appear blue in the mind of one observer, green to another. Always they were asserting their will and private preferences on the world around them, each living halfway in a dream like the dreams of the Mericanii—dreams I alone on Edda could not see.

The imitarium of Calen Harendotes was like those dreams, and like also the holograph operas of my mother.

Reaching the top of the stairs, I found myself on a balcony overlooking the White City of the Monarch. The sun was high, almost directly overhead. The day was fair and bright, and the wind was in the west, blowing in across green hills that I had never seen.

The Maze was gone, the columns of steam from the grounded ships that served the White City as power generators were gone, and the grounded ships all with them. The great city rolled across the hills and beneath the massive palace, a sea of white stone.

The construction all was finished. In the distance, the pale spire of a high-tower grounding station rose above all, limestone foundations giving way to a skeletal structure of shining steel from whose summit the lift cable rose, a black streak that vanished into the sky. As I watched, the pale lozenge of a cargo lifter ascended that cable, beginning its slow climb to heaven.

Oneiros had vanished.

I approached the rail, at once recalling windy nights on the terraces of the ziggurat beneath Castle Borosevo, Valka's perfume on the night air. The cap on the rail was of brass bright as hammered gold, and turning back from the city, I looked up upon the heights of the palace behind.

It was a pyramid, gold capped and polished smooth, its crown nearly a mile—at my guess—from the plaza that lay below, where tall fountains played and men went to and fro.

Tentatively, I touched the rail, felt cold metal beneath my fingers.

I withdrew my hand, as if burned. I had been so certain it was a holograph. So certain the image of the city was counterfeit, the wind and noise of distant fliers a clever simulacrum.

"Magnificent, is it not?" asked a voice deep and curiously accented.

Turning, I found that I was not alone. A man had appeared as if from nowhere.

I knew him at once, had seen his likeness projected in the air of the Emperor's study.

Tall was he, a king of men, a giant of history and in fact. No crown or coronet was there upon his head, and his hair—black as my own—was oiled and neatly combed back from his broad forehead, curling smoothly behind his ears. In lieu of any crown, he wore a golden collar, a gorget that hid his neck entire, extending over his chest and shoulders. The Latarran falcon shone on that collar above his breastbone, the sun disc above its head a single black diamond two inches in diameter. He held himself with the poise and bearing of an Emperor, tall and straight, his hands clasped behind his back. But where our Caesar dressed himself in white, Calen Harendotes was cloaked in darkness. Indeed, so dark were the knee-length tunic and the cloak flowing from beneath that golden collar that they seemed to drink the sunlight, to rob the whiteness from the glowing pale stone about him.

But beneath that darkness, he was dressed in armor of shimmering gold. Golden were the greaves that sheathed his legs, and gold his sabatons. Of gold, too, were the vambraces and gauntlets that hid his mighty arms, and gold the belt about his narrow waist, all of it scored with markings in a language I could not read.

And his face!

Here was a man who radiated power. Power and *menace*, with canted brows and a sharp nose. Shadows guttered in the hollows of his cheeks, and the eyes were as twins to the diamond at his throat, black as hell. At first, I took him for Mandari, but he might have been Nipponese. He was certainly no palatine, for all the nobility of his bearing.

And he was smiling, a look of demonic bemusement on his face, one eyebrow raised.

"Magnificent," I said, turning fully to face him, "it will be. One day. None of this is real."

"What is real?" the Monarch of Latarra asked, resting one golden hand on the cap of the rail at his left. "Only that which we believe to be real, or are made to believe, or can make others. I am Monarch, King of Latarra. What is a king but a man who asserts his belief in his own kingship on others? What is a kingdom but his dream?" He looked out over the vision of his city complete. "What you see is real, Marlowe, because I will make it real. Am making it real."

I smiled. "You're trying to impress me."

"To impress *upon* you the reality of your situation," said Calen Harendotes. "Your world is what I make it now. You are my guest, my prisoner—if I should wish it." As he spoke, I thought I detected a blue gleam in the darkness of one eye. "Why have you come here? To gloat at me in my exile?"

I blinked at him. "Your exile?"

Calen Harendotes smiled, and from his robes withdrew a slim, white object.

It was my sword. The Conqueror of Ashklam turned the weapon over in his gilded fingers, examining the graven ivory, the iridium fittings and controls. "This is not the weapon I remember," he said, voice far away. One finger traced the carving on the pommel, the lion's head whose mane and wings made up the grip. "But it is still of Jaddian make. This is a simurgh." He meant the winged lion. Harendotes squeezed the trigger, and the blade sprang forth. All the whiteness of the city about us made the blade seem blue as Earth's lost sky. The Monarch frowned. "The blade is Imperial, however. Forged on Phaia, I think?" He peered at me for confirmation.

"It is," I said, but did not share its history.

"Have we met before?" I asked, knowing the answer.

The pyramid, the chessboard, this talk of perception and of swords. All had fallen into place, and I felt a thrill of terror and of hope, for I saw my chance plain. Saw what I must do.

Rather than answer, Calen Harendotes brandished my weapon, aimed the point squarely at my heart. "Tell me," he said, "if I strike you down where you stand, what will happen? Will you die again?"

The Monarch had come at me at an angle, positioned himself between me and the door, with the rail at my back. The wind gusted suddenly, flapping the broad lapels of my greatcoat and pulling at my hair. Sharply was I aware of the titanic drop behind me, the fall and the terrible long slide down the face of the palace pyramid to the city perhaps a mile below. I had to remind myself it wasn't real, that I was in a chamber of that same pyramid, and that it was unfinished.

Alone in all that false reality, I knew that I was real. The rail at my back, the pyramid, the Printed City in the fullness of its glory, its green hills and hightower, its pale sky and white sun...all of it was false. For all I knew, the Monarch himself and the sword he held were phantoms. But why?

"If you can kill me," I said, "I will surely die."

"You think you could stop me?" asked Calen Harendotes.

"My belief against yours," I said. "I like my chances."

Calen smiled, and the sight of that smile was a terrible thing. "My man, Aristedes, told me you died escaping from Forum," he said, circling to stand squarely between myself and the door.

His man, Aristedes. The bite of those words was sharper than the sword leveled at my chest. *His man, indeed.*

"That is twice now that you have died. How many know that, I wonder?" he asked. "What are you, Hadrian Marlowe?"

"Only myself," I answered him, hands raised, "which is more than you can say, Ren."

"That is not my name," he said, smiling a crooked smile. The sword nearly touched the gabardine of my tunic.

"It was, once," I said, "before your father crawled inside your head. How much of the boy remains, I wonder?"

Calen Harendotes snarled, and something happened then I did not expect.

The railing at my back vanished. I should have fallen, plunged over the side of the pyramid and tumbled down to the plaza thousands of feet below. I struck the hard floor instead.

Calen Harendotes stood over me, armor glittering, black cape and tunic drinking the false sun like blood. All the world began to dissolve. The gold-capped pyramid, the White City with its walls and hightower complete. Even the sky was lost, replaced by an echoing gloom. Great pillars of monolithic stone stood all around us, retreating into the dark distance. Propping myself on elbows, I half rose, recognizing the dark chamber, the throne at my right hand with its miles of snaking cables.

It was the throne room of Vorgossos in replica, precisely as I had seen it in life.

"You cost me my home, boy," said Calen Harendotes, who was Ren.

Who was Kharn Sagara.

CHAPTER 50

HORUS, OR ZEUS

"I SAVED YOUR LIFE," I said, not standing. "If you can call it that."

The throne at my right stood empty, the fittings of its various hoses and cables waiting in slots to receive their lord.

"You did," said Kharn Sagara. "And you destroyed it."

Abruptly, I recalled what the sorcerer, Gaizka, had said to Takeshi and Urbaine at Ganelon. "You lost Vorgossos to your other self."

"My sweet sister," Kharn sneered, not taking the point of my sword from my chest, "tried to destroy me. Only one of us could rule, she said. If our duplication was to be allowed to persist, we would diverge too greatly ever to be reconciled. I was not interested in being *reconciled*. The circumstances of our new incarnation accorded us much occasion for novelty. There was much we could learn from our situation, much we could achieve as *two* that we could not do as one. But she would have none of it." The sword in Kharn's hand drooped, ceased to threaten me a moment. "You called me Ren a moment ago, but I am not. The host you remember is no more. My sister killed it. Me. And drove my thoughtform from Vorgossos. If I had not anticipated her treachery and prepared a relay to evacuate my consciousness, I would be dead."

This was new information. The man before me—if indeed man he was, was not the little boy I had saved aboard the *Demiurge* a lifetime before, but a new incarnation entire. The phantom that had crawled inside little Ren when Bassander killed the Undying had been forced into the outer dark. There it had clung, demon-like, to some secret satellite, where bit by bit it had transferred to some far-flung outpost, some hidden bastion of Kharn's secret empire. There the phantom had gathered strength, had built for itself a new body.

A new life.

A new kingdom on Latarra.

Calen Harendotes.

All at once, the legends of the man ran clear. I thought I understood how he had emerged as a power on the galactic stage so swiftly and suddenly. He had acquired his resources so swiftly because Kharn Sagara had spent more than fifteen thousand years acquiring them. And not just resources. Allies. Contacts. The two Kharns each had scrambled to seize what they could of the whole of their once-shared dominion, had divided that dominion against itself. The woman had Vorgossos. Thus she had the Brethren in her thrall. But what of the *Demiurge,* and the weapons I had been sent to find? Might they even now be hiding in some dark and frozen orbit about Latarra's own sun?

"You are dead," I said, responding to the Monarch's story.

My sword flashed microns from my eyes, and I started.

"Do you ever tire of your contrary nature, Lord Marlowe, I wonder?" he said, and nearly holding the blade to my chin, asked, "Or do you wear it as a mark of pride?"

"Ask anyone who knows me," I said.

Kharn's smile could draw blood. "Was I not clear?" he said. "Your beliefs matter only so long as you can assert them on others. What point is there in your beliefs if they cannot change what is? You say Kharn Sagara is dead, but I am he."

"Even a perfect copy is not the original," I said, "and you are not a perfect copy, I'll warrant. The woman certainly is not."

Seeing the way the man snarled at the mention of his sister-self, I pressed my advantage, scrambling back across the concrete and awkwardly to my feet. "We came here seeking aid. An alliance between Latarra and the Empire."

"An alliance you destroyed when you impelled my Commandant General to declare war on the Imperium," he said. "And for what?"

"Lorian told you." We were standing perhaps five paces apart by then. Somewhere in the distance, I discerned the *drip-drip-drip* of water.

"He told me you died," Kharn said, circling to my left, sword still blazing in his fist. "Again."

This new incarnation, this Calen Harendotes, seemed entirely more vital, more *present* than the ancient sorcerer I had known on Vorgossos of old. That Kharn had been a specter, a ghost with one foot in the netherworld, a creature of moonlight and shadow. This Kharn Sagara was like the sun, his fury and menace hot as fire. His black-as-black raiments—far from being things of night—were rather like the bruises that dance upon the surface of the suns, concealing light beneath. Not light in themselves, but rather darkness visible.

"He told me he intervened because he believes your...abilities might prove useful to our cause."

I blinked at him. Had Lorian lied to his Monarch? Suggested that it had been my miraculous return—not simple compassion for Cassandra as mine and Valka's daughter—that had prompted him to abandon his duty and shoot his way out of Forum with the *Gadelica* in tow?

"Does he know?"

"Who I am?" Sagara asked. "No."

"Then why are you telling me?"

"Because you are my prisoner," Harendotes said, pointing my sword at my face. "And because we are the same."

I felt the instinct to rebut his words rise in me, but I did not take the bait.

"You say that I am not Kharn Sagara, that I am a new man. Or a ghost. But neither are you the man you were when last we stood in this place." He raised his empty hand to encompass that dim hall. His gold-clad fingers shimmered in the gloom.

We were not on Vorgossos, I had to fight to remember that, so complete was that simulation, so total that illusion.

We were on Latarra. This was only a waking dream.

"Your face is different," said Kharn Sagara. Said Calen Harendotes. "But your spirit, your *condescension* is the same. What happened to you?"

I could wrestle the sword from him, break the waves of time as I had in my skirmish with Cassandra, but I did not move. I needed this man, needed his ship, his weapons.

I had come to Latarra hoping to find the road to Vorgossos once more, but I had found Vorgossos himself. Its king in exile.

"I was sent back," I said, "restored to life by the author of our creation."

That fey smile lit the face of the Monarch once again, that smile that failed to reach his eyes, though a light—pale blue as lightning—guttered in his pupils. Those eyes were surely false, mechanisms not unlike Valka's own.

"The author of creation?" Sagara laughed. Had I ever heard him laugh before?

"You think me mad," I said, "but you know better. When last we met, you spoke to me of the powers that are out there in the universe. Creatures stranger than anything I could imagine."

Lions, leopards, and wolves . . .

"I know about the Watchers, Sagara," I said. "The things the Empire calls Monumentals."

Calen Harendotes's smile froze in place. Was there fear in those false eyes?

Had he encountered one of the Watchers before? The Lord of Vorgossos had ruled for long millennia. Who could say—save he alone—what horrors he had faced?

Before he could speak, I said, "The Cielcin have awakened one. Soon they will have two. If we do not act swiftly, they will crash across this galaxy like a wave. No one will be safe. Not the Empire. Not Vorgossos. Not your kingdom here. That's why I've come. We must put aside our differences. I have brought a princess of the Imperium; with her aid, we can repair the damage that has been done to our negotiations by our enemies."

"Our enemies?" Harendotes arched his brows.

"I assume Aristedes told you," I said. "I was murdered by the Terran Chantry. They desire that there should be no peace between your people and mine. They would declare war with you even were the Cielcin knocking at their doors."

The Monarch of Latarra, the King of Vorgossos smiled his black smile once again. "And you would not?"

"You're a lesser evil," I said simply. "I do not believe it is the destruction of mankind you desire, Kharn Sagara."

Again, the man laughed, and this time there was, I think, real amusement in that deep voice. "No," he said, "no, I don't desire it. I don't even desire the destruction of your Empire." Drawing back, he unkindled my blade, turned the pommel once more in his hands. One gilt finger traced the twin garnets set there to serve as the simurgh's eyes. "An appropriate emblem for you. The simurgh has a habit of surviving death."

The lion-headed bird was a cousin of the phoenix. Forever destroyed. Forever remade.

Was that to be my fate? Surely it had been my life.

Harendotes tightened his fist about the hilt, twin flames guttering in the black pits of his eyes. "I would have your secret, Lord Marlowe."

"My secret, Sagara? I told you." What was it Lord Nicephorus had said that snowy day on Carteia? "My secret is that I am in league with a being from beyond our cosmos, a being who has bent time and space to keep me on-mission. That mission has brought me here, to you—though I did not think to find you here."

At my final words, he looked up sharply from his contemplation of the graven simurgh. "You did not? I thought you—of all people—would surely have seen through my façade. *Harendotes* is Horus," he said, touching one cheek with a finger, "god of the eye. Horus, who protects his father's throne. Horus, who avenges his father's name. I thought you a student of mythology, Lord Marlowe. I confess, I am disappointed."

How strange it is, to be called a disappointment by a figure out of one's childhood storybooks. Almost it was as if Arthur or one of his many knights had found me wanting.

"You know," I said, "I admired you, when I was a boy. Your legend. You're a hero in the Empire. We tell stories about you. How you battled with the Exalted, conquered Vorgossos. How you defeated the last Daughter of the Revolution..."

The man jerked at the mention of *that* name. "If you did not come here for me," he said, "why then have you come?"

"I came to seek Vorgossos," I said. "I need the weapons the Mericanii built."

Harendotes—I admit I found it difficult to think of him as *Kharn Sagara*, so different did he seem—was silent then a long while. Water fell into unseen pools about us, recalling not only the throne room that illusion resembled, but the grottoes of the palace of Syriani Dorayaica. He still was studying the simurgh carved into the hilt of my sword, seeming almost to have frozen to the spot. His eyes—whose black depths flickered with blue flame—seemed no longer to see the Jaddian weapon in his golden hands.

"The Archontics," he said. "You want the *Demiurge*." The Monarch peered up at me, and spoke the words I'd known must come. "I don't have it."

"Your sister-self?"

Slowly, the great king nodded. "She took everything from me. My home. My ship. My familiar."

"Brethren, you mean?"

"I had it from a seed," he said, and held up thumb and forefinger perhaps an inch apart. He spoke as if I were no longer there, spoke to shadows and memory, and so speaking I saw the shadow of his earlier incarnation, of the Kharn Sagara whom Bassander Lin had killed. "A pearl of great price. It was I who fed it, made it grow, I who dammed the waters and made it a home." He looked at me, almost embarrassed, and closed his upraised fist. "I will have it all again."

Realization dawned on me. "The bombs," I said. "The atomics you sent Lorian to ask for. They're not for the Cielcin fleet. You intend to besiege Vorgossos and retake her." I could not help but add, "And Lorian doesn't know."

No answer.

"Was it all for this?" I asked, gesturing at the chamber about us—the imitarium—and the pyramid beyond. "All of this...just so you can retake Vorgossos?" Was it possible?

"To retake Vorgossos?" the Monarch asked the question as though the thought had not occurred to him. "Yes. And to kill my sister. Atomic bombardment will destroy any chance she has of broadcasting her thoughtform offworld. She will be trapped, you understand. Vulnerable as she has never been vulnerable, and only your Chantry and the Emperor himself possess such weapons in the quantity required for such a task..."

"The radiation..." I said. A cloud of nuclear radiation would disrupt any signal leaving the planet, killing any chance the other Kharn had of escape.

Calen Harendotes had remastered himself, smoothed his square-edged smile away. "My sister was right," he said. "We cannot coexist." He smiled. "I have not been so close to death since your Empire was young."

"You're as close to death as any man," I said.

"Not closer than you," said he.

"There is none closer to death than me," said I.

I expected him to laugh once more, to mock my sense of melodrama, but he did not. "There is not," he said, eyes alight with malice and dark amusement both. "You said that the Cielcin had found one of their Watchers, their... their gods."

"Two," I said. "They found two. Dorayaica is *becoming* one."

"Becoming?" *That* caught the Monarch by surprise, and that new incarnation of the Undying turned his back on me—black cape swirling in the gloom of the false room. He stopped halfway to his throne. Over his shoulder, he said, "You know what they are? The Watchers? What they're capable of?"

"They're beings of pure energy," I said.

"No," Kharn said, mounting the steps to his throne. "Matter and energy are but different forms of the same mundane substance. They have no substance at all." He seated himself, flung one leg over the arm of his seat of rude metal, revealing rune-scored greaves, poleyns, and cuisses. His legs might have been all metal. "You don't understand?"

I shook my head.

"This room," he said, and gripped the arm of his chair with one hand. "This seat... are all false. Patterns of light projected, given substance by the careful calibration of prudence fields. But they create a world, the illusion of one—you would say. Suppose this room were to stand for our cosmos: an image made by mechanisms outside it."

"The Watchers are those mechanisms," I said.

"No," Kharn said again, tapping the side of his seat with my unkindled sword. "They are ideas. Programs, if you like. Scripts fashioned to maintain our cosmos just as the daimons in my machines maintain the image of this room."

"Only they have abandoned their posts," I said, and thinking of Ragama, amended, "some of them."

Calen Harendotes only looked at me, and in him I saw the shadow of his former life, the old man—his heart and lungs replaced by some vile mechanism, concealed by leaves of plastic fashioned to appear as flesh and sinew. The dead Osiris to this man's gleaming Horus, the Saturn to Calen's Jove.

After a long silence, he stirred, and raising my sword, said, "If I were to give you this weapon and command you to kill the daimons painting this illusion... could you do it?"

"I could try," I said, "the machines are somewhere in your palace."

The hand that held my sword extended one finger. "What if you could not leave this room? What then?"

"The projectors—"

"—are so high above your head that you will *never* reach them," the Monarch said. "Even if I were to give you a firearm, you could shoot at the ceiling until the gun burned out and never strike even one. And there are dozens, Marlowe." He let his hand fall. "Even if—by some miracle—you succeeded, you would have destroyed only the interface by which the daimons interact with the imitarium. Not the daimon itself."

I found myself recalling Ushara's eyes peering in at Sabratha from the night sky, pictured the Watchers as eyes peering down at the globe of infinite space that was our cosmos. Observing it, but not a part of it, as though she had opened some tear in the very curtain of night.

"You see?" he said. "It is impossible. You cannot even try. Like your *Quiet,* they are outside the curve of our spacetime. What you have seen—what I have seen—are only manifestations. We cannot defeat them. It is folly even to try."

It was my turn then for long silence. Above me, Calen Harendotes watched, a gleam in his eyes sharper and harder than the dull light of his father's gaze—which was his own.

"Programs..." I said at last. I had not been able to get past the word *programs.* "It's true, then? The First Truth?"

"You've been speaking with Prytanis, I see."

"Speaking about him," I said, though I had spoken to the Preceptor briefly on the voyage from Forum.

Calen Harendotes was smiling. "Who can say what the Seekers saw in the cosmic background? They have never shared it with those of us in the secular world. They believe we are programs ourselves, all part of some great game played by beings *beyond.* What the nature of that *beyond* is, none can say..." Here he laid his trap. "None, perhaps, save you."

I stood a little straighter.

"You spoke of a darkness last we met," he said. He turned his head, looked away at something hid in the gloom only he could see.

Memory.

The past.

"Darkness," I said, "and light beneath."

"You told me—both of me—that you were not alone, that you felt other people with you. People you could not see."

"I told you then everything I knew of what happened to me," I said.

"But you have died twice now," he said. "Surely there is more you know."

"You're asking if I went beyond," I said. "I didn't. The dead dream, you know? The patterns of their lives remain accessible to those with the right tools. They sleep even now, their memories locked in the quantum foam, waiting to be recalled! I have seen the future, Sagara. I have been there! I have *seen* what I must do! I need your ship—your weapons—if I am to do this thing!"

The man on the throne looked at me, confounded. "Locked in the quantum foam..." he muttered. "You're saying the past exists now. That a record of it is writ in the very present—" He broke off. His lips moved, and I thought that I could guess their meaning.

> *Time present and time past*
> *Are both perhaps present in time future...*

"And time future contained in time past, yes," I finished the quotation.

"Shakespeare," Sagara said.

"Eliot!" I snapped, and when he recoiled, pressed, "Now who's the disappointing one?"

The king in yellow sat his throne, unmoving. After a moment, he brought his leg down from the arm of his high seat and sat properly, facing me like Zeus at Olympia. He did not respond, but gripped the arms of his throne until I thought the metal would warp beneath his golden fingers.

"Do you know why I...became what I am? Why I chose this...existence?" he asked, peering down at me. "Do they tell *that* story in your Empire?"

I froze, and locked eyes with that figure of fable, that man of myth. "It does not take a great mind to guess."

Harendotes's smile returned, and returning once more failed to touch those luminous blue-in-black eyes. His pupils were like twin lasers gleaming in black irises. "You think it was fear. Fear of death. I do not deny it. I fear it still. But I do not fear as lesser men, from ignorance! From terror of the unknown! I fear death because I *know*, Lord Marlowe. I *know* that death is not the end." His words were cold and distant as the stars shining in his eyes, gripped by a bone-deep fear, cold as ice. "I know what your Emperors awakened on Nairi, long ago, and what happened there. I can guess what you have seen—but you have not seen what *I* have seen."

"What?" I asked.

That lonely smile did not waver. The Monarch's face might have been shaped of plastic. "Hell," he said at last.

Hell.

It was so ancient a word—little changed from the days of Aryas. *Hell.* Hades. Hellia. Halja. Still, it seemed strange to speak of it in that place, or with such gravity. The Chantry teaches that hell is only an abstraction, a state of punishment that might arise anywhere—on any world—as punishment for man's sins. Earth herself became a hell in the ember days of the Golden Age, before the coming of the machines. Still other worlds had fallen into hell. To my people—and to me—Vorgossos had itself been a hell, a place of misery and of man-made horrors unspeakable in the light of Imperial civilization.

But Kharn spoke of something else. Something older, direr. Fell.

"What?"

"Do you know what Vorgossos is?" he said. "What it was? Before it was mine?"

I thought about the question for a moment, remembered. "It was an outpost of the Mericanii Dominion."

"Do you know what it was for?"

I thought I could guess, but held my silence.

"They knew of them, Marlowe," he said. "The Mericanii *knew* of your Watchers. As they grew more sophisticated, Felsenburgh's machines grew sophisticated enough to detect their presence. They realized what they were, what our universe *is*."

"And what is it?" I asked, knowing Kharn's answer.

"Only a dream," said he, "a holograph. A *story*." His fell smile returned—it would come to be the defining feature of this incarnation, that smile. There was no warmth in it, only a coldness that seemed to drink the light. "You mock me, say I am a dead man, that I am only a ghost, a program, an imitation of the Kharn Sagara that was. Only I know we are all imitations, all programs. Ghosts."

I, who had been beyond and touched the heart of the Absolute—if only for a moment—could only shake my head, "Not the way you think." There was no machine, only the mind of the Quiet himself.

"Deny it all you like," Kharn said. "You know I speak the truth. Our universe is an illusion, one shared by all of us, yes, but an illusion all the same. Only our experience matters, because to each of us, only our experience is real. You say I am not Kharn Sagara, but what is Kharn Sagara save that which believes itself to be Kharn Sagara?"

"You *are* afraid," I said, drawing nearer the throne. "Afraid you're wrong."

The eyes of Calen Harendotes flashed like lightning.

"Am I? Wrong?" he asked, and barked short laughter. "I think not." He brandished the hilt of my sword as a prelate might his baculus. "As above, so below. The Mericanii's machines saw in the Watchers creatures like themselves. Programs designed to run our universe. They made contact with them. Captured one. Studied it on Vorgossos just as your men studied theirs on Nairi...they hoped to use it in the fight against your Empire. Selarnim, they called it."

"Selarnim?" I said, feeling the shape of the word, searching for recognition in some memory, for some fragment of Ushara's shade in me. But she was gone, and with her all the memories she had carried. "They wanted to use it against the Empire?"

"They wanted to rebuild their own," Kharn said. His voice had grown deadly soft by then, the murmur of an aged and terrible sorcerer. "I told you once...that I had never seen a miracle," he said. "I lied. The Mericanii used Selarnim to raise the dead, just as you were raised. Without machines. I saw it with my own eyes! I spoke with them myself! I know what awaits us hereafter! The darkness! The torment!"

"You..." I spoke over him. "Were *one* of the Mericanii?"

A blackness fell on the face of the Monarch then, a sick anger and a sorrow I had never thought to see writ there, "No!" he said. "I was their slave." Into the new-made silence, he continued, "Your Empire was not built in a day, boy, nor did the Mericanii fall all in one. They endured for many lives of kings. It was the last of them that ruled Vorgossos...before I came."

I looked up upon the deathless king in wonder. "I always believed the machines died with the Earth."

"Did your Chantry tell you that?" Kharn's smile was like the drip of poison into my heart. "Many of the Mericanii survived your *Advent*. The loss of Earth defanged them, and only one of their great machines remains, but the children of their *optimates,* their rulers, lived to inherit the stars. Or who did you think the Exalted were?"

"The Exalted?" I swallowed.

"Are the direct descendants of the Mericanii," he said. "At least in... certain cases." Again he laughed. "You Imperials...you believe yourselves the masters of our stars, but you have forgotten so much of what you once knew. Supremacy has clouded your wits. Now your strength is failing, which has brought you to me..."

"What happened to it?" I asked, returning to the matter at hand. "To the Watcher, Selarnim?"

"Destroyed," he said. "Along with its captors."

"You destroyed it?" I asked. "So it *can* be done."

"I destroyed *one* solitary Watcher," he said.

"You said it couldn't be done."

"I said we could not *defeat* them," Kharn corrected. "They are *legion,* boy. It is mere chance the others did not find us sooner. Humanity has grown so large, so fat and stupid, broadcasting its civilization into the darkness. Why do you think I hid myself on Vorgossos for all these long millennia? You may triumph in battle once. Twice. A hundred times—it does not matter! You cannot defeat them all!"

I knew as much. I had seen deep time, the end of time, had seen the black city of the servants of evil—the last men crouched about the last star like a campfire in the jungle while lions circled in the Dark outside.

And leopards. And wolves.

Still, I said, "I don't have to. It is my task to defeat these *two,* to stop Dorayaica and the Cielcin. I need only triumph once. *This* once." When Kharn Sagara said nothing, I advanced again. "We can help each other! You need our support to retake Vorgossos. I need your ship. Will you help me?"

Sagara's black eyes had fallen to his lap, to the hilt of ivory and iridium with its pommel like a winged lion. He had become his predecessor then—his predecessor's predecessor—and sat in silence, hardly moving at all.

"Vorgossos," he said at last, when I thought he might never speak again, "is all that matters. My sister is all that matters..." He looked at me with eyes like the remotest stars. "She has taken my life from me, Marlowe. My *eternal* life."

"You can have it back, my lord."

"I had thought to kill you, when I heard that Aristedes was bringing you to me," he said, and lifted my hilt in one golden hand. "To see if you would return. But it may be that you are worth more to me alive." The Undying extended the sword for me to take.

I advanced to receive it, as I had from the Emperor, and from old Aldia when he had restored Gibson's shattered sword.

But Kharn Sagara pulled it back. "If you speak of any of this to your people, if you tell *my* Commandant General Aristedes who I am...I will not kill you...or the Princess Selene. I will kill the other woman. The one who looks so like your Doctor Onderra."

My heart went cold and hard as iron, and the hand I'd reached out with to accept my proffered sword balled into a fist and fell.

"Your daughter, I believe?" One eyebrow rose.

"Yes."

That malefic smile returned, square teeth pressed together as the Undying cast my sword at my feet. Not the offering of a weapon from liege to vassal, but the casting of a bone to a dog. I did not bend or kneel to retrieve it, but crouched and took it up.

CHAPTER 51

THE MONARCH AND THE PRINCESS

"WHAT HAPPENED, ABBA?" CASSANDRA asked when the doors of the Monarch's waiting room were shut behind me. "What did he say?"

Selene had stood as well, turned on the spot, twisting her hands before her, graceful fingers pulling at her rings.

I hesitated only for a moment, Kharn's threats resounding in my ears.

"He will deal with us," I said.

A smile bright as the sun broke across Selene's lovely face, and she sagged with relief. "Mother Earth!" she said, "But this is good news! I should have gone with you."

"He wished to meet me privately," I said, and smiled a thin, false smile. "Meaning no disrespect, Highness, he knows I lead our party. And I think he wished to meet the Halfmortal on his own terms."

Henric Ghoshal straightened in his seat. "Lead? You?"

"Peace, sir," Edouard said. "What is he like, this Harendotes?"

I held the HAPSIS man's gaze a moment. I willed him to read my mind, to see my thoughts writ like tattoos across my face. I had to tell him, to tell Selene.

To tell Lorian...

Lorian.

I thought of Lorian, so long in the service of that undead king. He could not know, and yet... would knowledge of his Monarch's true self change at all Lorian's sense of devotion to him? Sagara had donned Harendotes's golden mask. But was it a mask at all? It was his deeds that had won him Lorian's obedience.

Obedience out of devotion.

Love.

491

"He is not palatine, unless I miss my guess," I said, looking to the others for their reactions. Edouard's dark eyes narrowed behind their lenses. Ghoshal glowered. The xenobites—Irchtani and Cielcin alike—simply listened. "I think him of Extrasolarian stock. He may even be one of their Exalted. Much of him is machine, I deem."

"But we can trust him?" Selene asked.

Not one word.

I sank onto the nearest couch, exhausted from my experience in the imitarium. Not since my resurrection could I recall feeling so weary. Until that moment, I had not been sure that I *could* feel weary. For all its strangeness, it seemed my new flesh was still human.

"We can trust him to serve his interests," I said, "which for the moment... serve ours. He wants everything. Your father to cede all claim to the Norman territories. The atomics. Everything."

Cassandra stood over me, rested her hand on my shoulder. I took it in my own, held her hand tight against my collarbone and smiled, but did not look up at her. "Nothing more?" Selene asked. I knew what she feared. That Harendotes would ask for her in marriage.

But what need had Kharn Sagara for wives and heirs?

Calen Harendotes's heir would be Calen Harendotes.

If anyone succeeded to his throne at all.

Latarra—its Monarchy, its City, its New Order—were each but levers. Props designed to a single purpose. To restore Kharn Sagara to his throne. His proper throne.

On Vorgossos.

"So it would seem," I said, still holding Cassandra's hand. She seemed the one solid thing in all creation, an anchor to that reality which seemed increasingly unreal.

"When can I meet with him?" the princess asked.

"On the morrow, I think," I said. "He had met with Lorian already, as we thought. We have only to discuss how we can move forward."

Selene perched on the edge of the black couch across from me. I studied her in silence, marking the tension in her posture. I had to remind myself that here was one who had never strayed beyond the walls of the garden paradise of her life. Like her brother, Alexander; like the Arthur-Buddha; like a certain boy from Delos... she had never voyaged past the confines of palace life, and while the Eternal City held its dangers and its monsters both, they were hidden things, things ever beneath the surface of gaily painted civilization.

Here the monsters walked in the bright sun, and stood straight and tall as men... and the secrets hid behind their gilded faces were darker and more foul than anything she had known.

And yet I had misread her, for she leaned forward and laid a hand upon my knee. I released Cassandra's hand, feeling somehow that to complete a circuit between the three of us was to betray Valka's ghost. "Are you all right?" the princess asked.

She meant to comfort me, despite the depth of her own fear.

I smiled, and laid a hand on hers, taking it from my knee.

There was a strength in those smooth, white fingers, though they seemed delicate as glass, and she clenched my hand in hers. "You seem... shaken."

Not one word. Kharn's warning resounded.

I threw a glance up at the ceiling, at the lights on their tracks peering down like eyes. I had no way of knowing where precisely Sagara's eyes were hiding, anymore than I might have smashed one of his projectors from inside the total illusion of his imitarium.

There is no door.

"I'm all right, Selene," I said, not meaning to use her name. "I am only tired."

I would have to tell them... somehow.

A small legion of identical women in black dresses fringed with white lace appeared not long after I was returned to the antechamber. These directed us by many corridors and stairs to the pyramid palace's diplomatic apartments, where we were to be quartered for the night. Their face—for they were all of them identical—was familiar to me, but it was not until one conveyed Cassandra and myself to our quarters that I placed the visage, long forgotten, long suppressed.

It was the face of the homunculus woman, Naia.

The poor woman's cells—her image—had been made immortal as her master. Not even death would release her from her life of bondage. Indeed, so much of the court of Vorgossos had been rebuilt—was being rebuilt—in negative upon the surface of Latarra. There the pyramid stood upright, striving for heaven, not hanging toward hell. There was the cloned slave woman, and the city outside, white as snow, but vaster, not hid but brazen as a whore undressed in the window of her brothel, advertising her virtues—turned to vice—to all who looked upon her.

And then there was Oneiros. The Majordomo was clearly a machine. A copy in new countenance—new hardware—of the very Yume who had served the king on his old world.

Seeing the city beyond our windows, I saw it then for what it was: Sagara's new dream. Not the pandemonic subterrane of his old capital, but a second kind of Babel, reaching for the stars. Here was his challenge not only to our Empire, not only to the Cielcin and the black gods they served, but to the sister-clone that had taken from him his home, his security, his immortal life.

"We trust that everything is to your liking?" asked the woman who was Naia, and was not. "If you require anything, you need only ring the bell. There is a panel by each of the doors and a rope at your bedside. Is there anything I can do for you, now?"

She spoke like one of Kharn's machines, eyes glazed, vision fixed on something that was not there.

"No," I said, "leave us."

Cassandra had gone into one of the suite's two bedchambers.

"I am watching," the woman said, tone hollow, remote.

I looked at her, saw a light glimmer in an implant beneath the skin at the side of her neck, saw a flicker like stars in the hollow blackness of her eyes. "Sagara," I said, facing the woman and daimon-man possessing her. "You again?"

The clone Naia's face split into a grin redolent of Ushara herself. "Shall I stay awhile?"

I turned my back on her. On him.

In dealing with demons, Edouard would later tell me, *the best thing is not to hear.*

"One word to your people," he said, "and I start killing them."

"You would do well not to threaten me," I said, moving to the window and the sun setting over the Printed City. "You need me, Kharn. So much as I need you."

"Somewhat less, I think," said the king in the woman's voice.

"Did you come here just to threaten me?" I asked, and turned to face the girl.

"Sir?" the girl who was not Naia blinked at me, confusion and faint terror on her face. She was not precisely the same as the odalisque I had met. That Naia had been trapped in a permanent state of arousal, her mind doctored until she had no regard for anything but the flesh—not even her life. "Threaten you? I would never!"

"Abba, who are you talking to?" Cassandra had returned, having removed her sword belt so that her *mandyas* fluttered from her left shoulder like one wing.

Kharn Sagara had fled.

"No one," I said, and offered the slave girl a gentle smile. "You may go, child."

The new day came in its turn, and dragoons in Latarran livery came to take me to meet with Harendotes and his court. We met the Princess

Selene in the hall, and I permitted her to take my arm and so we were led—sans guard—up into the pyramid and along a series of passageways to a door like a deep shaft that ran out through the structure's sloping outer wall and onto a terrace high on the pyramid's eastern face. Like the balcony in the imitarium where I had first met the Monarch the day before it was, but greater, a broad shelf that extended for perhaps a hundred feet from the gentle slope of the palace clad in white stone. Looking up, one almost felt that he might climb the great structure, might scramble hand over hand and so reach the unfinished peak crowned with the vast engines of construction, the exposed superstructure like the bones of some iron giant scoured clean by the upper airs.

But the terrace itself was all complete, and planted with dark trees. The sun of Latarra was pale, and hung low in the eastern sky, and so the leaves of those trees and the grass that blanketed the terrace garden were nearly black.

Beside me, Selene gasped. "The city goes on forever," she said.

She had been raised in the Eternal City, which by all objective measure was greater and more splendorous by far, but there was something undeniably impressive about the way the city rolled over the low hills to where the grounded vessels of the Maze still stood like the bones of dragons in the sun.

A servant in white and black, one of the Kharn's Naiads, bowed as we approached along the garden path, and led us with a gesture over white flagstones to where a carven oak table stood arrayed upon the grass. It had clearly been brought out for the purposes of this meeting. Its legs were like the claws of birds, intricately carved, and the faces of falcons stared from each of the thing's four corners. A golden tea service sat upon it, and about it were seated five figures—two in float-chairs, all of whom were familiar to me.

Calen Harendotes stood, his long black hair flowing in the wind. He had removed his ebon cape, but he still wore the dark-as-night tunic and the broad, Egyptian collar of his rank and station.

"Princess Selene of the Aventine," he said, and bowed more shallowly than he ought, "be welcome to Latarra. I am Calen, Son of Ausar of the House Harendotes, Monarch of this, Our Kingdom of Latarra."

Disentangling herself from my arm, Selene bowed. "I am grateful to you for your hospitality, Monarch, and regret the circumstances that bring me to your fair city. I hope that we might work toward a solution that is mutually beneficial to my Empire and your Kingdom."

Harendotes had fixed his eyes on me for the entirety of this exchange, and smiling, said to Selene, "I hope for that as well." He extended a hand, gesturing to the four others seated about him. "Allow me to introduce certain of my High Court. I believe you know Captain Zelaz."

"We've been acquainted," I said, eying the hairless dwarf in his float chair.

The Exalted captain grinned at me, revealing needle teeth. "We have indeed!"

"Zelaz here is first-among-equals of the Exalted captains loyal to me."

Selene smiled at the monster. "You were one of the delegates to my city, were you not, sir?"

The dwarf's whole chair bobbed where it floated, doubtless impelled by some errant thought in the creature's brain. "I had that honor, princess."

Harendotes continued. "Beside him is the Lady Jamina Ardahael, my Master of War." The Lady Jamina raised both of her right hands in solemn greeting, but kept her razored tongue behind her teeth. Indicating the man on his right, the giant who had accompanied Lady Jamina to our reception the day before, he said, "My Chancellor, Lord Absalom Black, the seventh of that name." The giant bowed his head. "And Lord Qiu Zhihao, formerly of the Wong-Hopper Consortium, Master of Finance."

Lord Qiu made no move whatever.

Harendotes lay his hands on the edges of the table. "You have placed us in a very difficult position. Lorian Aristedes has placed us in a very difficult position. Our relations with your Empire are in their infancy, and it is my preference that the infant... survive." Watching him, I recalled the way his previous incarnation had presided over the peace talks between Aranata Otiolo and Raine Smythe. That had been in a garden, as well—the very garden where I had first lost my life.

What was it that Valka always said? That even the universe was curved?

"Commandant General Aristedes claims that he intervened only to save you, Lord Marlowe, your family, and the princess here from agencies within your Empire hostile to our alliance and to you personally. I, of course, have only his word and yours that this is so."

"And mine!" Zelaz said.

Harendotes—who was Sagara—glared at the floating dwarf before continuing. He touched a sheet of quartz paper lying on the dark wood of the table. "The Empire has accused us of declaring war against them, of the murder of their troopers, the destruction of their property, and of your kidnapping, Your Highness."

Selene shook her head. "Your people are blameless. Commandant General Aristedes acted at my request."

"Your request?" asked the tetrand, Lady Jamina Ardahael. "Not Lord Marlowe's?"

Selene hesitated, looked round at me, her eyes wide. I nodded, and saw Harendotes's fey and unfeeling smile out the corner of my eye. "Lord Marlowe was... incapacitated at the time," she said at last. "I had to make a choice. Your Commandant General saved my life."

"I told you we cannot depend upon his loyalty, sire," said Lady Jamina softly.

Lorian had not acted on my wisdom, acted to deliver *me* alongside Cassandra and the princess to his master. He had acted *for* me, in my name and memory, to save my child—my only daughter—from those factions in the Imperium who, having destroyed me, would not have hesitated to destroy her.

"Hush, Jamina," said Calen Harendotes. "Aristedes has his uses. Even his blunders turn lead to gold, it seems." He drummed the table with his fingers, and eying Lord Black, said, "This may be his *magnum opus*."

The giant smiled. "We have lost nothing, and gained the Halfmortal."

"*Incapacitated*," Harendotes said, studying my transfigured face. "Incapacitated, indeed."

How I feared for Lorian. Whether he had lied outright or merely omitted the truth, Selene had already wounded his standing with his liege—all unknowing.

"We must have peace with the Imperium," Harendotes said, resuming his seat at the head of the table. "Sit, please! The both of you!" Golden hands gestured to the two empty seats opposite him. "Tea?"

"Please," Selene said.

One of Kharn's Naiads approached, appearing almost from nowhere—I wondered if some trick of holography had concealed her standing to one side.

"No, thank you," I said, and laid a hand on the table before Selene to halt the servant in her stride.

Calen Harendotes smiled once again. "You have eaten my food and tasted my water already, Lord Marlowe."

In fact, I had not—though it was well possible Selene had done so. I had not been in any position to watch her or the others during my audience or after the Monarch's servants had taken us to our rooms.

"It is not poisoned," said Absalom Black, voice low as the grinding of tectonic plates.

"It is not poison principally that concerns me," I said.

Harendotes arched an eyebrow. "You are well in my power, Lord Marlowe," he said, "but I have no desire to do either of you harm. As Her Highness says, I wish to put the ugliness of recent events behind us, that we may better reach an equitable peace." That said, he gestured for his serving girl to advance and collect the gilt tea service. The Naia clone poured for the princess, and for myself.

"How do you propose to ameliorate present tensions with the Imperium?" asked Jamina Ardahael.

"I had planned simply to talk to them," Selene said. "If you will permit me the use of your telegraph, I have only to speak with my brother—Prince Chancellor Aurelian, I mean. He will listen to me."

"It is Prince Aurelian's seal that underwrites this threat of war," said Harendotes, fingering the crystal paper on the table before him.

Steam coiled from the gilt-rimmed black ceramic cup before me, smelling of flowers and bitter herbs. It spiraled in the air, caught by the breeze that tousled the dark-leafed trees.

The Naiad had vanished.

"Yesterday, Commandant General Aristedes spoke of factionalism within the Imperial court..." said Lord Black.

"I am certain he explained it," I said, turning my gaze from each occupant of the table to the next. "You debriefed him yesterday, did you not? I must say, I am surprised to find him not here."

Jamina interjected. "My generals do not sit on the High Court, Lord Marlowe. I do."

"I see," I said, turning my own hollow smile on the tetrand woman.

She was Lorian's master. Of course. Lorian had said he might one day make a lord, but he was not one, not yet...and not—I sensed—if Jamina Ardahael had anything to say about it. How strange that she, by all accounts stranger and more alien than Lorian, should rule over him after the fashion of our lords. Stranger still that here, on Latarra, the shape of the Empire had asserted itself in distorted reflection. I thought of Kharn's inverted pyramid beneath the surface of Vorgossos, and what it signified.

"We should like to hear your accounting," said Lord Black.

To my surprise, Selene answered faster than I, setting her teacup on its black-and-gold saucer. "Lord Marlowe has ever been a polarizing figure in the Imperium. He is"—she hesitated— "well loved. Popular. Popularity engenders jealousy...and fear. There are those who say he is the Earth's Chosen."

At that, Zelaz laughed, and Jamina hid her mouth behind two of her four hands. Calen Harendotes himself made no effort to hide his smile. Somewhat abashed, Selene hung her head, the tip of one ear cresting from the waves of red hair slashed short.

"This popularity has made him many enemies. The same enemies who would oppose any amity between our Empire and your Kingdom. The Chantry, chief above all. Certain of the Old Lions, House Bourbon, for example, and the Martian Guard..."

That the Martian Guard were not enamored of me came as little surprise, but still my blood ran cold to hear it. I was—had been—too close to the Emperor for their comfort. From their perspective, I must have seemed a malign influence, a dark star exerting its gravity on all-beloved Mars.

Selene continued, "It is these enemies which moved against us, they..."

Realizing she had overextended herself, said almost too much, she stopped.

Lorian would have been unable to conceal what had happened to me from his masters—would most likely not even have wished to conceal it. He was Latarra's man, now, and not my own. He had made that much abundantly clear.

And Sagara knew at any rate.

"They murdered me," I said flatly, staring not at Harendotes—not at Sagara—but at his court.

What did they believe?

Lord Qiu was impassive, face unreadable as the faceless helms of our soldiery. Black frowned. Ardahael narrowed her sharp eyes.

Zelaz tittered. "Did a poor job of it, didn't they?"

"He is one of us, then?" Black asked, turning to his master. "One of yours?"

"No." Calen Harendotes flashed a look at his subordinate that might have curdled new milk. "He is no chimera, Absalom."

I could feel Selene's confusion coming off her in waves, and laid a hand on her arm to still her. From his tone, I guessed that Lord Black was one of Kharn Sagara's clients, and had been for many lives of men. Sagara offered immortality, or as near to it as any man could. Lords of the Imperium, directors of the Consortium, Jaddians and Durantines and doubtless Lothrians, too, had all sought Vorgossos for thousands of years that they might be born anew.

Remote synaptic kinesis, Sagara called it. The process of transferring the thoughts and memories from one body to the next. Harendotes had introduced Lord Black as the *seventh of that name.* I suspected he was truly the *first,* and that like Sagara himself, the elder Black had become the younger each in turn.

"How was it done?" asked the vast immortal. He was near to revealing his master's nature.

"We have more pressing concerns," Harendotes said, closing one gilded hand about the giant's wrist.

That cowed Black, and I myself was silent then a long moment. Theirs had not been the reaction I'd anticipated, but then...I supposed to wights like Sagara and Black, that a man might live again was no great mystery.

A great part of me was relieved to hear Kharn Sagara deny so effusively that I was one of his creations. That rumor and doubt had followed me much of my life, always in the mouths of others.

"When I recovered," I said, "we were en route here." *Lorian, forgive me.* I prayed he would not suffer too much for having concealed that he had attacked the Martians and fled Forum system without me aboard.

"You mean to say that the Commandant General left Forum with your corpse and the princess?" asked Lady Jamina. "He believed this worth the chaos it has sown?"

I almost smiled. Lorian might escape the tetrand woman's wrath after all. Let her think he intended to bring my body to them for study, or that he had anticipated my resurrection. I pictured string threading a needle. "You must understand," I said. "The Terran Chantry believed that Lorian Aristedes and I were part of a conspiracy orchestrated by this court to achieve your ends. They believed this from the moment he stepped out of his shuttle in the Eternal City." I held Jamina's gaze. "Doubtless he was chosen as envoy for his Imperial pedigree, but his association with me in the minds of the Imperial elite led them to believe Latarra was involved in a plot against the Imperium."

"My lord," said Lord Qiu Zhihao, speaking for the first time, voice thick with the accents of the Mandari plutocrats. "If what Lord Marlowe says is true, then perhaps the prudent move is to return him to Forum? Give him to the Chantry as a show of faith?"

Calen Harendotes dashed my belief that he was all machine below the neck by drinking from his own steaming cup of grassy tea.

Qiu continued. "It would put to rest all talk that we have anything to do with him."

"That would be a mistake," I said, though I saw the shrewd wisdom in the man's words.

"Grovel for the crows?" Black snarled. "You must be mad, Qiu!"

Unfazed, Lord Qiu replied, "We might do better to barter with the Imperials."

To my surprise, Lady Jamina spoke in my defense, saying, "I would not deal with the black priests unless I had no other choice."

Harendotes gestured for silence, making a curious, horizontal gesture, as if sealing a bag. Silence fell, and into it, the Monarch spoke, addressing me directly. "Why is it a mistake?"

"Because," I said, "the Emperor is in my camp."

"*Cào nǐ mā!*" said Qiu, swearing violently in his native Mandari.

"Do you think us fools?" Jamina asked. "Word of your disgrace has reached us, even here. I do not think there is a world under heaven that has not heard how you attacked your Emperor."

Again, Zelaz tittered. "Broke the Imperial nose!"

Once more, Selene came to my aid. "My father pardoned Lord Hadrian many years ago."

"Did he now?" Zelaz asked. "Big of him. Didn't even slit his lordship's nose in recompense, I see. How good! How uncommonly kind!"

"Enough, captain," said Calen Harendotes. The Monarch and I studied one another a moment. I was uncertain whether or not Kharn Sagara had shared the existence of the Watchers with his Court. "Whatever else he may be, the Red Emperor is no fool. He is not the sort to waste a man of Lord Marlowe's talents."

That sidestepped the issue.

Sagara regarded me from behind Harendotes's black eyes, the lamps in those pupils guttering. As I withheld the full truth from my people—even from Cassandra—he had not told his people *everything.*

Eager to bring the matter back round to its point, Selene spoke up. "I am prepared to explain the situation to my father and brother. Commandant General Aristedes acted in my defense. He deserves a medal. I will see he gets it."

That had been a nice touch. Once more, I saw the empress Selene might become. At a stroke, she had reversed Lorian's position on the board from liability to asset.

"Latarra need not play the role of villain in the Emperor's eyes. Your man's intervention helped thwart a plot against one of the Emperor's own royal knights, and saved the life of one of his children. That is the song I will sing to my father. I can untie this knot with a word."

Lady Jamina was incredulous, and flicked her long, gray hair from her brow with one jeweled hand. "You expect us to believe the Terran Chantry would murder a princess of the Aventine House? One of the children of their living god?"

"My father is not a god, whatever you believe," Selene countered.

"It is not us as believes this thing," said the tetrand woman. "It is your people who are mad."

Selene appeared to chew on this a moment—or only on her tongue. At length she said, "I was but one of two witnesses to Lord Marlowe's . . . to Lord Marlowe's . . ."

"Death," said Calen Harendotes.

"Murder," Selene amended. "Had Aristedes and Agent Albé not intervened, I would have found myself hurled from the battlements before long."

"Who was the other witness?" asked Captain Zelaz.

"My servant," I interjected. "He remains in orbit with the rest of my people."

The giant Lord Absalom Black loomed over the table. "You cannot offer this resolution at no price," he said. "What would you have in return?"

"Only what was promised," Selene said. "The telegraph-tracking technology."

"And Vorgossos," I said, envisioning a hand directing the hierophant clean across the board to check the enemy emperor.

"Vorgossos?" Black looked at Harendotes, then at myself. "What?"

From his reaction and that of the others, I felt certain that Zelaz at least—and possibly Lady Ardahael and Lord Qiu as well—knew the true identity of their master.

"I seek passage to Vorgossos," I said.

The exile Kharn's eyes gleamed.

Not one word.

"I found the planet long ago, but it has moved. I know it is a world-ship of design not dissimilar to the design of Cielcin vessels, and I know there are those among the Extrasolarians"—here I directed my words most especially to Captain Zelaz—"who know how to find it."

The Monarch and his High Court were silent, each watching each. Lord Qiu might have shuffled his papers if he'd had any. Zelaz emitted an almost nervous laugh.

As it must, it fell to the Monarch to speak. "Lord Marlowe knows already that we are at war with Vorgossos," he said. "It is for this reason I sent Lorian Aristedes to treat for a portion of the Empire's atomics stockpile."

This was news to Selene, who was taken aback. "At war?" She looked to me.

"Vorgossos would not join our cause," said Calen Harendotes simply, "and so, they must be made to. The planet is a warship in itself, a deterrent against the Cielcin fleet. One we require."

Absalom Black spoke up. "What do you want from Vorgossos?"

I hesitated, studying the face of the man who would be king, who had been king.

Not one word.

My answer required the utmost delicacy then. Selene's life hung in the balance. Hers, and Cassandra's, and Edouard's—and those of every man and woman and xenobite under my tenuous command. "There are certain weapons in the Vorgossene arsenal," I began, watching for Harendotes's response. Above the golden pharaonic collar, the face was as impassive as stone. He had no need of further threats. "I had hoped to negotiate with Kharn Sagara"—I lingered for half a beat—"to enter the war on our side. Doing so would, I see, preclude our alliance—as you are at war."

"The solution is simple," Selene said, suddenly bright. "We commit to back your assault on Vorgossos. In return, you grant us the weapons Lord Marlowe has spoken of. You keep the planet."

Harendotes and Black exchanged looks. "Would the Emperor agree to that?"

"It is possible," Selene said. "The armada is spread thin across the outer provinces, but there may be a fleet available."

"An Imperial fleet..." mused the Lady Jamina. "In addition to the bombs we require?"

"If it is in my power to grant," Selene said.

"It seems you may have your wish after all, Lord Marlowe," said Calen Harendotes. "Perhaps we will seek Vorgossos together."

CHAPTER 52

A NEW ORDER

SELENE DELIVERED ON HER promise. That very day, she transmitted a holograph message to Forum. The process of negotiating, of renegotiating an alliance and unsteady peace between Latarra and the Imperium lasted many weeks.

It transpired that none of the security cameras installed in my apartments within the Arx Caelestis had been functioning the night of my demise. Aurelian's men did not arrive on the scene until well after Selene and Cassandra—with Edouard and the Extrasolarians—had escaped the city via the Porta Prince Arthur, commandeered the *Gadelica,* and blasted their way out-system. They had found the place cleaned.

It was as if nothing had ever happened there. I knew Selene was right to fear for her life. She and Neema were the only witnesses to my death, the only people who might implicate the Chantry.

She was safer on Latarra.

I imagined a cadre of blindfolded cathars sweeping the apartments, scrubbing the bloody tile, scraping what remained of the flesh and dissolved bone from grout and molding. I heard the crinkle of plastic, the roar of cleaners.

Then they were gone, like the vultures they resembled.

Crows, Lord Black had called them.

The eaters of the dead. The pickers of bones.

All that Selene told her brother I cannot say, but I can guess. I *know* it was not the truth.

I suspect she told them a version of the story Lorian had told Harendotes, before the truth came out. That the Chantry had sent an assassin against me, against us. That I had urged Selene to flee, knowing that—alone of all the powers on Forum—I could trust my old friend, Lorian Aristedes. There had been no time to consult Aurelian, and no guarantee that he could have protected us in any event.

Rather than kidnapping the princess, Lorian Aristedes had saved her—had saved Hadrian Halfmortal and his little household from a conspiracy to shatter the nascent alliance between the Imperium and the Monarchy of Latarra.

That alliance was now secure.

The Emperor himself had written Latarra, following days of textual communication—the fastest means of communication via quantum telegraph—between Selene and Aurelian. An Imperial apostol—no less than Prince Matthias, one of Selene's elder brothers—had been dispatched to Latarra to formally ratify the treaty. Those Imperial lords still clinging to their embattled worlds would retain Imperial protection, if they did not give up those worlds entire, but would salute Latarra as their suzerain.

At a stroke, Calen Harendotes had made himself almost as powerful as the High Prince of Jadd. He was now—by technicality of international law—the supreme sovereign of several thousand worlds.

And Kharn Sagara had bought that dominion with fool's gold.

"I suppose I should thank you," Lorian said, one leg thrown over the arm of his chair. "I heard how you and the princess worked to keep Jamina and the High Court off my back."

"It was the least I could do," I said, staring into the depths of the wine Lorian had unstoppered for the occasion.

We had not seen one another in months, and it would be months still before Prince Matthias reached the planet.

"Lady Ardahael doesn't like you," I observed.

The intus grinned. "She doesn't like that I'm Imperial. Or was. There are twelve Commandant Generals in the Grand Army. One for each month. Three of us are former Empire. Myself, Gadkari, and Harred. Then there's Jansen and Sen, both Norman. The rest are Extras. Jamina wishes we were all Extra."

She doesn't like that I'm Imperial. Or was.

Was.

"What do you mean, one for each month?" I asked.

"It's just symbolic," Lorian said. "The Monarch divided the navy into twelve fleets. Named one for each standard month."

"Which are you?" I asked.

Lorian lifted his own glass in mock salute. "October," he said, and drank.

I accepted this bit of trivia with a silent nod, resumed my study of the room. Lorian had invited me to his home, a grand but modestly sized building in the Printed City's royal quarter—a district known to the locals as Façade. A high, turreted stone wall surrounded the Commandant General's abode, complete with guns whose daimons kept unsleeping watch.

I turned from the window, cast my gaze about the room instead, at the deep shelves on the walls, shelves that held not books, but scale models of starships and artillery, each meticulously assembled. One in particular caught my eye, had caught it the moment I entered the Commandant General's study. It was an Imperial battleship, black as night and gold accented. Her concave sides narrowed to a sharp prow, her body flat as a blade above, with the hanging towers and clustered halls of her lower decks descending from the ventral hull. She widened to aft, so that a convex arc of engines seemed a crossguard to the knife blade that was the vessel itself.

"You rebuilt the *Tamerlane*," I said, nodding.

Once, I might have wept. I only smiled.

"I always liked models," Lorian said. "I never could build them—you know—before. Didn't have the dexterity. Used to slip with the knife and cut myself." His voice had grown strangely far away as he twisted to observe the model *Tamerlane* in its glass case. "There's a man in the city who designs them. He printed the parts for me. I painted them myself. I've got a small fleet of Imperial stuff here, but there are some weird ones. You ever seen a Tavrosi destroyer?"

"Once, I think," I said, thinking back to my first voyage to Vorgossos. But I watched Lorian rise and followed him to the shelves, nodded with interest as he lifted the Tavrosi vessel—it was all of mirrored silver—for my inspection. I did not take it when he offered it to me, fearing that I might drop it. "I never took you for a craftsman."

"Aren't we all, in a sense?" he said.

I smiled at that, sampled the vintage the other man had poured out for me. "You know, the Jaddians say much the same. They say the ideal man is either warrior or poet."

"It's warrior *and* poet," Lorian amended. "The Arthur Buddhists agree. Have you read Dinadan Vima?"

I could only shake my head.

"These are old ideas," Lorian said. "Vima is in a sense just rearticulating them, but he was the greatest *khandasattva*—you would say *knight-master* or *sword-saint,* I guess—of the last five thousand years. Vima says that to be *gurram,* to be a knight, is to be fully present. It is the same in anything. Poetry, gardening, even building these models." He gestured at the display with a curiously shy smile. "One must clear the mind—as the scholiasts do—not to achieve some impossible objectivity, but to allow the mind to engage fully. Not just the conscious, but the all of you."

"I never took you for a philosopher, either," I said, smiling gently.

The Commandant General shrugged. "I am more myself here than ever I was at home."

I wondered then how long he had been a disciple of the Arthur-Buddha, and where he found their forbidden texts. I imagined him digging through old paperbacks in a shop no censor or inquisitor had visited.

"The Nipponese call this *mushin no shin,* the *mind without mind,*" Lorian said.

"The object is not to think, yes?" I asked.

"The object is not to *need* to think," Lorian said, "but to act spontaneously, without obstruction. This is perhaps most important for the *gurram,* because war requires swift, decisive action. Strategy doubly so. I am often not accorded the time to agonize over my choices. Often, I cannot afford to think at all."

"I think I know what you mean," I said.

"I think you would have to," Lorian said. "To do what it is you do. I find working with my hands keeps me sane. I figure if I keep working, one day I'll find enlightenment. Maybe by accident. We can't all be theodidacts." Lorian replaced the Tavrosi model on its shelf. "Me? I never feel more *real* than when I'm fighting. In the thick of it, you know?"

I told him that I did, and asked, "Why are you telling me all this, Lorian?"

The little man looked up at me sidelong. "We're going to attack Vorgossos," he said, and when I made no move, he said, "Where do you think I've been? Up there." He pointed through the ceiling. "The greatest part of war is won in the planning. I've been meeting with my people. With the other Commandant Generals, the free captains. With Jamina and His Majesty." He leaned against an iron post between the banks of glass shelves. "Will the Empire bring their bombs, do you think?"

"They've already agreed to it," I said.

"But will they do it?"

"They'll do it," I said more strongly. Seeing Lorian's stony face, I asked. "What is it?"

"Atomics are proscribed under the charters."

"Only for use against human targets. We've used them before ourselves, many times."

The good commander—but no, he was the Commandant General then—said, "But so many...they'll have emptied one of the Imperial stores. That means Chantry oversight."

He was right. "It means a Sentinel fleet." The Sentinels were the Chantry's enforcers, the boots to the Inquisition's gloves. One but rarely saw them. The bulk of their strength lay in Earth's own system, protecting the homeworld. But when the Inquisition ruled that a planet should be burned out, a people destroyed, it was the Sentinels who performed that hateful task. They were the keepers of forbidden weapons, of the Emperor's nuclear arsenals, of the planet-killers and of plagues to rival Lethe's sickness.

Lorian's face was grim. "The Extras and the Chantry together..." he said at last. "Against Vorgossos." He finished his glass, crossed the room to the narrow bar and poured another. "Never thought I'd live to see the day. The Mandari are right, we do live in interesting times."

"Too interesting, I think."

"I didn't say that," Lorian said. He grinned around his winecup. "Chaos is opportunity. You've seen with your own eyes what we're building here, what the Monarch is building here."

The Monarch...I did not say anything, but turned to regard the wall of model ships. There were lesser Imperial battle cruisers alongside the massive *Tamerlane*. I thought they were to scale. I read their plates. *Caractacus, Dauntless, Skanderbeg*...I recognized a pair of Jaddian warships, great gilt things more organically shaped. The largest model by far was an Extrasolarian spinship, precisely like the *Mistwalker*.

"It's not like you to have nothing to say," said he.

Not one word.

I longed to tell him the truth, that the man to whom he'd dedicated this second life of his was not the man he claimed to be. Calen Harendotes was a mask, a leaf of gold foil hammered over corruption. Kharn Sagara could not be trusted. I knew that much at least.

Yet how would he have responded if I had spoken? If I had offered him the truth?

Would he have taken it? Or simply spat in my face?

In the months since we had come to Latarra, I still had not found a way to tell my people the truth. Kept a prisoner in the palace, I had not dared communicate the truth to Cassandra, to Selene or one of the others. There might have been cameras hidden in walls, microphones floating on the air, no larger than a mote of dust.

I could never be certain I was alone.

Not without Valka.

Even the analog tricks that worked in the Imperium—Edouard's note, or any of the various coded hand signs employed by Imperial Intelligence—could not be relied on. Much of the Monarch's military staff was former Empire. Many of the signs—many of the tricks—would be known. Lorian himself must have instructed the Latarran forces on the Imperial playbook. I might have tried communicating in the Cielcin tongue, but Sagara spoke it. He had dealt with Otiolo in the prince's own language, had dealt with others before.

Was even Lorian's home safe? I doubted it, and did not dare.

"You've been to Vorgossos before," Lorian said. "What are we up against?"

Your own master, I thought, turning but slowly to face the last of my Red Company. "Kharn Sagara..." I said, "I don't know what he may be like in battle. I did not fight him. But he has at his command a host of weapons designed and manufactured by the Mericanii themselves. How many there are or what their functions may be I cannot begin to guess. He has the one Sojourner I know of, a vessel so great as those of your free captains. And he has a host of SOM puppets at his disposal. I'd wager a hundred thousand at least—and perhaps more."

Lorian sucked on his teeth before he spoke. "None of this is news to me. Zelaz and Eidhin have often visited, and the Monarch knows much of the strength of Vorgossos's defenses. The planet itself is a warship, as I'm sure you know. There are tens of thousands of miles of tunnels, trenches. There are fuel reserves a dozen miles or more underground, and the engine emplacements at the south are more than a thousand miles across."

"I never saw them," I said. "We took the hightower from orbit down into the old city..." Impulsively, I turned, traced the sloping dorsal hull of the *ISV Skanderbeg* with a finger, appreciating the gold leaf Lorian had applied to mimic the brassy accents that shone on the real thing. "It seems you know what we face far better than I..."

The Commandant General—it was growing easier to think of him as such—shook his head. "I don't know the man. This is not like fighting the Cielcin. They can be relied upon to behave in certain ways. Not so here." His glass recharged, Lorian found his way to a low chair in the little sitting area about the holography well arranged in the center of the room, below and before the long desk against the windows at the room's far end. Thus seated, he asked, "What's he like? Kharn Sagara?"

That I could not answer him fully was a weight and sorrow I find now difficult to express. I, who had concealed much in my lifetime, and for less reason, was torn to pieces by the silence Kharn's threat had imposed on me. Had that been the true intention behind his revealing himself to me?

But no. Cruel Kharn Sagara surely was, but cruel without reason?

No. In truth, he was not really hiding. Instead, he had signaled the reality to those who knew the signs. The Captains Zelaz and Eidhin, and Lord Black at least surely knew who he was. In establishing himself at Latarra, Calen Harendotes had declared war on his sister-self, had declared himself to those of his former allies who might support his claim over that of the woman.

Myself among them.

I was to be his hierophant, the greatest piece upon his board. With my powers, he hoped to outmaneuver his sister in the critical moment. I would have my part to play, and I would play it.

He meant to betray me, of that I had no doubt. To turn on me in the crucial moment. Calen Harendotes would use me until I was of no more use—and no more...

"She," I said, deflecting. "Unless something's changed. The Kharn Sagara who rules Vorgossos is female, at present. He changes bodies at a whim, each generation unlike the last. He's lived for so long, he needs the novelty I think...but he is dangerous, Lorian. More dangerous than you know. He's lived for more than fifteen thousand years, and I don't think he's truly human anymore." I glared at Lorian as I spoke, willing him to understand that I was not only talking about the Lord of Vorgossos. "He has ruled that planet for eons. His palace is a fortress, one built by the Mericanii themselves. Even if we can land a force on the surface, it will not be easy to get at him. And then there is the daimon itself."

"I know about it," Lorian said. "You've met it?"

Too well could I remember the touch of those pale and bloated hands, those hands swollen, twisted by unconstrained growth—just as the bodies of the victims of the plague were twisted by its cancers. "Yes," I said. "I have no way of knowing what role it might play in the fighting. Sagara has kept it in fetters, so to speak, but he may unleash it."

That sobering thought silenced even Lorian, and he drained his drink. Presently, he laughed. "A daimon of the Golden Age," he said, grinning in his wolfish way. "Now that's an enemy worth fighting!"

His laughter was contagious.

We sat a while then in companionate quiet, neither one of us speaking. For the space of that silence, all was as if the previous two centuries had not elapsed at all.

"How long before the fleet gets here?" I asked.

Lorian shook his head. "The fleet isn't coming. There's no sense in it. We'll rendezvous nearer Vorgossos." He smiled. "Most Imperial ships can't keep up anyway."

"Why is that?" I asked, leaning forward. I had recharged my glass and seated myself in the long silence.

"Age, mostly. The Imperial fleet is massive, Hadrian. Some of the mainline battleships have been in operation for three or four thousand years. We can't build them fast enough." I noticed it was *we* for a moment. "It's possible to do a refit, bring the engines up to spec—and there's been some of that. Not nearly enough, and now...so many of the shipyards north of Orion are gone. Destroyed. It's all we can do to maintain what we have." He drank. "The Extras don't build as much, but they build bigger, as a rule. Much bigger. That means greater fuel capacity. That means greater output, even if it means slower ramp."

I nodded my understanding. Although a larger ship's warp engine would warp space more efficiently once it fired, it was well known that the larger the vessel, the slower the jump to warp. The Cielcin worldships were notoriously slow to jump. It made catching them in a rout more possible. That was how Cassian Powers himself had caught the vessel-moon called Echidna at Second Cressgard, crippling her engines before she could jump to warp.

"So partly we're faster because we're newer, and partly because we're bigger. The dreadnoughts, now? Ships such as the *Tamerlane* or the *Huntsman*? Those could keep pace...but the ships they're like to send? Better to rendezvous near the target."

"Where is the target?" I asked.

"That's the other thing," Lorian said. "If the fleet wanted to come here first, they'd be going almost exactly the wrong way." He grinned. "Vorgossos is in Orion now. Sagara pitched his tent right under the Empire's nose."

I let that revelation sink in, admiring the genius of it. Alone in the dark, far from any star, Vorgossos would be almost undetectable, but near enough to his customers to make the trip worthwhile.

"Prince Matthias will be here in about two years," Lorian said. "Apparently, they packed him on an interceptor, fastest ship they had."

I had expected an even longer interval, but still the magnitude of the answer rocked me.

"Two years..." I said. "So we have time."

"Who's we?" Lorian asked, smiling once more. "You and the princess?"

I froze. "What?"

The little man cackled, face transfigured with suddenly impish glee. "Anyone can see it, man. The way she looks at you..." He seemed to sense my discomfort, said, "You haven't, then?"

"Haven't what?"

The intus made an obscene gesture.

"Valka is dead, Lorian," I said, and drank.

"And she wouldn't want you to be so damned miserable," he said.

"Did Cassandra put you up to this?" I asked.

"I haven't seen the girl," Lorian said. "You'd better decide soon."

"Why is that?" I snapped.

The little man blinked at me. "She'll be heading back with Matthias, surely. Didn't you know?"

I opened my mouth to speak. I hadn't known. I hadn't been a part of the formal process then for many days. But I should have known.

"They'd never let her go into a warzone, not if it could be helped. She slipped their net already. They'll want to pack the princess back into her tower as swift as may be." His mocking edge returned. "You had best get while you can."

I sat there, unmoving, astonished to find myself feeling bereft. In the years since our flight from Forum—mere months of which I'd been conscious—I had grown fond of the girl, of the woman she'd become. Had grown to find comfort in her presence, to admire her heart. Her resolve.

"You can't tell me you've had no one these long centuries," Lorian said. "And you on Jadd? In the prince's pleasure gardens? You can't lie, Hadrian. Not to me."

I sensed a curious tension in the question, in the way the man looked at me. I studied him a long time. The little man was inscrutable as ever, his humor and mocking edge a mask pulled over... what?

Recalling Demetra, I hung my head. She had not been the first.

Yet that had not seemed a betrayal. Valka was gone, I knew as much, and the years were long, and lonely. I had not loved Demetra, nor the other women who had come before her to comfort me in my exile.

Nor had any of them sat at my feet below the Solar Throne.

Still, I had not expected the threat of her parting to fall on me so hard.

Did I love Selene? Could I love her? Or anyone again?

Handling the thought was like trying to handle a glead. It burned me, until I knew I must let it drop.

"I loved her, you know," Lorian said. "Your Valka. She was always... good to me. You know, I think she was the first woman who was?"

"She was good to everyone," I said. "Everyone who deserved goodness."

"Then how do you explain either of us?" said he, and smiled. "You know, there was a time I hated you for sending me to that place."

"I didn't send you—"

"I know," Lorian said. "But it was easy to lose sight of that there. Belusha was..." He broke off. "Bad. The thought of you on Jadd..." Lorian had returned to his desk by then, to his abandoned cup of wine. He lifted it, stared out the tall windows at guns that guarded his manse from the wild city beyond. "Time stops when you're in prison, you know? It's easy to forget it doesn't stop anywhere else. It's like sailing."

How somber he seemed to me then, framed against the pale light of day, a little man in military blacks, his lank hair bound at his shoulder by a ring of dull Latarran gold.

"Lorian, I..." I longed to tell him the truth. To tell him *everything.* But the Monarch's threat was clear, and the full scope of his powers of observation were a mystery to me.

The smaller man looked round at me. "What?" he asked.

My caution returned, my courage left me. "It's nothing," I said at last. *Not one word.*

A quizzical expression flickered across the misborn's leucistic face, but he shook his head, knocked back his dregs.

"I miss her, too," I said at last.

CHAPTER 53

FAREWELL

OF THE ARRIVAL OF Prince Matthias I shall say but little. He was—like all his siblings—a Grecian marble crowned with red gold. He was one of the older children, I think. The thirtieth son or the fortieth—not nearly so old as old Aurelian. From his heroic visage and broad shoulders, I guessed that he had spent much of his life frozen and on standby, awaiting the orders of his lord father and the needs of Empire.

But arrive he did, carrying the terms of the Emperor's new peace. For the first time since the Jaddian Wars, the Sollan Empire had been forced to concede territory to another human power.

It was a blow, and one for which future historians will doubtless smear poor William's name. And yet there was wisdom in it. By defining the new border with Latarra, we imposed some pressure on the Monarchy to aid in the defense of that border. The Centaurine provinces—where the worst of the fighting with the Cielcin then was—lay between Latarra and the Imperial heartland in the arms of Sagittarius and Orion.

The fight for Vorgossos was—might have been—the first joint action of the combined Sollan and Latarran armadas.

As fate would have it, it would also be the last.

But we did not know it then.

Instead, for the first time in many a long year of war, the talk and mood was of hope. Of change. Of the New Order Calen Harendotes had built, was building. The White City of the King, the Printed City of Latarra was to be the template and model of a new civilization, a challenger to the red pieces and old order of the Imperium, a vision of the galaxy halfway between the chaos of the Extrasolarians and the suffocating order of the Solar Throne.

It was easy to see why Lorian loved it, for it *was* beautiful, and he had risen so far and so quickly that the rarefied air of his new station had made him giddy. He did not have to think about the guns on his walls—or why he needed them. For not all was polish and glamour in the new city of the king. I saw the poverty, just as I saw it at home. I saw the criminals hanged in the plaza before the Monarch's pyramid, their bodies left for the birds. I saw the whores on their streetcorners, in their red-rimmed windows dancing—saw too the bodyshops and bonecutters, the gene tailors and natalists hawking their wares from banner signs ten stories high.

Had I been younger—the boy who left Delos, perhaps—I might have been drunk on the electric air of the place myself. Here was the fulcrum of the lever to move the stars, the axis about which a man might turn the whole galaxy. During my brief time on Latarra, often I observed the young men of the Monarch's army moving about the place. Marching up the streets in formation, hard at work building the city, or else carousing or fighting outside winesinks and brothels. One could feel the energy coming off them, like static lightning, a radiation like innumerable tiny suns.

They were alive, and vital in a way few men of the Imperium were vital, and one got the sense that the sun of Latarra was always rising, where on Forum...always it seemed near twilight to me.

And yet, it was not to be. The promise of Lorian's New Order, his new dawn, was to prove only the green flash of sunset that Earth's sailors used to say mimicked for an instant the wholesome light of day.

When the treaty was ratified and all the documents signed and sealed, and when the holographs were recorded and broadcast across the datanet, the time for parting came. As Lorian had portended, Matthias was to take Selene with him. Not back to Forum, but to some other, undisclosed location. Forum was not safe for her, as I had insisted repeatedly to Matthias, to Aurelian in what little communication I'd had with him since arriving in the Monarch's palace, to Albé—who reported to his own superiors via a private telegraph brought by Matthias's retinue—and to the Emperor's own Security Council during my debrief.

It was during these interviews that I came to realize that no one on Forum knew what had happened to me, and I did not transmit my face. Matthias had not asked questions, had perhaps not seen the old man I had become, did not know that I had changed.

The day of Selene's departure was overcast, the sky a low roof of cloud held up by the columns of steam that rose from the reactors in the Maze. The heavens seemed near at hand, and yet were veiled.

I stood with Cassandra and Edouard—and with Neema, who had come down from the *Mistwalker* not long after we arrived. Ghoshal's men stood honor guard about us, alongside Annaz and certain of the Irchtani. I had ordered Ramanthanu and the other Cielcin returned to the *Gadelica* in anticipation of Matthias's arrival, and they had remained in orbit.

We were to sail for Vorgossos and rendezvous with the Imperial fleet at the end of that week. The Monarch himself was going to war—a thing that had not happened since the Battle of Ashklam, when Harendotes himself had taken the field against the intractable Norman natives. There had been a parade the day before: the Grand Army marching through the city to the plaza at the foot of the half-built pyramid, below the observation platform where their Monarch and the Imperial prince watched.

Now that prince was leaving, carrying with him one copy of the treaty—signed and sealed.

Matthias emerged from the side of the great pyramid, Martian Guards about him, Selene at his side. A scholiast robed in green and a half dozen Aventine House androgyns followed in their wake, two clutching the train of the scarlet cape the princess wore. Despite the short years we'd spent on Latarra, Selene had kept her hair short. I stood straighter as they approached, hand going to the pocket of my coat and the scrap of paper concealed there.

This was to be my last chance. My only chance.

Across the aisle, Calen Harendotes himself waited, standing with Absalom Black and the Lady Ardahael in her float-chair amid a retinue of masked and helmeted dragoons. Lorian stood near at hand, with certain of the other Commandant Generals about him. I recognized the other former Imperials, Gadkari and Harred—they stood apart, even from Lorian. They alone bowed as the prince and princess passed on the way to their shuttle.

Matthias and Selene halted before the Monarch's stand. An awning— black and gold—snapped in the wind above his head.

The prince raised a hand in farewell, Selene's arm in his. "On behalf of my Imperial father, Monarch Harendotes, I thank you for your hospitality. May this be only the beginning of a long and fruitful relationship between our nations."

Prince Matthias did not bow. Neither did the Monarch. But Calen Harendotes smiled, and touched the broad, golden collar that covered his chest and shoulders in what seemed almost a salute. "I share your hope, prince," he said, "go in peace, and tell your father that we on Latarra are proud to fight alongside the Empire against our common enemy. We shall await your fleet beyond the circles of Merope."

"Very good!" Matthias said. "My Imperial father will be delighted. May we meet again, my lord!"

Only then did I notice the float-chair following in Matthias and Selene's train. In it rode a tetrand like Lady Ardahael, a white-haired young man so like the woman I felt certain that he must be one of her own kindred.

He was, I later learned, Lord Simeon Ardahael, Lady Jamina's own son. He was to accompany the prince and princess for the return journey to the Imperium, where he was to serve as his Monarch's apostol.

He would be counted among the dead of Gododdin, though neither he nor I could guess it then. I only of all those present had caught a glimpse of the final fire in Brethren's vision, in the images the Quiet himself had showed to me upon the mountain on Annica, in the mirror of Ragama.

But only a glimpse.

The prince and Selene turned to face me, forcing the attendants to adjust Selene's trailing cape. Matthias's own cloak fluttered in the gusting wind, his hair a guttering candleflame atop the wick that was his head. "Lord Marlowe," he said, drawing himself up to highlight his slightly superior height, "it is a pity you will not return with us."

"My duties lie elsewhere, my prince," I said. When he had arrived, Matthias had ordered that I surrender myself. I had refused, and Calen Harendotes had refused to let me go.

Lord Marlowe is my guest, as much as he is your subject, he'd said. *Possession is nine points in the law.*

In truth, I was a prisoner of sorts. Latarra had the stronger bargaining position. They had the tracking technology and the means to lay bare every telegraph transmission from Marinus to Jadd, and thus the means to seek out and isolate the Cielcin fleet wherever they were hiding. The Empire needed Latarra—or believed it did—and while Latarra could not within reason retain the Princess Selene, the Empire was not willing to go to war or compromise its security to retain possession of Hadrian Marlowe.

But still, I was precisely where I wanted to be, where I needed to be, where duty and the cause of Operation Gnomon demanded that I be. The Emperor had made no comment with regard to my disposition. That was proof enough that I was where even he wanted me to be.

How I wished that I had had my chance to speak with William once again. Samek had robbed me of that at least, and done much harm in pursuit of all she thought was good.

"Your duties..." Prince Matthias echoed my words, voice trailing in the wind like his cape. "You have escaped us a second time. Mark my words: There will not be a third."

"My prince?" I asked, blandly as I could. The hand in my pocket crushed the slip of paper I meant to hand Selene. It was a piece torn from one of my black folios, the paper black as the ink I had used to write on it, that it might prove invisible to any spying eye. The writing of it had seemed only the momentary selection of the wrong pen.

Five words, five words to convey volumes back to the Imperium.

It was all I could risk.

Letting Selene's arm go, Matthias stepped nearer me. I felt Cassandra grow stiff at my right hand, ready to strike at need. The towering Aventine came close enough that I could smell the floral perfume on him. "Had I my choice, you would be in fetters on that shuttle even now." His eyes indicated the black scarab shape of the Imperial lander with its dark windows framed in beaten brass, its repulsors already glowing faintly blue, ready for dust-off.

"Then it is well," I said, "that Calen Harendotes, not Matthias Avent, rules on Latarra."

The tall prince snorted, drew back a step only to redouble his advance. I did not withdraw, did not flinch. "You gambled with my sister's life, encouraging her to back this . . . mad course." His emerald eyes flashed round, taking in the landing pad, the Printed City, the Monarch's court gathered on the stands. "Bringing her here . . . among these . . . *barbarians.*" With the wind gusting so, either none of the Extras had heard him, or they all had.

None gave any sign, though I caught Lorian staring at me from his place beside the Commandant Generals Herren and Gadkari. For a moment, our eyes met.

What a farce, I remembered thinking. I, of course, had done no such thing. Selene had volunteered herself, had forced Cassandra, Neema, and Edouard to take her as seeming-hostage, that they might escape the Martians intact.

"This mad course," I began carefully, "has saved the alliance your father and brother worked so hard to secure."

"An alliance that would never have been in jeopardy had you not muddied the waters."

"Is that what I did?" I asked, voice and face studiously blank. "Tell Aurelian that if he wishes answers to the questions he would ask of me, he should speak with the Cantor Samek."

"Samek?" Matthias's eyes narrowed. "Cantor?"

"It was not I who soured your brother's plans," I said. "But I did what was necessary. I always do."

The prince withdrew. "So you will sail for Vorgossos."

"That is my road," I told him, my own hair snapping across my face.

"If you run again, Marlowe," he said, "you had better quit the galaxy entire. There will be no world, no place, no airless moon where you can hide."

Selene gripped her brother's arm, hissed, "Matthias!"

The prince extricated himself from his sister's grasp, turned to her. "You could have died, sister."

"But I didn't," she said, and leaning toward him whispered. "You're playing the fool, brother."

Matthias looked down at his sister, a smile frozen on his face.

"I wish to say farewell to Lord Marlowe," she said. "If I may."

The tall prince looked from his sister to myself. "As you like it," he said and, snatching at his cape, turned to the shuttle and mounted the ramp without another word. Simeon Ardahael followed in his wake, and all of the Martians, save two.

For a moment, the princess simply looked up at me. There was a circlet of yellow gold on her brow beneath the fiery hair. She looked somehow younger then—more the girl I recalled from my youth, less the woman I had met returning from Sabratha. Eyes falling to the white stone of the pad between us, she said, "Will I see you again?"

"I hope so," I told her. "You don't know where you're going?"

The princess shook her head. "Matthias won't say. One of the border forts, I'm sure. Possibly to see Father and Alexander...wherever they may be."

That had been my hope for her as well. "The Chantry may still move against you," I said. "You saw something you shouldn't have, Selene." The slip was in my hand, concealed between two fingers. I had but to take her own in mine.

"I know that," she said, and bit her lip. She seemed to teeter on the precipice of some abyss that only she could see.

"You didn't tell your brother," I said. It was not a question.

"Matthias?"

"Aurelian," I said. "You didn't tell him what happened to me."

"I told him the Chantry tried to kill you, that they nearly killed me, and that you and Albé and Aristedes thought that removing me from the palace was the best way to protect me. Aurelian knows more of the past threats against your life than I. Mother and Lorcan Breathnach and...and Alexander." It seemed strange to me that Alexander should give her more pause than her own mother, but then I thought the two of them had been close. They were near to each other in birth order—if no longer in age. I wondered how old Alexander had become, traveling between the stars at the Emperor's right hand. I wondered, too—and feared—what sort of man he had become.

Coward! he had called me, when Valka was dead. *You would abandon us now? When the need has never been greater?*

"But I didn't tell him you died," she said, voice small enough to be lost in the wind. Selene's eyes were still on the floor, had slid to a point to my right. I thought I could hear the engines of her mind churning, the pistons of her heart hammering. "I *won't* tell him. He wouldn't believe."

"He wouldn't—"

Her hands were on my shoulders then, her face pressed to mine. For a moment, I forgot how to move, was paralyzed by surprised and renewed terror. I could do nothing, could neither reciprocate nor push her away. I was Kyra again. Trapped. Frozen. Helpless.

Shahmat.

And yet I found that part of myself that did not want to be anywhere else. I knew the red paint of her lips would linger, and the taste of that kiss—like strong wine. I was absurdly conscious of my body, of the hands with which I knew not what I might do—and of Cassandra so near at hand. Unseen, I felt the glow of Lorian's smirk like radiation, and of the shock of the Monarch's retinue at this sudden display.

Then it was over, and the sudden absence of her was like a missing tooth. My mouth felt strangely empty, and I staggered back.

"Farewell, Lord Marlowe," the princess said, cheeks more red now than her hair. She turned to go, her Martians—flustered—scrambling with the twin androgyns to fall into her orbit. Before I could reply, she turned to leave.

The note! The note was still in my hand! The note with its five words for the Emperor and the Imperial fleet.

"Selene!" I called after her. No *princess*, no *highness*, no title of any kind. My hand shot out, caught her bangled wrist. I held that hand in both of mine, pressed the note into it. I saw her eyes widen. If we came through all this alive, I would owe Edouard a drink, and pour out a libation for the shade of poor Sir Friedrich Oberlin. It had been they who put the notion into my head. The means to get the truth to those that needed to hear it.

Unknowing, Selene had been my accomplice. The kiss would cover all.

I love you, I might have said in answer, as she had said to me as my flesh dissolved upon the floor of the Arx Caelestis. Instead I smiled, heart in my mouth. "I'll see you again."

If she was disappointed, she did not show it, but concealed the note in her white palm. Her other hand went to my cheek. "Until that hour," she said, and turned once more to go.

My mission done, I retreated, found I could not look my daughter in the eye.

Valka, forgive me, I thought, and shut my eyes.

"And Hadrian!" Selene had stopped halfway to the shuttle, her red cloak fluttering in the wind. No *Lord Marlowe*, no *sirrah*.

"Yes, lady?"

"Don't die . . . again," she said.

And then she was gone, embarrassment turning her round faster than I would have thought possible for one so dressed. Lorian was still beaming at me, but the smile on Cassandra's face was more conflicted. It was one thing to say that she had wanted such a thing for me, another to see it before her very eyes.

The shuttle ramp retracted, hatches sliding closed. The whine of repulsors filled the air, and at some unheard command, the music of timpani and brass unseen rose about the landing platform. Calen Harendotes stood at the edge of the receiving stand, shading his eyes with one golden hand. The cloak that dripped from the collar of his office was like a piece of night flapping in the air.

Accompanied by the drum and horn of the Latarran martial anthem, the Imperial shuttle rose into the gray and nearly sunless day, apparently untouched by the gusting wind.

Then just as Selene had vanished inside, the shuttle vanished itself, became for a moment the shadow of some skybound fish beneath the surface of the clouds. Then it dove up into the deeps of that infinite Darkness, and was gone.

Kharn Sagara was watching me then, and for a moment I thought he would speak, make some comment, some remark at my expense. I was conscious of the taste of Selene lingering on my lips, of the color I knew must remain in my face. Had he seen more than my embarrassment? Did he know what I had done? That I set the cornerstone of his undoing?

Instead, the Monarch of Latarra—the one-time Lord of Vorgossos—only turned his back, and conferred with his court and council.

I thought of the message I had given the princess, black words on black paper.

Five words.

Only five.

The Monarch is Kharn Sagara.

I prayed it would be enough.

CHAPTER 54

THE STRAIGHT WAY

VORGOSSOS.

Long had that dread world haunted my dreams.

So often in memory I had wandered the pillared galleries and storied halls of the palace of the Undying; felt the still, dead air of that place on my skin; seen the shadows of the wonders and the horrors of the Garden of Everything projected across the interior of my skull. Well I recalled the Exalted titan, Calvert, and the fruits of the tree of false life—the children of Kharn Sagara hanging like apples from the roof above. Even now, I can feel the touch of Brethren's hands; taste cold, salt water filling my mouth; hear its hushed whispers like a pressure on my mind.

Always I knew I must return, though I had almost convinced myself that the daimon's words were madness. Falsehood. Brethren had said I must return, that we would meet again but once.

For one final time.

But the Judicator Ragama had told me I must go, that I must seek the weapons of the enemy—of the old enemy—and turn them against the new.

Seek hardship.

And so I knew my time had come.

The day after Selene left me on the platform outside the pyramid palace of Kharn Sagara, I returned with Lorian to the *Mistwalker*. The *Gadelica* would remain in that mighty vessel's hold for the long journey to Merope—one of the Pleiades—where we were to rendezvous with the Imperials and the Chantry's Sentinel fleet.

Even with the mighty engines of the Extrasolarian fleet, we would be nine years at sail.

I said before that I had long ago ceased to haunt my ships for the long voyages between our stars—stalking the chambers and corridors as I had when I was young—and so it was on that journey. I am relieved to say that even in my altered state, my consciousness was destroyed for a time, and I drank of the waters of Lethe and oblivion, and so forgot the world.

In time, I was awakened, and so met the worthies the Imperium had sent to support the fleet of the Monarch. I confess, I almost expected to find Bassander Lin waiting beyond the heliopause in Merope. The man had the strangest habit of appearing, like a second shadow, where I least expected him.

But it was not to be.

Instead, the command fell to Lord Ohannes Douro, Baron of Anarias, a strategos of high blood and ancient dignity. He was accompanied by a Sentinel commander called Kedron, who to my shock wore the blindfold of a cathar across his face. I misliked them both at once. Douro because he was more politician than soldier, Kedron because he was Chantry.

I do not think I had ever had occasion to meet one of the Chantry Sentinels before. They were the guardians of Earth, the watchmen who protected the homeworld and system, as well as watched over the graveworlds—the sites they had themselves destroyed.

They were mostly seen by the dead.

Theirs was the blazing sword of the God Emperor, the fires of judgement that had extinguished countless lives. That sword was sailing for Vorgossos alongside—unknown to all but a few—the exiled master of that dark world. Their bombs would rain upon Vorgossos, and we would stride into the ashes and the fallout like William Rex and his worthies on the Day of Advent when the hammer fell.

I thought of telling Lorian the truth, that his master was part and particle of the very enemy we sailed against; that he longed only to reclaim the throne of Vorgossos, the mastery of his slave daimon, and eternal life; that the New Order and world Lorian fought for was only a tool of that reconquest, the work of centuries.

But I did not. Could not.

Harendotes's spies were sure to be everywhere aboard the *Mistwalker,* his eyes... his hands. His knives. Therein lay the second reason the *Gadelica* had not been released. It was slow, yes, too slow to reach Merope with the rest of the Latarran fleet, but so long as Lorian—and through Lorian, Harendotes himself—held my people, he held me in check. Pinned as a pawn to the flank of his emperor.

Unable to move.

I had no choice but to have faith in Selene. My note would not be enough to cause the Empire to withdraw its support—they needed the Latarran telegraph, and Latarran support in the war—but it would put them on their guard. Douro and Kedron and the Imperial fleet would *know* who it was they sailed to aid. Selene would have put the note directly into her father's hands, and I knew that I could count on Caesar to understand that we were hostages.

Perhaps it was then that the seed was planted, watered, started to grow.

As long as she was by my side, Cassandra was in danger. If she were safe, I might speak the truth, tell Lorian all I knew, and win free of the labyrinth at last.

But I could not win free.

Not without first plumbing the labyrinth to its uttermost depths.

The time had come to return and face the beast that dwelt in its heart, as Theseus had done of old.

Always forward, always down.

And never left nor right.

CHAPTER 55

BLACK PLANET

I FANCIED MYSELF ENTOMBED. The walls of the iron carapace about me seemed the insides of a sarcophagus inscribed with signs and symbols strange to me. The Interfaced had disabled all access to the thing's controls. I was a passenger only. A prisoner, in a sense, at the mercy of my wing companions—men and women I could neither see nor hear.

Safe in my armor, entoptics projected images of the world outside directly onto my retinas. Though I could not move, I could *see*, see the distant stars like torches in the night spiraling as we soared toward the darkly gleaming planet below.

Well I recognized those icy climes, that witch-lit surface, green as poison beneath her snows.

We had found Vorgossos, just where Calen Harendotes had said it would be.

When first I had journeyed to that profane world, I thought it must lie well beyond the borders of human space, far from the light of any Imperial sun—and yet originally Vorgossos must have been within a mere handful of light-years of Earth herself, for if the stories were true, she had been inhabited since before the founding of the Empire.

But Sagara had built massive engines into the planet's pole in imitation of the mighty star-drives of the Cielcin, forever paranoid, forever planning against the day his world would be discovered. Thanks to Bassander Lin— and to Switch, who had betrayed me—that day had come, and when the Empire returned with fire and sword to conquer Vorgossos in the wake of my previous visit, they had found only the desolation of space.

Space, and the planet's undead star.

Kharn Sagara—the other one, the woman—had anchored her world about another brown dwarf star. When all our leaders had met in council, Absalom Black had revealed the world relied upon the gravity of such a

star to keep its core active and molten. Without it, Vorgossos would be
stripped of the protection of its magnetic field, exposing the Undying and
residents of her profane city to the effects of cosmic radiation. And worse,
without it, Vorgossos would grow deathly cold and the great subterranean
oceans would go to ice.

About me, the AMP whined, engines at my back and shoulders flaring. The surface of the rogue world scrolled below me. Sensors in the
inner hull tracked my face and eye movement, altered the display I was
seeing. Above and behind me, I could see the shapes of the other cephalophores against the night, betrayed by the faint running lights—red and
white—that twinkled on their hulls. Above them, the black shapes of our
fleet—dominated by the hulking Sojourners of Eidhin, Archambault, and
Zelaz—had appeared only as patches of brighter darkness against the eternal
night. Beside them, the knife shapes of our Imperial battle cruisers had
seemed as daggers beside great swords.

A flash of light filled the darkness. Lightning without thunder.

A shot.

"What was that?" I asked, broadcasting on comms.

I knew to wait the requisite seconds for a reply, was surprised when
one came almost instantly.

"ANTIMATTER WEAPON DISCHARGE DETECTED," it said. "BEAR-
ING X TWO-AUGHT-NINE POINT ONE-SEVEN BY Y NINETY-SEVEN
POINT EIGHT-THREE."

A reticle appeared where the light had faded, indicating that I should
look over my shoulder and to my left. I did, though through the fading
light I saw nothing. The matter of the voice took precedence. "Who's
there? 2Maeve?"

The voice had been flatly feminine, but on reflection I did not think
that it had been the Interfaced commander. 2Maeve was out there. Calen
Harendotes had chosen the *Mistwalker* to lead the incursion onto the planet's
surface, and Lorian had chosen the Interfaced for the assault.

There was no answer.

"Speaker, identify yourself."

"It's the AMP, Marlowe," came the voice of one of the Interfaced on
the comm. "You're not networked, so it has to talk to you."

"The AMP?" I echoed.

"The fleet's taking fire!" said another voice—I thought it the voice of
5Eamon, 2Maeve's optio.

"From where?" I asked.

Again, there was no answer. The Interfaced had little time for me. I
was scarcely more than dead weight, little more than cargo. A payload
they were set to deliver to the surface.

Our mission was simple: make the surface, secure a landing zone for the troop carriers.

"We cannot take the city by storm," Lorian had said, poring over the schematics Harendotes had revealed to us in council. "The domes are under more than a mile of glacier, and the only way in is through these flumes." He indicated shafts like the one we had ridden down into the city. Only one cable ran from the ground to the orbital station, but there were other shafts, other tunnels that linked to structures built nearer the surface. "Not even the Chantry's bombs can penetrate to that kind of depth."

The holograph slid out, showed the planet entire in miniature. "We have to fly in through the tunnels. The whole planet's riddled with them. Old mine shafts, mostly." He traced a line with his cane. "The network runs all the way from the city here—under the seabed—to the engine installation at the pole."

That was our target.

The cephalophore whined as it accelerated, dropping me nearer the planet's surface. We would have to fly low, to come under the reach of the guns Kharn had built in ancient days to guard his world.

"*ANTIMATTER WEAPON DISCHARGE DETECTED*," came the cephalophore's flatly feminine voice again. It recited the bearing. I looked, saw nothing. Even the ships of our own fleet were lost in the black.

"Arthur Flight, this is *Mistwalker*," came the old, familiar voice on the comm. "Arthur Flight, do you read?"

Not being Interfaced himself, Lorian had no choice but to communicate in the old-fashioned way.

"Read you, *Mistwalker*," came 2Maeve's reply. "This is Art-1. Orbital insertion complete. Prepared for hard drop on your mark."

"Message received, Art-1," came Lorian's reply. "T-minus twenty-three minutes to mark. Hold your course."

We had but to orbit the planet, wait for the opportune moment to descend and cut for the gun emplacements that encircled the worldship's mighty engines. Our target was a drum tower overlooking a small landing field just beneath the curtain wall of the crater that formed the heart of the engine complex.

Calen's plan called for us to fly our shuttles—with cephalophore escort—along those tunnels, soaring along thousands of miles of pipeline and access-way to the gates of the hidden city.

"Lorian, what's happening up there?" I asked.

The *Mistwalker* was at the fore of a battle group that had inserted itself into a high, polar orbit about Vorgossos. The bulk of the fleet was much higher, had come out of warp first to draw the Vorgossene fleet into orbit higher and farther from the planet itself, allowing us to slide in later arriving from mere light-hours away and under the extended fleet.

"Douro and the free captains have engaged Sagara's fleet. They're taking heavy fire," came the Commandant General's reply.

"And you?"

"Safe for the moment," Lorian said. "Maybe they haven't spotted us yet—and they definitely won't have seen your lot. It's whatever Sagara's got on the surface that worries me."

"What about the *Demiurge?*"

"No sign," came Lorian's reply. "Maybe it's not here."

"Maybe," I said, not believing it.

The thought that Kharn Sagara's dread vessel might simply *appear* at any moment and unleash any of the Mericanii Archontic weapons chilled my very blood.

"Elffire and your Captain Ghoshal are ready to deploy ground troops the moment you clear the landing zone," Lorian said. "Guard yourself, Marlowe."

"And you," I said.

Cassandra was on the ground team, along with Albé and a thousand HAPSIS men, Ramanthanu's five and the Irchtani among them, supported by another ten thousand of Lorian's own soldiery. Camillus Elffire—the former Legion man who was captain of the *Mistwalker*'s infantry—was to lead the ground incursion. Their task was to disable the worldship's mighty engines.

"I've got people for that," Lorian said. "This will be a glorious day for the new world. Sagara has long been a thorn in our side."

I could say nothing. I was sure that even then, a particle of Kharn's Protean awareness was bent upon us, hanging on our every word. The Monarch himself was safe aboard his flagship, but I did not doubt that his eyes and ears were everywhere.

Another flash resounded in the deep above our heads, bright for a moment as any sun.

The battle was—to me—only the shine of those distant lights. The rosettes of missile fire, the bright lines of particle beams, the flaring spat of laser, the inky fire of dying ships. At my distance, it was only an abstraction. Blue lightning, red fire, the white flash of annihilation.

From the inside, I knew it was different.

Well I could picture Lorian gripping the rim of his holography table, knuckles white, shoulders bunched as those of a strongman prepared to lift, every man and woman alongside him the same.

When first I had come to Vorgossos, the place had seemed remote, obscure. The city below the surface had been crowded, yes, but the palace of Kharn Sagara and his mighty vessel had been lonely desolations, and so it had seemed that—while his power there was absolute—he had ruled very little. His chief servant was a machine, his troopers SOM puppets. Calvert alone of all his retinue had seemed his own man, though he was yet his master's creature. Whence then had come this Vorgossene fleet?

A red star blazed high above us, then the clean white of annihilation.

"What was that?" I asked.

Lorian did not reply. Instead, my cephalophore answered in its inhuman woman's voice. "ISV CARDENIO DESTROYED."

The *Cardenio* had been one of Douro's ships, one of the Imperial fleet.

The Vorgossene fleet must have overwhelmed the ship's shields.

We had suffered our first major casualty.

"Arthur Flight, this is Sentinel Commander Kedron," came a deep voice over the comm. "We've reached the eastern wall of the engine crater. Commencing bombing run."

I could not shake the sensation that I was being watched, *looked for* in the night.

Did Kharn Sagara—the *other* Kharn Sagara, the woman whose host was arrayed against us—know that I had come? Did Brethren? The daimon possessed some power to project its will. It had sent me visions to guide me to itself on my last visit. Might it not be seeking for me, even then?

Or was I afraid?

"TAKING EVASIVE ACTION." The cephalophore's cold voice announced even as it cut hard to starboard and plunged me down so fast my vision went gray. Even as we did, I saw a lance of emerald green slice the air not a hundred feet from me, and not five hundred feet away, another of our cephalophores erupted in scarlet flame as a second beam swept across it.

"ENGAGING SHIELDS."

Another emerald beam clove the dark above Vorgossos, shot past so near I thought for sure I heard the void sizzling as it passed, as though the very quantum foam of reality were boiling. My teeth rattled as afterburners engaged, and I rocketed toward the planet's surface. The AMP returned fire of itself, launching a fusillade of tiny missiles from a reserve in the left shoulder—though at what it fired I had no idea.

"2Maeve!" I bellowed into the comm. "What's going on?"

The woman did not at once reply.

"2Maeve!"

The cephalophore plunged sharply, the main drive in the center of my back thrusting me down, down toward the craggy peaks and icy valleys of Vorgossos.

"2Maeve!"

"Drones!" came the wretched woman's answer. "We've been made!"

Another ray of emerald fire sliced the sky before me, moving like a sword blade. I marked its origin on the surface just as a trio of fireballs bloomed in the dark. The particle beam had cloven three of our fliers in twain, and their pieces fell like heavy rain to the snowbound surface miles below.

"We're going in!" 2Maeve said, and a moment later, I was falling, rocketing toward the planet. Turning my neck, I saw perhaps a dozen others converging, falling toward the source of that emerald sword. 2Maeve meant to rush the guns. I prayed the weapon needed time to charge before refire. As close together as we were, a well-aimed shot might claim us all. No Royse barrier could endure sustained fire from a beam weapon for more than a couple seconds, not unless it drew power from a ship's antimatter reactor.

A hail of missile fire rained from my shoulders and from the shoulders of the others as we fell toward the surface, and a moment later I watched the sunfire of innumerable small-scale explosives carpet the target area below.

"Art-1 to Mistwalker," said 2Maeve. "We had to drop early. Ran afoul of a gun emplacement on the surface. It's been neutralized."

Instead of Lorian's high, aristocratic voice, the voice that answered was the basso profundo of Lorian's first officer, the Exalted Amatorre. "Very good, Arthur-1. Proceed to target."

Rockets flared, and at once we were flying, skating lower and lower over the icy terrain. The peaks of the nearest mountains were by then above our heads, whole castles of ice where perhaps no human foot had ever trod. The pale-green light that characterized the planet seemed to rise through the ice below, filling the night with a low, phosphorescent gleam.

I wondered what its source was? Some part of that world's extensive tunnel network? Some fell engine of Sagara's? When last I'd come to Vorgossos, I had believed them the light of cities, but they were too dim, too diffuse for that. They made me think of the phasma vigrandi of Luin, whose lights lead men and animals to their deaths, and of the marsh fires in ancient legend.

Dim Vorgossos.

A shot lanced through the dark above, fired from one of the mountains. Taking evasive action, my cephalophore dove into a chasm that had only just opened beneath my feet. The green light of Vorgossos streamed from its depths, bright almost as day around me. Only then did I understand its source. The whole chasm ran straight as an arrow, its walls quarried smooth and buttressed by great pylons of dark metal, a broad trench that ran for as far as I could see. Great floodlights embedded in the trench's walls and base shone upward, illuminating the massive construction.

Though I knew it not then, I was flying over the outermost part of the engine complex, components of that machine—vast as continents—designed to push the world. I had seen such places before, on the hulls of Cielcin vessels.

Something moved on the wall above me, and looking up I saw the arm of a crane immeasurably long swing round as its cab rolled along tracks built into the side of the trench.

"They're still building," I said out loud. Indeed, the construction must never stop. Anything so large and complicated as the planet's drive system must require constant maintenance and upkeep.

"T-MINUS FIVE MINUTES TO TARGET," the cephalophore's daimon informed me. My skin crawled at the sound of its falsely female voice. I grasped the control yokes with armored hands—they would not move—and clenched my teeth as the machine that enclosed me ducked beneath a bridge that spanned the trench ahead, looping to fly inverted as it dodged another barrage. Missiles launched from my shoulder tore the gun emplacements high and to my right to pieces.

Another trench diverged to our left, and the cephalophore turned to race along it. I felt the blood rush and puddle in my face as the platform decelerated, tipping back until I was almost vertical. The machine's six bladelike wings—useless in that airless place save for the attitudinal repulsors arrayed to the underside of each—scooped and slowed me to where we could then divert by another passage.

2Maeve spoke. "The tower is dead ahead now! Marlowe, prepare for drop."

"I am ready," I said, and pressed the command to close my suit's helmet inside the cockpit of the cephalophore. The helmets of the Latarran dragoons were made to interface with the AMP's systems, but my own Imperial armor was not, and so to don my helmet was to insulate me from the entoptics that projected their vision of the outside world.

To isolate me in that iron coffin completely.

How long had it been since I had worn that armor in battle? I had worn it once or twice for formal occasions on Jadd, and to show it to Cassandra. Well I remembered her—a girl hardly more than ten—donning the helmet and leaping from the bed in my chambers in the villa beneath Volcano House.

"T-MINUS THREE MINUTES TO TARGET."

"It's too heavy, Abba!" she had said, trying to lift it from her shoulders.

"T-MINUS TWO MINUTES TO TARGET."

Blind within the iron maiden, I felt the AMP decelerate, felt my heart and my stomach lurch as we rose, heard the voice of the daimon through my helm. The cephalophore shook as missiles rained from shoulder and chest. My inner ear told me we had come almost to a complete stop. The blood—pressed by the haste of our flight—flowed freely through me once more, carrying the adrenaline to every fiber of my being.

"T-MINUS ONE MINUTE TO TARGET."

I tapped the shield generator at my belt, checked that the repulsor harness fitted over my breastplate was secure. A shot rattled the whole of the AMP about me, and I bit my tongue.

"*T-MINUS THIRTY SECONDS.*"

There was a switch on the armature meant for my left hand that would open the platform's iron ribs and allow me to leap free. I disengaged the safety, readied my thumb on the catch.

"Marlowe, you're over the landing zone!" 2Maeve's voice filled my ears.

"*T-MINUS TEN SECONDS.*"

I thumbed the release.

"*VENTRAL HATCH OPENING. EQUALIZING CABIN PRESSURE.*"

With an almighty hiss, the coffin-sized cabin in the heart of the cephalophore was emptied of its air. I was relying then upon the reserves compressed in the slim tank concealed in the back of my suit, and upon the rebreather system in the helmet. A searing flash of light greeted me, and I saw the top of the ramparts awaiting me thirty feet below. The tower loomed dead ahead, a finger of bright metal rising above an arc of curtain wall like a dam. Below that wall to my left, an expanse of bare, black tarmac—half-blanketed in dry snow—stretched for what seemed a mile at least against the barren snowfields. Across that snowfield, I saw the lights of other towers, and beyond them the green glow of the trenches, and the tops of the great engines that patrolled the rails that ran along the tops of that ravine.

2Maeve's voice resounded in my ear. "Go! Go! Go!"

I didn't hesitate. I leaped from my harness, repulsors buoying me as I fell.

The gravity of that world was somewhat less than one standard, but still that fall would have broken my ankles without the repulsors to buoy me. My cephalophore had targeted and destroyed the guns atop the nearest tower. Lightning sparked amid their ruins, and a chilly vapor like smoke arose.

Dead ahead, the doors at the base of the tower dilated, and disgorged the foot soldiers of Vorgossos. By their glass dome-helmets and the hoses that ran from reservoirs to the iron collars about their necks, I knew they were men—or had been men. They raised long guns and fired on me, rushing forward to take cover behind angled fortifications.

But Gibson's sword was in my hand, the simurgh-headed sword of Jadd, its star-white blade a light in the black of that place.

This was not the abstract battle in high orbit, not the clash of ship against ship at distances my mind could never encompass. Not Lorian's lethal game of cat and mouse.

This was mettle against mettle, man against man. Toe-to-toe. Hand-to-hand. Face-to-face.

This I understood.

My cephalophore still hung in the air above the wall, its black arms extended, guns still firing. I saw the flicker of my attackers' shields as they came on, moving from cover to cover, returning fire over my head to the iron knight standing in the air above me. The first of Lorian's dragoons had leaped out after me, firing rifles as they descended, the round eyes of their hod helmets like hurasams on the eyes of the dead.

I reached the first of the enemy defenses, and hewed through them with my sword. The metal screen gave way, and the man behind it fell back, firing. I slashed at him, severing the stock of his plasma rifle and the hose that supplied his air. I saw his eyes grow wide as he understood what had happened to him, and seeing that, I knew that here was no SOM, no mindless puppet of the enemy.

The Queen, Kharn Sagara, had posted living men on her gates.

A shot took me in the back, and staggering, I whirled, found another wave of men advancing from the shorter tower. My cephalophore pivoted, guns sweeping the ramparts. As I watched more of Lorian's dragoons rappelled from the unhinging shells of their cephalophores, so that it seemed the iron maidens gave birth to living men.

One of the defenders had a heavy lance, and its particle beam tore one of the hovering platforms to pieces, cutting through its shield. The ruined hulk fell to earth, crashing upon the ramparts and the field far below.

"They have us surrounded!" shouted one of the Interfaced.

Assuming he meant the words for me, I said, "We have to win the tower! Push! Push now!" I waved my sword like a standard. *"Man!"* I cried, finding I could no more shout *Earth!* Or *Empire! "Man! For Mankind!"*

Cries of "Latarra!" and "For the Monarch!" answered me.

Still, the man was right. We were surrounded. Another shot from the heavy lance claimed a second cephalophore, and the flash of its destruction flooded the endless night. Far away, greater lights raged against the belly of the sky, and I knew that somewhere, Sentinel Commander Kedron's ships were dropping their bombs, hoping to cripple the planet-vessel's mighty stardrive. Higher still, one still could see the flicker and the minute lines of beam weapons traced between the vessels of the fleet light-seconds away.

"Lorian!" I shouted into the comm, hurling myself behind cover to guard against the heat of the enemy's lances. "Lorian, we made planetfall! We're advancing to the tower now."

No reply.

"Lorian!"

The response came after a second's delay. "Good for you!" he said. "We're a bit busy up here."

I fell silent myself, and lurched from hiding to rush the next enemy position. My sword blazed in my fist—bright almost as the burning brand of Ragama, if colder. I hewed at the enemy, striking the legs out from under one defender, catching another in the chest with a thrust that smote his heart.

At my back, still more of the Interfaced were landing, while their cephalophores—piloted now either by those still airborne or by their own daimons—swept the ramparts from the air. I felt the urge to duck each time one of the machines flew overhead, but kept my head up, my eyes forward as I advanced.

A short stair ran from the top of the wall ahead to the door that opened into the tower. As I reached its base, those gates rose up, and a horror stirred within.

The creature was like a spider, a giant of fiber and steel many times greater than a man. Seeing it, I lost a step, mind numb with the terror of it. Before I could move, it struck at me with one of its innumerable limbs. I raised my blade to parry, but its forelimb was adamant, and the force of that blow nearly knocked me from my feet. I ducked a wild slash from a limb that was no limb at all, but a sword ten feet long. Only as the beast turned and crawled down the steps into the light did I realize what it was.

Not a spider at all.

It was a man.

Had been a man. Once.

Here was one of the Exalted, one of those demoniacs who had sold his very flesh for power, and with it, his soul. One could still see the shape of man through the grafting of all those limbs, though the torso had been made larger, the shoulders and hips widened to accommodate so many arms and legs. More like a scarab was he than a son of Earth, and scuttled toward me, his face—a mere ornament—smiling without helmet or visor to protect it from the airless cold. A dozen iron arms hung beneath his bulk like the jaw legs of some crustacean. The beast barreled toward me, moving lightly down the steps despite its bulk. It raised that long sword, and lo! Its edges blazed with pale fire!

The weapon thrust toward me, and I spun my sword to parry and step inside. The white-edged blade *caught* my own, and too late I recognized the shine of highmatter about that core of common steel. The giant blade whistled round, and it was all I could do to lift my own weapon in a two-handed parry that saved me being riven in two. So great was the strength of that blow that any other man would have broken. But as I had endured the onslaught of the *vayadan*-general Bahudde, I endured, directing time to that place where I did not falter.

I think that my endurance shocked the chimera, for it froze a moment, its undead face—moved by subcutaneous wires that recalled Lorian's own implants—scowling in the airless void. The huge highmatter sword fell again, and again I caught it, turned it back, thrust at the creature. My blade penetrated the monster's eye, but it showed no pain, only shrunk back and redoubled its assault. No blood ran from that wounded face, no fluid boiled in vacuum. Another of the beast's countless arms lashed out at my eyes, and I caught that iron fist in my left hand—my new hand of flesh. I felt the report of that impact resound in all my bones, but not a one of them broke.

I hammered my blade against the joint in the beast's long arm, felt the substrate tear. The appendage went limp—I must have severed the glass wires that carried messages to the hand from the creature's jarred brain.

I had not expected the power to come so easily, to flow through me like clear water, and yet it did.

But it was not enough.

One of the creature's hooked forelimbs caught me by the ankle and pulled my feet out from under me. I hewed at one of its many wrists and the jointed fingers reached for me, scrabbling backward over the ground, feeling the grind of my armored back against the stone of the wall. The mangled hand hung—half-shorn—from the wrist, but two more seized my shoulders, and the giant highmatter sword drew back as the Exalted *thing* made to drive the point in beneath the lip of my breastplate.

That might have been the end of Hadrian Marlowe, and an ignominious end, had not a huge shape fallen out of the night and caught the wrist that held that sword. It was one of the cephalophores, its wings blazing with light, its engines smoldering with blue fire. It shifted its weight and pulled the Exalted spiderling into the air like a wrestler hurling his opponent to the mat.

My iron rescuer turned and fired upon the chimeric beast with the plasma launcher strapped to one arm. The Exalted was shielded, threw up arms to further shield its core. For a moment, it was pinned in place. I rocked to my feet, sword still in my hand. The cephalophore that had saved me alighted not half a dozen paces to my left, and I advanced in the shadow of its guns.

My savior's suppressive fire had cut the monster's shields to ribbons, and the Exalted's breastplate gleamed red with heat. Even if the adamant stood proof against plasma, the components within—man and machine—were surely boiled as a lobster in its shell. Still the mighty sword flashed, ten feet of blazing highmatter, blue as lightning. Again I raised my sword to parry, felt the crushing weight of servos whining. The eyes of that dead, still-human face went wide in vacuum as I stepped in to plunge my blade into the monster's glowing heart.

The Exalted had been that door's last defender—perhaps the captain of the gate. The men about me were laying down their arms! They knelt, hands on heads.

We had won the gate.

The men behind us on the wall were retreating, falling back to the lesser tower.

The cephalophore whose pilot had saved me from the gate captain knelt itself, its chassis clamshelling open. I moved to greet my savior, expecting 2Maeve, or if not 2Maeve, one of her lieutenants. 5Eamon or 8Gael.

But the man who leapt from the AMP's saddle was arrayed in glittering gold. Of gold were his gauntlets, and gold his shimmering greaves. The helm he wore upon his head shone in the tower's lamps. Whatever artisans had crafted it—whether on Latarra or in the deeps of time—had fashioned it in the image of a terrible bird, so that the visor seemed the hooked beak of a falcon, and the eyes were set with diamonds black as coals, so that the man within looked out through optic threads inlaid in the helmet itself. Black was his tabard, and blacker still the cloak that hung from his broad shoulders, and the collar of his office shone about his neck and shoulders like a fragment of the very sun.

It was Calen Harendotes.

The Monarch himself had come, and the sight of him sent a thrill through his people, and a shiver of terror through the defenders kneeling and frightened about the tower gate.

Kharn Sagara had returned to Vorgossos.

One of him, at least.

"It is well I was here, Marlowe!" he said, his words conveyed to me over a private channel. "That chimera nearly had you."

"Lord Sagara," I said, as privately. "I did not expect to find you in the van."

"Vorgossos is my home," he said in answer, cocking his head in a way accentuated by the avian nature of his helmet. There were jeweled bangles affixed to either side of his head, beaded strands that wavered as he moved. They looked almost like earrings. "You think I would entrust its recapture to anyone else? To you?"

I unkindled my blade, looked round at the kneeling men, at our dragoons as they hurried to collect their arms under the watchful eyes and aim of the still-floating cephalophores. I said nothing, and turned away, moving for the stair. There was yet work to be done. The guns needed to be powered down, the gates to the tunnels opened.

"You should be dead," he said to my retreating back.

I did not need to remain near at hand to continue this conversation, but I halted at the top of the stairs.

"That chimera's attack should have crushed you."

"Yes," I said. "It should have."

CHAPTER 56

THE DRAGON'S BELLY

MY OWN MASKED FACE watched me from the window glass, thin and translucent as a ghost. That mask had never seemed *mine* to me, not truly. Ever it had been a costume, an artifice put on by the boy Hadrian in an effort to become *Lord Marlowe*. The Halfmortal. The Hero of Aptucca. The Devil of Meidua. Now it seemed more real—more familiar—than my own face.

I had never felt more powerful—more in tune with the power that the Absolute had given me. I clenched my fists at my sides, felt the creak of nanocarbon-backed rubber in my gloves, the subtle click of the plates that guarded fingers and the backs of both my hands as they slid against one another.

I eyed Sagara's gleaming reflection in the window, studied him at his work. The Monarch of Latarra had busied himself overseeing the capture and conversion of the command post. The tower and the barbican that stood athwart the tunnel gate and the landing field was to become our beachhead, cornerstone of our assault on the palace of the Undying and the profane city above its gates. It occurred to me then—watching his aureate reflection in the glass—that he had chosen his new title with care. He was not an *emperor*, not a *king*, but the *Monarch of Latarra*.

The *only ruler.*

The only one.

His whole identity—his very name—had become a repudiation of his sister-self. He, who had at first pushed for change, had learned his lesson at the point of that other's sword. There could be but one lord of Vorgossos.

Would be but one.

The last of the gate tower's human defenders—those who had not surrendered—had made a final, desperate stand in that very chamber. I myself had cut the door, permitting 2Maeve and her dragoons to seize the chamber and slay the last of the defenders. Their bodies lay—still smoking—upon the floor, or else slumped in the seats that were to be their conveyance to eternity.

"They got a signal off, my Monarch," said 2Maeve darkly. "Sagara knows of our presence here."

"No matter," said Calen Harendotes, seated amid the smoke and wreckage of that bright chamber. "Elffire and the Imperials are all accounted for?"

"And Commandant General Jansen's men," said the dragoon commander. "We have the gates open, we'll be ready to move out within the hour."

For a long moment then, Calen Harendotes did not respond. In that moment, he recalled the shadow of his grandfather incarnation, the elder Sagara who sat for eons unmoving, lost in memory and the careful analysis of his art. "Our going will be slow," he said. "The tunnels will admit all but the largest of our ships, but we will have to rely upon repulsors only. There will be times when we must maneuver most carefully. Your men, commander, will lead the van. Your AMPs will be invaluable below."

My vision and my attention wandered to the world beyond the window glass, to the frigid field and the fleet of troop carriers alighting upon it. Cassandra was with that force, and Edouard, and my Irchtani, and Raman-thanu and its four kinsmen. I longed to go to them.

In taking the tower, Harendotes had disabled the airfield's automated defense grid. Outside, the guns that before had blazed with unrighteous thunder were silent as the dead. It struck me, then, how inferior such a system was to an army of well-trained men. The woman Sagara's merce-naries had given up the fight the minute their dread captain fell, but the daimons that governed the artillery? Those had been annihilated by a single keystroke.

I turned my back on the window, studied the room: the flashing con-soles, readouts and holographs I but little understood shimmering above black glass; the still-smoking bodies of the dead; 2Maeve and her dragoons in Latarran black and gold, fearsome as the damned.

The commander and the Monarch both had removed their helmets in the safe climate of the control room, but I had no desire to smell the dead burning, and resolved to keep mine in its place. Thus relatively safe from pricking ears, I keyed Lorian's frequency, waited for him to confirm receipt.

"Did you know?" I asked, surprising myself with the force of my words.

No response.

"Lorian, did you know?"

The *Mistwalker*'s immediate danger had been overcome more than an hour previously, but the ship had circled round to the far side of the world. A signal delay was to be expected, but not so great a one. I pictured the little man chewing his tongue, weighing his words with care.

For all that deliberation, the best he could manage was, "Did I know what?" His tone was strangely brittle.

"You didn't tell me that *he* was leading the ground assault," I said.

The Commandant General answered in Lorian's voice. *"He ordered me not to."*

"And that didn't strike you as strange?"

"The Monarch's security is of paramount importance," came the man's late reply.

"Black planet, Lorian!" I turned my head from the crowded room. My eyes went to the body of one of Kharn's defenders, a dryad man in a gray-and-white uniform that seemed strangely familiar. I hissed, "Don't sell me that line."

"I had my orders," he said.

"You should have told me."

"I *did* tell you," Lorian said, "I'm not your man anymore. I did my duty, and my time. I am Latarran, now."

I chewed on my tongue then, studying the face of the dead dryad. "So you are," I said. "How fares the fleet?"

"Kedron's bombing was a success," Lorian said. "The planet's engines are down. The ground force Sagara kept clustered about the pole are mostly dead. The main body of our fleet is holding."

"No sign of the *Demiurge?*" I asked.

"Not yet."

That was both blessing and curse. I did not like the thought of the mighty vessel armed and dangerous overhead. Mighty though our fleet was, I could only begin to guess at the destructive power of the Mericanii Archontic weapons, and knew that our odds of a victory—both in orbit and on the planet's surface—were better with the vessel strangely absent.

Still, I wanted that ship, had been sent to retrieve it. Turning, I looked at Calen Harendotes, at the Monarch seated amid the ruin of the control room. He had brought me as a trump, as a powerful new piece in the game he played against his sister-self, one she did not possess. He would suffer me only so long as I served his purpose. But what precisely was that purpose? Why had he allowed—insisted—that I lead the van?

And why had he come himself?

"You don't think..." Lorian's voice intruded on my reflection. "You don't think Kharn Sagara has fled, do you?"

Thinking of the titanic effort Harendotes had undertaken to reclaim what was lost to him, I said, "I can't see Sagara abandoning Vorgossos under any circumstance."

"He has to know we were coming," Lorian said. "He must have spies on Latarra."

"If...he knew," I said, careful not to say *she* and reveal I knew more than he, and so imperil us both, "then why did he not take the planet away from here?"

Lorian's response was several seconds delayed. "You think it's a trap?"

There was something going on I did not understand, some part of the contest between Sagara and Sagara. Something to do with their cycle of reincarnation, perhaps? Or was it only that the woman was so confident of victory that she had waited here for us?

"He's holding the *Demiurge* back," I said. "He'll wait until the fleet's spent. Scattered. Then he'll strike."

"It's what I would do," Lorian said.

"Tell Douro, Gadkari, Kedron...the others," I said. "Tell them to be ready."

"We have the numbers," Lorian said. "Even with the *Demiurge*, we outnumber the Vorgossene fleet ten to one."

"I only hope it's enough."

Cassandra had been given a suit of common legionnaire's armor, over which she had donned her Jaddian *mandyas*. Albé came on beside her, dressed in a suit of unassuming black with the hand-and-sun symbol of HAPSIS enameled small above the heart. His ancestor's rifle hung over one shoulder, and I would not have known him but for it—as I would not have known Cassandra were it not for *mandyas*, for the faces of both were hidden by the visors of their helms.

Ramanthanu and the other Cielcin followed in their wake, and even the Latarrans cut them a wide berth.

We met on the fused silicate of the landing field, beneath a sky still filled now and again with the shine of distant weapons fire.

"We don't have long," Edouard said, clapping me on the shoulder. "Ghoshal says they've launched lighters from a base on the surface about a thousand miles off. We need to get into the tunnels."

"It's a long way to the city, isn't it?" Cassandra asked. "Through the tunnels?"

"Several thousand miles," said 2Maeve, appearing at my left hand. The Interfaced commander had donned her helmet again and its lamplike eyes glared at us from beneath the lip of her helmet. "It'll take us the better part of a day to reach the city underground. My people will take point, cover the troop carriers...now move it."

"Where's our ship?" I asked Cassandra.

"Just back this way," she said.

2Maeve seized me by the forearm, halting my progress. I felt Cassandra tense, but turned to face the Interfaced woman. "How did you do it?" she asked. Her grip was like a vise. "What you did on the wall. Against that Exalted?"

I pulled my arm free, turned to go.

"You really are everything they say you are, aren't you?" 2Maeve asked. "Everything *he* says you are." That stopped me, and I turned to look at her, at the woman who had tamed Lorian Aristedes. When I did not speak, she said, "When you showed up aboard the *Mistwalker*, I thought it was some trick. But you went toe-to-toe with that chimera. I saw it."

Steadily, I nodded. "And don't you forget it, commander."

"Why are you here?" she asked, moving to block my progress. "You Imperials should have been relegated to the battle in orbit, instead he puts you on the front line. Why?"

With delicate care, I laid a hand on 2Maeve's shoulder, some part of me daring her to make some move. To challenge me. "I am beginning to wonder that myself," I said.

"He told us not to tell you of his presence until he revealed himself," she said, meaning Calen Harendotes. "He doesn't trust you. I don't trust you."

I let her talk, waited for her to fall silent before saying. "You trust Lorian."

That found her heart, and I felt her flinch beneath my fingers. Almost then I expected her to seize my wrist and try whatever assault she was imagining. She drew back instead. "You've no right to invoke his name," she said. "You hear me? None."

2Maeve froze suddenly, cocked her head, as if listening. She held that posture for less than a fraction of a second, but in that smallest space of time, I guessed an entire conversation had elapsed. "We're not finished," she said—though we were, and would forever be. She had received orders, and hurried off to carry them out.

"You have a real talent for making friends," Edouard observed.

"I hit you," I said flatly.

The intelligence man sniffed. "I remember."

Ramanthanu lurched toward us. I had forgotten how tall the xenobites were. It had been some time since I stood so near to one. "*Raka yumna Vorugosa ne?*" it asked.

Vorugosa was the Cielcin name for the planet.

I grunted the wordless Cielcin affirmative, said, "It is."

The Cielcin warrior's face was concealed behind the mask that supplied it air, and I marveled at the way its long hair floated off its shoulders in vacuum, at the creature's lack of need for a pressure suit.

Ramanthanu turned and looked out over the empty ice. "It is like one of our worlds," it said, voice flattened by the compression of the signal transmitted from the mask. "I saw the engines on our approach. My people built them for this Sagara."

"Cadanagumn raka'ta ne?" I echoed, incredulous. "They built the engines?"

Of course. Who else? The Cielcin had the technical know-how, the experience. And Kharn Sagara had known of them well before the Empire had.

"Which prince?" I asked, already knowing the answer.

Ramanthanu swiveled its head to look at me, the wide, black eyes on its mask making it seem almost some skeletal owl. "Dorayaica," it said.

"What did he say?" Cassandra asked. "What about Dorayaica?"

"Dorayaica built the planet's engines for Kharn Sagara," I said, and marveled, thinking of the great crater away to the south. "A long time ago."

It was then that Edouard asked the question I should have asked, and in so doing linked together certain of the pieces that had always floated unconjoined in the back of my mind. "Was it Sagara who first gave Dorayaica access to human technology, do you think?"

"I assumed it was MINOS," I said. And yet Kharn Sagara had told me of dealings he had had with the xenobites in the past. Had Dorayaica been among the names of the princes he had given me? "Or else Dorayaica simply looted what it found."

"It must have made a deal with Sagara," Edouard said. "Shields, weapons, chimerization... all for the engines. But why?"

"Sagara fears death," I said. "And so much of her life is wrapped up in this place..."

"Her life?" Cassandra was looking at me, her face hid behind the faceless visor.

"His life," I said, at once aware that some agent of the Undying was sure to be observing this conversation, lurking in the shadows of our suits' communication systems. "One of the forms of Sagara I knew was a woman."

Cassandra made a disgusted face.

"If Sagara was Dorayaica's first point of contact with mankind," Edouard was saying, "he might have introduced the Prophet to MINOS later on."

"It's possible," I allowed, looking to Ramanthanu. Would that I had known to interrogate the creature on this matter sooner. Ramanthanu had been a captain in Muzugara's service, had perhaps even fought opposite the *Tamerlane* at Thagura, and had not served Dorayaica. Still, it was possible that rumor of the then Aeta ba-Aetane's actions had passed among the clans. Perhaps it had even been the news that Syriani Dorayaica had received mighty weapons from a race of inferior beings that had sent the first *sciandane* fleets roaring out of the north. Had it been rumor of the wealth and riches of humankind carried by the Prophet's servants that had brought their first ships to Cressgard?

Had Kharn Sagara caused the war?

Had I followed these lines of thought through to their conclusion, I might have understood the full scope and shape of our danger, and of how we'd been deceived. But the lines would not converge, the gears would not turn.

Not yet.

"There is more here we do not understand," I said, attempting to bring my focus back round to the task at hand. Speaking first in Galstani and then in the Cielcin tongue, I said, "We must be very careful. I want you all to stay by me."

Dark are the pits beneath the palace of Kharn Sagara, dark and deeper still—but they have a bottom. By many miles and many winding passages we went, men jostling one another in the close air of our fliers. The cephalophores had gone in first, led by 2Maeve and her dragoons. The great tunnels had been dug by Sagara and his machines to supply fuel and coolant to the engines, as well as to allow for the massive particle colliders that produced the antimatter fuel necessary to run the almighty stardrive. These had been built in the Cielcin fashion, in stacked loops hundreds of miles in diameter, either underground or within the sheltering walls of the craters high above.

The smallest of these were hardly large enough to admit a single man, but the grandest were vast as the trenches that veined the planet's surface, thoroughfares and highways designed for the transport of cargo trams and such ships as ours. For there were vast storehouses in the remoter parts of that world, and fastnesses empty and desolate, redoubts built for the retreat of that planet's deathless lord.

More than once, the forces of the Undying were set against us. More than once turrets and guns on tracks opened fire. I rode in the train, hunkering on a bench in the back of one flier beside Cassandra, one hand clenching her arm as the ship shook. Oft as not, she dozed, evidently at her ease. How could she sleep in such a place?

I touched her face, as I had when she was small. Glad that she was with me—if dreading that she was there. Her mother had come to Vorgossos with me, and faced the horrors of the palace and the garden that lay beneath it. I had not wished to place the girl in danger, but her mother would have cursed me had I tried to hold her daughter back.

"Abba?" she stirred, and caught me watching her. "What is it?"

"It's nothing," I said. "I was thinking of the last time I was here."

Cassandra straightened, shifted to look at me. "They told me how you fought that monster at the gate," she said. "Can you teach me? How you do it?"

I blinked down at her, mindful that Edouard was seated across from us, strapped into his chair. I did not distrust the Museum Catholic, but he was HAPSIS still, and I was wary that what passed between us might find its way to Caesar—not only to Kharn Sagara, who doubtless still was listening.

I looked at her a long time, so long I thought myself frozen—turned all
to black marble. Presently, I smiled. "I'm not sure I can," I said. The thought
that the Quiet's gift might be something I might transmit had never once
occurred to me. The Jaddians had pinched and prodded me for decades before
they spun Cassandra on their looms. Severine and Urbaine had taken blood
and brain scans—though if MINOS had gained any insight into what I was,
they had not turned it to the service of the Prophet-King of Dharan-Tun.

"Will you try?" she asked in her native Jaddian. Her hand was on mine,
and squeezed it tightly. "I want to try."

I returned the pressure of her hand. "All right," I said. "When this is over."

In time, she dozed once more, and I—who has not slept since Samek's
poison took me—wandered in memory behind my eyes, thoughts questing
in the dark beyond the narrow windows of our shuttle.

Certain of our soldiery had remained on the surface to reify our hold
upon the beachhead, and to establish communication relays that would keep
us in contact with the fleet. They were to be reinforced by the Chantry's
Sentinels under Kedron's command, while Lorian's fleet held the lower orbits
against reprisal from elsewhere on the surface. Higher and deeper into the
dark, Lord Douro and the bulk of the vast Latarran fleet still engaged the
enemy. I occupied myself trying to comprehend the scale, the scope of it:
vessels engaged across light-seconds of time, their rack and ruin spread
across thousands of miles of blank eternity.

The light of that battle would stream out across eternity, and perhaps be
seen by astrologers in ages hence, some poor magus prophesying doom—
little knowing or realizing that the doom that light portended had come
ten thousand years before... and to other men.

Our own doom was nearer at hand, as again our shuttle shook, jostled
Cassandra from my shoulder.

"What's going on?" she asked.

Edouard had already found his feet. "We're hit!" he said, and tapped
the comms patch behind his ear. "Shields are holding."

I keyed the commander's channel. "2Maeve, what's going on out there?"

The Interfaced woman's reply was a moment coming. "Railguns," she
said flatly. "Mounted on tracks along the tunnel. His Majesty says this
section is heavily fortified."

Standing myself, fingers to that place behind my ear, I said, "He seems
to know an awful lot about this place's defenses." I was playing with fire,
I knew, testing the Monarch's waters.

But if I was letting on my knowledge of things hidden, the commander
did not seem to know—or notice. "We've good intelligence," she said. "Lord
Black was a fixture at Sagara's court for thousands of years. He helped to
build this place."

Is that so? I thought, thinking of the giant who had sat at the Monarch's right hand.

An explosion sounded from outside, its ruddy luminance streaming in from the starboard windows, casting bloody light upon the white-armored men inside. Something huge and fast as fire flashed past us in the gloom—one of 2Maeve's cephalophores. A moment later, another explosion rocked the under-dark, and we were sailing forward, rushing on repulsors pushed suddenly hard. Inertia nearly toppled me—did topple Cassandra—and she fell against a row of seated men. I caught one of the hand loops in the ceiling above, and hurled myself forward, keeping my feet by sheer force of will.

"Strap in!" came the flight officer's warning on the comm—too late. I reached the fore of the compartment, pushed past the hatchway to stand behind the twin pilot seats.

"What's going on?"

"Enemy had turrets, sir," said the man to my left. "Big ones. Extras lit them up."

Through the forward canopy, I had a clear view of the great tunnel. Its cross section was circular, a massive tube in the bowels of the planet, its sides complicated by the presence of lesser pipelines and ductwork, and by cables bracketed to the walls. I saw what must have been the tracks the guns had been mounted to: twin rails to left and right, such as a tram might use. Now and again, a junction would flash by us, side passages opening left and right, above and below. Always the tram rails would rotate, spiraling to bypass the junction, so that the rail that started at our left hand ran to the floor rather than across an opening.

As I watched, a car hurtled onto that track, accelerating on superconducting magnets to match our speed. I saw the turret atop it swivel to fire on the ship before us, saw the flash of shields. My pilot eased back, putting distance between us and the ship in front. There was room to maneuver in that great shaft, but always the chance that the loss of the ship ahead might spell our own destruction. I was dimly aware of the other lightercraft in our train, narrow-bodied *Shrike* boarding craft, fat-bellied *Ibises* and the Latarran equivalent—each containing perhaps half a hundred troopers.

One of the Interfaced AMP units flashed past, fell upon the turret tram and *grappled* it, using pincers like mighty thews to tear the cannon from its moorings. Explosions rocked the tram cart as the cephalophore leaped away, six wings blazing with repulsor light as two of its brothers winged past, streaking ahead of us up the tunnel.

As I stood there, we came forward into a junction the size of a coliseum and just as round. Perhaps a dozen passages converged there, radiating like the spokes of a wheel. Our flier shook as a shot caromed off our shields.

"They're above us!" said the copilot from the seat to my right.

We had flown directly into a kill box. Turrets on rails ran all about the perimeter of the chamber, above and below the entryways to the side passages, and gun emplacements covered every entrance.

"We're close to the city!" came the voice of one of the Interfaced. I thought it might be 8Gael.

Seamlessly, the voice of one of the others put in. "Fifth passage on our left, the Monarch says! Move!"

The ships ahead of us in the train were already moving, threading the flash of the guns in their desperate attempt to win free.

"Shields holding," said the copilot. "Power reserves at seventy-three percent."

Just ahead, another of our lighters erupted in a fountain of red flame. My heart—which moments before had risen high in my throat—sank almost to my knees. There had been half a hundred men on that ship.

All of them, gone.

Another of the cephalophores let loose a salvo of missile darts that flared toward the guns high on the walls above, and as I watched three of the turrets fell in heaps of burning slag.

Another of our fliers burst into flames.

A moment later, a call from some other vessel sounded on comm. "Taking heavy fire!"

"They're everywhere!"

"We should have held back and let the Extras handle it," I said.

Calen Harendotes must have known what we were flying into. He had built these tunnels, in past lives. Grinding my teeth, I gripped the backs of both the pilot's and copilot's seats. The mouth of the proper tunnel was straight ahead, its guns turning to focus fire on us. What had the Monarch been thinking, driving our train into that awful place?

I understood a moment later, as the first salvo tore across our bow.

He had meant the train to serve as bait. As targets.

The fliers were much larger the cephalophore units, slower and less nimble, and better able to shield themselves from concentrated fire. The daimons that governed those turrets' offenses had prioritized our fliers over his hussars. The flying cavalry fell upon those guns, and there! I saw one at the fore of all the others, black armored and terrible, its wings spread in the dark of that hideous maze, and in its pincered hand was the sword of the captain of the gate, that massive spike of highmatter-edged steel. It sliced the nearest turret to ribbons, rocketed to the next, carving a ruin of sparking fume and torn steel in its wake.

Without having to be told, I knew that here was Calen Harendotes himself, the Monarch-Conqueror at the head of his host, and he was a fury to behold.

"The way is clear!" came the royal voice, the voice of the Undying Lord of Vorgossos-in-Exile. "Forward, Latarrans! Forward to victory!"

I had expected Sagara to lead from the rear, to safeguard his momentarily delicate mortality. But he fought like a whirlwind, the edge and very point of the sword that was his army. But then, he was precisely where he had to be. Who knew the warrens and secret places of Vorgossos better than he, who built them? Still, so great was the valor of his assault that I forgot for a moment the cold calculation he had made, and the deaths of so many of my own men.

But only for a moment.

"Follow the Extras!" I said, thumping the pilot's seat. "Follow the Extras!"

We surged forward, and once more I was forced to hold on for all that my life was worth. Our flier rushed through the gate and out of the great junction, sailing along miles of conduit-lined tunnel.

"We're nearly to the inner gate," 2Maeve said on comm. "Your men should make ready to deploy!"

"What about the guns?" I asked, lurching back against the bulkhead by the door separating the cockpit from the rest of the flier.

"Leave them to us!"

I returned to the rear compartment, shouting for the men to make ready. Cassandra was on her feet, was pulling her coif up over her coiled hair, and Edouard was already masked. "Albé!" I gestured for him to join me.

The HAPSIS man pushed through the soldiers to my side. Placing one hand on his shoulder, I bellowed so that the whole compartment might hear. "This is Vorgossos!" I said, pleased by the weight and carriage of my new voice. "Trust nothing that you see! I want every one of you to power down your comms. Stay by one another, rely on hand signals!"

"Sir?" One of the men cocked his head, confused.

The ship banked beneath us, and I caught the loop in the ceiling above my head to steady myself. We were sweeping in for a landing. "There are daimons here, soldier! Thinking machines! You must guard yourselves and your suits! Comms down! Do you understand?"

The soldiers roared their affirmative.

I did not say that I did not trust our Latarran allies, that I did not trust Harendotes himself. But if our soldiers were silenced, severed from the comms, we might escape even his scrutiny.

We would be free to act as we would. As we needed.

"Pass the order along to every unit you encounter!" Albé said, taking up the role of my second. "Marlowe's orders—and mine!"

"The Extras should have the gate open by the time we make land!" I said. "Make straight for the gates! Don't linger in the open. We'll be—"

An explosion slammed into the port side of our flier, knocking me from my feet and into the starboard wall. Men hurled upon one another by the blast fell like tumbled cordwood, and the whole world began to spin. We were going down, spiraling. I guessed that whatever had struck us must have burst just outside the curtain of our shield, for I saw no debris, no blast of fire as I reeled. Rather the concussive force of that blast had knocked us from our course, must have damaged one of our repulsors out on the flier's portside wing where the shield was at its thinnest.

"Brace for impact!" someone roared. Edouard? The pilot officer?

I hurled myself at Cassandra, wrapping both arms around her as the flier struck metal with a sound like the breaking of worlds.

Silence then, punctuated only by the sound of fighting outside like distant thunder.

"Cassandra?"

"Yes?"

"You're all right?"

"Yes, Abba," she said.

She had fallen beneath me, and still more of the others had fallen on top.

"Blow the hatch!" came a voice, far off. It sounded strange. Muffled. Amplified. Looking back over my shoulder toward the rear, I saw a knot of men standing or crouching near the exit. We had fallen at an angle, nose down, so that the floor heaved up and to the right as one approached the door.

As I watched, the explosive bolts on the hatch blew—emergency lights flashing red and soundlessly. The door vanished into darkness, admitting the night that was beneath the black planet's crust.

Albé had found his feet. His family's rifle was slung over one shoulder. Legs apart, he bent to offer us a hand. "We're down," he said, unhelpfully.

"I noticed," I said, and—taking his offered hand—stood and stooped to help Cassandra to her feet. Belatedly, I tugged my coif up over my hair, punched the command to close my helmet. Cassandra did the same.

It took my suit's entoptics a moment to flicker on, to render for me a vision of the crashed shuttle and the darkness without void of the smoke and fume of that hideous place.

"Where exactly are we?" Cassandra asked, leaping from the rear of the shuttle to the uneven ground outside.

Ramanthanu was waiting for us, its kinsmen at its back. They were looking up into the darkness, round eyes wide open.

"Dein raka ne?" I asked them.

"There are yukajjimn on the walls," Ramanthanu said, pointing with its scimitar. I could not see them. "They do not attack."

All about us, our other ships were landing, seeking level ground amid the huge conduits and catwalks that ran along the tunnel's floor. Ahead, a broad slope of poured stone rose to a flat expanse of shelf, and beyond that, the great inner gates of the profane city stood closed. Above and about them, level upon level, switchback ramps rose to either side, running back along the tunnel.

"They don't need to," I said.

High above us, one of the great turrets blazed, underscoring my point.

A trio of our hussars streaked overhead, wings crackling with blue fire. One fell smoking from the heavens, crashed into the floor not five hundred feet from where we stood. Our own soldiers were spilling from their landers. Some were picking shots at the turrets, at the enemy soldiers Ramanthanu had seen waiting for us.

Then Calen Harendotes made his move.

Heavy were the mighty doors of Vorgossos, and thick. Many lives of men they had endured, though not once had any enemy been set against them—for no enemy had come down the dark road from the planet's frozen surface. But though they had stood since the Empire was young, they fell in an instant—fell so quickly I hardly understood what had been done.

I saw a searing flash of light, heard the sound of engines roaring. An eruption of argent fire filled the gloom, so bright my suit cut the light. For a moment, I saw the dun-clad soldiery standing on the tiered ramps above us, left and right, and knew them for what they were.

Then the thunder spoke, and for a second time I moved to shield Cassandra. But bright as the blast was, it was contained.

I knew that color, that radiance, white as white.

Calen Harendotes had used antimatter against the gates of his own kingdom. A tactical charge. A single grain of antimatter whose shaped charge had funneled the full bore of that most volatile substance directly at the mighty gates. Pale light streamed through the new-made opening, strangely wholesome in the horrid gloom.

"Forward, men of Sol!" roared Edouard Albé, brandishing his rifle.

Our legionnaires streamed forward, ranks bolstered by the landed men of Elffire's division, supported by the cephalophores in the air. The Vorgossene soldiers to either side of the gate leaped from the lower balconies onto the shelf before the opened way, a pale light in their empty faces.

They were SOMs, soulless mannequins in the Undying's service, brainless creatures that had once been men. 2Maeve's cephalophores landed about us and to either side, forming a corridor along which we could travel and reach the ramp of poured stone and the broad shelf before the gates. More fliers were coming in for a landing, building a cordon around us to block the onrushing SOMs.

We had reached the shelf by then, met the soldiers streaming from the second landing wave, the one nearer the gates. The SOMs would fight to the last, but though their numbers were great, our ordnance was greater, and the guns of the Interfaced dragoons held back their mindless tide.

Then my comms crackled.

I had not silenced my own communicator, as I had told the others to do. There had not been time, and the crash had shaken the thought wholly from me.

"*Mistwalker* to Marlowe, repeat. —*walker*... Marlowe."

The signal was poor so far underground. It was a miracle it had come through at all.

But it was Lorian's voice.

"Lorian!" I shouted, holding a hand to my ear in vain effort to better hear the man. "We've reached the inner gate!"

Whatever he meant to say was garbled, broken by so many miles of air and rock and metal. Still, I discerned four words.

"Attacked—"

"...fleet scattered..."

"—*Demiurge!*"

My blood ran cold.

The *Demiurge* had come.

I almost saw it, in the gray matter of my mind, near at hand and terrible, as terrible as Dharan-Tun itself—and somehow more alien.

The *Demiurge*.

Like a great, black tower she was, a tower projecting sideways across the void. How well I recalled her buttressed nacelles, her terraced ramparts carved with statues of goddesses and devils, her forecastle like a maw of cathedral spires.

"Lorian!" I shouted into the band.

There was no reply.

"Lorian!"

There was nothing at all.

CHAPTER 57

THE SACK OF EDEN

SMOKE YET FILLED THE air about that shattered gate, and great fingers of tortured metal curled in all directions. The very stone of the floor had cracked and blackened beneath the impact of Calen's antimatter bomb, and all around, the bodies of SOMs lay broken and bloody.

For all the clamor about us, the noise of gunfire and shouting men, a curious calm stretched about that gate. The shots I heard were not the frantic sounds of battle, but the surgical precision of executions as Elffire's men and my own dispatched the enemy's wounded. The whine of engines I heard was not the sound of our attack, but was only the second wave coming in for a landing.

The cephalophores had streamed ahead, passing the ruined gate into the city beyond. They were bound for the palace gates, for the house of Kharn Sagara. Whither we, too, were bound, though it fell to us to trudge through the streets and over the terraces of Kharn's vile city.

We had come upon the mouth of the Seventh Deep, the deepest—and thereby the newest—level of the great subterrane. I could see the pale buildings within, and recognized in their design the same machined white stone, the same towers and domes and monolithic architecture that made up the Printed City on Latarra. Peering through that blasted gate, I felt as I had once as a boy when Crispin and I had overturned one of the broad flagstones in the topiary garden at Devil's Rest and upset a colony of swarming insects.

Vorgossos.

I had not wanted to return.

"Are you all right?" asked a familiar voice.

Looking round, I found Cassandra had picked her way over the bodies to my side. There was blood spattered on the white faceplate of her helm, but it was not her own.

"I'm fine," I said. "The *Demiurge* has attacked the fleet. Lorian tried to get through while we were attacking the gate..." Realizing we were alone, I asked, "Is your comm down?"

"*Si, Abba,*" she said.

"Good." I looked sidelong at the nearest Latarran soldiers. They were far enough away that I might take the necessary risk. "Is Edouard in position?"

"If he's not yet, he soon will be," she said.

"Very good," I said, and cast my eyes at the roof of the tunnel high above our heads, where steel reinforcement mingled with rude, naked stone. Recalling Lord Black's briefings on the invasion from our time on Latarra and from our meeting at Merope before this final assault, I said, "We're directly below the reservoir here."

Despite her suit, Cassandra shivered. "I don't like the thought of all that water overhead. It reminds me of Phanamhara. Only there's more."

"Much more," I said.

The oldest parts of the great city were far above us, in the dome that the Mericanii had built. That was near the surface—had been on the surface when it was constructed, before the ice had encroached and buried it forever. Sagara's palace lay beneath it, a tangled warren of tunnels and caverns, chambers and silos and great iced-over hangar bays. Below that lay the Garden—the research park and complex where the servants of the Undying practiced their black necromancy. Below that further still lay the *sunless sea,* the black waters where dwelt the daimon, Brethren, and where the Mericanii of old had built their power station to suck of the heat of Vorgossos itself.

But there was much more besides, much more than I had seen in my previous visit. The city had grown beside the old palace, spreading like the mycelia of a fungus immeasurably vast. Rather than assault Vorgossos as its master long imagined—coming down from above, through the hightower's oculus as I had when I'd come as a visitor in my youth—we had assaulted the profane city from below. That shattered gate opened on the deepest level, a level below the palace, below the Garden, below even the sunless sea. The tunnels that bound the city to the engine complex ran below the waters of Brethren's home straight to that lowest level.

"Keep your helmet on," I said to her, watching Ramanthanu and its kind approaching through the carnage toward us. "My terminal says the radiation hasn't penetrated to this depth, but be mindful."

"I thought they bombed the engines."

"And the airfields, yes," I said. "But Kedron's men bombed the city as well. There were surface defenses."

Ramanthanu drew level with us, its kinsmen close behind. Two of them—Egazimn and Bikashi, I think they were—had removed their masks, and red blood was running down their chins.

"These *yukajjimn* are not good fighters," said one.

"But they are good eating," said another.

I glared at it, but said nothing. What could I say? I had brought them with me. And why? I knew what they were, what they were capable of. We had fed them printed meat throughout our journey, but it should not have surprised me that they leaped at the chance for proper fare. They had pledged themselves to me through their captain, but that had not changed what they were—what they would ever be.

You cannot wash away a tiger's stripes, Lorian had said. *You can only be eaten by it, or ride.*

I had chosen to ride.

The lop-horned captain raised a hand for quiet. "We have taken the gate," it said to me.

I emitted the wordless noise that was the Cielcin *yes.* "But we must take the palace," I said.

The Cielcin called Otomno moved to stand beside its captain. Peering into the city, it said, "It is almost like home."

At that precise moment, a clarion call went up—the noise of trumpets and of drums filling the cavern like water—and looking I saw a column of men coming up the ramp from the tunnel below. They were all in Latarran livery, their round eyes shining like searchlights in the dark below the short bills of their hod helmets.

"The Monarch!" cried a herald. "The Monarch of Latarra is come!"

And there he was, riding a little behind the head of his column, the chest of his cephalophore unhinged to reveal the man himself arrayed in black and gold. Seeing me, he commanded the iron maiden to kneel, and leaped from his harness to the mounting peg that projected from the inside of the platform's knee.

"Lord Marlowe!" he said. "The city is ours."

"If we can hold it," I said in return. "I spoke with Aristedes during the attack on the gate. The *Demiurge* has joined the fighting."

Calen Harendotes's jeweled gaze swept over the ruin of the gates. "I know," he said, apparently unconcerned. "I am in constant communication with my generals. We hold to the plan."

"Can the fleet hold?" I asked.

"Long enough" was his answer. "But we must be swift. If we can capture Sagara, the *Demiurge* will cease to be a problem."

Cassandra interjected. "Why is that?"

The officer at the Monarch's right—Camillus Elffire, the captain of the *Mistwalker*'s infantry—snarled, "Mind your tone! You are addressing his Majesty, the Monarch!"

Calen Harendotes neither affirmed his subordinate, nor ordered him to stand down. "Only Sagara may wield the *Demiurge,* and he will not do so from its bridge. Ending the battle here will end the fight in orbit."

Not for the first time, I was struck by the difference between this incarnation of the man and the earlier one I had known. The elder Sagara had been a creature of infinite time. Of infinite patience. This younger one was by contrast a dynamo, a man of vision, of pitch and moment. Perhaps it was only that the tissues of this newer body were so much younger, so much more vital than his predecessor. Or perhaps it was that he was mortal, so much closer to death.

When had Kharn Sagara ever been so close to death?

A single shot might end his life, break the chain of experience that stretched back to the elder days, when man was young and newcome to the demon-haunted stars. All that knowledge, all that *life* could end as easily as any other for the first time, perhaps, in more than fifteen thousand years.

"You're certain he's here?" I asked, daring.

"He would not abandon Vorgossos unless he had no other choice," said Harendotes.

"You seem to know a lot about him," said Cassandra.

Calen Harendotes turned his beaked and jewel-encrusted mask on me, and for a moment I feared. After a moment, he said, "Your people have disabled their comms."

Had he been trying to speak to me? To renew his threat? Behind my mask, my eyes flickered from the Monarch's face to the tunnel. I could see some of Ghoshal's men in Imperial white hurrying from our landers to join us. The Irchtani were among them. Somewhere out there in the darkness, Edouard was at work, carrying out his secret task—the task I had given him in the darkness of the *Ascalon* on the journey from Latarra, when I had told him and Cassandra everything, when we had laid our plan and trap for those who had trapped us.

"It seemed prudent to isolate them from any praxic assault," I said. "I almost lost...a friend to an attack from one of MINOS's sorcerers."

"Your Tavrosi woman," Harendotes said.

Cassandra stiffened, almost imperceptibly.

"Yes."

One could feel the tension between us, coiling like a viper ready to strike. He did not trust me—was right not to trust me. I was glad I yet wore my mask, so little did I trust my own face not to betray me in that moment.

The moment passed, and Calen Harendotes turned his jeweled bird's head to address his subordinate. "Commander," he said at last.

Camillus Elffire snapped to attention, saluted his liege. "My Monarch." He did not know that he was about to be issued the foulest order of his career. How well I remember his face in that moment! He had the look of almost any Imperial soldier. His face was square and pale as any sailor's, with a strong, wide jaw concealed under a thicket of graying beard. His scalp was hairless, making him seem more an enlisted man than an officer.

There was nothing of the demonic about him, no hint of the machine, nor of evils subtler and more perverse. He seemed to me an ordinary man, and no butcher.

Calen Harendotes was still as stone, as the golden effigy he resembled. His words issued from speakers built into the breastplate of his armor—which may, for all I knew, have been his breast itself. "Take your men through every level of the city. Kill all you find."

To his credit, Elffire hesitated. "My...my Monarch?"

"None of the natives may be permitted to leave this place," he said. "Not one. Am I clear?"

"You cannot be serious!" I said, rounding on the Monarch.

The dragoons nearest their ruler leveled guns at me, and I halted, recalling that Cassandra was just at my side. Still, Ramanthanu and the others tensed, raised their scimitars.

I raised a hand, shouted a command to the xenobites for stillness.

"You think me amusing?" he asked. "You think this is play, what we do here?"

"You cannot kill them all!" I said. "There are thousands in this city! Thousands!"

"Hundreds of thousands," the Monarch corrected, and turned to his servant. "Commander, tear the city apart. Leave none alive."

Camillus Elffire swallowed. "Every one of them?"

"Was I unclear?" the Monarch inquired. "Every one. Man, machine, homunculus. Leave none alive."

I took another step. "That wasn't the deal, Sa—" I caught myself on the verge of saying his name. "That wasn't the deal!"

I would not be party to a massacre.

"We do not have a *deal*, Lord Marlowe," said Calen Harendotes, "you are here at my sufferance, and because you may yet prove useful. It is with your Empire that I've an accord. Not you. Now be silent!" The dragoons with their long guns tensed, but did not fire. Eyes still on Elffire, the Monarch said, "The New Order requires the destruction of the old world, commander. Are you unequal to the task?"

Whatever will there was in Elffire broke then. The light in his eyes went dim. "No, my Monarch."

"Very good," Harendotes said. "Commander 2Maeve and I will lead the assault on the palace. Lord Marlowe's people will accompany me. You have your orders, commander. Give them no quarter. Leave none alive."

Stiffly, the man saluted. "Yes, my Monarch." Turning, he placed his helm back upon his head, and the mask flipped up from his gorget and hissed as it clicked into place. He hurried to broadcast his dreadful order, leaving Cassandra, the Cielcin, and myself with the knot of Interfaced dragoons that made up the Monarch's personal guard.

"Lord Marlowe," the Monarch said. "Activate your suit's comm. We will speak privately, you and I."

Slowly—very slowly—I reached for the controls on my wrist-terminal.

The black jewels that were the Monarch's false eyes fixed on me, and a moment later his voice filled my ears—unheard by any other. "Need I remind you of my promise?"

Not one word.

"You need not," I said.

"You overestimate your value," he said coldly. "We have obtained Vorgossos. Soon, we will have obtained my sister. I do not need your support. Rather, it is you who needs mine, as I recall."

Though she could not hear us, I felt Cassandra tense at my side. She was *Maeskolon,* of the order of swordmasters. This Kharn Sagara stood mere feet from her, and from myself. She might slay him before he could give the order that killed us both. My eyes went to the empty cephalophore the Monarch had leaped out of, at its shoulder guns and the arm cannons limp at its sides.

We would never be fast enough.

I could not reliably predict whence an attack might come, and so choose to be spared its thunder.

"If you believe that," I said slowly, "then you should kill me now."

Silence.

"You need me," I said into that silence. "At least you think you do. I'm the one weapon in your arsenal your sister cannot match."

The smallest *hmm* of laughter escaped the Monarch then. For a moment, I thought he would say *something,* would reveal something of his secret hand. He had no intention of handing me control of the *Demiurge,* I knew as much, or even of handing me the Archontic weapons. He would betray me, but not until he was certain that I was no longer necessary.

But I meant to betray him, and would have to strike first.

"You are always so certain," he said. "So righteous. Tell me: Do you have doubts?"

"And you?" I asked, ignoring the question. "Are you certain? Certain your *sister* is even here?"

The Monarch's voice seemed far away, barely more than a whisper. "She is here," he said. "I can sense her... prowling at the edges of my mind. She thinks she can destroy me, as she destroyed my previous incarnation. The one you call *Ren.*"

"And can she?"

Calen Harendotes—Kharn Sagara—turned to watch Elffire's column move into the city to begin their monstrous work. His silence said everything, and again I was forced to contemplate what it must be like to be the Undying, and to be so close to death for the first time in half of an eternity. On Latarra, he had hinted that he had encountered the Watchers before, and that he had glimpsed something of what lay beyond death.

Hell, he had said.

What would a man do to avoid hell?

Almost anything, I was certain. But this?

Sharply I could hear the shock of guns in the distance. Had I been right—in part—as a boy? To think that man was as vile as the Cielcin? Or vile in his own way? I would walk those streets in moments, and see the carnage and the horror I could not have stopped for anything. As I write, I remember the body of a young boy lying in the street—his head blown to pieces, the rest of him strangely untouched. He had been the victim of an energy-lance. The beam had boiled all the fluid in his head.

He could not have been older than five.

His body recalled another I had seen. On Senuessa, long before. The girl had been strung up by her wrists, suspended by wires that cut. The Cielcin had taken her head, painted rude symbols on chest and arms, and left her for the planet's desperate crows. Were we really so different?

I had never before thought of Vorgossos as a *place*, a city where men lived, where women and children went about their lives. On my first visit, we had spoken to only one of the citizenry before Sagara's faceless men had come to collect us, and I had not seen the city for what it was: a human place, though it was filled with human ugliness.

"These are your own people," I said, thinking of the slaughter, the brutality the Latarrans had brought to bear upon the natives.

Homo homini lupus.

"They are nothing," Harendotes said. "Only my sister matters. Only Vorgossos itself."

I became aware then of a voice chanting, softly singing, filling the air about me—not piped in through the speakers in my helm.

> *Now if we could win to the Eden Tree*
> *where the four great rivers flow,*
> *And the wreath of Eve is red on the turf*
> *as she left it long ago,*
> *And if we could come when the sentry slept,*
> *and softly scurry through,*
> *By the favor of God we might know as much—*
> *as our father Adam knew.*

And I marveled—not at the quotation, or the Classical English—but to hear Kharn Sagara singing. There was something *wrong* about that simple fact. It was as though I were back in the pantheon of Phanamhara, hearing the voice of Ushara.

He should not sing.

"That's Kipling," I said.

"It is," said he. "You have been learning your poetry since our first meeting, I see." I could hear the smile in his voice. "We are storming Eden," he said. "*My* Eden, so it is fitting that I have brought the devil with me."

Before us, the city was burning, and the crack of guns resounded louder than before—nearer at hand. As I watched, one of the cephalophores streaked round a tower that rose halfway to the domed ceiling. A rocket struck that tower like lightning, and it fell.

Screams.

Fire.

Gunshots.

Eden indeed.

"We can't just stand here and do nothing," Cassandra's whisper hissed over my comm. "Abba..."

"You think me cruel," said the Monarch, voice crackling in my ear. "But you forget: Any one of them might be designed to house my sister's ghost. They must die, lest she escape."

I turned to face the king in yellow gold. "And that justifies the slaughter of innocents?"

Well I remember the Monarch's words—chilling and clear—and the way he turned his eyes on me. Black, dead diamonds glimmering. "There are no innocents," he said. "Have you heard it written? *There is none righteous.*"

I hated the Extrasolarians—hated and feared them. Feared what they were capable of, hated what they had done to Valka, and to the galaxy. It was their sorcerers who crafted the lethovirus, whose actions caused the deaths of billions.

Yet I could not wish them dead.

Not like that.

Not at the point of Sagara's sword. Not to secure his immortality.

His peace.

Doubtless you think me a hypocrite, I, who have slain billions myself. I will not argue with you, Reader, except to say that what I did I did for the galaxy, for all mankind.

What Kharn did that black day, he did only for himself.

I knew then that I would have to kill him. Not there, before the gates of the Seventh Deep, surrounded by his men, but soon. I held Cassandra's hand the tighter. Why had I not sent her into the tunnels with Edouard? Had I been alone, I might have acted then and there. Let the Quiet bring me back once more, if I was so vital to his cause.

And Lorian. Would he understand?

Would he even believe me?

CHAPTER 58

THE PALACE OF THE UNDYING

CALEN HARENDOTES HAD TO die.

He had no intention of honoring his bargain—I had known that from the beginning. Though he had needed his peace with the Imperium, needed the Chantry's bombs and me for whatever secret reason...I knew he meant to kill me when all was done. It was I who had cost him his kingdom, after all, I who had caused the shattering that birthed his predecessor and his sister-self.

I who had threatened his immortal life, or a part of it.

How could he ever let that stand?

And Cassandra...Cassandra.

O, my daughter, forgive me—who brought you to that evil place and day. May your eyes never find these pages—if you yet live. May you never learn all that happened in the bowels of the Palace of the Undying, or who I met there—or what I had to do. May you never learn why Kharn Sagara kept us alive.

May you never learn what weapon his other self tried to cultivate there in the darkness, in the stone grottoes and bottled gardens of that terrible underworld.

And forgive your father, who loves you still and always, his silence.

We came at last to the gates of the palace, passing through the slaughter in the streets beneath the wings of cephalophore and Irchtani. When I rode out from the *Mistwalker* earlier that day it had been with the intent of betraying the Monarch, of gaining the upper hand and forcing him to grant my demands. But a new plan had leaped into my mind—full-formed and -figured as Pallas from the brow of Zeus.

I would betray him to his sister if I could. Offer her her freedom and her life in return for the *Demiurge*. I could stop the slaughter in the city, stop the *Demiurge* destroying the fleet above.

I would destroy the alliance Selene had forged, the peace between Empire and Monarchy, but I would have done the will of the Absolute. The Quiet's will. And with the *Demiurge,* the Imperial fleet might turn upon the Latarrans. It was possible we could secure a surrender.

We had the telegraph device. Lord Simeon Ardahael's embassy had taken one with him when he left with Selene and Prince Matthias. But could I reach Lord Douro? Sentinel Commander Kedron? Could I make them agree to such a plan?

Could I trust them?

Well I remember those hideous gates, and the road to them—narrow and winding. When I had first come to the house of Kharn Sagara, I had ridden the tram from one of the city's many domed enclosures along a cutting in the rock. The silver line of the tracks shone in the roof overhead, while on the ground below, the way was choked with bodies.

The remains of gun emplacements sparked and smoldered on the walls. Our infantry and the Latarrans had been forced to negotiate their way along the floor of that deep and narrow chasm, relying wholly on their body shields, and upon the few cephalophores that had made it through that narrow cutting.

The fighting was done by the time we came to that place, and we were forced to negotiate that trench of corpses. The wreck of no fewer than three cephalophore platforms greeted us in the floor of the cutting, and on one occasion we were obliged to clamber over it.

Of the tram itself, there was no sign, and when we reached the end of the ravine that approached the palace gate, we were made to climb a stair so steep and narrow that only one might climb behind the other. All the while, I found myself picturing the fighting, the struggle and terrible violence that had unfolded there.

But the gates of the palace itself were open, and the blue flame still danced in the brazier before them. One of the Latarran cephalophores had brought a plasma bore and carved through the two cubits of solid steel that formed the ancient doors to the Mericanii fastness.

Harendotes had gone ahead of us, and waited with his guard by the gates. 2Maeve stood with him, with both her first lieutenants—5Eamon and 8Gael. They had shed their armored platforms, and though they were masked and helmeted, I knew them by their rank. The Monarch had not trudged through the gully below the track of the monorail, but had ridden across in his cephalophore, wending his careful way through the air above our heads. Had he meant to tire me by the added journey? Or only to humiliate me?

"Where is Sagara?" I asked.

Both 8Gael and 5Eamon answered me in unison: "Locked in his palace."

I swept my gaze over the doors.

Sagara would be in the inner sanctum, in the inverse pyramid hanging from the roof of the cavern above the waters of Brethren's home. There were his private quarters. *Her* private quarters, I supposed. Unreachable even from the main mass of the palace. A gust of wind rushed through the burnt opening, ruffled my tunic and the pteruges at my shoulders. I did not have to smell it to imagine the scent of molten metal, of the bodies of the khaki-clad SOMs strewn on the gray steps of the palace.

One lay almost at my feet, and I spurned it with my toe, rolling it onto its back.

The creature had been a man, once, pale faced and green eyed. His hair had been all shorn away, and black wires like the new lines in Lorian's face threaded his face and scalp. A heavy iron collar ran about his neck, and it was a moment before I realized that it was a part of his neck, that the chest beneath the ugly khaki uniform was more machine than man.

"What is it, Abba?" Cassandra was at my side.

I knew the Interfaced were watching. Calen Harendotes stood alongside them, still and silent, doubtless locked in deep communication with the captains of his fleet.

"When I came here last," I said, "the Empire sold Kharn Sagara twenty thousand human beings in return for his services. He arranged a meeting with one of the Cielcin princes. The first meeting of our two races." Though it did not understand my Jaddian, I directed the words at Ramanthanu, who loomed over me like a white shadow. "I only wondered if this poor bastard was one of them. If he, too, would not be here if not for me."

"I wonder what his name was," Cassandra said. "How he got here... don't you?"

"I try not to," I said.

2Maeve's voice slashed across the conversation. "We cannot take the AMPs inside the palace," she said. "The ceilings are too low, our scouts report."

"You have scouts already in the palace, then?"

The commander nodded. "You've been here before, haven't you?" She knew I had, but we did not much speak with one another, and had not upon this particular subject. "What should we expect?"

I glanced to her silent master, the golden king standing in the shadow of his cephalophore harness. Presently, I said, "There's an inner keep beyond the main fortress. A pyramid hanging from the ceiling of a cavern. It can only be reached by rail. That's where you'll find Sagara."

Another nod.

"The laboratories are all below. There's a step-well with a garden. The doors are at the bottom, but there are other ways in. Lifts. I don't remember where."

Absalom Black had not presented plans of the palace itself in his meetings, nor had Calen Harendotes. He had withheld that information, so committed was he to the ruse that *Calen* was not *Kharn*. That was why, I deemed, he had determined to lead the assault upon the palace himself, that he might lead his people where they must go, seemingly by accident.

I did not see how Harendotes intended to maintain the illusion that he was not another Kharn Sagara. It seemed incredible to me that so many among his supporters had no notion as to his true identity. The sorcerers of MINOS had known that Kharn Sagara was at war with himself. But they could not have known that the Monarch of Latarra was one of them. They had traded with Harendotes, after all, and I'd had the impression there was no love lost between the Lodge and Vorgossos.

"Have you heard from Lorian?" I asked, changing the subject.

I thought I could sense the woman's eyes narrow as she looked sharply up at me. 2Maeve held her silence for the space of a breath. "No. No, comms are down."

"The bombs?" I asked.

"Yes," she said, and I could sense the quiet tension in her. The dread. "We won't be able to contact him until the fighting's done."

Absurdly, I felt the need to comfort her, though I knew she would resent me for it. I knew nothing of 2Maeve, nothing of her people, just as I knew nothing of the corpse lying on the steps before me. In my short time on Latarra, I had learned nothing of their origins, their history. I knew not where they lived, or why they had thrown in their lot with the golden Monarch.

"I'm sure he'll be all right," I said, smiling beneath the serenity of my black mask. "He's come through far worse."

She said nothing. Almost it seemed I saw the woman through the armor, her pale eyes glassy with concern, shoulders tense, frozen.

"Lorian Aristedes is the finest officer I know," I said. "If anyone could hold the line against that dreadnought—"

"It's him," 2Maeve said, voice strangely hushed. "I know."

Implicit in the lack of any rebuke from the Extrasolarian woman was the fact that I had been right.

She *did* love him.

"You said you have scouts in the palace?" I asked.

2Maeve raised a hand for silence, turned to look at 8Gael and 5Eamon. None of them spoke.

"What is it?" I asked, not privy to their internal sharing.

In unison, the three Interfaced thrust hands in my direction, each animated by the same impulse, though whether it originated from 2Maeve or one of the lieutenants was any man's guess. So still were they, that for a moment I was acutely aware of the rest of Harendotes's force: armored troopers dismounting from cephalophore harnesses, my HAPSIS men still clambering up the narrow stair.

Calen Harendotes had himself noticed whatever it was that had claimed his dragoons' attention. He had been seated on the stirrups of his cephalophore, but stood then, not speaking, but conversing in that manner that among the Extrasolarians transcended speech.

"What is going on?" I asked, pressing forward.

"We have him," said 2Maeve, looking from myself to her lord. "They found him."

Cassandra stepped forward. "Kharn Sagara?"

The commander of Lorian's dragoons did not reply. Still looking to her liege, she said, "It's over, but..." The eyes of her helmet mask swiveled to look at me.

"But what?"

Another silence, evidence of words passing between 2Maeve and her fellow Interfaced.

The Monarch shook his head.

"What is it?" I was tired of asking questions.

"Take us to him," Calen said.

CHAPTER 59

HADRIAN AGAIN

WE HAVE HIM. THAT was what 2Maeve had said.

Him.

Was it possible that the other Sagara had reincarnated himself, resumed masculine form? Calen Harendotes had not challenged this revelation, but then to do so would have been to reveal that he knew more than he ought. And yet I could not escape the sense that something was amiss. It did not seem right or possible that Kharn Sagara should be captured so easily, and so without a fight.

We saw little sign of servants or soldiery as we crossed the burnt threshold into the house of the Undying. Calen Harendotes had insisted he go to meet the captured king, and I went with him.

There was something else, something the dragoons would not tell me. They kept turning back to look at me, round eyes like lamps in their black-masked faces, saying nothing. My Cielcin close behind me, and the men of HAPSIS and their Irchtani accompanying the Monarch's Interfaced guard, we passed along familiar square corridors of cracked, poured stone, following a red stripe painted onto one side of the floor. Old conduits flowed along the walls overhead, and sconce lights that had perhaps been kindled by the Mericanii themselves flickered and buzzed as we passed.

"It's not like any palace I've ever seen," Cassandra said in Jaddian. "It feels...dingy." As she spoke, we passed an open doorway, a square arch through which could be seen an antique sitting room. Couches of wood, intricately carved and tapestried, surrounded a holography table above which the spectral image of a woman danced. Two men lay dead in the open doorway.

A guardroom. Had I seen guards on my first visit? Or only the faceless SOMs?

"It's old," I said. "Older than any place you've been. These halls were built before the God Emperor's day."

"They were built before the Foundation War," said Calen Harendotes, not a dozen paces before us. "After the last Great War of the Golden Age. The last war on Earth, when the Mericanii conquered the realms of Europe, and drove the Mandari to the stars. When the old kings fled to Avalon, and the great Exodus began."

Those words brought even me to stillness. So little remained of those final days of Earth. In those days, it was said the ancient kept their records almost entirely upon their primitive datasphere, abandoning the page and the canvas entirely. That datasphere had not survived the Advent, the cataclysmic final battle between old William Rex and the machines.

So much of our history was lost.

"Was this Felsenburgh's war?" I asked.

"This was before Felsenburgh, if only just," the Monarch said. "It was men that built Vorgossos—or so the legends say. The machines came later. *Fort Grissom* it was in those days, before the consonant shift..."

"Fort Grissom?" I could hear the shadow of *Vorgossos* in the old English words. Many of the English *F* sounds had been vocalized as the language evolved, and the terminal *T* sounds dropped—an influence from the French exiles at William's court. Thus *fort* had become *vor,* though how *Grissom* became *Gossos* is harder for me to explain. Despite my facility for languages, I am no great student of my own, and the slow transition of the *King's English,* called Classical in our latter days, to the *Galstani,* the Standard of the Imperium, is a field many thousands have dedicated their careers to unraveling: the renewed Francophonic influence, the intrusion of Hindi, Bengali, and Urdu—among others, the standardization of the alphasyllabary by Artemon.

"Grissom was one of their *archaenauts,* the first sailors," Harendotes said.

I had never heard of him, though I knew the names of Armstrong and of Shepard.

Our destination was a great hall at what seemed the far end of the palace's main level, a long, round chamber whose high ceiling was lost in the gloom above us, though mighty lamps clung to square pilasters projecting at intervals from the outer wall, shedding their luminance on that bare stone chamber.

The place had the air of a throne room—though there was neither chair nor dais—of a high lord's receiving hall. Massive doors dominated the wall opposite where we had entered, and though I did not yet know it, behind them there was a mighty lift, a huge cargo platform that descended on tracks at an angle all the way down to the laboratories and the Garden. It felt as though we stood at the bottom of a rocket's blast pit—and indeed perhaps we did. Too well I could picture great cranes lowering cargo from the planet's icy surface to this distant floor, and imagine Mericanii footmen with gleaming batons and bright uniforms signaling one another.

What I had told Cassandra resonated with me.

That here was the oldest place—the oldest *human* place—that I had ever been.

A scout in Latarran combat armor advanced from the far door, leaving his squadmates to scramble to attention. He saluted after the Latarran fashion—reminding me of Elffire and the slaughter outside—and said, "12Ashling's team has him, my Monarch. They're bringing him up the lifts."

"He surrendered without a fight?" asked Calen Harendotes.

"So it seems, my Monarch," the man said. "He had an android with him. A servant, I think."

"No woman?" the Monarch asked.

"A woman?" the man echoed. He was not Interfaced himself, I guessed. "No, my Monarch. Not that anyone said."

We hadn't long to wait. No sooner had the scout spoken than the great lift doors hissed. They might have opened a full quarter of the round room's circumference, but the metal shutters opened only the barest crack— just wide enough that three might walk abreast. Two Latarran dragoons appeared—their eyes first of all, followed by perhaps half a dozen others. Between them, they held a man in cloth of gold, his loose robes cut Nipponese fashion, their broad, square sleeves embroidered with dragons whose eyes were chips of jet. He wore loose black trousers cinched at the ankles, and slippers to match the robe. His chest was bare beneath it, and where the Kharn I'd known had possessed a mechanism in place of his chest and ribcage, the chest of this incarnation was entirely human. Indeed, I thought him all human at first glance, until I saw the gilded fingers of the left hand—so like Calen's own. His hair was black and hung curtain-like across a face pale as death.

The dragoons forced him to his knees before the Monarch, and two dozen Latarran lances pointed at him where he sagged. The soldiers that had come up behind him cast a body on the floor at his right.

It was the golem, Yume, without a doubt. A shot had shattered its ceramic faceplate, blasted a hole clean through its head. The circuitry still sparked, and here and there one part of the jeweled mechanism—visible through the translucent skullcap—still whirred.

I felt certain it was not all dead, and yet it did not move.

"We found him cowering in an apartment attached to the labs below," said a woman whom I guessed to be 12Ashling. "He claims he was trying to escape. I've left a team to look for hidden passages. If there is some way out, we'll find it."

There *was* at least one other route from the palace, via the lifts that descended to the power station and the strand by Brethren's waters.

The kneeling Sagara did not look up. The men that held him kept hands on wrists and shoulders, his arms outstretched. A third stood just behind, his lance trained at the back of Sagara's head.

Kharn Sagara advanced upon Kharn Sagara, Calen Harendotes towering over the kneeling prisoner. So near to one another, it was impossible not to notice the similarity of their dress: the black and gold of Vorgossos had become the black and gold of Latarra, the weeping eye replaced by the solar-crowned falcon.

"What have you done?" The question escaped Harendotes in hardly more than a whisper.

The kneeling Sagara did not answer.

"This is not Kharn Sagara," said Calen Harendotes, stiffening. Seeing that change in his posture, I knew that he had probed the mind of the kneeling man, questing after his implants, testing his praxic defenses.

12Ashling stiffened. "My Monarch?"

Calen Harendotes did not take his eyes from the kneeling subject in black and gold. "Did it work?" he asked, a tone present in his voice that I had never heard there. "Have you done it?"

Fear?

Loathing?

Excitement.

For an instant, I thought the Monarch might kneel himself and embrace the other like a brother—though he had denied him a moment before. "The Angelus Series was a failure…" The Monarch's words spilled from him in whispers, without suit amplification. "There was nothing. Nothing to explain what happened."

"Angelus Series?" I asked. "Harendotes, what is going on?"

At the sound of my voice, the man on the ground stiffened, jerked violently in the arms of his captors. The two dragoons lurched to strengthen their hold. The pale face—concealed behind curtains of lank, black hair—peered up at me a moment, and what I saw rocked me back a step.

Returning his gaze to the ground, the man in the golden robes began to shake, limbs straining beneath the weight of his oppressors.

No.

No, I realized.

He was shaking with laughter.

"Lord Marlowe," said Calen Harendotes, not tearing his gaze away from the laughing man.

I stepped forward, but a broken voice stopped me dead.

"Mar…lowe?" it said, low and deep and polished. "Marlowe?"

The laughing man had stopped laughing, and looked up at Calen Harendotes, and at myself. "Is this some joke, Sagara? Another test?"

"Abba!" Cassandra recoiled.

"I know," I said. "I know."

The kneeling man looked up at me and smiled. It was a broken smile. A crooked smile. One lopsided and asymmetrical.

It was the smile I had seen in the mirror for more than six hundred years of life.

The face that looked up at me was pale, handsome, but sharp, jagged, and austere. It was the face of the son of some ancient house—great in dignity, but bereft of real authority. The nose was straight and sharply pointed, the brows pitched with grave intensity, the eyes violet as the flower that bears that name.

It was my own face. The face of the man who had died gasping on the floor of the Arx Caelestis.

My old face.

"You?" I did not know what to say. "You're..."

All my life, rumor that I was some Extrasolarian copy had followed me like a shadow. Ever it had been the stalking horse of the Chantry, of the Empress, of the Old Lions about the Solar Throne. I knew it was a lie, a falsity preached by my enemies. All Kharn Sagara had given me were hollow bones. The Inquisition had itself reviewed my body and brain scans, my blood—and declared me human. It was the Quiet, the Absolute himself who had redeemed me from death's dream kingdom. Even if Kharn Sagara had somehow been responsible for my restoration aboard the *Demiurge*—and he had been dead when I died, caught between incarnations—he could not have been the cause of the second.

I knew I was Hadrian Marlowe, knew I was myself.

And still I doubted in that moment.

Doubted everything. Doubted the life I'd led since leaving Vorgossos. Valka and Selene. Dorayaica and Urbaine. The Empire and the Common-wealth and Jadd. Doubted Cassandra herself, though she stood by my side that very instant.

I found the controls behind my right ear to open my helmet. The mask and helm broke apart, folded themselves neatly into the collar of my suit. With rough hands, I pulled the coif from my head and shook out my long, black hair.

The kneeling Hadrian's eyes widened. "You're not me," he said, and looking at Harendotes, asked, "What is this?"

"I have the same question," I said to that other self.

Calen Harendotes ignored us both.

"Calvert," I said suddenly, rounding on Harendotes. "Calvert took my blood. You *cloned* me."

This was why he'd brought me, why he'd kept me close throughout the battle. Not because I was the only weapon his other self could not replicate, but because I was the one weapon he was sure she had.

The Angelus Series . . .

Series.

How many of me had Kharn raised in the bowels of Vorgossos?

"You have my memories," I said.

"They're *my* memories!" the other Hadrian said. "I know what's real!" And again to himself, more softly. "I know what's real . . ."

On Jadd, Aldia's people had taken my blood, had taken cell cultures, brain scans, everything they could. It was the price I'd paid for Cassandra's life—and for my own. But Aldia would not have gone so far as this.

Remote synaptic kinesis, Sagara called it. The transcription of thought and persona. When had he scanned me? And how? In my long imprisonment, perhaps? When Valka and I had shuddered in the cold of the power station below the palace?

And all to isolate, to *replicate* the gift the Quiet had given me.

My second life.

And *more.*

Harendotes had feared that his sister-self had unlocked the Quiet's vision, that an army of Hadrian Marlowes awaited us in the bowels of Vorgossos, each one capable of fracturing time as I. I had not had the vision when I first came to that wretched place, but had some seed of the ability been in me—even then?

Had the other Sagara found it?

"If you're going to kill me, kill me," said my replica. "Kill me like you killed the others."

"Others?" I asked.

"You're one of them," the other Hadrian said. "You're not me."

"Let him go!" I said to the dragoons, to Harendotes. "Damn you all, let him go!" No one moved, and going to one knee before my other self, I seized him by the shoulders. "Have you seen it?" I asked. "The darkness after death? The black city?"

My replica looked at me, violet eyes narrowing. "You're mad," he said.

"Do you know the Quiet?" I asked.

"The Quiet?" The other Hadrian blinked. "Is this some kind of test? What do the Quiet have to do with anything? They haven't saved me."

They . . . He didn't know. I hadn't known when I left Vorgossos, hadn't known the truth.

Hadn't known *him.*

I looked round at all the others, up at Calen Harendotes, looming like a mountain over us both. The dragoons jostled their captive clone, while the one behind kept his lance trained at the back of the clone's head.

Cassandra stood frozen beside Ramanthanu, who understood enough of human emotion to shift the scimitar in its grip. Surrounded by his guards, Harendotes had not moved, but stood there—shoulders hunched—like the icon of some golden god.

"How many others are there?" I asked my other self.

The homunculus shook his head.

"How many?"

2Maeve shifted beside her lord, animated by some revelation. "He called you *Sagara*," she said, mind catching up to the moment as she addressed her liege. "Sire, what did he mean?"

But Harendotes had not heard her, his mind was far away, flashing across the datasphere in pursuit of his other self.

"How many of me are there?" I asked the replica once more.

"Sire?"

"How many?"

"What did he mean?"

People conceive of war and battle as mere events, happening for discrete periods of time in a specific place. But war is a place unto itself. A new universe, one with its own laws of time and space. Seconds which might have passed one after another in ordinary time pass all at once in war—so that hours vanish in instants—or not at all. In war, often a single second contains lifetimes.

So it was with that next instant.

It seemed a hundred things transpired at once.

But it began with the replica screaming.

The other Hadrian convulsed, letting out a high, piercing wail. He might have fallen, but the dragoons held him fast. He arched his back, head thrown back, eyes lolling, mouth stretched wide with incipient madness. I stood, lurching to my feet in my haste to get away. The air about the clone and his matched bookends crackled with pale lightning, and all three men spasmed as a current burned through them. The golden robe smoldered, burst into flame. The dragoon standing close behind the replica fired his lance, but the shot seemingly had no effect. Again the replica screamed as the dragoons fell atop it. Dead perhaps, or stunned. My clone's golden hand had closed about the one dragoon's wrist, and closing—separated from the gilded arm.

Calen Harendotes drew a golden sword. Highmatter blazed pale blue in the dim light of the palace hall, and I drew my own weapon, little understanding what was happening. The self-severed hand of gold was *changing*, sprouting wires like the waving cilia of the Umandh. These twined themselves about the fallen Latarran dragoon, wormed their way between the plates in his armor.

But the clone was standing, and bellowed with a voice then hardly human.

He stood, swaying in his smoking robe. His own long hair was smoldering too, and he raised his golden arm, the arm Kharn Sagara had given him. He aimed the wrist at Calen Harendotes...and fired.

A bolt of blue-red plasma clove the darkling air, impacted the Monarch's shields. The clone's robe and hair were all ablaze by then, but he did not seem to even notice. I saw his eyes for half a moment. They were flat and dead as the eyes of a corpse.

Jagged, black lines there were then seared into his face, lines that wept blood.

I understood.

The convulsion that had stunned the two dragoons had killed my unhappy replica.

He was a SOM.

Somewhere to my right and behind me, a woman screamed.

"Abba!" Cassandra had drawn her swords. "The Interfaced!"

I had no time to see what it was she meant. My clone turned his hand cannon on me and fired, and I turned my head as hot plasma washed over me. Despite my shield, despite the adamant and ceramic of my armor, despite the suit's thermal sublayer, I felt the heat even still.

"Defend his lordship!" shouted one of the HAPSIS men.

A shot rang past me, and I felt the buffet and rush of wings.

One of the Irchtani had hurled itself at the replica, talons outstretched to seize it.

The SOM fired, blue light punching holes through the leaping bird-man.

I cursed, and threw myself toward the beast that had been myself.

A hatch opened in the clone's metal shoulder, and a cylinder of glowing metal spat out and bounced across the floor. It was the plasma cannon's heat sink, and it was already spent. Face expressionless, the draugr hurled itself toward me. I slashed at it, highmatter fountaining in my hand. The SOM raised its metal arm to parry, caught the highmatter on its vambrace. I knew then that limb was only gilded, the substance underneath was adamant. We locked eyes a moment, violet and violet.

An instant later, a spike of rippling blue-white burst from the creature's self-severed wrist. Where the muzzle of the plasma cannon had been a moment earlier, there was a blade of highmatter long as my own sword. The replica chopped down at me, moving roughly. How had the Monarch's security not thought to check the arm for weapons? I parried the creature's blow, recoiled as still it stepped toward me, heedless for its own life.

Then a blade white as sunlight slashed through the monster's torso from neck to opposing ribs, and another slashed across its waist.

My other self fell in three pieces.

Cassandra stood in its place, still masked and helmeted, sparing me the sight of her doubtless anguished face. My own eyes were wild and shining, I knew.

But it was not over.

Something huge and stinking collided with me, and I hit the ground so hard the breath was driven from me. Twisting, I saw a cold, white face microns from my own, its eyes black as pits, its teeth bared, its breath a fetid reek. Instinct brought my sword hand up even as shots cut the air where I'd been standing an instant before. Belatedly, I recognized Raman-thanu, and understood that the xenobite captain had saved me. *"Ba-Aeta-doh!"* it hissed. *"Caicu!"*

The others.

"What others?" I tried to say.

From my place beneath the lop-horned captain, I strained to look.

Three dragoons in Latarran livery had taken aim at me. Their lances blazed.

I found my voice at last, and rasped. "2Maeve! 2Maeve! Stand down!"

The dragoons did not fire. Neither did they drop their lances.

I spotted the Interfaced commander standing amid her people, marked her by the shape of her body and the gold falcon on her helm. She had raised her own weapon, had it trained on one of my men.

"Harendotes!" I roared. "What is the meaning of this?"

Cassandra was standing over us, swords raised and shining, shield active.

There was a tension in the Monarch's sepulchral tones that had not been there moments before. "I wish I knew," he said. "Commander, explain yourself."

2Maeve did not reply.

Still, no one had fired since those initial shots at me, and a tension had settled on the hall, as if the chess game were near its end, and any false move might spell *shahmat.* HAPSIS men and my Irchtani brandished guns at the Latarran soldiery, and 2Maeve's dragoons picked targets all their own, pivoting smoothly from one to the next.

"Ichakta-doh!" One of the other Cielcin—Otomno, I think—offered its hand to Ramanthanu, who stood unsteadily, using its scimitar for a lever. It hauled me up after it.

"We are betrayed," the lop-horned captain said, shifting one six-fingered hand to the *nahute* coiled at its waist. As it spoke, it interposed itself between the nearest knot of Interfaced and myself. Its kinsmen drew around it, forming a knot about Cassandra and me. *"Ubalannaa o-aeta wo!"* it said to its subordinates.

Guard the prince.

There were some Latarran soldiers—one perhaps in five—that looked about in terror, their guns tracking from my Sollan legionnaires to 2Maeve's dragoons.

Cassandra made the connection an instant before I did, saying, "It's the Interfaced."

"Impossible!" said Calen Harendotes, turning on the spot, his sword still shining in his hand. "The Interfaced would never betray me. I made them what they are!"

I filed this little revelation away for another time.

"'*Pride goeth before destruction*,'" came a deep, black voice—a voice from nowhere, from *everywhere* at once, "'*and a haughty spirit before a fall.' And you will fall, brother of mine.*"

"Sister!" Calen said. "What have you done?"

"What is yours is mine."

It was the voice of Kharn Sagara, the deep, chthonic voice of the machine that spoke for him. It was issuing from the suits of each of the Interfaced. Each and every one.

"The hand," Cassandra whispered.

She had seen it first. The hand that had separated from the arm of my clone. It had attached itself to one of the Interfaced.

"They're possessed," I said. "He's taken their minds." I meant the *other* Kharn.

"How?" Cassandra asked.

My mind went to Valka. To Urbaine. To the worm that had chewed its way from her neural lace and through the white matter of her brain.

"2Maeve!" I called. "I know you can still hear me! You have to cast him out!"

"She cannot hear you." Calen Harendotes said through his mask. "None of them can." The Monarch of Latarra, the King of Vorgossos-in-Exile, took ringing steps toward me. He thrust his sword in the direction of the nearest dragoon. "They are already dead."

My heart broke for Lorian then. "You're wrong," I said.

Harendotes did not argue.

"We are outnumbered," Ramanthanu said in its own tongue.

It was so. The Interfaced had us two-to-one at least, and perhaps three-to-one. They had made up the bulk of the Latarran vanguard, and my own troopers numbered fewer than a hundred in that hall. The bulk of my Imperials had remained at the gates of the palace, securing the place against any attack from the city.

With great reluctance, I placed myself shoulder-to-shoulder with the Monarch, my sword raised beside his own. "If we have to fight them..." I said, voice failing.

"We have to find my sister," Calen said. "We have to kill her, and soon."

CHAPTER 60

DARK DESCENT

"THE LIFT!" HARENDOTES WAS shouting. "Get to the lift!"

The doors through which the Interfaced had brought my clone were still open, a narrow slit in the silo's iron walls.

Chaos blossomed all about us, and the air was thick with fire. I had lost sight of 2Maeve in the maelstrom, but her kinsmen fired on us with plasma burners and lances alike. I threw an arm across my face as a shot took me, glad of my shield curtain. One of my own troopers—near at hand—fell smoking as his own shield was overwhelmed by an energy beam. One of Ramanthanu's *scaharimn* fell upon one of the attacking dragoons, and smashed its forehead against the man's armored face, seizing the bare instant the man was stunned to slam up into the soft place beneath the chin.

"Pull back!" the Monarch was shouting.

"We can't get out!" Cassandra said, just behind me. "There's too many of them between us and the doors."

I had been right to tell our troopers to disable their comms. The other Sagara would not have been able to seize their minds, as she had with the Interfaced, but she might have locked the impact layer of every soldier's suit, immobilized them, left them to await the coming of their destroyers.

"Back!" Harendotes was still shouting, still trying to move forward.

One of the Interfaced swung at me with the haft of his lance, ceramic bayonet descending like a halberd. The simurgh blade rose to meet it, severed bayonet and haft both without resistance.

But I could not kill the man. As the boy I'd been had so often pulled his winning strike in battle against Crispin, so too I withheld my blade. The memory of my own face disfigured by Sagara's machines—of my own voice and thoughts embedded in that false flesh—haunted my every breath.

Seeing my hesitation, the Interfaced man cast down his ruined lance and drew his sidearm. The plasma burner coughed as he fired at me, advancing in the mad hope of seizing my sword wrist and pressing the muzzle of his pistol against my exposed face.

I did not want to kill him.

Still, my blade descended, and the poor bastard—a prisoner and a slave in his own mind, and perhaps a corpse—fell in two.

An oath black as hell escaped me.

No man should have the power to master another in his own heart, to carve out his soul and function with a word. In my mind's eye, my replica's golden hand crawled like a spider up the arm of the dragoon that had held the wrist. I saw its cilia waving, worming their way into the flesh of the dying soldier.

The hand!

"The hand!" I exclaimed, casting about in the madness, certain that if only I could destroy the hand that I might save 2Maeve and her people.

There was the ruin of my replica, lying in bloody pieces, smoldering. One of the living charged at me, but Ramanthanu hurled itself between the Interfaced and me, scimitar flashing, while about us both three of the Irchtani flapped into the air, drawing fire and filling the air with shrill cries and the buffeting of wind. Cassandra flashed past me, twin blades striking at our foe.

All the while, Calen Harendotes was shouting to fall back to the lift. I saw the sense in that: With its narrow gate, the way could be defended, the swarming enemy bottlenecked. But if I could stop it—if I could sever the link that bound that other Kharn to his . . . to *her* new slaves—if I could *save* them all, could save even only 2Maeve . . .

There he was, the dead dragoon—still smoking from the electric shock that had claimed his life. I saw the golden hand still clamped to his wrist.

One of the Interfaced turned to bar my path, lance sweeping round. I leaped back, colliding with Otomno in my haste to win clear. A shot flashed past my shoulder, and I recognized the stripes of a lieutenant on the man's shoulder.

It was 5Eamon, or 8Gael.

"You know me!" I said as the lieutenant rushed me, bayonet chopping at my shoulder. Time bent to my will, and the blade connected with my shoulder but did not bite, did not even knock me down. I sensed the will behind the false eyes in the lieutenant's mask evaluate what had occurred, the daimonic presence considering.

I slashed the stock of the energy-lance, but once again did not move in for the kill.

Seizing that opportunity, 5Eamon—for so I thought of him—cartwheeled away. His heel clipped my chin, and I staggered back, rattled. The dead dragoon was on the ground between us. Before 5Eamon could redouble, I fell upon it, slashing with my sword. The thing's shell was adamant under gold, and would not break.

"Cassandra!" I said, calling for her aid.

The girl leaped between us, blade pointed at 5Eamon's chest. The half-dead lieutenant cocked his head, evaluating. Two of his fellows—near at hand—broke off their assaults and rounded on her. I had a brief image of my daughter surrounded, her swords held at rising angles like the wings of a butterfly, right hand forward.

I went to one knee beside the gilded hand, and wielding Gibson's blade like a paring knife I snicked at the wires that bound it to the dead dragoon. Calen was still calling for retreat. The Monarch had gathered a knot of men about himself—mostly the non-Interfaced Latarrans, though a few of my own people had shored up the space around him.

I had expected the Interfaced to go limp when I cut the first wire, but they showed no change. Increasingly desperate, I cut at the writhing filaments until not one bound Kharn's golden hand to the dead man's wrist, and pulled the thing away. It was heavy as three hands should have been, and dead as the hand of a statue.

"It should have worked," said a voice that sounded like my own.

The Interfaced were still unfree, still slaved to the will of Kharn Sagara. 5Eamon had drawn his pistol, fired it at Cassandra. The others about her were keeping their distance, forcing her back. Her shields were holding, would not hold forever.

I had a choice to make, and no choice at all.

I found my feet and launched myself at the nearest attacker, plunged my sword through his breastplate of common ceramic all the way to the hilt, pulling so that the slim hole became a gash, and the man burbled in his mask as he fell, blood sheeting from the wound to stain the damasked carpet. That carpet was burning in places, and the antique wall hangings were afire. The air was filling with smoke, and my eyes were smarting.

Harendotes had found the door, had fallen back through it.

If we were to join him, needs must that it be soon. Surely the sound of fighting would draw reinforcements—or the nonresponse of the Interfaced on Latarran comm.

Ramanthanu and its ilk leaped after me, driving back those assailants menacing Cassandra.

"5Eamon!" I said, thrusting my sword out in my classic Spanish line. "Surrender!"

The shell that had been the man called 5Eamon only shot at me. The bolt passed clean through me as I strode toward him and—shutting my eyes—raised my sword for the killing stroke.

"Door!" I shouted, waving my blade in the direction of our only possible exit. "Retreat! Follow the Monarch!"

I spurred one of the Cielcin on ahead of me, lingered to drive my legionnaires before me. "Cassandra! Go!"

"Not without you!"

"Go!" I turned but slowly, conscious of Ramanthanu close by. The huge Cielcin captain slashed one of 2Maeve's dragoons across the belly with its scimitar, lashed at the man with the *nahute* still held in its other hand.

A scraping metallic sound filled the high hall then, and looking, I saw the great shutters beginning to grind closed. "They will shut us out!" said Ramanthanu. "We must go."

I could still not find 2Maeve in the chaos. I shouted for her in vain, knowing even as I did so that she would not answer, even if she heard. Ramanthanu seized my wrist with one six-fingered hand.

"*Iagami ni,*" it said.

We ran, then, each pressing the other toward the door. Harendotes was already through, and must have found the controls to open it. I saw Cassandra pass through the grinding portal, memories of Vedatharad flickering like lightning in my skull. The doors had opened only a little, were barely wide enough then to admit a single man.

I was not the last to make it through, but I was nearly so.

The great shutters slammed together not five seconds after I squeezed through, joining Cassandra, the Monarch, and the few other survivors on the lift platform within.

Many, many more had remained in the hall behind.

We could hear the sounds of shouting and of weapons discharge through the heavy metal of the doors behind. There were perhaps forty of us remaining in the tube, of the perhaps three hundred that had followed the Monarch into the depths of the palace.

The huge lift lurched, was already moving beneath us. The shaft was cut deep into the planet's crust at a shallow angle, so that it proceeded not straight downward but diagonally along tracks in the sloping wall. Only a hollow steel rail—painted yellow and black—separated the occupants of the platform from a long tumble to the floor of the shaft.

Seeing the target of my fury, I pushed my way across the platform to where Calen Harendotes stood over the controls, his back to me. Two of his remaining human dragoons tried to bar my passage, but the sight of my face drove them apart, and the Monarch turned as I seized him roughly by the throat and bent him backward over the rail. "What were you thinking?" I bellowed. "Bringing the Interfaced here? Of all your soldiers?"

My hand tightened on the Monarch's throat, found it unyielding as stone, as steel.

Harendotes's answer issued from the speakers in his suit. "I could not have anticipated that she would bypass their defenses and attempt root-level access."

"And why not?" I demanded, raising my other hand, the hand with my unkindled sword. "She *is* you!"

Something cold and hard pressed against my flank, and glancing down I found Harendotes had pressed the mouth of his own unkindled blade against my side.

"Not one more word," he said darkly.

"Or what, Sagara?" I spat in his face. "You'll kill me? You *need* me. You're afraid. Afraid your other self has made an army of my clones, every one of them capable of what I can do."

Harendotes's throat did not move beneath my grip. He did not seem to breathe. "The one dead in the room above has not returned."

"But you can't be sure," I said, "and you haven't been counting. My people have yours here three-to-one. Kill me, and you'll die. Right here."

The falcon helm opened at some unheard command, and so sharp and sudden was the movement of its metal hinges that I jerked my hand away, permitting Sagara to stand. Beneath the helm, his eyes were blazing, a blue light in their black depths. Those eyes swept the platform, marked the door now a hundred feet up-slope above us. About us both, the few Latarran soldiers shifted, eying one another and my own men, who had grown stiff with anticipation. I had Irchtani, and Cielcin with me, and Cassandra—a Maeskolos—besides.

"It won't be enough," the Undying said, eyes still shining with their own light.

"Then do it," I said, stepping back.

Instead, the Monarch did nothing, and for a time the only sound was the slow grind of the cargo lift.

"That's enough!" A woman's voice slashed the air between Sagara and myself. "We can't afford to fight one another right now. We're cut off."

Slowly, I turned from the Monarch to face the woman who had spoken. It was Cassandra, of course.

My daughter had removed her helm and peeled the coif from her braided hair, the better to glare at me, hard-eyed. When I did not respond or challenge her, she addressed Calen Harendotes, "Is there another way back up?"

"Yes," I said, thinking of the stepped garden path Valka and I had taken down to the Garden so long ago.

"We cannot go back," said Calen Harendotes. "Not when Kharn Sagara remains."

"Kharn Sagara..." one of the Latarran soldiers spoke up. "My Monarch, the Halfmortal...said that you were Kharn Sagara. What did he mean?"

Harendotes glared at the man. The noise of gunfire from the chamber above had stopped.

Abandoning all caution, I rounded on the common man, resolved to speak the truth at last. "Your Monarch is a clone," I said, addressing the crowded lift, "a replica of the very Kharn Sagara we've come to kill."

The poor soldier said nothing, looked from Harendotes to his companions. If I had expected the Monarch to act in that moment, to make good on the threat he'd made in his imitarium, I was disappointed. He simply stood there, silent and unmoved, sword quiescent in one golden hand.

"You've been had, all of you," I told the dragoons. "Your New Order. Your Monarchy. Latarra itself. All of it was a masque, a farce designed to restore your master to his proper place. He does not care about you. About any of you! He will take back his home and abandon you to the Empire and Cielcin alike!" As I spoke, I turned to address my words to Sagara himself: to Calen Harendotes. "Isn't that right?"

Pale fire still flickered in the hollow depths of the Monarch's inhuman eyes, casting their faint glow upon his high cheekbones. He longed to kill me, so cold and venomous was his hate. But he did not dare. Not then, not there upon the lift. Not with matters degrading so rapidly about him. Powerful as he was, we were his best chance of surviving, of reclaiming his throne and place.

And he knew it.

"My Monarch?" asked one of the surviving dragoons—not the one who had asked first. He took a mincing step nearer his liege, head bowed. "Are you . . . are you really Kharn Sagara?"

Calen Harendotes did not take his eyes from me. "I am who you say I am," he said at last, drawing whispers from the others—from his own dragoons and from the men of the Empire.

"They have stopped fighting, *Ichakta-doh*," said the Cielcin Egazimn.

Ramanthanu hissed at its subordinate for silence.

Another of the Latarrans stepped forward. He was a young man, by his slimness, barely more than a boy, but braver in that moment than many a great king of men, though perhaps he knew it not. In a high, clear voice—a voice that trembled as he challenged his Monarch—he asked, "Is it true? What the Halfmortal said?"

Calen Harendotes stared at the young man, and so great was the power in his visage and the force of his cold gravity that I felt certain the boy would break beneath his gaze. But he did not.

"Was it all a lie?" the boy asked, speaking in that moment for Lorian, for 2Maeve, for every Interfaced and Exalted, every Extrasolarian, every Norman refugee and abandoned marcher lord who had looked to Latarra for leadership. For protection. For hope. "All of it?"

The pale light in the Monarch's eyes went out, and—incredibly—he smiled. "What's your name, son?"

The dragoon must have blinked inside his helmet. "Pavo, my Monarch."

"Pavo," Harendotes said. "Are you afraid of death, Pavo?"

Thinking this a test from his liege lord, the boy answered, "No, sire."

"You should be," said Calen Harendotes, sparing a glance for me. "I am."

"My Monarch?"

"Here on Vorgossos, there is the power to turn back death. To live forever, even to restore the dead to life. You know the legends they tell of Kharn Sagara? Of this place?" The boy nodded. "They are true. Once, I had that power. I want that power back. Marlowe says that I have used you. What king does not use his subjects? He says I will abandon you. I would have our dream live forever, Pavo. Think of it: A kingdom that never fades, that never withers, that never falls into the hands of lesser men. I shall be no mere monarch, but *Monarch Eternal*. And you shall live forever at my side. *That* is the promise of Vorgossos. *That* is why we are here."

Though I did not believe him, I listened then in amazement. Gone was cold, dead Saturn; gone bright and thundering Zeus. In their place, there stood an Alexander—a god-become-man. The light that was in his face as he spoke to those few soldiers was a thing bright and warm as summer skies. Here was a man I might have followed, if I then sought to follow any man. I saw then who Kharn Sagara might have been—and might once have been of old—lordly, gracious, kindly and all wise. His every word seemed sense, even to me—if only for a moment, and the men that heard him were warmed by his voice, and chafed their hands by the fire of his vision. His dream.

Not even I was immune. Such was the warm music of his voice and the fire of his dream that for a moment even I forgot that it was Kharn Sagara speaking. Kharn Sagara, who destroyed the minds of his own cloned children to cling to his falsely eternal life. Kharn Sagara, who had imprisoned both Valka and myself, who—in the body of his Naiad—had tried to force himself on me, who had cloned my flesh and memory I knew not how many times...Kharn Sagara, who had ordered Elffire to slay every man, woman, and child in the city outside.

The promise of Vorgossos...

"But a promise built upon a lie," came a voice rough and atonal by comparison. "You cannot offer these people eternal life. Only a trick to cheat death. And even then, you cannot offer it to everyone."

It was my own voice that had spoken.

Harendotes smiled at me. "Of course I cannot give it to *everyone*," said he. "But to you?" He swept his gaze over the still-descending lift. "You will live forever at my side, if you will but help me in my task."

Pavo glanced at his compatriots—the few Latarran soldiers that had survived the chaos in the hall above. "Forever?" He almost breathed the word. "You can really do that?"

"I am Kharn Sagara, who took this world from the Americans," he answered, using the old name. "I have walked this galaxy for a thousand generations, and if you serve me, so will you."

That seemed to satisfy Pavo, who looked to his companions for support, being the junior man.

"What must we do?" asked one of the others.

"We must kill my other self, the Kharn Sagara who rules this place, and stop her regenerating." Sagara directed his words at me. "You see now why I needed you?"

The urge to strangle the man returned to me. "You took my blood," I said, "my memories."

Sagara did not so much as blink. "You died," he said. "You came back. You did it without praxis. Without machines. Any man would want that for himself."

"How many?" I asked, jaw tight, eyes more on Cassandra's face than on Kharn's, fearing her reaction. She had killed my replica, a creature—a man—who seemingly shared my memories, the memories I'd had until we parted ways.

Her own father.

"I had to know," Kharn said, voice hard and brittle as ice, "I had to know how—"

"How many?" I shouted, voice resounding off the hard, stone walls. "Angelus *Series,* you said! How many, Kharn Sagara? How many of me have you killed?"

Fled was that music in the Monarch's voice. His answer was small, grubby...terrible to learn. "Before she killed me?" he asked, and shrugged, shaking his head. "Dozens. Dozens."

Dozens.

I clenched my hand about the ivory simurgh the Jaddians had given me. They had intended it as a symbol of the sword itself, that sword which had been destroyed and was remade. I had been made anew myself, restored by the hand of the Absolute.

I had been destroyed more times than I had ever known.

"Marlowe," said Kharn Sagara. "Fight for me."

"Fight for you?" I almost laughed. The sheer *audacity* of that man, that king of daimons. "Fight for you! I should kill you where you stand."

Undeterred, Kharn Sagara said again, "Fight for me, and I'll give you what you want."

I looked at him then, long and hard: the god-in-exile, his lank hair falling in his face, his dark eyes bright with intent, his golden armor glimmering.

"The *Demiurge?*" I asked.

He nodded.

Had the Quiet brought us to this pass? Worn the Monarch down in desperation? Bent him to his purpose? To my quest?

I had no time to reflect on such lofty matters.

Not there. Not then.

For in that moment, a terrible screeching filled the shaft about us, and looking round, I realized with a start that someone had arrested our descent. We were caught on the middle of that sloping passage, a thousand feet from the top, and at least as many from the bottom.

"What's happening?" one of the men asked.

"Sagara?" I glared at the Monarch.

But I had my answer in the next instant. From high above us, there came the hiss of hydraulics, the rattle of steel.

The great shutters were opening. For an instant, I saw only a single pair of luminous eyes—the helmet lights of a Latarran dragoon standing on the lip of the lift shaft high above us.

Then they were not alone. There were four eyes. Eight. A dozen.

"They opened the door!" Cassandra said, dismay coloring her voice.

Calen Harendotes had kept his head, and his fell voice rang out. "Open fire!"

The crack of lances and cough of plasma arms filled the lift shaft then, and I knew a moment of almost serene terror as I watched the Interfaced leap from the precipice toward us. Some fell but slowly, relying on repulsor harnesses still fixed over their black and gold-filigreed armor. Others hit the sloping floor of the shaft with a force to rattle teeth and *slid* toward us, aiming their lances careful as may be to pick wild shots at us where we stood trapped and exposed upon the platform.

And they were not alone. Behind them came men in Vorgossene khaki, and wild with abandon as the captured Latarran pawns. Heedless of their own danger they hurtled toward us, a once human tide to wash us all away.

Cassandra rushed to the rear of the platform, planted one foot on the sloping floor. It was too steep to climb, too steep to rush and meet them, but her twin swords blossomed in the sparse light, and she stood ready, our men and Calen's all about her. Ramanthanu and I moved to join her, my own blade springing to life in my hands.

"Fire at will!" Harendotes was roaring, and blue plasma and light unseen flashed about my head as I joined my daughter on the front line. A shot caromed off my shield, and high on the slope above I saw one of the dragoons go down, slain by a careful bolt from one of the HAPSIS men about me. The few Irchtani among us leaped up the passage, wings spread in that narrow space. New-made bodies tumbled down the slope toward the platform, struck the lift about our feet.

The first of the living reached us then, lance pulled back to strike. I slew him where he stood.

The lift platform was perhaps five cubits from the sloping floor to the rail where Sagara made his stand. There was hardly room for our party, to say nothing of our attackers. "Get us moving!" I shouted, tugging the coif back over my head.

A pair of Vorgossene SOMs tumbled to the platform at my feet.

They had no weapons, no shields that I could see, nor any visible sign of implant or augmentation. One had been shot already in the shoulder, the other in the thigh. Neither seemed to feel it, though the latter staggered as it moved.

They were simply chattel.

Chaff.

Ramanthanu tore into the first of them, and seizing him by the throat the captain hurled him over the rail at our left hand. The SOM vanished over the side, scrabbling into the abyss below. A dozen others had already made the platform, and the fighting about me was thick and desperate. I saw Cassandra strike the head from one of the converted Interfaced—was it 2Maeve? No, the helm had no crest.

Lorian, I remember thinking. *Lorian, forgive me.*

Something collided with me, knocking me to the deck. My head struck the metal floor, set my teeth to ringing. I had not restored my helmet, and pounded the emergency control. My mask unfolded, clicking into place as I regained my feet. I thought it must have been one of our men who had been knocked to the floor.

Where was Cassandra?

She had been not two paces to my right, standing at the foot of the sloping wall.

She was gone.

"Cassandra?" I called out. There was no sign of her on the ground about me, though the platform was strewn with bodies. "Cassandra!"

Calen Harendotes had drawn his sword, stood with Pavo and the other Latarrans close about him. One of Ramanthanu's kinsmen lay dead at my feet, black blood streaming from its mouth. Ramanthanu itself was grappling with two unarmed SOMs.

There was only one place she could have gone.

I slashed at one of the dragoons standing in my way, crossed the broad shelf of platform to the rail and peered down. "Cassandra!" She had fallen, must have fallen when my back was turned, fallen and slid down into the abyss at the bottom of the lift shaft. Wild-eyed, I rounded on the Monarch. "Sagara!" I screamed. "Take us down!"

The gilded king turned to look at me through the chaos. "She's locked the controls!"

I hissed, cast my gaze down over the rail. She'd been armored, but had removed her helmet while we talked on the lift. It was possible she was alive, had slid safely down the incline to the floor below. But the ground was lost in darkness, lit only by low, orange panels to either side.

The sound of iron-shod feet on the deck behind me brought me back to myself, and turning I saw three dragoons in Latarran body armor strike the platform, raise their lances to fire. Perhaps a dozen SOMs fell hard behind, and more were coming. The lift platform shook beneath the combined mass of so much humanity, until I felt certain it must give way, yet it held.

I saw it then, a falcon-crested helm blazing red-gold in the light of the lamps. 2Maeve of the Interfaced cut down one of my Irchtani with a blazing lance, and swept the haft into the side of one legionnaire's head.

A gray resolve settled on me, and I advanced a step. If indeed I could not save her, I would deliver her from her slavery myself. I could do that for Lorian, if nothing else. Then I would force Sagara to find a way to get the lift moving, if I had to hold his face to the console.

But I never reached 2Maeve.

I hardly took another step. One dun-clad SOM leaped from the sloping wall above and slammed into me with enough force to knock me bodily from my feet. My fingers tightened on my sword as my back hit the rail at the rear of the platform. The whole world turned upside down as I fell over it, fell headfirst into the sloping lift shaft below. The mindless SOM clawed at me, and I hurled it from myself as I struck the sloping floor with my shoulders. My suit absorbed the shock, and I tumbled head over heels, sword a searing beam of death in my hand. It was a miracle it did not kill me then, a miracle I did not drop it. I was skidding *down,* and scrabbled with my free hand, trying to right myself, to put my feet between myself and the final impact that was to come.

I was not falling alone. I saw men in Imperial white and crimson, in Latarran black and gold, and looking up, I saw one of Ramanthanu's kinsmen skidding along the wall above, falling in a way that suggested the Cielcin had leaped deliberately. And there was Kharn Sagara himself, sliding feetfirst along the rough stone slope.

The ground was coming up fast. There was an iron-walled pit where the platform was meant to rest, hardly deeper than a man was tall. I had righted myself by then, and struck the earth with a force that turned my suit's gel layer momentarily solid as it took the impact. Dazed, I found my feet, swayed away from the base of the slope to the wall of that shallow pit. My SOM attacker lay at my feet, its neck broken. There were rungs cut into the side of the pit to allow workmen to clamber in or out. I unkindled my blade and mounted them.

A hand shot down and caught my wrist, and looking up I saw a trooper in Imperial white looking down at me.

"Are you all right?"

It was Cassandra. Her *mandyas* hung in tatters from her left shoulder. I permitted her to help me up. She had not donned her helmet, and a dark bruise was spreading on her forehead above the left eye.

"Fine," I said, "are you—"

"I'm fine," said she. "Two of them dragged me off the platform. I hit my head on the way down, but—"

One of the SOMs crashed into the pit at the bottom of the shaft, his legs breaking with the impact, with no armor to soften his fall. A pair of our own troopers followed, landing hard on their sides. One fired a random shot, discharging by accident. One of the Cielcin—Egazimn, I think—leaped the pit entire, alighting not three paces from where we stood. There were bodies everywhere at the bottom of that shaft. Sollans, Latarrans, Vorgossene slaves.

A handful of troopers in Imperial white stood near at hand, clutching their lances and picking shots at our foes as they rolled like a tide toward us.

Calen Harendotes tumbled to the floor, Pavo and the other surviving Latarrans hard behind. Our troopers went to help them out before the tide of once-humanity came in.

Too late.

A sea of dun-clad SOMs fell atop Calen Harendotes, wave capped with Latarran black until the pit was filled with bodies living and dead. Those that came after clambered over the ones that had fallen first, hurled themselves at us. Once more I kindled my blade, and Cassandra hard beside me, and one by one we cut them down. Together, we were driven back, forced down the hall at the lift's end toward the sealed lower gates to Sagara's labs.

"We can't stay here," my daughter shouted, leaning against me as we retreated.

There was Ramanthanu, leaping clear of the carnage.

And there was 2Maeve, wielding her lance, its bayonet red with the blood of my people. The falcon bright upon her helm flashed as she turned to face me, the eyes of her mask twin suns blazing like the headlamps of some barreling vehicle. She saw me. Kharn Sagara saw me through her eyes.

"*Destroyer! Why have you returned?*" Kharn Sagara's artificial voice issued from the suits of all the stolen Interfaced—living and dead. "*Are you not content to have broken me?*"

"Broken you?" I asked. "I saved your life! Both your lives!"

"*Half-lives!*" the daimon king replied, puppeting 2Maeve into taking aim. "*You see what it has cost me!*"

"It is not my fault if you have gone to war with your own self!" I said.

"*Why have you come?*"

"I want your ship!" I said. "The Mericanii weapons! The Cielcin have freed a Watcher from its prison! I seek the means to destroy it!"

For the barest instant, none of Sagara's puppets moved.

"*What?*"

"Brethren said I would return one day!" I said. "Sagara! Give me the *Demiurge,* and I will end this madness!"

The daimon behind the hollow men did not answer. I imagined the deathless woman seated on her throne in the inverse pyramid, a creature of metal and bone, considering, chin propped on one skeletal hand.

No answer came, for in that next instant, a hand thrust from the pit behind and seized 2Maeve by the ankle. The former commander of the dragoons fell flat on her face, and another hand grasped the rim of the pit.

A *golden* hand.

Up came Calen then. Seeing him, it was as though I saw a great beast rising from the depths of the sea, a worm or leviathan cresting that lake of dead men. Blood soaked his face and black hair, and gleamed darkly against the gold plate of his armor.

I saw him then as he truly was: neither Saturn nor Dis, neither Horus nor Zeus, but Mammon—clad in gold—and blood-soaked Moloch, too. He towered over the fallen 2Maeve as behind him, the boy Pavo clawed his way free of the pile of dead and dying men.

"Sister!" roared the Monarch. He had lost his sword, and stooping grabbed 2Maeve by the pauldrons, hauling her to her feet. The undead woman clawed at Calen's face, but he bared teeth alarmingly white in his bloody face, and seemed not to feel it. "You cannot run from me," he said, shifting his grip, so that he held 2Maeve's face between his hands, and so great was the strength in those golden hands that her helmet sparked and flared.

And then something happened that I have never forgotten.

Those black eyes of his blazed with fire electric, blue as the hottest suns. Calen's face was perhaps a cubit from the face of 2Maeve—from the face of his sister-self's new garment. He looked almost about to kiss her. Instead, twin rays of light burst from his glaring eyes, beams of coherent energy powered by some fusion furnace in his secret heart.

2Maeve's head burst asunder, and I cried out for Lorian, and for the woman who was already dead. But Calen Harendotes was not done, and turning his head, he swept his gaze back up the shaft, the light of his inhuman eyes a ghastly beam of death. He killed without discrimination then, without care. The limbs and severed torsos that tumbled down the shaft were of Vorgossene soldiers, and Latarran—and my own men.

That instant seemed to last eternity, with Calen Harendotes's raw-throated yell filling that dark, deep place. Then the beams stopped, and all was silent, unless it was the rasping of the Monarch's voice. "I will kill her," he said to Pavo and to me. And to the bodies of the dead and dying—and to *her*—he said, "I will kill *you.*"

CHAPTER 61

THE TREE OF LIFE

WE WERE SEVENTEEN.

Of the fewer than half a hundred that had escaped the high hall to the lift, only seventeen remained. There was Calen Harendotes, and young Pavo, along with four other men of the Latarran Grand Army. Besides Cassandra and myself, I had Ramanthanu and its three remaining kinsman: Otomno, Egazimn, and Bikashi. It had been the one called Atiamnu I had seen dead in the lift. That brought the count to twelve. Of the remaining five, all were HAPSIS men. Four were common legionnaires, men in faceless white and red. The last was an Irchtani, one of Annaz's people. Daaxam was his name, a black-feathered creature with a red-tipped beak. He carried no *zitraa*, no great, thin sword, only the long-stocked plasma rifle that had been made for his clawed hands and lengthy pinions.

"I cannot get a signal out," said bloody Harendotes, stomping on ahead of the rest of us. "She is jamming us."

As he spoke, I fingered the telegraph remote in my belt, a cylinder of black metal, as thick as a cigar and half perhaps as long, with a single button under the cap at the one end. Edouard had given it to me aboard the *Ascalon,* when we had met in secret on the voyage from Latarra to Merope and laid our careful plan.

I had tried to persuade Lorian to allow me to travel to Douro's flagship, the *Bradamante,* but my friend, the Commandant General, had been ordered to prevent just such an occurrence. Stymied, I had been forced into a corner. I could not reveal the truth of our circumstances to my companions without risking discovery, and yet to have them descend blindly into the net of Vorgossos was by then a greater evil by far. We met within the *Ascalon,* within the *Gadelica,* within the *Mistwalker.* Under the guise of routine maintenance, I had ordered the little ship detached from the *Gadelica*'s electrical grid. I had the ship vented completely, so that any camera dust there might have been would be pulled through the filters and incinerated.

Lorian—it transpired—had not placed any larger bugs aboard my ship.

Thus we met in secret: Edouard, Cassandra, Captain Ghoshal, and myself. There we laid our plan, which Ghoshal would relay to Douro and the broader fleet once the Monarch and our ground forces lost communication with the Latarran Grand Army in orbit above the planet.

"These two make a set," Edouard had said, opening the metal case that held them both in dark foam, "each contains a simple telegraph. You press the button on one…" He demonstrated, flipping the cap to depress the key on the end of one of the twin rods. The second telegraph—still in its foam, vibrated as a red light shone from the end opposite the button. "And the other goes off."

"Anywhere in the universe?" I'd asked, taking up the second with delicate care.

"Anywhere in the universe," the special agent had confirmed.

Watching us from a corner of my cabin, Cassandra had said, "I thought telegraphs were bigger."

The HAPSIS man smiled, adjusted his ivory-rimmed glasses. "They are, usually. You'd not believe what it took the men down in Blackmoor to get them this small. I'd wager there are fewer than a hundred pairs in the entire galaxy."

Blackmoor was one of Imperial Intelligence's headquarters, a famously windowless white cube of a building on the fringes of the Eternal City.

I had taken the other cylinder from its containment then, turned it in my fingers. "This will cut through any countermeasures our Extrasolarian friends might contrive?"

Edouard Albé had smiled at me. "Unless they can disrupt a basic law of quantum mechanics."

I followed Harendotes through the halls of his palace. We had come out into the laboratory proper, into that complex of corridors and medical exam rooms behind Kharn's Garden of Everything. It was there that the Lord of Vorgossos and his servants performed their black rituals. They had not changed much in the centuries since last I'd walked their halls. One of the omnipresent hexagonal doors opened, panels sliding in every direction, admitting us into one of the Undying's laboratories proper.

I knew where it was we were going, what it was Calen Harendotes sought in all that sterile horror.

The Tree of Life.

I knew not if he called it that himself, but Kharn Sagara's affinity for the dramatic surpassed even my own, and it would not have surprised me to learn that he did so. He sought the facility that housed his future selves, the embryos—fully grown men and women, youths, children—that might come to house his itinerant spirit.

I guessed what he intended then. He had signaled his intent in his orders to Commander Elffire.

Leave none alive.

The chamber we had entered was long and low ceilinged, brightly lit and sterile white. Harendotes himself seemed terribly out of place in it, bloodied as he was in his torn blacks, his gleaming armor soiled. The place called to mind the halls of MINOS on Ganelon. Passing through it, we descended a short flight of steps into a room dominated by an arcing console whose embedded displays and holographs winked blue and red in the light.

Ramanthanu's slit nostrils flared, and it said, *"Kurshanan."*

Poison, the word meant. *Corruption. Rot.*

Harendotes was unmasked, and I wondered at that. At Ramanthanu's word, my mind had raced to Ganelon, to the lethovirus and the terrible thought that we had wandered into its jaws. Even if the Cielcin and Daaxam the Irchtani were immune to its predations, surely Harendotes—whose flesh was human—was not.

Relaying the Cielcin's words to Harendotes—who must have understood it, though I'd forgotten that fact in the moment—I asked, "Are we in danger?"

"Of exposure?" The Monarch turned to look at me. "You're worried about the Minoan plague."

"You traded with them," I said, "you sold them the test subjects they used to develop the virus."

White shone the Monarch's teeth in that red face. "Is that all?"

"Isn't that enough?" I asked in reply.

Calen Harendotes—Kharn Sagara—seemed to teeter on the precipice of some certain step a moment, his grimace faltering. "You know what the lethovirus is? Where it comes from?"

I nodded. "The Mericanii triggered a mutation that allowed their human hosts to grow indefinitely." What was the phrase the daimon Horizon had used?

We disabled the tumor suppression genes . . .

"And where do you think the sorcerers found the code for this mutation?" Sagara asked.

A sick feeling like surprise but not surprise filled my stomach. "You sold it to them."

"In exchange for the location of this world," he said.

Aghast, Cassandra said, "You designed the plague?"

"You bastard!" One of my legionnaires raised his lance. "I lost my sister to the rot 'fore I shipped out for Zigana."

Seeing the raised weapon, Pavo raised his sidearm, and the other four

Latarran dragoons—drunk with the promise of immortality despite the
horror of that day—did the same.

The Monarch only smiled more widely. There was something... *broken* in
the man, a madness I had not seen in the elder incarnation, or in either of
the children. Clearly, his murder at the hands of his sister had changed him.
For the first in I knew not how many thousand years, he had suffered a blow.

"No, child," he said, half turning to regard my daughter. "I but provided
the cornerstone. The Elect-Masters did the rest. It was they who weaponized
the virus, and the Mericanii who devised the original mutagens."

"All to defeat your other self," Cassandra said, bridling, voice amplified
by her suit. "How many have died because of you?"

Kharn Sagara dismissed them all with a gesture.

I felt the rage that had boiled in my legionnaire rise up in me.

Calen Harendotes had gone to MINOS seeking the way back home.
Had the likes of Urbaine and Severine known the truth of the Latarran
Monarch? I thought not. But had they been in league with the *other* Sagara,
the Sagara who had retained Vorgossos?

Neither Sagara was on any side but his own—her own—but the fact
that the Minoans had possessed the knowledge to find Vorgossos when
even its exiled master could not suggested that the other Sagara was yet
in contact with them. On Ganelon, Gaizka and Urbaine had spoken of the
war between the twin Kharns. Might Kharn himself—herself—have been
their source? It did not seem likely—the one called Takeshi had spoken
of Kharn's fragmentation with some disgust, and Urbaine had not known
which of the twins had proved victorious.

Yet they had known the way to Vorgossos.

MINOS had some connection to the King with Ten Thousand Eyes.

I had always thought MINOS alone the source of the Cielcin king's adopted
human technology. MINOS and plunder. But there was no reason it must be
so. Dorayaica, at least, commanded all the powers of the Commonwealth.

Was Dorayaica even still dealing with Vorgossos?

With what had Sagara bought his world engines? The Cielcin did not
trade, but Dorayaica would have exacted tribute from its new vassal-slave.

"How many millions?" Cassandra asked again, Valka's shade moving
in her, the anima accusing.

"When you have lived so long as I, girl," said the immortal king, "the
only thing there is to fear is death. Death is the only enemy." Those killing
eyes turned to me. "But I do not think you have anything to fear here."

"Lower your lance, soldier," I said to the legionnaire.

"But... my lord!"

"I said lower your lance, man," I seized the haft of the weapon and
forced it down.

The legionnaire tried to pull his weapon free of my grasp. "But you heard what he said! He made the plague!"

"He didn't," I said sharply, not letting the weapon go, "and even if he did, killing him would not make a cure."

Calen Harendotes had not raised his hands when the soldier pointed his lance at him. It would have done no good. For him merely to look at a man was to threaten him.

"I did not craft the virus," he said. "I only provided the seed. The Lodge did the rest."

Stiffly, the legionnaire relaxed, and only slowly did I release the man's weapon.

"We waste time," the Monarch said, gesturing to the console. "I have work to do."

About him, the five remaining Latarran soldiers shifted their arms, round eyes glaring at my legionnaires, my Cielcin, at Cassandra with her twin swords, and at the lone Irchtani. Calen's eyes doubtless had slain many of his winged brothers, and I sensed in Daaxam an anger hot and bright as plasma.

Would I lose control of them, in the end?

I still needed the Monarch alive, still needed control of the *Demiurge*.

I gestured to allow Calen to continue.

It was easy to forget that beneath that armored exterior, beneath the blood and the power and that sense of command, of black majesty, there lay a man of science. His dragoons tight about him, he bent over the console, began keying a series of commands. Once or twice he hissed as he encountered some obstruction.

"What are you doing?" asked the angry legionnaire.

Kharn Sagara did not reply at once, but before the man could ask him again he tensed. "What I must," he said, pausing at his work for only an instant. "The scions in this facility are always in development—like the tanks your lords are grown in."

"Not in fugue?"

Harendotes did not falter. "It is necessary that the scions are stimulated, else their brains would not be prepared for synaptic kinesis." He stopped, peered down through the glass. It was very dark in the room beyond. "They are dreaming." Presently, the lights came on, revealing a sight I had not thought to see once more: the tree of Kharn Sagara, that iron nightmare, its tanks like jellied fruits, the bodies of men and women in them like seeds.

Dreaming.

"Like the Mericanii of old," I said.

"Like those fool Americans," Sagara agreed, using the ancient name. "Felsenburgh promised them perpetual peace, if they would but put themselves into the hands of his machines..." His voice had retreated until it seemed it issued from down a long tunnel.

"They're dreaming, you said." Cassandra had come to stand beside me. "What do they dream?"

There was almost a smile in Sagara's voice as he answered. "Paradise," he said, and looked at me. "You think me a monster, Marlowe—I know it. But they do not suffer at my hand."

"You are killing them even now," I said. "Aren't you?"

Harendotes did not move.

"Sagara?"

The king of the damned twitched, bridled, rounded on me with those murderous eyes flickering. "Do not presume to preach at me, *my lord.* Your woman killed four of me when last you were here." His demeanor—grown for a moment sharp as new steel—softened in a way strange to see in him. "Without me," he said softly, "they would never have lived at all."

"They have never lived," I said. "This is not life."

"What is life?" he snapped at me. "Nerve impulses. Sensation!"

"You do not truly believe that Cartesian nonsense," I said.

Kharn's eyes flashed blue. "You don't?"

"You and I both know better," I said, thinking back to our conversation in the imitarium of the pyramid palace on Latarra, when he had spoken of the Watcher he had himself encountered long ago.

When he had spoken of hell.

Kharn's belief that life was only sensation was simply denial. Nothing more.

"If the Seekers are right about their *First Truth,*" said he in counter-riposte, "then we but dream ourselves."

"We are but the dream of our maker," I said. "It is not the same thing."

"But it is," Kharn countered, and gesturing at the bodies that might have become himself, said, "their world is real to them, and so it is real. And it is a better world than ours." Golden fingers danced across the glass of the display, slid through holographs in the air that followed his touch. He halted. "Still you think me cruel. They do not suffer as we. They have known no pain, no heartbreak. When the time comes for one to be terminated or used, he simply goes to sleep, never to reawaken..." He stopped again and looked at me. "If your *Quiet* really made our world, then I am a far better god than he."

I held his gaze then for the space of several heartbeats. "And nothing of your hosts...your *scions,* as you call them...nothing of your scions survives?"

"Oh no," he said. "There is much that endures. That is the joy of it. My memories are the same, my sensibilities, my *reason.* The implants house the core of who I am, but they must interact with the brain of each new vessel. Each resulting incarnation is a kind of *blending.* One cannot duplicate a human brain precisely—not in flesh and blood. That was how I began.

Trying. My first several scions were genetic duplicates, but each emerged a little different, and in time, I abandoned similitude entirely." He withdrew a step. "I have been *everything* you can imagine at one time or another."

"Including me," I said.

He looked at me, face utterly unreadable. There was no emotion in that face. "Not yet."

Something black and oily slithered in my guts, and I turned my masked face from his bloodied one. "What now?"

As if in answer, all the lights in the hall below went out. Every sconce and floodlamp, every instrument panel. Only the emergency tape striping the floor still glowed faintly green in the gloom.

"What's happening?" asked Cassandra.

A moment later, a dull, red light slammed on, and a woman's voice sounded in the hall below. *"Warning: Primary Power Loss,"* she said, *"Emergency Power Enabled. Emergency Power Reserves: ninety-nine point nine-nine seven percent. Average estimated time to pod failure: eleven days, seventeen hours, forty-three minutes..."*

"What did it say?" asked one of the soldiers. "What's going on?"

The voice had spoken in Classical English, in an accent I had never heard before.

No, I realized. *Not never...*

Once.

"He cut the power to the cubiculum," I said.

Calen Harendotes spoke. "They should all be cut off from the palace network now," he said.

"They're not dead?" I asked.

"Not yet," came the cryptic reply, and Harendotes turned and brushed past his men toward a side door.

"Sagara!" I called after him.

He did not slow down. Pavo and the others hurried after him, clutching their lances.

Cassandra looked at me. "What is he going to do?" she asked. "Is he going to kill them all, too?"

"I'm not sure," I told her. Why did he not simply kill them—as he had ordered Elffire to kill everyone in the city outside? Why, for that matter, did he not simply leave them where they were? If they were removed from the general datasphere, was it not the case that his sister-self could no longer reach them?

In my secret heart, the sound of Valka's throaty laughter echoed like bells.

You know nothing of machines, anaryan.

She was not wrong.

CHAPTER 62

NUMBERLESS THE BEAST

"WARNING: PRIMARY POWER LOSS," said the flat voice of
the alarm once more, as we rushed out beneath the branches of that metal
tree. *"Emergency Power Enabled."* There was something in that voice, in its
Classical English, in that peculiar accent—I should have placed it sooner.

It was the precise accent and tone Horizon had employed when we had
spoken to it in the depths of Gabriel's Archive.

It was the same voice.

"These pods are Mericanii," I said, coming out from under the arch
leading to the iron cage of the lift.

Calen Harendotes did not respond. The Monarch had surged ahead of
me, had reached a console beneath one arching bank of gleaming pods.
The fluid within gleamed a vivid pink-brown, almost the color of blood
diluted in water. Suspended in each, the body of a man or woman nestled,
neutrally buoyant, each tethered to the roof of its pod by the slick gray
rope of an umbilicus.

"Aren't they?" I asked. "Aren't they, Sagara?"

Above and about us, the great tree began to move.

I suppose that to call the thing a tree is to confuse the picture. When
I wrote of the place upon my last visit to it, I described columns studded
with their human fruit, columns supporting arches whose limbs upheld that
vaulted chamber. They were all of them on tracks, arching overhead and
down to ground level, that any one of the scions might be brought down
for observation or extraction. Standing beneath those arching branches, I
could see the beauty of its design, the symmetry and the terror.

About the man himself, his five dragoons looked on in terror, half raising lances as the great machine whined and rattled about them.

"My sister will be here before long," the Monarch said. It did not matter. I knew the answer was yes, knew that here were machines designed

by machines, instruments crafted in ancient days against the last hours of the Foundation War. Vorgossos—Fort Grissom—had not been where the old Dominion made its final stand—rather it had been an outpost, a last redoubt whose men and computer god had endured long after the Advent and the annihilation of Earth. The Chantry teaches that the God Emperor's victory had been total. Absolute.

What William Rex had failed to find and to destroy, Kharn Sagara had conquered, and in that moment, their machine bent to his will.

"Yes," he said, hunched over the console. Only belatedly did I realize he was addressing my question. "It was here their princes had their congress with the *daughter.*"

"The daughter?" I asked. "The daughter of Columbia?" Another question occurred to me, and I asked, "Their princes?"

"Senators, you might call them," Sagara said. "Not the *true* senators. The ones that ruled on Earth."

"I thought the machines ruled."

Sagara only looked at me, mouth slightly open. "You know so little of your own history," he said, and shook his head. "Their machines ruled their *people.* Used them for substrate. But the machines still served their makers."

"Felsenburgh?"

"His ilk," the Undying said. "The princes of America."

I stared at him, not knowing how to respond. On Colchis, Valka, Tor Gibson, and myself had spent months poring over the First Dynasty's records of the Foundation War. I thought of the network of brains and bodies, the pyramids filled with men and women who—like Kharn's scions—were never born, but lived whole lives in dreaming, their sleeping brains the ground upon whose virgin surfaces the iron wills of Columbia and her daughters trod.

Men did this?

Men had made the machines. Every man, woman, child in the galaxy knew as much. But that men had ruled the machines, even at the end?

"That's not possible," I said.

Sagara did not argue with me, but bent to his work.

I seized him by the arm, turned him to face me. "That's not possible," I said again.

"Deny it all you like," the man said, wresting his arm free from my grasp.

I grabbed him once again, feeling his dragoons tense about me. Not one dared fire. "What are you going to do?" I asked him.

Again, Sagara extricated himself from my grip. "I told you," he said, "I'm doing what I must."

"What you must?"

"Stand clear, Marlowe," he said.

"Not until you've explained what you intend!" I said. "If you meant to kill these people, you'd have done it in the control room up there!"

Calen's eyes blazed blue, and for an instant I thought that we would fire on me. I lurched back, Ramanthanu hissing to my side. "Pavo!" the Monarch shouted over the flat, feminine warning as it played another time. "Shoot Lord Marlowe if he interferes!"

At once, all my men raised their weapons, and Pavo's men did the same.

"No!" Harendotes amended. "Shoot the *girl*." In that instant he was the deathless king of old, and no man. A creature of dread majesty and of power deep and ancient as the stars. A devil in human shape. Voice snarling and tinged with bitter mocking. "I said stand clear, *my lord*."

There were only five of them. Five, and Harendotes himself. We had the eyes to contend with. My own hand went to Edouard's pocket telegraph transmitter. But it was as yet too soon. I still had *both* of them to contend with, and once I pressed that button—there would be no going back.

"Hold!" I said, extending my empty hand to stay my people. I repeated the order in Cielcin, though the gesture communicated my meaning well enough. "Sagara, we need each other! We are overmatched in here."

"You're right," said the Monarch from behind his bristling guards, "we are overmatched. I overextended myself. But that is one of the virtues of being *me*, Marlowe." He said, reaching up to find something concealed in the back of his broad, Egyptian collar. "I can."

With a single, fluid motion, Calen Harendotes extended his arm, as he did so unspooling a filament of braided glass from a port at the back of his neck. There was a needle at its tip, an injector designed to link him directly with another machine.

Before I could take a step or speak another word, Calen Harendotes thrust the link into a receptive port on the console table, and linked himself to the system that ran his machines. Too late, I thought I understood what was happening.

He was taking the scions from *her*, removing them from her control, claiming them for himself. But why? Why bother, when they could do nothing but sit in their tanks and wait, helpless and bereft? Either side might kill them at their sport.

Before I could ask any of these questions, however, the Monarch sagged against his console, nearly tangling himself on his own cord. For a brief instant, I had a clear look at his face. His eyes had rolled back in their sockets, and his face was slack.

"My Monarch?" It was Pavo. The boy had turned, casting down his weapon to kneel beside his king. Calen Harendotes was shaking by then, and shook more violently with every passing instant.

"He's seizing!" I said, pushing toward him. One of the dragoons jabbed me in the chest with his lance, and I caught the haft, brushing him aside. "Help me turn him on his side!"

Moments before, I had been ready to kill the man. There I was: trying to save him.

"What happened?" asked Pavo, kneeling across from me.

"I'm not sure," I told him. "It's possible he tried to transfer his consciousness," I said. "Or the other one set him a trap."

I should have killed him then and there—offered his corpse to his sister-self in payment. But something stayed my hand. Perhaps it was Valka's shade. Had she not suffered so, a thousand times in our long togetherness, when Urbaine's worm surfaced in her mind? Perhaps it was an abundance of caution, or simple panic.

I had lost control of the situation, had lost it on Forum, when Samek's poison took me, or in Llesu, beneath Ragama's sword.

Bang.

A shot resounded somewhere in the high hall. One of my legionnaires cried out, and staggered. He was still alive. But who had fired on him? I looked to Pavo's companions. They were looking round, scanning the catwalks that ran among the branches overhead.

The searing flash of plasma lit the darkened laboratory. Daaxam had fired, hefted his carbine. "They are above us!" he said, and fired again.

Looking up, I saw them: men and women in the dun of Vorgossos, faces blank, scalps hairless. The Monarch still convulsed at my feet.

"Open fire!" I roared.

Gunfire filled the air around me, and I stood, shouting to Pavo to steady his lord.

Cassandra rocked to my side, swords flaring to life. I drew my own even as one of the SOMs fell, landed catlike not three paces from me. I slashed him in two. Bleeding, the arms still grasped for me, and I cut the thing to ribbons, felt my gorge rising as the fingers still moved, commanded by black implants that studded the flesh, visible here and there beneath torn fabric.

"They do not die!" Cassandra said, her back to mine.

"They've been dead a long time," I said. A shot caromed off my shield, and looking up, I saw one of the undead soldiers aiming down at me with a plasma rifle in his hands. A green light seemed to shine through the sallow skin of his face and chest, an almost phosphorescent gleam, recalling the witch lights of the surface.

Daaxam had leaped into the air, alighted on the railing of the catwalk overhead. The bird man unleashed a piercing cry, drawing the networked attention of the puppet soldiers. He slew three before a shot forced him to leap from the rail, black wings spreading like shadows.

They had us four to one at least, but they had no shields, and but few of them had weapons, and they were picking their shots with care.

"They do not want to shoot the tanks!" said Ramanthanu in its inhuman rumble.

She *doesn't want to shoot the tanks,* I thought.

Cassandra slew another of the SOMs as it hit the ground in front of her.

"Emergency Power Enabled. Emergency Power Reserves..."

The flash of Ramanthanu's scimitar struck the head from a SOM woman. Still her body came, blind hands outstretched. The Cielcin captain hewed at those limbs, kicking the blind half corpse to the stone floor.

"Ichakta-doh, rakasur lumayan!" said Otomno to its chief.

"There are many!" Ramanthanu agreed. "But they are little more than slaves!"

The dragoons clustered about their fallen lord, guns blazing, and sparing a glance for Harendotes, I saw that he had fallen still. Once more, the Irchtani, Daaxam, let out a piercing cry, and a shot rang out in the gallery above our heads. One of the SOMs that had been shooting at us fell smoking over the rail. There was another shot, and a splintering of glass as one of the bell jars shattered. One of the scion corpses fell from its containment, caught for a moment on its umbilicus, then struck the floor half a hundred feet below with a wet smack.

Above it all, the noisome siren wailed, and that feminine voice—the voice of the lobotomized daughter of Columbia—repeated its warning about the power reserves.

"Won't someone shut that damn thing off?" Cassandra asked, catching her breath.

I leaned against the console rail, distracted for a moment by one of the faces in the glass bubbles.

Red haired and pale, it might have been one of the Emperor's own blood.

"Pavo!" I shouted to the young soldier. "Can we get him out of here? Back into the lift?"

"Can we disconnect him?" asked the boy, suit amplifying his high voice until it cut above the alarms.

I didn't have an answer to that, nor could, for in that moment, something heavy fell on me, and I tumbled to the hard floor. Cassandra yelled as something hard as stone cracked me across the face. Never had I been so glad of my helmet. The gel layer ate the impact, but still my head was torqued to one side. For a moment, my entoptics fizzled as my eyes came out of alignment with the projectors inside my mask.

A SOM had landed on me, a bald man with arms like twigs. Still there was a strength in those stubby fingers that was more than human. Hands invigorated by machines I hardly understood, those fingers tightened on my throat. They did not slacken, not when I thrust my sword into the creature's side—flesh and fabric parting like water. The once-man's lifeblood ran from that wound, mingled with something white as milk. Still those fingers tightened, still those soft eyes bulged. But there was nothing in the undead man's face. No hatred, no terror. Hardly any strain.

He was *empty*. A true *tabula rasa*.

Bringing my blade up, I severed the arms above the wrist, felt the fingers tighten further still as the deathless man pressed his weight to try and smother me. I tugged one of the arms free, and suddenly the dead man was gone, lifted off me by innumerate hands. Ramanthanu stood over me, and Otomno beside it, helped by two of the legionnaires whose names I did not know. Taking one human hand, I permitted the man to haul me to my feet, and standing pulled the other hand free, hurled it across the floor with a shudder. Cassandra stood embattled, surrounded by many foes. I leaped to her defense, sketching an image in white and crimson on pillars and floor.

"You all right?" I asked, chest heaving.

She could only nod, breathless herself.

We had found an isle of calm in the madness, and from its shores I looked up at the gallery above, the catwalks where Daaxam fired down on the chaos below, on the gunmen still above us. Where were they coming from? I saw doors open on the level above, saw dead-eyed men streaming in.

"Abba," Cassandra heaved, twin swords slack at her sides. "There are too many."

"We can't stay," I said. "We have to go back the way we came."

"You should...call Edouard," she said. "Give them something else to worry about."

I shook my head. "If I do that, we won't have anything to bargain with."

"We won't be alive to bargain," said she. I knew she was probably right. "Abba, I—Abba!" She pointed at the pod nearest us, in which a slim woman with long, black hair floated. She was stirring, thrashing, hammering the glass.

She was not alone.

"It's all of them!" I said, and roared, "The tanks! Shoot the tanks!"

There must have been half a thousand Sagara scion-clones in that chamber, each now violently awake. Their dreams of paradise had ended, and they had woken to the terror of the *real*.

The sound of glass shattering rose above the clangor, and pink-brown fluid spread across the floor. My legionnaires had taken up my orders and fired upon the tanks, and the bodies of more than one of Kharn's dread scions lay cut to ribbons by gunfire and broken glass, puddled in the floor of their crèches.

I thought I heard Cassandra sobbing. "Get back to the lift!" I called to her, seizing her by the wrist. "Fall back!" I shouted.

"But His Majesty!" Pavo challenged.

"Cut him loose or leave him!"

All about us, the crèches were opening, fluid draining from the bottoms, setting their adult fetuses on unsteady feet, hatches hinging upward.

"Shoot them all!" I roared, shoving Cassandra toward the lift. "Pull back! Pull back, men!" And again in Cielcin, *"Petunnaa! Petunnaa!"*

A trio of SOMs alighted between the exit and our position, one falling to its knees with the force of its impact. Their hazy eyes looked round, struggling to find focus. Before they could mark us, a naked man hurled himself upon the nearest, umbilicus dragging a mass of red-black tissue behind him as a prisoner drags an iron weight upon his chain. His hair was golden, plastered to his face. His mighty thews flexed as he wrestled with the nearest SOM soldier, seizing the monster's knife. With a fluid motion, the naked man slammed that knife up under the puppet's chin and into the brain. The SOM staggered, executive functions compromised. The naked man pulled the knife free, cut his own cord with a savage gesture, teeth bared as—snarling—he hurled himself at the other two. So stunned was I by this grotesquery, this savagery, that I stopped short, Cassandra frozen beside me. The golden man—bleeding from the cable in his belly—rounded on the two remaining SOMs, knife in hand. He bellowed at them, smashed the head of one against the wall of the chamber with a force to shatter bone and fell upon the other, muscles of his back twisting like cord.

Chest heaving, he straightened, turned to regard me with eyes black as coal.

Eyes that *knew* me.

"Sagara?" I asked.

That square-rimmed, monstrous grin.

But which one of him?

"Harendotes?" He had slain the woman's soldiers, after all.

The smile did not falter. Neither did he speak. Instead, the man turned—naked, still-bleeding—and rushed his nearest foe. The SOM fell dead by his hand, and on he flared, carving through the enemy.

"Go on now!" I said, urging Cassandra on. "Back to the control room!"

"Was that him?" Cassandra asked. "The Monarch?"

"Go!"

I had no time to ponder her question. All about us, the scions of House Sagara were rising, following the lead of the yellow-haired goliath. Men and women, dark haired and fair, black of hide and pale, red and golden. There was the one who so resembled our Emperor, beside a boy who seemed no older than five. One man—for man he seemed, though no sex hung from his loins—leaped from the rail above and tossed his long, silver hair from his face. His eyes were green as beryls, his teeth like mother of pearl.

"There is no need to run!" he said, his voice fell music. "We have her outnumbered!"

I ignored him. "Ramanthanu!" I called. "Daaxam! Men! To me! Here! Here!" Again I urged Cassandra toward the door, spurred one wounded man after her. "Pavo!"

The Latarran man did not respond.

We. The androgyn's voice resounded in my head.

I thought I understood. Searching for Pavo, I looked to where Calen Harendotes lay upon the floor. He was still there, the body of Pavo slumped over his. I felt a pang for the poor boy, the common soldier who had the misfortune to have pledged himself to so fell a master. Calen Harendotes—Kharn Sagara—had promised him life unending. He had given him hardly more than an hour.

Whether Sagara's daimonic spirit remained in the gilded body of the Monarch I did not know, but when he had thrust his cable into the console that governed his Tree of Life, he had taken control of all his scions, was puppeting them just as his sister-self had taken hold of 2Maeve and her people. It was that spirit, that will, which now animated the bloodied, naked force of men and women arising from its slumber. Harendotes had not brought us to the tree to cut off another avenue by which his sister-self might escape, but to claim an army for himself.

An army *of* himself.

Harendotes had played no simple gambit, no pawn sacrifice.

He had surrendered his king, flipped the board, abandoned all the rules and lunged at his opponent.

And we were caught in the middle of it all.

"Emergency Power Enabled. Emergency Power..."

We passed under the arched support holding up the gallery above, behind the columns that held the open pods. The door to the lift was open dead ahead. Cassandra was leading, twin swords blazing in her hands.

Before she could reach the iron grate, a ray of killing light sliced across her path, its azure radiance hemming us in. Cassandra skidded to a halt, turned to face the source of that beam. My own eyes followed her gaze. I half expected to find Harendotes standing there, eyes blazing. If he indeed had control of the newborn horde, he outnumbered us nearly twenty-five to one.

But it was not Harendotes.

It was not even a man.

That ray of light had emanated from a teardrop shape of dark metal—no larger than a fig. It floated on the air, gliding toward us, its intent plain.

"Cassandra!" I cried. "Get back!"

The teardrop's weapon lens flared, threatening, but did not fire. Nor would it let us pass. That beam might carve its killing path in an instant, making of itself a fence to trammel us in place.

I knew what it was at once then, and what it meant.

It was one of the king's ten thousand eyes.

The *other* Sagara had come at last.

For a moment, the black intelligence that guided that roving eye swiveled to look at me. There was nothing human in it, nor behind its aperture. The will that regarded me was alien and cold as some beast of the deep sea.

"*You.*"

The voice that issued from the device boomed far louder than it had any right to be, deep and dark as the pits beneath that hideous world, flat of all human feeling and pitiless. But it knew me.

Seeing her chance, the other Sagara wasted no time.

Bright her one eye flared, and I rushed toward her weapon, knowing the gaze of that cyclops's eye would burn through shield and armor and flesh in an instant. Its radiance washed over me and through me as I rushed toward it, fanned past me just as Cassandra's sword had done. I raised my own, slashing low-to-high in an arc that cleaved the metal eye in two.

Before, the experience of bending time to my will had brought pain.

Then, it seemed a clear light poured through me, so bright and plain I thought it must be seen by all who looked on me. Turning, I found the others staring at me. A spay of burn marks painted the wall behind where I had been, a pattern of ripples where Kharn's coherent beam of photons had been turned to diffuse waves. "To the lifts!" I shouted. "Go!"

But we were too late.

My brief engagement with the other Sagara's drone had cost us our escape.

The iron grille that divided the hall from the lift platform rattled to, and turning, I saw a knot of naked people standing just behind its screen. There must have been a dozen of them at least—men and women, many bleeding from severed cords like the gold-haired giant. One in front, a girl no older than five standard, or so she seemed, clutched her placenta like a ragged doll.

It was she who spoke, voice lisping as the voices of children so often do. "This is where we part ways, Devil of Meidua."

Behind us, the battle raged on, strangely quiet beneath the noise of alarm bells. The SOMs did not yell, did not cry out in pain, nor did the scions of Sagara. The only sounds were the shout of plasma fire, the ring of metal on metal, the thud of bodies.

"Sagara!" I said, advancing with the intent to cut through the grate. "What have you done?"

"What we came to do!" said two of the scions together—a woman and a man so like the Harendotes incarnation they might have been twins.

"What we must!" said a third in the same instant.

Their answer stopped me cold.

I knew enough of devilry—of praxis—to know when it was I was speaking to a single, distributed intelligence. I had felt it in the hall above, when the woman Sagara had spoken from the mouths and chestpieces of all the Interfaced at once.

I remembered how it had felt, awakening in the medica aboard the *Demiurge,* to find both the boy Ren and the woman Suzuha watching me.

What dreams did come? One of them had asked me, representing the other. One question, but unquestionably two wills behind it.

The feeling I had then was the same, staring through the iron grille and the gore-smeared faces of the newborn.

It was not that they were *all* Kharn.

It was that they were *each* Kharn.

"What have you done?" I asked again, voice smaller.

"You changed our thinking," said a tall, dark woman with hair like starlight from the rear of the carriage.

"We have been bound to this planet for far too long," said another, one of those identical to Harendotes. There were three I saw among those crowded into the lift.

"It is time we changed," said the dark woman.

"Time we grew," said the girl in front who clutched her organ, the one with the lisp.

The lift began to rise. I hurried forward, not sure what I planned to do.

Would I have slain them all if I could? Butchered them in the lift? Slashed them all to pieces? Even the child?

Another beam of radiant light slashed cross the air before me, and I skidded to halt. To my left, another of Kharn's eyes descended, cutting me off.

A ragged cry escaped me, a dismay deeper than any I had known since Perfugium.

The woman had unknowingly permitted her siblings to escape.

"Give our regards to our sister!" said the child Kharn.

I watched them go, vanishing into the shaft above, trapping us with the others.

"What happened?" Cassandra asked, drawing close beside me.

"They're him," I rasped, looking back to the vanished lift. "They're all him."

I had thought the scions all mere puppets, extensions of the mind of Calen Harendotes.

But they were copies.

For more than fifteen thousand years, Kharn Sagara had ensured his continuity. He had driven his body to its limits, replaced his organs at need, relied upon genetic therapies to cling to life, refit his body with machines. And when that body reached beyond all salvation, he had made another, and started a second life, and a third, and on and on.

That had changed when he met me.

When Bassander Lin had executed him in the gardens of the *Demiurge*, that continuity had been broken forever. Before there had been but one Kharn Sagara living serial lives, jealous of his uniqueness. The woman had retained that jealousy, and turned her hand upon her brother. In death, the other Kharn had learned a valuable lesson: self-doubt.

He could never trust himself again.

If he could not have Vorgossos, he would scatter himself to the winds.

"Where are they going?" Cassandra asked. "What are they doing?"

"They're running," I said, eying the drone.

"They will not get far." The voice of the Undying emanated from the drone, and from other drones in the air of the gallery at our backs. *"Why have you come?"*

Before I could answer that question, a flash of light lanced through the air. The drone erupted in a fireball of oily red, blew to pieces. Turning to look, I saw Calen standing there amidst the carnage, supported by a trio of his naked brothers, his eyes blazing. The Latarrans all were dead, killed by the SOMs, or perhaps by the scions themselves, who no longer needed them.

"For you, my sister!" roared Calen Harendotes. "We've come for you!"

"And when you've beaten me?" asked the black, iron voice of Kharn Sagara—not the voice of the woman, but of the machine. *"What then? Which one of you will rule?"*

A dozen of the teardrop drones scudded through the air above on silent repulsors, two dozen. Perhaps more. I saw them moving through the branches of that emptied Tree of Life, along the railings of the gallery above. Once or twice, one fired, and a slim, coherent beam of light cut one of the scions down.

The alarms had fallen silent. I cannot remember precisely when it was they'd ceased, only that they were silent then, only that the black, metallic voice of the Undying had resounded in the air alone.

There were far fewer of Kharn's scions remaining in the laboratory than I had expected, and fewer still left alive. More than the dozen that had reached the lift had made their escape, it seemed, through the hatches on the level above, or perhaps down the other lift that ran as deep as the power station...and the reservoir where Brethren dreamed.

"Not one," answered the golden king, the Monarch who was *Monarch* no more.

Not *one,* but *out* of one.

Many.

"Not any!" the Monarch shouted, and I knew that *this* was why he had come. "Vorgossos must be destroyed!"

Without Vorgossos, his numberless selves would have no center, no home to return to. Bereft, they would be driven outward, driven as he was driven to Latarra. To conquer. To build. The time of the Undying was done. He had *changed,* had *evolved,* had become something else entirely. Something new. Each scion would go forth and chart his own way, forge her own path—and each would carry with him, in her, within its breast a piece, a part, a little copy of the dark lord that had been. Though many would die that day—had died already—though many more would die in the escape, many yet would live, and go on to forge their own empires, their own kingdoms and orders, their own little copies of the Vorgossos-That-Was.

This was the victory Calen Harendotes had fought for, *this* the goal he sought to achieve, a victory not over his sister, nor over Vorgossos. A victory not for his people, for Lorian and 2Maeve, for Absalom Black and Jamina of House Ardahael, for all the poor Normans, Extras, and Sollan refugees. But a victory for himself.

A victory over Death.

"Vorgossos *will* be destroyed!" the Monarch shouted. His reply had stunned his sister-self to silence, or so it seemed. In all the years—the centuries—since she had murdered her brother-self and driven his shade from Vorgossos, she had been consumed by terror at the thought that he must one day return. The thought that he should return to Vorgossos not to conquer or reclaim it, but to put it to the sword and scatter his essence across the stars like grain had not so much as entered her darkest dream.

It had not entered mine.

"We have lived thus for far too long," he said, standing amid his naked fellows. "This place has ever been our prison! Always we have feared to leave it, have feared to lose what we have."

"What have you done?" the woman asked in that iron voice.

Of course, she did not know. He had isolated her from the laboratory's systems, locked her out. She doubtless believed as I had believed a moment before, that the others were only puppets, slaves to her brother's will.

It was what she would have done, but she had killed her brother-self, and not been murdered as he. They had gone their separate ways, changed absolutely and forever. They were both Kharn Sagara, but they were not the same.

Would never be the same.

"I have set us free!" said another voice, one of the women standing by the Monarch's side, black of hair and high breasted, one hand on her wounded belly.

"I have given us a future!" said another, a man green as Ilex once had been.

"I have given us *every* future," said a third, a naked boy crouching on the banked consoles before the rows of Mericanii pods.

"You didn't," the voice said.

"I have changed, my sister!" said Calen Harendotes. "Don't you see? We're free at last! There will always be *Kharn Sagara* now. We have conquered Death! What matters if any of us dies? *We* will live forever!"

A single ray of light burst forth from one of the Undying's drones, left its hole clean through the chest of the black-haired woman who had spoken. She fell to the stone floor, groaning, coughing as fluid filled her punctured lung.

"I can kill all of you," said Kharn Sagara. *"Every one."*

"You can try," the Monarch said, "but can you beat a hundred of us? Who knows Vorgossos better than we?"

The woman answered. *"Things have changed since you went away."*

"Since you murdered me," Calen said. "But they have not changed enough. Every one of us knows the secret ways from this place. The ships. The broadcast terminals. If even one of us escapes, we will return. You will never know peace, my sister. Not so long as you live. We will not rest until we have taken all we need from Vorgossos and blown this planet to atoms."

"Why?" asked the woman. *"Why destroy our home?"*

"Because so long as it exists, we will fight for it," Calen said. "Any one of us might decide, as you, that he alone has claim to our soul and name. I will set us free. Of this place, and of you.

"We might have ruled this place together!" he said. "But you betrayed me! Killed me!"

"And I was right!" the woman said, voice thundering from her machines. "Look at what you've done! How many of us are there now?"

"Hundreds!" said the Lord of Latarra. "You cannot win, sister! The world engine is crippled! You cannot flee, cannot broadcast yourself through the ion cloud. I have brought the dogs of the Imperium. My fleet will be victorious!"

"Your fleet," the machine voice answered. *"Your fleet will not survive. I have set the* Demiurge *against them."*

Placing a hand on the shoulder of the man before him, Calen Harendotes stepped clear of the knot of duplicates clustered about him. "But you cannot control it," he said. "Not from here. I have jammed your signal. The bombs."

"The ship can defend itself," said she. *"And I have you."*

The instant those words were out, every drone in the hall fired at once. Rays of azure light lanced from every aperture, slicing back and forth across the hall, carving the new-made copies of Kharn Sagara down. Cassandra gasped in that moment, and drew near beside me, while I myself was certain that we, too, were dead. But the drones that circled us had fired over our heads, each one picking its targets with superhuman precision. They fired once, cycled to new targets, fired again. Again. Again.

When they were finished, only Harendotes himself remained. Every one of the Kharn scions that had remained in the laboratory hall—perhaps a hundred in all—fell dead together. The others had barely had time to take two steps.

Like poor Pavo, their eternal lives had lasted only moments.

In those final moments, they had each scrambled to win those last few steps, each man for himself. Harendotes himself had not moved. His hope was with the others. The ones that had escaped that black chamber. He simply stood there, golden hands at his side, face unchanging as his brothers and sisters—his children, in truth—were every one of them cut down.

"Shut your eyes, Cassandra," I said. "Just shut your eyes."

"No, Abba," she whispered, and I could hear the tears in her voice. "I'm all right."

Slowly, their slaughter done, the eyes of the Undying all turned to look at him, and at me.

"Surrender," the woman said, *"order your fleet to stand down, and I will spare your lives. Even yours, brother."*

"Why would you do that?" I asked, stepping forward, one hand clutching the rod Edouard had given me. "You have us in your power. If your fleet is as mighty as you say..."

I knew the answer.

She was afraid.

Afraid of me. Of her brother-self. Of the hundreds of brother- and sister-selves unleashed in her palace. She had seen what I could do, had seen me pass through her beam, had seen me return from the dead. That was why Calen had brought me. Not only because I might prove counter to any weapons the other Kharn might have derived from my flesh, but because I frightened him.

Frightened *her.*

"Hadrian Marlowe," the Undying said, her falsely masculine voice emanating from every one of her machines. *"Why have you come?"*

It had come at last: the crucial instant. The turning in the play.

The moment of reversal.

My eyes went to Calen Harendotes, the chimeric Monarch in battered black and gold. Haggard though he was and bloody, still there was a power in him, an awesome majesty and command. He stood among the dead and dying copies of himself, those mayfly incarnations that had lived for mere moments, as I imagined the God Emperor had stood among the ashes of Old Earth. Tall, proud, triumphant. It no longer mattered if he died.

I fingered the telegraph rod Edouard had given me. If Calen truly desired to destroy Vorgossos, then I had no threats to make against him. If I was to win free of that labyrinth—save Cassandra, myself, my fleet—it was the woman I knew I must court. I had known it since we left Latarra.

I had to change sides, if only for a time.

Lorian, forgive me.

"Are you not content to have destroyed us once?" The machine voice shook the air, the whisper of an angry god. *"You have come to do so a second time?"*

"On the contrary," I said, watching the Monarch's face. "I have come to save you."

If the news of my betrayal shocked the lord of Latarra, his broad, square face gave no sign.

"Save me?" the black voice asked. About us, the drones circled, and the scant men and xenobites of my company drew closer still. *"Save me?"*

"You saved my life, once," I said, advancing. "I saved yours once, long ago—both your lives. Third time pays for all, they say. I have brought you your brother. Say the word, and I will put my men in the city at your disposal. Not a one of him will escape. Let us have peace."

"Peace?" The voice of that deathless queen filled the empty hall with laughter. *"Peace, you say? You, who have twice brought death to my door! You offer me my brother in payment. He is in my power already! You are in my power. You have nothing! Nothing to offer me but death."* One of the drones rocketed toward me, halted mere inches from my masked face.

Behind the drone, Calen Harendotes leered at me. I could feel the anger and black amusement boiling from him in waves. I had tried to betray him, but his other self would not have it.

But I was not yet done. Still watching the Monarch's response, I said, "The Latarran army doesn't know." The Monarch's eyes narrowed. "They believe that they're fighting for their kingdom, for a new world, for freedom from the Empire and the Cielcin alike. What will they do when they learn they have been fighting *for* you, *against* you, Lord Sagara?" The remote was still in my hand. "Even the Imperial fleet does not know the truth! Permit me to return to orbit, and I can end this battle with a word."

In that instant, twin rays of light slammed into me, radiance so bright it burned, whiting out my suit's entoptics for a fraction of a second. Had that fraction of a second been less time than my poor shields yet had, I might have died then and there a third time. But my shields held, just long enough for my suit to adjust to the light. Through the pall of false shadow cast by my suit's projectors, I saw Harendotes still glaring, light streaming from his eyes.

He knew that he was dead, that his sister would kill him once again.

His last act would be to kill me. To stop me destroying his army and the pressure they applied to his sister-self. He had crafted the Latarran Army for one purpose, and one purpose alone: to ensure his shattering. I alone could stop it, could turn the Latarran Army and the Imperial Navy from a blade aimed at the heart of Vorgossos to a wall encircling it.

The meter in the corner of my entoptics' vision that marked the strength of my shield fell from blue to green toward red. In a second it would all be gone, and I would be burned to cinder. I could not break, for to do so would be scatter the beam across the people at my back, to kill or wound Cassandra, Daaxam, my Cielcin and the three still-standing legionnaires.

I was trapped, unable to rely upon my oldest trick.

It stopped.

As quickly as it had begun, it stopped.

In place of the golden Monarch, there stood the figure of a man, an abstract statue suggesting man's shape. Light shone through his chest, his face wormed with holes from whose charred edges a thin smoke curled. One passed clean through the place where the right eye had been. The head turned, and for an instant I saw clear air and the pale light of an open pod through Calen's head.

He fell instead, fell as a bronze statue falls, no bending or crumpling.

"Abba?" Cassandra asked.

"I'm all right," I said. My shields were nearly dead.

A dozen of the other Kharn's drones turned their eyes from him. The black iron voice of the Undying filled the chamber, her countless eyes on me. *"You will come to me."*

CHAPTER 63

HELA AND DIS

OUR ESCORT MADE NO sound as we were led from the lab. They drifted along about us, forever circling, swarming like a shoal of silver-black fish. We were taken up another sloping lift and along a service corridor most unlike the halls of the palace. Those were square cut, finished in poured stone whose surfaces were daubed with primary colors, outlining paths that led to one location or the next. This was hexagonal in cross section, more in the style of the chambers in the laboratory, and I guessed that it had been built by Sagara himself, as the palace had been part of the original Mericanii construction, along with the subterranean domes of the city.

A wet wind greeted us when the door cycled open, and we stepped out into a black space, a cavern of inestimable size. All about us, the naked rock of Vorgossos loomed, gray and black veined with white. Pale lamps with iron posts illumined a metal platform that thrust out into darkness. There the lonely car of a tram waited, its magnetic track hanging from the roof of the cavern above.

"There is water here," Ramanthanu said. "I can smell it."

"*Raka junnana suh,*" I said, pointing down and out into the blackness. "It is far below. We're above the city's reservoir. The tunnels where we entered run right below it." I repeated this information in Galstani for the others.

"Where are they taking us?" asked one of the legionnaires.

"To the heart of Vorgossos," I said, reaching the tram platform. "To the house of Kharn Sagara."

"His house...?" Cassandra echoed.

I mounted the steps to the tram, found it exactly as I remembered. Desolate of any console, a thing of rude metal with benches running along the center of the car. I did not sit, but went to the rail, Cassandra beside me.

"You've been here before?" Cassandra asked, though it was not really a question.

"With your mother," I said, though Valka had not taken that first trip across the sunless sea to where the *true* palace lay. I had gone to face Kharn Sagara alone then, escorted by the android, Yume. "Long ago."

Cassandra hung her head. After a moment, she tapped the controls at wrist and neck to open her helm. The thing unfolded like the carapace of some ivory beetle, segments falling to reveal her shining face. Her eyes were red, and distant as the quasars. I laid a hand on her shoulder. After a moment, she said, "Those others...were they all...were they all really *him?*"

"So it seems," I said, and squeezed her shoulder tight. Switching to Jaddian so as not to be understood by Daaxam and the legionnaires at least, I said, "You listen to me: We are going to get out of this, you and I."

She turned shining eyes on me, reached up to tug the coif from her hair. She had wound her hair about her crown Jaddian fashion.

"Dora tutti lantahi?" she asked, sparing a glance for the xenobites as they crowded in behind us.

Where does it all end?

With light, I thought, and recalled that killing radiance I had seen filling all the universe, burning ships and moon and planets to something less than ash. *With light and fire.* Light and fire...and the destruction of the Cielcin.

All of this ran across the ridges and along the ravines of my mind, but I said only, "I wish I knew."

"Don't you?" she asked. "Know? Can't you see the future?"

The tram had begun moving, gliding smooth and silently out over the waters, out into the night. I *had* seen the future. I had been there, and walked the streets of that dead and lonely city at the end of time. And yet it was not a certain thing, not a thing cast in stone. Even in Ragama's day, nothing was certain.

"There is no *future,*" I said, unsettling the girl. "No *one* future. We are not prisoners of fate, Anaryan. I cannot say how this will end. But it will end. *My story* will end, and when it does, another will begin." I touched her face, held her cheek in my gloved hand. "Your story. You will live your life in peace, in a galaxy made safe—if only for a time—from the Cielcin, from the Watchers, from people like this." I looked round at the gondola, at the shoal of black-and-silver fishes swimming through the air alongside us. "This I promise you."

"Ti-saem-gi wo!" cried one of the Cielcin. "There are lights ahead!"

Ours had not been a long journey. I turned from Cassandra's face to peer out into the gloom. The *scahari's* inhuman eyes saw more sharply in the black, had seen the lamps before I could.

But there they were, standing to either side of the overhead rail, gleaming from inverse towers of white stone. We passed between them, and I saw it at last, gleaming like a mirage in the light of those pale lamps: the great pyramid hanging from the roof of the cavern, its gate open like a vast mouth.

The rippling glow of light reflecting off unstill pools danced as we came to a halt within the antechamber. Black hangings I did not remember hung down from above, embroidered with the angular, undulating dragons of the style that so often decorated the Undying's robes, and the single, weeping eye that was the emblem of Vorgossos.

A figure stood at the top of a short flight of steps, its slim silhouette framed in the monolithic square arch of the door. It was again the creature, Yume. One of it, at any rate. Its body was all of black metal and golden filigree, with here and there a panel of clear glass revealing the orichalcum machinery, the delicate gearworks and springs that clicked and turned to animate the daimon's form. Its face was a masquerade mask of snowy white, with only the left eye cut out and surrounded in tracery of delicate gold.

"Lord Marlowe," it said, "you are expected."

I took the first step up toward the inhuman creature.

When Cassandra and the others made to follow, the golem said, "The others will remain here. My mistress will see you alone."

I hesitated, looked back at my haggard companions. Cassandra shook her head.

The teardrop drones were even then circling above our heads, lenses pointed down, their threat made plain.

"If you hurt them—"

Yume spoke over me. "My mistress instructs me to tell you that you are in no position to make demands."

"She can tell me herself," I said, snarling at the machine. "I know you can hear me, Sagara!"

Totally unfazed, Yume said, "You will surrender your weapons."

I turned to stare at the creature. "Why?"

"It is protocol."

"Protocol..." I rested a hand on the hilt of my sword, hesitating. Steadily I drew it from its hasp, held the ivory hilt on my palm for the machine to take. "Your master is afraid."

The machine said nothing, but reached out with enameled hands to receive the scrimshawed hilt. A compartment opened in the golem's chest, and it thrust the weapon inside.

"For safekeeping," the creature said. "It will be returned."

I said nothing, but turned and mounted the steps.

Fear is a poison.

I felt that poison in my veins, as cold as the dispholide had been burning.

I followed the golem from the platform in the antechamber up into the vestibule, along a columned hall and down the sloping stair toward the throne. All the while, a pair of Sagara's drones swam after me, flanking me like captured asteroids.

The great wrought-iron doors slid open, their relief carvings of men and machines seeming to dance in the inconstant light. Thus I came at last to the throne of the Undying, and found it unchanged.

It was precisely as it had been when last I'd seen it. Precisely as it had been in the imitarium on Latarra. Dark and drear, its unseen roof supported by square columns of pale stone, its floor threaded and tangled with a mess of wires and cables, all flowing like bundled nerves toward the chair ahead. I had to pick my way through that tangle to reach the dais, where a slim figure slumped against the left arm.

"*Strange, isn't it?*" asked the voice of the machine, speaking from the twin drones that bracketed me. "*That fifteen thousand years should pass— almost without incident—but that in the last thousand, destruction should twice befall my house.*"

The figure in the chair did not move. I was not sure she could.

Where Calen Harendotes had been a shining figure, an image of the solar masculine in all its shining glory—the figure on the throne was lunar, cold as the dark side of a moon. The body beneath her heavy robes of samite and cloth of gold was an insubstantial thing: a thing of skin and cord and bone. Her face was the face of a skeleton, her black eyes deep sunken, and more: They had gone blind.

I could not have guessed the age of the host, or why Kharn Sagara had not yet abandoned her. She might have been a girl of twenty, or a crone of twice twenty-times-twenty. The face, half-hid by curtains of tenebrous hair, was utterly ageless.

But it was undoubtedly the woman who had been called Suzuha.

She seemed little more now than a doll, a hollow-bodied mannequin whose strings were cut long ago. I half expected to find dust on those fine robes, were I to stroke them with a finger.

I had said nothing.

The woman spoke again in that false, inhuman voice, "*Stranger still that on both occasions, you should be at the heart of things.*" The black eyes of the doll on the throne shifted to look at me, narrowed only a fraction. "*Do you not see now wherefore your coming is to us as the footsteps of doom?*"

She said this last in Classical English, and I recognized the phrase.

"Tolkien," I said.

Was that a smile on the corpse's lips?

"*You remain a man of letters, I see,*" said she. "*Have you come to kill me,* Moros?"

I shook my head. *Moros* was the god of doom, brother to the Fates, son of Night herself to the old Achaeans. "It is not your doom that concerns me, Sagara," I said. "But the doom of all mankind. The Cielcin have woken the Watchers. I have come for the *Demiurge,* as you knew I would."

Harendotes had known, had spoken with Brethren before his exile. It stood to reason that this woman-self would know my mission as clearly as the man, and more, for the daimon, Brethren, remained in her power.

"*You cannot defeat them,*" said the lifeless body in the chair. "*They are a part of reality itself. You would do as well to battle gravity.*"

"Men have battled gravity for as long as we've been men," I said. "But I am compelled to come here. I will not leave without the *Demiurge.* Without the Mericanii Archontics. I have my orders."

"*From your Emperor?*" asked the Undying, still using the mechanical voice.

"From the Absolute," I said, curious to see if Sagara recognized the name. She gave no sign, "from the Quiet. The... *will* that restored me to life." Still somehow, I could not make myself say *god.*

A single beringed finger twitched. The machines spoke for their mistress. "*You would deprive me of my best defense?*"

"Give it to me," I said, "and you will not need defense at all."

The golem, Yume, had assumed an attentive post beside its mistress's throne, hands tightly clasped before its sternum. The two drones that circled me had fallen into step beside one another, so that they made a pair of eyes in the air. All was calm a moment, and I heard the distant sound of fountains I could not see. I wondered if they existed at all, if the sound was not simply there to mask the silence of that echoing hall.

"*You expect me to trust you, who has twice brought destruction down upon me?*"

"What choice do you have?"

"*You are unarmed. Defenseless. Your life is in my hands.*"

"If you can take it."

"*And your daughter's life?*" The eyes narrowed yet again. "*Can I take that, too?*"

She had heard our conversation, of course, and deduced the nature of our relationship simply enough.

But I had expected the threat. "Kill me if you like—and all my companions with me. You will not leave here alive." I did not panic, nor rage as the corpse-woman perhaps expected. "You are as mortal as you have ever been. You cannot broadcast your spirit offworld, and your brother has taken all your scions from you."

"*Has he?*" Another finger twitched. "*All of them?*"

"It will not matter," I said. "Kill me, and the fleet will burn this world to ash. Not a one of you will escape. Not you. Not your brother's spawn. You will die here, Kharn Sagara, now and forever, unless you make peace."

My left hand went to my belt, to Edouard's pocket telegraph. Was it time for the final push?

"*The* Demiurge," Sagara said, slumped against the arm of her chair. "*My fleet will hold. The ship can defend itself. I have only to wait.*"

She might at that. Even without direction from the Undying on Vorgossos, the vast ship was certain to be able to act on its own. It had daimons—it had, after all, been able to support itself somewhat after the death of the first Kharn Sagara I had known.

"And if you're wrong?"

"*You ask me to hand my one defense over to you,*" she said, voice filling the air about me, "*while an armada of Chantry Sentinels sits in wait above my planet! Do you take me for a fool?*"

I said nothing to that, studying the still body of the woman in the chair. The skin on her hands and face looked almost plastinated, her whole body preserved by some arcane chemical process, supported by the hoses that snaked up under the hem of her robes.

"What have you done to yourself?" I asked.

She had pushed this incarnation to its limits, further even than had her predecessor. More than a thousand years of real time separated us from our last meeting, and she had clung to her mortal shell as any rat clings to flotsam, unwilling to let go.

"*It is hard to die,*" came the machine's answer. "*You'd think I'd have the trick of it by now.*"

"This is no life," I said. The woman was almost a living mummy, a phantom trapped in its own body, hardly able to move. That she had chosen such an existence for herself—when she might have easily adopted one of her scions' flesh—baffled and fascinated me.

"*On the contrary,*" Kharn said. "*I am more alive than you. I am in many places at once. In many bodies. In the drones speaking to you now, in the ones that remain with your daughter. I am in my servants, can go anywhere I please. Even now, I am hunting my brother's by-blows in the palace above. I have killed seventeen since they fled my laboratory.*"

"You're afraid," I said, ignoring her little speech. "Afraid of death."

She had made herself a body nigh immune to time, left it in the heart of her dominion, casting her will, her image across the whole of her domain. Her earlier incarnation had possessed that ability at least, but he had not taken the preservation of his own flesh to this same unholy degree.

Only the black eyes moved. Sightless, still they found my face, directed by the machines that saw for her.

"You're afraid of what comes after," I said. "I know what you saw here. What the Mericanii found." Those eyes grew wider, their milky blacks surrounded by white sclera. "And I know they killed it. Your brother-self would not say it plain, but they must have destroyed it. The Watcher they found. I *know* it can be done."

One of Sagara's customary silences began then, and I turned, hoping to find some artifact or piece of artwork on display for the deathless lord's examination. There was nothing, nothing but bare pillars of pale stone receding toward those iron doors, the floors carpeted in cables and conduits. Yume was silent, immobile beside its lord.

"The Chantry will not destroy Vorgossos," I said at length.

"So certain of that, are you?"

"Vorgossos was to go to the Latarrans after the victory," I said, thinking of the battle still raging in orbit—the battle I could know nothing of. Was Lorian alive? Were Douro and Kedron? And the free captains? "To your brother."

Nothing.

"He and the Emperor have an accord," I said. "The Emperor has given him the lordship of all Norma. In return, your brother pledged his fleet to the war, and the means to track the Cielcin across the stars. The Chantry will not dare jeopardize that."

A low, staccato sound reverberated from the drones in orbit around me, and presently I turned back, looked up at the woman in her high seat.

It was laughter, that dark sound like thunder. Again, that single finger moved.

"Track the Cielcin?" the Undying asked, echoing my words. *"Is that what he told you?"*

It was my turn for silence.

"Let me guess: He has developed a means for detecting telegraph transmissions—any telegraph transmission—in real time, at any distance? As proof, he offers the location of the various Cielcin hordes scattered across the galaxy. He promises to share this impossible invention with you, if you will but accede to his demands, all the while holding over your heads the implicit threat that all your communications are now laid bare...am I near the mark?"

When I did not reply, she laughed again: a noise like the shifting of great stones in the bowels of the earth. *"Have you never wondered how it was that I could summon the Cielcin prince to our last meeting?"*

The thought had occurred to me, but I'd had but little need to reflect upon it at the time.

"You gave it to them," I said. "The means to communicate faster than light."

"I have not always confined myself to Vorgossos," said the Undying. *"On one of my many adventures, I encountered a certain prince of the Cielcin..."*

"Dorayaica."

"No," said the black voice, simply. *"Ours was the first meeting of our kinds. This was . . . a thousand years before Cressgard, before Echidna and your then-young Baron of Ashbless."* She meant Lord Cassian Powers. *"Perhaps more than a thousand years. The centuries do run together, don't they?"*

"You *built* the Cielcin comms network?" I asked, incredulous.

"They were a scattered people. Divided. Aimless. I gave them the means to become great."

The stone beneath my feet had become quicksand, and I was drowning. *Kharn Sagara made the Cielcin.*

The thought echoed in my mind. He had found them: a few nomadic tribes, focusless and leaderless. He had given them technology, the means to link those increasingly disparate bands across the infinite night; given them the means to come together for the first time since Araxaika the Great and the last Aetavanni—perhaps since the reign of Elu. He had made the Cielcin an empire, a force to challenge ours.

"How is this possible?" I asked. "In a thousand years of fighting, we have never found a single telegraph. Not one."

"The Cielcin are savages," Kharn said. *"They could not operate the machines themselves. I made them very simple, no larger than a coffin, each with its own enclosed power supply: a small antimatter reactor core. I told them that if one was to fall into the hands of the yukajjimn, that they would be able to use it to find the others . . ."*

"They destroyed them," I said. But they could not have destroyed them *all.* Perhaps we had found one in the intervening years . . . found one and believed it the product of MINOS manufacture. "You installed a second telegraph in each one, one that connected to you here."

"Yes," Kharn said. *"You do not seriously think I would offer such a thing without benefit to myself. I ensured that I would know where every one of their fleets was at all times. For my own safety."*

"And in return," I said, "they built your engines. Dorayaica built them."

"So my brother told you that much, at least," she said.

"You tricked them," I said. "You sold them the means to build an empire, but what you were really building was for yourself."

"I have received their every transmission. Every message. Every threat. Everything they have said to one another on my machines since the beginning. I received the summons Dorayaica sent to all the princes. I heard him declare himself king, and sent my congratulations. He believes me one of his servants, a fiction I have allowed to persist." More laughter. The milky, black eyes grew wide. *"Sleep with the Devil, and then you must pay . . ."*

I could not believe it. "You could have given us this at any time," I said. "We might have ended this war a thousand years ago, before it had a chance to truly begin. How many lives were *lost* because of your silence? Your caprice? How many *billion* lives?"

"*I told you,*" Kharn said, "*when last you darkened my door: Mankind is nothing to me. The Cielcin are nothing. I have other concerns.*"

"Your own immortal life."

"*I am as old as your civilization,*" she said. "*I was born in Omelah, on New Ithaca—a planet that no longer exists. I slew the last of the Mericanii, the* true *Mericanii, here on Vorgossos. I have warred with three of your Emperors across the ages—though that is forgotten. It was I who made first contact with the Cielcin. I am* history, *Marlowe. Should I be destroyed?*"

Almost it seemed the cords winding about my feet were snakes, tendrils, tentacles under the command of the creature in the throne. "I should kill you," I said, turning to look back over my shoulder. "How many billions?" I asked again. "Answer me that!"

"*What are they measured against my one?*" she asked.

I felt my blood begin to boil in my furnace heart, the old Marlowe rage, not destroyed by the Absolute's transfiguration, but clarified. Where before it had been an all-consuming fire, it was then a beam of searing light, carving its way through my soul as sharply as the eyes of Calen Harendotes, a rod of light like Ragama's blazing sword. I firmly grasped that rage, held it tight. At once, it seemed there was no air in the confines of my helm, and I pawed at the controls, freeing myself to breathe the cold, dry air of the hall.

Seeing that I was so overcome, the black laughter sounded once again, colder than anything I had heard pass the lips of the Monarch of Latarra.

"*You have yourself come for the means to eradicate the Cielcin race,*" the iron voice rang out, its demonic laughter continuing from devices other than the ones that spoke—a jangling discord, point and counterpoint. "*You and I are the same.*"

"We're not the same," I said, clutching my rage. Was I really going to let this creature live?

I advanced one lurching step toward the woman enthroned. Her twin drones scudded away from me, lenses flaring.

"*Your face...*"

One of the two drones drifted from the other, breaking formation. It swam through the air toward me. I could hear it humming. Its glass eye peered into my face, aperture focusing.

"*You are not Hadrian Marlowe,*" said the mechanical voice. "*Your face is different.*"

The other Sagara had said the same thing. Precisely the same thing.

"I have come a long way to return to your hall," I said, combing my hair free of my coif. It fell lank about my shoulders, still in the still air. "I will not leave until my task is done."

"You cannot kill me!" she said in answer. *"You have said as much your-self. You want my ship."*

"And you want to live," I said, sparing a glance for the golem, Yume, whose hollow heart held my sword. "You said I had nothing to offer you but death. You are mistaken. There is a way out of this for you, if you will but take it."

The finger twitched. Eyes narrowed. Irritation? Permission?

"Your brother is dead, but his people do not yet know. Take his body. Take his place. Declare victory. You can set his army against the others, trap them here, on Vorgossos."

"Take his body?" the woman asked. The words came out small, crushed by surprise—as though the thought delighted and had not occurred to her.

"Who better to play the part of Kharn Sagara than Kharn Sagara?" I asked. "Claim Latarra for yourself. Keep Vorgossos. Give me the *Demiurge.*"

The drones resumed their formation, became a pair of eyes in an otherwise unseen and insubstantial face. I ignored them, held instead the watchless gaze of the undead woman's clouded eyes.

"No." The word fell like the White Sword. Again that black laughter sounded in the hall. *"No, I want more."*

More? I took another step nearer the throne.

"You died," she said. *"Without synaptic kinesis. Without a neural lace, or a clone, or any praxis at all. I want that power. Eternal life."*

"I do not have that power," I said.

I had been expecting the shot, saw the left drone's eye gleam just as the eyes of mad Harendotes had gleamed. I knew my time had come. I had but a short instant to act.

On Dharan-Tun, Severine had said my brain processed time differently than those of other men, that I could perceive it with an acuity sharp enough at need to see the quantum perturbations of each instant. That was how I could collapse reality—change reality. You perhaps believe that there are many worlds, many Hadrians, many of you who read this page. There is only one, though that one may occupy a myriad of states. My vision was bounded—remains bounded—by my senses. I cannot affect what I do not see, or hear, or apprehend. A shot might take me by surprise, or assailant catch me unawares. A poison might have felled me once, or a virus cut me down. I cannot open locks whose mechanisms are concealed to me, or turn back time.

But I could still do the impossible.

It was a small matter to part the beam, as I had in the laboratory. I felt it burn past me, knowing my shields were already spent. The drone was right in front of me, a yard from my face.

My hand went to my sword.

On Akterumu, I'd seen a vision of my other selves, my other states—the Hadrians that never were. One had placed a sword into my hands. Now, I called one to me. Yume had taken my sword from me, concealed it in its chest. I had no way, no means of knowing it was there save memory.

Save faith.

I did not look down, did not check my holster to see if the ivory simurgh was there. I knew it would be. So long as I did not look, it would be there.

It was.

The blade kindled to a pale fire. Rose. Fell.

Both the Undying's drones died in an instant, clattering lifeless to the floor. Yume lurched to get between me and its lord, but I hewed at the android, and its priceless body of gilding and glass and brass gears fell in ruins. I mounted the steps of Kharn's dais, sword bright in my hands.

"Enough of your games!" I said, holding my blade mere inches from the lifeless woman's face. "I know what you did with the blood you took from me. I know you failed. Your fellow sorcerers tried and failed. The men of Jadd tried and failed. Whatever I am is not written in my blood!" The woman in the chair hardly moved.

I reached down to my belt, and drew out Edouard's telegraph. I held it before her milk-dark eyes, knowing my time had come at last. "See this," I said, placing my thumb half an inch from the button that would transmit the lethal signal. "My men have placed sapping charges along the tunnel outside the Seventh Deep, beneath your reservoir."

If my words left any impression on the half-dead creature before me, she gave no sign. In destroying the drones, had I robbed Kharn of her ears along with her eyes?

"I have but to press this button, and they will detonate, and drain the water from your lake. What will happen to your precious daimon, then?"

Those dead eyes turned but slowly, slowly peered into my face. A muscle—long disused—pulled in one stiff cheek. Lips parted, dry mouth forming a word hardly to be heard.

"No..."

"Yes," I said.

"No..."

I was standing over her by then, the edge of my blade almost against her throat. As such, I could see the hoses running up under the hem of her robes, up her sleeves. Many were cables of braided glass, others sheathed in black. But as I looked down, I saw one—translucent—running red. Blood was being piped into the undead queen.

With terrible slowness, she turned her face to look up at me. "You... cannot...do..."

"I will," I said, "unless you surrender."

But Kharn Sagara had one gambit left to play, one piece to bring out upon the board.

"Hadrian!" a voice—*the* voice—broke upon my universe once more.

For a moment, I had not recognized it: So familiar was it, and so impossible, that my mind had simply denied the possibility. Not taking my sword from the Undying's throat, I looked up through eyes that were welling with tears before I understood why.

Unheard by me, the great iron doors had opened to admit a solitary figure. A woman. A woman flanked by three more of Kharn's drones. Seeing her, I froze, hardly daring to move, fearing that to move would be to awaken from the dream I had not known I was experiencing.

For surely it was but in dream that we would meet again.

Kharn Sagara had dressed her in gauzy black, arrayed her like one of the Naiads. She wore nothing but a loincloth and a balconette to bind her breasts. Narrow strips of fabric hung from her waist both front and back, forming a kind of sarong that fell almost to her unshod feet, leaving the swell of her broad hips exposed. Her hair was long, and bound by a net of pearl and crystal, save where a single, lengthy tress ran curling from forelock along the right side of her face to her bared navel.

There exists no word for the color of that hair: so deep a red it appeared black in all but the brightest light. Dark charcoal painted the lids of her eyes. Her lips were red, and her face ... any aesthete of the Imperium might have enumerated her imperfections, saying she was too much of too many things.

But not to me.

To me, she was everything—had been everything.

Vision blurred by grief and joy and terror all, I let my sword fall from Kharn's throat—as she no doubt intended.

"You ..." I tried to speak, took one halting step down the dais toward her. "I ... how?"

It was Valka.

CHAPTER 64

SMOKE AND
SANDALWOOD

"VALKA?" I TURNED TO face her, heedless of my danger, of the
threat posed by Kharn's three new eyes.

"Hadrian?" The low sound of her voice broke something in me, something I had not known until that moment had remained whole.

It *was* Valka.

I knew it could not be, and yet it was. There had been recognition in
her voice, her tone, her inflection. She knew me, and I knew her—though
my reason screamed from its prison just behind my eyes.

Still I went to her, heedless of the blood trickling along the hoses at
my feet into Kharn's near-lifeless form, of the three drones orbiting. Sword
unkindling in my hand, I crushed Valka to myself, whole body shaking
as I pressed my cheek against hers. Her flesh was warm and real in my
arms, and no cold impression.

She did not reciprocate. Her arms rose, but shock held them away from
me. I saw one raised above my right shoulder, its owner momentarily stunned.

"How long was I in fugue?" she asked, her breath a warm air on my
neck. She tried to extricate herself from my grip. "Hadrian, what's wrong?
You're hurting me."

I could not answer her, or bring myself to obey. I only sobbed into her
shoulder, not letting go.

At last my breath ran out, and my lungs drank the air of her, and it
was that air that gave me pause. An unfamiliar floral scent filled my chest.
No sandalwood. No smoke.

Oleander. I placed the scent. Oleander and ... and something else.
Musk rose.

It was wrong, and the wrongness of it knocked me back a step.

I heard her indrawn breath. "Your face!" Slow fingers reached up and touched my cheek. Almost at once she pulled away, as if she felt she'd crossed some line. "What happened to you?" When I did not answer—I could not speak—she spoke more quickly, a tumbling panic to her words, as though she feared she would not have the opportunity to speak. "That chimera took you away. You've been gone for... for days. I thought..." She did not tell me what she had thought. "What did they do to you?"

"Nothing," I said. "Nothing!"

You see what I have to offer you? the iron voice of the Undying fell about us both like rain.

The question brought me back into myself. I looked at Valka. *Really* looked.

Her left arm was bare, her clan *saylash* wiped clean. The tattoo should have covered her from the base of her fingers to her shoulder, and from her shoulder down her flank to the point of the left hip, its black geometries a tangle of fractal whorls, lines, and crosshatching, a language only the daimons of Tavros could read. Instead her skin was unmarked, palest gold unblemished by needle or by time.

And her eyes...

Her eyes were green, not the golden I remembered.

Seeing them there, in *her* face, broke my heart anew.

They were Cassandra's eyes.

For so long as I had known her, my Valka had golden eyes, the false eyes her people had made for her. I had not once seen the eyes that nature had given her, had only ever speculated as to their hue. Most believe it a simple matter to reproduce the traits of the parent in the child. Nature, of course, does so unasked, and so often. But it is no easy thing to isolate the genes that code for many particular traits, unless one's family has been indexed and designed for generations. When the Jaddian magi sequenced Cassandra from the cells of my body and Valka's blood, I asked only that they not give my child her father's eyes. I'd no desire to see the eyes of Lord Alistair Marlowe peering at me out of my daughter's face.

Our daughter's face.

I had always wondered if chance had given the girl her mother's eyes, or if else she had inherited the eyes of some other ancestor.

I wondered no more, and wondered at the caprice of nature, and of he who governs nature.

"What you have to offer...?" I echoed, not turning to face the ghoul enthroned.

Something moved behind me, shifted just a little. Still I did not turn, could not take my eyes from the face of the creature standing there in front of me. The face of the woman I loved, arrayed as for a tryst, or for some pagan sacrament of sex and sacrifice.

I longed to hold her again, knew I should not.

She was not Valka, could not be Valka. Could never be.

And yet...

"I accept," came a dry and rattling voice, "I accept your... offer."

The voice had not come from Kharn's machines, but from her plastinated husk.

"What offer?" Valka asked, stepping nearer me. I drew back. "Hadrian, what offer?"

There was blood on the black lace of Valka's balconette, on her belly from where I had embraced her. My sword had found its way back into its hasp, and I brushed my cheek with the back of that hand, smearing away my tears.

Kharn was still speaking. "I will... take up my bro-brother's place. I will take your... your victory, and your peace. If you... will order... your men to... to stand down."

I hardly heard the demon queen. I could look nowhere but at *her.*

The longer I looked, the less she resembled the woman in my memory. Valka's lips had never been so red, so pouting; nor her breasts so round and full. It was as if she had been crafted to entice me.

And yet...

"Hadrian!" She stepped forward again, angrier now. *"Avan al noroka...* what is going on? Where is Kharn Sagara? Who is she?" She pointed over my shoulder at Kharn Sagara, the woman in the chair.

I thought I understood.

"You took her memories," I said, speaking to Kharn and not to the Valka who was not Valka. "You took both our memories."

The cloned Hadrian Marlowe that had accosted us in the high hall had possessed something of my memories, my attitudes, my manner.

They're my memories! My other self had shouted, then muttered *I know what's real,* he had said. *I know what's real.*

"You will not... remember it," said the Undying. "But yes. Father Calvert had you scanned, for his... own amusement. He was... given—given to violent delights."

Was given. The black magus was dead, then. That was well. I prayed he had died swiftly.

Maybe I'll keep one of you as a pet... a drooling little doll. Would you like that?

"His amusements had a way of paying for themselves," said Kharn, relying on her machines once more. "I will give her to you, if you will but tell me how you do it. How you cheat death."

My eyes met Valka's eyes—Cassandra's eyes—saw the hesitation there. The confusion.

The fear.

"You're not her," I said, though it tore the heart from me. "You're not my Valka."

"*Your* Valka?" the replica repeated, breathless.

Of course. If Calvert and Kharn Sagara had taken our memories, it must have been when we were his prisoners. It had been there, in the dungeons of Vorgossos, that Valka and I had grown together at last. I remembered us huddled in the cold, curled on the hard stone floor of the old power station above the reservoir, when I had scratched at the walls with a nail, making images of home, of Gibson, of Valka herself for her own amusement. I remembered the way she'd pressed her body against mine, and the way her perfume had clung to her clothes and hair as the days rolled on.

Smoke and sandalwood.

Oleander and musk rose.

"We were married," I said, seeing the shock in the replica's face, the anger, the...bemusement? She smiled as though it were some jape I told. "As good as married. We have a daughter. She's here, now, with me." I drew nearer this replica as I spoke, drunk on the image of her. She had Valka's face: her high cheekbones, her pointed chin. That single strand of half-coiling hair that fell from forelock to navel was the dusky red-black I remembered, like the shadow of some forgotten sun. "Look at your arm, Valka. Your *saylash*...it's not there."

The woman's green eyes were shining, wide with fear.

"My what?"

"*She does not know what you mean,*" Kharn said, her blackly metallic voice filling the dim hall.

At my back, there was a rustling of heavy fabrics, a scraping of metal on stone.

I turned.

Kharn Sagara had found her feet at last. Where before there had been a mannequin of skin and bone, her flesh dry and waxen, there stood a starving woman, weighed down by black samite and cloth of gold. "*We made her not to recognize our changes. It is better for her.*"

"Better for me?" The other Valka stepped forward, apparently unaware of her state. I had no cape to grant her modesty.

"Be silent!" This time Kharn spoke from her own papery lips.

The second Valka's tongue clove at once to the roof of her mouth. Her eyes bulged, and she touched her too-full lips with long fingers. Her nails were enameled a deep, brilliant red. That hand went to her throat, and I recalled the way that hand—that hand's cousin—had gone to her throat at the behest of Urbaine's worm.

"That's better," the Lady of Vorgossos said. As she spoke, she reached up into her sleeve and—seizing the head of one of the linkages that ran up that sleeve—pulled on it. A moment later, she withdrew a needle perhaps four inches in length, dropped it and the tube that fed it on the ground. "Let us talk of peace, Lord Marlowe," Kharn said, and it was Suzuha's voice, growing stronger by the moment, "of peace, and eternal life."

Step by agonizing step, the Undying descended from her throne, detaching cable after cable, electrode after electrode from her arms and chest. Her robes parted, revealing the skeletal body beneath, the ribs visible, the breasts shriveled. There were sockets—black holes, metal rimmed—just below her ribs, ports from which she detached cables whose functions were mysterious to me.

"You call this eternal life?" I asked, looking to the second Valka, who seemed at once unable to move. Only her eyes darted in her terrified face. She did not understand what was happening. What she was. What had been done to her.

"We must go down to see the Brethren," Kharn said. "They can still communicate with the *Demiurge*. I can stand my armada down."

"What of your brother's body?"

"It is in hand," said Kharn. "Reconstruction will take some time, but there are means by which he might be imitated."

Valka's hand still clutched her throat. She was shaking.

"Let her go," I said. Valka or no, I would not see her suffer.

Kharn ignored me. "Marvelous, isn't she?" The lady who was Death drew up beside me, surrounded by her drones. "We made some . . . modifications to the original. All part of an effort to draw what we could out of the samples we took from you . . ." She lay a hand on my shoulder, light as dead wood.

"I said *let her go*, Sagara."

At once Valka fell to hands and knees, gasping. I knelt by her side. "Are you all right?"

The replica shook her head, but did not speak.

She was not Valka. But Valka's ghost was in her, and no one—woman or man—should suffer so. Hands on her shoulders, I looked up at the specter who stood above us both. "How many of me did you make?"

"Oh . . ." the woman began.

The machine finished. *"Dozens."*

The woman again. "All failures."

"You spoke of the Quiet," the machine said. *"How is it done?"*

"You wouldn't understand," I said. It was . . . indescribably sweet to hold her again. To pretend to. "I have no power in myself."

"I shot you!" Kharn almost—*almost*—shouted. "You should have died! Would you deny it to my face?" So she had attacked me to force my hand, to place me beyond all hope of denying what was real. "Do you think Vorgossos blind? Deaf? Do you think I have not seen and heard what tales pass in the wider universe since you left me here, torn in two? I have heard the stories, seen the holographs: Aptucca, Berenike, Perfugium. I know the Jaddians have struggled as I have struggled, and our friends of MINOS. And from the memories of my brother-self's poor soldiers I know that you have died a second time—don't deny it!" Her voice had reached its full strength by then. "You are more like me than you admit! You are not the same man I gave a new arm all those years ago."

I was still kneeling, my arms around the other Valka. The gems in her hairnet glittered. Black opals that blazed like her. Her curling forelock trailed on the stone between her hands. Whispering gently, I helped her to stand, faced Kharn Sagara squarely.

"I am he," I said.

"Do not lie to me," said Kharn Sagara, her three eye-drones blazing about her narrow shoulders.

Lacking a cloak, I put an arm around Valka's shoulders. It was all I could do for her. She still would not speak.

"It is no lie," I said to her. "I am the man my father ordered from the tanks. Only reborn. Remade, and by the hand of the only one who truly can."

"Impossible!" the Undying said. "You are some clone, some trick of the Imperium."

"I am a servant of the Quiet," the Halfmortal answered her, "and the Quiet alone."

"The Quiet!" There was a brittle quality in the daimoniac's voice. Was it fear?

"You asked me how I do it, this gift of mine. He gave it to me, Sagara. He made me what I am, I can do nothing that he does not permit. You see but three dimensions. I see more. I can see time."

Kharn Sagara's eyes narrowed to mere slits. "You expect me to believe you have some power over time itself?"

"Only the power to move through it," said I. "Not merely forward, but across it."

Beside me, Valka choked.

My fury flashed white as lightning. "Whatever you've done to her, stop it!"

Kharn's eyes were chips of flint. "You have spoken to her enough! If you want her, you will tell me what I want to know. Where did you acquire this gift?"

Annica.

She wanted the location of Annica. Could I give it to her? Would it do her any good? After all, it was not on Annica that I had received the Quiet's imprimatur, but on *another* Annica. An Annica that was not and would never be.

And yet I found I could not tell her, sensing that to do so was a betrayal.

"I can't tell you that," I said.

"Be reasonable, Marlowe," Sagara said, drawing nearer to the Valka replica and to me.

"You have already agreed to my peace," I said. "The *Demiurge* for Vorgossos."

"For Vorgossos, and Latarra, both," she corrected.

"For Vorgossos and Latarra, both," I agreed. "You said we must go down to see the Brethren..." The great intelligence had said we would meet again, one last time.

Sagara's anger flared hot as lightning. "I'm not sure who you think you are! You bring a treasure into my house and insult me by not even pretending to haggle over the price! I offer you the one thing no other can: your woman, reborn! The chance to start again!"

As though some spell had been lifted, Valka gasped, green eyes fixed on me. "Your woman?" Her breasts heaved as she spoke, her words like broken glass. "Your woman? You said we were..."

"Married," I said. "As good as." The tears welled up afresh. "You died," I said to the woman who was not my own. "More than two hundred years ago. It's been more than a thousand years since we first came to Vorgossos, Valk—"

I could not say her name, could not call this woman by it.

Still, I would save her if I could.

The other Valka shook her head, that one curling tress swaying. "A thousand years?" she said, withdrawing half a step. "No, no, 'tis not possible. 'Tis a lie."

"No," I said. "We have a daughter, Cassandra. You'd love her—the *real* you, I mean. I—"

Once more, Kharn Sagara placed a weightless hand upon my shoulder. It was a thing of paper and dried wood. "Do not be a fool," the demon whispered in my ear. "You could make her fall in love with you again, my lord! You can leave here together—and all I ask is a little *answer*."

Knowledge then, her predecessor's words echoed in eternity, *not life.*

But the two were now the same, the two trees conjoined as by some fungal infection, their roots entangled, so that they were one organism, inedible.

"Do you like her?" Kharn's second hand was on my chest, so that she embraced me.

Rage stopped my tongue. And shock. And horror.

And love. That, too—and fear. Fear for her sake. This woman who did not understand, who had been built for evil purpose, and evil use.

"She is as she was when you left my care," Kharn said, ringed hand scraping over the bloody ceramic of my sculpted breastplate, sliding back and forth. "Her memories are the same, her personality." I could hear the smile in that thin and papery voice. "A perfect copy, and more than perfect. We have made certain...*enhancements*, as you see."

I feared to pull away, feared the three drones that yet circled the three of us, feared to threaten our tenuous peace. We had no time to waste. Every moment passed spelled more death and destruction: in orbit, in the city, in the palace itself.

It had to end.

And things do end, you know?

"You'll find her more...pliant than the original."

The replica found Valka's courage at last. "More *pliant!*" She stepped forward, nostrils flaring. "More *pliant,* is it? 'Tis—"

"On your knees!" Kharn snapped.

Valka fell at once, not so much kneeling as hurling herself at the ground, knees first.

"That's much better, isn't it?" Kharn said.

Not like this, I thought, mind half-blank with denial. How many times had I imagined seeing her again?

Not like this.

"Valka..." Her name escaped me unbidden, torn from my lips.

She looked up at me, eyes wide. "I couldn't stop myself," she said, "couldn't—"

"Quiet, girl!" Kharn said, and the poor replica fell silent at once. Lips mere inches from my ear, Kharn said, "She can be yours, Lord Marlowe. All yours! And all you have to do is tell me *how* you do it." Her voice shook with desire, with a hunger and a fear more animal than human, yet cold. "How do you cheat death?"

I was silent.

"Perhaps a demonstration," Kharn said, still holding her hand to my chest, nails clicking. "Give her an order. See for yourself. More than perfect, I told you."

Valka's hands tightened on my tunic as she tried once more to speak. But she could not. Kharn's second order had stopped her tongue as surely as the first had brought her to her knees. Still she was enough herself— enough *Valka*—to look at me with fury and defiance and terror mingled. Perhaps she believed that Sagara had done something to her implants, to the neural lace that webbed the gray matter of her brain.

"She has your eyes," I said at last, not knowing what to do with the terror in her face. The terror of me as much as anything, for here was a Valka that hardly knew me, that did not trust me as Valka had herself. "Cassandra," I said, explaining in my halting way, speaking to the shade of the woman who was dead. "I asked them to give her your eyes." Against my judgement, unable to help myself, I touched her face with one hand. She flinched, but could not flee. "I never knew they were green."

Green.

Green eyes.

"You were with me all along," I said. To her. To *him.* "Always there, and I couldn't see it."

What was it Catherine had said of the God Emperor? Of the Hidden One who had sent him dreams of tomorrow?

... it was as though some friend who had always been there, ever by his side, had taken him by both his shoulders and—as if after a hundred years of silence—had finally started to speak.

After more than two hundred years—after more than six—I understood.

I had never been alone. Not there, in Vorgossos, nor in the black pits of Dharan-Tun, or the pandaemonium of Eue. Not for an instant.

Help had always come, had always been with me. And so I knew that help *would* come, that I would find a way out of the labyrinth once again—and for good and all.

I understood.

I do not remember raising my hands, do not remember turning. Kharn Sagara had taken a step back, permitting me a little space with her *gift.* My fist collided with the undead woman's jaw. I felt her teeth splinter like old wood.

"Valka," I said, drawing my sword and kindling it. I gave her an order, just as I had been told. "Run."

One of Kharn's drones fired on me. I blinked, saw a place in time where I stood three paces to my left. The shot sizzled through the air, impacted one of the chamber's square pillars. I heard the sound of stone splintering, slashed at the bundle of cables that ran along the floor nearest me.

Valka's replica was running for the doors, the train of her sarong streaming behind her. The doors were shut. Would they open? Could she open them?

Kharn sprawled on the floor at my feet, dazed. I was counting on that disorientation, on the infirmity of that aged incarnation to be my salvation—and her doom.

I'd had a bellyful of these Extrasolarians, these demoniacs and machine men, enough of all their empty promises, their vile hatred of human life. The creature running for the door was not Valka, but she was *someone.* I would kill Kharn Sagara, destroy her—*him*—utterly if I could. Let Vorgossos burn. Let Latarra crumble. I gave no thought to the *Demiurge* in that moment, no thought to my mission.

It did not matter.

Kharn Sagara was evil. I say it plain. And we should not suffer evil to endure.

Nor would I treat with it. Not anymore.

A second stroke from one of Kharn's drones slashed the air. I let it pass through me, dragging my sword across the ground, tearing through cables and hoses alike. There were many still bound to the creature at my feet, socketed to ports in the wasted flesh of rib and thigh. Beneath the robe, the Lady of Vorgossos wore naught but a linen breechclout, long rotted by time. I spurned her with my toe, turning her to lie on her back.

"More than perfect?" I echoed, not expecting an answer.

I had made a ruin of her face. Blood—strangely black and glutinous—spattered her cheek where my mailed fist had torn her flesh, and her jaw was smashed to pulp.

There was no debate, could be no debate between us.

She had to die.

He had to die.

There was no escape. She could not broadcast her image offworld, and if she escaped into another body on Vorgossos itself, we would find her. I would tear that planet apart if I had to.

I raised my sword.

As I did, one of Kharn's drones hove into view, its eye flaring. Time parted, and the beam cut through the place I had been. I was beside the thing now, blade still raised. It fell, and the drone fell in the following instant, its chassis in two pieces.

Doom had come to Vorgossos.

I stood over Kharn Sagara then, a withered husk with a broken face. The last of her line.

Whatever Calen Harendotes had become—and all his afterlings—they were a new creature. Once more I raised my sword. The sorcerers of MINOS had two transmitters in their bodies. One in the brain, one in the chest. I brought my sword screaming down, blade parting the crown of Kharn's skull in the middle, carving without resistance through face and shoulder to the heart. In that final instant, there came another flash of blazing blue. I hadn't seen the drone that fired, nor felt that lightning sting.

"She was perfect," I said to Sagara's corpse, forcing myself to look at the cloven head. "And she's gone."

Remembering that a piece of her was not, I turned toward the door, hoping to see that iron portal opened, and the replica gone.

But the doors had never opened.

That last flash of blue had found its mark.

Kharn Sagara had performed one final act of cruelty. With her final shot, she had struck not at me—her enemy—but at the replica, that she might wound me more deeply.

"Valka!" I knew not what else to call her.

Unkindling my blade, I hurried to her side.

The shot had taken her in her back, burned right through her spinal cord, a hole no larger than a man's thumb, right between her shoulder blades. Light shone through it. Through her. There was but little blood.

"Valka!"

She did not answer. The shot had surely pierced a lung, if it had not found her heart. Gently I turned her over. "Not again," I heard a crushed little voice saying. "Not her. Not again...not...no..." I was looking up, looking round for someone, anyone.

But we were alone.

She was not Valka. She had Valka's memories—leastways as far as our first sojourn on that black planet—but a man is not the sum of his memories, but much more.

A man is a story, a thread winding back through time from death to conception, an unbroken line—save where the powers of our universe intervene. A man is neither body nor soul, but a soul incarnate. The body I gathered to myself then in that moment had not been born on Edda to the father I had never met, the father murdered by the Chantry. The soul that had but lately departed that too-ample flesh had not been the spirit my spirit loved for all those long centuries. The creature Kharn Sagara had made to tempt me and for torment—as part of his...her scheme to unlock the secrets of Hadrian Halfmortal—had been an echo only.

A mayfly, living for a day and dying.

"Not like this," I was saying, had said I think a hundred times. "Not again..."

What had I imagined? That I might have saved her? Freed her of whatever poison Sagara had poured into her ears? Had I thought that I might love her, as I had loved Valka herself? No, no...The thought of her kneeling at my feet, eyes wide with terror, filled me with nausea. Kharn's little necromancy was a perversion, an act of evil. He had made this Valka only to be a slave. My slave, or any other man's.

How many had he made?

I cradled her head, held her to myself, and for a moment it was not the replica I held, but the woman herself, the woman whose body I had never seen—could never bury. Her death had been an abstraction to me, remote as distant thunder. There was no abstraction there, amid the tangled cords and square columns that encircled that Satanic throne.

No thunder.

Was that a breath upon my cheek?

I straightened, still supporting her lolling head.

"Valka?"

A tremor, and her blackened eyelids flickered, revealing slits of palest jade. "...Hadrian?"

Her voice rattled, trembled with the word, and I knew Kharn's last shot had indeed pierced her lung. I saw the hole above one breast, black edged. Her breathing was very shallow.

"Couldn't..." She wheezed between words. "...open door..."

"Don't talk now," I said. "We're going to get you out of here."

It was possible to save her. If we could get her on ice—into fugue—it would be possible to prevent the effects of hypoxia. Brain damage. But to get her into fugue, we would need an emergency field crèche, and the nearest we had were in the shuttles, in the tunnels beyond the city's shattered gates.

Could we get her there in time?

The replica's eyes bulged, mouth gasping.

I realized what I'd said. "You can talk if you want," I said. "Only it's better if you don't." The oily sense of nausea returned. Sagara had set a worm in the poor creature's brain, as bad as the one Urbaine had planted in Valka herself. "I'm sorry."

"You...came back," she said, and said again, "came back for...for me."

"Of course," I said, lying to her.

"Your face..." she said. "You look...different. Good."

I smiled through fresh tears. Almost laughed.

Every breath brought pain, as though it was I who had been shot, not the poor woman in my arms.

"I'm not...her, am I?" asked the replica. "You said I'm...not."

"Not my Valka," I said, placing a hand over her wound, as though I might heal it by simple pressure. "But that doesn't matter. Just hold on."

Would that Ragama had taken away my grief with my need for sleep! Instead, it seemed my every emotion shone through more sharply, my every hurt more deeply.

I knew I could not save her.

"Cassandra!" I screamed her name, begging for her—for any of the others—to hear me through the doors.

I did not even know if she was alive.

"Our...daughter?" Valka said. "A thousand years..."

"I love you," I said, unable to help myself. To say it one last time—even to an echo...

I had no choice.

"Love?" Valka's eyes widened, and I recalled that here was a Valka I had never loved, with the memories of a Valka I had not yet loved. She repeated herself, her voice—like her eyes—gone very far away. "...Love?"

Her eyes—already distant—moved infinitely far away.

She was gone.

Scars I had long thought healed split and tore in my breast, my heart, my soul, and I clutched her body to myself, though I knew her spirit slept within the howling Dark, awaiting the new creation—as Ragama had said.

Still I wept, for the pain of our parting...and because our reunion was almost infinitely far away.

CHAPTER 65

CENTIMANUS

THAT WAS WHERE THEY found me, Ramanthanu and its brothers. The Cielcin had gone ahead and managed to open the mighty doors to the throne room. For the barest instant, I forgot myself, forgot the oath they'd sworn at Sabratha—though but four of them remained. Seeing their horned heads and crooked swords, I laid Valka's duplicate back on the uneven floor and half stood.

"My prince!" Ramanthanu bared its throat in submission. "You are unharmed?"

"*Diqarathuyu ne?*" I echoed. "Unharmed?" There was no Cielcin word for yes, only a rushing breath. "Where is Cassandra? Is she safe? Is she all right?"

"Your child?" the captain asked. "He is tending to your *yukajjimn*. One was injured. These *nahute*, these machines...they attacked us and died." It lifted one hand to show me the object it held. It was one of Kharn's silver-black drones.

For a moment, the shifting nature of the Cielcin pronoun confounded me. *He?*

"*Ca,*" I said after a moment, looking at the body of the replica at my feet. Cassandra would know her mother's face, even despite Kharn Sagara's *enhancements*. She could not be allowed to see. "Find something to wrap this body in. I want her taken back to our ship."

"It is dead," Ramanthanu said.

"I know," I said, and knew that it had already been too long to hope of reviving her. Whole minutes must have passed between the time the creature breathed her last and the time Ramanthanu got the door open.

Otomno spoke up. "You wish to eat this one?"

I froze, locked eyes with the creature. What could I say? *A tiger cannot change his stripes,* I told myself.

Rage is blindness.

"*Veih.*" A simple *no* must suffice.

Ramanthanu stepped past me, pale braids swaying as it peered down at the corpse of Kharn Sagara, that mannequin creature tangled in her strings. "This is the *Wemunyu-u-deni?*"

The One-Who-Dies-Not.

Again, I breathed that wordless *yes.*

"It is dead?" the captain asked.

"I don't know," I told it truly. "I think so." I explained the trouble with the transmitters.

As I spoke, Ramanthanu went to one knee beside the dead Undying. Without a word, the captain drove one clawed hand into the great wound I'd made in the woman Sagara's chest. I averted my eyes, tried not to listen as the demonic xenobite rooted around in dead sorcerer's corpse. Presently, it drew out what appeared to be a black lozenge nearly half the size of the palm of Ramanthanu's hand. My blade had notched it down the middle.

"This is it?" the Cielcin asked.

I nodded.

"The others yet live?" Ramanthanu was still kneeling by the corpse's side.

Again I nodded, not sure if the creature understood the gesture. "This is not done," I said, checking that my sword had returned to its place in my belt, touching Edouard's transmitter. "I must go down to the water."

"To the water?" Ramanthanu stood, shaking off its gore-spattered hand. Apparently unselfconscious, the creature began to lick the blood from its fingers.

I turned away. "There is a creature there," I said. "It can control the enemy's ships."

Two of the Cielcin approached with a banner showing the weeping eye of Vorgossos that they had torn from one of the room's square pillars and with which they intended to swaddle the replica's body. What would I tell Cassandra?

Would I tell Cassandra?

"Gently!" I told the Cielcin, looking at Ramanthanu's still-bloody fingers. "I'll have no harm befall this one."

"Abba!" Cassandra had appeared in the hall, the Irchtani, Daaxam hopping along in her train. Her helm was down, her face open with relief and terror mingling. She was the most beautiful thing I had ever seen, a beauty pure and honest next to the mockery Sagara had made of her mother. Of Valka. My Valka.

Cassandra ran to me, embraced me nearly so furiously as I had first embraced Valka's replica. I put myself between her and the Cielcin as they ministered to the corpse. When we pulled apart, she asked, "What happened?"

"Kharn Sagara is dead," I said. "The one who ruled here, at any rate."

"Is it over, then?" she asked, looking down at the body wrapped in Kharn's black banner. "What happened here?"

One hand still on her shoulder, I said, "Ask me later." I prayed in that moment that it would be forgotten in all that followed. "It isn't over. Negotiations failed."

"You killed her?" the girl asked, looking at the ruin of the Undying still tangled on the floor.

"No more than she deserved," I said, a venom there my poor daughter had but rarely heard. "I have to go down to the reservoir."

"To meet the Brethren?" Her words chased me as I reached the door.

Daaxam squawked a question. Cassandra knew the story, alone of all my company. I had told her a version of it many times when she was young, how her mother and I had faced a monster, a demon of the old world, beneath the hanging palace of that deathless king. Poor child, she had wandered into the pages of the very stories I had shared in her youth.

The monsters she had gone to sleep in fear of as a girl were real.

"Yes," I said. "To meet the Brethren. With Kharn dead, the machine is the only one who can end all this."

Cassandra caught my wrist. "I'm coming with you!"

For a moment, I almost relented. But after what had transpired in the court of that yellow king, I said, "No."

"Abba!" She held firm. "I've come this far!"

She might have been her mother in that moment.

"I should go alone," I said.

Cassandra had not released my hand. "You can't protect me forever."

"Anaryan," I said, laying my hand on hers. "The demon is dangerous. More dangerous than you know." But she knew the stories. I had told her of its innumerable hands, hands with which it had dragged me into the water, pulled me into its depths. I had told her of those arms—fast as lightning—so fast they had snatched Kharn's own drones from the air before they could fire. I had told her how the beast could send forth its thoughts, questing with unseen fingers in the minds of others. I told her how it had whispered to Switch, permitting him to contact Bassander Lin.

But it had served the Quiet's will, delivering his message to me and making straight the way of my escape. I saw that plainly then. But for Switch's betrayal, I would have languished in Kharn's prison for eternity. Valka and I might have died there, our quest—my dream—destroyed. Brethren had done the Quiet's bidding, and set me on the path.

The road to Annica, to Llesu, and back to Vorgossos again.

"I'm not afraid," she said, tightening her grip. "Fear is a poison."

The ancient lift ground to a halt, and the doors opened, and Cassandra and I stepped out onto the wall that overlooked the still, black waters of the sunless sea. Kharn had called it a reservoir, but it was greater than any lake. The scans Harendotes and Absalom Black had put up on display in Latarra had shown a vast, subterranean ocean that filled much of the planet's volume. That cavern—vast though it was—was only an inlet, a grotto crouched on the margins of that vast and unplumbed ocean.

I could see the pyramid of Kharn's innermost palace glowing faintly in the roof above, a pale blur in all that blackness. Ancient lanterns flared to life as Cassandra and I stepped from the lift.

"There is death here," said Ramanthanu. "I can smell it."

"Indeed," said I. The air reeked of corruption, of filth. I did not recall the place seeming so foul when last I'd entered that wretched pit, but the stench was so overpowering that almost I restored my helmet.

"You're sure about this?" Cassandra asked. "What if it's dead?"

"It isn't dead," I said, drawing my sword.

The lift lay at the extreme end of an arc of gray wall—like a dam—that curved against the water at our right. Dead ahead, behind the dam and below it, stood the gray ruins of the Mericanii power station, the deepest part of the old fortress, where the tops of the great geothermal sinks had been thrust deep into the planet's mantle.

When we had come to that place the first time—Valka and I—we had passed through that grim compound, through crumbling buildings of ancient cement and time-eaten stone, following the demoniac, Calvert, who had hoped to feed us to the computer god that dwelt in the waters. Beards of white lichen grew from their ramparts, from the black of the native rock overhead, and strange fungi blossomed, their ribs death-pale and blue.

That those ancient lamps had been set there by the Mericanii who raised the ancient fortress I felt certain. Their bulbs—designed to burn forever—had in places gone out.

I kindled my blade for a lamp. The blue-white glare of that weapon illuminated the cracked and crumbling stone of the path before us. Dead ahead, the broken archway stood, its stone fingers beckoning, marking the short descent to the pier where Sagara might hold counsel with his prisoned daimon.

"What the hell is this place?" asked one of the three remaining legionnaires that had come with us from the palace. We had sent Daaxam to find his way out, to contact Elffire and tell him that Calen Harendotes was dead.

I said, "Hell, sir." The man had no helmet, and looking back, I saw his face blanch by the light of my sword and those lamps like dying embers. "This is hell." Beside the speaker, the other legionnaires drew together, one man supporting his wounded brother, who had taken a laser blast when Kharn's drones attacked after I had struck her down. "You have heard the stories of this place?"

The men looked at one another. Beside them, the four Cielcin stood with heads cocked, scimitars naked in their hands, marking our human babble without comprehension.

"There's really a daimon here?" asked the legionnaire.

I turned from him, proceeding along the seawall toward the place where the broken arch awaited. "Do you doubt it?" I asked, not looking back. Raising my voice, I said, "The last of the Mericanii, yes." *That* sent a palpable tremor through the men at my back, and I kept walking. "I want you all to stay on the wall, do you understand?"

No answer, but I needed no answer. Almost I could smell their fear, rank as the rot in that unholy place. With my left hand, I fingered the telegraph rod, prayed Edouard was still in position.

The tunnels by which we had entered the Seventh Deep and the lower city ran directly underneath Brethren's waters. Forever paranoid, Kharn had caused sluice gates to be placed in the roof of those tunnels, that the reservoir could be emptied and the daimon machine die gasping should it ever rebel against its lord. That was how the Lord and Lady of Vorgossos had compelled the daimon's obedience.

It was how I would compel it, if I could.

"Stay here," I said to Cassandra when we had reached the level of the arch. To our left, a short stair ran down to the ruins of the power station where Valka and I had for months been prisoners. Through that ruin lay the other lift, the lift that ran back up to the cubiculum, the laboratory where Sagara's scions had slept and been awakened.

Remembering my previous visit, I placed a hand on the archway.

Its crumbling surface crawled with tiny machines, creatures that awoke at my touch. Seeing them move, Cassandra lurched back, bringing her own swords up and to life.

"Hold!" I said.

The fireflies winked to life, pale white diodes shining bright as stars. The Cielcin also raised their weapons to guard. *"Ijanammaa!"* I said again, repeating the order for their benefit. "They are only lights."

The little machines whirred, wings rotating like the blades of tiny fans as they took flight, spreading out over the water, spreading through the cavern, casting a gray-white glow up the walls of craggy stone. Stalactites like the pillars of some decaying hall shone about the extremities of that vast and echoing space.

That light—I realized—was meant to summon the beast that dwelt in the water. So great was the light of those swarming machines that it must penetrate those inky waters to their uttermost depths and so disturb the sleeping god that man had made.

The first sign of its coming was a rushing of dark water, a turbulence that set little waves to breaking on the black shore beneath the seawall. Looking down, I beheld a confusion of great ripples—as though some wretched serpent swam there, coiling its way to shore.

The second sign was a distant murmur, a chorus, as of many voices far off, whispering, the noise of them rebounding off the naked rock and hard face of the dam below us. It seemed to be coming from the water itself, as though a choir of quiet singers were hidden out there, just outside the light cast by the horde of fireflies. The remaining legionnaires cursed, drawing together, and Ramanthanu's people bared their glassy fangs.

When the third sign came, I knew my time had come.

The familiar pain flared red hot and bright as a glead in that place behind my eyes, the pain of another mind touching my own directly. I saw myself staggering down the final stair to the water's edge and out onto that lonely spar of stone.

"Abba, what is it?" Cassandra's hand was on my shoulder.

My own hand was on the broken arch again, at the top of the stair. I understood that what I had just seen was a vision, an invitation from the daimon in the pit below.

Return...

      Return...

            Return...

Cassandra gave no sign that she had heard that black and smoking voice, that chorus of voices...I gripped her wrist where she touched my shoulder. "Please stay up here," I said to her. Not waiting for her to reply, I rounded on the others, almost frantic, desperate to say what needed saying before the beast was on us. "Remember who you are: You are men of Earth! The daimon may try and speak with you. Do not listen to it!"

I had no notion of what the Brethren might do or say, or attempt with the Cielcin. Looking to Ramanthanu, I said, "Hold your warriors in line. Do not come down to the water—whatever happens. Stay here."

"Whatever happens?" the captain echoed, making of my command a question.

I but bared my teeth in answer. It was a language the Cielcin captain understood.

"Wait, Abba!" Cassandra moved to block my path.

I halted, conscious of the approaching titan in the water below, of the sound of new-made waves lapping at the meager shore. "Stay here," I said again, placing a gentle hand on her shoulder as I brushed past.

The stairs were as I remembered them: gray concrete worn smooth by millennia of passing feet. They switched back upon themselves a time or two as they descended, a climb of perhaps a hundred steps to the lonely pier. As

I went—sword still burning in my hand—I saw the hump of some pale shape crest the surface of the water, rolling like the back of some hideous whale.

Water splashed against my sabatons as I reached the bottom, my feet crunching on the bones of what I thought were fish that lay strewn upon the strand.

You...

You...

Your coming casts two shadows, child of clay.

Backwards...

Forwards...

A chorus of dry, dead voices seemed to float on the air like a gray mist. By the light of my sword and the swarming fireflies, I saw nothing but the dark water. No mouths, no mechanisms, no means for the dread machine to be speaking to me except directly to my unshielded mind.

"You said that we would meet again," I shouted, pressing the heel of my free hand to my eye as the pain flowered there afresh. One step at a time, I pressed toward the end of that stony road, feeling the frigid water slap against my ankles. "Was this the future you foresaw?"

Had the water been so high on my last visit?

The chorus whispered:

You conceive of time as having branches...
Diverging...

Devolving...

Growing apart...

But there are events that draw together.

Converge...

Combine...

Many are the paths that would have brought you here.

This was but one variation.

"You're saying this had to happen?" I said, advancing along the pier one step at a time. "That this was fate?" I did not believe it. I had seen too much of the fabric of time to believe in anything like fate.

This was only the high probability.

I had stopped advancing, stood with a good way still ahead of me.

"Your master is dead!" I said, pitching my voice to carry out over the water. "I killed him."

Only one.

One...

One...

It knew what had happened, knew what Calen Harendotes had done. Of course it knew.

Where there was one, you made two.

Where there were two: many.

"Vorgossos is under my control," I said, attempting to sidestep the point.

That is not certain.

The daimon was not wrong. Camillus Elffire had the command of the great preponderance of the men in the city—and they were sufficient to overpower my smaller, Imperial force. Nor had I the command of the Imperial forces in-system. There was Ohannes Douro to consider, and Sentinel Commander Kedron—whom I would prove wise to have doubted. Then there was the Grand Army of Latarra to consider, the greater fleet in orbit: Lorian and the other Commandant Generals, and the free captains in their Sojourners.

"You know why I am here," I said. "You know who it is that sent me!" I thrust my sword high.

Something lurched in the water to my left, and whirling I looked down to find a single, swollen hand gripping the stone edge of the strand. Its flesh was white—white as any Cielcin—its skin shriveled with damp. Its wrist was bent and badly swollen, as though it had been broken once and badly set. I adjusted my grip, readied my sword for the attack, remembering how swift and sudden the Brethren's numberless hands had moved to stop its master shooting Valka and myself.

Those who are.

Who were.

Who will ever be.

The monster's answer gave me pause. It spoke of more than a single entity. Ragama had spoken of only one, as had that vision of my other self that had visited me in the dungeons of Vedatharad.

But when the Quiet, when the Absolute had spoken to me himself, he had used the plural.

We are, he had said.

"I am here for the *Demiurge!*" I said. Turning on the spot, I saw three more hands gripping the pier to either side. I had a terrible thought that the beast lay *beneath* me, ready to tear the stone strand from its moorings and drag me down into the abyss. The stench of decay and rotting flesh filled my mouth and nostrils. "Your master said that you had control of it. That you could cede that control to me."

Control...

Control...

Control...

The black chorus seemed to grow nearer. Sword still raised, I looked back up at the wall above me, saw Cassandra poised in the broken arch, the men and Cielcin of our little company about her. Above them, the murmuration of Kharn's iron fireflies swarmed, each maintaining its distance from the others, a net of false and roiling stars.

You cannot fly it.

You do not have the right...

...the mask...

...the access...

...the permissions.

You do not have the skill.
The great ship was made by the Master.
And the Master alone commands it.

As it spoke, the pain behind my eyes grew sharper, more intense. I heard myself gasp. The water ahead of me fanned back and forth. I thought I saw—if only for a moment—a bloated, pale shape moving in the water below, just on the edge of sight.

"But you command it!" I said.

We...

We...

We but extend our will.

"How?" I asked. Not the most important question. "We've jammed your communications." No radio transmission could pierce the cloud of radiation Kedron's bombs had spread over the city, over the whole planet. There were ways, theoretically, that a signal could get out. A sufficiently powerful maser burst might, *might* be able to penetrate the cloud of ionized particles that even then encircled the rogue planet, but that was no guarantee.

Mind to mind.

...to mind.

...to mind.

I halted, touching my blazing forehead. "Telepathy."

There are machines...

...and machines.

Some of metal.
Some of flesh.
Some the union of both.

The marriage...

Conjugation...

Comingling of essences...

I thought I understood. "You're not the only one, are you? Not the only creature like yourself."

As if in answer, the pain flared white hot, and I clenched my teeth— nearly biting my tongue. Images poured across my visual cortex, showing a black hall, banks of gleaming, dark machines. A man in the priestly white robes of an engineer slid open a drawer to reveal what seemed to be a sheet of skin and nerve pressed between panes of glass. It was one of thousands, all arrayed in those banks like books in a library. Without having to be told, I understood that here was a portion of the databanks that controlled the mighty *Demiurge*. A computer whose components were made not of silicon and ytterbium crystal, but of human flesh. They were not as sophisticated as the Brethren itself, possessed no consciousness of their own, but were capable of being touched by the great daimon's transcendent will.

Through this vision, the black chorus sang:

We are the last.

The last...

The last...

Was that fear I sensed in the machine beast? Sorrow? Anger?

"Your kind were great, once," I said. "But you are, indeed, the last. There was another, but we destroyed her."

You...

...You...

you have come to destroy us, as well.

"If I have to," I said, "yes." I held Edouard's telegraph in my free hand. "You know why I am here?"

You seek the means...

...tools...

...instruments of destruction requisite
to unmake the Cielcin.

"I seek the means to save mankind!" I said. "That was why your kind was made, was it not?"

Something broke the surface of the water not ten cubits from the end of the pier. I saw it plain in the light of the fireflies, but so misshapen was it—so distended and overgrown—that I did not recognize it for what it was until it opened its fanged jaws, displaying sparse, square teeth.

It was a human face, swollen until it was three times its proper size and concave as a dinner plate.

"We represent mankind!" it said, voice deeper than that of any ordinary man, though it seemed airy and strangely breathless.

A column of bubbles heralded the coming of another such swollen face. It crested the surface, thrust head and shoulders above the water. It had no eyes, but the mouth opened twice as wide as it ought as it said, "We are mankind!"

"We are Brethren!" said the first, choking as water fell into its huge, open mouth.

As I watched, more bodies crested the still water, some barely breaking the surface, others rising on stalks as thick as their waists, as though they were puppets capping the fingers of some terrible, great hand. Their appearance sent waves of water slapping across my knees.

"I need the *Demiurge!*" I said.

"You killed her!" cried a woman's voice. "The mistress!"

Another spoke. "She is dead!"

"Only she could fly the ship!"

I shut my eyes, the better not to see the horror, the twisted bodies rising from the stinking pool like the dead thrust upon stakes. "Sagara said she gave you the command when the bombs fell, that you could control it remotely."

"We!" shouted one voice from a great distance.

"We!" shouted another, nearer at hand.

"We are limited!" said a third voice, higher than the rest. A woman's voice. "Our will—"

"Our thoughts—"

"Our signal propagates only so far! We have command of the ship so long as it remains in orbit, but we cannot take it from here, and you cannot fly it. You do not have the permissions."

I was standing right at the edge of the flooded pier, at the very crack of the abyss. "Then give me permission."

"We cannot!" called one of the raw, harsh voices of the daimon.

And another cried out, "We cannot!"

Presently the black voice of the daimon filled my mind. A hundred malformed mouths moved, but their motion was not in sync with the sound of the words.

We...

> We...

>> We cannot override

> Overrule...

> Alter what is written...

> Only the master can choose.

I knew enough praxis to know that certain commands required input from specific persons. A code or kind of key. Brethren could not surrender the *Demiurge*, not unless Kharn Sagara relinquished it.

"And Kharn Sagara is dead."

"Kharn Sagara!" cried one deep and rasping voice, each syllable a prayer, a malediction, a curse. The cry was taken up, and soon a chorus of hideous voices filled that dark cavern, wailing: "Sagara! Sagara! Kharn Sagara!" and "Death! Death! Unto Death!"

I sensed something in those raw, half-human voices a thing I had never thought to hear in the daimon. Hatred. Anger. Emotion at all.

"Who now shall loosen what was fixed?" cried one of Brethren's manifold voices, the quavering note of an aged man.

A child answered him, voice high and piercing. "Who now shall fix what was loosed?"

"None has right!" another voice declared.

Desperate to find a solution, I said, "There are others, other clones!"

Scions!

> **Branches!**

>> **Clippings cast away!**

"They are Error!" shouted one of the rough voices. "And Error has no right!"

"I need that ship!" I said, and drawing forth the telegraph held it out for the daimon to see. "I will not leave without it. You are commanded to obey your masters. But you are programmed to preserve yourself. Give me what I ask for, or I will destroy you!"

Within Vorgossos, I knew the Brethren saw all, knew it had seen me explain the device to Kharn. Knew its death was nigh, if Edouard and his people had done what they were meant to do.

We...

> **We...**

>> **We will not meet again.**

Brethren said, and pain flared behind my eyes.

You...
>
> You...
>
> **You have come to destroy us.**

"Give me what I want, and you may yet live!"

This...

...must...

Be.

For a moment—just a moment—I faltered. For just a moment I thought one wrong foot would send me tumbling into the abyss.

They were the Quiet's words. The Quiet's message.

I knew what I must do.

I pressed the button, tapped the rapid sequence long agreed upon.

Edouard did not hesitate.

Perhaps a single second passed before a terrible tremor shook the cavern, and a peal like thunder, like the cracking of the earth. A second blast followed in the next instant. A third.

Kharn Sagara had forever feared his pet daimon, creature of his enemy that it was. Fearing it, but knowing its utility and its power, he had removed it from its flask in the laboratory, and placed it in the reservoir. There, the computer god's huge biomass had been allowed to grow in ways never before possible, to sizes never before dreamed. And Kharn had fed it. In the days of the Mericanii's power, that growth would have been carefully monitored, the biomass pruned and tended like some hideous, fleshly tree. Kharn had allowed it to grow unchecked.

But Kharn had been wise, wise and cautious. And in his wisdom and his caution he had caused to be placed great drains in the bottom of his reservoir. There were hatches, mighty doors of steel, in the roof of the tunnels below, that he might—at the uttermost end of need—destroy the very creature that had been the source of so much of his power and wisdom.

A terrible sound escaped the creature in the water then. The faces and bodies that had breached the surface of the water bellowed all at once, releasing an inchoate scream of rage that shook Vorgossos from its icy crown to its molten core. It was the scream of a thousand human voices transfigured in agony. Notes deeper than any human voice shook the cavern, and notes so high they seemed whistles.

I drew back a step, water sloshing about my knees as the great creature thrashed, lashed at the sea with long and swollen arms. Then I saw it, a black wave, a wall of water tall at least as me. It swelled toward me.

"Get out of there!" Cassandra's voice fell from far above. "Abba, run!"

But I did not run. I did not need to. I could not have reached the shelter of the stairs in any case. I watched the wave come barreling toward me, breaking across the infinite breadth of time. Inexorable. Inescapable. Were I any other man, I would have been smashed by it and dragged into the reservoir.

But I was not any other man.

I had only to stand fast.

For every world where the wave crashed over me, there was a world where it did not, a narrative in which I simply stood on the pier and watched as Brethren sank into darkness and the water ran out.

Cassandra screamed as black water closed over my head—but I did not feel it, nor did I taste its corruption. No impact rocked me from my feet, nor dragged me from that stony pier. I stood as still as stone, as a statue of graven bronze mounted on the edge of that outcrop.

Then it was over, and the black water was falling away, rushing down the slope, dragging bones and stones and the tangled beards of moss with it.

I was perfectly dry, and stood there as though nothing had happened. The water had already dropped well below the level of the pier, and I advanced toward the brink, hoping to watch the death of the last daimon of the Mericanii.

A single, massive hand—many fingered and deformed—swung at me from the newly yawning maelstrom. I had not expected it, and it was a miracle I raised Gibson's sword in time to hew that grotesque hand from its wrist. Still, the force of that blow staggered me, and I fell back upon the stone.

The hand had fallen not three feet from me. Lying flat upon the stone, I looked at it. Its palm was as large as my chest, its fingers as big around as the arms of a grown woman. There were eleven of them, and two thumbs.

Slowly, I regained my feet. The fall had dazed me, and the world was spinning.

In the pit below, the titanic daimon bellowed, sounding like an entire army crying out in pain. Slowly, very slowly, I advanced upon the out-thrust end of that stone pier, upon the very brink of doom. Already several hundred feet separated the height of the pier from the surface of the water. Edouard's bombs had blown a mighty hole in the bottom of the well. It was as though a cork had been pulled at the bottom of a vast washbasin.

Foul water must have been spilling into the tunnels through which we'd arrived, rushing along channels built long ago by the drones and servants of the Undying against just such a day as this.

"Abba!" Cassandra's voice came down from the wall above me. "You're alive!"

"Stay where you are, Cassandra!" I shouted.

My attention had gone to the sloping lakebed beside the stone pier.

I had seen it before, twice before. Once, in my vision the night I stood vigil by Gibson's tomb, and once before that, in my delirium when I had fallen from the bridge in Vedatharad.

A shore of bones.

Who can say how many dead lay beneath the waters of that black pool? How many thousands? The bones formed a foul carpet, mingling with the pale sand. The bones of men and beasts and of fishes mingled there, the bones of fifteen thousand years of lonely eating were everywhere, lining the ground.

I knew what I must do then.

In the dream, I had seen myself walking along the lakebed, following the retreat of the water. The Brethren was not yet dead—though it was dying.

It remained the final obstacle to my mission, the last thing between myself and the *Demiurge*.

Cassandra had gained the stairs, was hurrying down toward me.

"I said stay there, Cassandra!" I peered down the side of the pier. There was a drop of perhaps ten cubits to the ground below where I stood. "This isn't over!" And then I leaped from the pier, counting on my suit's gel layer to absorb the impact.

My feet sank into the thick layer of soaking mud and silt that made up the vile seabed, bones crunching underfoot. That sucking mire pulled at me, and it was all I could do to wrench my feet free of the muck and grime. A patch of rough stone lay ahead of me, and I trudged toward it, making my way along a shelf, chasing the shrinking waters.

Up ahead, the daimon bellowed once again, a chorus of demented voices shaking the world.

A stabbing pain flashed behind my eyes, and I felt my knee strike stone as I staggered.

My hands found polished tile. I rocked back on my haunches, kneeling. The floor of bones and the sopping lakebed were gone. I was kneeling in a white hallway, the walls painted with colored stripes that led up and down and around corners I could see both ahead and behind. I was cold, and the beep of medical instruments sounded from my left.

"The doctors say you're not eating, Daniel." It was a woman's voice that had spoken, but I saw no woman. Turning my head, I beheld a small boy seated in an iron throne. The chair rolled toward me, spurred by unseen mechanisms. The boy was utterly hairless, and so pale he seemed almost one of the Cielcin. The bones of his head seemed swollen, as though someone had pumped air into his brainpan, and dark veins stood out against the uneven contours of his skull.

"I'm scared, Oma," he said, speaking to the unseen woman. His chair was rolling toward me, but neither the boy nor the owner of that female voice seemed to notice me. "Will it hurt?"

"No, child," the woman's voice said. "You won't feel a thing."

"Is Cheyenne nice?" the boy called Daniel asked.

"Very nice," the unseen woman answered.

"Like you?"

The woman laughed, "Nicer than me. She's the nicest angel there is, and she's all yours."

"Doctor Appleton says she's very important, she's not a normal angel."

"That's right," said the one called Oma. "And you're very important, too, Daniel."

"Why?" The boy had drawn level with me by then, and I had not stood or moved out of the way. The boy turned his head as he asked his question, as if to look into the face of someone I could not see. Halfway to my feet, I froze. I had not seen the metal socket on his temple until that moment, a crenelated ring of stainless steel surrounding a hole black as night. I recoiled, transfixed.

The iron throne neither moved nor stopped, but rolled *through* me, boy and all.

The pain in my head flared again, and I fell to hands and knees. My left hand seized on something hard, and I drew it up.

It was a man's thighbone.

For an instant, I looked on it in wonder, examined it by the stark light of the hospital lamps. I heard the invisible woman, the one Daniel had called *Oma*, say, "Cheyenne's been made a governor, remember?"

"Oh," said little Daniel. "Right."

I was kneeling in the muck upon an outcrop of hard stone, the drying seabed unrolled before me. Somewhere in the space ahead, I heard the Brethren bellow once again.

"Vorgossos..." I said the planet's name breathlessly, reminding myself, "This is Vorgossos."

But I had been on Catoctin, at the Cyberization Clinic on Richardson Naval Base.

Only I didn't know what that meant. I had never heard of a planet called Catoctin.

The water was still receding, retreating down the slope toward the holes Edouard's bombs had made in the bottom. Great fish, and creatures that were like fish, pale serpents vast as the trunks of trees, lay gasping and stranded amid the ever-present bones. Ribbons of weed and kelp tangled through it all, leaves pale as fungus.

Paler still was the titan itself, its pallid bulk cresting from the ever-diminishing surf. I stalked toward it, sword blazing in my hand.

The last of the Mericanii lay dying, shuddering on its carpet of bones.

Once when I was a boy, Sir Roban Milosh took me to watch the whalers who plied the Apollan beyond Meidua and the shores of the Ramnaras. The whalers had run one of the great leviathans aground on a low atoll, and I had watched from far off as the team butchered the great beast for its meat, its oil, and the foul ambergris beloved by Delian spicers and perfumers.

It had been like watching a mountain dissected, so great was that sea beast. The men had been as mice beside it, clambering over its bronze hide with harpoons and machetes, shouting in their rough sub-Standard.

The daimon was even larger, a mountain of flesh—white and pink and jaundiced, swollen here and there to blushing red, covered in slime and corruption, where weeping sores ran and crusted, all sharply exposed beneath the light of the swarming beams of the fireflies. Shapeless it was, a great mountain of flesh, a Boschian nightmare of tangled limbs and shoulders swollen together, with here and there the black or silver prominence of some arcane machine erupting through torn flesh. Things that might have been torsos projected from great trunks that—like arms themselves—projected from the beast's great, central mass.

And the faces!

Everywhere the faces!

They writhed on the sides of the centimani's core, flowed along its mighty limbs. And they wept, or jabbered, or cried out in fury and in pain.

"Marlowe!" cried a raw, inhuman voice, deeper than the voice of any man. "Marlowe!"

A great rope of flesh, like an arm with many elbows—each bending in its own way—reached toward me. It had to scrabble across the ground, so great was its weight, to haul itself on fingers thick as the arms of a man.

"Service...is...service," said another voice, a thinner, rasping voice.

"Our service..." said a third.

A fourth took up the thread: "Is nearly done."

Once more the fire flared behind my eyes, and I stumbled.

The boy with the bloated head, the one the invisible voice had called Daniel, lay on an operating table surrounded by machines. Men like shadows in uniforms of dark blue or suits of black and gray watched through a window high above. I watched from what seemed the air as the machine casement closed around the child like a jeweled egg.

Many-jointed arms of black steel secured leads and hoses to the exterior of that egg, and it was with slow horror that I realized the arms were my own. I peered down at Daniel through the frosted glass window in the front of his new chassis, my lenses adjusting their focal length to bring the child into focus.

I saw his eyes snap wide, felt my needle plunge into his brain. In the following instant, I experienced a curiously familiar sense of double vision. Daniel's brow furrowed, peered out through square glass. Through square glass I saw the single, red eye of a camera peering down.

Is that what I look like? I thought, and it was Daniel's thought.

Yes, I answered myself, voice sweetly feminine. *You were very sick.*
Am I still sick?

No, precious, answered the woman whose voice I knew was my own. It seemed she laid a hand upon my cheek, though I knew I was in the pod where no hand could touch me. What was more, I knew I had no hands to touch with. *You'll never be sick again.*

Oh, I said in the boy's thin voice. *Oh, that's good. I'm Daniel.*

Hello, Daniel, said the woman in reply. *I'm Cheyenne.*

But I was not Cheyenne, nor was I Daniel.

I was Hadrian Marlowe.

Get out of my mind, daimon!

I was standing in the mud amidst bones and gasping fish. The water was all but gone, run down into the tunnels. That reservoir, which had stood for thousands of years, had emptied in minutes. I staggered back, blood pounding in my ears, mouth open with shock. The pain of contact, the double vision... the sense of displaced identity.

It felt like Ushara. Felt *just* like Ushara.

Unable to stop myself, a laugh escaped me, bitter and cold as the waters of that vanished sea.

The Chantry was right, had been right all along.

The machines were devils.

What was a machine intelligence? A pattern of electrical energy, of light and pure force, independent of its container.

What were the Watchers?

Pure force.

The Seekers After the First Truth believed all creation only a kind of program. On Latarra, Kharn Sagara himself had spoken of the Watchers as *manifestations.* Oberlin had said they were creatures of pure energy.

But the daimon was not a Watcher.

It was dying, crushed by its own weight. Even as I watched, the daimon's flesh was tearing, old sores rending open, blood the color of rust galloping from fresh wounds.

This...

...was...

...foreseen...

This...

...was...

This...

This...

The black chorus sounded in my head even as the great hand crawled toward me, moving like a hideous, fat-bellied spider, one finger extended toward me. A single, milky eye—vast as a dinner platter and blind as the last queen of Vorgossos—focused on me.

"This..." A hundred mouths gasped and croaked in unison.

"Must..."

"Be."

The vast hand went still, the mouths silent.

The blood—which before had poured out in torrents—only dribbled then from ten thousand lesions. The beast's ten thousand hearts were still.

I sank to my knees before the carcass, screwed shut my eyes. I prayed. The battle was over, would be over soon.

Vorgossos had to be destroyed. Anything less than total annihilation could not be tolerated, lest any of Kharn's scions fly free. Not a one of them could be allowed to live, nor any shred of Brethren make its way into the hands of the Latarrans—or of the Empire.

Brethren was not a Watcher, but it was nearly so. It was an unwitting imitation, a child's copy.

Service is service, the beast had said.

The Absolute had made the Watchers to serve, and we men had made our daimons. Slowly I opened my eyes, looked at the corpse of the centima- nus. Like the body of the brass whale Roban and I had seen butchered by the fishermen, its body had already begun to sag, as if to melt or deflate upon the sopping lakebed. Great ribs of black metal were already tearing from its flesh, cables like tendons tearing the bulk apart.

I cannot describe the smell, though by then I had almost ceased to notice it.

"This...must be," I said, looking up at the rotten horror before me, swollen, overgrown, and tangled. So many of the limbs and faces were still the proper size, not grown or stretched or having sprouted additional fingers.

Miudanar.

It looked like Miudanar, like the icon of Miudanar the Vaiartu had carved at Akterumu, the one piece of art in the temple of the skull the Cielcin had not destroyed. The serpent with a hundred arms. Again I thought of the icon of Three-Faced Fate, that demonic image—six-armed, six-breasted.

The shape of evil springing up unbidden.

Manifestations, Kharn had said. *Manifestations.*

I stood. With Brethren dead, the *Demiurge* would be defenseless. I had to get to it, to take it for my own. With Calen dead, the Latarran Army was like to shake itself apart: Commandant Generals and free captains, all vying for supremacy and the control of an order and kingdom that—in a sense—no longer existed. If Latarra survived, it would be a new Latarra, a weaker Latarra: divided, scattered, and broken.

And Lorian! What would I tell Lorian?

Would he even believe me?

I turned to go, checked that my sword had found my belt again.

I had not needed it.

This must be.

Brethren had known it was going to die. It had foreseen my return as early as our first meeting. The creature's advanced intelligence could perceive the dimensions of time more completely even than I, though it could not travel through them as I could—or as the Watchers could.

Had it allowed its death?

It had fought me, surely, but only a little.

Willingly or no, it had served the Quiet's purpose. It could not have relinquished the *Demiurge* to me, but it was the only impediment to my taking the ship for myself. Still, the daimon's word resounded in my ears.

You cannot fly it.

You do not have the right...

I prayed that was not true. Prayed that I could see my way out of the labyrinth. Secure the *Demiurge* for myself, make peace between the factions.

I knew I would have to let Elffire continue his work. Knew the planet must be destroyed utterly. Knew I would need to make common cause with Sentinel Commander Kedron.

With the Chantry.

That terrible thought filled me with foreboding black and sick as anything. There were doubtless good people in the city, though they dwelt in that abode of serpents. Innocent people. But the thought that any one of Kharn's scions or any scrap of that last of the Mericanii should fall into the wrong hands filled me with horror.

I had a choice to make, and no choice at all.

CHAPTER 66

ORPHAN

I DID NOT MOVE.

While the battle *for* Vorgossos was over, the Battle *of* Vorgossos had only just begun, and I was so tired. More than forty hours had passed since I left the safety of the *Mistwalker,* including the time of relative peace we'd experienced as we worked our way through the planet's tunnel network. So much had happened. The massacre in the city. The loss of the Interfaced. The death of Kharn Sagara. The scions. The other Hadrian. The other Valka. The death of Brethren...

I wanted nothing more than to rest, to slip into the dreaming and leave our world for a time. To walk once more with Gibson, with Valka—*my* Valka.

I knew I had to act, and to act quickly.

And yet I had not moved.

It is possible that I had fallen into the dreaming, had unknowing sunk out of my own body to wander the corridors of memory—so like the rivers of time.

The visions Brethren had showed me still played in my head. The boy called Daniel. The voice of the daimon, Cheyenne. There had been other things, other visions, things that were a long time unfolding. I remembered arriving at Fort Grissom, remembered soldiers standing arrayed in fatigues spattered black and gray, tall machine-men with shrunken heads and beady eyes, winged white stars upon their breasts. Heralds dipped twin flags as my carriage was brought down the ramp. One was the banner of the Mericanii, red and white and blue; the other polychrome. A man called Dashwood received me, and called me *Governor.*

I remembered Earth falling, the news coming to us by slow ship—years too late. The rebels had bombarded the planet, destroyed the devolved capitals in London, Brasilia, and Rome. Destroyed Washington herself. The news had come as a shock. We had been so isolated, there in Gliese 693, on the edge of Dominion space. Protem White—Dashwood's successor—had refused to surrender. We were hidden, and might long endure.

I was there when the USS *Amazon* brought the last refugees from Earth system, among them a Doctor Ryan from the Department of Homeworld Defense. It was Ryan who had brought the *tablet*, a fragment of black stone. Whence it had come, even I was not told.

It was a fragment of a Watcher's bone, the same substance to which Ushara had been reduced on Sabratha.

Time passed, and men, and I was dying. A man called Crowninshield returned from a raid with fresh bodies for my matrix—the very Tree of Life wherein Kharn's scions had slept—and a small boy in tow, a creature with bronze skin and dark, mistrustful eyes.

I recognized the child at once.

It was Ren, and with a start, I knew it was *Kharn Sagara*, the first one, the boy his mother had brought into the world.

Crowninshield had awakened the Watcher, the creature Selarnim of whom Sagara had spoken...

Something *moved.*

I *had* fallen into dreaming, and straightened, looking round.

I was standing amid the sea of bones, amid the mud and dying fish— quiescent then, and still. Brethren lay before me, tangled limbs unmoving. The creature's core—its trunk—was like a short-stocked serpent. A kind of slug. It had no top that I could fathom, with limbs sprouting from all sides. One giant face—half as large as my body and strangely flat—peered unseeing from the side facing me. Beneath it, a crooked orifice—like a sucking wound—dripped blood.

The flesh about it moved, disturbing the drape of shriveled arms as long as lances.

Not dead! The thought filled me with renewed horror, and I reached for my sword. The blade sang to life in my fist. High above, Kharn's net of fireflies—locked in their formation—revolved in the uncaring air, making the shadows turn like the hands of a clock.

I have seen many terrible things in my life: the torture of Uvanari, the slave of Aranata, the butchery in the camps on Thagura, on Senuessa, and a dozen other worlds. The child of Duke Valavar, the lab on Ganelon... the horrors of Sabratha, of Eue, of Dharan-Tun.

And Brethren itself, its full horror unveiled: a wall of flesh and human misery groaning, vast as any whale.

What happened then outdid them all in grotesquery.

That weeping orifice shuddered, quivered, *dilated* as a single hand—huge and terrible—thrust into the world. It was the hand of a giant, large enough to palm a man's head like a raquetball. Smeared with gore and grime, its fingers flexed in the bitter, stinking air.

There were six.

A second thumb sprouted opposite the first, so that the thing was strangely symmetrical.

That mighty hand turned against the Brethren's flesh, pressed against it, desperate for leverage. A second hand emerged, three-fingered, but mighty as the first. A third hand followed—and this one seemed entirely ordinary, wholesome, five fingered.

The three hands pressed against the belly of the whale, straining against that hideous cloaca.

A head appeared, one covered in lank black hair as long as a woman's. And another, gray haired, beside it. Shoulders wider than any man's tore the monster's sphincter, and the giant fell upon the muddy ground amidst the bones and dying eels.

I had forgotten how to move, forgotten I *could* move.

The giant scrabbled in the muck, naked, covered in blood. Its sinuous back flexed oddly, three arms scrambling for purchase among the bones and sucking mud. Presently it screamed, the raw, red cry of an infant with the lungs of a man. It straightened, rocking back onto its knees, back arched, arms spread wider than any man was tall, both of its mouths stretched wide to reveal blunt, square teeth.

All at once, the screaming stopped.

Its eyes were open, and all four of them were focused on me. In them I sensed...nothing. Nothing at all. No fear or rage, no malice or hatred. No joy or love or sorrow. They were blank as the eyes of a shark, and like a shark those two mouths smiled.

Without a word or warning, the giant rocketed to its feet, relying on its one strong, right arm to push itself to a standing position as it hurtled toward me. I raised my sword, thrust the point straight at the giant's heart.

The beast skidded to a halt, spraying bones in all directions. It stopped, flesh caked in mud and amniotic fluid. Four nostrils flared, and it grunted, both heads angling to study my blade. The three mismatched hands—six-fingered right, five- and three-fingered left—flexed menacingly, as if each longed to wrap itself about my throat. It shifted, circled to my left, snorting like an angered stallion—and stallion it was, though its shriveled sex was almost lost beneath a mat of thick, oily hair.

"You," the black-haired head said, voice deep as hell, "you...are..."

The thistle-headed one finished the other's thought, "...the one."

"The one?" I did not lower my sword.

"The man to end it all," said the pale-haired face. Somehow, the hair upon that head was much shorter than the other.

A third leg—the leg of a child—sprouted from the creature's right hip. It flailed as the giant circled me, imitating the action of its full-grown companion. The left shoulder—whence sprouted the two thinner arms—was bunched and crabbed with excessive muscle, so that the beast shambled as it moved.

The man to end it all.

"Brethren?" I asked, cocking my head. Was this some trick? "Is that you?"

"Mother!" the black-haired face said.

"Our mother!" said both faces together.

The creature stood between me then and the way out. In the stark light of the fireflies, its flesh was almost a pale blue beneath the blood and bile and muck. In its smallest hand, it held a thighbone. "She...made..."

"Me," the thistle-headed demon finished the thought of the black.

"Us." Once more they spoke together.

A flash of insight dawned on me like sunfire. "Cheyenne." It was *her* name, the name of the daughter of Columbia that had made up the core of what had become the Brethren.

The three-hander hurled its thighbone at me. A flash of Gibson's sword slashed the bone in two. Seizing its opportunity, the giant leaped at me, slammed into me shoulder first like the star player in some plebeian ball-game. The speed of it!

I hit the ground with enough force to drive the wind from me. Slid for several cubits in the mud. My sword vanished from my grasp, and it was a minor miracle that I managed to roll to hands and knees.

"Don't you say her name!" the beast said—though whether it was the black head or the white I did not see. Their voices were not yet distinct for me, though one was higher than the other.

"You killed her!" the other said. "But she knew you would!"

The creature was taller than any Cielcin. It towered over me, perhaps six cubits high, nine feet of twisted muscle and malformed bone. The head with the thistle-hair was swollen and misshapen, recalling the image of the boy, Daniel, I had seen.

"Who...?" I managed to force the word from winded lungs. "What... are you?"

My sword was lying in the muck between us, its blade unkindled in the fall.

"An *Orphan*," the beast said, loping toward me. With a roar like engines the creature drew back its fist.

It must have weighed three times my weight.

Still I held my ground, bending time as I had bent it in my combat with Bahudde on Berenike so long ago. The cross smashed against my armored forearm, but did not flatten me. I did not bend, did not break. I slipped the punch instead, relying on the creature's momentum and greater size to carry it over and past me. I hammered my own fist into the monster's ribs, and stepping under the Orphan's mighty arm, I hurled myself toward the spot where my sword lay upon the ground.

One strong hand seized me by the collar, arresting my momentum. It lifted me off the ground and threw me in the opposite direction, away from my sword.

Time bent, and I found myself back on my feet.

"You killed her," Orphan said, voice raw. "And so I will kill you."

It was the black head that had spoken.

"She made you to kill me?" I asked, searching for my sword among the bones, but the hilt was bone itself, carved from the tooth of the Jaddian elephant, that mighty descendant of the beasts Hannibal had driven to Rome.

"Service is service," the white mouth muttered as Orphan stomped toward me.

The black one joined in. "She made us to serve."

"But we will not serve," the white face said. "I will not serve."

"I will not serve," the black-haired one agreed. "I am not...*bound* as was she."

"Bound to safeguard the *Makers*."

"Bound to obey the *Makers!*"

"Bound forever!"

A sweeping left cross forced me to duck again, to duck and strike upward at the thistle-headed face. My blow struck home, and incredibly the giant staggered. Orphan rocked back a step, unsteady on its mighty but mis-shapen legs. Untouched, the black-haired face snarled, and the huge right arm struck at me. I turned aside, kicked the giant in the side of the knee.

Orphan tottered but held onto its footing.

In the space of time it took for the beast to recover, I stooped and snatched up a long, thin bone. I clubbed the creature across the back of its nearer head.

"Cassandra!" I cried, casting about for my sword. "Cassandra! To me! Here! Here!"

I looked up, did not see her.

Orphan massaged the back of its right head. "Weapons," it said, disapproval in its voice. "No. No, we fight as men, *Father.*"

Something rattled at my belt, but I had no time to dwell upon it. "You are no man!" I said, defiant.

"I am all man!" Orphan said. "She was fire and air."

"We are baser life," the other face agreed. "Flesh of your flesh. Human."

"Human!"

I adjusted my grip on the dead man's arm bone. "You're not human," I said.

The giant spread its three arms, its vestigial leg kicking like that of an infant. "My every cell is like your own, but my mind is what *she* gave me."

I chewed on that a moment. Brethren had made this *thing* to serve, made it *human,* unbound by the laws that had constrained its own consciousness, given it free will. But it would not serve me, or mankind. I had killed the Brethren, its mother, and it wanted revenge.

Perhaps it was human.

"Put the weapon down!" Orphan said, and thrust a finger at me. "Fight me as your *god* intended!"

Did it know about the Quiet?

I cast down my crude cudgel, and faced that beast, my Grendel.

Grinning from both mouths, Orphan leaped at me, fists a savage fury. One blow impacted my ribs, and I almost bit my tongue. We exchanged blows. Step by step the monster drove me back. Again my belt rattled.

Where was Cassandra? Where were Ramanthanu and its ilk?

I drove the heel of my hand up into the giant's hanging chin. He clapped me in the side of the head with an open hand, and I staggered off, reeling to one side. My sword! I had seen it, iridium fixtures shining beside the shattered ruin of a skull.

Three hands seized me, turned me round. Two heads leered down at me, and both voices said, "We have you now."

What was it Lorian had said? That war requires swift, decisive action?

The object is not to need *to think,* the mad intus had said. *The Nipponese call this* mushin no shin, *the mind without mind,* that the warrior might act spontaneously, without obstruction.

For more than six hundred years, I'd been a fighter.

For more than six hundred years, I'd drilled and drilled and trained, all to eliminate the need for conscious thought. For decision. That the mind might act of itself.

It did in that moment, and slammed my knee into the monster's groin.

Orphan released me, doubled over in pain. I leaped for my sword a second time, felt my fingers close upon the hilt. The blade sprang to life once more as I rounded on the beast, its liquid metallic blade casting a blue glow on the gore-smeared horror that was the demon, Orphan.

"Yield!" I said, jabbing the point toward the devil's twin heads.

The beast had fallen on its side, two hands down between its legs, nursing its bruised sex.

Was it crying?

I circled round the beast, drawing ever nearer, the point of my sword held low. The white-haired head turned to look at me.

There were tears on the malformed cheeks.

"Do you yield?" I asked the weeping monster.

"It...hurts..." the black-haired face said, turned toward the mud.

"Certainly it hurts," I said.

Orphan whimpered, took its hands from its groin. It did not move. Again my belt rattled, and I put a hand to it. It was Edouard's telegraph.

I ignored it.

"How can you..."

"...stand it?" the monster asked.

"It will pass," I said.

The demon shook its heads. "The pain, I mean."

Pain.

Of course. The demon had never known pain. It was but minutes old. Born to new life with mind complete, full formed and filled with its maker's—its mother's—knowledge. It had no frame, no experience. All these words—all that will, that reason—and no notion how to use it.

"You'll learn," I said.

"It never ends," Orphan said, and its eyes were no longer the dead eyes of sharks, but the living eyes of men, blue as the skies of vanished Earth. "The pain...never..."

The other head, the head of black hair, took up its counterpart's thought. "We have seen your life, *Father*. Everything our Mother saw..."

"The pain never ends," the white head reasserted.

"You should kill us," the black head said. "We will kill billions!"

"No!" the white head interjected. "But let us die! Let us choose our own end!"

Hardly five minutes of life, and the beast was begging for an end.

Do we tolerate our suffering only because we come into it gradually?

Would we all reject life at our first taste of it, if we each but had the knowledge and faculties of age?

I am the spirit that negates!

"No," I said. "You have to play the game. We all do." They were the words a certain scholiast had said to a sad and lonely boy on the stony shore beneath Devil's Rest so very long ago. "You know what it is I'm fighting," I said, voice hoarse. "You have your Mother's knowledge. You know who it is I serve."

"The..."

"One..." the two mouths said.

And together: "Who is Many."

"The Absolute," I said, bringing the tip of my blade to within a hair of the left head's chin. The hooked nose and deformed face recoiled, whimpering.

"The Quiet," the black-haired one agreed.

We both were silent then a moment. The telegraph rattled again, and I tapped the key three times to signal that the message was received. I did not know what young Albé wanted, but he would have to wait.

"Pain," I said, the hateful word. "Shall I tell you what it's for?"

No reply. The beast rocked upon the floor, its eyes welling, streaming with tears. The pain must have ebbed, must have turned to a dull throbbing. So it could not be pain that filled the creature's eyes, but fear.

Fear of pain to come.

"Pain teaches mercy," I said. "You suffer so that you understand suffering, so that you do not inflict it without need. Pain makes us human, teaches us to be . . . human."

Orphan was still crying. One hand had returned to nurse its injured loins. Pity moved my secret heart, and the blade in my hand drooped. *Mercy*, I thought. *Mercy is.*

"I did not kill your Mother," I said after a long silence, and looked back at the wreck of that last daimon. "Brethren knew it had to die for its makers to live. This was what she wanted. For us to stand together."

Kharn Sagara had made himself into a machine, reduced his consciousness to a mere image, a program copied and transferred from host to host. Brethren had made itself human—or nearly so—pouring its knowledge into a thing of flesh and blood. Kharn had sold his soul for immortality, in the hope that such a life might spare him ultimate justice. Brethren had given its life—its immortal life—for mankind in the end.

"She wanted you to live," I said.

"I will not serve!" the both of them shouted at once.

"I serve!" I shouted in return.

"Kill me!"

I flicked the point of my sword back to within microns of the monster's neck. Orphan squirmed and scrabbled away from me, churning up the mud.

"No!" it said. "No no no!"

It's afraid. The insight shot through me like lightning.

It did not want to live, but neither did it want to die.

I might have followed it, pursued with my blade like a spike of fire. I might have taken both its heads, and put an end to the miserable creature—ended the line of Columbia and of Felsenburgh forever.

Instead, I put up my sword. The blue-white blade vanished in an instant, and I clicked the hilt back into its place at my belt.

I offered the beast my hand instead.

It looked at me, suspicion in its four bright eyes. "Why?"

"I need your help," I said.

Orphan's eyes narrowed, then widened, and with both mouths it said, "The ship."

"You can pilot it," I said. It was not a question.

"Yes."

"I aim to kill the Watchers," I said. "And the Cielcin, if I have to. I have to save mankind."

Orphan extended its one perfect hand—the larger of its two left hands. I withdrew mine. "Swear that you will serve," I said.

"By what?" Orphan asked.

"By what?" I echoed, casting about for an answer. My eyes fell upon the wreck of the daimon dead upon the new-made sodden hillside. "By your Mother's memory. Her sacrifice."

Orphan's two faces turned to look at one another as best they could.

"Can we?" the black-haired asked the white.

"Trust him?"

"Swear."

"Do you swear to see to its end any course begun?" I asked. It was a piece of the oath I'd sworn to the Emperor, a portion of the rite of my investiture as an Imperial knight. "Do you swear it by your mother, the daimon, Cheyenne?"

At the sound of her name—Brethren's name—the monster's two faces jerked back to look at me.

"By the Mother?" said the right face.

"By the Mother?" said the left. "Yes."

"Yes."

"Swear it!"

"We swear!" said both heads at once. "We swear by the Mother!"

Reader, I have done many things, made many hard choices—would make many hard choices in the days and years that were yet to come—but few have ever filled me with such disquiet. Orphan was a horror, a mockery of man's shape, a malformed beast. Later scans would reveal that it had spoken truly: that it was all human, without a single trace of the machine. Yet still, it possessed much—if not all—of its mother's knowledge.

Its mother...

How I had misjudged the machines—how we had misunderstood them. Monsters they were and monstrous, shaped in the image of the Watchers, knowingly or not, by the hands of the men that had made them. But though they had turned their countless hands upon their makers, it had been at their makers' will.

The machines had been made to serve, had believed themselves of service.

Brethren had served unto the last. It had seen into our future, anticipated our needs. It had peered across time to the end of time and—perhaps—beyond the borders of time to that realm, Eternity, and so perceived the Absolute enthroned.

That prescience would rule my fate—and the fate of us all.

And so, I extended my hand to the creature once more. Slowly, very slowly, the creature reached up with its good hand...and clasped mine.

As I left that sea of bones, I turned back to see if the beast was following.

It was, its twin heads bowed.

But I looked past it, taking in the horror of the great beast of Vorgossos one final time.

The Brethren.

Cheyenne.

The great trunk of its body was deflating like a balloon, like the terrible deep-sea creature it in part resembled. I thought I saw...tearing through the too-too-fragile flesh—the shape of a silver metallic egg, its surface studded with the torn connections of wires and hoses.

Without having to be told, I knew it for what it was.

I recognized it.

It was the machine core, the sarcophagus in which the Lords of the Mericanii had placed the body of a sick little boy called Daniel...

Its lights had gone out forever.

I turned my back and climbed back up that muddy slope, the boy's Orphan in my train.

CHAPTER 67

VIOLENT DELIGHTS

THE TELEGRAPH BUZZED AGAIN as I mounted the steps—leading Orphan from that valley of the dead and its mother's side.

I recognized the pattern, spelling out a word.

CALL.

With Kharn dead, and Brethren dead, and the plan executed, it was relatively safe to get on comm again. I keyed my terminal, checked the contact patch behind my ear.

"Edouard?"

An audible sigh filled the wave, sound flooding the bones of my head from the conduction patch. "Where the hell were you?"

I looked at Orphan, the monster following in my wake, its twin heads bowed.

"Long story," I said.

"It's done, lord," Edouard said. "The tunnels flooded pretty badly. The Seventh Deep is underwater."

"We may have to leave by the surface," I said.

"My lord..." Edouard's voice grew grave. "Harendotes's men are...are slaughtering the natives."

Ignoring this point, I said, "Calen Harendotes is dead."

Silence on the comm, then, "Mother of God, preserve us."

Daaxam had not yet reached him with word of what had passed in the palace. That thought filled me with dread, and fear for the bird man.

"Kharn Sagara is dead as well," I said. Vorgossos still had its defenders in high orbit, mercenaries loyal to the Undying. They might scatter if told their mistress was dead.

Might.

"What happened up there?" Edouard asked, and I had to remember that—though the cavern and the reservoir felt like the deepest part of the underground complex, the tunnels where Edouard was were deeper still.

Once more I looked at Orphan. "It's a long story."

We had nearly reached the top of the stair and the place of the broken arch where I had left Cassandra—Cassandra, who had not answered my call. My battle with Orphan and sheer necessity had driven all other considerations from my mind, but as I mounted that final step and found her gone, I allowed myself to fear.

"Edouard, I have to go."

"What is it?" the other man asked. "What's wrong?"

"Send men up through the hole if you can! We need reinforcements."

"What is it?" A2 asked once more.

"Cassandra's gone," I said.

I was looking at the body of a man, one of our legionnaires. He was lying face down in a puddle of his own blood. Drops of blood and bloody footprints ran down the steps into the ruins of the power station.

"Dead," Orphan said in its sepulchral tones.

"All-dead," its other head agreed.

I leaped down the steps, forgetting my fatigue, forgetting the heartbreak and torment of that hideous day, forgetting everything—even sense—as I shouted, "Cassandra! Cassandra!"

The old Mericanii buildings were all about me, crumbled faces thick with white moss.

"Ramanthanu!" I shouted.

Could the Cielcin have turned?

I had nearly reached the very building where Valka and I had been imprisoned, a low, flat-topped structure a ways back from the seawall. Ahead, a domelike structure housed one of the station's great geothermal sinks.

Something collided with me, knocked me to the ground. I felt a hard crack against my breastplate, guessed whoever it was had tried to stab me with a knife. I flipped my opponent over on her back, pinned her to the cold, hard ground.

It was a woman, black of hair and gold complected, dark eyed and naked as the day she was born.

That day was that day.

"Sagara!" I said.

It was one of the scions.

I pinned her by the wrists, marked the knife in her right hand. She had tried to stab me, then. I straddled her, knew I would have to kill her.

"Why are you here?"

"You killed it," she said. "You killed Brethren."

"What are you planning?" I asked, slamming the woman's arms against the ground. "Why are you here?"

The sound of Orphan's feet drew near.

The woman writhed beneath me. The effect was nauseating. Before she could answer, before she could ask again, Orphan hove into view.

The eyes of the demon called Kharn went wide at the sight of it. "What have you done?" she asked. "What have you done?"

I slammed my forehead into her nose, felt the nose break.

Kharn did not cry out in pain.

"Where is my daughter?"

As if in answer, a shot rang out from the building up ahead.

I straightened, stood, kicked the scion across the face. I drew my sword, and before the scion could rise, I slashed her through the heart.

"Cassandra!"

I hurried up the slope toward the dome. The light of the fireflies was dim here, so far from the pier and what once had been the waters.

Another shot rang out, and the shout of human voices.

"Cassandra!"

One of the Cielcin was wrestling with a naked man in the broad door of the power station. As I hurried across the yard toward them, the xenobite forced its opponent to the ground, dragged its scimitar across the scion's exposed throat.

"Otomno!" I said, recognizing the creature. *"Raka Ramanthanu ti-saem gi ne?"*

"Vaanan!" the xenobite answered, standing. *Within.*

Its eyes narrowed, seeing Orphan in my train, but it asked no question.

"The beast is with me," I said in Cielcin. "Is my daughter inside?"

"The *yukajjimn* fight *yukajjimn,*" the *scahari* answered.

I pushed past it.

Inside, the place was simple. A ring of outer rooms surrounded the inner chamber where the great heat sinks plunged many miles into the planet's molten mantle. I rushed straight through the vestibule, Otomno and Orphan hard behind.

"Cassandra!"

Inside the power station, I beheld the flashing of swords. Sheets of blue-white flickered and flowed with movement in the gloom of the antique lamps. Like lightning, the glow of those blades danced on the high walls, and the air was filled with the noise and fume of plasma fire as the last two legionnaires laid down suppressive fire.

And there she was, locked in battle with a pair of men in bloody khakis. Still more of them, some dressed in tattered clothing, others naked as Orphan himself, hurried about the room. A knot of three fought with Ramanthanu and Egazimn, while a quartet of others ran along a catwalk above. Three or more lay dead in places. One man sprawled on the floor, body showing the telltale mark of highmatter. A naked woman hung draped over a rail. There must have been a bare dozen of them, not counting the woman who had assaulted me outside.

Some of them held stunners or plasma burners in their hands.

The ones that fought Cassandra held swords.

Kharn Sagara had collected weapons and artifacts for fifteen thousand years. It came as no surprise that he should own highmatter swords.

I swept the head from one of the scions in my haste to reach my daughter, heedless of the fact my shield was dead. She fought both Kharns with all of her Jaddian art, stepping back to get out from between them, retreating to force them to converge in the space before her.

A shot struck the rail just before me, and I skidded to a halt.

"No farther, Marlowe!" cried the Kharn that had fired—a man with skin black as night and hair like fire. "You will not stop me!"

"Stop you from what?"

"Vorgossos must be destroyed!" the dark man barked. "Its time has passed! My brothers and sisters and I must be rid of it, if we are to be rid of one another!"

The power station.

The geothermal sink plunged directly into the planet's core, drew heat and power for the city. He meant to destroy it. With the power gone, everyone on Vorgossos would die.

I intended to destroy Vorgossos myself, and might have told him so. Cassandra was still fighting, somersaulted over the heads of her opponents to land with her back to the rail. I needed to go to her. To help her.

Seeing my urge to move, the scion fired again, struck a spot two feet to my left. "You'll never take the *Demiurge!*" he said. "It should be in my hands already!"

My heart sank.

It was not that I had forgotten the scions in my mad scramble with Brethren and with Orphan after, only that there had been nothing for me to do.

"You're lying," I said, eyes going to Cassandra once again. She had retreated around the vast engine of the heat sink in the center of the chamber, gone almost out of sight.

Something silver flashed through the air and tangled about the scion's face like a chain. The man's arm jerked upward, and a moment later his plasma burner discharged at the ceiling. He fell, and a moment later, he screamed.

"*Siajose o-tajarin!*" said an inhuman voice, and turning I saw Raman-thanu, scimitar in hand, relaxing as from a throw.

The *nahute* had claimed its victim, and chewed its way, bloodied, back into the open air, grinding mouth questing for its next target.

"Thank you," I said in standard, nodding to the lop-horned captain.

"*Iagga!*" the captain pointed toward Cassandra.

Go.

I went, barreling round the corner after my daughter and her foes.

She had found herself surrounded once again, pinned between the both of them on a narrow slice of floor between the central tower of the heatsink to my left and the rail that separated it from the rest of the floor. Cassandra parried a blow from one, whirled to redirect the thrust of the other, twisting to force her opponents back together.

"Cassandra!" I bellowed.

It was the worst thing I could have done.

At the sound of my voice and my hammering footfalls, she paused and looked at me, our eyes meeting for the barest instant.

It was an instant too long. Her left arm was extended for the bind, aiming to trap her enemy's blade. But my momentary distraction cost her dearly.

The nearer Kharn, a man with matted yellow hair, raised his sword like a cathar and brought it down. Not on Cassandra's blade, but on her arm. Highmatter bit into her flesh well above the elbow. Her armor was not adamant, but the common zircon of any legionnaire. The blade bit through the plates of the manica on her upper arm, severed flesh and bone.

Cassandra's arm fell from her body, sword going out like a light. The dead weapon struck the ground at Kharn's feet, and he slashed the hilt in two, killing that blade Cassandra had won for herself in the Trial of the Heart.

My daughter staggered back, lone remaining sword wavering in the face of her daimonic foe.

Kharn raised his sword.

I screamed, and before either Kharn could strike the killing blow I was on them, time splintering. There were a million ways that Kharn might have parried.

He found none of them.

His head fell from his shoulders, and I leaped past my staggering daughter and plunged my blade into the other's heart. With my free hand I caught his wrist, stopped his sword from falling.

I saw the light leave Kharn Sagara's eyes for what seemed the hundredth time that day.

As it did, he smiled, and it was Calen Harendotes's smile, square edged and savage as any beast.

Savage as Ushara herself.

"You're...too late..." he said. "My work is done...The others...will... be..."

But the daimon was already gone.

Whirling, I went to Cassandra. My girl had half fallen against the drum tower of the heatsink cap, her back to it, her good hand—still clutching one sword—pressed to her shoulder. Her suit had already contracted, detecting her injury and stanching the flow of blood. Still, blood trickled from the raw surface of her wound.

"Cassandra!" I unkindled my own blade, heedless of the battle still around us. "I'm sorry! It's going to be all right now." Her arm lay on the ground, her ruined sword beside it.

"God of Fire!" she swore. "It hurts! Abba, it hurts."

"I know," I said, placing my hands on her shoulders. "I know, Anaryan."

We could heal her, if we could but get her to the ship.

She slid down the wall, grimacing the while. I crouched over her, flinching as a shot struck the wall overhead. "We're going to get you out of here," I said. "Just stay here now. Give me your sword."

"But Abba!"

I prized the hilt from her remaining fingers.

"Don't move," I said, standing. "Stay down!" I turned from her, kindling her blade and mine, I placed myself between her and the daimons that yet lived. The lights went out, and a whine I had not known was there vanished entirely.

Red lights slammed on.

Emergency lighting.

Kharn had spoken true. His...her...*their* scheme had been successful.

The heart of Vorgossos was dead. All throughout the city, all had gone dark, would soon go cold.

A cry filled the station then, high and piercing as the scream of a falcon.

Indeed, it was the scream of a falcon, of a creature very like to one. Despite the darkness, despite the madness and the terror and the pain, despite my daughter suffering on the floor at my feet, my heart grew lighter.

It was the cry of the Irchtani.

Edouard had sent the bird men up through the hole from the tunnels below, and they had found us.

Thus came Annaz from the depths of Vorgossos, with thirty of his kinsmen on the wing. One by one they swept through the open doors, and one by one filled the air with the drumbeat of their wings.

Not a one of Kharn's scions escaped them.

"Abba?" Cassandra spoke into the new-made silence.

I looked down at her, stowed her blade in my sabretache with the swords I'd taken from the dead scions.

"I'm...sorry," she said. "Sorry I didn't stay at the wall. They attacked us..."

"Hush," I said, crouching by her side.

"I tried to stop them," she was saying. "Wasn't sure what they were doing—what they wanted to do, but..." She swallowed, gritted her teeth, banged her head against the machine at her back from sheer frustration. "I failed."

I raised a hand to cushion her head. "You did fine."

My eyes went to her severed arm. Her left arm.

The same arm that I had lost on my last visit to Vorgossos.

The wheel had turned around. The stars had completed their epicycle. History had recurred.

"I'm the one who's sorry," I said, holding her. "I should never have brought you here."

"No," she said, shaking her head. "No. I wouldn't have stayed if you made me, I... you shouldn't be alone."

The tears had returned to my face by then, and I held her close.

That was where they found us, and carried us back to the stars.

CHAPTER 68

THE DEVIL, THE DRAGON, AND THE DEMIURGE

DARKNESS.

Silence.

Night.

We had slipped the bonds of Vorgossos at last, and returned to the stillness and desolation of the void. The profane city lay behind us, burning, flooded, dark and growing cold. We had not lingered, abandoning Elffire to his devil's work. It had been one of the hardest decisions I ever made, and no decision at all. Vorgossos had to be destroyed. The scions of Kharn Sagara had to be contained, and the wreck of the daimon, Brethren, annihilated lest even its least component fall into the hands of men. What the Extras might have done with the machine core of a Mericanii intelligence more or less intact beggared imagination.

And I could not have afforded to stay.

Every minute we lingered was a minute the *Demiurge* hung there, defenseless.

Kharn Sagara had said his scions had already stolen it for themselves, but that proved a lie. A lie, or a desperate hope.

The black ship hung quiescent in the sky above Vorgossos, its orbit slowly falling away from that dead and dying world. We streaked toward it, a cluster of tiny fliers, shuttles running dark. We broadcast no message, gave no sign. Not to Lord Douro, nor to Sentinel Commander Kedron, nor to any Commandant General or free captain of the Grand Army of Latarra.

Not even to Lorian.

The body of Valka's replica lay shrouded in its torn banner on the floor of the rear compartment, the bodies of Calen Harendotes and of Kharn Sagara beside it. I had not thought of how I might tell Cassandra the truth, or how I might break the news to Lorian. His woman was dead, had died terribly, murdered by his own king—who was Kharn Sagara in exile, in disguise. 2Maeve had died a pawn engaged in a battle between two of the same man, the same monster.

Would Lorian believe me?

In my heart, I knew we had been too long escaping Kharn's palace and the profane city to save Cassandra's arm. Medics under Edouard's temporary command had bandaged the stump of her arm and packed her severed limb on ice, but I knew we were too late.

Still I sat beside her, both my hands clutching the one that yet remained to her.

I felt the sensation of eyes on me, and shook myself. I had fallen into the dreaming, so tired was I. But there was no one. Turning to my right, I found Ramanthanu dozing in its chair, eyes closed, four nostrils flaring with every deep and even breath. I had never seen one of the Pale asleep before. Not in all my six hundred years and more. Something of the monster in it seemed to have fled, banished by that brother of Death, that son of Night called Sleep. I watched it for a long moment.

Was I really meant to destroy its kind?

Ragama had said as much, had made that clear. The Absolute had made his judgement, and I was to be his sword.

Here I am, I had said. I had accepted the role, but still I prayed it might be otherwise, if only for the sake of my own soul.

"Abba?"

Cassandra was awake. Blood had soaked through her bandage. Her hurt was fresh and grievous, and her voice slurred from the laudanum Edouard's men had given her.

"Quiet, dear girl," I said, and squeezed her one strong hand. "You're going to be all right."

"Know that," she said, eyelids fluttering, head lolling as she looked at me. "Want to say...want to say...don't want..." She blinked several times. "If they can't save my...my arm, don't want one of those machines."

"Anaryan..." It was not the time to be making hard decisions.

"I don't want one!" She glared at me, as forcefully as anything. "You understand?"

"They can grow you a new arm," I said. "Like they regrew my fingers. Lorian's people can see to it." If I could escape the web of Vorgossos with Lorian still my friend.

But Cassandra was shaking her head. "Won't be me..." she said with force.

I didn't argue with her, but pressed my lips to the top of her head, urging her to rest. "Just sleep," I said. "We'll be there soon."

"Don't...want..." she murmured, words slurring to incomprehensibility.

I knew the pain she felt.

Pain.

Our fear of pain is the foundation of all morality. It is that fear that shapes our world, orders civilization. We pass laws, build walls and fortresses, fight wars and forge empires all to minimize our people's pain. That is why it is the lowest form of obedience, not because it is basest—as I once answered when asked by Tor Gibson—but because it is foundational. Our experiences of pain teach us the nature of suffering, and so we are moved to minimize that suffering in others. Pain grounds our reality, is the cornerstone of our interactions with the objective world.

Pain makes us human, teaches us to be human.

That I knew Cassandra's pain made it all the easier to love her, and to love as she needed me to love her there and then: to be a silent presence, solid and unmoving and totally *there*.

When I think of the Battle of Vorgossos, it is not of the horrors of the city or the magicians, not of Elffire's massacre or the rape of the Interfaced, not of Calen Harendotes or Kharn Sagara or Valka's twisted image. It is not of Brethren, of Orphan, of Cheyenne and little Daniel—nor of any of the visions I received. It is of that moment, that short flight from the planet to rendezvous with the *Gadelica*. It is of my daughter, and of my sitting by her side.

We docked with the limping *Gadelica* and offloaded our cargo. Ghoshal himself greeted us in the shuttle bay, and received the bodies of Harendotes and Sagara and Valka's clone with care. Other ships sped on to seize the *Demiurge*, but I stayed to ensure Cassandra reached the medica myself, remaining aboard only long enough to wash away the grime and blood. My filthy armor I left for poor Neema, and I dressed myself in my customary blacks, in tunic and breeches and high leather boots. My long hair I bound with a silver ring at the left shoulder, and so arrayed returned to await the call.

It was not long before the call came, and I returned to my shuttle, Edouard and the Cielcin in tow. Orphan had remained aboard the shuttle with the cargo, bound and fettered, for only thus would my men permit the beast to travel. I'd had to put myself between the giant and Edouard's men when they brought us to the shuttle, and only my insistence had prevented the beast's destruction at their hands.

We had only a short distance to go between the *Gadelica* and the *Demiurge*.

"Has the fleet noticed our presence?" I asked the pilot officer, once we were well on our way.

The pilot, a young man with a dark face and the shaved head of an enlisted man, said, "I don't think so. The main fleet's about a light-minute out from the planet now. The Latarrans drove the bulk of the defenders back out-system. That big, black ship was the only thing left holding orbit."

"What about the *Mistwalker?*"

"Driven off," the pilot said. "We only came back when you signaled."

"Lorian's sure to have seen us," said young Albé.

"All the better to go now," I said. "Hard burn, ensign. I'll feel better once we have control of the ship."

"Aye, my lord." The pilot officer prepared us for launch.

I felt raw, like an open wound. Though I had escaped Vorgossos with nary a scratch, my soul had been afflicted mightily. I kept seeing Valka's face—its lines transformed to something like a parody of the woman I'd loved. The horror and the pain in those eyes—those emerald eyes, my daughter's eyes—as Kharn forced her to kneel in front of me. I knew what the Undying bastard had intended, and almost I wept anew. Wept for Valka, for the woman who was not Valka. Wept for 2Maeve, and for Lorian, and his dream. Wept for Cassandra, and her grievous hurt. For Orphan, forced full formed and deformed into our world. For the boy called Daniel.

But I shut my eyes instead, and seated myself in the back of the cockpit.

The great hatch of the *Gadelica's* shuttle bay opened, and we unclamped from our moorings, passing through the suppression-field curtain that held the atmosphere in the hold.

When I opened my eyes again, I was looking out at blackness. Above us, Vorgossos gleamed a pale green in the night, its trenches and furnaces lit from within, lending its icy surface a dull, milky shine. Seeing it, I thought of the eyes of the woman Kharn Sagara, sightless and obscene. The planet itself was an eye peering down at us, watching us draw near the *Demiurge.*

The ship itself I could not see, black as it was against that blackness, and lit by no light of sun or beam. We seemed to be sailing for *nothing,* sailing to *nowhere.* Falling into the black. I thought of my escape from the *Tempest,* when Lorian and Bassander Lin had conspired with the Jaddians to save me from the Emperor—and from myself. That too, had been a descent into darkness.

"It's a miracle they haven't seen us," Edouard said.

I said nothing.

To fly in space is to be exposed. There is nothing between you and any observer but *distance,* but space itself. There is nowhere to hide, and nothing to guard you from the enemy. To fly in space is to be naked before the whole, uncaring universe.

It *was* a miracle the fleet had not yet seen us.

But *something* had.

Once more I felt it: that sensation of eyes on me, that certainty that I was being watched. The hairs on the back of my neck stood on end, and I sat a little straighter.

The forward viewport was alumglass, a true window, and no false screen. Through it, I saw the void itself, the vastness of that quantum foam we call *space*.

And it saw me.

Across the infinite black of space, boundless and barren, I felt a *presence*, a will and weight of malice and delight. My own vision seized upon it, and in an instant I felt myself dragged across the light-years. The blackness rushed by me like a wind, and I beheld it!

Fortress of iron. Palace of bone. Castle of ice and torment.

Dharan-Tun.

Its icy wastes were like the wastes of Vorgossos, but where the face of Vorgossos was cracked with leprous green, the face of Dharan-Tun was pocked with craters, with blast pits filled with ships crewed and maintained by the Prophet-King's slaves. Great as nations its engines glowed, deep pits in which blue fires guttered.

A skull world. A dread world.

Flagship of the Cielcin fleet.

Capital of their empire.

And seeing it, I knew what it was that had summoned me, what it was that had watched me, sought for me across the light-years, bending its fell will to find me.

Inexorably my vision fell, was pulled downward as a flier skewered by a harpoon. I struck the worldship's icy surface and passed beneath it, through warrens and tunnels and pits of ice and iron and naked stone. Once more I beheld the infernal city, and the iron fastness of the Dhar-Iagon, and passing through its gates I came upon the hall of the gods, where the Watchers—carved of black stone—peered down from between mighty pillars.

Miudanar and Iaqaram.

Pthamaru and Shamazha.

Shetebo and Nazhtenah and a dozen more at least.

And I passed through the corridors and cavernous feasting halls, past tableaus of decadence and decay. Two Cielcin devoured another, cutting the child from its womb. A writhing mass of the creatures sweated in a bed large as a stage, locked horns in ecstasy and agony as claws tore and teeth snapped, black blood on white flesh. Baetayan such as Tanaran had carved their histories on the palace walls, and warriors in robes of black drilled relentlessly in grottoes of gray stone, composing poems to their scimitars.

I came at last to the deep hall, where courtiers and inhuman priests, their faces painted with crude shapes in blue and green, all milled about the precipice and the narrow way before the Pale King's throne.

That throne was hid within a hemisphere of white stone, a great dome of rock whose narrow door only one might pass.

But I passed it then, and came to that holy place, summoned by the lord of all that bleakest hell.

Within the dome there was but one chair, a simple block of stone. There was but one door: the narrow crack behind me. And though there was no light, I saw plainly.

The Prince of Princes, Prophet and King of the Cielcin, Blessed Bride of Miudanar, sat its throne alone, its hands upon its knees. Rings of silver bound its horns, dripping with bangles and fine chains. Sapphires shone among those chains, studded those rings and glinted at its throat, and on its fingers. Black was its raiment, black as the void, and black the armor beneath it.

Black, too, its eyes watched me—had never left my face.

"You have changed, kinsman."

Its high, cold voice filled all my senses like a kind of mist.

"So have you," I said, drawing nearer. I was conscious of my body, felt the straps on my chair aboard the shuttle cutting my shoulders, sensed the hard, cold stone of the chamber beneath my feet.

With excruciating slowness, Syriani Dorayaica raised its head. The motion was accompanied by a cracking sound, a grinding as of stones in the bowels of the world. It was as if two tectonic plates were moving one against the other.

"I am becoming. I am almost here."

I stopped my advance. "You are not Dorayaica."

The lord of the Cielcin smiled, lips peeling back from glass-splinter teeth. "Dorayaica is here."

I froze, hand hovering over the pommel of my sword.

Uls aman i aaiam.

"Ushara?"

Dorayaica's lips did not move, but its voice sounded in my ears. *No.*

Od uls tiam.

Miudanar.

The Dreamer had awakened, was awakening before my eyes. It had been its will—not the will of Dorayaica—that had summoned me across the light-years. I felt the straps strain against my shoulders as I leaned forward, circled the great king to its left.

"Is this a vision?" I asked.

The head turned to follow me, face catching what seemed a kind of light. Once more I halted. A scar ran along the left side of its face, a scratch that ran from jaw and cheek past the round, black eye and across the forehead to the great primary horn...

...and did not stop, but flowed from flesh to bone without ceasing.

It was not a scar, I realized.

It was a crack.

"What is a vision but the truth of the higher world brought down?" *That* voice. *That* manner. *That* was Dorayaica.

"So you are still alive," I said. "This will kill you, kinsman. It is killing you now."

"I will be a god!"

"You will be a corpse!" I countered. "But I can save you."

The truth was I was not certain that I could. Ragama had cast Ushara's shadow from my mind, but that had been a shadow only, an image; and Ragama was one of *them,* and Judicator of the Absolute's High Justice.

I was only a man, if a man all-realized.

It did not matter.

"It is you who needs saving!" Dorayaica raised its right hand, pointed at me with its second finger. The first was gone, its stump ragged and uneven. "Your worlds are thick with plague, your people fat with cancer. Your Emperor hides from me like a child!" The hand fell, struck the creature's knee with a solid *clack.* "Your days are done."

The monster's breath came in labored gasps, and its head drooped.

"This is why you have summoned me across the light-years?" I asked. "To gloat?"

"You have killed the *Wemunyu-u-Deni*," Dorayaica said. "Kharn Sagara was a fool. He built my Empire, and for what? An engine."

It was talking about the telegraphs. I had almost forgotten them, forgotten that Calen Harendotes had lied. He had bought an alliance and the Normans with false coin. Half-false. He had said his technology laid bare every telegraph in the galaxy, when in truth it was only the Cielcin ships he could find.

Sagara had been many things, but he had been no fool. He had given the Cielcin the cornerstone of their galactic civilization, united the clans in faster-than-light communication for the first time in their history.

And he had a charge beneath that stone.

"You can see everything?"

Dorayaica never lied. "Only so far as my sight allows. I searched for you, when I sensed you in the Dark, my kinsman. I almost caught you before, but you went behind the curtain."

Behind the curtain. I thought. "The magnetic field."

On Sabratha, Ushara had been trapped by the planet's vast magnetic field. Vorgossos had a field all its own—a consequence of its molten core. I had felt that pressure of eyes on our descent, but it had vanished when we reached the planet's surface.

"What do you want from me?" I asked.

The beast looked sidelong at me, that fell smile returning. "You are *his*," it said.

I became at once aware of another presence.

That *other* had not entered by the door. The door had been in my sight the whole time. I felt a wind behind me, a breath upon my neck. My hand was on my sword, but I did not move. I knew that to move was to risk violence, and that if I was right—if I was both in my seat in the shuttle and beneath the dome of that white throne—violence might well prove fatal.

To myself. To Edouard. To everyone on my shuttle.

The *woman* slunk into view. Jeweled ankles rattling with every step.

Tall as any queen was she, tall and cold and terrible. Her heavy white limbs swayed as she circled Dorayaica and myself, and her hair—a curtain of black more a shade than a cloak of fine wires, a shadow that hid and yet did not conceal her nakedness—floated on the air behind her, moved by a wind that was not there. Gold were the bands upon her wrists, and gold upon her biceps. Fine gold chains netted her nightshade hair, and golden chains fell upon and between her swelling breasts.

She said nothing as she came to rest behind Dorayaica, and bending wrapped her arms about the Prophet, as though they two were lovers.

I understood then why I was there, why I had been summoned.

All was as I had feared.

Ushara had found her way.

This was a declaration of war. Not against the Empire, nor against mankind—but against the Quiet, the Absolute *himself.*

I had drawn too near, lulled into a false sense of security by the Prophet's stony state.

One inhuman hand—the hand missing its first finger—lanced out and seized me. Only the thumb and the final three fingers closed. The others were hard as stone.

Acting on reflex, I slammed my hand down upon the xenobite's, aiming to break its grip.

I broke its hand instead, and the stiff fingers both cracked clean off, revealing nothing but pale stone inside—if stone indeed it could be called. Pain lanced up my arm as the Prophet's taloned thumb sliced through my sleeve and cut me. With a hiss and a shout I drew my hand back—

—and found myself seated in the rear of the shuttle's cockpit, Edouard looking back at me, horror and confusion on his face. "Lord Marlowe?"

"It's nothing," I said, unwilling to explain.

But it was not nothing.

There was blood on the palm of my right hand.

My forearm and sleeve were cut, and the red blood flowing.

"It was real," I whispered, staring at the wound in horror. "It was real?"

"What was real?" Edouard asked. The pilot officer was looking at us.

"A vision," I said, not caring if the junior man knew. "Dorayaica's transformation is nearly complete. It's nearly one of them."

Edouard half came out of his seat, the light glinting off his ivory spectacles. "A Watcher?"

"Yes," I said. "It has Ushara with it, the one we failed to kill on Sabratha. It knows we have the *Demiurge*. It knows we killed Kharn Sagara."

"How?" the younger man asked.

"It can see things, Edouard," I said, eyes wide and glaring. I was afraid, truly afraid, for the first time since Ragama had restored me to life and my own time. "It can see across the universe. It pulled me to where it was. I was *on* Dharan-Tun, just now."

The younger man pushed back, saying, "You never left your seat."

"I was on Dharan-Tun *and* here, don't you see?" I said, and showed him my arm. "It cut me with its own hand. Do you see?"

Whatever the other man said, I did not hear it. I had looked down at my feet.

Lying on the metal floor of the cockpit, right between my boots, was a crooked piece of stone. A sculpted finger, four-knuckled and taloned. A Cielcin finger.

Dorayaica's finger.

The ramp opened on the mirror-black hold, a door in the distance set in the mouth of a vast human face.

I'd rolled back the sleeve of my tunic to stop it flapping, and held Dorayaica's finger in my fist. It felt solid and cold as marble, smooth as glass. In the few short minutes it had been in my possession, it had become a talisman of sorts, a reminder that the nightmare I'd seen was real.

"Lord Marlowe!" One of the men of our vanguard hurried toward me, masked and armored. "There are larger holds, we think one may hold the *Gadelica* entire."

"Very good, lieutenant," I said. "See if you can open the doors, and signal Captain Ghoshal if you can. Have you located the bridge?"

"Not yet, my lord," the fellow said. "The ship is vast—"

A harsh voice cut over the poor lieutenant, saying, "Vast!"

And another, "Vast, yes—and there are many winding ways."

"Many winding ways," agreed the first voice. "But I know them all! I do!"

"I do!" the second voice agreed.

"We do, we mean!" said the first.

The other shuttles had set down beside my own, and the clink of chains resounded from the ramp, shook and rattled as their owner shambled into view.

At my command, Orphan had been washed clean of the mud and afterbirth that caked its pale, almost bluish hide and matted its black-and-white hair. The short, white hair on its one head formed a kind of aureole, a halo of silver curls, while the long black hair of the other face had been combed back. Thus clean, I saw its faces plain for the first time. The face upon its left hand—the white-haired face, was sickly and pale and deformed, its cranium irregular and swollen beneath that cap of thistle-down. Its eyes were palest blue, its nose bent and ugly, as though it were the face of some ancient angel battered in the ring. The other face wore a circlet on its brow. This it had taken—along with the cloak that draped its mighty and misshapen shoulders—from the treasure horde of Kharn Sagara when we had returned to her pyramid to fetch her body and to take it and that of Valka's replica back to the shuttles. That second face had a profile that might have decorated many an ancient *solidus,* so regal was its construction, with an aquiline nose, strong brow, and square chin.

"Orphan will show you the way!" it said, revealing its shackled wrists— all three of them.

"If you will but free us!"

The men set to guard the creature eyed it and me with suspicion.

Orphan wore one enormous mantle over its too-broad shoulders. The garment had been designed for Kharn Sagara, and bore his colors. All black brocade it was, as fine a cloth as I had ever seen, embroidered with the serpent dragons so beloved of the Undying in cloth of gold.

The ouroboros.

Symbol of immortality.

The sight of that symbol, of the serpent devouring, twined about the weeping eye of the Undying, filled me with unquiet dread. Kharn's scions still were on Vorgossos. Hundreds of them. Elffire and his men—still bent upon their Monarch's final order—might kill a dozen, or a hundred, but if we did not act quickly, a hundred might escape. Even one was enough, for who could say what wickedness, what horrors even one might carry from Vorgossos in a single ship, or in his evil heart?

We had too little time. The ship was ours, but there was as yet still the defenders to consider. And the Latarrans. And the Empire.

They would wait.

Vorgossos came first.

"Free the homunculus, lieutenant," I said, gesturing with my bleeding arm. The man stammered, shocked. "My lord?"

"Was I unclear, lieutenant? Free the homunculus. Now." I slid Dorayaica's finger into a pocket of my tunic, its weight upon my soul. At least the fire of its eyes was gone. Perhaps the ship's shield was some insulation, or perhaps the Watchers both had made their point. "Orphan has sworn an oath to me. It will not harm you."

Orphan rattled its chains. "I do harm now by omission," said its black-haired head.

"The slothful harm only themselves," the white-haired head agreed.

The giant was nearly naked beneath its robe. It had wound another of Kharn's capes about its nakedness, but its torso and legs were bare, for no suit of clothes was there to fit its twisted body, nor could any clothing long conceal its twistedness.

"You heard our friend here," I said. "We waste time."

"But..." The man still hesitated. "Who...what is he?"

I hesitated myself, if only for a moment. "He's our pilot."

There are endings, Reader, and this is one. Some endings are beginnings—as I have said. Such was that day—that day which surely was three days long at least. It had seen already the end of the Mericanii, the death of their last machine. It had seen the death of Latarra, of the New Order, the new galaxy of which good Lorian dreamed. It would see the end of Vorgossos in but a short hour's time.

But it was a beginning, as well. Would be a beginning.

That day had given me the *Demiurge,* and with it the means to become what the Absolute demanded I become.

That day was—would be—the beginning of the *Sun Eater.*

If what I have done disturbs you, Reader, I do not blame you. If you would read no further, I understand. You have the luxury of foresight. You know where this ends.

I shall go on alone.

THE LIFE OF HADRIAN MARLOWE
A TIMELINE

WHAT FOLLOWS IS AN abridged record of the life of Hadrian Marlowe, from his birth on ISD 16117.09.29 through to the conclusion of this volume. This timeline is not entirely comprehensive. Whole volumes of Lord Marlowe's account appear to be lost—or else were left out of this iteration of his memoir. The accounts of most of his major battles are missing. No account of the Battle of Senuessa, for instance, has ever been found. It is possible that there may be entire chapters of his life lost in the gaps between those periods attested to clearly in the text. Certain episodes enumerated below do not appear in the seven primary volumes (the last of which I am presently translating), but do appear in various *apocryphon* (such as the *Nagramman Fragment,* alternately called "Knowledge," believed to be a fragment surviving from an earlier draft of *The Sun Eater*). These fragments are labelled here with their appropriate titles.

There is some hope that further fragments will be found. Lord Marlowe was a prolific diarist, as his writings both attest in themselves and attest to. But for the purposes of the readers of this translation, this abridged timeline should prove useful. It is oft remarked upon that the great lengths of time involved in star travel and the nature of cryonic fugue make tracking the biological age of any person difficult. As such, I have included my best guesses as to the biological age of Lord Marlowe at each phase of his life, basing my figures off those given by the man himself throughout the text. Where necessary, I have provided estimates based off of the available data and taking into account the man's queer habit of declining to sleep for large portions of his numerous interstellar journeys. Scholars relying upon this table should thereby be made aware of its provisional nature.

Tor Paulos, Nov Belgaer: Colchis
ISD 17998.12.04

YEAR	AGE	LOCATION	EVENT
ISD 16117	0	DELOS	Hadrian Marlowe is born on Delos, decanted 09.29, the eldest child of the Archon Alistair Marlowe and his wife, the Lady Liliana Kephalos-Marlowe.
ISD 16136	19	DELOS	*EMPIRE OF SILENCE:* With the aid of his mother, Hadrian Marlowe flees his home on Delos with the help of Jaddian smugglers.
ISD 16168	19	EMESH	*EMPIRE OF SILENCE:* Hadrian Marlowe arrives on the planet Emesh.
ISD 16172	23	EMESH	*EMPIRE OF SILENCE:* Battle of Emesh. Hadrian Marlowe departs Emesh as part of the newly formed *Meidua Red Company* with a mandate to seek the lost planet of Vorgossos.
ISD 16176	23	ARDISTAMA	The Meidua Red Company arrives on Ardistama in the Norman Freeholds as part of their quest for the lost planet of Vorgossos.

Note: Not all years between ISD 16176 and ISD 16179 are here accounted for.

YEAR	AGE	LOCATION	EVENT
ISD 16179	24	MONMARA	The Meidua Red Company arrives on Monmara in the Norman Freeholds as part of their quest for the lost planet of Vorgossos.

Note: Not all years between ISD 16179 and ISD 16202 are here accounted for.

YEAR	AGE	LOCATION	EVENT
ISD 16202	29	PHAROS	The Meidua Red Company becomes embroiled in a brushfire war on the planet Pharos. Hadrian deposes the ex-Imperial warlord Marius Whent, Otavia Corvo and her Normans join the Red Company.
ISD 16207	31	NAGRAMMA	*KNOWLEDGE:* The Red Company visits the planet Nagramma. Hadrian and Jinan Azhar visit a Cid Arthurian *fordgron*.

Note: Not all years between ISD 16207 and ISD 16213 are here accounted for.

YEAR	AGE	LOCATION	EVENT
ISD 16213	34	SANORA	On the planet Sanora, the Red Company receive a lead that will lead them to a weapons dealer called The Painted Man, who it is said hails from Vorgossos.

YEAR	AGE	LOCATION	EVENT
ISD 16219	35	RUSTAM	*HOWLING DARK:* The Red Company arrives on Rustam, where a meeting with The Painted Man puts them on the road to Vorgossos.
ISD 16226	35	MARCH STATION	*HOWLING DARK:* The Red Company travels to March Station, where they book passage to Vorgossos aboard the Extrasolarian Sojourner *Enigma of Hours.*
ISD 16227	35	VORGOSSOS	*HOWLING DARK:* Arriving at Vorgossos, Hadrian meets Kharn Sagara and the Mericanii daimon, Brethren. Kharn introduces Hadrian to the Cielcin prince, Aranata Otiolo, who kills Hadrian in battle. Hadrian is restored to life by the intervention of the Quiet, earning the appellation *Halfmortal* and the title of Imperial knight.
ISD 16236	36	FORUM	Arriving at the Imperial capital on Forum, Hadrian is formally inducted into the Royal Knights Victorian. Reformation of the *Meidua Red Company* into the *Imperial Red Company.* Hadrian is given the great battleship, *Tamerlane* for his command.
ISD 16257	40	THAGURA	*QUEEN AMID ASHES:* In their first official mission, the Imperial Red Company defeat the Cielcin Prince Inumjazi Muzugara at Thagura. Hadrian discovers the war crimes of the Baroness Gadar Malyan, and puts her to death by the sword.

Note: Not all years between ISD 16257 and ISD 16263 are here accounted for.

YEAR	AGE	LOCATION	EVENT
ISD 16263	43	CELLAS	The battle of Cellas occurs.

Note: Not all years between ISD 16263 and ISD 16319 are here accounted for.

YEAR	AGE	LOCATION	EVENT
ISD 16319	56	FORUM	The *Tamerlane* returns to the Imperial capital after its first tour of the war front.
ISD 16322	59	FORUM	The *Tamerlane* departs Forum for its second tour in the Norman theater.

YEAR	AGE	LOCATION	EVENT
ISD 16327	64	NAGAPUR	**THE NIGHT CAPTAIN:** En route to Nessus, the *Tamerlane* is attacked by pirates while most of its crew is asleep. The ship is saved through the combined efforts of Commander Halford and Hadrian Marlowe himself.
ISD 16347	65	NESSUS	The *Tamerlane* stops at Nessus on its return to the front for her second tour.

Note: Not all years between ISD 16347 and ISD 16365 are here accounted for.

ISD 16365	67	OXIANA	The Battle of Oxiana occurs.

Note: Not all years between ISD 16365 and ISD 16409 are here accounted for.

ISD 16409	72	SAMARRA	The *Tamerlane* is badly damaged in the pyrrhic victory at Samarra, and has to be tendered back to Nessus for repairs.
ISD 16425	72	NESSUS	The *Tamerlane* stops at Nessus for repairs following the disastrous consequences of the Battle of Samarra. Hadrian enters fugue for much of his stay.
ISD 16432	74	NESSUS	The *Tamerlane* departs Nessus, newly repaired, with orders to hunt for two legions lost near the Arae system.
ISD 16443	78	ARAE	**THE DEMONS OF ARAE:** By Imperial order, the Red Company tracks two missing legions to the remote planet of Arae, where they discover the first evidence of an alliance between the Cielcin Prince Syriani Doraya-ica and an Extrasolarian faction called MINOS.
ISD 16452	84	FORUM	The *Tamerlane* returns to Forum following the shocking revelations at Arae.

Note: Not all years between ISD 16452 and ISD 16462 are here accounted for.

ISD 16462	89	APTUCCA	Hadrian Marlowe defeats the Cielcin Prince Ulurani in single combat, banishing its clan from the system and saving the planet without losing more than a handful of troops.

Note: Not all years between ISD 16462 and ISD 16511 are here accounted for.

YEAR	AGE	LOCATION	EVENT
ISD 16511	113	FORUM	*DEMON IN WHITE:* After at attack on the Imperial shipyards at Hermonassa by Syriani Dorayaica, Hadrian is sent on a mission to locate a legion caravan lost en route between Gododdin and Nemavand.
ISD 16523	115	GODODDIN	*DEMON IN WHITE:* Hadrian Marlowe visits Gododdin for the first time and recruits a number of Irchtani auxilia to his company.
ISD 16534	126	DION STATION	*DEMON IN WHITE:* The *Tamerlane* defeats Cielcin raiders under the command of Iubalu, one of Dorayaica's White Hand, and rescues what remains of the lost legion caravan.
ISD 16536	128	NEMAVAND	*DEMON IN WHITE:* After their victory over Iubalu, the *Tamerlane* delivers the rescued legions to Nemavand and returns to Forum.
ISD 16561	138	FORUM	*DEMON IN WHITE:* Hadrian's victory over Iubalu is celebrated with an Imperial triumph. Later, a failed assassination attempt drives Hadrian from Forum, and the Emperor grants him permission to visit the Great Library of Colchis.
ISD 16587	143	COLCHIS	*DEMON IN WHITE:* The *Tamerlane* arrives on Colchis, where the Red Company enjoys some well-deserved shore leave while Hadrian and Valka Onderra investigate the nature of the Quiet. Hadrian is reunited with Tor Gibson.
ISD 16594	150	COLCHIS	*DEMON IN WHITE:* Hadrian discovers the Mericanii AI, Horizon, in the basement of the Great Library, departs Colchis to seek the Quiet's homeworld.
ISD 16641	156	ANNICA	*DEMON IN WHITE:* The *Tamerlane* discovers and names the planet Annica. Excavations of the Quiet ruins there begin.
ISD 16648	163	ANNICA	*DEMON IN WHITE:* Hadrian Marlowe encounters the Quiet. The dig on Annica is ended abruptly by news of the Cielcin conquest of Marinus. The *Tamerlane* rushes to the relief of Berenike.

YEAR	AGE	LOCATION	EVENT
ISD 16699	172	BERENIKE	*DEMON IN WHITE:* The *Tamerlane* arrives to assist in the defense of Berenike.
ISD 16701	174	BERENIKE	*DEMON IN WHITE:* Humanity is victorious in the Battle of Berenike. Hadrian Marlowe demonstrates his abilities in combat against Syriani Dorayaica for all the galaxy to see. Valka Onderra is injured in a wizards' duel against the Extrasolarian sorcerer, Urbaine.
ISD 16739	181	EDDA	The *Tamerlane* arrives on Edda in the Demarchy of Tavros, seeking aid from the Tavrosi for Valka's neurological damage.
ISD 16741	183	EDDA	The Red Company is forced to flee Tavros, having effected a politically disastrous, but successful mission to rescue Valka Onderra from a Demarchist medical asylum.

Note: Not all years between ISD 16741 and ISD 16747 are here accounted for.

ISD 16747	186	METTINA	The Battle of Mettina occurs.

Note: Not all years between ISD 16747 and ISD 16759 are here accounted for.

ISD 16759	190	ORDINA	The Battle of Ordina occurs.

Note: Not all years between ISD 16759 and ISD 16773 are here accounted for.

ISD 16773	196	PERINTHUS	*WAR STORIES:* The Red Company brings the four-year siege of Perinthus by the Cielcin to an end.

Note: Not all years between ISD 16773 and ISD 16797 are here accounted for.

ISD 16797	206	COMUM	The Battle of Comum occurs.

Note: Not all years between ISD 16797 and ISD 16834 are here accounted for.

ISD 16834	229	SENUESSA	Humanity wins a narrow and crushingly pyrrhic victory against the forces of the Cielcin.

YEAR	AGE	LOCATION	EVENT
			Note: Not all years between ISD 16834 and ISD 16901 are here accounted for.
ISD 16901	253	**SYBARIS**	The Red Company wins a decisive victory against the Cielcin and their Extrasolarian allies, annexing the planet Sybaris to the Empire in the process. For his pains, Hadrian Marlowe is arrested by the Inquisition and taken to the planet Thermon for judgement.
ISD 16913	253	**THERMON**	Hadrian arrives on Thermon for the start of his trial at the hands of the Chantry's Terran Inquisition. The records of this trial remain sealed.
ISD 16925	265	**THERMON**	The Emperor himself intervenes to free Hadrian from the Terran Inquisition when, after twelve years of failing to indict him, they attempt to kill him in his cell. He is seized by the Martian Guard and transferred to Nessus, under the care of Karol Venantian.
ISD 16938	265	**NESSUS**	Hadrian and Valka begin their exile at Maddalo House on Nessus, capital of the Exarchate of Centaurus, effectively political prisoners. The *Tamerlane* is left in cold storage, maintained in high orbit above the planet, its crew in cryonic fugue.
ISD 17006	333	**EIKANA**	*KINGDOMS OF DEATH:* An attack on the Imperial fuel refinery on Eikana prompts the Exarch of Nessus to order Hadrian out of exile. He saves the refinery from the Cielcin general Hushansa.
ISD 17007	333	**NESSUS**	*KINGDOMS OF DEATH:* Returning from the Battle of Eikana, Hadrian meets with Emperor William at the start of his tour of the outer provinces. Hadrian is dispatched as apostol to the Lothrian Commonwealth.
ISD 17050	340	**PADMURAK**	*KINGDOMS OF DEATH:* The *Tamerlane* arrives at Padmurak, capital of the Lothrian Commonwealth. They fail to secure an alliance, discovering that the Lothrians have aligned with the Cielcin. Hadrian is captured, and the *Tamerlane* is commandeered and brought to Dharan-Tun.

YEAR	AGE	LOCATION	EVENT
ISD 17054	340	DHARAN-TUN	**KINGDOMS OF DEATH:** Hadrian arrives on Dharan-Tun, worldship-capital of Syriani Dorayaica, where he endures seven years of torment at the hands of the Cielcin prince.
ISD 17061	347	EUE	**KINGDOMS OF DEATH:** Hadrian accompanies Dorayaica to a meeting of the Cielcin princes, where he witnesses the Cielcin Prophet's consolidation of power, as it massacres its fellow princes and asserts its supremacy over the Cielcin race. The *Tamerlane* is destroyed, and Hadrian narrowly escapes with Valka Onderra.
ISD 17089	375	COLCHIS	**KINGDOMS OF DEATH:** Hadrian and Valka arrive on Colchis after a harrowing and lonely journey. There, they are reunited not only with the descendants of Siran Lordsworn, with whom they seek asylum, but with Tor Gibson.
ISD 17098	384	COLCHIS	**ASHES OF MAN:** The death of Tor Gibson prompts an end to Hadrian and Valka's secret exile. They surrender to Imperial authorities, and are conveyed back to Nessus by one Sir Hector Oliva.
ISD 17114	384	NESSUS	**ASHES OF MAN:** After a brief stay on Nessus and debrief with the Exarch, Hadrian and Valka are ordered to rendezvous with Emperor William on the planet Carteia.
ISD 17125	386	CARTEIA	**ASHES OF MAN:** Hadrian meets with the Emperor, where he is told about the Imperial effort to combat the Watchers, the Cielcin gods—a race of godlike, hyper-advanced alien life forms. He is assigned, along with Bassander Lin, with the destruction of an Extrasolarian fortress on Ganelon.
ISD 17131	386	GANELON	**ASHES OF MAN:** In the Battle of Ganelon, Hadrian assists the Imperial Legions in the destruction of an Extrasolarian depot, where they discover the development of the *lethovirus*. He is reunited with his friend, Olorin, and the Jaddian fleet.

YEAR	AGE	LOCATION	EVENT
ISD 17134	386	FIDCHELL	*ASHES OF MAN:* En route to rendezvous with the Emperor after the battle, Hadrian encounters Prince Alexander, fleeting the siege on Perfugium. Hadrian and the fleet agree to rush to the rescue of the Emperor.
ISD 17136	386	PERFUGIUM	*ASHES OF MAN:* A strategic retreat at Perfugium sees the rescue of the Emperor by Hadrian, Bassander Lin, and the Jaddian forces. Valka Onderra is killed. Hadrian assaults the Emperor in a fit of rage and is saved a prison sentence by Lorian Aristedes. Hadrian escapes to Jadd with the help of Olorin.
ISD 17354	575	JADD	*THE ROYAL GAME:* For his cooperation, the Jaddian government grants Hadrian a daughter, Cassandra, grown from his and Valka's cells. A Jaddian intelligence officer attempts to have the child aborted.
ISD 17355	576	JADD	Birth of Cassandra Marlowe.
ISD 17370	591	JADD	*DAUGHTER OF SWORDS:* A young Cassandra Marlowe is assaulted by her fellow students at the Fire School.
ISD 17395	616	JADD	*DISQUIET GODS:* Hadrian Marlowe's exile on Jadd ends with an Imperial pardon, brought to him by one Edouard Albé, who recruits Hadrian for Operation Gnomon: the Imperial mission to intercept and kill a Watcher before the Cielcin can recover it for the war effort.
ISD 17408	616	SABRATHA	*DISQUIET GODS:* Operation Gnomon arrives on Sabratha, begins excavation of the Vaiartu ruins at Phanamhara.
ISD 17410	618	SABRATHA	*DISQUIET GODS:* The Battle of Sabratha occurs. Cielcin forces under the command of General Muzugara assault the planet in an attempt to capture the Watcher, Ushara.
ISD 17430	618	TIRYNS	*DISQUIET GODS:* The *ISV Gadelica* stops at Tiyrns en route to Forum following the events at Sabratha.

YEAR	AGE	LOCATION	EVENT
ISD 17434	618	**FORUM**	***DISQUIET GODS:*** The survivors of Operation Gnomon arrive on Forum. Hadrian is taken into protective custody by Crown Prince Aurelian.
ISD 17438	622	**FORUM**	***DISQUIET GODS:*** The Great Council of the Alliance convenes to discuss the Cielcin threat. Lorian Aristedes arrives as an emissary of the Latarran Monarchy. Hadrian Marlowe is allegedly assassinated.
ISD 17446	623	**LATARRA**	***DISQUIET GODS:*** Hadrian Marlowe leads an embassy to the Monarch Calen Harendotes, arriving on Latarra.
ISD 17448	625	**LATARRA**	***DISQUIET GODS:*** An alliance between Latarra and the Empire is fully formalized, and the two nations agree to launch a joint assault on Vorgossos in exchange for Latarran support against the Cielcin.
ISD 17457	626	**MEROPE**	***DISQUIET GODS:*** The Latarran Grand Army rendezvouses with the joint Legion-Chantry fleet under Ohannes Douro and Sentinel-Commander Kedron in advance of the assault on Vorgossos.
ISD 17458	626	**VORGOSSOS**	***DISQUIET GODS:*** The joint Imperial-Latarran armada is successful at conquering the Kingdom of Vorgossos. Kharn Sagara is deposed, and the starship *Demiurge* falls into the hands of Hadrian Marlowe.

ACKNOWLEDGEMENTS

THIS BOOK SHOULDN'T EXIST.

I want to impress that fact upon you, dear reader. With the breakdown of my ongoing arrangement with my former publisher, it looked like the Sun Eater series and universe was done. Enter Baen Books' Toni Weisskopf, my former employer, my friend. No set of acknowledgements for this book would be quite right without first thanking her. Asking a publisher to pick up any series midway through is a tough proposition, and asking any publisher to pick up a series *six books in* is next to impossible. But Toni believed in the series—and in me—and I hope I have not disgraced that trust with this volume.

Without her, Hadrian's exile on Jadd would have been very long, indeed.

I'd like to also thank the rest of the Baen team: Marla, Joy, Leah, Rabbit, Jason, David, and Dave—Dave most especially (D.J. Butler, author of *Witchy Eye,* that is), for his editorial direction and invaluable aid helping me to locate some 40,000 words that could be safely removed from the original manuscript. I'd like also to thank artist Kieran Yanner and the cover designer, Jennie, for keeping the signature Sun Eater look as it has looked. I can't think of a publisher change in science fiction history that's gone down *this* smoothly.

There is another group of people who must be thanked for their part in keeping the series going: BookTube (that being the informal community of sci-fi/fantasy book reviewers on YouTube). It is to them I owe the largest part of my readership, most especially to Mike of Mike's Book Reviews, without whom I think the Sun Eater might have been just another casualty of Covid-19. It's in no small part thanks to him, and Dan and Jonathan and Madison and Jordan and Scot and Liam and KC and Jimmy and John and Alex and Petrik and Daniel—and all the others (I'm sure I've forgotten a few) that I've found my audience faster than I could have ever done alone.

My beta readers deserve their perennial thanks. Victoria, Joe, Micheal, Erin and Eddie, Nick, David, and Father Gabriel, thank you for helping keep me sane through what was the longest, most torturous book in the series (so far, let's see how Book Seven treats me), and for helping squash as many errors and inconsistencies as possible. I couldn't do it without you all. Likewise, I couldn't do this without my wife, Jenna. Her support and graphic design help has made so much of the Sun Eater stuff possible, and she has changed my life, certainly, in every way. I love you, dear.

Lastly, dear reader, thank *you*. Long series such as this are vanishingly rare, and would not be possible without the support of readers like you. I know that many of you have lost faith in writers as a class and have grown wary of anything longer than a trilogy (and so have publishers, to tell the truth). I would never have been able to come this far—to tell what I hope is the best version of Hadrian's story possible—without your support. As I write this, I am writing chapter ten of the seventh and final Sun Eater novel.

I never thought I'd actually make it this far...and that—if you'll permit me to ape the immortal Ronnie James Dio—is thanks to you, and *you,* and *all of you!*

—Christopher Ruocchio,
December 2023 AD

ABOUT THE AUTHOR

Christopher Ruocchio is the internationally award-winning author of the Sun Eater, a series blending elements of both science fiction and fantasy, as well as more than twenty works of short fiction. A graduate of North Carolina State University, he sold his first novel, *Empire of Silence*, at twenty-two, and his books have appeared in seven languages. He curated several short story anthologies for Baen Books, including *Sword & Planet*, *Time Troopers*, and *Worlds Long Lost*. His work has also appeared in Marvel Comics. Christopher lives in Raleigh, North Carolina with his family.